OLD ENOUGH TO BE USED, YOUNG ENOUGH TO BE BROKEN

Sassinak was twelve when the raiders came. That made her just the right age: old enough to be used, young enough to be broken. Or so the slavers thought. But Sassy turned out to be a little different from your typical slave girl. Maybe it was her unusual physical strength. Maybe it was her friendship with the captured Fleet crewman. Maybe it was her spirit. Whatever it was, it wouldn't let her resign herself to the life of a slave. She bided her time, watched for her moment. Finally it came, and she escaped.

But that was only the beginning for Sassinak. Now she's a Fleet Captain with a pirate-chasing ship of her own, and only one regret in her life: *not enough pirates.*

THE PLANET PIRATES

BAEN BOOKS by ANNE McCAFFREY

Sassinak
(with Elizabeth Moon)
The Death of Sleep
(with Jody Lynn Nye)
Generation Warriors
(with Elizabeth Moon)
The Planet Pirates
(with Elizabeth Moon & Jody Lynn Nye)

PartnerShip
(with Margaret Ball)
The Ship Who Searched
(with Mercedes Lackey)
The City Who Fought
(with S.M. Stirling)
The Ship Who Won
(with Jody Lynn Nye)

THE PLANET PIRATES

ANNE McCAFFREY
ELIZABETH MOON
JODY LYNN NYE

THE PLANET PIRATES

This is a work of fiction. All the characters and events portrayed in this book are fictional, and any resemblance to real people or incidents is purely coincidental.

The Planet Pirates has been published in slightly different form as *Sassinak*, copyright © 1990, *The Death of Sleep*, copyright © 1991, and *Generation Warriors*, copyright © 1992, by Bill Fawcett & Associates.

A Baen Books Original

Baen Publishing Enterprises
P.O. Box 1403
Riverdale, NY 10471
www.baen.com

Cover art by Stephen Hickman

First hardcover printing, December 2000

The Library of Congress has already catalogued the trade paperback edition as follows:

    McCaffrey, Anne—
    The Planet Pirates / Bill Fawcett & Associates
    p.   cm.
    ISBN 0-671-72187-9 : $15.00
    I. Moon, Elizabeth II. Nye, Jody Lynn III. Title

                           93-207-01
                              CIP

ISBN: 0-671-31962-0
Hardcover, $26.00

Distributed by Simon & Schuster
1230 Avenue of the Americas
New York, NY 10020

Printed in the United States of America

10 9 8 7 6 5 4 3 2 1

Table of Contents

Book I

THE DEATH OF SLEEP

For another survivor,
Lida Sloan Moon

PART ONE

✧ CHAPTER ONE

The single engaged engine of the empty spherical ore carrier thrummed hollowly through the hull. It set the decks and bulkheads of the personnel quarters vibrating at a frequency which at first, depending on one's mood, could be soothing or irritating. After four weeks aboard the Tau Ceti registered mining vessel *Nellie Mine*, Lunzie Mespil had to think about it to remember that the hum was there at all. When she first boarded, as the newly hired doctor for the Descartes Mining Platform Number 6, the sound drove her halfway to distraction. There wasn't much to do except read and sleep and listen, or rather, feel the engine noise. Later, she discovered that the sound was conducive to easy sleep and relaxation, like being aboard a gently swaying monorail passenger carrier. Whether her fellow employees knew it or not, one of the chief reasons that the Descartes Mining Corporation had so few duels and mutinies on delivery runs was due to the peace-inducing hum of the engines.

The first few days she spent in the tiny, plain-walled cubicle which doubled as her sleeping quarters and office were a trifle lonely. Lunzie had too many hours to think of her daughter Fiona. Fiona, fourteen, lovely and precocious in Lunzie's unbiased opinion, had been left behind in the care of a friend who was the chief medical officer on the newly colonized planet of Tau Ceti. The settlement was surprisingly comfortable for one so recently established. It had a good climate, a biosphere reasonably friendly toward humankind, marked seasons, and plenty of arable land that allowed both Earth-type and hybrid seeds to prosper. Lunzie hoped to settle down there herself when she finished her tour of duty on the Platform, but she wasn't independently wealthy. Even a commodity as precious as medical expertise wasn't sufficient to buy into the Tau Ceti association.

She needed to earn a stake, and there was little call on an atmos-phere-and-gravity world for her to practice her specialty of psychological space-incurred trauma. There was no help for it: she was compelled to go offplanet to earn money. To her great dismay, all of the posts which were best suited to her profession and experience — and paid the most — were on isolated facili-ties. She would not be able to take Fiona with her. After much negotiation, Lunzie signed on with Descartes for a stint on a remote mining platform.

Fiona had been angry that she couldn't accompany her mother to the Descartes Platform, and had refused to accept the fact. In the last days before Lunzie's departure, Fiona had avoided speak-ing to her, and stubbornly unpacked Lunzie's two five-kilo duffels as often as her mother filled them up. It was an adolescent prank, but one that showed Lunzie how hurt Fiona felt to be aban-doned. Since she was born, they had never been apart more than a day or so. Lunzie herself was aching at the impending separa-tion, but she understood, as Fiona would not, the economic necessity that caused her to take a medical berth so far away and leave Fiona behind.

Their spacefare to Tau Ceti had been paid on speculation by the science council, who were testing the viability of a clone breeding center on the newly colonized planet. Lunzie had been approached by the ethics council to join them, their interest stemming from her involvement as the student advisor on a simi-lar panel during her days in medical school which had resulted in an experimental colony. Surprisingly, the data on that earlier effort was unavailable even to the participants on the panel. Her former term-husband Sion had also given her his recommenda-tion. He was becoming very well known and respected in genetic studies, mainly involved in working on controlling the heavy-world human mutations.

There were four or five meetings of the ethics council, which quickly determined that even so altruistic a project as fostering a survival-oriented genome was self-defeating in just a few genera-tions, and no further action was taken. Lunzie was out of work in a colony that didn't need her. Because of the classified nature of the study, she was unable even to explain to her daughter why she wasn't employed in the job which they had traveled to Tau Ceti to take.

After the fifth or sixth time she had to repack her case, Lunzie knew by heart the few possessions she was taking with her, and locked her luggage up in the poisons cabinet in the Tau Ceti medical center to keep Fiona away from it.

By then, the protests had degenerated into a mere sulk. With love, Lunzie watched Fiona patiently, waiting for her to accept their parting, placing herself where she would be available to the troubled youngster when she decided she was ready to talk. Lunzie knew from experience that it was no good chasing Fiona down. She had to let Fiona come to her in her own time. They were too much alike. To force an early confrontation would be like forcing a nuclear pile to overload. She went about her business in the medical center, assisting other medical personnel with ongoing research which the colony had approved.

At last, Fiona met her coming out of the medical center one sunny day after work, and presented her with a small wrapped package. It was a hard triangular cylinder. Lunzie smiled, recognizing the shape. Under the paper was a brand new studio hologram of Fiona, dressed in her feastday best, an outfit in the latest style for which she had begged and plagued her mother to supplement the amount she'd saved to buy it from her allowance on their last planetary home. Lunzie could see how much of her own looks were reflected in Fiona: the prominent cheekbones, the high forehead, the warm mouth. The waves of smooth hair were much darker than hers, nearer black than Lunzie's golden brown. Fiona had long, sleepy eyes and a strong chin she inherited from her father that made her look determined, if not downright stubborn, even as a baby. The ruby-colored frock enhanced the girl's light skin, making her exotic and lovely as a flower. The translucent flowing cape which fell from between the shoulders was in the very height of fashion, a field of stars in pinpoint lights which whirled like a comet's tail around Fiona's calves. Lunzie looked up from the gift into her daughter's eyes which were watching her warily, wondering what she would say. "I love it, darling," Lunzie told her, gathering her close and tucking the hologram safely into her zip pouch. "I'll miss you so much."

"Don't forget me." A broken whimper was muffled against Lunzie's tunic front.

Lunzie drew back and took her daughter's tear-stained face

between her hands, studying it, learning it by heart. "I never could," Lunzie promised her. "I never will. And I'll be back before you know it."

During her remaining days planetside, she had turned over her laboratory work to a co-worker so she could spend all her time with Fiona. They visited favorite spots, and together moved Fiona's belongings and the rest of her own from their temporary quarters to the home of the friend who would be fostering the girl. They asked each other, "Do you remember this? Do you remember that?", sharing precious memories as they had shared the events themselves. It was a glowing, warm time for both of them, too soon over for Lunzie's taste.

A silent Fiona walked her to the landing bay where the shuttle waited to transport her to the *Nellie Mine*. Tau Ceti's pale lavender-blue sky was overcast. When the sky was clear, Lunzie could often see the sun glint off the sides of visiting ships high above Tau Ceti in parking orbit, but she was just as happy that she could not now. She was holding back on her emotions. If there was any way to spare Fiona her own misery, she would do it. Lunzie promised herself a really good cry once she was shipside. For one moment, she felt like ripping up her contract and running away, telling Descartes to chuck it, and pleading with the Tau Ceti authorities that she would work at any job, however menial, to stay here with Fiona. But then, good sense took over. Lunzie remembered crude financial matters like making a living, and assured herself that it wouldn't be that long before she could return, and they would have a comfortable life thereafter with what she'd earned.

"I'll negotiate for an asteroid miner as soon as I can afford it," Lunzie offered, breaking the silence. "Maybe I'll stake a few." Her words echoed among the corrugated metal walls of the spaceport. There seemed to be no one there but themselves. "We'll strike it rich, you'll see. You'll be able to go to any university you like, or go for officer training in Fleet, like my brother. Whatever you want."

"Mm," was Fiona's only comment. Her face was drawn into a mask so tragic that Lunzie wanted to laugh and cry. Fiona hadn't used any makeup that morning, so she looked more childlike than her usual careful teenaged self.

It's manipulation, I know it, Lunzie told herself severely. I've got to make a living, or where's our future? I know she's grieving, but I'll only be gone two years, five at the most! The girl's nose was turning red, and her lips were white and pressed tightly closed. Lunzie started to offer another pleasantry, and then realized that *she* was trying to manipulate her daughter into foregoing her legitimate feelings. I don't want to make a scene, so I'm trying to keep her from acting unhappy. She pressed her own lips shut. We're too much alike, that's the trouble, Lunzie decided, shaking her head. She squeezed Fiona's hand tighter. They walked in silence to the landing bay.

Landing Bay Six contained a big cargo shuttle of the type used by shippers who hauled more freight than passengers. This craft, once nattily painted white with a broad red band from its nose to tail, was dinged and dented. The ceramic coating along the nose showed scorching from making descents through planetary atmospheres, but the vehicle seemed otherwise in good shape and well cared for. A broad-shouldered man with black curly hair stood in the middle of the bay, waving a clipboard and dispensing orders to a handful of coveralled workers. Sealed containers were being forklifted into the open top hatch of the shuttle.

The black-haired man noticed them and came over, hand out in greeting.

"You're the new doctor?" he asked, seizing Lunzie's free hand and wringing it companionably. "Captain Cosimo, Descartes Mining. Glad to have you with us. Hello, little lady." Cosimo ducked his head to Fiona, a cross between a nod and a bow. "Are those your bags, Doctor? Marcus! Take the doctor's bags on board!"

Lunzie offered Cosimo the small cube containing her contract and orders, which he slotted into the clipboard. "All's well," he said, scanning the readout on his screen. "We've got about twenty minutes before we lift off. Hatch shuts at T-minus two. Until then, your time's your own." With another smile for Fiona, he went back to shouting at one of his employees. "See here, Nelhen, that's a forklift, not a wee little toy!"

Lunzie turned to Fiona. Her throat began to tighten. All the things she wanted to say seemed so trivial when compared to what she felt. She cleared her throat, trying not to cry. Fiona's eyes were aswim with tears. "There's not much time."

"Oh, Mama," Fiona burst out in a huge sob. "I'll miss you so!"

The almost-grown Fiona, who eschewed all juvenile things and had called her mother Lunzie since early childhood, reverted all at once to the baby name she hadn't used in years. "I'll miss you, too, Fee," Lunzie admitted, more touched than she realized. They clutched each other close and shed honest tears. Lunzie let it all out, and felt better for it. In the end, neither Lunzie nor any member of her family could be dishonest.

When the klaxon sounded, Fiona let her go with one more moist kiss, and stood back to watch the launch. Lunzie felt closer to her than she ever had. She kept Fiona in her mind, picturing her waving as the shuttle lifted and swept away through the violet-blue sky of Tau Ceti.

Now, with the exception of today's uniform, one music disk, and the hologram, her baggage was secured in the small storage chamber behind the shower unit with everyone else's. Lunzie had cropped her hair practically short as most crew members did. She missed the warm, fresh wind, cooking her own food from the indigenous plant life, and Fiona.

Without other set duties to occupy her, Lunzie spent the days studying the medical files of her future co-workers and medical texts on the typical injuries and ailments that befall asteroid miners. She was looking forward to her new post. Space-incurred traumas interested her. Agoraphobia and claustrophobia were the most common in space-station life, followed by paranoid disorders. Strangely enough, frequently more than one occurred in the same patient at the same time. She was curious about the causes, and wanted to amass field research to prove or disprove her professors' statements about the possibility of cures.

She'd used her observations from the medical files to facilitate getting to know her fifteen shipmates. Miners were a hearty lot, sharing genuine good fellowship among themselves, but they took slowly to most strangers. Tragedy, suffered on the job and in personal lives, kept them clannish. But Lunzie wasn't a stranger long. They soon discovered that she cared deeply about the well-being of each of them, and that she was a good listener. After that, each of the others claimed time with her in the common dining recreation room, and filtered through her office, to pass the time between shifts, making her feel very welcome. With time, they began to open up to her. Lunzie heard about this crewman's broken romance, and that crewwoman's plan to open a satellite-based saloon with her savings, and the impending eggs of a mated pair of avians called Ryxi, who were specialists temporarily employed by the Platform. And they learned about her early life, her medical training, and her daughter.

The triangular hologram of Fiona was in her hand as she sat behind the desk in her office and listened to a human miner named Jilet. According to his file, Jilet had spent twelve years in cryogenic deepsleep after asteroids destroyed the drive on an ore carrier on which he and four other crewmen had been travelling. They'd been forced to evacuate from their posts, Jilet in one escape capsule near the cargo hold, the others in a second by the engine section. The other four men were recovered quickly, but Jilet was not found for over a decade more because of a malfunction in the signal beacon on his capsule. Not surprisingly, he was angry, afraid, and resentful. Three of the other crew presently on the *Nellie Mine* had been in cold sleep at least once, but Jilet's stint had been the longest. Lunzie sympathized with him.

"The truth is that I know those years passed while I was in cold sleep, Doctor, but it is killing me that I can't remember them. I've lost so much — my friends, my family. The world's gone round without me, and I don't know how to take up where I've left off." The burly, black-haired miner shifted in the deep impact lounger which Lunzie used as a psychoanalyst's couch. "I feel I've lost parts of myself as well."

"Well, you know that's not true, Jilet," Lunzie corrected him, leaning forward on her elbows attentively. "The brain is very protective of its memory centers. What you know is still locked up in there." She tapped his forehead with a slender, square-tipped finger. "Research has proved that there is no degeneration of memory over the time spent in cold sleep. You have to rely upon what you are, who you are, not what your surroundings tell you you are. I know it's disorienting — no, I've never been through it myself, but I've taken care of many patients who have. What you must do is accept that you've suffered a trauma, and learn to live your life again."

Jilet grimaced. "When I was younger, my mates and I wanted to live in space, away from all the crowds and noise. Hah! Catch me saying that now. All I want to do is settle down on one of the permanent colonies and maybe fix jets or industrial robots for a living. Can't do that yet without my Oh-Two money, not even

including the extra if I want to have a family — a *new* family — so
I've got to keep mining. It's all I know."

Lunzie nodded. Oh-Two was the cant term for the setup costs
it took to add each person to the biosphere of an ongoing oxygen-
breathing colony on a non-atmosphered site. It was expensive:
the containment domes had to be expanded, and studies needed
to be done to determine whether the other support systems
could handle the presence of another life. Besides air, a human
being needed water, sanitary facilities, a certain amount of space
for living quarters and food synthesis or farming acreage to support him. She had considered one herself, but the safety margins
were not yet acceptable, to her way of thinking, for the raising of
a child.

"What about a planetside community?" Lunzie asked. "My
daughter's happy on Tau Ceti. It has a healthy atmosphere, and
community centers or farmland available, whichever you prefer
to inhabit. I want to buy in on an asteroid strike, so that Fiona and
I can have a comfortable home." It was a common practice for
the mining companies to allow freelancing by non-competitive
consortia from their own platforms, so long as it didn't interfere
with their primary business. Lunzie calculated that two or three
years worth of her disposable income would be enough for a tidy
share of a miner's time.

"Well, with apologies, Doctor Mespil, it's too settled and set on
a domeless world. They're too — complacent; there, that's the
word. Things is too easy for 'em. I'd rather be poor in a place
where they understand the real pioneering spirit than rich on
Earth itself. If I should have a daughter, I'd want her to grow up
with some ambition . . . and some guts, not like her old man . . .
With respect, Doctor," Jilet said, giving her an anxious look.

Lunzie waved away the thought that he had insulted her courage. She suspected that he was unwilling to expose himself to the
undomed surface of a planet. Agoraphobia was an insidious complaint. The free atmosphere would remind him too much of free
space. He needed to be reassured that, like his memories, his
courage was still there, and intact. "Never mind. But please, call
me Lunzie. When you say 'Doctor Mespil,' I start to look around
for my husband. And that contract ended years ago. Friendly
parting, of course."

The miner laughed, at his ease. Lunzie examined the flush-set desk computer screen, which displayed Jilet's medical file. His anger would have to be talked out. The escape capsule in which he'd cold slept had had another minor malfunction that left him staring drugged and half conscious through the port glass at open space for two days before the cryogenic process had kicked in. Not surprisingly, that would contribute to the agoraphobia. There was a pathetic air of desperation about this big strong human, whose palpable dread was crippling him, impairing his usefulness. She wondered if teaching him rudimentary Discipline would help him, then decided against it. He didn't need to know how to control an adrenaline rush; he needed to learn how to keep them from happening. "Tell me how the fears start."

"It's not so bad in the morning," Jilet began. "I'm too busy with my job. Ever been on the mining platform?" Lunzie shook her head. The corners of Jilet's dark eyes crinkled merrily. "You've a lot to look forward to, then, haven't you? I hope you can take a joke or two. The boys are full of them. Don't get to liking this big office too much. Space is tight in the living quarters, so everyone gets to be tolerant of everyone else real fast. Oh, it's not like we're all mates right away," he added sadly. "A lot of the young ones first coming along die quickly. It only takes one mistake . . . and there you are, frozen or suffocated, or worse. A lot of them leave young families, too."

Lunzie gulped, thinking of Fiona, and felt her heart twist in her body. She knew the seals and panels of her atmosphere suit were whole and taut, but she vowed to scrutinize them carefully as soon as Jilet left. "What are your specific duties?"

"We all take turns at whatever needs doing, ma'am. I've got a knack for finding lucky strikes when I'm on scout duty, so I try to draw that one a lot. There's a bonus for a good find."

"Maybe you're the one I'll pay to make my daughter's fortune for her," Lunzie smiled.

"I'd be proud to have your trust, D— Lunzie, only why don't you see if I can cut it, eh? Well, every asteroid's got ore, large and small, but you don't waste your time on everything you see. The sensors in a scout are unidirectional. Once you've eyeballed something you like the look of, either on visual or in the navigational scanning net, you can get a detailed readout of the asteroid's makeup. Scouts aren't very big. They're fit for one man only, so he'd better like being by himself for days or weeks, even months, at a time. It's not easy. You've got to be able to wake up cold-eyed if the scanner net alarm goes off to avoid collisions. When you find a potential strike, you lay claim to it on behalf of the company, pending computer search for other claims of ownership. If it's small, like a crystal mass, you can haul it back behind you to the platform — and you'll want to: there's always a bonus on crystals. You don't want anyone jumping claim behind you. The mediums can be brought in by a tug. The big ones a crew comes out to mine on the spot. I don't mind being in a scout, because I'm looking straight down the 'corridor' between fields in the net, and inside of the ship is small enough to be comfortable. It starts to bug me when I'm fixing one of the rotating tumbling shafts, or something like that out in free-fall." Jilet finished with his brows drawn down and his arms folded tightly across his chest.

"Focus on the equipment, Jilet. Don't catch yourself staring off into space. It was always there before. You just didn't pay attention to it then. Don't let it haunt you now. What matters is what you are working on at the moment." Lunzie hastened to calm him. She wanted him to verbalize the good facets of his job. It was impossible to heal the mind without giving it something positive to hang on to, a reason for healing. Half the battle was won, whether Jilet knew it or not. He had the guts to go back to his post on the Mining Platform. Getting back on the horse that threw him. "What do you look for when you're scouting?"

Jilet's body gradually relaxed, and he studied the ceiling through his wiry black eyebrows. "What I can find. Depending on what's claiming a good price dirtside, you'll see 'em breaking down space rock into everything from diamonds to cobalt to iron. If the handling don't matter, they slag it apart with lasers and shove it into the tumbling chutes for processing. If how it's handled makes a difference, a prize crew'll strip it down. As much as possible is done in vacuum, for safety, conservation of oxygen, and to keep the material from expanding and contracting from exposure to too many temperatures. Makes the ore tough to ship if it has been thawed once. It'll split up, explode into a million shards if it warms too quickly. I've seen mates of mine killed that way. It's ugly, ma'am. I don't want to die in bed, but I'd rather not go that way, either.

With a rueful smile for her precise clinical imagination, Lunzie dismissed thoughts of trying to reconstruct a splintered miner's body. This was the life she was moving toward, at just under the speed of light. You won't be able to save every patient, you idealist. Help the ones you can. "What's a crystal strike look like? How do you find one?"

"Think I'd give all my secrets away, even to a friendly mind-browser like you?" Jilet tilted one eyebrow toward her. Lunzie gave him an affable grin. "Well, I'll give you one clue. They're lighter than the others on the inside. Sounding gives you a cross-section that seems to be nearly hollow, bounces your scan around its interior. Sometimes it is. Why, I had one that split my beam up in a hundred different directions. The crew found it was rutilated with filaments of metal when they cut it apart. Worthless for communications, but some rich senator had it used for the walls of his house." Jilet spat in the direction of the nameless states-man.

They were getting off the track. Regretfully, for Jilet was really relaxing with her, Lunzie set them back on it. "You've also com-plained of sleeplessness. Tell me about it."

Jilet fidgeted, bent forward and squeezed his forehead with both hands. "It's not that I can't sleep. I — just don't want to fall asleep. I'm afraid that if I do, I won't wake up."

" 'Sleep, the brother of Death,' " Lunzie quoted. "Homer, or more recently, Daniel."

"Yes, that's it. I wish — I wish that if I wasn't going to die they'd've left me asleep for a hundred years or more, so that I'd come back a complete stranger, instead of everything seeming the same," Jilet exploded in a sudden passionate outburst that surprised even him. "After only a dozen years I'm out of step. I remember things my friends have forgotten long since, that they laugh at me for, but it's all I've got to hang on to. They've had a decade to go on without me. They're older now. I'm a freak to them, being younger. I almost wish I had died."

"Now, now. Death is never as good as its press would have you believe. You've begun making new friends in your profession, you're heading toward a job right now that makes the best use of your talents, and you can learn some new techniques that didn't exist when you started out mining. Give the positive aspects a chance. Don't think of space while you're trying to sleep. Let your mind turn inward, possibly to a memory of your childhood that you enjoyed." A chime sounded, indicating Jilet's personal time was at an end, and he needed to get back to his duties. Lunzie stood up, waited for Jilet to rise. He towered easily a third of a meter over her. "Come back and talk to me again next rest period," Lunzie insisted. "I want to hear more about crystal mining."

"You and half the youngsters that come out to the Platforms," Jilet complained good-naturedly. "But, Doctor, I mean Lunzie, how can I get to sleep without having this eating away at me? We're still so far out, but the feelings are keeping me awake all over again."

"I'd rather not give you drugs, though I will if you insist after you try it my way first. For now, concentrate on what is here, close by and around you. When you're in the rec area, never look out the window, always at the wall beside it." Lunzie smiled, reaching out to press Jilet's hand warmly. "In no time, you'll be so bored with the wall that mere yearning for something new will set you to gazing at the stars again."

After Jilet left, Lunzie got a carafe of fresh hot coffee for herself from a synthesizer hatch in the corridor, and returned to her office. While her observations on Jilet's case were still fresh in her mind, she sat down at her desk to key in data to her confidential files. She believed that in time he would recover completely. He'd obviously been counselled by experts when he first came out of cold sleep. Whoever the psychology team was that had worked with him, they were right on the ball when it came to rehabilitation counseling.

Jilet's agoraphobia had been triggered by an occupational hazard. Lunzie wondered uneasily how many latent agoraphobics there were in space who simply hadn't been exposed to the correct stimuli yet that would cause it to manifest. Others in the crew could be on the edge of a breakout. Had anyone else shown symptoms?

Immediately, Lunzie put the thought away. Wryly, she decided she was frightening herself. "I'll have to treat myself for paranoia soon, if I'm not careful." But the feeling of uneasiness persisted. Not for the first time, Lunzie wished Fiona was here to talk to. She had always discussed things with Fiona, even when she was an infant. Lunzie turned the hologram in her hands. The girl was growing and changing. She was already as tall as her mother.

"She'll be a woman when I get back." Lunzie decided that her dissatisfaction was because she was spoiling for a good chat with someone. Her remote cubicle was too lonely. Since "office hours" were over, she would run down the corridor to the rec area and see if anyone else was on break.

Abruptly, Lunzie realized that the everpresent hum of the engine had changed, sped up. Instead of the usual purr, the sound had an edge of panic to it. Two more growling notes coughed to life, increasing the vibration so much Lunzie's teeth were chattering. They were trying to fire up the dorsal and ventral engines!

"Attention, all personnel," Captain Cosimo's voice blared. "This is an emergency alert. We are in danger of collision with unknown objects. Be prepared to evacuate. Do not panic. Proceed in an orderly fashion to your stations. We are attempting to evade, but we might not make it. This is not a drill."

Lunzie's eyes widened, and she turned to her desk screen. On the computer pickup, the automatic cutoff devolved to forward control video, and showed what the pilot on the bridge saw: half a dozen irregularly shaped asteroids. Two that appeared to be the size of the ship were closing in from either side like pincers, or hammer and anvil, with more fragments heading directly for them. There wasn't room for the giant ship, running on only one of its three engines, to maneuver and avoid them all. Normally, asteroid routes could be charted. The ship's flight plan took into account all the space-borne debris to be avoided. At the last check, the route had been clear. These must have just crashed into one another, changing their course abruptly into the path of the *Nellie Mine*. The huge freighter was incapable of making swift turns, and there was no way to get out of the path of all the fragments. Collision with the tumbling rocks was imminent.

One of the asteroids slipped out of view of the remote cameras, and Lunzie was thrown out of her chair as the huge ship fired all its starboard boosters, attempting to avoid collision. Crashing sounds reverberated through the corridor, and the floor shook. Some of the smaller fragments must have struck the ship.

The red alert beacons in the corridor went off. "Evacuate!" the captain's voice shouted. "We can't get the engines firing. All personnel, evacuate!"

As the klaxon sounded, Lunzie's mind reached for Discipline.

She willed herself to be calm, recalling all her training on what to do in a red alert. The list scrolled up in her mind as clearly as it would do on a computer screen. Make sure all who are disabled or too young to look after themselves are safe, then secure yourself — but most importantly, waste no time! Lunzie paused only long enough to grab Fiona's hologram off the desk and stow it in a pocket before she dashed out into the corridor, heading for her section's escape capsule.

The crew section was a curved strip one level high across the equator of the spherical freighter. When the ship was making a delivery run, she could carry as many as eighty crew in the twenty small sleeping cubicles, ten on either side of the common rooms. At intervals along the corridor, round hatchways opened onto permanently moored escape capsules. Lunzie's office was at the far left end of the crew section.

The ship rocked. They'd been struck again, this time by a big fragment. There was a gasp of life-support fans and compressors speeding up to move the air in spite of a hull breach. All the lights in the corridor went out, and in the center of one wall, a circle of bright red LEDs chased around the hatch of the escape capsule, which irised open as Lunzie ran toward it.

She waited at the hatch, staring down the long corridor toward the center of the crew section to see if anyone was coming to board this escape shuttle with her. Her heart hammered with fear and impatience. The capsule iris would close and launch automatically thirty seconds after a body entered the hatchway, so she forced herself to wait. Lunzie wanted to be certain that there was no one else in this section that she would be abandoning if she took off alone in the capsule.

There was a deafening bang, and then a roar like thunder echoed in the corridor. A section of rock the size of her head burst through the bulkhead less than a hundred feet down the passage, cutting her off from the rest of the crew. Lunzie ducked the splinters, and grabbed with both hands at the edge of the hatchway, as the vacuum of space dragged the ship's atmosphere out through the tear in the hull. Gritting her teeth tightly, she clung to the metal lip, and watched furniture, clothing, coffee cups, atmosphere suits fly through the air toward the gap. The air dropped to near freezing, and frost formed swiftly on her rings and sleeve fasteners, and on her eyelashes, cheeks, and lips. Her hands were growing numb with cold. Lunzie wasn't sure how long she could hang on before she, too, was sucked out into space through that hole. This was death, she knew. Then: a miracle.

She heard a rending sound, and her desk and chair flew out of her office door, ricocheted off the opposite corridor wall with individual bangs, and collided in the tear in the hull. The tornadic winds died momentarily, blocked by her office furniture. Lunzie grabbed the opportunity to save herself. She dove through the hatchway headfirst, tucking and rolling to land unhurt between the rows of impact seats. She arched up from the floor to punch the manual door control with her fist, then crawled to the steering controls, not bothering to right herself before sending the pod hurtling into space.

The capsule spun away from the side of the *Nellie Mine*. Lunzie was flung about in the tiny cabin. She caught hold of the handloops, yanked herself into the pilot's seat, and strapped in.

The lumpy shape of the mining ship looked like another asteroid against the curtain of stars. The brief strip of living space raised across a 60-degree arc of the ship's midsection bloomed with other pinpoints of light as the rest of the crew evacuated in vessels like hers. She regretted that there hadn't been opportunity for anyone else to join her in the escape pod, company until rescue could reach them, but Space! when the alarm sounds, you go, or you die.

She could see where the gigantic asteroid had struck the *Nellie*. It had torn away a large section of the crew quarters at the opposite end of the strip from hers, creased the hull deeply, and sailed away on a tangential course. The second asteroid, the size of a moon, would do far more damage. The ship, still on automatic pilot, was slowly turning toward her, firing on all the steering thrusters down one side, so the jagged rock would take it broadside instead of a direct strike. She watched, fascinated and horrified, as the two immense bodies met, and melded.

Her little pod hurtled outward at ever-increasing speed, but much faster still came the explosion, the overtaxed inner engine kicking through the plating behind the living quarters, imploding the shells and then kicking the debris forward of the directionless hulk. Pieces of red-hot hull plating shot past her, some missing her small boat by mere yards. The planetoid deflected away, its course changed only slightly.

Lunzie let go of the breath she had been holding. The disaster had happened so quickly. Only minutes had gone by since the alert was broadcast. Her Discipline had served her well — she had acted swiftly and decisively. She was considered by her masters a natural Candidate, who had already achieved much on her own. Basic training in Discipline was recommended for medics and Fleet officers of command rank and above, especially those who would be going into hazardous situations — much like this. Over the years, Lunzie had achieved Adept status. It was a pity she hadn't been able to go on with her lessons since reaching Tau Ceti. Lunzie was grateful for the instruction, which had probably saved her life, but she realized that her capsule was still at least two weeks travel away from the Mining Platform. She switched on the communication set and leaned over the audio pickup.

"Mayday, Mayday. This is *Nellie Mine* Shuttle, registration number NM-EC-02. I repeat, Mayday."

A wave of static poured out of the speaker. Underneath it, she could hear a voice. The static gradually died, and a man's voice spoke clearly. "I hear you, EC-02. This is Captain Cosimo, in EC-04. Is that you, Lunzie?"

"Yes, sir. Is everyone else all right?"

"Yes, dammit. All present and accounted for but you. We thought we'd lost you when Damage Control reported a punch-through in your wing. That was one hell of bang. I knew it would happen one day. Poor old *Nellie*. Are you all right?"

"I'm fine."

"Good. We've been signalling, but there's no one in immediate range. Before the blast, we sent off a message to Descartes 6 advising them to send someone out for us. Lock in your beacon to 34.8 and activate."

Lunzie found the controls and punched in the command. "How long will it take for them to reach us, Cosimo?"

There was more static, and the captain's voice broke through it, fainter than before. " . . . flaming asteroid interference. It'll be at least two weeks before the message reaches them, and I'd estimate it'll take them four more weeks to find us. I am ordering cold sleep, Doctor. Any comments or objections?"

"No, sir. I concur. It would be an emotional strain for so many people to spend six weeks awake in such close quarters, even providing the synthesizers and recyclers hold out."

"That's for certain. There are two crew on this shuttle, including the Ryxi, who're squawking about their damned eggs and claustrophobia. I wish you were here to oversee the deepsleep process, Doctor. Hypodermic compressors make me nervous." Cosimo didn't sound in the least distressed, but Lunzie was grateful to him for keeping the mood light.

"Nothing to it," she said. "Just remember, pointed end down."

With a hearty laugh, the captain signed off.

Inside the shuttle's medical supply locker were several vials containing medicines: depressants, restoratives, and the cold sleep preservative formula alongside its antidote. Lunzie removed the spraygun from its niche and loaded in a vial of the cryogenic. She would have only moments before the formula took effect, so she prepared a cradling pad from stored thermal blankets, and wadded up a few more under her head as a pillow. She fed instructions to the ship's computer, giving details of her identity, allergies, next of kin, and planet of origin for use by her rescuers. When all was prepared, Lunzie lowered herself to the padded deck. She could feel the adrenaline of the Discipline state wearing off. In moments, she was drained and exhausted, her strength swept away. In one hand she held the spraygun. In the other, Lunzie clutched the hologram of her daughter.

"Computer," she commanded. "Monitor vital signs and initiate cold sleep process when my heart rate reaches zero."

"Working," the metallic voice responded. "Acknowledged."

Her order was unnecessary, since the module was programed to complete the cold sleep process on its own, but Lunzie needed to hear another Standard-speaking voice. She wished someone had been close enough in the corridors of the damaged carrier to have boarded the pod with her. For all her theoretical training, this was the first time she would experience the cryogenic process. Lunzie gazed into the lucite block, smiled into the image of Fiona's eyes. "What an adventure I'll have to tell you about when I see you, my darling." She pressed the nozzle of the spray against her thigh. It hissed as the drug dispersed swiftly through her body. Where it passed, her tissues became leaden, and her skin felt hot. Though the sensation was uncomfortable, Lunzie knew the process was safe. "Initiating," she told the computer indistinctly. Her jaw and tongue were already out of control. Lunzie could sense her pulse slowing down, and her nervous responses became lethargic. Even her lungs were growing too heavy to drag air in or push it out.

Her last conscious thoughts were of Fiona, and she hoped that the rescue shuttle wouldn't take too long to answer the Mayday.

All lights on the shuttle except the exterior running lights and beacon went down. Inside, cold cryogenic vapor filled the tiny cabin, swirling around Lunzie's still form.

PART TWO

✧ CHAPTER TWO

When his scout ship was just two days flight out of Descartes Mining Platform 6, Illin Romsey began to pick up hopeful signs of radioactivity. He was prospecting for potential strikes along what his researches told him was a nearly untapped vector leading away from Platform 6. He was aware that in the seventy years since the Platform became operational, the thick asteroid stream around the complex had had time to shift, bringing new rock closer and sweeping played-out space rock away. Still, the explorer's blood in his veins urged him to follow a path no one else had ever tried.

His father and grandfather had worked for Descartes. He didn't mind following in the family tradition. The company treated its employees well, even generously. Its insurance plan and pension plan alone made Descartes a desirable employer, but the bonus system for successful prospectors kept him pushing the limits of his skills. He was proud to work for Descartes.

His flight plan nearly paralleled a well-used approach run to the Platform, which maintained its position in the cosmos by focusing on six fixed remote beacons and adjusting accordingly. Otherwise, even a complex that huge would become lost in the swirling pattern of rock and ice. It was believed that the asteroid belt had originated as a Uranian-sized planet, destroyed in a natural cataclysm of some kind. Some held that a planet had never been formed in this system. The sun around which the belt revolved had no other planets. Even after seven decades of exploration, the jury was still out on it, and everyone had his own idea.

Illin held a fix on the vector between Alpha Beacon and the Platform. It was his lifeline. Ships had been known to get lost within kilometers of their destination because of the confusion thrown into their sensors by the asteroid belt. Illin felt that he was different: he had an instinct for finding his way back home. In more than eight years prospecting, he'd never spent more than a day lost. He never talked about his instinct, because he felt it would break his luck. The senior miners never twitted him about it; they had their own superstitions. The new ones called it blind luck, or suggested the Others were looking after him. Still, he wasn't cocky, whatever they might think, and he was never less than careful.

The clatter of the radiation counter grew louder and more frenzied. Illin crossed his fingers eagerly. A strike of transuranic ore heretofore undiscovered by the busy Mining Platform — and so close by — would be worth a bonus and maybe a promotion. Need for other minerals might come and go, but radioactive elements were always sought after, and they fetched Descartes a good price, too. What terrifically good luck! He adjusted his direction slightly to follow the signal, weaving deftly between participants in the great stately waltz like a waiter at a grand ball.

He was close enough now to pick up the asteroids he wanted on his scanner net. Suddenly, the mass on his scope split into two, an irregular mass that drifted gently away portside, and a four-meter-long pyramidal lump that sped straight toward him. Asteroids didn't behave that way! Spooked, Illin quickly changed course, but the pyramid angled to meet him. His rad counter went wild. He tried to evade it, firing thrusters to turn the nippy little scout out of its path. It was chasing him! In a moment, he had the smaller mass on visual. It was a Thek capsule.

Theks were a silicate life-form that was the closest thing in the galaxy to immortals. They ranged from about a meter to dozens of meters high, and were pyramidal in shape, just like their spacecraft. Illin's jaw dropped open. Theks were slow talking and of few words, but their terse statements usually held more information than hundreds of pages of human rhetoric. Not much else was known about them, except their inexplicable penchant for aiding the more ephemeral races to explore and colonize new planetary systems. A Thek rode every mothership that the Exploratory and Evaluatory Corps sent out. What was a Thek doing way out here? He cut thrust and waited for it to catch up with him.

He was suddenly resentful. Oh, Krims! Illin thought. Did I come all this way just for a Thek? The other miners were going to have a laugh at his expense. He tapped his rad counter and aimed the sensor this way and that. It continued to chatter out a high-pitched whir, obviously responding to a strong signal nearby. Were Theks radioactive? He'd never heard that from anyone before. Had he discovered a new bit of interesting gossip about the mysterious Theks to share with the other miners? Yes, it would seem so. But to his delight, the signal from the asteroid he'd spotted continued. A strike! And a concentrated one, too. Should be worth a goodly handful of bonus credits.

In a few minutes, the Thek was alongside him. The pyramidal shape behind the plas-shield was featureless, resembling nothing so much as a lump of plain gray granite. It eased one of its ship's sides against the scout with a gentle bump, and adhered to the hull like a flexible magnet. The cabin was filled then with a low rumbling sound which rose and fell very, very slowly. The Thek was talking to him.

"Rrrrreeeeeee . . . ttrrrrrrrrriieeeeevvve . . . ssssshhhhuuuuuutttt . . . ttttlllleee."

"Shuttle? What shuttle?" Illin asked, not bothering to wonder how the Thek was talking to him through the hull of his scout.

For answer, the Thek moved forward, dragging his ship with it.

"Hey!" Illin yelled. "I'm tracking an ore strike! I've got a job to do. Would you release my ship?"

"Iiiiimmmm . . . perrrrrrr . . . aaaa . . . ttttiiiiivvvvvveee."

He shrugged. "Imperative, huh?" He waited a long time to see if there was any more information forthcoming. Well, you didn't argue with a Thek. Resigned but unhappy, he allowed himself to be towed along at a surprising speed through a patch of tiny asteroids that bounced off the Thek craft and embedded themselves into the nose of his ship. The outermost metal layer of a scout's nose was soft, backed by a double layer of superhard titanium sandwiching more soft metal, to absorb and stop small meteorites or slow and deflect bigger ones. Illin had only just stripped the soft layer and ground out the gouge marks in the hard core a week ago. It would have to be done all over again when he got back from rescuing this shuttle for the Thek — would anyone believe him when he told them about it? He scarcely believed it himself.

Behind him the starfield disappeared. They were moving into the thickest part of the asteroid belt. The Thek obviously knew where it was going; it didn't slow down at all, though the hammering of tiny pebbles on the hull became more insistent. Illin switched on the video pickup and rolled the protective lid up to protect the forward port.

A tremendous rock shot through with the red of iron oxide rolled up behind them and somersaulted gracefully to the left as the Thek veered around it, a tiny arrowhead against its mass. Illin's analyzer showed that most of the debris in this immediate vicinity was ferric, and a lot of it was magnetic. He had to recalibrate continually to keep his readings accurate. They looped around a ring of boulders approximately all the same size revolving around a planetoid that was almost regular in shape except for three huge impact craters near its "equator."

Nestled in one of the craters was a kernel-shaped object that Illin recognized immediately. It was an escape pod. As they drew closer, he could read the markings along its dusty white hull: NM-EC-02.

"Well, boy, you're a hero," he said to himself. Those pods were never jettisoned empty; there must be sleepers aboard. The beacon apparatus, both beam and transmitter, was missing, probably knocked off by the meteor that had shoved the pod into the cradle it now occupied. He didn't recognize the registry code, but then, he wasn't personally familiar with any vessels large enough to be carrying pods.

The Thek disengaged and floated a few meters away from his scout. It hadn't extruded any eyes, or anything like that, but Illin felt it was watching him. He angled his ship away from the escape pod. The magnetic line shot out of the scout's stern and looped around the pod. The tiny dark ship twisted in his wake, showing that the net had engaged correctly.

Moving slowly and carefully, Illin applied ventral thrusters and steered his ship upward, over the ring of dancing giants. The Thek floated next to him.

He followed the small pyramid out of the thick of the field and back to his vector point. As soon as they were clear, he bounced messages to the beacons: Scout coming in, towing escape pod NM-EC-02, intact, beacon damaged. Thek involved. He grinned jauntily to himself. That short message would have them fluttering on the Platform all right. He couldn't wait to see what a fuss he was stirring up.

Descartes Mining Platform 6 had changed a great deal in the many years since the first modular cylinders had been towed into the midst of the asteroid field and assembled. While the early employees had had to make do with barrackslike communal quarters, families could now claim small suites of their own. Amenities, which were once sold practically out of the backpacks of itinerant traders, could be found in a knot of shops in the heart of the corridors joining the cylinder complex near the entertainment center. With the completion date for the residential containment dome only five years away, Descartes 6 could almost claim colony status. And would.

Ore trains consisting of five to eight sealed containers strung behind a drone crossed back and forth between the ships ranged out along the docking piers. Some carried raw rock from the mining vessels to the slaggers and tumblers whose chutes bristled from the side of the Platform. Some carried processed minerals to the gigantic three-engine ore carriers that were shaped like vast hollow spheres belted top to bottom by thruster points. Those big slow-moving spheres did most of the hauling between the Platform and civilization. In spite of their dowdy appearance and obvious unwieldiness, the Company had never come up with anything better with which to replace them.

Ships belonging to merchants from the Federated Sentient Planet worlds were easily distinguished from the Mining Company's own vessels by their gaudy paint jobs. They were here to trade household goods, food, and textiles for small and large parcels of minerals that weren't available on their own planets, hoping to get a better price than they would get from a distributor. As Illin watched, one moved away from its bay with four containers in tow, turning toward the beacon that would help guide it toward Alpha Centauri, many months travel from here even at FTL. A personal shuttle with the colors of a Company executive shot out of an airlock and flew purposefully toward a large Paraden Company carrier that lay in a remote docking orbit somewhere over Illin's left shoulder.

Illin transmitted his scout's recognition code as he approached the Platform. The acknowledgment tone tweetled shrilly in his headphones.

"Good day, Romsey. That your Thek behind you there at .05?" Flight Deck Coordinator Mavorna said cheerfully from Illin's video pickup, now tuned to the communications network. She was a heavyset woman with midnight skin and clear green eyes.

"It's not my Thek," Illin said peevishly. "It just followed me home."

"That's what they all say, pumpkin. You've hooked yourself a geode, I hear."

"That's so," Illin admitted. A "geode" was a crystal strike that was deemed promising but couldn't be cracked in the field. Some of them panned out well, others proved to be deeply disappointing to the hopeful miner who found one. "I don't know who's in it. The Thek didn't say. It's still sealed."

"The Thek didn't say — ha, ha! When do they ever? I've got a crew and medics on the way down to the enclosed deck to meet you. Set down gently, now. The floor has just been polished. Remember, wait until the airlock siren shuts off before you unseal."

"Have I got a tri-vid team waiting to talk to me, too?" Illin asked hopefully.

"Sonny, there's more news than you happening today. Wait and see. You'll get the whole picture when you're down and in. I haven't got time to gossip."

With a throaty chuckle, Mavorna signed off. Her image was replaced on the screen with the day's designated frequency for the landing beacon. Illin tuned in and steered up toward the opening doors through which bright simulated daylight spilled. The Thek sailed silently behind him.

Tiny gnats were buzzing near her ears. "Lnz. Lnz. Dtr Mspw." She ignored them, refusing to open her eyes. Her skin hurt, especially her ears and lips. Gingerly, she put out her tongue and licked her lips. They were very dry. Suddenly, something cold and wet touched her mouth. She started, and cold stuff ran across her cheek and into her ear. The gnats began whining again, but their voices grew slower and more distinct. "Lunz. Lunzie. Doctor Mespil. That is your name, isn't it?"

Lunzie opened her eyes. She was lying on an infirmary bed, in a white room without windows. Three humans stood beside her, two in white medic tunics, and one in a miner's jumpsuit. And there was a Thek. She was so curious about why a Thek should be in her infirmary ward that she just stared at it, ignoring the others. The tall male human in medical whites leaned over her.

"Can you speak? I'm Doctor Stev Banus. You're on Descartes Platform 6, and I am the hospital administrator. Are you all right?"

Lunzie drew a deep breath, and let out a sigh of relief. "Yes, I'm fine. I'm very stiff, and my head is full of sawdust, but I'm all right."

"Iiiiinnnnnn-taaaaaaaaaccct?" the Thek rumbled. The others listened carefully and respectfully, and then turned to Lunzie. It must have been a query directed at her. She wished that she had more personal experience with the Theks, but none had ever spoken to her before. The others seemed to known what it was asking.

"Yes, I'm intact," she announced. She wished it had a face, or any attribute that she could relate to, but there was nothing. It looked like a hunk of building stone. She waited for a response.

The Thek said nothing more. As the humans watched it, the featureless pyramid rolled swiftly toward the door and out of the room.

"What was that Thek doing here?" Lunzie asked.

"I don't know," Stev explained, puzzled. "I'm not sure what it was looking for out there in the asteroid field. They're not easy to communicate with. This one is clearly friendly, but that's all we know. It was instrumental in finding you. It pointed you out to young Miner Romsey."

"I'm sorry I didn't thank it," Lunzie said flippantly. She pulled herself up into a sitting position. The human in white tunics rushed forward to support her as she settled against the head of the bed. She waved them away. "Where am I? This is the Mining Platform?"

"It is." The female medic smiled at her. She had perfectly smooth skin the color of coffee with cream, and deep brown eyes. Her thick black hair was in a long braid down her back. "My name is Satia Somileaux. I was born here."

Lunzie looked at her curiously. "Really? I thought the living quarters on the Platform were less than fifteen years old. You must be at least twenty."

"Twenty-four," Satia confessed, with a friendly and amused expression.

"How long was I asleep?"

The two doctors looked at each other, trying to decide what to say. Lunzie stared at them sharply. The dark-haired young man in the coverall shifted uncomfortably from one foot to the other and cleared his throat. Banus shot him a sly, knowing look out of the corner of his eye and turned to face him. "I haven't forgotten you, Illin Romsey. There's a substantial finder's fee for bringing a pod in, you know that."

"Well," the young man grinned, squinting thoughtfully. "It'll make up for losing that strike. Just. But I'd'a brought her in anyway. If I was shiplost, I sure hope someone would feel the same about bringing me home."

"Everyone is not so altruistic as you, young man. Self-interest is more prevalent than your enlightened attitude. Computer, record Miner Romsey's fee for retrieving escape pod . . . ?" The tall doctor looked to Lunzie for assistance.

"NM-EC-02," she said.

" . . . and verify by my voice code. If a check is necessary, refer requests to me."

"Acknowledged," said the flat voice of the computer.

"There you go, Miner," Stev said. "There's no security classification, so if you want to beat the rumor mill with your news . . . "

Illin Romsey grinned. "Thanks. I hope all's well for you, Doctor Mespil." The young man dropped a courteous bow and left the room.

Stev returned to Lunzie's side. "Of course, the fee is nothing compared to the back salary that is owing to you, Doctor Mespil. You were in the Company's employ at the time you underwent deepsleep. Descartes is honest about paying its debts. Come and talk to me later about your credit balance."

"How long have I been asleep?" Lunzie demanded.

"You must understand where the miner found you. Your capsule was not recovered when the other two pods from the, er, 'Nellie Mine' were brought in. Even they were difficult to locate. The search took more than three months."

"Is everyone else all right?" she asked quickly, immediately concerned for the other fourteen members of the Nellie's crew. Jilet had been so frightened of going into deepsleep again. She regretted not having ordered a sedative for him before he took the cryogenic.

Dr. Banus swiveled the computer screen on the table toward

him and drew his finger down the glass face. "Oh, yes, everyone else was just fine. There are normally no ill effects from properly induced cryogenic sleep. You should be feeling 'all go and on green' yourself."

"Yes, I do. May I make use of the Communications Center? I assume you notified my daughter, Fiona, when we escaped from the *Nellie Mine*. I'd like to communicate with her that I've been found. She's probably been worried sick about me. Unless, of course, there is an FTL shuttle going toward Tau Ceti soon? I must send her a message."

"Do you think she's still there?" Satia asked, frowning at Stev.

Lunzie watched the exchange between the two. "It's where I left her, in the care of a friend, another medical practitioner. She was only fourteen. . . . " Lunzie paused. The way the doctors were talking, it must have been a couple of years before they found the shuttle. Well, that was one of the risks of space travel. Lunzie tried to see Fiona as she might be now, if she continued to grow into her long legs. The adolescent curves must be more mature now. Lunzie hoped her daughter's mentor would have had the clothes-sense to guide the girl into becoming fashions instead of the radical leanings of teenagers. Then she noticed the over- whelming silence from the others, who were clearly growing more uncomfortable by the minute. Her intuition insisted some- thing was wrong. Lunzie looked suspiciously at the pair. When an FTL trip between star systems alone could take two or three years, a cold sleep stint at that length would hardly provoke worry in modern psychologists. More? Five years? Ten?

"You've very neatly sidestepped the question several times, but I won't allow you to do that any more. How long was I asleep? Tell me."

The others glanced nervously at each other. The tall doctor cleared his throat and sighed. "A long time," Stev said, casually, though Lunzie could tell it was forced. "Lunzie, it will do you no good to have me deceive you. I should have told you as you were waking up, to allow your mind to assimilate the information. I erred, and I apologize. It is just such an unusual case that I'm afraid my normal training failed me." Stev took a deep breath. "You've been in cryogenic sleep for sixty-two years."

Sixty-two — Lunzie's brain spun. She was prepared to be told that she had slept for a year, or two or three, even twelve, as Jilet had done, but sixty-two. She stared at the wall, trying to summon up even the image of a dream, anything that would prove to her that amount of time had passed. Nothing. She hadn't dreamed in cold sleep. No one did. She felt numb inside, trying to contain the shock. "That's impossible. I feel as though the collision occurred only a few minutes ago. I closed my eyes there. I opened them here. There is no gap in my perception between then and now."

"You see why I found it so difficult to tell you, Lunzie," Stev said gently. "It isn't so hard when the gap is under two years, as you know. That's generally the interval we have here on the Platform, when a miner has an accident in the field and has to send for help. The sleeper falls a little behind in the news of the day, but there's rarely a problem in assimilation. Working cryogenic technology is slightly over a hundred and forty years old. Your . . . er, interval is the longest I've ever been involved in. In fact the longest I've ever heard of. We will help you in any way we can. You have but to ask."

Lunzie's mind would still not translate sixty-two years into a perception of reality. "But that means my daughter . . ." Her throat closed up, refusing to voice her astonished thoughts. Fumbling, her hand reached for the hologram sitting on the pull-out shelf next to the bed. She could have accepted a seventeen- or eighteen-year-old Fiona instead of the youth she left, but a woman of seventy-six, an old woman, more than twice her age? "I'm only thirty-four, you know," she said.

Satia seated herself on the edge of the bed next to Lunzie and put a hand sympathetically on her arm. "I know."

"That means my daughter . . . grew up without me," Lunzie finished brokenly. "Had a career, boyfriends, children . . ." The smile in the Tri-D image beamed out at her, touching off memories of Fiona's laughter in her ears, the unconscious grace of a leggy girl who would became a tall, elegant woman.

"Almost certainly," the female doctor agreed.

Lunzie put her face in her hands and cried. Satia gathered her in her arms and patted her hair with a gentle hand.

"Perhaps we should give you a sedative and let you relax," Stev suggested, after Lunzie's sobs had softened and died away.

"No!" Lunzie glared at him, red-eyed. "I don't want to go to sleep again."

What am I saying? she thought, pulling herself together. It's just like Jilet described to me. Resentment. Fear of sleep. Fear of never waking again. "Perhaps someone could show me around the Platform until I get my bearings?" She smiled hopefully at the others. "I've just had too much relaxation."

"I will," Satia volunteered. "I am free this shift. We can send a query to Tau Ceti about your daughter."

The Communications Center was near the administrative offices in Cylinder One. Satia and Lunzie walked through the miles of domed corridors from the Medical Center in Cylinder Two. Lunzie was taking in the sights with her eyes wide open. According to Satia, the population of the Platform numbered over eight hundred adult beings. Humans made up about eighty-five percent, with heavyworlders, Wefts, and the birdlike Ryxi, along with a few other races Lunzie didn't recognize, making up the rest.

Heavyworlders were human beings, too, but they were a genetically altered strain, bred to inhabit high-gravity planets that were otherwise suitable for colonization, but had inhospitable conditions for "lightweight" normal humans. The males started at about seven feet in height, and went upward from there. Their facial features were thick and heavy, almost Neanderthal in character, and their hands, even those with proportionately slender fingers, were huge. The females were brawny. Lightweight women looked like dolls next to them. They made Lunzie nervous, as if they were an oversize carnival attraction. She had an uncomfortable feeling that they might fall over on her. Their pronounced brow ridges made many of the heavyworlders look perpetually angry, even when they smiled. She warily kept her distance from them.

Satia kept up a cheerful chatter as they walked along, pointing out people she knew, and talking about life on the Platform. "We're a small community," she commented cheerfully, "but it's harder to get away when you're feuding with someone. Privacy centers are absolutely inviolable on a deepspace platform. They help at most times, but Descartes really does detailed personality analyses to weed out the people who won't be able to get along on the Platform. There are community games and events every rest period, and we have a substantial library of both video and text. Boredom is one of the worst things that can happen in a closed community. I get to know everyone because I organize most of their children's events." Numbly, Lunzie kept pace with her, murmuring and smiling to Satia's friends without retaining a single name once the face was out of sight.

"Lep! Domman Lepke! Wait up!" Satia ran to intercept a tall, tan-skinned man in a high-collared tunic who was just disappearing between the automatic sliding doors. He peered around for the hailing voice, and smiled broadly when Satia waved.

"Lep, I want you to meet a new friend. This is Lunzie Mespil. She was just rescued from deepsleep. She's been lost for over sixty years."

"Oh, another deadtimer," Lepke said disapprovingly, shaking hands. "How do you do? Are you a 'nothing's changed' or an 'everything's changed'? Listen, Satia, have you heard the latest from the Delta beacon? Heavyworlders have claimed Phoenix. It must have been pirated!"

Satia, her mouth open to rebuke Lep for his insensitivity, stopped, her eyes widening with horror. "But that was initiated as an inhabited human colony, over six years ago."

"They claim now that the planet was empty of intelligent life when they got there, but there should be lightweights on that planet right now. No sign of them, or their settlement, *or* any clue as to what happened to them. Wiped clean off the surface, if they ever made it there in the first place. The FSP are releasing a list of settlers — the usual: 'anyone knowing the last whereabouts,' and so on." Lepke seemed pleased to have been the first to pass along the news. "Possession and viability make a colony, so no one can deny their claim if there's no evidence the planet was inhabited before they got there. The Others only know who's telling the truth."

"Oh, sweet Muhlah! It must have been pirated! Come on, Lunzie. We'll hear the latest." Pulling Lunzie behind her, the slim pediatrician raced toward the Communications Center.

When they arrived, there was already a large group of people gathered around the Tri-D field, talking and waving arms, tentacles, or paws.

"They had no right to take over that world. It was designated for lightweight humans. They're adapted to the high-G planets. Let them take those, and leave the light worlds to us!" a man with red hair expostulated angrily.

"It is not the first planet to be stripped and abandoned," said a young female with the near-perfect humanoid features a Weft shapechanger usually assumed when living among humans. Lunzie looked around quickly to find the Weft's co-mates. They always travelled in threes. "There was the rumor of Epsilon Indi not long ago. All its satellites were attacked at once. Phoenix is just the most recent dead planet brought to light."

"What happened to the colonists assigned to Phoenix?" a blond woman asked.

"No one knows," the communications tech said, manipulating the controls at the base of the holofield. "Maybe they never made it there. Maybe the Others got 'em. Here, I'll run the 'cast again for those of you who missed it. I'm patching down files as quickly as I can strip them off the beacon." The crowd shifted, as viewers who had already seen the report went away, and others pressed closer.

Squeezing between a broad-shouldered man in coveralls and a lizardlike Seti in an Administrator's tunic, Lunzie watched the report, which featured computer imaging of the new colony's living quarters and their industrial complex. What had happened to the other colonists? They must have relatives who would want to know. Humans weren't raised in a vacuum. Each of these was somebody's son. Or somebody's daughter.

"The FSP's official report was cool, but you could listen between the lines. They are horribly upset. Something's breaking down in their system. The FSP is supposed to protect nascent colonies," the blond woman complained to the man standing beside her.

"Only if they prove to be viable," the Weft corrected her. "There is always a period when the settlement must learn to stand on its own."

"It was their gamble," the Seti said, complacently, tucking its claws into the pouch pockets on the front of its tunic. "They lost."

"See here, citizens, if the heavyworlders can make a go of it, let them have the planet." This suggestion was promptly shouted down, to the astonishment of the speaker, a florid-faced human male in coveralls.

"It's a good thing the FSP don't have an attitude like yours," another growled. "Or your children won't have anywhere to live."

"There are plenty of new worlds for all out there," the coveralled man insisted. "It's a big galaxy."

"Look at us, we're all acting like this is news," the red-haired man grumbled. "Everything we get is months or years old. There's got to be a faster way to get information from the rest of civilization."

"Speed of light's all I've got," the tech smiled wryly, "unless you want to pay for a regular FTL mail run. Or talk the Fleet into letting us install an FTL link booster on the transmitter. Even that's not much faster."

Lunzie peered into the tank at the triumphant face of the Phoenix colony's leader, a broad-faced male with thickly branching eyebrows that shadowed his eyes. He was talking about agreements made for trade between Phoenix and the Paraden Company. All that was needed for a colony to be approved by the FSP was a viable population pool and proof that the colony could support itself in the galactic community. " . . . although this planet appears to be poor in the most valuable minerals, transuranics, there are still sufficient ores to be of interest. We have begun manufacture of . . . "

"The heavyworlders shouldn't claim that planet, even if the first colonists didn't survive," Satia declared. "There are many more planets with a high gravity than there are ones which fall within the narrow parameters that normal humans can bear."

"In my day," Lunzie began, then stopped, realizing how ridiculous she must sound, using an elder's phrase at her apparent physical age. "I mean, when I left Tau Ceti, the heavyworlders had just began colonizing. They were mostly still on Diplo, except for the ones in the FSP corps."

"You know, there must be a connection there somewhere," the red-haired man mused. "There was never planet-pirating before the heavyworlders started colonizing."

A huge hand seized the man's shoulder and spun him around. "That is a lie," boomed the voice of a heavyworlder-born man in a technician's tunic. "Planets have been found stripped and empty long hundreds of years before we existed. You want to blame someone, blame the Others. They're responsible for the dead worlds. Don't blame us." The heavyworlder glared down from his full seven feet of height at the man, and included Lunzie and Satia in his scorn. Lunzie shrank away from him. With a heavyworlder in its midst, the lightweight crowd began to disperse. None of the grumblers wanted to discuss Phoenix personally with one of the heavyweight humans.

The Others. A mysterious force in the galaxy. No one knew who they were, if indeed a race of Others, and not natural cataclysm, had caused destruction of those planets. Lunzie suddenly had a cold feeling between her shoulder blades, as if someone was watching her. She turned around. To her surprise, she saw the Thek that had rescued her waiting on the other side of the corridor. It had no features, no expression, but it drew her to it. She felt that it wanted to talk to her.

"Cccccccooooooooouuuuurrrrr . . . aaaaaaaaagggggggeee . . . Sssuurrrrrr . . . vvvviiiiiiiivvvveee . . . " it said, when she approached.

"Courage? Survive? What does that mean?" she demanded, but the pyramid of stone said nothing more. It glided slowly away. She wanted to run after it and ask it to clarify the cryptic speech. Theks were known for never wasting a word, especially not on explanation to simple ephemerals such as human beings.

"I suppose it meant that to be comforting," Lunzie decided. "After all, it saved my life, leading that young miner to where my capsule was lodged. But why in the Galaxy didn't it rescue me sooner, if it knew where I was?"

In her assigned room, Lunzie made herself comfortable in the deep, cushiony chair before the cubicle's computer screen. She glanced occasionally at the bunk, freshly made up with sweet-smelling bedding, but avoided touching it as if it was her dreaded enemy. Lunzie wasn't in the least sleepy, and there was still that nagging fear at the back of her mind that she would never wake up again if she succumbed.

Better to clear her brain with some useful input. Once she had run through the user's tutorial, she began systematically to go through the medical journals in Descartes library. She made a database of all the articles on new topics she wanted to read about. As she pored over her choices, she felt more and more lost. Everything in her field had advanced beyond her training.

As promised, Stev Banus had sat down with her and discussed the credits owed to her by Descartes. It amounted to a substantial balance, well over a million. He recommended she take it and go back to school. Stev told Lunzie that a position with Descartes was still open, if she wanted to take it. Even without up-to-date training, he felt that Lunzie would be an asset to his staff. With refresher courses under her belt, she could be promoted to department head under Stev's administration.

"We can't restore the years to you, but we can try to make you happy now you're here," he offered.

Lunzie was flattered, but she wasn't sure what to do. She resented having her life interrupted so brutally. She needed to come to terms with her feelings before she could make a decision. Stev's suggestion to seek further education made sense, but Lunzie couldn't make a move until she knew what had happened to Fiona. She went back to the file of medical abstracts and tried to drive away her doubts.

✧ CHAPTER THREE

"Did you sleep well?" Satia asked Lunzie the next morning. The intern leaned in through the door to Lunzie's cubicle and waved to get her attention.

Lunzie turned away from the computer screen and smiled. "No. I didn't sleep at all. I spent half the night worrying about Fiona, and the other half trying to get the synthesizer unit to pour me a cup of coffee. It didn't understand the command. How can I get the unit fixed?"

Satia laughed. "Oh, coffee! My grandmother told me about coffee when I was off-platform, visiting her on Inigo. It's very rare, isn't it?"

Lunzie frowned. "No. Where, or rather when, I come from it's as common as mud. And sometimes has a similar taste. . . . Do you mean to say you've never heard of coffee?" She felt her heart sink. So much had changed over the lost decades, but it was the little things that bothered her most, especially when they affected a lifelong habit. "I usually need something to help me wake up in the morning."

"Oh, I've *heard* of coffee. No one drinks it any more. There were studies decrying the effects of the heavy oils and caffeine on the nervous and digestive systems. We have peppers now."

"Peppers?" Lunzie wrinkled her nose in distaste. "As in capsicum?"

"Oh, no. Restorative. It's a mild stimulant, completely harmless. I drink some nearly every morning. You'll like it." Satia stepped to the synth unit in the wall of Lunzie's quarters, and came back with a full mug. "Try this."

Lunzie sipped the liquid and felt a pervasive tingle race through her tissues. Her body abruptly forgot that it had just spent an entire shift cramped in one position. She gasped. "That's very effective."

"Mm — Sometimes nothing else will get me out of bed. And it leaves behind none of the sour aftertaste my grandmother claimed from coffee."

"Well, here's to my becoming acclimated to the future." Lunzie raised her cup to Satia. "Oh, that reminds me. The gizmos in the lavatory have me stumped. I figured out which one was the waste-disposer unit, but I haven't the faintest idea what the others are."

Satia laughed again. "Very well. I ought to have thought of it before. I will give you the quarter-credit tour."

Once Lunzie had been shown how to work the various conveniences, Satia punched up a cup of herbal tea for them both.

"I don't understand these newfangled things perfectly yet, but at least I know what they do," Lunzie said, wryly self-deprecating.

Satia sipped tea. "Well, it's all part of the future, designed to make life easier. So the advertisements tell us. My friend, what are you going to do with your future?"

"The way I see it, I have two choices. I can search for Fiona, or I can take refresher courses to fit me to practice medicine in this century, and then try to find her. I had the computer research information for me on discoveries that were just breaking when I went into cold sleep. Progress has certainly been made. Those breakthroughs are now old hat! I feel like a primitive thrust into a city without even the vocabulary to ask for help."

"Perhaps you can stay and study with me. I am completing my internship here with Doctor Banus. I may do my residency off-platform, so as to give me a different perspective in the field of medicine. Specifically, I am studying pediatrics, a field that is becoming ever so important recently — we're having quite a population explosion on the Platform. Of course, that would mean leaving my children behind, and that I do not wish to do. Nonya's three, and Omi is only five months old. They're such a joy, I don't want to miss any of their childhood."

Lunzie nodded sadly. "I did the very same thing, you know. I'm not sure what I want to do, yet. I must work out where to begin."

"Well, come with me first." Satia rose and placed her cup in the disposer hatch for the food processor. "Aiden, the Tri-D technician, told me he wanted to talk to you." Lunzie put her cup aside and hastened after Satia.

"I sent your query to Tau Ceti last shift, Doctor," the technician said, when they located him at the Communications Center. "It'll take several weeks to get a reply out here in the rockies. But I wanted to tell you — " the young man tapped a finger on the console top, impatiently trying to stir his memory. "I think I've seen your surname before. I noticed it, I forget where . . . in one of the news articles we've received recently. Maybe it's one of your descendants?"

"Really?" Lunzie asked with interest. "Please, show me. I'm sure I have great-nieces and -nephews all over the galaxy by now."

Aiden keyed in an All-Search for the day's input from all six beacons. "Here it comes. Watch the field." The word "MESPIL" in a very clear, official-looking typestyle, coalesced in the Tri-D forum, followed by "FIONA, MD, DV." Other words in the same font formed around it, above and below.

"My daughter! That's her name. Satia, look! Where is she, Aiden? What's this list?" Lunzie demanded searching the names. "Is there video to go with it?"

The technician looked up from his console, and his expression turned to one of horror. "Oh, Krims, I'm sorry. Doctor, that's the FSP list. The people who were reported missing from the pirated Phoenix colony."

"No!" Satia breathed. She moved to support Lunzie, whose knees had gone momentarily weak. Lunzie gave her a grateful look, but waved her away, steady once again.

"What happens to people who were on planets that have been pirated?" she asked, badly shaken, trying not to let her mind form images of disaster. Fiona!

The young man swallowed. Bearing bad news was not something he enjoyed, and he desperately wanted to give this nice woman encouragement. She had been through so much already. He regretted that he hadn't checked out his information before sending for her. "Sometimes they turn up with no memory of what happened to them. Sometimes they are found working in other places, no problems, but their messages home just went astray. It happens a lot in galactic distant communications; nothing's perfect. Mostly, though, the people are never heard from again."

"Fiona can't be dead. How do I find out what became of her? I must find her."

The technician looked thoughtful. "I'll call Security Chief Wilkins for you. He'll know what you can do."

Chief Wilkins was a short man with a thin gray mustache that obscured his upper lip, and black eyes that wore a guarded expression. He invited her to sit down in his small office, a clean and tidy cubicle that said much about the mind of the man who occupied it. Lunzie explained her situation to him, but judged from his knowing nods that he knew all about her already.

"So what are you going to do?" he asked.

"I'm going to go look for her, of course," she said firmly.

"Fine, fine." He smiled. "Where? You've got your back pay. You have enough money to charge off anyway in the galaxy you wish and back again. Where will you begin?"

"Where?" Lunzie blinked. "I . . . I don't know. I suppose I could start at Phoenix, where she was last seen. . . ."

Wilkins shook his head, and made a deprecatory clicking sound with his tongue. "We don't know that for certain, Lunzie. She was expected there, along with the rest of the colonists."

"Well, the EEC should know if they arrived on Phoenix or not."

"Good, good. There's a start. But it's many light-years away from here. What if you don't find her there? Where next?"

"Oh." Lunzie sank back into the chair, which molded comfortably around her spine. "You're quite right. I wasn't thinking about *how* I would find her. All her life, I was able to walk to any place she might be. Nothing was too far away." In her mind, she saw a star map of the civilized galaxy. Each point represented at least one inhabited world. It took weeks, months, or even years to pass between some of those star systems, and searching each planet, questioning each person in every city. . . . She hugged her elbows, feeling very small and helpless.

Wilkins nodded approvingly. "You have ascertained the first difficulty in a search of this kind: distance. The second is time. Time has passed since that report was news. It will take more time to send out inquiries and receive replies. You must begin at the other end of history, and find out where she's been. Her childhood home, records of marriage or other alliances. And she must have had an employer at one time or another in her life. That will give you clues to where she is now.

"For example, why was she on that planetary expedition? As a settler? As a specialist? An observer? The EEC has records. You may have noticed" — here Wilkins activated the viewscreen on his desk and swiveled the monitor toward Lunzie — "that her name is followed by the initials MD and DV."

Lunzie confronted the FSP list once more, trying to ignore the connotation of disaster. "MD. She's a doctor. DV — " Lunzie searched her memory. "That denotes a specialty in virology."

"So she must have gone to University somewhere, too. Good, you would have wanted her to opt for Higher Education, I am sure. What did she do with her schooling? You have a great many clues to work with, but it will take many months, even years, for answers to come back to you. The best thing for you is to establish a permanent base of operations, and send out your queries."

"Stev Banus suggested I go back to school and update myself."

"A valid suggestion. While you're doing that, you'll also be accomplishing your search. If one line of questioning becomes fruitless, start others. Ask for help from any agency you think might be of use to you. Never mind if they duplicate your efforts. It is easier to have something you might have missed noticed by a fresh, non-involved mind. And it will be less expensive than running out to investigate prospects by yourself. It will be a costly search in any case, but you won't be in the thick of it, trying to make sense out of your incoming information without the perspective to consider it."

"I do need perspective. I've never had to deal on such a vast basis before. Her father and I corresponded regularly while she was growing up. It simply never occurred to me to think about the transit time between letters, and it was a long time! It's faster to fly FTL, but for me to think of travelling all that distance to a place, when I might not find her at the end of the journey . . . Fiona is too precious to me to allow me to think clearly. Thank you for your clear sight." Lunzie stood up. "And, Wilkins? Thank you for not assuming that she's dead."

"You don't believe she is. One of your other clues is your own insight. Trust it." The edges of the thin mustache lifted in an encouraging smile. "Good luck, Lunzie."

The child-care center was full of joyful chaos. Small humans chased other youngsters around the padded floor, shouting, careening off foam-core furniture, and narrowly missing the two adults who crouched in one of the conversation rings, trying to stay out of the way.

"Vigul!" Satia cried. "Let go of Tlink's tentacle and he will let go of your hair. Now!" She clapped her hands sharply, ignoring the disappointed "Awwwwww" from both children. She relaxed, but kept a sharp eye on the combatants. "They are normally good, but occasionally things get out of hand."

"They're probably acting up in the presence of a stranger — me!" Lunzie said, smiling.

Satia sighed. "I'm glad the Weft parents weren't around to see that. He's so young, he doesn't know yet that it's considered bad manners by his people to shape-shift in public. I'd rather that he learn to be himself with other children. It shows that he trusts them. That's good."

Beside Lunzie in his cot, Satia's infant son Omi twisted and stretched restlessly in his sleep. She picked up the infant and cradled him gently against her chest, his head resting on her shoulder. He subsided, sucking one tiny fist stuffed halfway into his mouth. Lunzie smiled down at him. She remembered Fiona at that age. She'd been in medical school, and every day carried the baby with her to class. Lunzie joyed in the closeness of the infant cradled in the snuggle pack, heartbeat to heartbeat with her. That perfect little life, like an exotic flower, that she'd created. The teachers made smiling reference to the youngest class member, who was often the first example of young humankind that an alien student ever encountered. Fiona was so good. She never cried during lectures, though she fretted occasionally in exams, seeming to sense Lunzie's own apprehension. Harshly, Lunzie put those thoughts from her mind. Those days were gone. Fiona was an adult. Lunzie must learn to think of her that way.

Omi snuggled in, removing the fist from his mouth for a tiny yawn and popping it back again. Lunzie hugged him, and shook her head aggressively. "I refuse to believe that Fiona is dead. I cannot, will not give up hope." She sighed. "But Wilkins is right. I've got to be patient, but it'll be the hardest thing I've ever done." Lunzie grinned ruefully. "None of my family is good at being patient. It's why we all become doctors. I have a lot to learn, and unlearn, too. Schoolwork will help me keep my mind in order."

"I'll miss you," Satia said. "We have become friends, I think. You'll always have a home here, if you want one."

"I don't think I'll ever have a home again," Lunzie said sadly, thinking of the vastness of the star map. "But thank you for the offer. It means a great deal to me." Gently, she laid the baby back in his cot. "You know, I went to see Jilet, the miner I was treating for agoraphobia before the *Nellie Mine* crashed. He's still hale and healthy, at ninety-two, good for another thirty years at least. His hair is white, and his chest has slipped into his belly, but I still recognized him on sight. Illin Romsey is his *grandson*. He prospected for some fifty years after his shuttle was rescued, and now he's working as a deck supervisor. I was glad to see him looking so well." Her lips twitched in a mirthless smile. "He didn't remember me. Not at all."

Astris Alexandria University was delighted to accept an application for continuing education from one of their alumni, but they were obviously taken aback when Lunzie, dressed very casually and carrying her own luggage, arrived in the administration office to enroll for classes. Lunzie caught the admissions secretary surreptitiously running her identification to verify her identity.

"I'm sorry for the abrupt reception, Doctor Mespil, but frankly considering your age, we were expecting someone rather more mature in appearance. We only wanted to make sure. May I ask, have you been taking radical rejuvenative therapy?"

"My age? I'm thirty-four," Lunzie stated briskly. "I've been in cold sleep."

"Oh, I see. But for our records, ninety-six years have passed since your birth. I'm afraid your ID code bracelet and transcripts will reflect that," the registrar offered with concern. "I will make a note for the files regarding your circumstances and physical age, if you request."

Lunzie held up a hand. "No, thank you. I'm not that vain. If it doesn't confuse anyone, I can live without a footnote. There's another matter with which you can help me. What sort of student housing, bed and board, can the University provide? I'm looking for quarters as inexpensive as I can get, so long as it still has communication capability and library access and storage. I'll even share sanitary facilities, if needed. I have few personal possessions, and I'm easy enough to get along with."

The registrar seemed puzzled. "I would have thought . . . your own apartment, or a private domicile. . . . "

"Unfortunately, no. I need to leave as much of my capital

resources as possible free to cope with a personal matter. I'm cutting back on all non-essentials."

Clearly, the woman's sense of outrage regarding the dignity and priorities of Astris Alexandria alumni was kindled against Lunzie. She was too casual, too careless of her person. Her only luggage was the pair of small and dowdy synth-fabric duffles slung across the back of the opulent office chair in which she sat. Not at all what one would expect of a senior graduate of this elite seat of learning.

To Lunzie's relief, her cases had been kept in vacuum temperatures in remote storage on the Mining Platform, so that none of her good fiber-fabric clothes were perished or parasite-eaten. She didn't care what sort of state the University wanted her to keep. Now that she had acknowledged her goals, she could once more take command of her own life as she had been accustomed to doing. Austerity didn't bother her. She preferred a spare environment. She had felt helpless on the Descartes platform, in spite of everyone's kindness. This was a familiar venue. Here she knew just exactly how much power the authorities had, and how much was empty protest. She kept her expression neutral and waited patiently.

"Well," the woman allowed, at last. "There is a quad dormitory with only a Weft trio sharing it at present. There is a double room with one space opening up. The tenant is being graduated, and the room will be clear within two weeks, when the new term begins. One room of a six-room suite in a mixed-species residence hall. . . . "

"Which is the cheapest?" Lunzie asked, abruptly cutting short the registrar's recitation. She smiled sweetly at the woman's scowl.

With a look of utter disapproval, the registrar put her screen on Search. The screen blurred, then stopped scrolling as one entry centered itself and flashed. "A third share of a University-owned apartment. The other two current tenants are human. But it is rather far away from campus."

"I don't mind. As long as it has a roof and a cot, I'll be happy."

Juggling an armful of document cubes and plas-sheet evaluation forms as well as her bags, Lunzie let herself into the small foyer of her new home. The building was old, predating Lunzie's previous university term. It made her feel at home to see something that hadn't changed appreciably. The old-fashioned textboard in the building's entryhall flashed with personal messages for the students who lived there, and a new line had already appeared at the bottom, adding her name and a message of welcome, followed by a typical bureaucratic admonishment to turn in her equivalency tests as soon as possible. The building was fairly quiet. Most of the inhabitants would have day classes or jobs to attend to.

Her unit was on the ninth level of the fifty-story hall. The turbovator *whooshed* satisfyingly to its destination, finishing up on her doorstep with a slight jerk and a noisy rattle, not silently as the unnerving lifts aboard the Platform had. Neither of her roommates was home. The apartment was of reasonably good size, clean, though typically untidy. The shelves were cluttered with the usual impedimenta of teenagers. It made her feel almost as if she were living with Fiona again. One of the tenants enjoyed building scale models. Several of them were hung from the ceiling, low enough that Lunzie was glad she wasn't five inches taller.

A little searching revealed that the vacant sleeping chamber was the smallest one, closest to the food synthesizer. She unpacked and took off her travel-soiled clothes. The weather, one of the things that Lunzie had always loved about Astris Alexandria, was mild and warm most of the year in the University province, so she happily shed the heavier trousers she had worn on the transport, and laid out a light skirt.

The trousers were badly creased, and could use cleaning. Lunzie felt she would be the better for a good wash, too. She assumed that all the standard cleaning machinery would be available in the lavatory. She gathered up toiletries, laundry, and her dusty boots.

In the lavatory, Lunzie stared with dismay at the amenities. Instead of being comfortably familiar, they were spankingly brand new. The building's facilities had been very recently updated, even newer and stranger than the ones Descartes furnished to its living quarters. If it hadn't been for Satia's patient help on the Platform, she would not now have the faintest idea what she was looking at. There were enough similarities between them for her to figure out how to use these without causing a minor disaster.

While her clothes were being processed, she slipped on fresh garments and sat down at the console in her bedroom. She logged on to the library system, and requested an ID number which would give her access to the library from any console on the planet. Automatically, she applied for an increase in the standard student's allotment of long-term memory storage from 320K to 2048K, and opened an account in the Looking-GLASS program. If there was any stored data about Fiona anywhere, the Galactic Library All-Search System, GLASS, as it was fondly known, would find it. As an icon to luck, she set Fiona's hologram on top of the console.

LOOKING-GLASS LOG-ON (2851.0917 Standard) scrolled up on her screen.

She typed in *Query Missing Person* NAME *Fiona Mespil* DOB/RACE/SEX/S,PO *2775.0903/human/female/ Astris Alexandria* She had been born right here at the University, so that was her planet of origin. *Current location requested.* LOCATION SUBJECT LAST SEEN? Lunzie paused for a moment, then entered: *Last verifiable location, Tau Ceti colony, 2789.1215. Last presumed location, Phoenix colony, 2851.0421.* The screen went blank for a moment as GLASS digested her request. Lunzie entered a command for the program to dump its findings into her assigned memory storage and prepared to log off.

Suddenly, the screen chimed and scrolled up a display of dates and entries, with the heading:

MESPIL, FIONA
TRANSCRIPT OF EDUCATION (REVERSE
  CHRONOLOGICAL)
2802 GRANTED DEGREE CERTIFICATE IN
  BIOTECHNOLOGY, ASTRIS ALEXANDRIA
  UNIVERSITY
2797 GRANTED DEGREE CERTIFICATE IN
  VIROLOGY, ASTRIS ALEXANDRIA UNIVERSITY
2795 ASTRIS ALEXANDRIA UNIVERSITY,
  GRADUATED WITH HONORS, M.D. [GENERAL]
2792 GRADUATED MARSBASE SECONDARY
  SCHOOL EDUCATION SYSTEM, GRADUATED
  GENERAL CERTIFICATE
2791 TAU CETI EDUCATION SYSTEM, TRANSFERRED
2787 CAPELLA PRIMARY SCHOOL EDUCATION
  SYSTEM, GRADUATED

Following was a list of courses and grades. Lunzie let out a shout of joy. Records existed right here on Astris Alexandria! She hadn't expected to see anything come up yet. She was only laying the groundwork for her information search. The search was beginning to bear fruit already. *Save*, she commanded the computer.

"I should have known," she said, shaking her head. "I might have known she'd come here to Astris, after all the hype I'd given the place." The first successful step in her search! For the first time, Lunzie truly felt confident. A celebration was in order. She surveyed the apartment, and advanced smiling on the food synthesizer. One success deserved another.

"Now," she said, rubbing her hands together. "I am going to teach *you* how to make coffee."

An hour or so later, she had a potful of murky brew that somewhat resembled coffee, though it was so bitter she had to program a healthy dose of a mellowing sweetener with which to dilute it. There was caffeine in the stuff, at any rate. She was satisfied though still disappointed that the formula for coffee had disappeared from use over the last sixty years. Still, there was a School of Nutrition in the University. Someone must still have coffee on record. She considered ordering a meal, but decided against it. If the food was anything like she remembered it, she wasn't that hungry. Synthesized food always tasted flat to her, and the school synth machines were notoriously bad. She had no reason to believe that their reputation — or performance — had improved in her absence.

When time permitted, Lunzie planned to treat herself to some real planet-grown food. Astris Alexandria had always produced tasty legumes and greens, and perhaps, she thought hopefully, the farm community had even branched out into coffee bushes. Like all civilized citizens of the FSP, Lunzie ate only foods of vegetable origin, disdaining meats as a vestige of barbaric history. She hoped neither of her roommates was a throwback, though the Housing Committee would undoubtedly have seen to it that such students would be isolated, out of consideration to others.

Following the instructions of the plas-sheets, she logged into the University's computer system and signed up for a battery of tests designed to evaluate her skills and potential. The keyboard had a well-used feel, and Lunzie quickly found herself rattling along at a clip. One of the regulations which had not existed in her time was registration qualification: enrollment for certain classes was restricted to those who qualified through the examinations. Lunzie noted with irritation that several of the courses which she wanted to take fell into that category. The rationale, translated from the bureaucratese, was that space was so limited in these courses that the University wanted to guarantee that the students who signed up for them would be the ones who would get the most out of them. Even if she passed the exams, there was no guarantee that she could get in immediately. Lunzie gave a resigned shrug. Until she had a good lead on finding Fiona, she was filed here. There was no hurry. She started to punch in a request for the first exam.

"Hello?" a tentative voice called from the door.

"Come?" Lunzie answered, peering over the edge of the console.

"Peace, citizen. We're your roommates." The speaker was a slender boy with straight, silky black hair and round blue eyes. He didn't look more than fifteen Standard years old. Behind him was a smiling girl with soft brown hair gathered up in a puffy coil on top of her head. "I'm Shof Scotny, from Denmarkis. This is Pomayla Esglar."

"Welcome," Pomayla said, warmly, offering her hand. "You didn't have the privacy seal on the door, so we thought it would be all right to come in and greet you."

"Thank you," Lunzie replied, rising and extending hers. Pomayla covered it with her free hand. "It's nice to meet you. I'm Lunzie Mespil. Call me Lunzie. Ah . . . is something wrong?" she asked, catching a curious look that passed between Shof and Pomayla.

"Nothing," Shof answered lightly. "You know, you don't look ninety-six. I expected you to look like my grandmother."

"Well, thank you so much. You don't look old enough to be in college, my lad," Lunzie retorted, amused. She reconsidered asking the registrar to put an explanation on her records.

Shof sighed long-sufferingly. He'd obviously heard that before. "I can't help it that I'm brilliant at such a tender age." Lunzie grinned at him. He was hopelessly cute and likely accustomed to getting away with murder.

Pomayla elbowed Shof in the midriff, and he let out an

outraged *oof!* "Forgive Mr. Modesty. They don't bother teaching tact to the Computer Science majors, since the machines don't take offense at bad manners. I'm in the Interplanetary Law program. What's your field of study?"

"Medicine. I'm back for some refresher courses. I've been . . . rather out of touch the last few years."

"I'll bet. Well, come on, granny," the boy offered, slinging a long forelock of hair out of his eyes. "We'll start getting you up to date this millisecond."

"Shof!" Pomayla shoved her outrageous roommate through the door. "Tact?"

"Did I say something wrong already?" Shof asked with all the ingenuousness he could muster as he was propelled out into the turbovator.

Lunzie followed, chuckling.

Looking-GLASS turned up nothing of note over the next several weeks. Lunzie submerged herself in her new classes. Her roommates were gregarious and friendly, and insisted that she participate in everything that interested them. She found herself hauled along to student events and concerts with them and their "Gang," as they called themselves, a loose conglomeration of thirty or so of all races from across the University. There seemed to be nothing the group had in common but good spirits and curiosity. She found their outings to be a refreshing change from the long hours of study.

No topic was sacred to the Gang, not physical appearance, nor habits, age, or custom. Lunzie soon got tired of being called granny by beings whose ages surely equaled her own thirty-four Standard years. The subject of her cold sleep and subsequent search for her daughter was still too painful to discuss, so she lightly urged the conversation away from personal matters. She wondered if Shof knew about her search, seeing as he had already unlocked her admissions records. If he did, he was being unusually reticent in not bringing it up. Perhaps she managed to lock her GLASS file tightly enough away from his prying gaze. Or perhaps he just didn't feel it was interesting enough. In most cases when someone started a query, she would carefully reverse the flow and launch a personal probe into the life of her inquisitor, to the amusement of the Gang, who loved watching Lunzie go into action.

"You ought to have taken up Criminal Justice," Pomayla insisted. "I'd hate to be on the witness stand, hiding anything from you."

"No, thank you. I'd rather be Doctor McCoy than Rumpole of the Bailey."

"Who?" demanded Cosir, one of their classmates, a simian Brachian with handsome purple fur and reflective white pupils. "What is this Rompul?"

"Something on Tri-D," Shof speculated.

"Ancient history," complained Frega, another of the Gang, polishing her ebony-painted nails on her tunic sleeve.

"Nothing I've ever heard of," Cosir insisted. "That's got to have been off the Forum for a hundred Standard years."

"At least that," Lunzie agreed gravely. "You could say I'm a bit of an antiquarian."

"And at your age, too!" chortled Shof. He clutched his hands over his narrow belly. He tapped a fist on it and pretended to listen for the echo. "Hmm. I've gone hollow. Let's go eat."

Lectures were, on the whole, as dull as Lunzie remembered them. Only two courses kept her interest piqued. Her practicum in Diagnostic Science was interesting, as was the required course in Discipline.

Diagnostic science had changed enormously since she had practiced medicine. The computerized tests to which incoming patients were subjected were less intrusive and more comprehensive than she would have believed possible. Her mother, from whom Lunzie had inherited the "healing hands," had always felt that to be a good doctor, one needed only a thoroughgoing grasp of diagnostic science and an excellent bedside manner. Her mother would have been as pleased as she was to know that Fiona had followed in the family tradition and pursued a medical career.

Diagnostic instruments were no longer so cumbersome as they had been in her day. Most units could be carried two or three in a pouch, saving time and space in case of an emergency. Lunzie's favorite was the "bod bird," a small medical scanner that required no hands-on use. Using new anti-gravity technology, it would hover at any point around a patient and display its readings. It was especially good for use in zero-G. The unit was very popular among physicians who specialized in patients much larger than themselves, and non-humanoid doctors who considered extending manipulative digits too close to another being as an impolite intrusion. Lunzie liked it because it left her hands free for patient care. She made a note of the "bod bird" as one of the instruments she would buy for herself when she went back into practice. It was expensive, but not completely out of her range.

Once data had been gathered on a subject's condition, the modern doctor had at her command such tools as computer analysis to suggest treatment. The program was sophisticated enough that it gave a physician a range of choices. In extreme but not immediately life-threatening cases, recombinant gene-splicing, chemical treatment, or intrusive or non-intrusive surgery might be suggested. It was up to the physician to decide which would be best in the case. Types of progressive therapy now in use made unnecessary many treatments that would formerly have been considered mandatory to save a patient's life.

Lunzie admired her new tools, but she was not happy with the way attitudes toward medical treatment had altered in the last six decades. Too much of the real work of the physician had been taken out of the hands of the practitioner and placed in the "hands" of cold, impersonal machines. She openly disagreed with her professors that the new way was better for the patients because there was less chance of physician error or infection.

"Many more will give up the will to live for lack of a little personal care," Lunzie pointed out to the professor of Cardiovascular Mechanics, speaking privately with him in his office. "The method for repairing the tissues of a damaged heart is technically perfect, yes, but what about a patient's feelings? The mood and mental condition of your patient are as important as the scientific treatment available for his ailment."

"You're behind the times, Doctor Mespil. This is the best possible treatment for cardiac patients suffering from weak artery walls that are in danger of aneurysm. The robot technician can send microscopic machines through the patient's very bloodstream to stimulate regrowth of damaged tissue. He need never be worried by knowing what is going on inside him."

Lunzie crossed her arms and fixed a disapproving eye on him. "So they're not troubled by asking what's happening to them? Of course, there are some patients who have never known anything but unresponsive doctors. I suppose in your case it wouldn't make any difference."

"That's unjust, Doctor. I want what is best for my patients."

"And I want to do more than tending the machines tending the patient," Lunzie shot back. "I'm a doctor, not a mechanic."

"And I am a surgeon, not a psychologist."

"Well! It doesn't surprise me in the least that the psychology professor disagrees with your principles one hundred percent! You're not improving your patient's chances for survival by working on him as if he was an unaware piece of technological scrap that needs repair."

"Doctor Mespil," the cardiologist said, tightly. "As you so rightly point out, the patient's mental condition is responsible for a significant part of his recovery. It is his choice whether to live or die after receiving quality medical care. I refuse to interfere with free will."

"That is a ridiculous cop-out."

"I assume from your antiquated slang that you think I am shirking my duties. I am aware that you have published in respected scientific journals and have a background in medical ethics. Commendable. I have even read your abstracts in back issues of *Bioethics Quarterly*. But may I remind you of your status? You are my student, and I am your teacher. While you are in my class, you will learn from me. And I would appreciate it if you would cease to harangue me in front of your fellows. However many hands you wish to hold sympathetically when you leave my course is entirely up to you. Good afternoon."

After ending that unsatisfying interview, Lunzie stormed into the gymnasium for a good workout with her Discipline exercises.

Discipline was a required study for high-level physicians, medical technicians, and those who wanted to pursue deep-space explorations. The tests she'd taken showed her to have a natural aptitude for it but she dreaded having to set aside the hours necessary to complete the course. She had moved from the basic studies to Adept training years ago. Discipline was time-consuming but more than that, it was exhausting. She was dismayed to discover that her new teacher insisted that at least six hours every day be devoted to exercises, meditation, and practice of concentration. It left little time for any other activity. The short months since she had practiced Discipline showed in softened muscles and a shortened attention span.

After a few weeks, she was pleased to notice that the exercises had put more of a spring back in her walk and lessened her dependency on her ersatz coffee. She could wake up effortlessly most mornings, even after little sleep. She had forgotten how good it felt to be in shape. Meditation techniques made that sleep more refreshing, since it was possible to subsume her worries about Fiona by an act of will, banishing her concerns temporarily to the back of her mind.

Her memory retention improved markedly. She found it easier to assimilate new data, such as the current political leanings and policies as well as the new styles and colloquialisms, besides the data from her schoolwork. It was clear, too, that she was in better physical shape than she had been in years. Her bottom had shrunk one trouser size and her belly muscles had tightened up. She mentioned her observations to Pomayla, who promptly pounced on her and dragged her out to the stores to buy new clothes.

"It's a terrific excuse. I didn't want to mention it before, Lunzie, but your garb is *dated*. We weren't sure if that was the way fashions are on your homeworld, or if you couldn't afford new clothes."

"What makes you think I can now?" Lunzie asked calmly.

Pomayla, embarrassed, struggled to get her confession out. "It's Shof. He says you have plenty of credits. He really is brilliant with computers, you know. Um." She turned away to a synth unit for a pepper. With her face hidden from Lunzie, she admitted, "He opened your personal records. He wanted to know why you look so young at your age. Were you truly in cold sleep for sixty years?"

Lunzie refused to be shocked. She'd suspected something of the kind would happen eventually. "I don't remember anything about it, to be honest, but I find it difficult to argue with the facts. Drat Shof. Those records were sealed!"

"You can't keep him out of anything. I bet he knows how many fastenings you've got in your underthings, too. We get along as roommates because I treat him the same way I treat my little brother: respect for his abilities, and none for his ego. It's a good thing he has a healthy moral infrastructure, or he'd be rolling in credits with a straight A average. Oh, come on, let go of a little money. All you ever use it for is your mysterious research. Fashions have changed since you bought that outfit. No one wears trousers tight about the calves any more. You'll feel better about yourself. I promise."

"Well . . . " Shof must not have found her GLASS file yet. Thank goodness. There were other things in her records which she didn't want to have found, such as her involvement as a student on a clone colony ethics panel. Surely by now the laundered details of the aborted project had been made public, but she couldn't be sure how they would feel about her involvement in it. Clone technology was anathema to most people. Lunzie weighed the price of a few garments against the cost of data search. Perhaps she had been keeping too tight a hand on the credit balance. Even though she hated the flatness of synth food she had even been eating it exclusively to save the cost of real-meals. Every fraction of a credit must be available for the search for Fiona. Perhaps she was allowing her obsession to run her life. It wouldn't make all that much difference, with the interest her credits were earning, to spend a little on herself.

"All right. We can shop for a while, and you can drop me off at the Tri-D forum afterward. I want to see today's news."

Lunzie had taken to heart Security Chief Wilkin's advice to make use of every source of information she could. At the EEC office, she filled out hundreds of forms requesting access to any documents they had on Fiona, and asking how she was involved in the doomed Phoenix colony.

For doomed it was. In the interval since she had seen the first report about Phoenix, an independent merchant ship had made planetfall there to trade with the colonists and had its story to the Tri-D. The merchant brought back vid-cubes of the terrain, which showed the "smoking hole" where the lightweight camp had been. The merchant had also affirmed that the heavyweight humans now living there were possessed of no weapons of that magnitude and could not possibly have caused the colony's destruction. Lunzie, who had conceived a dislike for heavyworlders that surprised her, mistrusted such a blanket assurance, but the colonists had gone under oath and sworn the planet was vacant when they landed. In any case, they had proved the viability of their own settlement, and were now entitled to FSP privileges and protection. Looking-GLASS told her much the same thing.

The heavyworlders had their own disappointments, too. The original EEC prospect report, made twelve years before the original colony was launched, had stated that Phoenix had copious radioactive ores that could be easily mined because upthrust folds in the planet's surface had brought much of it in reach. Their rad counters didn't so much as murmur. The planet's crust had been swept clean of transuranics. If the Phoenix settlers were hoping to become a trading power in the FSP with a new source of the ever-scarce ores, they were frustrated. Rather than chalk the omission off to the unknown Others, as the Tri-D chat-show presenters were doing, the FSP was suggesting that the original report had been in error. Lunzie doubted it. Her resentment for the unknown planet pirates redoubled. Her hopes of finding Fiona alive were slipping away.

The University's Tri-D Forum was a public facility for use free of charge by any individual. Cheap entertainment on Astris was fairly limited beyond outdoor concerts and Tri-D, and Tri-D was the only one which was held in all weathers. The display field hovered several feet above the ground in a lofty hexagonal chamber lined with tiered benches. The Forum was seldom filled to capacity, except during reception of important sports events, but it was never completely empty. News broadcasts and reports of interest were received throughout the day and night, the facts recited in FSP Basic, with Basic subtitling over the videos of local language events. Astris University authorities tried to keep it from becoming a haven for the homeless, preferring to divert those luckless beings to shelters, but even at night there were usually a few citizens watching the broadcast: insomniacs, natural nocturnals, a few passing the time between night classes, or just those who were unwilling to let the day end. Lunzie noted that most of those who used the facility were older and more mature than the average. Entertainment Fora were available to the younger set who weren't interested in the current news.

Lunzie went there whenever sleep eluded her, but her usual time to view Tri-D was late morning, just before the midday meal. A dozen or so regulars smiled at her or otherwise acknowledged her presence when she came in after shopping with Pomayla. She kept her head down as she found her accustomed seat. Though she hated to admit it to herself, she was becoming addicted to Tri-D. Lunzie watched all the news, human interest stories as well as hard fact documentation. Nothing much had changed but the names in the sixty-two years since she was in the stream. Piracy, politics, disaster, joy, tears, life. New discoveries, new science, new prejudices to replace the old ones. New names for old things. The hardest thing to get used to was how old the world leaders and public figures of her day were now. So many of them were dead of old age, and she was still thirty-four. It made her feel as though there was something immoral in her, watching them, secure in her extended youth. She promised herself that when she was sufficiently familiarized with the news events of her lost years, she would quit stopping in to the Forum every morning, but she didn't count on keeping that promise.

The round-the-clock headline retrospective aired at midday. Lunzie always waited through that to see if there was any story that might relate to Fiona, and then went on with her day. She had arrived at the Forum later than usual. The headline portion was just ending as she entered the dim arena. "There is nothing new since yesterday," one of the regulars, a human man, whispered as he stood up to leave.

"Thanks," Lunzie murmured back. The Tri-D field filled the room with light as another text file appeared, and she met his eyes. He smiled down at her, and eased his way out along the bench toward the exit. Lunzie settled in among her parcels. Watching repeats of earlier broadcasts didn't bore her. She considered Tri-D in the light of an extracurricular course in the interaction of living beings. She was instantly absorbed in the unfolding story in the hovering field.

✧ CHAPTER FOUR

Lunzie had no classes that afternoon, so following her visit to the Forum, she decided to stop in at the EEC office. It had been nearly a Standard year since she filled out the forms requesting Fiona's records. So far, she hadn't been told anything, but every time she came in there were more forms to fill out. She was becoming frustrated with the bureaucratic jumble, smelling a delaying technique, and an irritating one at that. Her temper had reached the fraying point.

"You're just giving me more paperwork so you don't have to tell me you don't know anything," Lunzie accused a thin-faced clerk over the ceramic-topped counter between them. "I don't believe you've even advanced my query to the FSP databanks."

"Really, Citizen, such an accusation. These things take time . . ." the man began, patiently, glancing nervously at the other clerks.

Lunzie held on to her temper with all of her will. "I have given you time, Citizen. I am Doctor Mespil's next of kin, and I want to know what she was doing on that expedition and where she is now."

"This information will be sent to you by comm link. There is no need to come into this facility every time you have questions."

"Nothing ever gets answered anyway. I've never had information passed on to me even when I do come here in person. *Have* you sent my queries on to the FSP databank?"

"Your caseworker should be keeping you posted on details."

"I don't have a caseworker." Lunzie's voice rose up the scale from a growl to a shriek. "I've never been assigned one. I've never been told I *needed* one."

"Ah. Well, if you'll just fill out these forms requesting official assistance, I will see who has room in their caseload for you." The clerk blithely fanned a sheaf of plas-sheets before her, and disappeared through the swinging partitions before she could fire off an angry retort.

Muttering furiously to herself, Lunzie picked up the stylus and pulled the forms over. More of the same nonsense. Heartless bureaucratic muckshovelers. . . .

Some days later, she was back filling out yet another form.

"Excuse me, Doctor Mespil." Lunzie looked up to find a tall man standing over her. "My name is Teodor Janos. I'll be your caseworker. I . . . haven't we met?" He sat down across from her and peered at her closely. His straight black brows wrinkled together.

"No, I don't think so — Wait a milli." She blinked at him, trying to place him, then smiled. "Never formally, I'm afraid. I've seen you at the Tri-D."

Teodor threw his head back and laughed. "Of course. A fellow viewer. Yes. You leave before I do most days, I think. I saw you, only a short time ago, on my way out. Good, then we have something in common. I am supposed to relate to you as closely as I can. But not too much. Officially." His smile was warm, and slightly mischievous.

"You're new at this," Lunzie guessed.

"Very. I've only been in this position since the beginning of the year. Would you prefer a caseworker with more experience? I can find one for you."

"No. You'll do just fine. You're the first person with any life in you I've seen in this office."

That set him laughing again. "Some would say that is a disadvantage," Teodor admitted humorously, showing even, white teeth. "Let us see. You wish information on your daughter, also a doctor, whose name is Fiona, and who was involved in the Phoenix expedition, which ended in failure."

"That's right."

He consulted an electronic clipboard. "And the last time you had contact with her was when she was fourteen? And she is how old now?"

"Seventy-seven," Lunzie confessed, and braced herself for a jibing remark. "An accident to my space transport forced me into cold sleep."

To her surprise, Teodor only nodded. "Ah. So the dates in this record are accurate. Another thing which we have in common, Lunzie. May I call you Lunzie? Such an unusual name."

"Certainly, citizen Janos."

"I am Tee. Teodor to my parents and my employer, only."

"Thank you, Tee."

"So, let us go over your questions, please, if you don't mind. I promise you, it is the last time."

With a deep sigh, Lunzie started from the top of her now-familiar recitation. "When I disappeared, Fiona was sent from Tau Ceti to my brother Edgard on MarsBase. She finished school there, and came here to study medicine. Her first employer was Doctor Clora, affiliated with Didomaki Hospital. She went into private practice and got married. According to transmissions found for me by Looking-GLASS, she applied to the FSP a few years after that. And that is the last I've been able to discover. Everything else about her is locked up in the databanks of the FSP, and no one will tell me anything."

Tee frowned sympathetically. "I will get information for you, Lunzie," he promised. "Is your communications code here? I'll notify you whenever I find something."

With greater hope than she had felt in weeks, Lunzie walked out into the warm air. She was in such good spirits she decided to go back to her quarters on foot. It was a long walk, but the day was fine and clear. Her parcels bumped forgotten against her back.

She checked the message board automatically on her way into the residence hall. Beneath the school's notices and invitations for the three roommates from the Gang was a small, frantically flashing message: "Lunzie, call Tee," and a code number. Lunzie hurried up to the apartment, tossed her parcels onto her bed, and flew over to the Communications Center. She danced impatiently from one foot to the other, waiting for the connection to go through.

"Tee, I got your message. What is it?" she demanded of the image on the comset breathlessly. "What is it? What have you found?"

"Nothing, nothing but you, lovely lady," Tee replied.

"What?" Lunzie shrieked, disbelievingly. She couldn't have heard him correctly. "Say that again? No, don't — What has this to do with my investigation?"

"Only my eagerness to know the querent better: you. It occurred to me only when you had gone, that I would enjoy escorting you to dinner this evening. But it was too late to ask. You had already departed. So I called and left a message. You do not mind?" he inquired, his voice a soothing purr.

One part of Lunzie felt extremely let down, but the rest of her was flattered by the attention. "I don't mind, I suppose, though you could have been less cryptic in your message."

"Ah, but the mystery made you react more quickly." Tee smiled wickedly. "I finish work very soon. Shall I come by for you?"

"It's a long way out here. I'm at the tail end of the '15' Transportation Line. Why don't we meet?"

"Why not? Where?" Tee asked.

In spite of his audacity, Tee proved otherwise to be a courteous and charming companion. He chose the restaurant, one of Astris' finest, and stated unequivocally that he would pay for both their meals, but he insisted that Lunzie choose from the menu for both of them.

Lunzie, fond of good food and wine, and weary of student synth-swill, went down the list with a critical eye. The selection was very good, and she was pleased by the variety, exclaiming over a few of her old favorites which the restaurant offered. To the human server's obvious approval, she selected a well-orchestrated dinner in every detail from appetizers to dessert. "I have a heirloom recipe from my great-granny for the potatoes Vesuvio. If their dish is anything like hers, this meal will be worth eating."

"But you must also choose wines," Tee offered, temptingly.

"Oh, I couldn't," Lunzie said. "This will already cost the wide blue sky."

"Then I shall." And he did, choosing a wine Lunzie loved, one which wouldn't be overpowered by the garlic in the main course; and finishing up for dessert with a fine vintage blue Altairian cordial, the price of which he would not let Lunzie see.

Lunzie enjoyed her meal wholeheartedly, both the food and the company. Because of their common interest in Tri-D, she and Tee were able to converse almost infinitely on a range of subjects, including galactic politics and trends. Their opinions were dissimilar, but to her relief, not mutually exclusive. Beyond the outrageous compliments he paid her throughout the meal, which

Lunzie saw as camouflage fireworks for a sensitive nature that had been wounded in the past, Tee was otherwise an interesting and intelligent companion. They talked about cooking and compared various ethnic cuisines they had tried. Tee loved his food as much as she did, though his frame was the ectomorphic sort that would never wear excess weight for long. Lunzie looked down cautiously at the shimmering, teal tissue sheath that she had purchased that afternoon at Pomayla's urging. It was gorgeous, but outlined every curve. That wouldn't fit long if she indulged like this too frequently.

Tee was a man of expansive physical gestures. He waved his hands to underscore the importance of a point he was making, nearly to the destruction of the meals for the next table, being delivered at that moment by a server. Lunzie always noticed hands. His were long-boned but very broad in the palm, and the fingers were square at the tips. Capable hands. His thick dark brown hair fell often into his eyes, tangling in his eyelashes, which were shamefully long for a man's. Lunzie wished hers would look so good without enhancement. He was a handsome man. She wondered why it had taken her so long to notice that fact. It struck her too that it had been a long time since she'd been out for an evening with an admirer, not since she and Sion Mespil were courting. She rather missed the experience.

Tee caught her staring at him, and caught her hand up in his. "You haven't heard what I just said," he accused her lightly. He kissed her fingertips.

"No," she admitted. "I was thinking. Tee, what did you mean when you said in the EEC office that we had something more in common?"

"Ah, so that's it. We have in common lost time. I don't know whether cryogenics is a boon to the galaxy at large or not. It is not to me. I almost rather that I had died, or remained awake, than being closed away from the world. At least I would know what went on in my absence, instead of finding it out in a single moment when I returned."

Lunzie nodded sympathetically. "How long?"

Tee grimaced dramatically. "Eleven years. When my spacecraft was becalmed because of fuel-source failure, I was the leading engineer on the FSP project to perfect laser technology in space drive navigation systems and FTL communications. On the very cutting edge, you will pardon the joke. Light beams to send information more quickly and accurately among components than ion impulse or electron could. When I awoke two years ago, the process was not only old, but obsolete! I was the most highly trained man in the FSP for a skill that was no longer needed. They offered to retire me at full salary plus my back pay, but I could not stand to feel useless. I wanted to work. It would take too long to retrain me for space technology as it has evolved — so fast!" His hands described the flight of spacecraft. "So I took any job they offered me as soon as I could. They said I wasn't over the trauma yet, so I couldn't have a space-borne post."

"It's for your own safety. It takes on the average of three to five years to recover," Lunzie pointed out, thinking of her own days of therapy on the Descartes Platform and thereafter. Through the University clinic, she still had psychologists running her through periodic tests to check her progress. "It will be even longer for me, because I have more to assimilate than you did. I'm an extreme case in point. My own medical knowledge is as archaic as trepanning to these new people. The researchers consider me fascinating because of my 'quaint notions.' It's lucky that bodies haven't changed radically. But, there are more subgroups than before. There's so much that it might have been better if I'd started from scratch."

"Yes, but you can still practice your craft! I cannot. I worked in Supply for a year, pushing paper for replacement drive parts though I had no idea what they did. They called that an 'extension' of my previous job, but it was their way of keeping me safely out of trouble. The therapists pretended they were doing it for my sake. In the end, I transferred to Research, where I would be around people who did not pity me. Besides casework, I can also fix the laser computers. It saves a call to Maintenance when something breaks." Tee drummed moodily on the table. The diners next to them gave him a wary glance as they inserted their credit medallions into the table till and left.

Lunzie wisely remained silent. Introspection, personal evaluation, was an important part of the healing process. Muhlah knew she'd spent enough of her time doing just that. She just waited and watched Tee think, wondering what pictures were going through his mind. When the server approached, Lunzie caught his eye and signalled for more cordial to be poured. The ring of ceramic on crystal awoke Tee from his reverie. He reached over and pressed her fingers.

"Forgive me, lovely Lunzie. I invite you to dine with me, not watch me sulk."

"Believe me, I understand completely. I don't always brood in private, myself. It's been so frustrating hearing nothing from the EEC that I tell everybody my troubles, hoping somebody will help me."

"You will have no trouble in future, not with Teodor Janos making the search on your behalf. You must have guessed that assignment to a caseworker such as I is only made if they cannot make you go away."

Lunzie nodded firmly. "I guessed it. Oh, how I loathe bureaucrats. I'm proud of the stubborn streak in my family. Fiona has it, too — I'm sorry. I didn't mean to bring up business. I've had such a splendid time with you."

"As have I." Tee consulted his sleeve chronometer. "It grows late, and you have classes early tomorrow. I will escort you home in a private shuttle. No, no. It is my pleasure. You may treat next time, if you choose. Or apply your prodigious and discerning skills to prepare some of the delightful-sounding recipes you have hoarded in your family memory banks."

Lunzie was met at the door to the apartment by Pomayla, Shof, and half the Gang, who, by the look of things, had been studying together with the concerted assistance of processed carbohydrates and synthesized beer.

"Well, who was it, and what was he, she, or it like?" Pomayla demanded.

"Who was who?"

"Tee, of course. We've been wondering all evening."

"I told you it'd be a he," Shof called out, tauntingly, from his seat on the floor. He and Bordlin, a Gurnsan student, were working on an engineering project that had something to do with lasers. There was a new burn mark in the wall over their heads. "Ask Mr. Data, that's me." Bordlin shook his horned head, and searched the ceiling with long-suffering bovine eyes.

"You forgot to erase the message on the board down in the foyer," Pomayla explained. "Everyone read it as they came in. Our curiosity's been running out of control."

"Let it run," Lunzie said loftily. "It's good for you to wonder. I'm going to bed."

"True love!" Shof crowed as Lunzie closed her cubicle door on them. For once she did not have trouble relaxing into sleep. She remembered the gentle pressure of Tee's fingers on hers and smiled.

As Tee had promised, Lunzie began to get results from the EEC much more quickly with his help. Fiona's virology work for the FSP was largely classified. Her official rank was Civilian Specialist, and the grade had increased steadily over the years. Her pay records showed several bonuses for hazardous duty. She had worked for the EEC for several years before her marriage in positions of increasing responsibility. She took a furlough for eight years, and resumed field work afterward. Tee still hoped to track down her service record.

This quantity of news would have seemed small to her roommates, but Lunzie was overjoyed to have it. Her mood was lighter, and not only because the barrier between herself and her daughter was falling away. She was also seeing a lot more of Tee.

He changed his viewing time to coincide with hers. They sat together on the padded bench, drinking in the news of the day, saving up their observations to discuss later over synth-lunch. Tee was amused by Lunzie's economies, but acknowledged that the fees for remote retrieval of old documents and records were steep.

When Lunzie's classes or labs didn't interfere, they would meet for an evening meal. Tee's quarters were larger than hers, a quarter of a floor in an elderly former residence of higher-level civil servants. Besides the food synthesizer, there were actual cooking facilities. "An opulent conceit," Tee admitted, "but they work. When I have time, I like to create."

They tried to set aside one day a week for a real-meal, cooked with local ingredients. Lunzie retraced her steps to the Astris combine farms she had patronized decades before, and chose vegetables from the roadside stands and pick-it-yourself crops. Tee marveled at the healthy produce, far cheaper than it was in the population centers. How clever she was to know where to find such things, he told her over and over, and so surprisingly close to the campus!

"City boy," Lunzie teased him. A part of her that had been neglected reasserted itself and began to blossom again in the warmth of his devoted admiration. She was not unattractive, vanity forced her to admit, and she started to take more pleasure in caring for herself, choosing garments that were flattering to her figure instead of ones that just preserved modesty and protected her from atmospheric exposure. Pomayla was delighted to have Lunzie join her on restday shopping expeditions. Lunzie found she was also rediscovering the simple pleasures which gave life its texture.

After a good deal of friendly teasing and many unsubtle hints from her young roommates, Lunzie was persuaded to bring Tee back to the apartment to meet them.

"You can't keep him out of the Gang's way for long," Pomayla remarked. "He might as well join now and face the music."

Though he was eager to please Lunzie, Tee was reluctant to encounter her young suitemates. From the moment he entered the apartment, he felt nervous, and wondered if he would lose too much face if he decided to bolt.

"You live such a distance from town center I have had too much time to worry," he complained, straightening his tunic again as they swept upward in the turbovator.

"Come now, they're only children. Be a man, my son."

"You don't understand. I like youngsters. Ten years ago, I may have felt no discomfort, but . . . oh, you'll see. It has not happened to you yet."

Shof, Pomayla, and Pomayla's boyfriend Laren were waiting for them in their common living room. The apartment was clean. They had done a commendable job in making the place look neat, but Lunzie was uncomfortably aware for the first time how scholastically plain the apartment was. Though she knew Tee would understand why she chose to live in such cheap quarters, she wished illogically that it looked more sophisticated.

Tee, bless him, reacted in exactly the right way to make her feel comfortable once more. "This looks like a place where things are done," he cried, stretching his arms out, feeling the atmosphere. "A good room to work." He gave them a wide grin, encompassing them all in its sunshine.

"You're never at a loss anywhere you go, are you?" she asked, a small, cynical smile tweaking up the corner of her mouth.

"I mean it," Tee replied. "Some quarters are merely to sleep in. Some, you can sleep and eat in. This, you can live in."

"Sort of," Shof said grudgingly. "But there's no storage space to speak of, and Krim knows, you can't bring a date here."

"It would be easier to get around in if you didn't have models hanging everywhere," Pomayla told him.

"I've been in worse on shipboard, believe me," Tee said. "In which every bunk belongs to three crew, who use it in turn for a shift apiece. No sleeping late. No lingering in the morning to get to know one another all over again." He glanced at Lunzie through his eyelashes with an exaggerated look of longing, and she laughed.

"My lad, you should simply have gotten to know someone on the next shift, so then you could move on to her bunk."

Pomayla, who was shy about personal relations, promptly got up to serve drinks.

"Were you in the FSP?" Shof asked Tee.

"Only as a contractor. I helped to develop a new star navigations system. My specialty was computer-driven laser technology."

"Stellar, citizen," Shof said, enthusiastically. "Me, too. I built my first laser beam calculator out of spare parts when I was four." He held up his right hand. "Cauterized this index finger clean off. I've generally had bad luck with this finger. It's been regenerated twice now. But I've learned to use a laser director better since then."

"Laser director?" Tee asked. "You don't use a laser director to create the synapse links."

"I do."

"No wonder you burned off your finger, little man. Why didn't you simply recalculate the angles before trying to connect power?"

They bean to argue research and technique, going immediately from lay explanation, which the other three could understand, into the most involved technical lingo. It sounded like gibberish to Lunzie and Pomayla, and probably did to Laren, who sat politely nodding and smiling whenever anyone met his eyes. Lunzie remembered that he was an economics major.

"So," asked Shof, stopping for breath, "what's the new system based on? Ion propulsion with laser memory's faulty; they've figured that out now. Gravity well drives are still science fiction. Laser technology's too delicate by itself to stand up against the new matter-antimatter drives."

"But why not?" Tee began looking lost. "That was new when I was working for the FSP. The laser system was supposed to revolutionize space travel. It should have lasted for two hundred years."

"Yeah. Went in and out of fashion like plaid knickers," Shof said, deprecatingly. "Doppler shift, you know. Well, you've got to start somewhere."

"Somewhere?" Tee echoed indignantly. "Our technology was the very newest, the most promising. . . ."

Shof spread out his hands and said reasonably, "I'm not saying that the current system wasn't based on LT. Where have you been for the last decade, Earth?"

Tee's face, once open and animated, had closed up into tight lines. His mouth twisted, fighting back some sour retort. His involuntary passage with cold sleep was still a sore point with him. Lunzie suddenly understood why he was reluctant to talk about his past experiences with anyone. The experiential gap between the people who experienced time at its normal pace and the cold sleepers was real and troubling to the sleepers. Tee felt caught out of time, and Shof didn't understand. "Peace!" Lunzie cried over Shof's exposition of modern intergalactic propulsion. "That's enough. I declare Hatha's peace of the watering hole. I will permit no more disputes in this place."

Shof opened his mouth to say something, but stopped. He stared at Tee, then looked to Lunzie for help. "Have I said something wrong?"

"Shof, you can behave yourself or make yourself scarce," Pomayla declared.

"What'd I do?" With a wounded expression, Shof withdrew to arrange dinner from the synthesizer. Pomayla and Laren went to the worktable, and peeled and cut up a selection of fresh vegetables to supplement the meal. Tee watched them work, looking lost.

Lunzie rose to her feet. "Now that we have a natural break in the conversation, I'll give Tee the tenth-credit tour." She twined her arm with Tee's and led him away.

Once the door to Lunzie's cubicle had shut behind them, Tee

let his shoulders sag. "I am sorry. But you see? It might have been a hundred years. I have been left far behind. Everything I knew, all the complicated technology I developed, is now toys for children."

"I must apologize. I tossed you into the middle of it. You seemed to be holding your own very well," Lunzie said, contritely.

Tee shook his head, precipitating a fall of black hair into his eyes. "When a child can blithely reel off what a hundred of us worked on for eight years — for which some of us lost our lives! — and refute it, with logic, I feel old and stupid." Lunzie started a hand to smooth the unsettled forelock, but stopped to let him do it himself.

"I feel the same way, you know," she said. "Young people, much younger than I am, at any rate, who understand the new medical technology to a fare-thee-well, when I have to be shown where the on-off switch is! I should have realized that I'm not alone in what I'm going through. It was most inconsiderate of me." Lunzie kneaded the muscles at the back of Tee's neck with her strong fingers. Tee seized her hand and kissed it.

"Ah, but you have the healing touch." He glanced at the console set and smiled at the hologram prism with the image of a lovely young girl beaming out at him. "Fiona?"

"Yes." Lunzie stroked the edge of the hologram with pride.

"She's not very like you in coloring, but in character, ah!"

"What? You can see the stubborn streak from there?" Lunzie said mockingly.

"It runs right here, along your back." His fingers traced her spine, and she shivered delightedly. "Fiona is beautiful, just as you are. May I take this?" Tee asked, turning it in his hands and admiring the clarity of the portrait. "If I can feed an image to the computers, it may stir some memory bank that has not yet responded to my queries."

Lunzie felt a wrench at giving up her only physical tie to her daughter, but had to concede the logic. "All right," she agreed reluctantly.

"I promise you, nothing will happen to it, and much good may result."

She stood on tiptoe to kiss him. "I trust you. Are you ready to rejoin the others?"

Shof had clearly been chastised in Lunzie's absence. During dinner around the worktable, he questioned Tee respectfully about the details of his research. The others joined in, and the conversation turned to several subjects. Laren proved also to be a Tri-D viewer. Lunzie and he compared their impressions of fashion trends, amidst hilarious laughter from the other two males. Blushing red for making her opinions known, Pomayla tried to defend the fashion industry.

"Well, you practically support them," Shof said, wickedly, baiting her as he would a sister.

"What's wrong with garb that makes you look good?" she replied, taking up the challenge.

"If it isn't comfortable, why wear it?" Lunzie asked reasonably, joining the fray on Shof's side.

"For the style —" Pomayla explained, desperately.

Lunzie raised an eyebrow humorously. "We must suffer to be beautiful? And you call me old-fashioned!"

"I don't know where they get the ideas for these new frocks," Laren said. After a quick glance at Pomayla, "No offense, sweetheart, but some of the fads are so weird."

"Do you really want to know?" Lunzie asked. "To stay in style for the rest of your life, never throw out any of your clothes. The latest style for the next season — I saw it in the Tri-D — is the very same tunic I wore to my primary-school graduation. It probably came around once while I was in cold sleep, and here it is again. Completely new to you youngsters, and too youthful a fashion to be worn by anyone who can remember the last time it was in vogue."

"Can I look through your family holos?" Pomayla asked, conceding the battle with an impish gleam in her eye. "I want to see what's coming next year. I'll be seasons ahead of the whole Gang."

The remains of the meal went into the disposer, and Tee rose, stretching his arms over his head and producing a series of cracks down his spine. "Ah. That was just as I remember school food."

"Terrible, right?" Pomayla inquired, with a twinkle.

"Terrible. I hate to end the evening now, but I must go. As Lunzie said so truly, you are at the outer end of nowhere, and it will take me time to get home."

Lunzie ran for her textcubes. "I think I'll come in with you. My shift at the hospital begins in just four hours. Sanitary collection units won't wait. I might as well travel while I can still see. Perhaps I'll nap at your place."

Tee swept her a bow. "I should be glad for your company." He expanded the salute to include the others. "Thank you for a pleasant evening. Good night."

Pomayla and Laren called their goodnights to him from the worn freeform couch in the far corner of the room. Shof ran to catch up with them at the door. "Hey," he called softly, as they stepped into the turbovator foyer. "Good luck finding Lunzie's daughter, huh?"

Lunzie goggled at him. "Why, you imp. You know?"

Shof gave them his elfin smile. "Sure I know. I don't tell everything I find out." He winked at Lunzie as the door slid between them.

Lunzie's studies progressed well throughout the rest of the term. To their mutual satisfaction, she and the cardiology professor declared a truce. She toned down her open criticism of his bedside manner, and he overlooked what he termed her "bleeding heart," openly approving her grasp of his instruction. His personal evaluation of her at the end of term was flattering, for him, according to students who had had him before. Lunzie thought she had never seen a harsher dressing down ever committed to plas-sheet, but the grade noted below the diatribe showed that he was pleased with her.

The new term began. The Discipline course continued straight through vacation, since it was not a traditional format class. No grade was issued to the University computer for Discipline. Either a student kept up with the art, or he dropped out. It was still eating up a large part of Lunzie's day, which was now busier than ever.

Her new courses included supervised practical experience at the University Hospital. The practicum was worth twice the credits of other classes, but the hours involved were flexible according to need, and invariably ran long. Lunzie and her fellows followed a senior resident on his rounds for the first few weeks, observing his techniques of diagnosis and treatment, and then worked under him in the hospital clinic. Lunzie liked Dr. Root, a human man of sixty honest Standard years, whose plump pink cheeks and broad hands always looked freshly scrubbed.

Many patients who came to the clinics were of species that Lunzie had seen before only in textbooks, and some of them only recently. Under the admiring gaze of his eight apprentices, Root removed from the nucleus of a five-foot protoplasmic entity a single chromosome the size of Lunzie's finger, altered and replaced it, with deft motions suggesting he did this kind of thing every day. Even before he finished sealing the purple cell wall, the creature was quivering.

"Conscious already?" Dr. Root transmitted through the voice-synthesizer the giant cell wore around the base of a long cilium.

" . . . good . . . is good . . . divide now . . . good. . . ."

"No, absolutely not. You may not induce mitosis until we are sure that your nucleus can successfully replicate itself."

" . . . rest . . . good. . . ."

Root wrinkled his nose cheerfully at Lunzie. "Nice when a patient takes a doctor's advice, isn't it?"

Whenever Root held clinic, his students did the preliminary examinations, and, if it was within their capabilities, the treatment as well. Like Lunzie, the others were advanced-year students. Most would be taking internships next year in whichever of the University-approved hospitals and medical centers throughout the FSP would take them. Lunzie's own plan was to apply to the University Hospital each term for residency, until they took her, or the search for Fiona led offplanet at last. Her advisor reminded her that she didn't need to follow the curriculum as if she was a new student. Lunzie argued that she needed as much refreshment as she could get to regain her skills. The grueling pace of internship was the quickest way to be exposed to the most facets of new medicine.

The clinic's comm unit chirped during Dr. Root's demonstration of how to treat a suppurating wound on a shelled creature. The tortoiselike alien lay patiently on the examination table with probes hanging in the air around it and any number of tubes and scopes poked under the edge of its shell. With the help of a long-handled clamp and two self-motivated cautery units, Root was gently fitting a layer of new plas-skin over the freshly cleaned site, and watching his progress on a hovering Tri-D field. He handed the clamp over to one of the students. "Close up, please."

"Emergency code," Root announced mildly to the roomful of students after taking the call. "Construction workers from the spaceport. They are airlifting them in to the roof. Some nasty wounds, a lot of blood, patients likely to be in shock. To your stations, doctors."

Lunzie and her Brachian lab partner, Rik-ik-it, fled to treatment room C, scrubbed, and helped each other put on fresh surgical gear. They had just enough time to do a check on supplies and power before they heard the screaming.

"Muhlah, what are they?"

"I can scream louder than that," Rik scoffed.

"Don't," ordered Lunzie, listening. "Shh."

The door to their treatment room slid open, and two enormous men staggered in, one supporting the other. Heavyworlders. Lunzie looked up at them in dismay.

"Help me," Rik chittered, springing forward to help the more badly wounded man to the canted table. His tremendous strength supplemented that of the other heavyworlder and together they got the man settled on the gurney. Lunzie started to move toward him, when the other man brushed her away, and assisted Rik in laying his friend facedown onto the padded surface.

It was amazing that the prone heavyworlder had made it to the clinic on his feet. There was a tremendous tear through the muscles on his back. One calf was split down the middle, probably sliced by the same falling object. Blood was flowing and spurting from both wounds.

"What happened?" she demanded, pushing past the other two. She cut away the heavy cloth of the prone man's trouser leg and began cleaning the wound with sterile cleanser. By main strength, Rik tore open the slit in his tunic and began to search the wound with a microscopic device. Lunzie tossed the scraps of cloth to one side and put pressure on the pumping blood vessel. When the spurting stopped, she applied a quicksplint to it with an electronically directed clamp. Its edges forced together under the flexible tubeform splint, the tear would heal now by itself.

"Runway extension buckled, fell down on us," the other man said, clutching his arm. "Sarn it, I knew those struts were faulty. Trust Plasteel Corporation, the crew boss told us. Gurn shit! The machines'll tell us if any of the extrusions won't hold up. Uh-huh."

"I can handle this one now," Rik told Lunzie.

With a comprehending nod, Lunzie turned away from the

table to the other man. By the heavens, he was tall! He ground his teeth together, rasping them audibly. Lunzie knew that he was in tremendous pain.

"Sit down," she said, quickly, swallowing her nervousness. Her stomach rolled. She knew she was going to have to touch him, and she was afraid. These angry giants seemed more than human to her: larger, louder, more emphatic. They frightened her. In the depths of her soul, she still associated heavyworlders with the loss of Fiona, and she was surprised how much it affected her. She had to remind herself of her duty.

"It's my arm," the heavyworlder said, starting to unfasten the front closure of his tunic. Lunzie quelled her feelings and unsealed the magnetic seam running the length of his sleeve. She eased the fabric down, trying to avoid touching the swelling in the upper arm, and helped him ease the sleeve down over the injured limb. His hand, gigantic next to hers, clenched and twitched as she undid the wrist fastening, and the plas-canvas fabric flapped free against the man's ribs.

A quick glance told her that the right humerus was broken, and the shoulder was badly dislocated. "Let me give you something for pain," Lunzie said, signalling for the hypo-arm. The servomechanism swung the multiple injector-head down to her, and the LEDs on its control glowed into life. "Why not?" she demanded when the heavyworlder shook his head.

"You're not gonna knock me out. I don't trust bonecrackers. I want to see what you do."

"As you wish," Lunzie said, adjusting the setting. "How about a local? It won't make you drowsy, but it will kill the pain."

"Yeah. All right." He stuck his arm out toward her suddenly, and Lunzie jumped back, startled. The heavyworlder frowned at her, lowering his eyebrows suspiciously.

Made more nervous by his disapproving scrutiny, Lunzie stammered as she spoke to the hypo-arm control. "A-analyze for allergies and in-incompatibilities. Local only, right upper arm and shoulder. Implement." The head moved purposefully forward and touched the man's skin. The air gauge hissed briefly, then the unit rotated and withdrew. Lunzie felt the arm tentatively, examining the break. That bone was going to be difficult to set through the thick layers of muscle.

"Get on with it, dammit!" the man roared.

"Does something else hurt?" Lunzie asked, jerking her hands away.

"No, but the way you mince around makes me crazy. Put a rocket in it, lady!"

Stung, Lunzie paused for a moment to gather the resources of Discipline deep within her, as much for strength enough to set the arm as for mental insulation from her feelings against the heavyworlder. She would not allow herself to react in an adverse fashion. Her breathing slowed down until it was even and slow. She was a doctor. Many people were afraid of doctors. It was not unnatural. He was traumatized because of the accident and the pain; no need to take his behavior personally. But Lunzie kept seeing the newsvideo of Phoenix, the bare hollow where the human camp used to be. . . .

The burst of adrenaline characteristic of Discipline raced through her system, blanketing her normal responses, shoring up her weaknesses, and strengthening her sinews far beyond their unenhanced capability. Her hands braced against the heavyworlder's bunched muscle, spread out, and grasped.

The heavyworlder screamed and flailed at her with his free hand, knocking her backwards against the wall. "Suffering burnout, let go! Dammit, get me a doctor who's gonna treat me like a human being, for Krim's sake!" he howled. He clenched his hand around the wounded shoulder, and sweat poured down his face, which was white with shock.

"Is there a problem here?" Rik-ik-it asked, peering shortsightedly down on Lunzie. His silver-pupiled eyes blinked quizzically as he helped her up.

Furiously, the heavyworlder angled his chin toward Lunzie. "This fem is a klondiking butcher. She's torn my arm apart!"

Still held in Discipline trance, Lunzie backed away. She hadn't been hurt. The man's anger held no terror for her as long as she held her feelings in check under the curtain of iron control. What had gone wrong? She reviewed her actions with the perfect recall at her command. Two quick twists, one front to back, the other, in a leftward arc. She knew, as if an ultrasonic image had been projected before her, that the shoulder was once again in place and that the broken bone had been aligned. Discipline also increased the sensitivity of her five senses.

Rik examined the arm carefully, then read the indicators on

the hypo-arm. "There is nothing wrong here," he said calmly. "The doctor has set your arm correctly. It will heal well now. It is just that the anesthetic had not yet taken effect." He glanced at the clock on the wall. "It should be starting to work right now."

"I should have checked the time factor," Lunzie chided herself later when she and Tee were alone together. "But all I could think of was fixing him up and getting him out of there. It was a stupid mistake, stupid and embarrassing." She waved her hands helplessly as she paced, unable to light anywhere for long. "Rik says that I'm overreacting. He thinks that I have a — phobia of heavyworlders, otherwise I would have remembered the time factor." Miserably, she programmed herself a cup of ersatz coffee from the food synthesizer. "Look. I'm reverting. Maybe I should get therapy. I was in Discipline trance; I might have torn the man's arm off." She swallowed the coffee and made a wry face.

"But you didn't," Tee said, sympathetically, guiding her to sit close to him on the wide couch in the center room of his quarters. She looked away as he clasped her hand in both of his. She couldn't stand the pity in his eyes.

"I should quit. Perhaps I can go into research, where I can keep away from any life larger than a microbe." Her mouth quivered, trying to hold up the corners of a feeble little grin, though she still stared at Tee's knees. "I never suffer fools gladly, especially when one of them is myself."

"That doesn't sound like my Lunzie. She who is taking hold with bold hands in this new world. And she who persuades me not to be discouraged when small boys know more than I do about my hard-learned craft."

Her self-pity shot down, Lunzie had to smile. She met Tee's eyes for the first time. "That poor man kept shouting to me to hurry up, to fix his arm and be done with it. I knew he was scared of me because I am a doctor, but I was more scared of him! However Brobdignagian in dimension, he was just another human being! My daughter's father was involved in the genetic evolution of heavyworlders. I used to get intersystem mail from Sion, long after we parted, talking about the steps he and the other researchers were taking to better adapt their subjects to the high-grav worlds. I know a lot about their technical development, and nothing about their society. It's funny that humanity is the only species making fundamental changes on itself. Catch the Ryxi altering one feather of their makeup."

"Never. It must be our curiosity: what we can do with any raw material, including ourselves," Tee suggested. "You must not blame yourself so much. It is so pointless."

Lunzie wiped the corners of her eyes with a sleeve. "It isn't. I misused my training, and I can't forget that — mustn't forget it. I'm not used to thinking of myself as a bigot. I'm a throwback. I don't belong in this century."

"Ah, but you're wrong," Tee said, removing the ignored, half-empty cup from her hand and setting it down on the hovering disk at the end of the couch. "It was an accident and you are sorry. You don't rejoice in his pain. You are a good doctor, and a good person. For who else would have been so loving and patient with me as you have been? You have much you can teach these poor ignorant people of the future." Gently, his arms stole around her, and hugged her tightly. Between soft kisses, he whispered to her. "You belong here. You belong with me."

Lunzie wrapped her arms around his ribs and rested her head on his shoulder. She closed her eyes, feeling warm and wanted. The tension of the day melted out of her neck and shoulders like a shower of petals falling from an apple tree as his tiny kisses travelled up the side of her throat, touched her ear. Tee kneaded the muscles in her lower back with his strong fingers, and she sighed with pleasure. His hands encircled her waist, swept upward, still stroking, putting aside fastenings and folds of cloth until they touched bare skin. Lunzie followed suit, admiring the line of shadows that dappled the strong muscles of his shoulders. The springy band of dark hair across his chest pleased her with its silky texture.

One of Tee's hands drifted up to touch her chin. He raised her face. His deep-set, dark eyes were solemn and caring. "Stay with me always, Lunzie. I love you. Please stay." Tilting his head forward, he brushed his lips tenderly against hers, again and again.

"I will," she murmured, easing back with him into the deep cushions. "I'll stay as long as I can."

✧ CHAPTER FIVE

The hologram of Fiona held pride of place on the hovering disk table in the main room of Lunzie's and Tee's shared living quarters. Lunzie glanced up at it from time to time while she studied patient records. Fiona's beaming, never-fading smile beckoned her mother. Find me, it said. Sunlight shone through the image, sending lights of ruby and crystal dancing along the soft white walls of the room. Lunzie was coming to the end of her second full year on Astris. It was difficult to keep her promise to Chief Wilkins to be patient when she felt she ought to be out in the galaxy, looking for her daughter. In spite of the time Lunzie devoted to her many other activities and Discipline exercises, she never failed to check in with Looking-GLASS and her other sources of information in hopes of finding a trace of Fiona. She was spending a lot of money, but it had been a long time since she had learned anything new. It was frustrating.

It had been several months since she and Tee decided to live together, which decision coincided almost perfectly with Pomayla's timid request that her steady boyfriend be allowed to move into the apartment with her. Pomayla was overly shy about normal behavior between consenting adult beings. There was no stigma in present-day culture against "sharing warmth," as it was called, nor had there been for centuries. Students — in fact, all citizens — who participated in an open sex lifestyle were responsible for ensuring they were disease- and vermin-free or honestly stating that there was a problem, so there was no risk, just joy. Lovers who lied about their conditions soon found that they were left strictly alone: the word spread, and no one would trust them. Medical students especially were aware of what horrible things could happen if care was not taken to stay "clean," so they were scrupulous about it. Otherwise, one of their own number would eventually rake them over the philosophical coals later on when treatment was sought. Lunzie liked Laren, so she ceded him her own bedroom without a qualm, and moved her few belongings to Tee's.

Tee was a considerate, even deferential, suitemate. He behaved from the first day as if he considered it a favor bestowed by Lunzie that she had chosen to move in with him. Without offering his opinions first, so as not to prejudice her to his choices, he begged her to look around the roomy apartment and decide if she felt anything ought to be moved or changed to make her comfort greater. Everything was to be done for her pleasure. Lunzie was a little overwhelmed by his enthusiasm; she was used to the laissez-faire style of her roommates, or the privacy-craving nature characteristic of those who lived in space. Tee had few possessions of his own, except for a number of books on plaque and cube, and a great quantity of music disks. All of the furniture was secondhand, a commodity plentiful on a university world. Most of his belongings, he explained, had been divided up according to his previous will, automatically probated when he had remained out of touch with any FSP command post for ten years. It was a stupid policy, he argued, since one could be out of touch much longer than that in a large galaxy and still be awake!

Careful to consider his feelings, and perhaps out of her naturally stubborn reaction to his insistence, Lunzie changed as little as possible in his quarters. She liked the spare decor. It helped her to concentrate more than the homey clutter of the student apartment did. When Tee complained that she was behaving like a visitor instead of a resident, she had taken him out shopping. They chose a two-dimensional painting by a University artist and a couple of handsome holograph prints that they both liked, and Lunzie purchased them, refusing to let Tee see the prices. Together, they arranged the pieces of art in the room where they spent the most time.

"Now that is Lunzie's touch," Tee had exclaimed, satisfied, admiring the way the color picked up the moon in the predominantly white room. "Now it is our home."

Lunzie put down the datacube. She loved Tee's apartment. It was spacious, ostentatiously so for a single person's quarters, and it had wide window panels extending clear around two walls of the main room. Lunzie reached up for a tendon-crackling stretch that dragged the cuffs of her loose-knit exercise pants up over her ankles, and dropped wide sweatshirt sleeves onto the top of her head, mussing her hair, and stalked over to open the casements to let the warm afternoon breezes through. The irising controls of the window panels were adjusted to let in the maximum sunlight on the soft white carpeting. At that time of the afternoon, both walls were full of light. A pot of fragrant herbal tea was warming on the element in the cooking area, which was visible through a doorway. The food synthesizer, a much better model than she'd had in the University-owned apartment, was disguised behind an ornamental panel in the cooking room wall, making it easy to ignore. She and Tee still preferred cooking for one another when they had time. Lunzie was becoming happily spoiled by the small luxuries which were rarely available to students or spacefarers.

During this school term, Lunzie had been assigned as Dr. Root's assistant in the walk-in clinic. After she shamefacedly admitted having been upset by her heavyworlder patient, and voiced her concerns about its effect on her treatment to him, Root had counselled her and interviewed Rik-ik-it. It was his determination that there was nothing wrong with her that a little more exposure to the subjects wouldn't dispel. He dismissed her fears that she was a xenophobe.

"An angry heavyworlder," he assured her, "could easily intimidate a normal human. You may fear one with impunity."

She was grateful that he hadn't seen it as a major departure from normalcy, and vowed to keep a cooler head in the future. So far, she hadn't had to test her new resolve, as few heavyworlders made use of the medical facility.

The University Hospital clinic treated all students free of charge, and assessed only a nominal fee from outsiders. Accident victims, too, like the heavyworlder construction workers, were frequently brought directly to the University Hospital because the wait time for treatment was usually shorter than it was at the private facilities. Most of the Astris students Lunzie saw were of human derivation, not because non-humans were less interested in advanced education or were discriminated against, but because most species were capable of passing on knowledge to infants in utero or in ova, and only one University education per subject was required per family tree. Humans required education after birth, which some other member races of the FSP, particularly the Seti and the Weft, saw as a terrible waste of time. Lunzie felt the crowing over race memory and other characteristics to be a sort of inferiority complex in itself, and let the comments pass without reply. Race memory was only useful when it dealt with situations that one's ancestors had experienced before. She treated numerous Weft engineering students for dehydration, especially during their first semesters on Astris. Young Seti, on Astris to study interplanetary diplomacy, tended toward digestive ailments, and had to be trained as to which native Astrian foods to avoid.

It had been a slow day in the office. None of her case histories demanded immediate action, so she pushed them into a heap on the side of the couch and sat down with a cup of tea. There was time to relax a bit before she needed to report back to Dr. Root. He was a good and patient teacher, who only smiled at her need to circumvent the healing machines instead of chiding her for her ancient ideals. Lunzie felt confident again in her skills. She still fought to maintain personal interaction with the patient, but there was less and less for the healer to do. Lunzie sensed it was a mistake to learn to rely too heavily on mechanical aids. A healer was not just another technician, in her strongly maintained opinion. She was alone in her views.

The band of sunshine crept across the room and settled at her feet like a contented pet. Lunzie looked longingly across at her portable personal reader, which had been a thirty-sixth birthday gift from Tee, and small rack of ancient classical book plaques she had purchased from used-book stores. An unabridged *Works of Rudyard Kipling*, replacement for her own lost, much-loved copy, sat at the front of the book rack, beckoning. Though there wasn't time to page through her favorites before she needed to go in to work, there was, coincidentally, just enough to perform her daily Discipline exercises. With a sigh, she put aside the empty cup and began limbering up.

"Duty before pleasure, Kip," Lunzie said, regretfully. "You'd understand that."

The tight Achilles tendons between her hips and heels had been stretched so well that she could bend over and lay her hands flat on the floor and relax her elbows without bowing her knees. Muscular stiffness melted away as she moved gracefully through the series of dancelike fighting positions. Lunzie was careful to avoid the computer console and the art pedestals as she sprang lightly around the room, sparring with an invisible opponent. Discipline taught control and enhancement of the capability of muscle and sinew. Each pose not only exercised her limbs, but left her feeling more energetic than when she began the drills. Under conscious control, her footfalls made no sound. She was as silent as the black shadows limned on the light walls by the sun. She moved in balance, every motion a reaction, an answer to one that came before.

Holding her back beam-straight, she settled down into a meditation pose sitting on her crossed feet in front of the couch with the sunshine washing across her lap. She held her arms out before her, turned her hands palms up, and let them drop slowly to the floor on either side of her knees.

Lunzie closed her eyes, and drew in the wings of her consciousness, until she was aware only of her body, the muscles holding her back straight, the pressure of her buttocks into the arches of her feet, the heat of the sun on her legs, the rough-smooth rasp of the carpet on the tops of her hands and feet.

Tighter in. At the base of her sinuses, she tasted the last savor of the tea that she had swallowed, and felt the faint distension of her stomach around the warm liquid. Lunzie studied every muscle which worked to draw in breath and release it, felt the relief of each part of her body as fresh oxygen reached it, displacing tired, used carbon dioxide. The flesh of her cheeks and forehead hung heavily against her facial bones. She let her jaw relax.

She began to picture the organs and blood vessels of her body as passages, and sent her thought along them, checking their functions. All was well. Finally she allowed her consciousness to return to her center. It was time to travel inward toward the peace which was the Disciple's greatest source of strength and the goal toward which her soul strove.

Lunzie emerged from her trance state just in time to hear the whir of the turbovator as it stopped outside the door. Her body was relaxed and loose, her inner self calm. She looked up as Tee burst into the room, his good-natured face beaming.

"The best of news, my Lunzie! The very best! I have found your Fiona! She is alive!"

Lunzie's hands clenched where they lay on the ground, and

her heart felt as if it had stopped beating. The calm dispersed in a wash of hope and fear and excitement. Could it be true? She wanted to share the joy she saw in his eyes, but she did not dare.

"Oh, Tee," she whispered, her throat suddenly tight. Her hands were shaking as she extended them to Tee, who fell to his knees in front of her. He clasped her wrists and kissed the tips of her fingers. "What have you found?" All of her anxieties came back in a rush. She could not yet allow herself to feel that it might be true.

Tee slipped a small ceramic information brick from his pocket and placed it in her palms. "It is all here. I have proof in *three dimensions*. Grade One Med Tech Fiona Mespil was retrieved offplanet by the EEC shortly before the colony vanished. She was needed urgently on another assignment," Tee explained. "It was an emergency, and the ship which picked her up was not FSP — a nearby merchant voyager — so her name was not removed from the rolls of poor Phoenix. She is alive!"

"Alive . . . " Lunzie made no attempt to hold back the flood of joyful tears which spilled from her eyes. Tee wiped them, then dabbed at his own bright eyes. "Oh, Tee, thank you! I'm so happy."

"I am happy, too — for you. It is a secret I have held many weeks now, waiting for a reply to my inquiries. I couldn't be sure. I did not want to torture you with hope only to have bad news later on. But now, I am glad to reveal all!"

"Two years I've waited. A few weeks more couldn't hurt," Lunzie said, casting around for a handkerchief. Tee plucked his out of his sleeve and offered it to her. She wiped her eyes and nose, and blew loudly. "Where is she, Tee?"

"Doctor Fiona has been working for five years on Glamorgan, many light-years out toward Vega, to stem a plague virus that threatened the colony's survival. Her work there is done. She is en route to her home on Alpha Centauri for a reunion with her family. It is a multiple-jump trip even with FTL capabilities, and will take her probably two years to arrive home. I did not make contact with her directly." Tee grinned his most implike grin, obviously saving the best for last. "But your three grandchildren, five great-grandchildren, and nine great-great-grandchildren say they are delighted that they will get to meet their illustrious ancestress. I have holograms of all of them there in this cube."

Lunzie listened with growing excitement to his recitation, and threw her arms around him as he produced the cube with a flourish. "Oh! Grandchildren. I never thought of grandchildren. Let me see them."

"This is downloaded from the post brick brought from Alpha Centauri by the purser aboard the merchant ship *Prospero*," Tee explained as he tucked the cube into the computer console reader. Lunzie scrambled up onto the couch and watched the platform with shining eyes as an image began to coalesce. "There is only sketchy family information on all of these. The message is short. I think your grandson Lars must be a tightwad. It is his voice narrating."

The holographic image of a black-haired human man in his early fifties appeared on the console platform. Lunzie leaned in to have a closer look. The image spoke. "Greetings, Lunzie. My name is Lars, Fiona's son. Since I don't know when this will reach you, I will give the names and Standard birthdates for all family members instead of the current date. First, myself. I'm the eldest of the family. I was born in 2801.

"Here is Mother, the last image I have of her before she blasted off last time." The voice was reproving. "She is very busy in her career, as I guess you know."

And before Lunzie was the image of a middle-aged woman. It was clearly a studio picture taken by a professional, sharp and clear. Her dark hair, stroked only here and there with a gentle brushing of silver, was piled up on top of her head in a plaited bun. Standing at her ease, she was dressed in a spotless uniform tunic which in contrast to her stance was formal and correct to the last crease. There were fine, crinkly lines at the corners of her eyes and underscoring her lashes, and smile lines had etched themselves deeply between her nose and the corners of her mouth, but the smile was the wonderful, happy grin that Lunzie remembered best. She closed her eyes, and for a moment was back on Tau Ceti in the sunshine, that last day before she left for the Descartes Platform.

"Oh, my baby," Lunzie murmured, overcome with longing and regret. She pressed her hand to her mouth as she looked from the holo of Fiona as a teenager to the image she saw now. "She's so different. I missed all her growing up."

"She is fine," Tee said, halting the playback. "She was happy, see? Wouldn't you like to see the rest of your family?"

Shortly, Lunzie nodded and opened her eyes. Tee passed his hand over the solenoid switch, and the image of Fiona disappeared. It was followed by a very slim young man in Fleet uniform. "My brother, Dougal, born 2807," stated Lars' voice. "Unmarried, no attachments to speak of outside his career. He's not home much, as he is commissioned in the FSP Fleet as a captain. Sometimes transports Mother and her germ dogs from place to place. It's often the only time one of us gets to see her.

"My wife's camera shy, and won't stand still for an image." In the background, Lunzie could hear a high-pitched shriek. "Oh, Lars! Really!"

Lunzie grinned. "He has the family sense of humor anyway."

The image changed. "My daughter Dierdre, born 2825. Her husband, Moykol, and their three girls. I call them the Fates. Here we have Rudi, born 2843, Capella, 2844, and Anthea Rose, 2845.

"My other girl, Georgia, 2828. One son, Gordon, 2846. Smart lad, if his own grandfather does have to say so.

"Melanie, daughter of Fiona, born Standard year 2803." This was a stunningly lovely woman with medium brown hair like Lunzie's own, and Fiona's jaw and eyes. She had a comfortably motherly figure, soft in outline without seeming overweight for her slender bones. She stood with one arm around the waist of a very tall man with a sharp, narrow, hawklike face which looked incongruous under his mop of soft blond hair. "Husband, Dalton Ingrich.

"Their third son, Drew, 2827. Drew has two boys, who are away at Centauri Institute of Technology. I don't have a current holo.

"Melanie's older boys, Jai and Thad, are identical twins, born 2821. Thad, and daughter, Cassia, born 2842.

"This is Jai and his wife and two imps, Deram, 2842, and Lona, 2847."

There was an interruption of Lars' narration as the image of Melanie reappeared. She stepped forward in the holofield to speak, extending her hands welcomingly. "We'll be delighted to meet you, ancestress. Please come."

The image faded. Lunzie sat staring at the empty consolehead as the computer whirred and expelled the datacube.

Lunzie let out her breath in a rush. "Well. A moment ago I was an orphan in the great galaxy. Now I'm the mother of a population explosion!" She shook her head in disbelief. "Do you know, I believe I've missed having a family to belong to."

"You must go," Tee said softly. He was watching her tenderly, careful not to touch her before she needed him to.

"Why didn't they tell me where she is?" Lunzie asked. Tee didn't have to ask which "she."

"They can't. They don't know. Because her assignments deal with planet-decimating disease, who knows when a curiosity seeker might land, perhaps to get a story to sell to Tri-D."

Lunzie recalled the holo-story about Phoenix. "That is so true. He might spread the plague farther than his story might ever reach. But it is just so frustrating."

"Well, you will see her now. She will arrive home from the distant edge of the galaxy within two years." Tee looked pleased with himself. "You can be there waiting for her, to celebrate your reunion, and her new appointment, which was made public. That is how I found her at last, I confess, though it was because I was looking that I noticed the articles of commission. For long and meritorious service to the FSP, Doctor Fiona is appointed Surgeon General of the Eridani system. A great honor."

"Did you notice? A couple of the children look just like her." Lunzie chuckled. "One or two of them look like me. Not that these looks bear repeating."

"You insult yourself, my Lunzie. You are beautiful." Tee smiled warmly at her. "Your face is not what cosmetic models have, but what they wish they had."

Lunzie wasn't listening. "To think that all this . . . this frustration could have been avoided, if Phoenix could simply have transmitted word that Fiona'd left when she did. It was the one blocked path I couldn't find my way around, no matter what I did. The planet pirates are responsible for that, for two, almost three years I've spent — in anger, never knowing if I was hunting for a . . . a ghost. I think — I think if I had someone I knew was a pirate on my examination table with a bullet near his heart that only I could remove. . . . Well, I might just forget my Hippocratic oath." Lunzie set her jaw, furiously contemplating revenge.

"But you wouldn't," Tee said, firmly, squeezing her hand. "I know you."

"I wouldn't," she agreed, resignedly, letting the hot images fade. "But I'd have to wrangle it out with the devil. And I'll never forget the sorrow or the frustration. Or the loneliness." She shot Tee a look of gratitude and love. "Though I'm not alone now."

Tee persisted. "But you will go, of course? To Alpha Centauri."

"It would cost a planetary ransom!"

"What is money? You have spent money only seeking Fiona over the last many months, even though you are well off. You have saved every hundredth credit else. What else is it for?"

Lunzie bit her lip and stared at a corner of the room, thinking. She was almost afraid to see Fiona after all this time, because what would she say to her? All the time when she'd been searching for her, she played many scenes in her mind, of happy, tearful reconciliations. But now it was a reality: she was going to see Fiona again. What would the real one say to her? Fiona had told her when she left that she feared her mother would never come back. Once resentment faded, she must long ago have given up hope, believing her mother dead. Lunzie worried about the hurt she had caused Fiona. She imagined an angry Fiona, her jaw locked and nose red as they had been that last morning on Tau Ceti. Lunzie blanched defensively. It wasn't her fault that the space carrier had met with an accident, but did she have to leave Fiona at all? She could have taken a less distant post, one that was less dangerous though it paid less. But, no: for all her self-doubts and newly acquired hindsight, she had to admit that at the time she left Tau Ceti, the job with Descartes seemed the best possible path for her to take. She couldn't have foreseen what would happen.

She missed Fiona, but for her the separation had only been a matter of a few years. She tried to imagine how it would feel if it had been most of a lifetime, as it had for her daughter. She'd be a stranger after all these years. They'd have to become acquainted all over again. Would she like the new Fiona? Would Fiona like her, with the experience of her years behind her? She would just have to wait and see.

"Lunzie?" Tee's soft voice brought her back to herself. When she blinked the dryness from her eyes, she found Tee watching her with his dark eyes full of concern.

"What are you thinking of, my Lunzie? You are always so controlled. I would prefer it if you cry, or laugh, or shout. Your private thoughts are too private. I can never tell what it is you're thinking. Have I not brought good news?"

She took a deep breath, and then hesitated. "What — what if she doesn't want to see me? After all these years, she probably hates me."

"She will love you, and forgive you. It was not your fault. You began to search for her as soon as it was possible to do so," he stated reasonably.

Lunzie sighed. "I should never have left her."

Tee grabbed both of her arms and turned her so that he could look into her eyes. "You did the right thing. You needed to support your child. You wanted to make her very comfortable, instead of merely to subsist. She was left in the best of care. Blame the fates. Blame whatever you must, but not yourself. Now. Are you going? Will you meet with your daughter and your grandchildren?"

Lunzie nodded at last. "I'm going. I have to."

"Good. Then this is a celebration!" He swept back to the parcel he had carried home with him, and removed from it a bottle of rare Cetian wine and a pair of long-stemmed glasses. "It is my triumph and yours, and I want you to drink to it with me. You should at least look like you want to celebrate."

"But I do," Lunzie protested.

"Then wash that worried look from your face and come with me!" Switching the glasses to the hand that held the wine, Tee bent over, and with one effort, threw Lunzie across his shoulders. Lunzie shrieked like a schoolgirl as he carried her into their bedchamber and dumped her onto the double-width bed.

"I can't! Root is expecting me." She flipped over and looked at the digital clock in the headboard. "Oh, Muhlah, now I'm late!" She started to get up but he forestalled her.

"I will take care of that." Tee stalked out. The comm unit chimed as he made a connection. Lunzie had to stifle a giggle as he asked for Dr. Root and solemnly requested that she be allowed to miss a shift. ". . . for a family emergency," he said, in a sepulchral voice that made her bury a hoot of laughter in the bedclothes.

"There," Tee said, as he returned, shucking his tunic off into a corner of the room and kicking off his boots. "You are clear and on green, and he sends his concern and regards."

"I don't know why I'm letting you do that. I shouldn't play hooky," Lunzie chided, a little ashamed of herself. "I usually take my responsibilities more seriously than that."

"Could you honestly have stood and taken blood pressures with this knowledge dancing in your brain?" Tee asked incredulously. "Fiona is found!"

"Well, no . . ."

"Then enjoy it," Tee encouraged her. "Allow me." He knelt before her and grabbed one of her feet, and started to ease the exercise pants down her leg. When her legs were free, he started a trail of kisses beginning at her toes and skimming gently upward along her bare skin. His hands reached around to squeeze and caress her thighs and buttocks, and upward, thumbs stroking the hollow inside her hipbones, as his lips reached her belly. His warm breath sent tingles of excitement racing through her loins. Lunzie lay back on the bed, sighing with pleasure. Her hands played with Tee's hair, running the backs of her nails gently through his hair and along the delicate lines of his ears. She closed her eyes and allowed the pleasure to carry her, moaning softly, until the waves of ecstasy ebbed.

He raised his head and crept further up, poised, hovering over her. Lunzie opened her eyes to smile at him, and met an impish glance.

"Oh, no, you don't," she warned, as he descended, pinioning her, and dipping his tongue into her navel to tickle. "Agh! Unfair!"

He captured her arms as they flailed frantically at his head. "Now, now. All is fair in love, my Lunzie, and I love you."

"Then come up here and fight like a man, damn you." Lunzie freed her hands and pulled at his shoulders. Tee crawled up and settled on his hip beside her. She undid the magnetic seams of his trousers as he lifted himself up, and threw them into the corner after his tunic.

He was already fully aroused. Lunzie stroked him gently with her fingertips as they melted together along the length of their bodies for a deep kiss. He bent to run his tongue around the tips of her breasts, cupping them, and spreading his fingers to run his hands down her rib cage. Their hands joined, intertwined, parted, trailing along the other's arm to draw sensual patterns on the skin of throat and chest and belly. Tee rolled onto his back, taking Lunzie on top of him so he could caress her. She spread her palms along his chest, massaging the flesh with her fingers, and reached behind her to brace against the long, hard muscles of his thighs. She arched up, straddling him, moving so that their bodies joined and rocked together in a rhythm of increasing tempo.

At last, Tee dragged her torso down, and they locked their arms around one another, kissing ears and neck and parted lips as passion overcame them.

Lunzie held tightly to Tee until her heart slowed down to its normal pace. She rubbed her cheek against his jaw, and felt the answering pressure of his arms around her shoulders. Through the joy at having found the object of her search, she was sad at the thought of having to leave Tee. Not only was there a physical compatibility, but they were comfortable with one another. She and Tee were familiar with one another's likes and desires and feelings, like two people who had been together all their lives. She was torn between completing a quest she had set herself years ago, and staying with a man who loved her. If there was only a way that he could come with her — He wasn't denying her her chance to rebuild her life after her experiences with cold sleep; she mustn't deny him his. He had worked too hard and had lost so much. Lunzie felt guilty at even thinking of asking him to come with her. But she loved him too, and knew how much she was going to miss him.

She shifted to take her weight off his arm, and rolled into a hard obstruction in the tangled folds of the coverlet. Curiously, she spread out the edge of the cloth and uncovered the bottle of wine.

"Ah, yes. Cetus, 2755. Your year of birth, I believe. The vintage is only fit to drink after eighty years or more."

"Where are the glasses?" Lunzie asked. "This worthy wine deserves crystal."

"We will share from the bottle," answered Tee, gathering Lunzie close again. "I am not leaving this spot until I get up from here to cook you a marvelous celebratory dinner, for which I bought all the ingredients on the way home."

He fell back among the pillows, tracing the lines of her jaw with one finger. Lunzie lay dreamily enjoying the sensation. Abruptly, a thought struck her. "You know," she said, raising herself on one elbow, "maybe I should travel to Alpha as a staff doctor. That way I could save a good part of the spacefare."

Tee pretended to be shocked. "At this moment you can think of money? Woman, you have no soul, no romance."

Lunzie narrowed one eye at him. "Oh, yes, I have." She sighed. "Tee, I'll miss you so. It might be years before I come back."

"I will be here, awaiting you with all my heart," he said. "I love you, did you not know that?" He opened the bottle and offered her the first sip. Then he drank, and leaned over to give her a wine-flavored kiss.

They made love again, but slowly and with more care. To Lunzie, every movement was now more precious and important. She was committing to memory the feeling of Tee's gentle touch along her body, the growing urgency of his caresses, his hot strength meeting hers.

"I'm sorry we didn't meet under other circumstances," Lunzie said, sadly, when they lay quietly together afterward. The wine was gone.

"I have no regrets. If you didn't need the EEC, we would not have met. I bless Fiona for having driven you into my arms. When you come back, we can make it permanent," Tee offered. "And more. I would love to help you raise a child of ours. Or two."

"Do you know, I always meant to have more children. Just now, the thought seems ludicrous, since my only child is in her seventh decade. I'm still young enough."

"There will be time enough, if you come back to me."

"I will," Lunzie said. "Just as soon as things are settled with Fiona, I'll come back. Doctor Root said that he'd sponsor me as a resident — that is, if he'll still speak to me after my subterfuge to get a night off!"

"If he knew the truth, he'd forgive you. Shall I make us some supper?"

"No. I'm too comfortable to move. Hold me."

Tee drew Lunzie's head onto his chest, and the two of them relaxed together. As Lunzie started to drop off to sleep, the comm unit began chuckling quietly to itself. She sat up to answer it.

"Ignore it until morning," Tee said, pulling her back into bed. "Remember, you have a family emergency. I have asked for travel brochures from all the cruise lines and merchant ships which will pass between Astris and Alpha Centauri over the next six months. We can look over them all in the morning. I do not see you off gladly, but I want you to go safely. We will choose the best of them all, for you."

Lunzie glanced at the growing heap of plastic folders sliding out of the printer, and wondered how she'd ever begin to sort through the mass. "Just the soonest. That will be good enough for me."

Tee shook his head. "None are good enough for you. But the sooner you go, the sooner you may return. Two years or three, they will seem as that many hundred until we meet again. But think about it in the morning. For once, for one night, there is only we two alone in the galaxy."

Lunzie fell asleep with the sound of Tee's heartbeat under her cheek, and felt content.

In the morning, they sat on the floor among a litter of holographic travel advertisements, sorting them into three categories: Unsuitable, Inexpensive, and Short Voyage.

The Unsuitable ones Tee immediately stuffed into the printer's return slot, where the emulsion would be wiped and the plastic melted down so it could be reused in future facsimile transmissions. Glamorous holographs, usually taken of the dining room, the entertainment complex, or the shopping arcades of each line's vessels, hung in the air, as Tee and Lunzie compared price, comfort, and schedule. Lunzie looked most closely at the ones which they designated Inexpensive, while Tee paged through those promising Short voyages.

Of the sixty or so brochures still under consideration, Tee's favorite was the *Destiny Calls*, a compound liner from the Destiny Cruise Lines.

"It is the fastest of all. It makes only three ports of call between here and Alpha Centauri over five months."

Lunzie took one look at the fine print on the plas-sheet under the hologram and blanched. "It's too expensive! Look at those prices. Even the least expensive inside cabin is a year's pay."

"They feed, house, and entertain you for five months," Tee said, reasonably. "Not a bad return after taxes."

"No, it won't do. How about the Caravan Voyages' *Cymbeline*? It's much cheaper." Lunzie pointed to another brochure decorated with more modest photography. "I don't need all those amenities the *Destiny Calls* has. Look, they offer you free the services of a personal psychotherapist, and your choice of a massage or a trained masseuse. Ridiculous!"

"But they are so slow," Tee complained. "You did not want to wait for a merchant to make orbit because of all the stops he would make on the way; you do not want this. If you would pretend that money does not matter for just a moment, it would horrify your efficient soul to find that the *Cymbeline* takes thirteen months to take you where the *Destiny Calls* does in five. And it will not be as comfortable. Come now, think," he said in a wheedling tone. "What about your idea to work your way there on the voyage? Then the question of expense will not come up."

Lunzie was attracted by the idea of travelling on a compound liner, which had quarters for methane- and water-breathers, as well as ordinary oxygen-nitrogen breathers. "Well . . ."

Tee could tell by her face she was more than half persuaded already. "If you are taking a luxury cruise, why not the best? You will meet many interesting people, eat wonderful food, and have a very good time. Do not even think how much I will be missing you."

She laughed ruefully. "Well, all right then. Let's call them and see if they have room for me."

Tee called the comm unit code for the Destiny Line to inquire for package deals on travels. While he was chatting with a salesclerk, he asked very casually if they needed a ship's medical officer for human passengers.

To Lunzie's delight and relief, they responded with alacrity that they did. Their previous officer had gone ashore at the ship's last port of call, and they hadn't had time to arrange for a replacement. Tee instantly transmitted a copy of Lunzie's credentials and references, which were forwarded to the personnel department. She was asked to come in that day for interviews with the cruise office, the captain of the ship and the chief medical officer by FTL comm link, which Lunzie felt went rather well. She was hired. The ship would make orbit around Astris Alexandria in less than a month to pick her up.

✧ CHAPTER SIX

"Please, gentlebeings, pay attention. This information may save your life one day."

There was a general groan throughout the opulent dining room as the human steward went through his oft-recited lecture on space safety and evacuation plans. He pointed out the emergency exits which led to the lifeboats moored inside vacuum hatches along the port and starboard sides of the luxury space liner *Destiny Calls*. Holographic displays to his right and left demonstrated how the emergency atmosphere equipment was to be used by the numerous humanoid and non-humanoid races who were aboard the *Destiny*.

None of the lavishly dressed diners in the Early Seating for Oxygen-Breathers seemed to be watching except for a clutch of frightened-looking humanoid bipeds with huge eyes and pale gray skin whom Lunzie recognized from her staff briefing as Stribans. Most were far more interested in the moving holographic centerpieces of their tables, which displayed such wonders as bouquets of flowers maturing in minutes from bud to bloom, a black-and-silver-clad being doing magic tricks, or, as at Lunzie's table, a sculptor chipping away with hammer and chisel at an alabaster statue. The steward raised his voice to be heard over the murmuring, but the murmuring just got louder. She had to admit that the young man projected well, and he had a pleasant voice, but the talk was the same, word for word, that was given on every ship that lifted, and any frequent traveller could have recited it along with him. He finished with an ironic "Thank you for your attention."

"Well, thank the stars that's over!" stated Retired Admiral Coromell, in a voice loud enough for the steward to hear. There were titters from several of the surrounding tables. "Nobody listens to the damfool things anyway. Only time you can get 'em together is at mealtimes. Captive audience. The ones who seek out the information on their own are the ones who ought to survive anyway. Those nitwits who wait for somebody to save them are as good as dead anyhow." He turned back to his neglected appetizer and took a spoonful of sliced fruit and sweetened grains. The young man gathered up his demonstration gear and retired to a table at the back of the room, looking harassed. "Where was I?" the old man demanded.

Lunzie put down her spoon and leaned over to shout at him. "You were in the middle of the engagement with the Green Force from the Antari civil war."

"So I was. No need to raise your voice." At great length and corresponding volume, the Admiral related his adventure to the seven fellow passengers at his table. Coromell was a large man who must have been powerfully built in his youth. His curly hair, though crisp white, was still thick. Pedantically, he tended to repeat the statistics of each maneuver two or three times to make sure the others understood them, whether or not they were interested in his narrative. He finished his story with a great flourish for his victory, just in time for the service of the soup course, which arrived at that moment.

Lunzie was surprised to see just how much of the service was handled by individual beings, instead of by servomechanisms and food-synth hatches in the middle of the tables. Clearly, the cruise directors wanted to emphasize how special each facet of their preparations was, down to the ingredients of each course. Even if the ingredients were synthesized out of sight in the kitchen, personal service made the customers think the meals were being prepared from imported spices and produce gathered from exotic ports of call all over the galaxy. In fact, Lunzie had toured the storerooms when she first came aboard, and was more impressed than her tablemates that morel mushrooms were served as the centerpiece in the salad course, since she alone knew that they were real.

The diverse and ornamental menu was a microcosm of the ship itself. The variety of accommodation available on the huge vessel was broad, extending from tiny economy class cabins deep inside the ship, along narrow corridors, to entire suites of elegant chambers which had broad portholes looking out into space, and were served by elaborate Tri-D entertainment facilities and had their own staffs of servitors.

Lunzie found the decor in her personal cabin fantastic, all the more so because she was only a crew member, one of several physicians on board the *Destiny*. It was explained to her by the purser that guests might need her services when she was not on a duty shift. The illusion of endless opulence was not to be spoiled at any price, even to the cost of maintaining the doctors in a luxury surrounding, lest the passengers glimpse any evidence of economy. This way was cheaper than dealing with the consequences of their potential distress. Lunzie was surprised to discover that the entertainment system in her quarters was as fancy as the ones in the first-class cabins. There was a wet bar filled with genuine vintage distillations, as well as a drink synthesizer.

The computer outlet in the adjoining infirmary was preprogrammed with a constantly updating medical profile of all crew members and guests. Though she was unlikely to serve a non-humanoid guest, she was provided with a complete set of environment suits in her size, appropriate to each of the habitats provided for methane-breathers, water-breathers, or ultra cold- or hot-loving species, and language translators for each.

Dr. Root would have loved the infirmary. It had every single gadget she had seen listed in the medical supplies catalog. Her own bod bird and gimmick-kit were superfluous among the array of gadgets, so she left them in her suitcase in the cabin locker. She was filled with admiration for the state-of-the-art chemistry lab, which she shared with the other eight medical officers. The *Destiny* had remained in orbit for six days around Astris after taking on Lunzie and fifteen other crew, so she had had plenty of time to study the profiles of her fellow employees and guests.

The files made fascinating reading. The cruise line was taking no chances on emergencies in transit, and their health questionnaires were comprehensive. As soon as a new passenger came aboard, a full profile was netted to each doctor's personal computer console.

Lunzie turned to Baraki Don, the Admiral's personal aide, a handsome man in his seventh or eighth decade whose silver hair waved above surprisingly bright blue eyes and black eyebrows. "I'm not suggesting that I should do the procedure, but shouldn't he have his inner ear rebuilt? Shouting at his listeners is usually a sign that his own hearing is failing. I believe the Admiral's file mentioned that he's over a hundred Standard years old."

Don waved away the suggestion with a look of long suffering. "Age has nothing to do with it. He's always bellowed like that. You could hear him clear down in engineering without an intercom from the bridge."

"What an old bore," one of their tablemates said, in a rare moment when the Admiral was occupied with his food. She was a human woman with black and green-streaked hair styled into a huge puff, and clad in a fantastic silver dress that clung to her frame.

Lunzie merely smiled. "It's fascinating what the Admiral has seen in his career."

"If any of it is true," the woman said with a sniff. She took a taste of fruit and made a face. "Ugh, how awful."

"But you've only to look at all the medals on his tunic front. I'm sure that they aren't all for good conduct and keeping his gear in order," Lunzie said and gave vent to a wicked impulse. "What's the green metal one with the double star for, Admiral?"

The Admiral aimed his keen blue gaze at Lunzie, who was all polite attention. The green-haired woman groaned unbelievingly. Coromell smiled, touching the tiny decoration in the triple line of his chest.

"Young lady, that might interest you as you're a medical specialist. I commanded a scout team ordered to deliver serum to Denby XI. Seems an explorer was grounded there, and they started one by one to come down with a joint ailment that was crippling them. Most of 'em were too weak to move when we got there. Our scientists found that trace elements were present in the dust that they were bringing in on their atmosphere suits that irritated the connective tissue, caused fever and swelling, and eventually, death. Particles were so small they sort of fell right through the skin. We, too, had a couple of cases of itch before it was all cleaned up. Nobody was that sick, but they gave us all medals. That also reminds me of the Casper mission . . ."

The woman turned her eyes to the ceiling in disgust and took a sniff from the carved perfume bottle at her wrist. A heady wave of scent rolled across the table, and the other patrons coughed. Lunzie gave her a pitying look. There must be something about privilege and wealth that made one bored with life. And Coromell had lived such an amazing one. If only half of what he said was true, he was a hero many times over.

The black-coated chief server appeared at the head of the dining hall and tapped a tiny silver bell with a porcelain clapper. "Gentlebeings, honored passengers, the dessert!"

"Hey, what?" The announcement interrupted Coromell in full spate, to the relief of some of the others at the table. He waited as a server helped him to a plate of dainty cakes, and took a tentative bite. He leveled his fork at the dessert and boomed happily at his aide. "See here, Don, these are delicious."

"They have Gurnsan pastry chefs in the kitchen." Lunzie smiled at him as she took a forkful of a luscious cream pastry. He was more interesting than anyone she'd ever met or had seen on Tri-D. She realized that he was just a few years older than she was. Perhaps he had read Kipling or Service in his youth.

"Well, well, very satisfactory, I must say. Beats the black hole out of Fleet food, doesn't it, Don?"

"Yes, indeed, Admiral."

"Well, well. Well, well," the Admiral murmured to himself between bites, as their tablemates finished their meals and left.

"I should go, too," Lunzie said, excusing herself and preparing to rise. "I've got to hold after-dinner office hours."

The Admiral looked up from his plate and the corners of his eyes crinkled up wisely at her. "Tell me, young doctor. Were you listening because you were interested, or just to humor an old man? I noticed that green-haired female popinjay myself."

"I truly enjoyed hearing your experiences, Admiral," Lunzie said sincerely. "I come from a long line of Fleet career officers."

Coromell was pleased. "Do you! You must join us later. We always have a liqueur in the holo-room during second shift. You can tell us about your family."

"I'd be honored." Lunzie smiled, and hurried away.

"That's nasty," Lunzie said, peeling away the pantsleg of a human engineer and probing at the bruised flesh above and below the knee. She poked an experimental finger at the side of the patella and frowned.

"Agh!" grunted the engineer, squirming away. "That hurt."

"It isn't dislocated, Perkin," Lunzie assured him, lowering

the sonic viewscreen over the leg. "Let's see now." On the screen the bone and tendons stood out among a dark mass of muscle. Tiny lines, veins, and arteries throbbed as blood pulsed along them. Near the knee, the veins swelled and melded with one another, distended abnormally. "But if you think it's pretty now, wait a day or so. There's quite a bit of intramuscular bleeding. You didn't do that in an ordinary fall — the bone's bruised, too. How did it happen?" Lunzie reached under the screen to turn his leg for a different view, and curiously watched the muscles twist on the backs of her skeletal hands. This was state-of-the-art equipment.

"Off the record, Doctor?" Perkin asked hesitantly, looking around the examination room.

Lunzie looked around too, then stared at the man's face, trying to discern what was making him so nervous. "It shouldn't be, but if that's the only way you'll tell me . . ."

The man let go a deep sigh of relief. "Off the record, then. I got my leg pinched in a storage hatch door. It shut on me without warning. The thing is six meters tall and almost fifteen centimeters thick. There should have been a klaxon and flashing lights. Nothing."

"Who disconnected them?" Lunzie asked, suddenly and irrationally worried about heavyworlders. Perhaps there was a plot afoot to attack the Admiral.

"No one had to, Doctor. Don't you know about the Destiny Cruise Line? It's owned by the Paraden Company."

Lunzie shook her head. "I don't know anything about them, to be honest. I think I've heard the name before, but that's all. I'm a temporary employee, until we pull into orbit around Alpha Centauri, four months from now. Why, what's wrong with the Paraden Company?"

The engineer curled his lip. "I sure hope this room hasn't got listening devices. The Paraden Company keeps their craft in space as long as it possibly can without drydocking them. Minor maintenance gets done, but major things get put off until someone complains. And that someone always gets fired."

"That sounds horribly unfair." Lunzie was shocked.

"Not to mention hazardous to living beings, Lunzie. Well, whistle-blowing has never been a safe practice. They're Parchandris, the family who owns the company, and they want to squeeze every hundredth credit out of their assets. The Destiny Line is just a tiny part of their holdings."

Lunzie had heard of the Parchandri. They had a reputation for miserliness. "Are you suggesting that this starship isn't space-worthy?" she asked nervously. Now *she* was looking for listening devices.

Perkin sighed. "It probably is. It most likely is. But it's long overdue for service. It should have stayed back on Alpha the last time we were there. The portmaster was reluctant to let us break orbit. That's been bad for morale, I can tell you. We old-timers don't usually tell the new crew our troubles — we're afraid that either they're company spies working for Lady Paraden, or they'll be too frightened to stay on board."

"Well, if anything goes wrong, you'll be sure to warn me, won't you?" She noticed that his face suddenly wore a shuttered look. "Oh, please," she appealed to him. "I'm not a spy. I'm on my way to see my daughter. We haven't seen each other since she was a youngster. I don't want anything to get in the way of that. I've already been in one space accident."

"Now, now," Perkin said soothingly. "Lightning doesn't strike twice in the same place."

"Unless you're a lightning rod!"

Perkin relaxed, a little ashamed for having distrusted her. "I'll keep you informed, Lunzie. You may count on it. But what about my leg here?"

She pointed to the discoloration on his skin. "Well, then, except for the aurora borealis, and no one need know about that but you and your roommate, there will be nothing to draw attention to your, er, mishap," Lunzie said, resealing his magnetic seams. "There's no permanent damage of any kind. The leg will be stiff for a while until the hematoma subsides, and there might be some pain. If the pain gets too bad, take the analgesic which I'm programming into your cabin synthesizer, but no more than once a shift."

"Make me high, will it?" the engineer asked, pushing himself off the table with extra care for his sore leg.

"A little. But more importantly, it will stop up your bowels better than an oatmeal-and-banana sandwich," Lunzie answered, her eyes dancing merrily. "I never prescribe that mix for young Seti. They have enough problems with human-dominated menus as it is."

Perkin chuckled. "So they do. I had one working for me once.

He was always suffering. The cooks grew senna for him. Didn't know much about him other than that. They're the most private species I've ever known."

"If you like, I'll also give you a liniment to rub in your leg following a good hot soak."

"Thank you, Lunzie." Perkin accepted the plastic packet Lunzie handed him and slipped out the door past the next patient waiting to see the doctor.

After that day, Lunzie began to notice things about the ship which weren't quite right. It was hard to tell under all the ornamentation, but the clues were there for eyes paying attention. Perkin was right about the lack of maintenance on ship's systems. There was a persistent leak in the decks around the methane environment, which made various passengers complain of the smell in the hallway near the fitness center. Perkin and the other engineers shrugged as they put one more temporary seal on the cracks, and promised to keep the problem under control until they made the next port with repair facilities, months away at Alpha Centauri.

Lunzie began to worry whether there was a chance that the ship might fail somewhere en route to Alpha Centauri. The odds of meeting with a space accident twice in a lifetime were in the millions, but it still niggled at her. It couldn't happen to her again, could it? She hoped Perkin was exaggerating his concerns. With an uncomfortable feeling that ill fate was just past the next benchmark, Lunzie started listening more intently to the evacuation instructions. True to her word, she didn't mention Perkin's confidences to anyone else, but she kept her eyes open.

Seating arrangements in the dining room had been changed over the course of the last month. Lunzie, Admiral Coromell, and Baraki Don had been given seats at the captain's table, presided over at the early seating by the first mate. This was a distinguished woman of color who was probably of an age with Commander Don. First Mate Sharu was very small of stature. The top of her head was on a level with Lunzie's chin. Sharu wore a snugly cut long evening dress of the same regimental purple as her uniform. Her military bearing suggested that she had been in the service before coming to Destiny Cruise Lines. The ornate gold braid at the wrist of the single sleeve showed her rank, and hid a small, powerful communicator, which she employed to keep in touch with the ship's bridge during the meal. The other arm, which bore a brilliantly cut diamond bangle, was bare to the shoulder. To Lunzie's delight, Sharu, too, loved a good yarn, so Coromell had a responsive audience for his tales.

Not that he appeared to appreciate it. He was still grouchy at times, and occasionally snapped at them for humoring an old man. After a while, Lunzie stopped protesting her innocence and turned the tables on him.

"Maybe I am just humoring you," she told Coromell airily, who stopped in full harangue and glared at her in surprise. "I've gone to school lectures where there was more of a dialogue than you allow. We have opinions, too. Once in a while I'd like to voice one."

"Heh, heh, heh! Methinks I do protest too much, eh?" Coromell chortled approvingly. "That's Shakespeare, for all you beings too young to have read any. Well, well. Perhaps I'm at the age when I'm at the mercy of my environment, in a world for which I have insufficient say any more, and I don't like it. Rather like those poor heavyworlder creatures, wouldn't you say?"

Lunzie perked up immediately at the phrase. "What about the heavyworlders, Admiral?"

"Had a few serving under me in my last command. When was that, eight, ten years ago, Don?"

"Fourteen, Admiral."

Coromell thrust his jaw out and counted the years on the ceiling. "So it was. Damn those desk jobs. They make you lose all track of intervening time. Heavyworlders! Bad idea, that. Shouldn't adapt people to worlds. You should adapt worlds to people. What God intended, after all!"

"Terraforming takes too long, Admiral," Sharu put in reasonably. "The worlds the heavyworlders live on are good for human habitation, except for the gravity. They were created to adapt to that."

"Yes, created! Created a minority, that's what they did," the Admiral sputtered. "We have enough trouble in politics with partisanship anyway. Just when you have all the subgroups there are already getting used to each other, you throw in another one, and start the whole mess over. You've got people screaming about the Phoenix disaster, saying that the heavyworlders were dancing on the graves of the lightweights who were there before 'em, but you can bet they paid a hefty finder's fee to whoever helped them make landfall — probably a goodly percentage of their export income to boot."

"I've heard that planet pirates destroyed the first settlement," Lunzie said, angrily remembering the anguished two years she had spent believing that Fiona had been one of the dead on Phoenix.

"Doctor, you may believe it. Probably they cut off Phoenix's communications with the outside first, destroying their support system, traders and so on. Soon as a planet's population can't take care of itself, the rights go to the next group who can. My ship got the mayday from a merchant ship being chased by a pirate outside of the Eridani system. They had been damaged pretty heavily, but they were still hauling ions when we came on the scene. My Communications Officer kept up chatter with their bridge for three weeks until we could come to the rescue. Lose your spirit, lose the war, that's what I say!"

"Did you capture the pirate?" Lunzie asked eagerly, leaning forward.

The Admiral shook his head regretfully. "Sunspots, no. That'd have been a pretty star on my bow if we had. We engaged them as they streaked after the merchant ship, exchanging fire. That poor little merchant begged heaven's blessings down on us, and scooted! The pirate had no choice. He couldn't turn his back on me again. My ship was holed, but no lives were lost. The pirate wasn't so lucky. I saw hull plates and other debris shoot away from the body of his ship, and the frayed edges curled, imploded! Must have been an atmosphered chamber, which meant crew. I hope to heaven it didn't mean prisoners.

"Whatever they had in their engines, ours was better. We chased them outside the system into the radiation belt, we chased them past comets. Finally, my gunner struck their port engine. They spiralled in circles for a couple of turns, and got back on a steady course, but my gunner hit them again. Dead in the water. As soon as we relayed to them that we were going to board them with a prize crew, they blew themselves up!" The Admiral held out his hands before him, cupping air. "I had them like this, so close! No captain has ever succeeded in capturing a planet pirate. But I flatter myself, that if I couldn't, no man can."

"You do flatter yourself, Admiral," Sharu remarked flippantly. "But most likely, you're right."

Lunzie still joined the Admiral and his aide in the holo-room during the evenings after she held infirmary call. Coromell had two favorite holos he requested in the alcove in which he and Don spent the hours before turning in. The first was the bridge of his flagship, the *Federation*. The second appeared when Lunzie suspected that Coromell was in a pensive mood. It was a roaring fireplace with a broad tiled hearth and an ornamented copper hood set in a stone-and-brick wall.

The quality hologram system was equipped with temperature and olfactory controls as well as visual display. She could smell the burning hardwoods and feel the heat of the flames as she took a seat in the third of the deep, cushiony armchairs furnished in the alcove. Don stood up as she approached, and signalled a server to bring her a drink. As she suspected, Coromell sat bent with one elbow on his knee and a balloon glass in the other hand, staring into the dance of shadows and lights and listening to the soft music playing in the background. He hadn't noticed her arrive. Lunzie waited a little while, watching him. He looked pensive and rather sad.

"What are you thinking of, Admiral?" Lunzie asked in a soft voice.

"Hm? Oh, Doctor. Nothing. Nothing of importance. Just thinking of my son. He's in the service. Means to go far, too, and see if he doesn't."

"You miss him," she suggested, intuitively sensing that the old man wanted to talk.

"Dammit, I do. He's a fine young man. You're about his age, I'd say. You . . . you don't have any children, do you?"

"Just one, a daughter. I'm meeting her on Alpha Centauri."

"A little girl, eh? You look so young." Coromell coughed self-deprecatingly. "Of course, at my age, everyone looks young."

"Admiral, I'm closer to your age than to your son's." Lunzie shrugged. "It's in the ship's records; you could find out if you wanted. I've been through cold sleep. My little girl will be seventy-eight on her next birthday."

"You don't say? Well, well, that's why you understand all the ancient history I've been spouting. You've been there. We should talk about old times." The Admiral shot her a look of lonely appeal which touched Lunzie's heart. "There are so few left who remember. I'd consider it a personal favor."

"Admiral, I'd be doing it out of blatant self-interest. I've only been in this century two years."

"Hmph! I feel as though I've been on this ship that long. Where are we bound for?"

"Sybaris Planet. It's a luxury spa. . . ."

"I know what it is," Coromell interrupted her impatiently. "Another dumping ground for the useless rich. Phah! When I get to be that helpless you can arrange for my eulogy."

Lunzie smiled. The server bowed next to her, presenting a deep balloon glass like the one the Admiral had, washed a scant half inch across the bottom with a rich, ruddy amber liquid. It was an excellent rare brandy. Delicate vapors wafted out of the glass headily as the liquid warmed in the heat from the fire. Lunzie took a very small sip and felt that heat travel down her throat. She closed her eyes.

"Like it?" Coromell rumbled.

"Very nice. I don't usually indulge in anything this strong."

"Hmph. Truth is, neither do I. Never drank on duty." Coromell cupped the glass in his big hand and swirled the brandy gently under his nose before tipping it up to drink. "But today I felt a little self-indulgent."

Lunzie became aware suddenly that the background music had changed. Under the lull of the music was a discreet jingling that could have been mistaken for a technical fault by anyone but a member of the crew. To the crew, it meant impending disaster. Lunzie set down her glass and looked around the shadows.

"Chibor!" She hailed a mate of Perkin's staff who was passing through the immense chamber. She looked up at the sound of her voice and waved.

"I was looking for you, Lunzie. Perkin told me . . . "

"Yes! The alarm. What is it? You can speak in front of the Admiral. He doesn't scare easily."

Coromell straightened up, and set aside his glass. "No, indeed. What's in the wind?"

Chibor signalled for a more discreet tone and leaned toward her. "You know about the engine trouble we've been having. It was giving off some weird harmonics, so we had to turn it off and drop out of warp early. There's no way to get back into warp for a while until it's been tuned, and we jumped right into the path of an ion storm. It's moving toward us pretty fast. The navigator accidentally let us drift into its perimeters, and it's playing merry hell with the antimatter drives. We're heading behind the gas giant in the system to shield us until it passes."

"Will that work?" Lunzie asked her, her eyes huge and worried. She fought down the clutch of fear in her guts.

"May do," Coromell answered calmly, interrupting Chibor. "May not."

"We're preparing to go to emergency systems. Perkin said you'd want to know." Chibor nodded and rushed away. Lunzie watched her go. No one else noticed her enter or leave the holo-room. They were involved in their own pursuits.

"I'd better go up and see what is going on," Lunzie said. "Excuse me, Admiral."

The gas giant of Carson's System was as huge and as spectacular as promised. The rapidly rotating planet had a solid core deep inside an envelope of swirling gases thousands of miles thick. A few of her fellow passengers had gathered on the ship's gallery to view it through the thick quartz port.

The captain of the *Destiny Calls* increased the ship's velocity to match the planet's two-hour period of rotation and followed a landmark in the gas layer, the starting point of a pair of horizontal black stripes, around to the sunward side of the planet, where they stood off, and held a position behind the planet's protective bulk. The green-and-yellow giant was just short of being a star, lacking only a small increase in mass or primary ignition. The planet's orbit was much closer to the system's sun than was common with most gas giants, and the sun itself burned an actinic white on the ship's screens. Telemetry warned of lashing arms of magnetic disturbance that kicked outward from the gaseous surface. This was the only formed planet in this system, and ships passing by were required to use it when aligning for their final jump through the sparsely starred region to Sybaris. Still the planet's rapid rotation and the massive magnetic field it generated meant that here gases and radiation churned constantly, even on its dark side. Lunzie suspected they were closer to the planet, which filled half the viewport, than was normal, but said nothing. Other passengers, the more well-travelled looking ones, seemed concerned as well. The captain appeared a few minutes later, a forced smile belying his attempts to calm his passengers' fears.

"Gentlebeings," Captain Wynline said, wryly, watching the giant's surface spin beneath them. "Due to technical considerations, we were forced to drop out of warp at this point. But as a result, we are able to offer you a fabulous view seen by only a few since it was discovered: Carson's Giant. This gas giant should have been a second sun, making this system a binary without planets, but it never ignited, thereby, leaving us with a galactic wonder, for study and speculation. Oh . . . and don't anybody drop a match."

The passengers watching the huge globe revolve chuckled and whispered among themselves.

The *Destiny* waited behind the gas giant's rapidly spinning globe until they were sure that the particularly violent ion storm had swirled past and moved entirely out of the ecliptic. The first edges of the storm, which an unmanned monitor had warned them of the instant they had entered normal space, filled the dark sky around the giant with a dancing aurora.

"Captain!" Telemetry Officer Hord entered the gallery and stood next to the captain. "Another major solar flare on the sun's surface! That'll play havoc with the planet's magnetic field," he offered and then paused, watching to see how the captain reacted. The Chief Officer didn't seem overly concerned. "This will combine with the effects of the ion storm, sir," he added, when no response was forthcoming.

"I'm aware of the ramifications, Hord," the captain assured him and tripped his collar mike. He spoke decisively in a low voice. Lunzie noticed the change in his hearty tone and moved closer to listen. The captain observed her, but saw only another crew member, and continued with his commands. "Helm, try to maneuver us away from the worst of this. Use whatever drives are ready and tuned. Telemetry, tell us when the storm's passed by enough to venture out again. I don't like this a bit. Computer Systems, get the ceramic brick hard copies of our programming out of mothballs. Just in case. Inform Engineering. What's the period for magnetic disturbance reaching us from the sun, Hord?"

"Nine hours, sir. But the flame disturbances are coming pretty close together. I estimate that some are coming toward us already. There's no way to tell, too much noise to get anything meaningful from the monitor." Both officers looked worried now. The comm unit on the captain's collar bleeped. "Engineering here, Captain. We're getting magnetic interference in the drives. The antimatter bottle is becoming unstable. I'm bringing in portable units to step it up."

The captain wiped his forehead. "So it's begun. We can't depend on the containment systems. Prepare to evacuate the ship. Sound the alarms, but don't launch. Gentlebeings!" Everyone on the gallery looked up expectantly. "There has been a development. Will you please return immediately to your quarters, and wait for an announcement. *Now*, please."

As soon as the gallery cleared, the captain ordered the Communications Officer to make the announcement over shipwide comm systems. When Lunzie turned toward the gallery's door to go back to the holochamber, everything went dark, as the ship abruptly went onto battery. The emergency lights glowed red for a brief instant in the corners and around the hatchway.

"What the hell was that?" the captain demanded as the full lights came back on.

"Overload, probably from the solar flares," Hord snapped out, monitoring his readouts on his portable remote unit. "We'll lose the computer memory if that happens again. Watch out, here it goes!"

Lunzie dashed back toward her cabin through flickering lights. Interstellar travel is safer than taking a bath, less accidents per million, she repeated the often-advertised claim to reassure herself. No one was ever in two incidents, not in this modern age. Every vessel, even one as old as the *Destiny*, was double-checked and had triple back-ups on every circuit.

"Attention please," announced the calm voice of the Communications Officer, cutting through the incidental music and all the video and Tri-D programs. "Attention. Please leave your present locations immediately and make your way to the lifeboat stations. This is not a drill. Do not use the turbovators as they may not continue to function. Repeat, do not use the turbovators."

The voice was interrupted occasionally by crackling, and faded out entirely at one point.

"What was that?" A passenger noticed Lunzie's uniform and grabbed her arm. "I saw the lights go down. There's something wrong, isn't there?"

"Please, sir. Go to the lifeboat stations right now. Do you remember your team number?"

"Five B. Yes, it was Five B." The man's eyes went huge. "Do you mean there's a real emergency?"

Lunzie shuddered. "I hope not, sir. Please, go. They'll tell you what's going on when you're in your place. Hurry!" She turned around and ran with him to the dining hall level.

The message continued to repeat over the loudspeakers.

The corridor filled instantly with hundreds of humanoids, hurrying in all directions. Some seemed to have forgotten not only which stations they were assigned to, but where the dining hall was. Emergency chase lights were intermittent, but they provided a directional beacon for the terrified passengers to follow. There were cries and groans as the passengers tried to speculate on what was happening.

The crowd huddled in the gigantic holo-room near the metal double doors to the dining room, milling about, directionless, babbling among themselves in fear. The holo-room was the largest open space on the level, and could be used for illusions to entertain thousands of people. At one end of the room, several dozen humans, unaware that anything was going on around them, were fending off holographic bandits with realistic-looking swords. In a cave just next to the doors in the dining room, a knot of costumed cave dwellers huddled together over a stick fire. At that moment, the illusion projectors in the alcoves shut off, eliciting loud protests from viewers as their varied fantasies disappeared, leaving the room a bare, ghost-gray shell with a few pieces of real furniture here and there. The costumed figures stood up, looking around for ship personnel to fix the problem, and saw the crowds bearing down on them into the newly opened space. They panicked and broke for the exits. More passengers appeared, trying to shove past them into the dining hall, yelling. Fights began among them. Into the midst of this came the child-caretakers with their charges. The head of child care, a thin human male, spoke through a portable loudspeaker, paging each parent one at a time to come and retrieve its offspring.

"Listen up!" Coromell appeared from his alcove with Don behind him. "Listen!" His deep voice cut across the screaming, and the mechanical whine of overtaxed life-support systems. "Now listen! Everyone calm down. Calm down, I say! You all ignored the emergency procedures in the dining hall. Those of you who know what to do, proceed to your stations, NOW! Those of you who don't know what to do, pipe down so you can hear instructions over the loudspeakers. Move it! That is all!"

"The doors are shut! We can't get through!" a large human woman wailed.

"Just hold your water! Look! They're opening right now."

The engineers appeared in a widening gap between the huge double metal blast doors between the holo-room and the oxygen-breathers' dining hall. The crowd, considerably quieter, rushed through, grabbing oxygen equipment from crew lined up on either side of the doors. Stewards directed them to the irised-open hatchways of the escape capsules and ordered them to sit down.

Coromell, with Don's help, continued to direct the flow of traffic, pushing water-breathers in bubble-suits and frantically shapechanging Weft passengers toward the access stairway to the water environment.

"Attention, please, this is the captain," the Chief Officer's voice boomed over the public address system. "Please proceed calmly to your assigned evacuation pod. This will be a temporary measure. Please follow the instructions of the crew. Thank you."

In the midst of the screaming and shouting, Lunzie heard frantic cries for help. She forced her way through the press of beings to a little girl who had tripped and fallen, and was unable to get up again. She had nearly been trampled. Her face was bruised and she was crying. Shouting words of comfort, Lunzie picked her up high and handed her over the heads of the crowd to her shrieking mother. Don escorted the woman and child into the dining room and saw them onto a capsule. As the escape vehicles filled, the hatches irised closed, and the pods were sealed. It was an abrupt change from the leisurely pace of the luxury liner, and most people were not making the transition well. Lunzie hurried back and forth throughout the huge chamber with an emergency medical kit from a hatch hidden behind an ornate tapestry. She splinted the limbs of trampled victims long enough to get them through the door and slapped bandages on cuts and scrapes suffered by passengers who had had to climb out of the turbovators through accessways in the ceiling. She dispensed mild sedatives for passengers who were clearly on the edge of hysteria.

"Just enough to calm you," she explained, keeping a placid

smile on her face though she too was terrified. "Everything is going to be all right. This is standard procedure." Space accident! This could not be happening to her again.

"My jewelry!" a blue-haired human woman screamed as she was dragged toward the dining hall by a young man in formal clothing. "All of it is still in my cabin. We must go back!" She pulled her hand out of the young man's grip and made to dash back toward the cabins.

"Stop her!" the man shouted. "Lady Cholder, no!"

The woman was borne back toward him on the wave of panicked passengers, but still struggled to move upstream. "I can't leave my jewelry!"

Lunzie seized her arm as soon as it was within reach and pressed the hypo to it. The woman moved her lips, trying to speak, but she collapsed between Lunzie and the young man. He looked quizzically from Lady Cholder to Lunzie.

"She'll sleep for about an hour. The sedative has no permanent effects. By then, you'll be well into space. The distress beacon is already broadcasting," Lunzie explained. "Just try to keep calm."

"Thanks," the young man said, sincerely, picking up Lady Cholder in his arms and hurrying toward an escape capsule.

Lunzie heard rumbling and tearing behind her. She spun.

"There it goes again!" Two ship's engineers leaped toward the double doors, which were sliding closed on the hysterical crowd. The lights went out again. Along the ceiling the lines of red emergency lights came on, bathing all in shadow.

"Cut off that switch!" Perkin shouted at one of his assistants, pointing to the open control box next to the doorway. "It's only supposed to do that when the hull is breached."

"All the programming's messed up, Perkin!" The other engineer pushed and pulled at the levers on the control panel, trying to read the screen in the reduced light. "We'll have to try and keep it open manually."

"We've only got minutes. Get between 'em!" Perkin leaped between the heavy metal doors, now rolling closed, and tried to force one of them back. His men started to force their way through the crowd to help him, but they couldn't reach him before he screamed.

"I'm being crushed! Help!" The doors had closed with him between them.

Lunzie was galvanized by his cries. Mustering the strength of Discipline, she shoved her way through the crowd. Perkin's face was screwed up with pain as he tried to get out from between the doors which were threatening to cut him in half lengthwise. The adrenaline rush hit her just as she reached the front of the line. She and the other engineers took hold of the doors and pulled.

Slowly, grudgingly, the metal blast doors rolled back along their tracks. The crowd, now more frantic than before, rushed into the dining hall around Perkin, who was nearly collapsing. As soon as the doors had been braced open with chucks blocking the tracks, Lunzie rushed to catch Perkin and help him out of the way. He was almost unable to walk, and outweighed her by fifty percent, but in her Discipline trance, Lunzie could carry him easily.

She pulled open his tunic and examined his chest, hissing sympathetically at what she saw. Her fingers confirmed what her heightened perception detected: his left rib cage was crushed, endangering the lung. If she worked quickly, she could free the ribs before that lung collapsed.

"Lunzie! Where are you going?" the voice of Coromell demanded as she hurried to the access stairway leading to the upper decks.

"I've got to get some quick-cast from my office. Perkin will die if I don't brace those ribs."

"Admiral! We'd better go, too," Don shouted, urging him toward the doors.

Coromell pushed the aide's hands away. "Not a chance! I won't be shoved into one of those tiny life preservers with a hundred hysterical grand dames wailing for their money! They need all hands to keep this hulk from spinning into that planet. We can save lives. I may be old, but I can still do my part. The captain hasn't given the evacuation order yet." Suddenly he felt at his chest, and took a deep, painful breath. The color rushed out of his face. "Dammit, not now! Where's my medication?" With shaking fingers, he undid his collar.

Don led him to a couch at the side of the room. "Sit here, sir. I'll find the doctor."

"Don't plague her, Don," Coromell snapped, as Don pushed him down into the seat. "She's busy. There's nothing wrong with me. I'm only old."

Lunzie flew up the steps. As she rounded the first landing, she found herself in the way of another crowd of frantic passengers running down, heading to the dining hall from their cabins. She tried to catch the stair rail, but was knocked off her feet and shoved underfoot. Lunzie grabbed at the legs of the passing humans, trying to pull herself to her feet, but they shook her off. Still possessed of her Discipline strength, she forced her way to the wall and walked her hands upward until she was standing up. Keeping to the wall, Lunzie focused on staying balanced and pushed through the mob, paying no attention to the protests of the people in her way. Another herd of humans barreled past her, trying to climb over one another in their panic to get to safety. She knew she was as terrified as they were, but between Discipline and duty, she didn't — wouldn't — feel it.

The next level was practically deserted. The emergency hatch to the methane environment, normally sealed, had drifted open, dissipating the nauseating atmosphere through the rest of the ship. The rescue capsules on that level were gone. Gagging and choking on the stench, Lunzie ran to her office.

The power in this section had gone on and off several times. Hatchways held in place by magnetic seals had lost their cohesiveness and fallen to the ground, denting walls and floors. Lunzie dodged past them and physically pushed open the door to the infirmary.

With the corridors clearing, she could see that there were other victims of the tragedy. With Perkin's ribs correctly strapped and braced, he was out of danger. She left him on the soft couch to rest. Tirelessly, she sought out other injured members of the crew.

"Here, Lunzie!" Don waved her over to the dark corner where the Admiral lay unconscious. "It's his heart."

As soon as she saw the old man's pinched face, Lunzie gasped. Even in the red light she could tell his skin was going from pasty to blue-tinged white. She dropped to her knees and dug through the medical bag for a hypospray, which she pressed against Coromell's arm. She and Don waited anxiously as she peered at her scanner for his vital signs to improve. The Admiral suddenly stirred and groaned, waving them away with an impatient hand.

"I'm going to give him a vitamin shot with iron," Lunzie said, reaching for a different vial. "He must rest!"

"Can't rest when people are in danger," muttered Coromell.

"You're retired, sir," Don said patiently. "I'll help you walk."

"You'd better get to the capsules," First Mate Sharu called to them.

"Not going in capsules," Coromell wheezed.

"I'll stay and help, Sharu," Lunzie shouted back.

Sharu nodded gratefully, and signalled for the remaining capsules to close their doors. "Captain," she told her wrist communicator, "you may give the order."

"What can we do?" Don asked, as they helped the Admiral toward the stairs. "This situation will only worsen his condition. He'll want to help!"

"Let's get him to one of the cryogenic chambers. I'll give him a sedative, and he and the other critically injured crew can cold sleep it until we're rescued." Lunzie half carried the old man toward the infirmary ward, worrying whether he would survive long enough to be given the cryogenic drug.

There was another tremor in the ship's hull, and all the lights went off. This time they stayed off for several seconds. Only the corner emergency beacons came on in the great holo-room.

"That's it, then," Chibor groaned. "No more drives. Those lights are on batteries."

A crewman battered at the side of the control screen next to the doors. "The function computers are wiped. The programs'll all have to be loaded again from ceramic. It'll take months, years to get the whole ship running again. We could lose everything, power, life support. . . ."

"Concentrate on one section at a time, Nais, so we have partial environment to live in," Sharu ordered. "I suggest the hydroponics sections. For now there's plenty of fresh air for the few of us left. Set up mechanical circulation fans to keep it moving. Rig a mayday beacon."

"Telemetry said that we're too close to the planet. No one will be able to see us," Nais argued pugnaciously. His nerves were obviously frayed. "We're not supposed to be here anyway. The giant is only our landmark in this system. We're millions of kiloms from our proper jump mark."

"Don't you want to be found?" Sharu shot back, grabbing his shoulder and shaking him. "Check with Captain Wynline, see what he wants to do. He's up on the bridge."

"Yes, Sharu," Nais gasped and dashed toward the accessway.

"It'll be dangerous here until we regain systems stabilization," Sharu said to Lunzie, who had just returned to the holo-room. "Can I help in any way?"

"Get me a battery-powered light down here, and I can keep going." Lunzie was grateful that she hadn't become totally dependent on all the toys of modern medical technology. What would those fellow physicians of hers from Astris Alexandria do now without their electronic scalpels?

She was still working on the burst of adrenaline evoked from her Discipline training. When it wore off, she'd be almost helpless. Until then, she intended to help the wounded.

There was a sound like a muffled explosion behind her. Lunzie stood up to see what it was in the dimness. Only half visible in the gloom, the metal blast doors rolled slowly, inexorably closed on the empty dining hall.

"There go the chucks! The doors are closing!" Chibor cried. "Look out!"

A sharp-cornered weight hit Lunzie full in the chest, knocking her backwards. She slammed against the wall and slid down it to the floor, unconscious, over the body of her patient. Chibor ran to her, mopping the blood from Lunzie's cut lip, and felt for a pulse.

Sharu appeared a few minutes later, sweeping the beam of a powerful hand-held searchlight before her. "Lunzie, will this do? Lunzie?"

"Over here, Sharu," Chibor called, a formless shape in the red spotlights.

The first mate ran toward the voice. "Krim!" she sighed. "Dammit. Put her in the cold-sleep chamber with Admiral Coromell. We'll get medical attention for her as soon as somebody rescues us. Meantime, she'll be safe in cold sleep. Then let's get back to work."

PART THREE

✦ CHAPTER SEVEN

Lunzie opened her eyes and immediately closed them again to shut out a bright sharp light that was shining down on her.

"Sorry about that, Doctor," a dry, practical male voice said. "I was checking your pupils when you revived all of a sudden. Here" — a cloth was laid across the hand shielding her eyes — "open them gradually so you can get used to the ambient light. It isn't too strong."

"The door chuck hit me in the chest," Lunzie said, remembering. "It must have broken some ribs, but then I hit the back of my head, and . . . I guess I was knocked unconscious." With her free hand, she felt cautiously down the length of her rib cage. "That's funny. They don't feel cracked or constricted. Am I under local anesthetic?"

"Lunzie?" another voice asked tentatively. "How are you feeling?"

"Tee?" Lunzie snatched the cloth from her face and sat up, suddenly woozy from the change in blood pressure. Strong arms caught and steadied her. She squinted through the glaring light until the two faces became clear. The man on the left was a short, powerfully built stranger, a medical officer wearing Fleet insignia of rank. The other was Tee. He took her hand between both of his and kissed it. She hugged him, babbling in her astonishment.

"What are you doing here? We're ten light years out from Astris. Wait, where am I now?" Lunzie recovered herself suddenly and glanced around at the examination room, whose walls bore a burnished stainless steel finish. "This isn't the infirmary."

The stranger answered her. "You're on the Fleet vessel *Ban Sidhe*. There was a space wreck. Do you remember? You were injured and put into cold sleep."

Lunzie's face went very pale. She looked to Tee for

confirmation. He nodded quietly. She noticed that his face was a little more lined than it was when she had last seen him, and his skin was pale. The changes shocked and worried her. "How long?"

"Ten point three years, Doctor," the Fleet medic said crisply. "Your first mate was debriefed just a little while ago. She and the captain spent the whole time awake, manning the beacon. We very nearly missed the ship. It's about sixteen percent lower into the Carson's Giant's atmosphere than it was when they sent out the mayday and released the escape pods. The orbit is decaying. Looked like a piece of debris. Destiny decided it doesn't want to retrieve the hulk. In about fifty more years, it'll fall into the methane. Too bad. It's a pretty ship."

"No!" Lunzie breathed.

The medic was cheerful. "Just a little down time. It happens to about a fifth of Fleet personnel at one time in their careers. You should feel just fine. What's the matter?" He closed a firm, professional hand around her wrist.

"It's the second time it's happened to me." Lunzie sagged. "I didn't think it could happen to me again. Two space wrecks in one lifetime. Muhlah!"

"Twice? Good grief, you've had an excess of bad luck." He released her hand and quickly ran a scanner in front of her chest. "Normal. You've recovered quickly. You must be very strong, Doctor."

"You need exercise and food," Tee said. "Can I take her away, Harris? Good. Walk with me through the ship. We have recovered all forty-seven of the crew who stayed behind, and two passengers. It is because of one of them that we were able to come looking for you."

"What? Who stayed on board with us?"

"Admiral Coromell. Come. Walk with me to the mess hall, and I'll tell you."

"It was after you had been gone two years that I began to worry about you," Tee explained, dispensing a much-needed pepper to Lunzie. They programmed meals from the synthesizer and sat down at a table near the wall in the big room. The walls here were white. Lunzie noticed that the navy vessel ran to two styles of decoration in its common rooms, burnished steel or flat ceramic white. She hoped the bunkrooms were more inviting.

Tedium caused its own kinds of space sickness. "I knew something was wrong, but I didn't know what it could be. You had only written to me once. I found out from the AT&T operator that it was the only communication charged to your access code number in all that time."

Lunzie was feeling more lively after drinking the mild stimulant. "How did you do that? Astris Telecommunication and Transmission is notoriously uncooperative in giving out information like that."

Tee smiled, his dark eyes warm. "Shof and I became friends after you left. He and Pomayla knew how lonely I was without you, as they were. I taught him much about the practical application of laser technology, and in exchange he gave me insight to computer tricks he and his friends nosed out. He was very pleased to learn from me. I think he made some points with his technology teacher, being able to give detailed reports on the earliest prototypes of the system. Oh, he wanted me to let you know that he graduated with honors." He sighed. "That was eight years ago, of course. He gave me a ticket for the graduation. I went with the rest of the Gang who were still at the University, and we had a party later on, where your name was toasted in good wine. I did miss you so much."

Lunzie noticed the slight emphasis on "did," but let it pass. There seemed to be a distance between them, but that was to be expected, after all the time that had passed. Ten years didn't pack the same shock value as sixty-two, but at least she could picture the passage of that interval of time. "I'm happy to hear about Shof. Thank you for letting me know. But how did you get here?"

"It was the video you sent me, and the fact that you sent no more, which made me go looking for answers. You seemed to be very happy. You told of many things which you had observed on the ship already. The cabin in which you were living was the daydream of a rich man. The other physicians were good people, and all dedicated professionals. You had just delivered a baby to a dolphin couple underwater in the salt-water environment. You missed me. That was all. If you had meant to tell me that you had found someone else, and it was all over between us, you would have sent a second message. You were sometimes very mysterious, my Lunzie, but never less than polite."

"Well," Lunzie said, taking a forkful of potatoes gratinee, "I do hate being cubbyholed like that, but you're right. So my manners saved my life? Whew, this meal is a shock after the *Destiny's* cooking. It isn't bad, you understand."

"Not bad, just uninteresting. How I miss the apartment's cooking facilities!" Tee looked ceilingward. "So long as I live, I will never be entirely happy with synth-swill. Fresh vegetables are issued sparingly to us from the hydroponics pod up top. I never know when I will next see something that was actually grown, not formed from carbohydrate molecules."

"To us?" It registered with Lunzie for the first time that Tee was dressed in a uniform. "Are you stationed on the *Ban Sidhe*, Tee?"

"I am temporarily, yes, but that comes at the end of the story, not the beginning. Let me tell you what happened:

"I was not informed when the space liner first went missing. Whenever I asked the cruise line why I was not receiving messages from you, I was told that interstellar mail was slow, and perhaps you were too busy to send any. That I could accept for a time. It could take a long while for a message brick to reach Astris from Alpha. But surely, after more than two years, I should have heard from you about your meeting with Fiona. Even," Tee added self-consciously, "if it were no more than a thank you to me as your caseworker."

"Surely, if anyone does, you had a right to a full narration of our reunion. I owe you much more than that. Oh, I have missed you, Tee. Great heavens!" Lunzie clutched her head. "Another ten years gone! They were expecting me — Fiona might have had to leave again for Eridani! I must get in touch with Lars."

Tee patted her hand. "I have already sent a communication to him. You should hear back very soon."

"Thank you." Lunzie rubbed her eyes. "My head isn't very clear yet. I probably did have a concussion when they put me in the freezer. I should have your doctor scan my skull."

"Would you like another pepper?" Tee asked solicitously.

"Oh, no. No, thank you. One of those is always enough. So the cruise line said everything was fine, and it was just the post which was going astray. I smell a very nasty rat."

Tee disposed of their trays and brought a steaming carafe of herb tea to the table. "Yes. So did I, but I had no proof. I believed them until I saw on the Tri-D that *Destiny Calls* was supposed to have been lost in an ion storm. The Destiny Line had recovered the passengers, who were sent out in escape capsules. Some of them gave interviews to Tri-D. Even after that, I still hadn't heard from you. Then, I began to move planets and moons to find out what had happened. Like you with Fiona, I ran into the one block in my path. No one knew what had happened after the *Destiny Calls* left its first stop after Astris. The Destiny Line was eager to help, they said, but never did I get any real answers from them. I insisted that they pay for a search to recover the vessel. I told them that you must still be aboard."

"In fact I was. There were a lot of crew wounded when everything began to fall apart, and I couldn't leave them." Tee was nodding. "You know about it already?" Lunzie asked.

"The first mate had kept a handwritten log on plas-sheets from the moment the power failed, then kept files in a word processing program as soon as the terminals were reprogrammed. When we reached the *Destiny*, they had the most vital systems up and running, but the interface between engineering and the drives had been destroyed. I examined it myself. Even to me, the system was primitive."

"How did the Destiny Line get a military vessel involved in looking for a commercial liner?" Lunzie asked curiously, blowing on her cup to cool the tea.

"They didn't. I felt there was something false about the assurances they gave out that the search was progressing well. Using some of my own contacts — plus a few of Shof's tricks — I discovered that the Paraden Company had put in claims on the insurance on the *Destiny Calls*, using the testimony of recovered passengers to prove that the ship had met with an accident. The search was no more than a token, to satisfy the claims adjuster! The company had already written off the lives of the people still on board, you among them. I was angry. I went to the offices myself, on the other side of Astris, to break bones and windows until they should make the search real. I stayed there all day, growling at everyone who walked into the office to book cruises. I'm sure I drove away dozens of potential passengers. They wanted to have me removed because I was hurting business, but I told them I would not go. If they called for a peace officer, I would tell the whole story in my statement, and it would be all over the streets — and that would hurt their business far more!

"I was not the only one who had the idea to confront them personally. I met Commander Coromell there the next morning."

"Commander Coromell. The Admiral's son! I had no idea he was on Astris."

"It was the nearest Destiny Lines office when he got the news. He and I occupied seats at opposite ends of the reception room, waiting silently for one of the company lackeys to tell us more lies. Around midday, we began to converse and compare notes. Our missing persons were on the same ship. The day passed and it was clear that the Destiny Lines manager would not see us. We joined forces, and decided to start a legal action against the company.

"It was too late, you see. They had already been paid by the insurance company, and were uninterested in expending the cost of a search vessel. They were willing to pay the maximum their policy allowed for loss of life to each of us, but no more. Coromell was upset. He used political clout, based on his father's heroic service record, and his own reputation, to urge the Fleet to get involved. They commissioned the *Ban Sidhe* to make the search. Admiral Coromell is a great hero, and they did not like the idea of losing him."

"Bravo to that. You should hear some of his stories. How did you get aboard her? I thought you were still restricted from outer-space posts."

"More clout. Commander Coromell is a very influential man, in a family with a long, distinguished history in the FSP Fleet. He reopened my service file, and arranged for my commission. Commander Coromell gave me a chance to get back into space. It is the chance I was dreaming of, but I thought out of my reach for so much longer. I am very grateful to him."

"So am I. I never hoped to see you so soon," Lunzie said, touching Tee's hand.

"It isn't so soon," Tee answered sadly. "We made many jumps through this system, following the route *Destiny Calls* should have taken. It was my friend Naomi who noticed the magnesium flare near the planet. You should not have been there," Tee chided.

Lunzie raised an outraged eyebrow at him. "We were running from an ion storm, as I think you know," she retorted. "It was a calculated risk. If we'd jumped to this system only a little earlier or a little later, we wouldn't have been in the storm's path."

"It was the worst of bad luck, but you are safe now," Tee said, gently, rising to his feet and extending a hand to her. "Come, let's reunite you with the rest of the *Destiny*'s crew."

"Well, she's as good as scrap. Without a program dump from another Destiny Lines mainframe, we can't get the hulk to tell us all the places where it hurts, let alone fix them," Engineer Perkin explained, ruefully.

"Do rights of salvage apply?" One of the younger Fleet officers spoke up, then looked ashamed of himself as everyone turned to look at him. "Sorry. Don't mean to sound greedy."

"Hell, Destiny Lines had already abandoned us for dead," First Mate Sharu said, waving the gaffe away. "Take whatever you want, but please leave us our personal belongings. We've also laid claim to the insured valuables left behind by some of our passengers."

"I . . . I was thinking of fresh foodstuffs," the lieutenant stammered. "That's all."

"Oh," Sharu grinned. "The hydroponic section is alive and well, Lieutenant. There's enough growing there to feed thousands. The grapefruits are just ripe. So are the ompoyas, cacceri leaf, groatberries, marsh-peas, yellow grapes, artichokes, five kinds of tomatoes, about a hundred kinds of herbs, and more things ripening every day. We ate well in exile. Help yourselves."

The younger officers at the table cheered and one threw his hat in the air. The older officers just smiled.

"We'll take advantage of your kindly offer, First Mate," the Fleet captain said, smiling on her genially. "Like any vessel whose primary aim is never to carry unnecessary loads, our hydro section is limited to what is considered vital for healthy organisms, and no more."

"Captain Aelock, we owe you much more than a puny load of groceries. I'm sure when Captain Wynline comes back from the *Destiny*'s hulk with your men, he'll tell you the same. He may even help you strip equipment out personally. To say he's bitter about our abandonment is a pitiful understatement. Ah, Lunzie! Feeling better?" Sharu smiled as Lunzie and Tee entered, and gestured to the medic to sit by her.

"I'm fine, thanks."

"It seems we owe our rescue to the persuasiveness of Ensign Janos, is that correct?"

"In part," Tee said, modestly. "It is actually Commander Coromell that we all must thank."

"I'm grateful to everyone. I've set aside some of the salvage goods for both of you. Lunzie, do you fancy Lady Cholder's jewels? It's a poor bonus for losing ten years, but they're yours. I would say they're worth something between half a million and a million credits."

"Thank you, Sharu, that's more than generous. Am I the last awake?" Lunzie asked.

"No. The Commander's father and his father's aide were the last," Aelock answered. "I've asked them to join us here when they've finished in the Communications Center."

"I should have been consulted," Lunzie said, with some asperity. "The Admiral has a heart condition."

"We had that information from his son," Aelock said apologetically. "Besides, his health records are in the Fleet computer banks."

"Ah, there you are, Doctor," the senior Coromell said in a booming voice, striding into the room, followed by his aide. "If there is ever anything that I or my descendants can do for you, consider it a sacred trust. This young lady saved my life, Captain. I just told my son so." Lunzie blushed. The Admiral smiled on her and continued. "He's very grateful that I'm alive, but no more so than I. He spent a lot of air time ticking off his old man for heroics, and then said he'd probably have done the same thing himself. I'm to meet him on Tau Ceti. I'll take responsibility if anyone asks why the transmission on a secure channel was so lengthy."

"I have discretion in this matter, Admiral, but thank you," Aelock said graciously. "Now, what is to be done with all of you? Since Destiny Lines seems to have washed its hands of you. At least temporarily, that is. I shall be preferring charges in FSP court against them for reckless abandonment of a space vessel."

"With your permission," Sharu asked, "may I communicate with the head office? Since I have managed to live in spite of their efforts, I may be able to shame them into paying for our retrieval and continuing travel to our destination from wherever you may drop us off."

Captain Aelock nodded. "Of course."

❖ ❖ ❖

"Oh, and Doctor, there was a transmission for you on the FTL link, too," the Admiral told her when the meeting broke up. "You might want to take it in private." It was the softest voice she'd ever heard him use.

"Thank you, Admiral." Lunzie was puzzled by his uncommon solicitousness. He smiled and marched off down the corridor with Captain Aelock, with Don and Aelock's officers trailing behind.

"Come," Tee said. "It is easy to find. You should begin to learn the layout of the ship." They stood outside the meeting room in a corridor about two and a half meters wide. "This is the main thoroughfare of the ship. It runs from the bridge straight back to the access to engineering. It was considered unwise," he added humorously, "to have the engineering section directly behind the bridge. An explosion there would send a fireball straight through the control panels directing the ship."

"I can't argue with that logic," Lunzie agreed.

"I will give you the full tour later. For now, let's see what Lars has to say."

There was a small commotion when Tee led Lunzie into the Communications Center.

"So, this is the lady who launched a thousand rescuers, eh?" winked a human officer, twirling the ends of his black mustache.

"This is Lunzie, Stawrt," Tee acknowledged, uncomfortably.

"A pleasure," Lunzie said, shaking hands around. There were three officers on duty, the Communications Chief, Stawrt, and two Wefts, Ensigns Huli and Vaer. Huli, instead of wearing the standard humanoid form so widely used by Wefts in the presence of humans, had extruded eight or ten tentaclelike arms with two fingers each, with which he played the complicated board before him.

Huli tapped her with one of the attenuated digits on his fifth hand. "You would like to view your message? Would you care to step into that privacy booth?" Another hand snaked over to point at a door on an interior wall.

"Tee, would you come and listen, too?" Lunzie asked quietly, suddenly uneasy.

The private booth was a very small compartment with thick beige soundproofing on all walls, floor, and ceiling. Any words spoken seemed to be swallowed up by the pierced panels. In the center of the room was a standard holofield projector, with chairs arranged around it. Lunzie took a chair, and Tee settled down beside her. She half expected him to take her hand but he didn't touch her. In fact, except for when she'd practically fainted into his arms when she woke up, he hadn't touched her at all.

"Press this red button to start," Tee said, pointing to a small keypad on the arm of her chair. "The black stops transmission, the yellow freezes the action in place, and the blue restarts the transmission from the beginning."

Lunzie touched the red button, feeling very nervous.

In the holofield, the image of Lars appeared. He, like Tee, had aged slightly. His hair was thinner, he was getting thicker around the middle, and the pursed lines at the side of his mouth were deeper.

"Ancestress," Lars began, bowing. "I'm happy to hear that you have been recovered safely. When you didn't arrive on schedule, we were very concerned. Ensign Janos was kind enough to tell me the whole story.

"I am very sorry to tell you that Mother isn't here any more. She arrived, as scheduled, two years after we heard from you." The dour face smiled at his memories. "She was so delighted when we sent a message to her that you were expected. Ancestress, she waited eighteen months more for you. Since we had not heard further from you, we were forced to conclude that you had changed your mind. I know now that was an erroneous judgment. I am sorry. You will still be more than welcome if you come to Alpha Centauri. My grandchildren have been nagging me to make sure I remember to extend the invitation. Well, consider it extended.

"Before she left for Eridani, she recorded the following holo for you." Lars hastily blinked out, to be replaced by a larger image of Fiona's head and shoulders, which meant that the recording had been made on a communications console. Now, more clearly than before, Lunzie could see the resemblance in the older Fiona to the child. Age had only softened the beautiful lines of her face, not marred them. The hooded eyes were full of experience and confidence and a deep, welling grief that tore at Lunzie's heart. Her eyes filled with tears as Fiona began to speak.

"Lunzie, I guess that you aren't coming. What made you change your mind?

"I wanted to see you. Truly, I did. I resented like hell having you go away from me when I was a girl. I mean, I understood why you went, but it didn't make it any easier. Uncle Edgard came to get me after the shipwreck, and took me to MarsBase. It was nice. I roomed with cousins Yonata and Immethy, his two daughters. I worried so much about you, but then time went by and I had to stop worrying, and get on with my life. You know by now I went into medicine." The image grinned, and Lunzie smiled back. "The family vocation. I worked hard at it, got good grades, and I think I earned the respect of my professors. I would have given anything to hear you tell me you were proud of me. In the end, I had to be proud of myself." Fiona seemed to be having trouble getting the words out. Her eyes were bright with tears, too.

"I was proud of you, baby," Lunzie whispered, her mouth dry. "Muhlah, I wish you knew that."

"I got to be pretty good at what I did," Fiona continued. "I joined the EEC and racked up a respectable service record. Your mother's brother Jermold hired me; I think he's still working the same desk job in Personnel, even at his advanced age. I've been all over the galaxy in the service, though I've seen mostly new colony worlds in the worst possible condition — suffering from disease epidemics! — but I have had a great time, and I loved it. They think they're rewarding me by assigning me to a desk job.

"Lunzie, there are a thousand things I want to tell you, all the things I thought about when you went away. Most of them were the resentful mutterings of a child. I won't trouble you with those. Some were beautiful things that I discovered that I wanted to share with you. I wish you could have met Garmol, my husband. You and he would have gotten along so well, though we've always had itchy feet, and he was the original ground-bounder. But the most important thing I wanted to let you know is that I love you. I always did, and always will.

"I have to leave for Eridani now, and assume the duties of my office as Surgeon General. I've made them wait for me as long as I've dared, but now I must go.

"Lunzie . . . " Fiona's voice became very hoarse, and she stopped to swallow. She cleared her throat and raised her chin decisively, the image of her eyes meeting Lunzie's across the light years. "Mother, goodbye."

Lunzie was quiet for a long time, staring at the empty holofield long after the image faded. She shut her eyes with a deep-chested sigh, and shook her head. She turned to Tee, almost blindly, lost in her own thoughts.

"What should I do now?"

He had been studying her. She could tell that he, too, was moved by Fiona's message, but his expression changed immediately.

"What should you do?" Tee repeated quizzically. "I am not in charge of your life. You must decide."

Lunzie rubbed her temples. "For the first time in my life, I haven't got an immediate goal to work toward. I've left school. Fiona's given up on me. Who could blame her? But it leaves me adrift."

Tee's face softened. "I'm sorry. You must feel terrible."

Lunzie wrinkled her forehead, thinking deeply. "I should, you know. But I don't. I'm grieved, certainly, but I don't feel as devastated as I . . . think that I should."

"You should go and see your grandchildren. Did you hear? They want to see you."

"Tee, how will I get there now?" Lunzie asked in a small voice. "Where is the *Ban Sidhe* dropping us?"

"We are waiting for orders. As soon as I know, you will know."

Captain Aelock had already received the *Ban Sidhe's* flight orders, and was happy to share the details with Lunzie.

"We've been transferred to the Central Sector for the duration, Lunzie. Partly because of the Admiral's influence, but also because it is convenient to our mission, we're going to Alpha Centauri, then toward Sol. Would you mind if we set you down there? It'll be our first port of call."

Lunzie's eyes shone with gratitude. "Thank you, sir. It takes a great load off my mind. I must admit I've been worrying about it."

"Worry no longer. The Admiral was quite insistent that you should have whatever you needed. He's very impressed with your skill, claims you saved his life. You can assist our Medical Officers while we're en route. 'No idle hands' is our motto."

"So I've heard."

"With all the *Destiny* refugees aboard, things will be somewhat cramped, but I have discretion with regard to officers. You and Sharu will share a cabin in officer country. If there are any problems," Aelock smiled down on her paternally, "my door is always open."

"I was never so glad in my life to see anything as this destroyer popping out of warp just as we rounded the dark side of the planet," Sharu said, sipping fresh juice the next morning at mess with a tableful of the *Ban Sidhe*'s junior officers. Lunzie sat between the first mate and Captain Wynline. Tee was on duty that shift. "I had a magnesium bonfire all ready to go behind the quartz observation desk port. I lit it and jumped back, and it roared up into silver flames like a nova. The ship was sunk into the gravity well of the planet and was following its orbit instead of staying stationary. Because Carson's Giant spins so fast, our window of opportunity was very small. Our signal had to be dramatic."

"Magnesium?" declared Ensign Riaman. "No wonder that deck was slagged. It was probably red hot for hours afterwards.

"It was. I got burns on my arms and face. They're only just healing now," Sharu said, displaying her wrists. "See?"

"It was worth it," Captain Wynline said positively. "It worked, didn't it? You saw it."

"We certainly did," added Lieutenant Naomi, a blond woman in her early thirties. "A tiny spark on the planet's surface where nothing should have been. You were lucky."

"Oh, I know," Sharu acknowledged. "There has never been a prettier sight than that of your ship homing in on us. We have seen so many ships go by without seeing us. We did everything but jump up and down and wave our arms to get their attention. We were very lucky that you were looking the right way at the right time."

"We could have been planet pirates," Ensign Tob suggested.

He was shouted down by his fellows. "Shut up, Tob." "Who'd be stupid enough to mistake us for them? It'd be an insult to the Fleet."

"You were wounded when the ship was first evacuated," Ensign Riaman asked Lunzie, who was spreading jam on a slice of toast. "Was it a shock to wake up and find you had been in cold sleep?"

"Not really. I've been in cold sleep before," Lunzie explained.

"Really? For what? An experiment? An operation?" Riaman asked eagerly. "My aunt was put in cryo-sleep for two years until a replacement for a bum heart valve could be grown. My family has a rare antibody system. She couldn't take a transplant."

"No, nothing like that," Lunzie said. "My family is disgustingly ordinary when it comes to organ or antibody compatibility. I was in another space wreck once, on the way to take a job on a mining platform for the Descartes Company."

To her surprise, the young ensign goggled at her and hastily went back to his meal. She looked around at the others seated at the table. A couple of them stared at her, and quickly looked away. The rest were paying deep attention to their breakfasts. Dismayed and confused, she bent to her meal.

"Jonah," she heard someone whisper. "She must be a Jonah." Out of the corner of her eye, Lunzie tried to spot the speaker. Jonah? What was that?

"Lunzie," Sharu said, speaking to break the silence. "Our personal belongings are being brought aboard in the next few hours. Would you care to come with me and help me sort out the valuables that were left in the purser's safe? We'll package up what we aren't claiming for shipment to their owners when we make orbit again."

"Of course, Sharu. I'll go get freshened up, and wait for you." Hoping she didn't sound as uncomfortable as she felt, Lunzie blotted her lips with her napkin and hurried toward the door.

"Bad luck comes in threes," a voice said behind her as she went out the door, but when she turned, no one was looking at her.

"It's my fault. I should have warned you to keep quiet about the other wreck," Sharu apologized when she and Lunzie were alone. Before them were dozens of sealed boxes from the purser's strongroom and a hundred empty security cartons for shipping. "I've been in the Fleet so I remember what it was like. One space accident is within the realm of possibility. Two looks like disastrously bad luck. No one's more superstitious than a sailor."

"Sharu, what is a Jonah?"

"You heard that? Jonah was a character in the Old Earth Bible. Whenever he sailed on a ship, it ran into technical difficulties. Some sank. Some were becalmed. One of the sailors decided Jonah had offended Yahweh, their God, so he was being visited with bad luck that was endangering the whole ship. They threw him overboard into the sea to save themselves. He was swallowed by a sea leviathan."

"Ulp!" Lunzie swallowed nervously, pouring a string of priceless glow pearls into a bubblepack envelope. "But they wouldn't throw me overboard? Space me?"

"I doubt it." Sharu frowned as she sorted jewelry. "But they won't go out of their way to rub elbows with you, either. Don't mention it again, and maybe it'll pass."

Lunzie put the bubblepack into a carton and sealed it, labeling the carton FRAGILE — DO NOT EXPOSE TO EXTREMES OF TEMPERATURE, which made her think of Illin Romsey, the Descartes crystal miner who rescued her, and the Thek that accompanied him. She hadn't thought of that Thek in months. It was still a mystery to Lunzie why a Thek should take an interest in her.

"Of course, Sharu. I never knowingly stick my head into a lion's mouth. You can't tell when it might sneeze."

Among the jewels and other fragile valuables, she found her translucent hologram of Fiona. Lunzie was shocked to find that she was now used to the image of the grown woman Fiona, and this dear, smiling child was a stranger, a long-ago memory. With deliberate care, she sealed it in a bubblepack and put it aside.

Three days later, Lunzie waited outside the bridge until the silver door slid noiselessly aside into its niche. Captain Aelock had left word for her in her cabin that he wished to speak with her. Before she stepped over the threshold, she heard her name, and stopped.

" . . . She'll bring bad luck to the ship, sir. We ought to put her planetside long before Alpha Centauri. We might never make it if we don't." The voice was Ensign Riaman's. The young officer had been ignoring her pointedly at mealtimes and muttering behind her back when they passed in the corridors.

"Nonsense," Captain Aelock snapped. It sounded as though this was the end of a lengthy argument, and his patience had been worn thin. "Besides, we've got orders, and we will obey them. You don't have to associate with her if she makes you nervous, but for myself I find her charming company. Is that all?"

"Yes, sir," Riaman replied in a submissive murmur that did nothing to disguise his resentment.

"Dismiss, then."

Riaman threw the captain a snappy salute, but by then Aelock had already turned back toward the viewscreen. Smarting from the reproach, the ensign marched off the bridge past Lunzie, who had decided that she'd rather be obvious than be caught eavesdropping. When their eyes met, he turned scarlet to his collar, and shot out of the room as if he'd been launched. Lunzie straightened her shoulders defiantly and approached the captain. He met her with a friendly smile, and offered her a seat near the command chair in the rear center of the bridge.

"This Jonah nonsense is a lot of spacedust, of course," Aelock told Lunzie firmly. "You're to pay no attention to it."

"I understand, sir," Lunzie said. The captain appeared to be embarrassed that she had been affected by the opinion of one of his officers, so she gave him a sincere smile to put him at his ease. He nodded.

"We've been out on maneuvers trying to catch up with planet pirates, and they still haven't come down from the adrenaline high. After a while we were seeing radar shadows behind every asteroid. It was time we had a more pedestrian assignment. Perhaps even a little shore leave." Aelock sighed, shrugging toward the door by which the ensign had just left. "Though Alpha Centauri wouldn't be my first choice. It's a little too industrialized for my tastes. I like to visit the nature preserves of Earth myself, but my lads consider it tame."

"Have the pirates struck again?" Lunzie asked, horrified. "The last raid I heard of was on Phoenix. I once thought my daughter had been killed by the raiders."

"What, Doctor Fiona?" Aelock demanded, smiling, watching Lunzie's mouth drop open. "It may surprise you to know, Doctor Mespil, that we had the pleasure of hosting the lady and her dog act fifteen Standard years ago. As charming as yourself, I must say. I can see the family resemblance."

"The galaxy is shrinking," Lunzie said, shaking her head. "This is too much of a coincidence."

"Not at all, when you consider that she and I serve the same segment of the FSP population. We're both needed chiefly by the new colonies that are just past the threshold of viability, and hence under FSP protection. The emergency medical staff like her use our ships because we're the only kind of vehicle that can convey help there quickly enough."

"Such as against planet pirates?"

Aelock looked troubled. "Well, it's been very quiet lately. Too quiet. There hasn't been a peep out of them in months — almost a year since the last incident. I think they're planning another strike, but I haven't a clue where. By the time we reach Alpha, I'm expecting to hear from one of my contacts, a friend of a friend of a friend of a supplier who sells to the pirates. We still don't know who they are, or who is providing them with bases and repair facilities, drydocks, and that kind of thing. I'm hoping that I can make a breakthrough before someone follows the line of inquiry back to me. People who stick their noses into the pirates' business frequently end up dead."

Lunzie gulped, thinking of Jonahs and the airlock. The captain seemed to divine her thoughts and chuckled.

"Ignore the finger-crossers among my crew. They're good souls, and they'll make you comfortable while you're aboard. We'll have you safe and sound, breathing smoggy Alpha Centauri air before you know it."

✧ CHAPTER EIGHT

She didn't have time to worry about her new label of Jonah on the brief trip to Alpha Centauri. A number of the crew from the *Destiny Calls* broke out in raging symptoms of space traumatic stress. There was a lot of fighting and name-calling among them, which the ship's Chief Medical Officer diagnosed as pure reaction to danger. In order to prevent violence, Dr. Harris assigned Lunzie to organize therapy for them. On her records, he had noticed the mention of Lunzie's training in treating space-induced mental disorders and put the patients' care in her hands.

"Now that it's all over, they're remembering to react," Harris noted, privately to Lunzie, during a briefing. "Not uncommon after great efforts. I won't interfere in the sessions. I'll just be an observer. They know and trust you, whereas they would not open up well to me. Perhaps I can pick up pointers on technique from you."

Lunzie held mass encounter sessions with the *Destiny* crew. Nearly all the survivors attended the daily meetings, where they discussed their feelings of anxiety and resentment toward the company with a good deal of fire. Lunzie listened more than she talked, making notes, and throwing in a question or a statement when the conversation lagged or went off on a tangent; and observed which employees might need private or more extensive therapy.

Lunzie found that the group therapy sessions did her as much good as they did the other crew members. Her own anxieties and concerns were addressed and discussed thoroughly. To her relief, no one seemed to lose respect for her as a therapist when she talked about her feelings. They sympathized with her, and they appreciated that she cared about their mental well-being, not clinically distant, but as one of them.

The mainframe and drives engineers were the most stressed out, but the worst afflicted with paranoid disorders were the service staff. They complained of helplessness throughout the time they'd spent awake cleaning up the *Destiny Calls*, since they could do nothing to better the situation for themselves or anyone else. For the mental health of the crew at large, Captain Wynline had ordered stressed employees to be put into cold sleep. In order to continue working efficiently on the systems which would preserve their lives, the technicians had to be shielded from additional tension.

"But there we were on the job, and all of a sudden, we'd been rescued while we were asleep," Voor, one of the Gurnsan cooks, complained in her gentle voice. "There was no time for us to get used to the new circumstances."

"No interval of adjustment, do you mean?" Lunzie asked.

"That's right," a human chef put in. "To be knocked out and stored like unwanted baggage — it isn't the way to treat sentient beings."

Perkin and the other heads of Engineering defended the captain's actions.

"Not at all. For the sake of general peace of mind, hysteria had to be stifled," Perkin insisted. "I wouldn't have been able to concentrate. At least cryo-sleep isn't fatal."

"It might as well have been! Life and death — my life and death — taken out of my hands."

Lunzie pounced on that remark. "It sounds like you don't resent the cold sleep as much as you do the order to take it."

"Well . . . " The chef pondered the suggestion. "I suppose if the captain had asked for volunteers, I probably would have offered. I like to get along."

Captain Wynline cleared his throat. "In that case, Koberly, I apologize. I'm only human, and I was under a good deal of strain, too. I ask for your forgiveness."

There was a general outburst of protest. Many of the others shouted Koberly down, but a few agreed pugnaciously that Wynline owed them an apology.

"Does that satisfy you, Koberly?" Lunzie asked, encouragingly.

The chef shrugged and looked down at the floor. "I guess so. Next time, let me volunteer first, huh?"

Wynline nodded gravely. "You have my word."

"Now, what's this about our not getting paid for our down time?" Chibor asked the captain.

Wynline was almost automatically on the defensive. "I'm sorry to have to tell you this, but since the ship was treated as lost, the Paraden Company feels that the employees aboard her were needlessly risking their lives. Only the crew who were picked up with the escape pods were given compensatory pay. Our employment was terminated on the day the insurance company paid off the *Destiny Calls*."

There was a loud outcry over that. "They can't do that to us!" Koberly protested. "We should be getting ten years' back pay!"

"Where's justice when you need it?"

Dr. Harris cleared his throat. "The captain is planning to press charges against the Paraden Company to recover the cost of the deepspace search. You can all sign on as co-plaintiffs against them. We'll give statements to the court recorder when we reach Alpha Centauri."

Lunzie and a handful of the *Destiny's* crew watched from a remote video pickup in the rec room as the *Ban Sidhe* pulled into a stable orbit around Alpha Centauri. It was the first time that she'd been this close to the center of the settled galaxy. The infrared view of the night side of the planet showed almost continuous heat trace across all the land masses and even some under the seas, indicating population centers. She'd never seen such a crowded planet in her life. And somewhere down on that world was her family. Lunzie couldn't wait to meet them.

Two unimaginably long shifts later, she received permission to go dirtside in the landing shuttle. She took a small duffle with some of her clothes and toiletries and Fiona's hologram. After checking her new short haircut hastily in the lavatory mirror, she hurried to the airlock. Some of the *Destiny's* kitchen staff were already waiting there for the shuttle, surrounded by all of their belongings.

"I'm staying," Koberly declared, "until I can get the Tribunal to hear my case against Destiny Lines. Those unsanctioned progeny of a human union won't get away with shoving me into a freezer for ten years, and then cheating me out of my rights."

"I'm just staying," said Voor, clasping her utensil case to her astounding double bosom. "There are always plenty of jobs on settled worlds for good cooks. I plan to apply to the biggest and best hotels in Alpha City. They'd be eager to snap up a pastry chef who can cook for ten thousand on short notice."

Koberly shook his head pityingly at the Gurnsan's complacent attitude. "Don't be dumb. You're an artist, cowgirl. You shouldn't apply for a job just because you're fast, or because you supply your own milk. Let 'em give you an audition. Once they taste your desserts they will give you anything to keep you from leaving their establishment without saying yes. Anything."

"You're too kind," Voor protested gently, shaking her broad head.

"I agree with him," Lunzie put in sincerely. "Perhaps you should hold an auction and sell your services to the highest bidder."

"If you like, I will handle the business arrangements for you," said a voice behind Lunzie. "May I join you while you wait? It is my turn to go on shore leave as well." It was Tee, glowing like a nova in his white dress uniform. Lunzie and the others greeted him warmly.

"Delighted, Ensign," Voor said. "You saved my life. I will always be happy to see you."

"I haven't seen much of you for the last few days," Lunzie told him, hoping it didn't sound like a reproach.

Tee grinned, showing his white teeth. "But I have seen you! Playing the therapy sessions like a master conductor. I have stood in the back of the chamber listening, as first one speaks up, then another speaks up, and you solve all their problems. You are so wise."

Lunzie laughed. "In this case the complaint was easy to diagnose. I'm a sufferer, too."

Behind the burnished steel door came a hissing and the booming of metal on metal. Around the edge of the doorway, red lights began flashing, and a siren whooped. Lunzie and the others automatically jumped back, alarmed.

"It is only the airlock in use," Tee explained apologetically. "If there had been an actual emergency, we would be too close to it to be safe anyway."

With a hiss, the door slid back, and the shuttle pilot appeared inside the hollow chamber, and gestured the passengers inside. "Ten hundred hours. Is everyone ready?"

"Yes!" The pilot dived aside as his cargo rushed past him eagerly.

"Unrecirculated air!" Lunzie stepped out of the spaceport in Alpha City and felt the caress of a natural wind for the first time since leaving Astris. She held her face up to the sun and took a deep breath of air. And expelled it immediately in a fit of coughing.

"Wha— what's the matter with the air?" she asked, sniffing cautiously and wrinkling her nose at the odor. It was laden with chemical fumes and the smell of spoiling vegetation. She looked up at the sky and saw the sun ringed with a grayish haze that shimmered over the surrounding city.

"Some good news, and some bad news, Doctor Lunzie," a Fleet ensign explained. "The good news is it's natural, and it hasn't been reoxygenated by machines a million times. The bad news is what the humans who live on Alpha have been throwing into it for thousands of years. Airborne garbage."

"Ough! How could they do this to themselves? The very air they breathe!" Lunzie moaned, dabbing her streaming eyes with a handkerchief.

Tee picked up her bags and hailed a groundcar. "It shouldn't be as bad further from the spaceport. Come on." He hurried her down the concrete ramp and into the sealed car.

"Where are you going?" Lunzie demanded when she could speak. She blew her nose loudly into the handkerchief.

"With you. I would not miss your family reunion for the world. I have an invitation from Melanie."

"What is your destination?" the robotic voice of the groundcar demanded. "With or without travel guide?"

Tee reeled off an address. "What do you think, Lunzie? Do you want it to tell you about the sights we pass?"

Lunzie peered through the windows at the unending panorama of gray buildings, gray streets, and gray air. The only color was the clothing of the few pedestrians they passed. "I don't think so. It all looks the same, for kilometers in every direction, and it's so gloomy. I just want to get there and meet them. I wonder how they've all changed in ten years. Do you suppose there are new babies?"

"Why not? No travel guide," Tee ordered.

"Acknowledged."

Tee chatted brightly with her as they sailed along the super-highways toward Melanie's. Once they had disembarked from the *Ban Sidhe*, he was his old self, expansive and affectionate. Lunzie decided that it must be the military atmosphere of the Fleet ship which squashed his usually sunny nature. She was relieved that he was feeling better.

It was twilight when they finally arrived. The groundcar disgorged them in suburban Shaygo, only two hundred kilometers from Alpha City. Lunzie couldn't tell by watching when one city left off and the second one began. They had obviously grown together over the years. There was no open space, no parks, no havens for vegetation, just intertwining thoroughfares with thousands of similar podlike groundcars hurtling along them. The trail of air transports penned on the gray sky in white between the tall buildings. Lunzie found the sight depressing.

The house, one of an attached row, sat at the top of a small yard with trees on either side of the walk leading to the door. A twinkling bunch of tiny lights next to the door read "Ingrich." Except for the gardens, every house was identical. Melanie's was a riot of colorful flowers and tall herbs spilling out of their beds on the trim lawn, a burst of individuality on a street of bland repetition.

"Muhlah, I'd hate to come home drunk," Lunzie said, looking up and down the endless row. The other side of the street was the same. Three floors of curtained windows stared blankly down on them.

"The robot taxi would get you safely home," Tee assured her.

She heard noises coming from inside the house as they approached, and the door irised open suddenly. A plump woman with soft brown hair bustled out and seized each of them by the hand. Lunzie recognized her instantly. It was her granddaughter.

"You are Lunzie, aren't you?" The woman beamed. "I'm Melanie. Welcome, welcome, at last! And Citizen Janos. I'm so glad to see you at last."

"Tee," Tee insisted, accepting a hug in his turn.

"How wonderful to meet you at last," Lunzie exclaimed. "I'm grateful you wanted to extend the invitation to me, after I stood you up last time."

"Oh, of course. We wanted to meet you. Come in. Everyone has been waiting for you." Melanie wrapped an arm warmly around Lunzie's waist and led her inside. Tee trailed behind, looking amused. "Mother was so disappointed that you didn't come to our last reunion. But when we heard about the accident, we were devastated that she had left with the wrong impression. I sent a message to Eridani to let her know what happened and that you're all right, but it's so far away she may still be on her way there. I just have no idea! Only the gods of chaos know when the message will reach her. There's been a lot of service interruptions lately. And no explanation from the company!"

She led them into a well-lit room with white walls and carpets, decorated with colorful wall hangings in good artistic taste, and set about with cushiony furniture. In the middle of one wall was an electronic hearth, and in the middle of the other was a Tri-D viewing platform, surrounded by teenaged children watching a sports event. Lunzie noticed that the holographic image was purer and sharper than anything she'd ever seen before. There had obviously been strides made in image projection since she went into cold sleep.

Two slightly built men with dark, curly hair, identical twins, and two women, all of early middle age, who had been chatting when Lunzie entered, rose from their seats and came forward.

"Oh, what a lovely home you have," Lunzie said, looking around approvingly. "Is this your mate?"

The tall man sprawled on a couch set aside his personal reader and stood up to offer them a hand. "Now and forever. Dalton is my name. How do you do, ancestress?"

"Very well, thank you," she said, shaking hands. Dalton had a firm, smooth grip, but not at all bonecrushing, as she feared it might be after noticing the prominent tendons on his wrists. "But please, call me Lunzie."

"I'll tell everyone your wishes, but Lars might not comply. He can be very stuffy and proper."

"I communicated with them as soon as you let us know you were here. They'll arrive in a little while," Melanie said busily, urging them into the middle of the common room. "Now, may I get you anything before I show you where you're going to stay? Something to drink?"

"Juice would be welcome. The air is . . . rather thick if you're not used to it," Lunzie said, diplomatically.

"Mmmm. There was a smog alert today. I should have said

something when you communicated with us. But we're all used to it." Melanie hurried away.

"Just like her to forget the rest of the introductions," Dalton said indulgently as his mate left the room. He embraced Lunzie, and waved a hand at the others in the room. "Everyone! This is Lunzie, here at last!" The children watching the Tri-D stood up to greet her. Lunzie smiled at them in turn, trying to identify them from the ten-year-old holos. She could account for all but two. Dalton explained, "Not all of this crowd is ours, but we get the grandchildren a lot because our house is the largest. Lunzie, please meet my sons Jai and Thad, and their mates, Ionia and Chirli." The women, one with short red tresses, one with shining pale blond hair, smiled at her. "Drew is still at work, but he'll be joining us for dinner."

The twins shook hands gravely. "You look more like a sister to us than what? A great-grandmother?" one of them said.

"You'll have to forgive us if we occasionally slip up and don't show the respect due your age," the other said playfully.

"I'll understand," Lunzie said, hugging them, and pulling the two women closer to include them in the embrace. The children pressed in to take their turns. There were nine of them, four girls and five boys. Lunzie could see resemblances to herself or Fiona in all of them. She was so overwhelmed with joy, she was nearly bursting inside.

"How old are you?" asked the youngest child, a boy who seemed to be eleven or twelve Standard years of age.

"Pedder, that's not a polite question," Jai's red-headed wife said sternly.

"Drew's youngest," Dalton explained in his deep voice over the heads of the throng clustered around her.

"Sorry, Aunt Ionia. I 'pologize," the boy muttered in a sulky voice.

"I'm not offended," Lunzie insisted, winning the boy's admiration immediately. "I was born in 2755, if that's what you mean."

"Wo-ow," Pedder said, impressed. "That's old. I mean, you don't look like it."

"Brend and Corrin," Dalton pointed, "are Pedder's older brothers, and possessed, I hope, of more tact, or at least less curiosity. The eldest, Evan, isn't here. He's at work. Dierdre's youngest, Anthea, is at school."

"Oh, I'm delighted to meet you all," Lunzie said happily. "I've been replaying the holos over and over again." She squeezed Brend's hand and ruffled Corrin's hair. The boys blushed red, and drew back to let the other cousins through.

"I'm Capella," said an attractive girl with black hair styled in fantastic waves and loops all over her head. In Lunzie's opinion, the girl wore too much makeup, and the LED-studded earrings on her earlobes were almost blinding.

"You've changed since the last picture I saw of you," Lunzie said diplomatically.

"Oh, really," Capella giggled. "It has to be ten years, right? I was just a microsquirt then." Tee, standing behind Capella, smiled widely and raised his eyes heavenward. Lunzie returned his grin.

Pedder became distracted by the Tri-D program, where it appeared that one team was about to drive a bright scarlet ball into a net past the other team's defense. "Give it to 'em good, Centauri! Plasmic!"

A slim young woman with long hair in a ribbon-bound plait rose from the other side of the viewing field and made her way awkwardly over to Lunzie, holding out a hand. She was several months pregnant. "How do you do, Lunzie? I'm Rudi."

Lunzie greeted her warmly. "Lars' first granddaughter. I'm delighted to meet you. When is the baby due?"

"Oh, not soon enough." Rudi smiled. "Two and a half months. Since it'll be the first great-grandchild, everyone's helping me count the days. This is Gordon. He's shy, but he'll get over it, since you're family." Lars' only grandson was a stocky boy of eighteen whose short, spiky mouse-brown hair stuck straight out all over his fair scalp.

Lunzie took his hand and drew him toward her to give him a kiss on the cheek. "I'm pleased to meet you, Gordon." The boy reddened and withdrew his hand, grinning self-consciously.

With the last goal, the game appeared to be over. Dalton leaned across the crowd and turned off the Tri-D field under the disappointed noses of the boys. "Enough! No more holovision. We have guests."

Cassia and Deram, cousins born within two days of each other, claimed the seats on either side of Lunzie, as she was settled down into the deep couch with a tall glass of fruit juice.

"It almost makes us twins, you see, just like our fathers," stated Deram proudly. In fact, he and Cassia did look as remarkably alike as a young man and woman could.

"We've always been best friends, from birth onward," Cassia added.

"Ugh!" Lona, Deram's younger sister, a lanky seventeen, settled at their feet, and shook back her long, straight black hair. "How phony. Lie, why don't you? You fight like Tokme birds all the time."

"Lona, that's not nice to say," Cassia chided, looking nervously at Lunzie, but the teenager regarded her with unrepentant scorn.

Of all the grandchildren, Lona looked the most like Fiona. Lunzie found herself drawn to the girl over the course of the evening, feeling as though she was talking to her own long-lost daughter. It became a point of contention among the other cousins, who felt that Lona should fairly share the attention of the prized new relative.

Lunzie overheard the whispered arguments and realized that she was near to starting off a family war. She neatly changed the subject, directing her conversation to each cousin in turn. Everyone was smiling in satisfaction when the adults arrived.

Lars greeted her and Tee with great ceremony. "Five generations in the same house!" he exclaimed to the assembled. "Ancestress Lunzie, we are very pleased to have you among us. Welcome!"

Lars was a stocky man who had inherited Fiona's jaw and a smaller version of her eyes, which wore a familiar obdurate expression that Lunzie recognized as a family trait. His hair was thinning, and Lunzie estimated that he would enter into his eighth decade completely bald. His wife, Dierdre, was fashionably thin, but with a scrawny neck. She had not changed much since the first holo Lunzie had seen. Drew, Melanie's third son, was a stockier version of his cheerful older brothers. He greeted Lunzie with a smacking kiss on the cheek.

"We've also got a surprise for you," Lars added standing aside from the doorway to let one more man come in. "Our brother Dougal arrived home for shore leave only last week."

Dougal was handsome. He had inherited all of Fiona's good looks plus a gene or two from Lunzie's maternal grandfather, who had also been tall and slim with broad shoulders. His coloring was similar to Lunzie's: medium brown hair and green-hazel eyes, and he had her short, straight nose. His Fleet uniform was a pristine white, like Tee's, but it bore more wrist braid, and there was a line of medals on his left breast.

"Welcome, Lunzie. Fiona told me a lot about you. I hope this is the beginning of a long visit, and the first of many more."

Lunzie glanced back at Tee, who shrugged. "Well, I don't know. There're a few matters I might have to take care of. But I'll stay as long as I can."

"Good!" Dougal wrapped her up in an embrace that made her squeak. "I've been looking forward to exchanging stories with you."

Lars started to reproach his brother, when Melanie stepped between them.

"Dinner, boys." She gave them a look which Lunzie could only describe as significant, and led the way to the dining room.

"Melanie, I must say, you've inherited my mother's cooking arm. That was absolutely delicious," Lunzie said. She and Tee sat across from each other on either side of Dalton at one end of the long table. Lars sat at the other end and nodded paternally over the wine. "What spice was that in the carrot mousse? And the celeriac and herb soup was just delightful."

Melanie glowed at Lunzie's praise. "I usually say the recipes are a family secret but I couldn't keep them from you, could I?"

"I hope not. Truly, I'd love to take a look at your recipe file. I can offer some of my inventions in return."

"Take her up on the offer," Tee put in, gesturing with his spoon. "Do not let her change her mind, Melanie. Lunzie is a superb cook. As for me, I have been eating synthetic Fleet food for many years now, and this is like a divine blessing."

"I know what you mean, brother," Dougal said, noisily scraping the last of the spiced cheese and bean dish out onto his plate. "Depending on how long a ship is in space, the crew forget first the love they left behind them, then fresh air, then food. Between crises, I dream about good meals, especially my sister's cooking."

"Thank you, Dougal," Melanie acknowledged prettily. "It's always nice to have you home."

"I made dessert," Lona answered, getting up to clear the plates. "Is anyone ready for it yet?"

Pedder and his brothers chorused, "Yes," and sat up straight hopefully, but their mother shook her head at them. They sighed deeply, and relaxed back into their seats.

"We'll have dessert in the common room, shall we, Lona?" Melanie suggested, getting up to clear away the dishes.

"All right. Good idea," Lona agreed. "That way I can display everything artistically."

"Aw, who cares?" Corrin said rudely, pushing back. "It all gets chewed up and swallowed anyway."

"Fall into a black hole!" Lona swung at him with an empty casserole dish, but he evaded her, and fled into the common room. Lona threw a sneer after him and continued stacking plates. Lunzie automatically got up and began helping to clear away.

"Oh, no, Lunzie," Lars reproved her. "Please. You're a guest. Come with me and sit down. Let the hosts clean up. I've been waiting to hear about your adventures." He tucked Lunzie's arm under his own and propelled her into the common room.

"Dessert!" Lona called, pushing a hover-tray into the middle of the room.

The supports of the cart hung six inches above the carpet until Lona hit a control when it lowered itself gently to the ground.

"There." Melanie hurried around the tray, setting serving utensils and stacks of napkins along the sides. "It's beautiful, darling."

Rescued from Lars' relentless interrogation, Lunzie immediately stood up to inspect the contents of the tray. Lona had prepared tiny fruit tarts in a rainbow of colors. They were arranged in a spray which was half-curled around the three dishes of rich cream. "Good heavens, what gracious bounty. It looks like Carmen Miranda's hat!"

"Who?" Melanie asked blankly.

"Why, uh . . ." Lunzie had to stop herself from saying *someone your age would surely remember Carmen Miranda.* "Oh, ancient history. A woman who became famous for wearing fruit on her head. She was in the old two-D pictures that Fiona and I used to watch together."

"That's dumb," opined Pedder. "Wearing fruit on your head."

"Oh, we don't watch two-D. Flatscreen pictures don't have enough life in them," Melanie explained. "I prefer holovision every time."

"There are some great classics in two-D. I always felt it was like reading a book with pictures substituted for words," Lunzie said. "Especially the very ancient monochrome two-Ds. Easy once you get used to it."

"Oh, I see. Well, I don't read much, either. I don't have time for it." Melanie laughed lightly. "I have such a busy schedule. Here, everyone gather around, and I'll serve. Lunzie, you must try this green fruit. The toppings are sweet apricot, sour cherry, and chocolate. Lona made the pastry cream herself. It is marvelous."

The dessert was indeed delicious, and the boys made sure that leftovers wouldn't be a problem. They were looking for more when the empty cart was driven back to the food preparation room. Lona was given a round of applause by her happily sated cousins.

"Truly artistic, in every sense of the word," Dougal praised her. "That will fuel food dreams for me for the entire next tour. You're getting to be as good a cook as your grandmother."

Lona preened, looking pleased. "Thanks, Uncle Dougal."

"Oh, don't call me a grandmother," Melanie pleaded, brushing at invisible crumbs on her skirt. "It makes me feel so old."

"And think of how it would make Lunzie feel," Lars said, with more truth than tact. Lunzie shot him a sharp look, but he seemed oblivious.

"How are things at the factory?" Drew asked Lars, settling back with a glass of wine.

"Oh, the same, the same. We've got a contingent from Alien Council for Liberty and Unity protesting before the gates right now."

"The ACLU?" Drew echoed, shocked. "Can they close you down?"

"They can try. But we'll demonstrate substantial losses far beyond accounts receivable for the products, and all they can do is accept what we offer."

"What are they protesting?" Lunzie asked, alarmed.

Lars waved it away as unimportant. "They're representing the Ssli we fired last month from the underwater hydraulics assembly line. Unsuitable for the job."

"But the Ssli are a marine race. Why, what makes them unsuitable?"

"You wouldn't understand. They're too different. They don't mix well with the other employees. And there's problems in providing them with insurance. We have to buy a rider for every mobile tank they bring onto the premises to live in. And that's another thing: they live right on the factory grounds. We almost lost our insurance because of them."

"Well, they cannot commute from the sea every day," Tee quipped.

"So they say." Lars dismissed the Ssli with a frown, entirely missing Tee's sarcasm. "We'll settle the matter within a few days. If they don't leave, we'll have to shut the line down entirely anyway. There's other work they can do. We've offered to extend our placement service to them."

"Oh, I see," Lunzie said, heavily. "Very generous of you." It was not so much that she thought the company should drive itself into bankruptcy for the sake of equity as that Lars seemed quite oblivious to the moral dimension of the situation.

Lars leveled a benevolent eye at her. "Why, ancestress, how good of you to say so."

Melanie and Lars' wife beamed at her approval, also missing her cynical emphasis.

"Is it considered backward to read books nowadays?" Lunzie asked Tee later when they were alone in the guest room. "I've only been on the Platform and Astris since I came out of cold sleep the first time. I haven't any idea what society at large has been doing."

"Has that been bothering you?" Tee asked, as he pulled his tunic over his head. "No. Reading has not gone out of fashion in the last number of years, nor in the ones while you slept in the asteroid belt. Your relatives do not wish to expose themselves to deep thought, lest they be affected by it."

Lunzie pulled off her boots and dropped them on the floor. "What do you think of them?"

"Your relatives? Very nice. A trifle pretentious, very conservative, I would say. Conservative in every way except that they seem to have put us together in this guest room, instead of at opposite ends of the house. I'm glad they did, though. I would find it cold and lonely with only those dreary moralizers."

"Me, too. I don't know whether to say I'm delighted with them or disappointed. They show so little spirit. Everything they do has such petty motives. Shallow. Born dirtsiders, all of them."

"Except for the girl, I think," Tee said, meditatively, sitting down on a fluffy seat next to the bed.

"Oh, yes, Lona. I apologize to her from afar for lumping her with the rest of these . . . these closed-minded warts on a log. She's the only one with any gumption. And I hope she shows sense and gets out of here as soon as she can."

"So should we." Tee moved over behind Lunzie and began to rub her neck.

Lunzie sighed and relaxed her spine, leaning back against his crossed legs. He circled an arm around her shoulders and kissed her hair while his other hand kneaded the muscles in her back. "I don't think I can be polite for very long. We should stay a couple of days, and then let's find an excuse to go."

"As you wish," Tee offered quietly, feeling the tense cords in her back relax. "I should not mind escaping from here, either."

Lunzie tiptoed down the ramp from the sleeping rooms into the common room and the dining room. There was no sound except the far-off humming of the air-recirculation system. "Hello?" she called softly. "Melanie?"

Lona popped up the ramp from the lower level of the house. "Nope, just me. Good morning!"

"Good morning. Shouldn't you be in school?" Lunzie asked, smiling at the girl's eagerness. Lona was both pretty and lively; she looked like a throwback to Lunzie's own family, instead of a member of Melanie's conservative Alpha brood.

"No classes today," Lona explained, plumping down beside her on the couch. "I'm in a communications technology discipline, remember? Our courses are every other day, alternating with work experiences either at a factory or a broadcast facility. I've got the day off."

"Good," Lunzie said looking around. "I was wondering where everyone was."

"I'm your reception committee. Melanie's just gone shopping, and Dalton normally works at home, but he's got a meeting this morning. Where's Tee?"

"Still asleep. His circadian rhythm is set for a duty shift that begins later on."

Lona shook her head. "Please. Don't bother giving me the details. I flunked biology. I'm majoring in communications engineering. Oh, Melanie left you something to look at."

Lona produced a package sealed in a black plastic pouch. Curious, Lunzie pulled open the wrapping, and discovered a plastic case with her name printed on the lid.

"They're Fiona's. She left them behind when she went away," Lona explained, peering over Lunzie's shoulder as Lunzie opened the box. It was full of two-D and three-D images on wafers.

"It's all of her baby pictures," Lunzie breathed, "and mine, too. Oh, I thought these were lost!" She picked up one, and then another, exclaiming over them happily.

"Not lost. Melanie said that Fiona brought all of that stuff to MarsBase with her. We don't know who most of these people are. Would you mind identifying them?"

"They're your ancestors, and some friends of ours from long ago. Sit down and I'll show you. Oh, Muhlah, look at that! That's me at four years of age." Lunzie peered at a small two-D image, as they sat down on the couch with the box on their knees.

"Your hair stuck out just like Gordon's does," Lona pointed out, snickering.

"His looks better." Lunzie put that picture back in the box and took out the next one. "This is my mother. She was a doctor, too. She was born in England on Old Earth, as true a *sassenach* as ever wandered the Yorkshire Dales."

"What's a *sassenach*?" Lona asked, peering at the image of the petite fair-haired woman.

"An old dialect word for a contentious Englishman. Mother was what you'd call strong-minded. She introduced me to the works of Rudyard Kipling, who has always been my favorite author."

"Did you ever get to meet him?"

Lunzie laughed. "Oh, no, child. Let's see, what is this year?"

"Sixty-four."

"Well, then, next year will be the thousandth anniversary of his birth."

Lona was impressed. "Oh. Very ancient."

"Don't let that put you off reading him," Lunzie cautioned her. "He's too good to miss out on all your life. Kipling was a wise man, and a fine writer. He wrote adventures and children's stories and poetry, but what I loved most of all was his keen way of looking at a situation and seeing the truth of it."

"I'll look for some of Kipling in the library," Lona promised. "Who's this man?" she asked, pointing.

"This is my father. He was a teacher."

"They look nice. I wish I could have known them, like I'm getting to know you."

Lunzie put an arm around Lona. "You'd have liked them. And they would have been crazy about you."

They went through the box of pictures. Lunzie lingered over pictures of Fiona as a small child, and studied the images of the girl as she grew to womanhood. There were pictures of Fiona's late mate and all the babies. Even as an infant, Lars had a solemn, self-important expression, which made them both giggle. Lona turned out the bottom compartment of the box and held out Lunzie's university diploma.

"Why is your name Lunzie Mespil, instead of just Lunzie?" Lona asked, reading the ornate characters on the plastic-coated parchment.

"What's wrong with Mespil?" Lunzie wanted to know.

Lona turned up her lips scornfully. "Surnames are barbaric. They let people judge you by your ancestry or your profession, instead of by your behavior."

"Do you want the true answer, or the one your Uncle Lars would prefer?"

Lona grinned wickedly. She obviously shared Lunzie's opinion of Lars as a pompous old fogy. "What's the truth?"

"The truth is that when I was a student, I contracted to a term marriage with Sion Mespil. He was an angelically handsome charmer attending medical school at the same time I was. I loved him dearly, and I think he felt the same about me. We didn't want a permanent marriage at that time because neither of us knew where we would end up after school. I was in the mental sciences, and he was in genetics and reproductive sciences. We might go to opposite ends of the galaxy — and in fact, we did. If we had stayed together, of course, we might have made it permanent. I kept his last name and gave it to our baby, Fiona, to help her avoid marrying one of her half-brothers at some time in the future." Lunzie chuckled. "I swear Sion was majoring in gynecology just so he could deliver his own offspring. With the exception of the time we were married, I've never seen a man with such an active love life in all my days."

"Didn't you want him to help raise Fiona?" Lona asked.

"I felt perfectly capable of taking care of her on my own. I loved her dearly, and truth be told, Sion Mespil was far better at the engendering of children than the raising. He was just as happy to leave it to me. Besides, my specialty required that I travel a lot. I couldn't ask him to keep up with us as we moved. It would be hard enough on Fiona."

Lona was taking in Lunzie's story through every pore, as if it was a Tri-D adventure. "Did you ever hear from him again after medical school?" she demanded.

"Oh, yes, of course," Lunzie assured her, smiling. "Fiona was his child. He sent us ten K of data or so every time he heard of a message batch being compiled for our system. We did the same. Of course, I had to edit his letters for Fiona. I don't think at her age it was good for her to hear details of her father's sex life, but his genetics work was interesting. He did work on the heavyworld mutation, you know. I think he influenced her to go into medicine as much as I did."

"Is that him?" Lona pointed to one of the men in Lunzie's medical school graduation picture. "He's handsome."

"No. That one." Lunzie cupped her hand behind Sion's holo, to make it stand out. "He had the face of a benevolent spirit, but his heart was as black as his hair. The galaxy's worst practical joker, bar none. He played a nasty trick with a cadaver once in Anatomy . . . um, never mind." Lunzie recoiled from the memory.

"Tell me!" Lona begged.

"That story is too sick to tell anyone. I'm surprised I remember it."

"Please!"

Remembering the nauseating details more and more clearly, Lunzie held firm. "No, not that one. I've got lots of others I could tell you. When do you have to go home?"

Lona waved a dismissive hand. "No one expects me home. I'm always hanging around here. They're used to it. Melanie and Dalton are the only interesting people. The other cousins are so dull, and as for the parents . . . " Lona let the sentence trail off, rolling her eyes expressively.

"That's not very tolerant of you. They *are* your family," Lunzie observed in a neutral voice, though she privately agreed with Lona.

"They may be family to you, but they're just relatives to me. Whenever I talk about taking a job offplanet, you would think I was going to commit piracy and a public indecency! What an uproar. No one from our family ever goes into space, except Uncle Dougal. He doesn't listen to Uncle Lars' rules."

Lunzie nodded wisely. "You've got the family complaint. Itchy feet. Well, you don't have to stay in one place if you don't want to. Otherwise, it'll drive you mad. You live your own life." Lunzie punctuated her sentence with jabs in the air, ignoring the intrusive conscience which told her she was meddling in affairs that didn't concern her.

"Why did you leave Fiona?" Lona asked suddenly, laying a hand on her arm. "I've always wondered. I think that's why everyone else is allergic to relatives going out into space. They never come back."

It was the question that had lain unspoken between her and the others all the last evening. Unsurprised at Lona's honest assessment of her family situation, Lunzie stopped to think.

"I have wished and wished again that I hadn't done it," she answered after a time, squeezing the girl's fingers. "I couldn't take her with me. Life on a Platform or any beginning colony is dangerous. But they pay desperation wages for good, qualified employees and we needed money. I had never intended to be gone longer than five years at the outside."

"I've heard the pay is good. I'm going to join a mining colony as soon as I've graduated," Lona said, accepting Lunzie's words with a sharp nod. "My boyfriend is a biotechnologist with a specialty in botany. The original green thumb, if you'll forgive such an archaic expression. What am I saying?" Lona went wide-eyed in mock shame and Lunzie laughed. "Well, I can fix nearly anything. We'd qualify easily. They say you can get rich in a new colony. If you survive. Fiona used to say it was a half-and-half chance." Lona wrinkled her nose as she sorted the pictures and put them away. "Of course, there's the Oh-Two money. Neither of us has a credit to our names."

Lunzie considered deeply for a few minutes before she spoke. "Lona, I think you should do what you want to do. I'll give you the money."

"Oh, I couldn't ask it," Lona gasped. "It's too much money. A good stake would be hundreds of thousands of credits." But her eyes held a lively spark of hope.

Lunzie noticed it. She was suddenly aware of the generations which lay between them. She had slept through so many that this girl, who could have been her own daughter, was her granddaughter's granddaughter. She peered closely at Lona, noticing the resemblance between her and Fiona. This child was the same age Fiona would have been if all had gone well on Descartes, and she had returned on time. "If that's the only thing standing in your way, if you're independent enough to ignore family opinion and unwanted advice, that's good enough for me. It won't beggar me, I promise you. Far from it. I got sixty years back pay from Descartes, and I hardly know what to do with it. Do me the favor of accepting this gift — er, loan, to pass on to future generations."

"Well, if it means that much to you . . . " Lona began solemnly. Unable to maintain the formal expressions for another moment more, she broke into laughter, and Lunzie joined in.

"Your parents will undoubtedly tell me to mind my own business," Lunzie sighed, "and they'd be within their rights. I'm no better than a stranger to all of you."

"What if they do?" Lona declared defiantly. "I'm legally an adult. They can't live my life for me. It's a bargain, Lunzie. I accept. I promise to pass it on at least one more generation. And thank you. I'll never, never forget it."

"A cheery good morning!" Tee said, as he clumped down the ramp into the common room toward them. He kissed Lunzie and bowed over Lona's hand. "I heard laughter. Everyone is in a good mood today? Is there any hope of breakfast? If you show me the food synthesizer, I will serve myself."

"Not a chance!" Lona scolded him. "Melanie would have my eyelashes if I gave you synth food in her house. Come on, I'll cook something for you."

Lona's parents were not pleased that their remote ancestress was taking a personal interest in their daughter's future. "You shouldn't encourage instability like that," Jai complained. "She wants to go gallivanting off, without a thought for the future."

"There's nothing unstable about wanting to take a job in space," Lunzie retorted. "That's the basic of galactic enterprise."

"Well, we won't hear of it. And with the greatest of respect, Lunzie, let us raise our child our way, please?"

Lunzie simmered silently at the reproval, but Lona gave her the thumbs up behind her father's back. Evidently, the girl was not going to mention Lunzie's gift. Neither would she. It would be a surprise to all of them when she left one day, but Lunzie refused to feel guilty. It wasn't as though the signs weren't pointed out to them.

After three days more, Lunzie had had enough of her descendants. She announced at dinner that night that she would be leaving.

"I thought you would stay," Melanie wailed. "We've got plenty of room, Lunzie. Don't go. We've hardly had a chance to get acquainted. Stay at least a few more days."

"Oh, I can't, Melanie. Tee's got to get back to the *Ban Sidhe*, and so do I. I do appreciate your offer, though," Lunzie assured her. "I promise to visit whenever I'm in the vicinity. Thank you so much for your hospitality. I'll carry the memories of your family with me always."

✦ CHAPTER NINE

As they rode back into Alpha City in a robot groundcar the next morning, Tee patted Lunzie on the hand. "Let's not go back to the ship just yet. Shall we do some sightseeing? I was talking to Dougal. He says there is a fine museum of antiquities here, with controlled atmosphere. And it is connected to a large shopping mall. We could make an afternoon of it."

Lunzie came back from the far reaches and smiled. She had been staring out the window at the gray expanse of city and thinking. "I'd love it. Walking might help clear my head."

"What is cluttering it?" Tee asked, lightly. "I thought we had left the clutter behind."

"I've been examining my life. My original goal, when I woke up the first time, to find Fiona and make sure she was happy and well, was really accomplished long ago, even before I set out for Alpha Centauri. I think I came here just to see Fiona again, to ask her to forgive me. Well, that was for me, not for her. She's moved on and made a life — quite a successful one — without me. It's time I learned to let go of her. There are three generations more already, whose upbringing is so different from mine we have nothing to say to one another."

"They are shallow. You have met interesting people of this generation," Tee pointed out.

"Yes, but it's a sorry note when it's your own descendants you're disappointed in," Lunzie said ruefully. "But I don't know where to go next."

"Why don't we brainstorm while we walk?" Tee pleaded. "I am getting cramped sitting in this car. Museum of Galactic History, please," he ordered the groundcar's robot brain.

"Acknowledged," said the mechanical voice. "Working." The

groundcar slowed down and made a sharp right off the highway onto a small side street.

"You could join the service," Tee suggested as they strolled through the cool halls of the museum past rows of plexiglas cases. "They have treated me very well."

"I'm not sure I want to do that. I know my family has a history in the Fleet, but I'm not sure I could stand being under orders all the time, or staying in just one place. I'm too independent."

Tee shrugged. "It's your life."

"If it *is* my life, why can't I spend two years running without someone throwing me into deepsleep?" She sighed, stepping closer to the wall to let a herd of shouting children run by. "Oh, I wish we could go back to Astris, Tee. We were so happy there. Your beautiful apartment, and our collection of book plaques. Coming home evenings and seeing who could get to the food-prep area first." Lunzie smiled up at him fondly. "Just before I left, we were talking about children of our own."

Tee squinted into the distance, avoiding her eyes. "It was so long ago, Lunzie. I gave up that apartment when I left Astris. I have been on the *Ban Sidhe* for more than six years. You remember it well because for you it has been only months. For me, it is the beloved past." His tone made that clear.

Lunzie felt very sad. "You're happy being back in space again, aren't you? You came to rescue me, but it's more than that now. I couldn't ask you to give it up."

"I have my career, yes," Tee agreed softly. "But there is also something else." He paused. "You've met Naomi, yes?"

"Yes, I've met Naomi. She treats me with great respect," Lunzie said aggrievedly. "It drives me half mad, and I haven't been able to break her of it. What about her?" she asked, guessing the answer before he spoke.

Tee glanced at her, and gazed down at the floor, abashed.

"I am responsible for the respect she holds for you. I have talked much of you in the years I've been on board. How can she fail to have a high opinion of you? She is the Chief Telemetry Officer on the *Ban Sidhe*. The Commander let me go on the rescue mission on the condition that I signed on to work. He would allow no idle hands, for who knew how long it would take to find the ship and rescue all aboard her? Naomi took me as her apprentice. I learned quickly, I worked hard, and I came to be expert at my job. I found also that I care for her. Captain Aelock offered me a permanent commission if I wish to stay, and I do. I never want to go back to a planet-bound job. Naomi confesses that she cares for me, too, so there is a double attraction. We both mean to spend the rest of our careers in space." He stopped walking and took both of her hands between his. "Lunzie, I feel terrible. I feel as though I have betrayed you by falling in love with someone else before I could see you, but the emotion is strong." He shrugged expressively. "It has been ten years, Lunzie."

She watched him sadly, feeling another part of her life crumble into dust. "I know." She forced herself to smile. "I should have understood that. I don't blame you, my dear, and I couldn't expect you to remain celibate so long. I'm grateful you stayed with me as long as you did."

Tee was still upset. "I am sorry. I wish I could be more supporting."

Lunzie inhaled and let out a deep breath. She was aching to reach out to him. "Thank you, Tee, but you've done all that I really needed, you know. You were by me when I woke up, and you let me talk my head off just so I could reorient myself in time. And if I hadn't had someone to talk to while I was in Melanie's house, I think I would have jetted through the roof! But that's over, now. It's all over, now," Lunzie said, bitterly. "Time has run past me and I never saw it go by. I thought that ten years of cold sleep would have been easier to accept than sixty, but it's worse. My family is gone and you've moved on. I accept that, I really do. Let's go back to the ship before I decide to let them put me in one of those glass cases as an antiquarian object of curiosity."

They arrived just in time for Tee to resume his usual duty shift, and Lunzie went back to her compartment to move the rest of her things down to the BOQ at the base down on Alpha. No matter what she let Tee believe, she had lost a lot of the underpinnings of her self-esteem in the last few days, and it hurt.

Sharu wasn't there, so Lunzie allowed herself fifteen minutes for a good cry, and then sat up to reassess her situation. Self-pity was all very well, but it wouldn't keep her busy or put oxygen in the air tanks. The shuttle was empty except for her and the pilot.

Thankfully, he didn't feel like talking. Lunzie was able to be alone with her thoughts.

The base consisted of perfectly even rows of huge, boxlike buildings that all looked exactly alike to Lunzie. A human officer jogging by with a handful of document cubes was able to direct her to the Bachelor Officers' Quarters, where the stranded employees of the Destiny Lines would stay until after they gave their statements to the court. When she reached the BOQ, she took her bags to quarters assigned for her use, and left them there. The nearest computer facilities, she was told, were in the recreation hall.

Using an unoccupied console in the rec room, she called up the current want ads network and began to page through suitable entry headings.

By the middle of the afternoon, Lunzie was feeling much better. She was resolute that she would no longer depend on another single person for her happiness. She added a "reminder" into her daily Discipline meditation to help increase her confidence. The wounds of loss would hurt for a while. That was natural. But in time, they would heal and leave little trace.

She realized all of a sudden that she had had nothing to eat since morning, and now it was nearly time for the evening meal. Her bout of introspection, not to mention the taxing Discipline workout, had left her feeling hollow in the middle. Surely the serving hatches in the mess hall would be open by now. She went back to her quarters, put on fresh garments and pulled on boots to go check.

"Lunzie! The very person. Lunzie, may I speak to you?" Captain Aelock hurried up to her as she stepped out into the main corridor of the building.

"Of course, Captain. I was just on the way to get myself some supper. Would you care to sit with me?"

"Well, er," he smiled a trifle sheepishly, "supper was exactly what I had planned to offer you, but not here. I was hoping to have a chance to chat with you before the *Ban Sidhe* departed. I am very grateful for the help you've given Doctor Harris since you came aboard. In fact, he is reluctant to let you go. So am I. I don't suppose I can persuade you to join us? We could use more level-headed personnel with your qualifications."

Aelock would be a fine commander to serve under. Lunzie

almost opened her mouth to say yes, but remembered Tee and Naomi. "I'm sorry, Captain, but no, thank you."

The captain looked genuinely disappointed. "Ah, well. At any rate, I had in mind to offer you a farewell dinner here on Alpha. I know some splendid local places."

Lunzie was flattered. "That's very kind of you, Captain, but I was only doing my job. A cliché, but still true."

"I would still find it pleasant to stand you a meal, but I must admit that I have a more pressing reason to ask you to dine with me tonight." The captain pulled her around a corner as a handful of crew members walked by along the corridor.

"You have my entire attention," Lunzie assured him, returning the friendly but curious gazes shot toward her by the passing officers.

Aelock tucked her arm under his and started walking in the opposite direction. "I remember when I mentioned planet pirates to you, you were very interested. Am I wrong?"

"No. You said that one of the reasons you were here was to get information as to their whereabouts." Lunzie kept her voice low. "I have very personal reasons for wanting to see them stopped. Personal motives for vengeance, in fact. How can I help?"

"I suspect that one operation might be based out of Alpha's own spaceport, but I haven't got proof!" Lunzie looked shocked and Aelock nodded sadly. "One of my, er, snitches sent me a place and a time when he will contact me, to give me that information. Have dinner with me at that place. If I'm seen dining alone, they'll know something is up. My contact is already under observation, and in terror of his life. You're not in the Fleet computers; you'll look like a local date. That may throw off the pirates' spies. Will you come?"

"Willingly," she said firmly. "And able to do anything to stop the pirates. How shall I dress?"

Aelock glanced over the casual trousers and tunic and polymer exercise boots Lunzie was wearing.

"You'll do just as you are, Lunzie. The food is quite good, but this restaurant is rather on the informal side. It isn't where I should like to entertain you, you may be sure, but my contact won't be entirely out of place there."

"No complaint from me, Captain, so long as supper's soon," Lunzie told him. "I'm starving.

The host of Colchie's Cabana seated Lunzie and Aelock in the shadow of an artificial cliff. The restaurant, a moderately priced supper club, had overdone itself in displaying a tropical motif. All the fruit drinks, sweet or not, had kebabs of fresh fruit skewered on little plastic swords floating in them. Lunzie nibbled on the fruit and took handfuls of salty nut snacks from the baskets in the center of their table to cut the sugary taste.

Lunzie examined the holo-menu with pleasure. The array of dishes on offer was extensive and appetizing. In spite of the kitschy decor and the gaudy costumes of the human help, the food being served to other diners smelled wonderful. Lunzie hoped the rumbling in her stomach wasn't audible. The restaurant was packed with locals chatting while live music added to the clamor.

"Have you had a good look at the corner band?" Lunzie asked, unable to restrain a giggle as she leaned toward Aelock, hiding her face behind the plas-sheet menu. "The percussionist seems to be playing a treestump with two handfuls of broccoli! That does, of course, fit in the general decor very well."

"I know," Aelock said with an apologetic shudder. "Let me reassure you that the food is an improvement on the ambience. Well cooked and, with some exceptions, spiced with restraint."

Despite the casual clothes he was wearing, the captain's bearing still marked him for what he was, making him stand out from the rest of the clientele. Lunzie had a moment's anxiety over that, but surely off-duty officers might dine here without causing great comment.

"That's a relief," Lunzie replied drily, watching the facial contortions of a diner who had just taken a bite of a dish with a very red sauce.

The man gulped water and hurriedly reached for his bowl of rice. Aelock followed her eyes and smiled.

"Probably not a regular, or too daring for his stomach's good. The menu tells you which dishes are hot and which aren't. And ask if you want the milder ones. He's obviously overestimated his tolerance for Chiki peppers."

"Will you have more drinks, or will you order?" A humanoid server stood over them, bowing deferentially, keypad in hand. His costume consisted of a colorful knee-length tunic over baggy trousers with a soft silk cape draped over one shoulder. On his head was a loose turban pinned at the center with a huge jeweled clip. He turned a pleasant expression of inquiry toward Lunzie who managed to keep her countenance. The man had large, liquid black eyes but his face was a chalky white with colorless lips, a jarring lack in the frame of his gaudy uniform. Except for the vivid eyes, the doubtless perfectly healthy alien looked like a human cadaver. Diners here had to have strong stomachs for more than the food.

"I'm ready," Lunzie announced. "Shall I begin? I'd like the mushroom samosas, salad with house dressing, and special number five."

"That one's hot, Lunzie. Are you sure you'd like to try it?" Aelock asked. "It has a lot of tiny red and green capisca peppers. They're nearly rocket fuel."

"Oh, yes. Good heavens, I used to *grow* LED peppers."

"Good, just checking. I'll have the tomato and cheese salad, and number nine."

"Thank you, gracious citizens," the server said, bowing himself away from the table.

Lunzie and Aelock fed the menus back into the dispenser slots.

"You know, I'm surprised at the amount of sentient labor on Alpha," Lunzie observed as the human server stopped to take drink orders from another table. "There were live tour guides at the museum this morning, and the customs service is only half-automated turnstiles at the spaceport."

"Alpha Centauri has an enormous population, all of whom need jobs," Aelock explained. "It is mostly human. This was one of the first of Earth's outposts, considered a human Homeworld. The non-humanoid population is larger than the entire census of most colonies, but on Alpha, it is still a very small minority. In the outlying cities, most children grow up never having seen an outworlder."

"Sounds like an open field for prejudice," Lunzie remarked, remembering Lars.

"Yes, I'm afraid so. With the huge numbers of people in the workforce, and the finite number of jobs, there's bound to be strife between the immigrants and the natives. That's why I joined the Fleet. There was no guarantee of advancement here for me."

Lunzie nodded. "I understand. So they created a labor-intensive system, using cheap labor instead of mechanicals. You'd be overqualified for ninety percent of the jobs and probably unwilling to do the ones which promise advancement. Who is the person we're waiting for?" she asked in an undertone as a loud party rolled in through the restaurant door.

Aelock quickly glanced at the other diners to make sure they hadn't been overheard. "Please. He's an old friend of mine. We were at primary school together. May we talk of something else?"

Lunzie complied immediately, remembering that secrecy was the reason she was here. "Do you read Kipling?"

"I do now," Aelock replied with a quick grin of appreciation. "When we had him in primary school literature, I didn't think much of Citizen Kipling. Then, when I came back fresh from my first military engagement in defense of my homeworld, and the half-educated fools here treated me with no more respect than if I'd been a groundcar, I found one of his passages described my situation rather well: 'It's Tommy this, an' Tommy that, an' 'Chuck him out, the brute!'"

"Mmm," said Lunzie, thoughtfully, watching the bitterness on Aelock's face. "Not a prophet in your own land, I would guess."

"Far from it."

"I've been fervently reciting 'If' like a mantra today, particularly the lines 'If you can meet with Triumph and Disaster, And treat those two impostors just the same . . . '" Lunzie quoted with a sigh. "I hate it when Rudy is so apt."

The relative merits of the author's poetry versus his prose occupied them until the appetizers arrived. The server swished his billowing cape to one side to reveal the chilled metal bowl containing the captain's salad and the steaming odwood plate bearing Lunzie's appetizer.

"This is delicious," she exclaimed after a taste, and smiled up at the waiting server.

"We are proud to serve," the man declared, bowing, and swirled away.

"Flamboyant, aren't they?" Lunzie grinned.

"I think everyone in a service job needs to be a little exhibitionist," the captain said, amused.

He took a forkful of salad, and nodded approvingly. Lunzie smelled fresh herbs in the dressing. Another gaudily dressed employee with burning eyes appeared at their table and bowed.

"Citizen A-el-ock?" The captain looked up from his dish.
"Yes?"

"There is a communication for you, sir. The caller claimed urgency. Will you follow me?"

"Yes. Will you excuse me, my dear?" Aelock asked gallantly, standing up.

Lunzie simpered at him, using a little of the ambient flamboyance in her role of evening companion. "Hurry back." She waggled her fingers coyly after him.

The dark-eyed employee glanced back at her, and ran a pale tan tongue over his lips. Lunzie was offended at his open scrutiny, hoping that he wasn't going to make a pest of himself while Aelock was away. She didn't want to attract attention to them by defending herself from harassment. To her relief, he turned away, and led the captain to the back of the restaurant.

Alone briefly, Lunzie felt it perfectly in character to glance at the other diners in the restaurant, wondering which of them, if any, could be the mysterious contact. She didn't notice anyone getting up to follow Aelock out, but of course the snitch would have been careful to leave a sufficient interval before having him summoned. She also didn't notice anyone surreptitiously watching their table, or her.

She was a minor player in a very dangerous game in which the opponents were ruthless. Lunzie tried not to worry, tried to concentrate on the excellence of her appetizer. One life more or less was nothing to the pirates who slaughtered millions carelessly. But if the captain's part was suspected, his life would be forfeit. When Aelock reappeared at last through the hanging vegetation, she looked a question at him. He nodded guardedly, inclining his head imperceptibly. She relaxed.

"I was thinking of ordering another drink with the entree. Will you join me?"

"A splendid notion. My throat is unaccountably dry," Aelock agreed. "Such good company on such a fine evening calls for a little indulgence." He pushed the service button on the edge of the table. He had been successful.

Lunzie controlled a surge of curiosity as discretion overcame stupidity. It was far wiser to wait until they were safely back on the base.

"By the way, what do you plan to do next, now that you're no longer employed by Destiny Cruise Lines?" Aelock asked. "Most of the others are already on their way to other jobs. That is, the ones who aren't staying here to sue the Paraden Company."

Lunzie smiled brightly. "In fact, I've just been checking some leads through the base computer," she said and summarized her afternoon's activities. "I do know that I absolutely do not want to stay on this planet — for all the reasons you gave, and more, but especially the pollution. I have this constant urge to irrigate my eyes."

Aelock plucked a large clean handkerchief out of his pocket and deposited it before Lunzie. "I understand completely. I'm a native, so I'm immune, but the unlucky visitor has the same reaction. Tell me, did you enjoy working as a commercial ship's medic?"

"Oh, yes. I could get to like that sort of a life very easily. I was very well treated. I was assigned a luxury cabin, all perks, far beyond this humble person's usual means. Not to mention a laboratory out of my dreams, plus a full medical library," Lunzie replied enthusiastically. "I got the chance to copy out some tests on neurological disorders that I had never seen before in all my research. Interesting people, too. I enjoyed meeting the Admiral, and most of the others I encountered during those two months. I wouldn't mind another stint of that at all. Temporary positions pay better than permanent employ."

Aelock grinned and there was something more lurking in his eyes that made Lunzie wonder if this was just casual conversation.

"Hear, hear. See the galaxy. And you wouldn't have to stay with a company long if you don't care for the way they treat you."

"Just so long as I don't get tossed into deepsleep again. I'm so out of date now that if I go down again, no one will be able to understand me when I speak. I'd have to be completely retrained, or take a menial position mixing medicines."

"It's against all the odds to happen again, Lunzie," Aelock assured her.

"The odds are exactly the same for me as anybody else," Lunzie said darkly — "and bad things come in threes," she added suddenly as she remembered the whisperers in the officers' mess.

The captain shook his head wryly. "Good things should come in threes, too."

"Gracious citizens, the main course."

Their server appeared before them, touching his forehead in salute. Lunzie and Aelock looked up at him expectantly. Apparently not entirely familiar with his waiter's uniform, the server swirled aside his huge cape with one hand as, with the other, he started to draw a small weapon that had been concealed in his broad sash.

But Aelock was *fast*. "Needlegun!" he snarled as he threw his arm across the table to knock Lunzie to the floor and then dove out of the other side of their seat in a ground-hugging roll.

Startled, the pale-faced humanoid completed his draw too late and the silent dart struck the back of the seat where Aelock had been a split second before. With a roar and a flash of flame, the booth blew up. The ridiculous cloak swirling behind him, the server turned and ran.

The frightened patrons around them leaped out of their seats, screaming. With remarkable agility, the captain sprang to his feet and pursued the pasty-faced man toward the back of the restaurant. There was a concerted rush for the door by terrified diners and the musicians. Smoke and bits of debris filled the room.

Summoning Discipline, Lunzie burst out from under the shadow of the false cliff where Aelock's push had landed her, intending to follow Aelock and help him stop his would-be assassin. As she gained her feet, someone behind her threw one arm around her neck and squeezed, grabbing for her wrist with the other hand. Lunzie strained to see her assailant. It was the other pale-faced employee, his eyes glittering as he pressed in on her windpipe.

She tried to get her arms free, but the silk folds of his costume restricted her. Polymer boots weren't very suitable for stomping insteps so she opted for raking her heel down the man's shins and ramming the sole down onto the tendons joining foot and ankle. With a growl of pain, he gripped her throat tighter.

Lunzie promptly shot an elbow backward into his midsection, and was rewarded by an *oof!* His grip loosened slightly and she turned in his grasp, freeing her wrist. Growling, he tightened his arms to crush her. She jabbed for the pressure points on the rib cage under his arms with her thumbs, and brought a knee up between his legs, on the chance that whatever this humanoid's heritage, it hadn't robbed her of a sensitive point of attack.

It hadn't. As he folded, Lunzie delivered a solid chop to the back of his neck with her stiffened hand. He collapsed in a heap, and she ran for the door of the restaurant, shouting for a peace officer.

The local authorities had been alerted to the fire and disturbance in Colchie's. A host of uniformed officers had arrived in a groundvan, and were collecting reports from the frightened, coughing patrons milling on the street.

"An assassin," Lunzie explained excitedly to the officer who followed her back into the smoke-filled building. "He attacked me but I managed to disable him. His partner tried to shoot my dinner companion with a needlegun."

"A needlegun?" the officer repeated in disbelief. "Are you sure what you saw? Those are illegal on this planet."

"A most sensible measure," Lunzie replied grimly. "But that's what blew up our booth. There, he's getting up again! Stop him!"

She pointed at the gaily costumed being, who was slowly climbing to his feet. In a couple of strides, the peace officer had caught up with Lunzie's attacker and seized him by the arm. The assassin snarled and squirmed loose, brandishing a shimmering blade — then folded yet again as the officer's stunner discharged into his sternum. The limp assassin was carried off by a pair of officers who had just arrived to back up their colleague.

"Citizen," the first one said to her, "I'll need a report from you."

While Lunzie was giving her report to the peace officer, Captain Aelock came out the front of the restaurant with the other assassin in an armlock. The captain's tunic was torn, and his thick gray hair was disheveled. She noticed blood on his face and streaking down one sleeve.

The assassin joined his quiescent partner in the groundvan while the captain took the report officer and made a private explanation.

"I see, sir," the Alphan said, respectfully, giving a half salute. "We'll contact FSP Fleet Command if we need any further details from you."

"We may leave, then?"

"Of course, sir. Thank you for your assistance."

Aelock gave him a preoccupied nod and hurried Lunzie away. He looked shaken and unhappy.

"What else happened?" she demanded.

"We've got to get out of here. Those two probably weren't alone."

Lunzie lengthened her stride. "That's not all that's bothering you."

"My contact is dead. I found him in the alley behind the building when I chased that man. Dammit, how did they get on to me? The whole affair has been top secret, need-to-know only. It means — and I hate to imagine how — the pirates must have spies within the top echelons of the service."

"What?" Lunzie exclaimed.

"There's been no one else who could have known. I reported my contact with my poor dead friend only to my superiors — and I have told no one else. It must mean Aidkisagi is involved," Aelock muttered almost to himself in a preoccupied undertone.

They turned another corner onto an empty street. Lunzie glanced behind them nervously. Yellow city lights reflected off the smooth surfaces of the building façades and the sidewalk as if they were two mirrors set at right angles. Each of them had two bright-edged shadows wavering along behind them which made Lunzie feel as if they were being followed. Aelock set a bruising pace for a spacer. They heard no footfalls behind them.

When he was sure that they had not been followed, Aelock stopped in the middle of a small public park where he had a 360-degree field of vision. The low shrubs twenty yards away offered no cover.

"Lunzie, it's more imperative than ever that I get a message to Commander Coromell on Tau Ceti. He's Chief Investigator for Fleet Intelligence. He must know about this matter."

"Why not give it to the Admiral? He told me he was going to visit his son."

In the half shadow of the park, Aelock's grimace looked malevolent rather than regretful. "He would have been ideal but he left this morning." Aelock gazed down hopefully at Lunzie and took hold of her wrists. "I can't trust this message to any ordinary form of transmission, but it must get to Coromell. It is vital. Would you carry it?"

"Me?" Lunzie felt her throat tighten. "How?"

"Do exactly what you were going to do. Take a position as Medical Officer. Only make it a berth on a fast ship, anything that is going directly to Tau Ceti as soon as possible. Tomorrow, if you can. Alpha is one of the busiest spaceports in the galaxy. Freighters and merchants leave hourly. I'll make sure you have impeccable references even if they won't connect you with me. Will you do that?"

Lunzie hesitated for a heartbeat in which she remembered the devastated landscape of Phoenix, and the triple column list of the dead colonists.

"You bet I will!"

The look of intense relief on Aelock's face was reward in itself. From a small pocket in the front of his tunic, he took a tiny ceramic tube and put it in her hands. "Take this message brick to Coromell and say: 'It's Ambrosia.' Got it? Even if you lose this, remember the phrase."

Lunzie hefted the cube, no bigger than her thumbnail. " 'It's Ambrosia,' " she repeated carefully. "All right. I'll find a ship tomorrow morning." She tucked the ceramic into her right boot.

Aelock gripped her shoulders gratefully. "Thank you. One more thing. Under no circumstances should you try to play that cube. It can only be placed into a reader with the authorized codes."

"It'll blank?" she asked.

Aelock smiled at her naivete. "It will explode. That's a high-security brick. The powerful explosive it contains would level the building if the wrong sort of reader's laser touches it. Do you understand?"

"Oh, after tonight, I believe you, even if this whole evening has been like something from Tri-D." She grinned reassuringly at him.

"Good. Now, don't go back to the BOQ. They must not realize that you're with me. It could mean your life if they think you are connected with the Fleet. They killed my friend, a harmless fellow, a welder in the shipyard. His family had been at Phoenix. Couldn't hurt a fly, but they killed him." Aelock shuddered at the memory. "I won't tell you how. I've seen many forms of death, but that sort of savagery . . . "

Lunzie felt the Discipline boost wearing off and she'd little reserve of strength. "I won't risk it then, but what about my things?"

"I'll have them sent to you. Take a groundcar. Go to the Alpha Meridian Hotel and get a room. Here's my credit seal."

"I've got plenty of credits, thank you. That's no problem."

Aelock saw a groundcar, its "empty" light flashing, and hailed it. "That one ought to be safe, coming from the west. Someone will bring your things to the hotel. It will be someone you know. Don't let anyone else in." He opened the car hatch and helped her in. He leaned over her before closing the car. "We won't meet again, Lunzie. But thank you, from the bottom of my heart. You're saving lives."

Then he slipped away into shadow as yellow streetlights washed across the rounded windows of the rolling groundcar. Lunzie buckled herself in and gave her destination to the robot-brain.

The Alpha Meridian reminded Lunzie of the *Destiny Calls*. In the main lobby, there were golden cherubs and other benevolent spirits on the ceiling holding up sconces of vapor-lights. Ornate pillars with a leaf motif, also in gold, marched through the room like fantastic trees. A human server met her at the door and escorted her to the registration desk. No mention was made of her casual clothing, though she appeared a mendicant in comparison to the expensively dressed patrons taking a late evening morsel in cushiony armchairs around the lobby.

The receptionist, who Lunzie suspected was a shapechanging Weft because of the utter perfection of her human form, impassively checked Lunzie's credit code. As the confirmation appeared, her demeanor instantly altered. "Of course we can accommodate you, Citizen Doctor Lunzie. Do you require a suite? We have a most appealing one available on the four-hundredth-floor penthouse level."

"No, thank you," Lunzie replied, amused. "Not for one night. If I were staying a week or more, certainly I would need a suite. My garment cases will follow by messenger."

"As you wish, Citizen Doctor." The receptionist lifted a discreet eyebrow, and a bellhop appeared at Lunzie's side. "One-oh-seven-twelve, for the Citizen Doctor Lunzie." The bellhop bowed and escorted her toward the bank of turbovators.

Her room was on a corridor lined with velvety dark red carpet, and smelled pleasantly musky and old. The Meridian was a member of a grand hotel chain of the old style, reputed to have brought Earth-culture hostelry to the stars. The bellhop turned on the lights and waited discreetly at the door until Lunzie had stepped in, then withdrew on silent feet. In her nervous state, she flew to the door and opened it, to make sure he had really gone. The bellhop, waiting at the turboshaft for the 'vator to come back, threw her a curious glance. She ducked back into her room and locked the door behind her.

"I must calm down," Lunzie said out loud. "No one followed me. No one knows where I am."

She paced the small room, staying clear of the curtained window, which provided her with a view of a tiny park and an enormous industrial complex. The bedroom was panelled in a dark, smooth-grained wood with discreet carvings along the edges near the ceiling and floor. The canopied bed was deep and soft, covered with a thick, velvety spread in maroon edged with gold trim that matched the smooth carpeting. It was a room designed for comfort and sleep but Lunzie was too nervous to enjoy it. She wanted to use the comm unit and call the ship to see if Aelock had made it back safely. A stupid urge and dangerous for both of them. Shaking, Lunzie sat down on the end of the bed and clenched her hands in her lap.

Someone would be coming by later with her clothing and possessions. Until that someone came, she couldn't sleep though her body craved rest after the draining of Discipline. The hotel provided a reader and small library in every room. Hers was next to the bed on a wooden shelf that protruded from the wall. She was far too restless to read, the events of the evening on constant replay in her mind. Even if the two assailants had been captured, that didn't mean they had been alone, or that their capture would go unremarked. That left a bath to fill in her time and that at least was a constructive act, helping to draw tension out of her body and ready it for the sleep she so badly needed.

While the scented water was splashing into the tub, Lunzie kept imagining she heard the sound of knocking on her door and kept running out to answer it.

"This is ridiculous," she told herself forcefully. "I can take care of myself. They would scarcely draw attention to themselves by leveling the hotel because I'm in it. I must relax. I will."

Her clothes were dirty and sweat-stained and there was a large blot of sauce on the underside of one forearm. She tossed them in the refresher unit, and listened to them swirl while she lay in the warm bath water.

The bathroom was supplied with every luxury. Mechanical beauty aids offered themselves to her in the bath. A facial cone lowered itself to her face and hovered, humming discreetly. "No, thank you," Lunzie said. It rose out of her way and disappeared into a hatch in the marble-tiled ceiling. A dental kit appeared next. "Yes, please." She allowed it to clean her teeth and gums. More mechanisms descended and were refused: a mani-cure/pedicure kit, a tonsor, a skin exfoliant. Lunzie accepted a shampoo and rinse with scalp massage from the hairdressing unit, then got out of the tub to a warmed towel and robe, pre-sented by another mechanical conveyance.

It was close to midnight by then and Lunzie found that she was hungry. Her entree at Colchie's had turned out to be an assassin with a needlegun. She considered summoning a meal from room service but she was loath to, picturing chalky-faced waiters in silk capes streaming into the tiny room with guns hid-den in their sashes. She'd been hungrier than this before. Wearing the robe, Lunzie climbed into bed to wait for the mes-senger with her bags.

Most of the book plaques on the shelf were best-sellers of the romance-and-intrigue variety. Lunzie found a pleasant whodun-nit in the stack and put it into the reader. Pulling the reader's supporting arm over the bed, Lunzie lay back, trying to involve herself in the ratiocinations of Toli Alopa, a Weft detective who could shapechange to follow a suspect without fear of being spot-ted.

Somewhere in the middle of a chase scene, Lunzie fell into a fitful dream of pasty-faced waiters who called her Jonah and chased her through the *Destiny Calls*, finally pitching her out of the space liner in full warp drive. The airlock alarm chimed insis-tently that the hatch was open. There was danger. Lunzie awoke suddenly, seeing the shadow of an arm over her face. She screamed.

"Lunzie!" Tee's voice called through the door and the door sig-nal rang again. "Are you all right?"

"Just a moment!" Fully awake now, Lunzie saw that the arm was just the reader unit, faithfully turning pages in the book plaque. She swept it aside and hurried to the door.

"I'm alone," Tee assured her, slipping in and sealing the locks behind him. He gave her a quick embrace before she realized that he was wearing civilian clothes. "Here are your bags. I think I have everything of yours. Sharu helped me pack them."

"Oh, Tee, I am so glad to see you. Did the captain tell you what happened?"

"He did. What an ordeal, my Lunzie!" Tee exclaimed. "What was that scream I heard?"

"An overactive imagination, nothing more," Lunzie said, self-deprecatingly. She was ashamed that Tee had heard her panic.

"The captain suggested that you would trust me to bring your possessions. Of course, you might not want to see me . . . " He let the sentence trail off.

"Nonsense, Tee, I will always trust you. And your coming means that the captain got safely back. That's an incredible relief."

Tee grinned. "And I've got orders to continue to confuddle whoever it is that sends assassins after my good friends. When I leave here, I am going to the local Tri-D Forum and watch the news until dawn. Then I am going to an employment agency to job hunt." Tee held up a finger as Lunzie's mouth opened and closed. "Part of the blind. I go back to the ship when you are safely out of the way and no connection can be made between us. Now, is there anything else I can do for you?"

"Yes indeed," Lunzie said. "I never got past the appetizer and I haven't eaten since you and I had breakfast this morning. I don't dare trust room service, but I am positively ravenous. If the wooden walls didn't have preservative varnishes rubbed into them, I'd eat them."

"Say no more," Tee said, "though this establishment would suffer terrible mortification if they knew you'd gone for a carry-out meal when the delights of their very fancy kitchens are at your beck and call." He kissed her hand and slipped out of the room again.

In a short time, he reappeared with an armful of small bags.

"Here is a salad, cheese, dessert, and a cold bean-curd dish. The fruit is for tomorrow morning if you still feel insecure eating in public restaurants."

Lunzie accepted the parcels gratefully and set them aside on the bedtable. "Thank you, Tee. I owe you so much. Give my best to Naomi. I hope you and she will be very happy. I want you to be."

"We are," Tee smiled, with one of his characteristic wideflung gestures. "I promise you. Until we meet again." He wrapped his arms around her and kissed her. "I always will love you, my Lunzie."

"And I, you." Lunzie hugged him to her heart with all her might, and then she let him go. "Goodbye, Tee."

When she let him out and locked the door, Lunzie sorted through her duffel bags. At the bottom of one, she found the holo of Fiona wrapped securely in bubblepack. Loosening an edge of the pack, she took the message cube out of her boot. At the bottom of the bubblepack were two small cubes that Lunzie cherished, containing the transmissions sent her by her daughter's family to Astris and the *Ban Sidhe*. One more anonymous cube would attract no attention. Unless, of course, someone tried to read it in an unauthorized reader. She hoped she wouldn't be in the same vicinity when that happened. She could wish they'd used a less drastic protection scheme; what if an "innocent" snoop were to get his hands on it? She would have to be *very* careful. *Hmm* . . . she mused. Maybe that was the point.

Lunzie tried to go to sleep, but she was wide awake again. She put on the video system and scrolled through the Remote Shopping Network for a while. One of the offerings was a security alarm with a powerful siren and flashing strobe light for travellers to attach to the doors of hotel rooms for greater protection. Lunzie bought one by credit, extracting a promise from the RSN representative by comm link that it would be delivered to the hotel in the morning. The parcel was waiting for her at the desk when she came down early the next day to check out. She hugged it to her as she rode down to the spaceport to find a berth on an express freighter to Tau Ceti.

✧ CHAPTER TEN

Two weeks later, Lunzie disembarked from the freighter *Nova Mirage* in the spaceport at Tau Ceti and stared as she walked along the corridors to the customs area. The change after seventy-five years was dramatic, even for that lapse of time on a colony world. The corrugated plastic hangars had been replaced by dozens of formed stone buildings that, had Lunzie not known better, she would have believed grew right out of the ground.

She felt an element of shock when she stepped outside. The unpaved roads had been widened and coated with a porous, self-draining polyester surface compound. Most of the buildings she remembered were gone, replaced by structures twice as large. She had seen the Tau Ceti colony in its infancy. It was now in full bloom. She was a little sad that the unspoiled beauty had been violated although the additions had been done with taste and color, adding to, rather than detracting from their surroundings. Tau Ceti was still a healthy, comfortable place, unlike the gray dullness of Alpha Centauri. The cool air she inhaled tasted sweet and natural after two weeks of ship air, and a week's worth of pollution before that. The sun was warm on her face.

Lunzie appreciated the irony of carrying the same duffel bags over her shoulder today that she had lugged so many decades before when she had left Fiona there on Tau Ceti. They'd all showed remarkably little visible wear. Well, all that was behind her. She was beginning her life afresh. Pay voucher in hand, she sought *Nova Mirage*'s office to collect her wages and ask for directions.

The trip hadn't been restful but it had been fast and non-threatening. The *Nova Mirage*, an FTL medium-haul freighter, was carrying plumbing supplies and industrial chemicals to Tau Ceti. Halfway there, some of the crew had begun to complain of a hacking cough and displayed symptoms that Lunzie recognized as a form of silicosis. An investigation showed that one of the gigantic tubs in the storage hold containing powdered carbon crystals had cracked. This wouldn't have mattered except that the tub was located next to an accidentally opened intake to the ventilation system; the fumes had leaked all over the ship. Except for being short fifty kilos on the order, all was well. It was merely an accident, with no evidence of sabotage. A week's worth of exposure posed no permanent damage to the sufferers, but it was unpleasant while it lasted.

Lunzie had had the security alarm on her infirmary door during her sleep shift. It hadn't let out so much as a peep the entire voyage. The hologram and its attendant cubes remained undisturbed at the bottom of her duffel bag. None of the crew had sensed that their friendly ship's medic was anything out of the ordinary. And now she was on her way to deliver it and her message to their destination.

"I'd like to see Commander Coromell, please," Lunzie requested at Fleet Central Command. "My name is Lunzie."

"Admiral Coromell is in a meeting, Lunzie. Can you wait?" the receptionist asked politely, gesturing to a padded bench against the wall of the sparsely furnished, white-painted room. "You must have been travelling, Citizen. He's had a promotion recently. Not a Lieutenant Commander any more."

"Admiralties seem to run in his family," Lunzie remarked. "And I'll be careful to give him his correct rank, Ensign. Thank you."

In a short time, a uniformed aide appeared to escort her to the office of the newly appointed Admiral Coromell.

"There she is," a familiar voice boomed as she stepped into the room. "I told you there couldn't be two Lunzies. Uncommon name. Uncommon woman to go with it." Retired Admiral Coromell stood up from a chair before the honeywood desk in the square office and took her hand. "How do you do, Doctor? It's a pleasure to see you, though I'm surprised to see you so soon."

Lunzie greeted him with pleasure. "I'm happy to see you looking so well, sir. I hadn't had a chance to give you a final checkup before they told me you'd gone."

The old man smiled. "Well, well. But you surely didn't chase me all the way here to listen to my heart, did you? I've never met a more conscientious doctor." He did look better than he had when Lunzie saw him last, recently recovered from cold sleep, but she longed to run a scanner over him. She didn't like the look of his skin tone. The deep lines of his face had sunken, and something about his eyes worried her. He was over a hundred years old which shouldn't be a worry when human beings averaged 120 Standard years. Still, he had been through additional strain lately that had no doubt affected his constitution. His outlook was good, and that ought to help him prolong his life.

"I think she came to see me, Father."

The man behind the desk rose and came around to offer her a hand in welcome. His hair was thick and curly like his father's, but it was honey brown instead of white. Under pale brown brows, his eyes, of the same piercing blue as the senior Coromell's, bore into her as if they would read her thoughts. Lunzie felt a little overwhelmed by the intensity.

He was so tall that she had to crane her head back to maintain eye contact with him.

"You certainly do tend to inspire loyalty, Lunzie," the Admiral's son said in a gentle version of his father's boom. He was a very attractive man, exuding a powerful personality which Lunzie recognized as well suited to a position of authority in the Intelligence Service. "Your friend Teodor Janos was prepared to turn the galaxy inside out to find you. He certainly is proficient at computerized research. If it were not for him, I wouldn't have had half the evidence I needed to convince the Fleet to commission a ship for the search, even with my own father one of the missing. It's nice to finally meet you. How do you do?"

"Very well, Admiral," Lunzie replied, flattered. "Er, I'm sorry. That's going to become confusing, since both of you have the same name, and the same rank."

The old man beamed at both of them. "Isn't he a fine fellow? When I went away, he was just a lad with his new captain's bars. I arrived two days ago and they were making him an admiral. I couldn't be more proud."

The young admiral smiled down at her. "As far as I'm concerned, there's only one Admiral Coromell," and he gestured to his father. "Between us, Lunzie, my name will be sufficient."

Lunzie was dismayed with herself as she returned his smile.

Hadn't she just vowed not to let anyone affect her so strongly? With the painful breakup with Tee so fresh in her mind? Certainly Coromell was handsome and she couldn't deny the charm nor the intelligence she sensed behind it. How dare she melt? She had only just met the man. Abruptly, she recovered herself and recalled her mission.

"I've got a message for you, er, Coromell. From Captain Aelock of the *Ban Sidhe*."

"Yes? I've only just spoken with him via secure-channel FTL comm link. He said nothing about sending you or a message."

Lunzie launched into a explanation, describing the aborted dinner date, the murder of Aelock's contact, and the attempted murder of the two of them. "He gave me this cube," she finished, holding out the ceramic block, "and told me to tell you. 'It's Ambrosia.'"

"Great heavens," Coromell said, amazed, taking the block from her. "How in the galaxy did you get it here without incident?"

The old Admiral let out a hearty laugh. "The same way she travelled with me, I'll wager," he suggested shrewdly. "As an anonymous doctor on a nondescript vessel. Am I not correct? You needn't look so surprised, my dear. I was once head of Fleet Intelligence myself. It was an obvious ploy."

Coromell shook his head, wonderingly. "I could use you in our operations on a regular basis, Lunzie."

"It wasn't my idea. Aelock suggested it," Lunzie protested.

"Ah, yes, but he didn't carry it out. You did. And no one suspected that you were a courier with top secret information in your rucksack — this!" Coromell shook the cube. He spun and punched a control on the panel atop his desk. "Ensign, please tell Cryptography I want them standing by."

"Aye, aye, sir," the receptionist's voice filtered out of a hidden speaker.

"We'll get on this right away. Thank you, Lunzie." Coromell ushered her and his father out. "I'm sorry, but I've got to keep this information among as few ears as possible."

"Well, well," said the Admiral to an equally surprised Lunzie as they found themselves in the corridor. "May I offer you some lunch, my dear? What d'you say? We can talk about old times. I saw the most curious thing the other day, something I haven't seen in years: a Carmen Miranda film. In two-D."

✦   ✦   ✦

Lunzie passed a few pleasant days in Tau Ceti, visiting places she'd known when she stayed there. It was still an attractive place. A shame, on the whole, that there hadn't been a job here for her seventy-four years ago. The weather was pleasant and sunny, except for a brief rainshower early in the afternoon. By the hemispheric calendar, it was the beginning of spring. The medical center in which she worked had expanded, adding on a nursing school and a fine hospital. None of the people she'd known were still there. Flatteringly enough, the administrator looked up her records and offered her a position in the psychoneurology department.

"Since Tau Ceti became the administrative center for the FSP, we've seen a large influx of cases of space-induced trauma," he explained. "Nearly a third of Fleet personnel end up in cryogenic sleep for one reason or another. With your history and training, you would be the de facto expert on cold sleep. We would be delighted if you would join the staff."

Tempted, Lunzie promised she'd think it over.

She also interviewed with the shipping companies who were based on Tau Ceti for another position as a ship's medic. To her dismay, a few of them took one look at the notation in her records indicating that she had been in two space wrecks and instantly showed her the door. Others were more cordial and less superstitious. Those promised to let her know the next time they had need of her services. Three who had ships leaving within the next month were willing to sign her on.

She spent some time with old Admiral Coromell, talking about old times. She also found it affected her profoundly to be in a familiar venue in which no one remembered many of the events that she did. To her, less than four years had passed since she had left Fiona there. The Admiral was the only other one who recalled events of that era and he shared her feelings of isolation.

Two weeks later, Coromell himself stopped by to see her at the guest house where she had taken a room.

"Sorry to have booted you and Father out of the office the other day," he apologized, with an engaging smile. "That information required immediate attention. I've been working on nothing else since then."

"My feelings weren't hurt," Lunzie assured him. "I was just incredibly relieved that I'd got it to you. Aelock had impressed its importance on me. Several ways." The assassin's grim face flashed before her eyes again.

Coromell smiled more easily now. "Lunzie, you're a tolerant soul! To cross a galaxy with an urgent message and find the recipient is brusque to the point of rudeness. May I make amends now that all the flap is over and show you around? Or, perhaps, it's more to the point that you show me around. I know you'd been here when Tau Ceti was just started."

"I would enjoy that very much. When?"

"Today? With the nights I've been putting in, they won't begrudge me an afternoon off. That's why I came over." He held the door open and the sunlight streamed in. "It's too nice a day, even for Tau Ceti, to waste stuck indoors."

They spent the day in the nature preserve which had been Fiona's favorite haunt. The imported trees, saplings when she left, were mature giants now, casting cool shade over the river path. Following her memory, Lunzie led Coromell to her and Fiona's favorite place. The brief midday showers had soaked the ground and a heady smell of humus filled the air. In the crowns of the trees, they could hear the twitter of birdsong celebrating the lovely weather. Lunzie and Coromell ducked under the heavy boughs and clambered up the slope to a stone overhang. At one time in the planet's geologic history, stone strata had met and collided, shifting one of them up toward the surface so that a ledge projected out over the river.

"It's good for sitting and thinking, and feeding the birds, if you happen to have any scraps of bread with you," Lunzie said, half lying on the great slab of sun-warmed stone to peer down into the water at small shadows chasing each other down the stream. "Or the fishoids."

Coromell patted his pockets. "Sorry. No bread. Perhaps next time."

"It's just as well. We'd be overrun with supplicants."

He laughed, and settled next to her to watch the dappled water dance over the rocks. "I needed this. It's been very hectic of late and I get to spend so little time in planetary atmosphere. My father has talked of no one else but you since he got here. He married late in life and doesn't want me to make the same mistake. He's lonely," Coromell added, wistfully. "He's been working on throwing us together."

"I wouldn't mind that," Lunzie said, turning her head to smile at him. Coromell was an attractive man. He had to be on the far side of forty-five but he had a youthful skin and, out of his official surroundings, he displayed more enthusiasm than she supposed careworn or rank-conscious admirals usually did.

"Well, I wouldn't either. I won't lie to you," he replied carefully. "But be warned, I can't offer much in the way of commitments. I'm a career man. The Fleet is my life and I love it. Anything else would run second place."

Lunzie shrugged, pulling pieces of moss off the rock and dropping them in the water to watch the ripples. "And I'm a wanderer, probably by nature as well as experience. If I hadn't had a daughter, I'd never have been trying to earn Oh-Two money to join a colony. I enjoy travelling to new places, learning new things, and meeting new people. It would certainly be best not to make lifetime commitments. Nor very good for your reputation to have a time-lagged medic who's suspected of being a Jonah appearing on your arm at Fleet functions."

Coromell made a disgusted noise. "That doesn't matter a raking shard to me. Father told me about the chatter going on behind your back on the *Ban Sidhe*. I should put those fools on report for making your journey harder with such asinine superstitious babbling."

Lunzie laid a hand on his arm. "No, don't. If they need shared fears and experiences as a crutch to help them handle daily crisis, leave it to them. They'll grow out of it." She smiled reassuringly, and he slumped back with a hand shielding his eyes from the sun.

"As you wish. But we can still enjoy each other as long as we're together, no?"

"Oh, yes."

"I'm glad. Sure I can't persuade you to join up?" Coromell asked in a half-humorous tone. "It'll improve your reputation considerably to be a part of Fleet Intelligence. You could go places, meet new people and see new things while gathering information for us."

"What? Is that a condition for seeing you?" Lunzie asked in mock outrage. "I have to join the navy?" She raised an eyebrow.

"No. But if that's the only way I can get you to join up, maybe

I'll have the regulations altered," he chuckled wryly. "Do stay on Tau Ceti for a while. I'm stationed here, flying a desk in this operation. I hope to persuade you to change your mind about the service. You could be a true asset to the Fleet. Stay for a while, please."

Lunzie hesitated, considering. "I wouldn't feel right hanging around waiting for you to get off work every day. I'd be useless."

Coromell cleared his throat. "Didn't you speak to the Medical Center about a job? You could be employed there, until you decide what to do. They, um, called me to ask if your services were available. They seem to think you're Fleet personnel already. You have other unsuspected valuable traits. You listen to my father, who would be so happy to spend time with you. At his age, there are so few people he can talk to." Coromell looked wistfully hopeful, an expression at odds with both uniform and occupation.

Her last protests evaporated. How well she understood old Admiral Coromell's dilemma. "All right. None of the current prospects at the spaceport appeal to me. But that's not why I'm staying. I'm enjoying myself."

"I like you, Doctor Lunzie."

"I like you, too, Admiral Coromell." She squeezed his hand, and they sat together quietly for a while, simply enjoying the brook's quiet murmur and the sound of birdsong in the warmth of the afternoon.

Thereafter, they spent some time together whenever possible. Coromell's favorite idea of a relaxing afternoon was a stroll or a few hours listening to music or watching a classical event on Tri-D. They shared their music and literature libraries, and discussed their favorites. Lunzie enjoyed being with him. He was frequently tense when they met, but relaxed quickly once he had put the day behind him. Their relationship was different from the one she had had with Tee. Coromell expected her to offer opinions, and held to his own even if they differed. He was perfectly polite, as was appropriate to an officer and a gentleman, but he could be very stubborn. Even when they got into a knock-down-drag-out argument, Lunzie found it refreshing after Tee's selfless deferral to her tastes. Coromell trusted her with his honest views, and expected the same in return.

Coromell's schedule was irregular. When pirates had been

sighted, he would be swamped with reports that had to be analyzed to the last detail. He had other duties which had not yet been reassigned to an officer of lesser rank that could keep him at the complex for four or five shifts on end. Lunzie, not wishing to take a permanent job yet, found herself with time on her hands that not even her Discipline training could use up.

Coromell knew that she had passed through the Adept stage of Discipline. At his urging, and with his personal recommendation to the group master, she joined a classified course in advanced Discipline taught in a gymnasium deep in the FSP complex.

There were two or three pupils in the meditation sessions, but no names were ever exchanged, so she had no idea who they were. Her guess that they were upper echelon officers in the Fleet or senior diplomats was never verified or disproved. The master instructed them in fascinating types of mind control that built on early techniques accessible even to the first-level students. Using Discipline to heighten the senses to listen and follow the development of a subject's trance state, one could plant detailed posthypnotic suggestions. The shortened form of trance induction was amazing in its simplicity.

"This would be a terrific help in field surgery," Lunzie pointed out at the end of one private session. "I could persuade a patient to ignore poor physical conditions and remain calm."

"Your patient would still have to trust you. A strong will can counteract any attempt at suggestion, as you know, as can panic," the master warned her, gazing into her eyes. "Do not consider this a weapon, but rather a tool. The Council of Adepts would not be pleased. You are not merely a student-probationer any more."

Lunzie opened her mouth to protest that she would never do such a thing, but closed it again. He must have known of cases in which students had tried to rely on this single technique to control an enemy, only to fail, perhaps at the cost of their lives. Then she smiled. Perhaps the technique worked too well and she had to learn to apply it correctly and with a fine discrimination for its use.

One delightful change which had occurred while she was in her second bout of cold sleep was that coffee had had a renaissance. On a fine afternoon following her workout, Lunzie came back from the spaceport and programed a pot of coffee from the synth unit. The formula the synthesizers poured out had no caffeine, but it smelled oily and rich and wonderful, and tasted just like she remembered the real brew. There was even real coffee available occasionally in the food shops, an expensive treat in which, with her credit balance of back pay, she could afford to revel. She wondered if Satia Somileaux back on the Descartes Platform would ever try any.

The message light on her comm unit was blinking. Lunzie wandered over to it with a hot cup in her hands and hit the recall control. Coromell's face appeared on the screen.

"I'm sorry to ask on such short notice, Lunzie, but do you have a formal outfit? I'm expected to appear at a Delegate's Ball tonight at 2000 hours and your company would make it considerably less tedious an affair. I will be in the office until 1700 hours, awaiting your reply." The image blinked off.

"Gack, it's 1630 now!"

Bolting her coffee, Lunzie flew for her cases and rummaged through them for the teal-tissue sheath. The frock was easily compressed and didn't take up much room, so it was difficult to find. Yes, it was there, and it was clean and in good condition, needing only a quick wrinkle-proofing. She communicated immediately with Coromell's office that she would be free to come and hastened to set the clothes-freshener to Touch Up. She tossed the sweat-stained workout clothes in a corner and dashed through the sonic cleanser.

"Much more modest than I remembered." Approvingly, she noted her reflection in the mirror, making a final twirl. She smoothed down the sides of the thin fabric which shimmered in the evening sunlight coming through her window, allowing herself to admire the trim curves of her body. "You wouldn't think I was interested in this man, with the fuss I'm making to look good for him, would you?"

Lunzie fastened on her favorite necklace, a simple copper-and-gold choker than complemented the color of her dress and picked up becoming highlights in her hair and eyes.

Coromell arrived for her at 1945, looking correct and somewhat uncomfortable in his dark blue dress uniform. He gave Lunzie an approving once-over as he presented her with a corsage of white camellias. "Earth flowers. One of our botanists grows them as a hobby. How very pretty you look. Most becoming, that shimmery blue thing. I've never seen that style before," he said as he escorted her out to his chauffeured groundcar. "Is it the latest fashion?"

Lunzie chuckled. "I'll tell you a secret: it's a ten-year-old frock from halfway across the galaxy. It's surely the latest vogue somewhere."

The party had not yet begun when they arrived at the Ryxi Embassy, one of an identical row of three-story stone buildings set aside for the diplomatic corps of each major race in the FSP. Lunzie was amused to observe the resemblance between the embassies and the BOQ barracks on the Fleet bases. A flock of excitable two-meter-tall avians stood at the entrance greeting their guests, flanked by a host of silent Ryxi wearing the crossed sashes of honor guards.

"Great ones for standing on their dignities, the Ryxi," Coromell said in an aside as they waited in turn to pass inside. "Excited they forget everything, and I shouldn't like to tangle with an enraged birdling."

A storklike Ryxi stepped forward to bow jerkily to Coromell. "Admirrral, a pleasurre," he trilled. The Ryxi normally spoke very fast. They expected others to comprehend them but occasionally, as on this festive evening, they slowed their speech to gracious comprehensibility.

Coromell bowed. "How nice to see you, Ambassador Chrrr. May I present my companion, Doctor Lunzie?"

Chrrr bowed like a glass barometer. "Welcome among the flock, Doctorrr. Please make yourrrself frrree of the Embassy of the Rrryxi."

"You're very kind," Lunzie nodded, beating back a temptation to roll the one r like a Scotsman.

With their stiff legs, Ryxi preferred to stand unless sitting was absolutely necessary. For the convenience of humans, Seti, Weft, and the dozen or so other species represented that night, their great hall had been provided with plenty of varied seats for their comrades of inferior race.

"That's what they consider us," Coromell murmured as they moved into the hall, "or any race that hasn't a flight capability."

"Where do they rank Thek?"

"They ignore them whenever possible." Coromell chuckled. "The Ryxi don't think it's worth the time it takes to listen."

An elderly Seti, who was the personal ambassador from the

Seti of Fomalhaut, held court from the U-shaped backless chair which accommodated his reptilian tail. He made a pleasant face at her as she was introduced to him.

"Sso, you were graduated from Astriss Alexandria," he hissed. "As was I. Classs of 2784."

"Ah, you were four years behind me," Lunzie calculated. "Do you remember Chancellor Graystone?"

"I do. A fine administrator, for a human. How curious, elder one, that you do not appear of such advanced years as your knowledge suggests," the Seti remarked politely. Seti were very private individuals. In Lunzie's experience, this was the closest that one had ever come to asking a personal question.

"Why, thank you, honored Ambassador. How kind of you to notice," Lunzie said, bowing away as Coromell swept her on to the next introduction.

"I'm surprised there aren't any Thek here," Lunzie commented as they acknowledged other acquaintances of Coromell's.

He cleared his throat. "The Thek aren't very popular right now among some members of the FSP. Even though the ordinary Ryxi never seem to care what anyone else thinks, the diplomatic corps are sensitive to public feeling."

"That makes them unusual?" Lunzie asked.

"You have no idea," Coromell said dryly.

"Why, Admiral, how nice to see you. And who is your charming companion?"

Lunzie turned to smile politely at the speaker and took an abrupt step back. A dark-haired female heavyworlder with overhanging brow ridges was glaring down at her. But she had not spoken. Seated in front of the huge female in an elegant padded armchair was a slight human male with large, glowing black eyes. He was apparently quite used to having the massive woman hovering protectively behind him. Lunzie recovered herself and nodded courteously to the man in the chair.

"Ienois, this is Lunzie," Coromell said. "Lunzie, Ienois is the head of the well-known Parchandri merchant family whose trade is most important to Tau Ceti."

"This humble soul is overwhelmed by such compliments from the noble Admiral." The little man inclined his head politely. "And delighted to meet you."

"The pleasure is mine," Lunzie responded as composedly as

she could. It would never do to display her distrust and surprise. She knew the reputation of the Parchandris. Something about Ienois made her dislike him on the spot. Not to mention his taste in companions.

Ienois indicated the heavyworlder woman behind him. "My diplomatic aide, Quinada." She bowed and straightened up again without ever taking her eyes off Lunzie. "We haven't had the pleasure of seeing you before, Lunzie. Are you a resident of Tau Ceti?"

"No. I've only just arrived from Alpha Centauri," she answered politely. Coromell had assured her there was no reason to hide her origins beyond the dictates of simple good taste.

"Alpha Centauri? How interesting," intoned the Parchandri.

"My daughter's family lives in Shaygo," Lunzie replied civilly. "I had never met them and they invited me to a family reunion."

"Ah! How irreplaceable is family. In our business, we trust family first and others a most regrettably distant second. Fortunately, ours is a very large family. Alpha Centauri is a marvelously large world with so many amenities and wonders. You must have found it hard to leave."

"Not very," Lunzie returned drily, "since the atmosphere's so polluted it's not fit to breathe."

"Not fit to breathe? Not fit?" The Parchandri bent forward in an unexpected fit of laughter. "That's very good. But, Lunzie," and he had suddenly sobered, "surely the air of a planet is more breathable than that of a ship?"

Lunzie remembered suddenly the engineer Perkin's warning about the owners of the Destiny Cruise Lines. They were a Parchandri merchant family called Paraden. She didn't know if Ienois was a Paraden but preferred not to provoke him or arouse his curiosity. What if he was one of the defendants in the case against Destiny Cruise Lines? Coromell might need this man's goodwill.

"Lunzie was shipwrecked on her way to Alpha Centauri," Coromell said, completely surprising Lunzie with this remark delivered in the manner of keeping a conversation going.

"I see. How dreadful." The Parchandri's large eyes gleamed as if it were not dreadful to him at all and, in some twisted way, she became more interesting to him. That was a weird perversion. "Were you long in that state?" the Parchandri pressed her. "Or were your engineers able to make repairs to your vessel? It is quite a frightening thing to be at the mercy of your machines in deep space. You appear to have survived the calamity without trauma. Commendable fortitude. Do tell this lowly one all!" His eyes glittered with anticipation.

Lunzie shrugged, not at all willing to gratify this strange man. Coromell would not have placed her in jeopardy if this Ienois was a Paraden and possibly one of the defendants in the case against Destiny Cruise Lines.

"There's not much to tell, really. We were towed in by a military ship who happened to pass by the site of the wreck."

"How fortuitous a rescue." Ienois' eyes glittered. His . . . minder — no matter if he called her a diplomatic aide, she was a bodyguard if ever Lunzie had seen one — never wavered in the stare she favored Lunzie. "Stranded in space, landed on Alpha Centauri, and now you're here. How brave you are."

"Not at all," Lunzie said, wishing they could move away from this vile man and his glowering "aide" but Coromell's hand on her elbow imperceptibly restrained her. Strange that he failed to notice that she had given no details about her ship. Did Ienois already "know"? "Travel is a fact of life these days. Ships and rumors traverse the galaxy with equal speed."

Ienois ignored her flippancy. "Admiral," he turned to Coromell, "have you tried the refreshments yet? I do believe that the Ryxi have brought in a genuine Terran wine for our pleasure. From Frans, I am told."

"France," Coromell corrected him with a bow. "A province in the northern hemisphere of Earth."

"Ah, yes. This is one world to which I have not yet been. The Ryxi have truly provided a splendid repast for their guests. Raw nuts and seeds are not much to my liking, but there are sweet cream delicacies that would serve to delight those far above my humble station. And the cheeses! Pure ambrosia." The Parchandri kissed the back of his hand.

In spite of her shield of will, Lunzie flinched involuntarily. Ambrosia. It was a coincidence that the Parchandri should use that word. Having carried and cherished it like an unborn child for the better part of three months, Lunzie was sensitive to its use. She caught both men looking at her. Coromell hadn't reacted. He knew the significance of the word, but what of the merchant? Ienois was studying her curiously.

"Is the temperature not comfortable for you, Doctor?" Ienois asked in a sympathetic tone. "In my opinion, the Ryxi keep the room very warm, but I am accustomed to my home which is in a mountainous region. Much cooler than here." He beckoned upward to his gigantic bodyguard. They whispered together shortly, then Quinada left the room. Ienois shrugged. "I require a lighter jacket or I will stifle before I am able to give my greetings to my hosts."

Ienois drew the conversation on to subjects of common interest on which he held forth charmingly, but Lunzie was sure that he was watching her. There was a secretive air about the little merchant which had nothing to do with pleasant surprises. She found him sinister as well as perverted and wished she and Coromell could leave. Lunzie was made uncomfortable by Ienois' scrutiny, and tried not to meet his eyes.

Finally, Coromell seemed to notice Lunzie's signals to move on. "Forgive me, Ienois. The Weftian ambassador from Parok is here. I must speak to him. Will you excuse us?"

Ienois extended a moist hand to both of them. Lunzie gave it a hearty squeeze in spite of her revulsion and was rewarded by a tiny moue of amusement. "Can we count on seeing the two of you at our little party in five days time?" the merchant asked. "The Parchandri wish to reignite the flame of our regard in the hearts of our treasured friends and valued customers. Will you brighten our lives by attending?"

"Yes, of course," Coromell said graciously. "Thank you for extending the invitation."

The Parchandri was on his feet now, bowing elaborately. "Thank you. You restore face to this humble one." He made a deep obeisance and sat down.

"Must we go to the party of the unscrupulous Parchandri?" Lunzie asked in an undertone as they moved away.

Coromell seemed surprised. "We do have to maintain good relations. Why not?"

"That unscrup makes me think he'd sell his mother for ten shares of Progressive Galactic."

"He probably would. But come anyway. These do's are very dull without company."

"There's something about him that makes my very nervous.

He said 'ambrosia.' Did you see his stare at me when I reacted? He couldn't have failed to notice it."

"He used the word in an acceptable context, Lunzie. You're just sensitive to it. Not surprising after all you've been through. Ienois is too indolent to be involved in anything as energetic as business." Coromell drew her arm through his and led her toward the next ambassador.

"She lied," Quinada muttered to her employer as she bowed to present a lighter dress tunic. "I checked with the main office. According to our reports from Alpha Centauri covering those dates, no disabled vessel was towed in. However, numerous beings in civilian garb were observed disembarking from a military cruiser, the *Ban Sidhe*. One matches her description. That places her on Alpha at the correct time, and with a false covering story."

"Inconclusive," Ienois said lightly, watching Lunzie and Coromell chatting with the Weftian ambassador and another merchant lord. "I could not make a sale with so weak a provenance. I need more."

"There is more. The man in the restaurant to whom the dead spy reported had a female companion, whose description also matches our admiral's lady in blue."

"Ah. Then there is no doubt." Ienois continued to smile at anyone who glanced his way, though his eyes remained coldly half-lidded. "Our friends' plans may have to be . . . altered." He pressed his lips together. "Kill her. But not here. There is no need to provoke an interplanetary incident over so simple a matter as the death of a spy. But see to that she troubles us no further."

"As your will dictates." Quinada withdrew.

A live band in one corner struck up dance music. Lunzie listened longingly to the lively beat while Coromell exchanged endless stories with another officer and the representative from a colony which had just attained protected status. Coromell turned to ask her a question and found that her attention was focused on the dance floor. He caught her eye and made a formal bow.

"May I have the honor?" he asked and, excusing himself to his friends, swept her out among the swirling couples. He was an excellent dancer. Lunzie found it easy to follow his lead and let her body move to the beat of the music.

"Forgive me for boring you," Coromell apologized, as they

sidestepped between two couples. "These parties are stamped out of a mold. It's a boon when I find any friends attending with whom I can chat."

"Oh, you're not boring me," Lunzie assured him. "I hope I wasn't looking bored. That would be unforgivable."

"It won't be too much longer before we may leave," Coromell promised. "I'm weary myself. The tradition is for the hosts giving the party to toast the guests with many compliments, and for the guests to return the honors. It should happen any time now."

The dance music ended, and the elderly Ryxi made his way to the front of the room with a beaker in one wingclaw. He raised the beaker to the assembled. At his signal, Lunzie and the others hastened to the refreshment table. Coromell poured them both glasses of French wine.

When everyone was ready, the ambassador began to speak in his mellow tenor cheep. "To our honored guests! Long life! To our fellow members of the Federated Sentient Planets! Long life! To my old friend the Speaker for the Weft!"

Coromell sighed and leaned toward Lunzie. "This is going to take a long time. Your patience and forbearance are appreciated."

Lunzie stifled a giggle and raised her glass to the Ryxi.

"I can't wear the same dress to two diplomatic functions in a row," Lunzie explained to Coromell over lunch the next day. "I'm going shopping for a second gown."

When she had arrived on Tau Ceti, Lunzie had marked down in her mind the new shopping center that adjoined the spaceport. Originally the site had been a field used for large-vehicle repair and construction of housing modules, half hidden by a hill of mounded dirt suitable for sliding down by the local children.

The hill was still there, landscaped and clipped to the most stringent gardening standard. Behind it lay a beautifully constructed arcade of dark red brick and the local soft gray stone. In spite of the conservative appearance, the high atrium rang with the laughter of children, five generations descended from the one Fiona had once played with. Lunzie overheard animated conversations echoing through the corridors as she strolled.

Most of the stores were devoted to oxygen-breathers, though at the ground level there were specialty shops with airlock hatches instead of doors to serve customers whose atmosphere differed from the norm. Lunzie window-shopped along one level and wound her way up the ramp to the next, mentally measuring dresses and outfits for herself. The variety for sale was impressive, perhaps too impressively large. She doubted whether there were three stores here which would have anything to suit her. Some of the fashions were very extreme. She stood back to peruse the show windows.

In the lexan panes, she caught a glimpse of something very large moving toward her from the left. Lunzie looked up. A party of heavyworld humans was stumping down the walkway, angling to get past her. She recognized the somber male at the head of the group as the representative from Diplo, whom Coromell had pointed out to her at the Ryxi party. They took up so much of the ramp walking two abreast that Lunzie scooted into Finzer's Fashions until they passed.

"How may I assist you, Citizen?" A human male two-thirds of Lunzie's height with elegantly frilled ears approached her, bowing and smiling. "I am Finzer, the proprietor of this fine outlet."

Lunzie glanced out into the atrium. The party was gone, all except for one female who had stopped to look into one shop window across the corridor. And she wasn't one of the Diplo cortege. It was the Parchandri's bodyguard, Quinada. The heavyworld female turned, and her dark eyes met Lunzie's with a stupid, heavy gaze. Lunzie smiled at her, hoping a polite response was in order. Quinada stared expressionlessly for a moment before walking away. Puzzled, Lunzie glanced back at the shopkeeper, who was still waiting by her side.

"I'm looking for evening wear," she told Finzer. "Do you have something classic in a size ten?"

Finzer produced a classic dress in dusty rose pink with a bodice that hugged Lunzie's rib cage and a full evening skirt that swirled around her feet.

Two evenings later, she held the folds of the dress bunched up on her lap as she and Coromell rode toward the Parchandri's residence.

"I'm not imagining it, Coromell," Lunzie said firmly. "Quinada's been everywhere that I've gone these past two days. Every time I turned around, she was there. She's following me."

"Coincidence," Coromell said blithely. "The area in which the Tau Ceti diplomatic set circulate is surprisingly small. You and Quinada had similar errands this week, that's all."

"That's not all. She stares at me, with a look I can only describe as hungry. I don't trust that perverse unscrup she works for any further than I could toss him. Didn't you see how his eyes glittered when I said I'd been spacewrecked? He's got nasty tastes in amusement."

"You're making too much of coincidence," Coromell offered gently. "Certainly you're safe from perversion here in Tau Ceti. Kidnapping is a serious breach of diplomatic immunity, one a man of Ienois' status and family position would hardly risk. As for that aide of his, you told me yourself that you have a deep-seated fear of heavyworlders."

"I do not have a persecution complex," Lunzie said in dead earnest. "Putting aside my deep-seated fear, once I got to thinking that Quinada might be following me, I tried to lose her. Tell me why she was in four different provisions stores without buying a thing! Or three different beauty salons! Not only that, she was waiting outside the FSP complex when I finished my Discipline lessons."

Coromell was thoughtful. "You're convinced, aren't you?"

"I am. And I think it probably has to do with ambrosia, even if you won't enlighten me on that score." Coromell smiled slightly at the reference but said nothing, which further annoyed her in her circumstances. Ambrosia must be a classified matter at the highest level, and she was only the envelope which had delivered the letter, not entitled to know more. Stubbornly, she continued. "I don't think Ienois' reference was as casual as you do, despite his unassailable diplomatic status. In any event, I find his aide's surveillance sinister."

"On a personal level, there's not much I can do to discourage that, Lunzie. However," and he cocked his head at her, a sly gleam in his eyes, "enlist in Fleet Intelligence and you have the service to protect you."

Lunzie cast a long searching look at his handsome face to dispel the unworthy thought that popped into her head. "To what ends *would* you go, Admiral Coromell, to get me into Fleet Intelligence?"

"I do want you in FI — you'd be a great asset, and frankly it would be wonderful having you around — but not at any cost. I can't compromise Fleet regulations, not that you'd want me to, and I can't give you any special consideration, not that you'd accept it anyway. The most important thing of all, Lunzie, is that you're willing to join. Even if I could press you into service, that's not the kind of recruit we want. I do know that you'd be ten times better as an operative than someone like Quinada . . . if you do decide to volunteer."

Lunzie hesitated, then nodded. "All right. I'm in."

Coromell smiled and squeezed her arm. "Good. I'll see to your credentials tomorrow morning. There will be a follow-up interview, but I have most of the details of your life on disk already. I hope you won't regret it. I don't think you will."

"I'm feeling more secure already," Lunzie said, sincerely.

"Good timing. We've arrived."

The Parchandri mansion lay on the outskirts of the main Tau Ceti settlement. Ienois and a group of Parchandri were waiting on the steps to greet their guests in the deepening twilight. Pots to either side of the wide doors swirled heavily scented and colored smoke into the air. Two servants met each vehicle as it pulled up. One opened the door as the other ascertained who was inside and announced the names to the hosts. Lunzie caught a passing glimpse of burning dark eyes in pasty-white faces and gulped. The unexpected appearance of representatives of the same race as the assassins in the Alpha Centauri restaurant was unsettling to say the least. The burning eyes, however, held no flicker of recognition. But then, why should they? She was getting overly sensitive to too many coincidences.

Ienois greeted them warmly, introducing Coromell to members of his family. Each was dressed in garb of such understated elegance Lunzie found herself trying to estimate the value of their clothes. If her guess was correct, each Parchandri was wearing more than the value of the clothes on the entire party of diplomats. As the evening weather was fine, drinks were circulated under the portico by liveried servants.

"Admiral Coromell! And Lunzzie, how very niccce to sssee you again," said the Seti ambassador, wending his way ponderously up the front stairs from the welcoming committee. "Admiral, I had hoped to sssee you a few days ago, but I missssed my opportunity."

Knowing a hint for privacy when she heard one, Lunzie excused herself. "I'll just find the ladies' lounge," she told

Coromell, placing her drink on the tray of a passing servant.

Asking directions from one of the Parchandri ladies, Lunzie made her way into the building. Ienois had given her no more than a disinterested "Good evening," which reassured her. Maybe her assumption was only part of her heightened awareness since that disastrous evening with Aelock. She was pleased to have escaped his attention. Rumors she had heard since the Ryxi party confirmed her feelings about his proclivities and the reality was worse than she had imagined. Discounting half of what she'd heard, he was still far too sophisticated in his perversities.

Lunzie found herself in the Great Hall, a high-ceilinged chamber in an old-fashioned, elegant style. The ladies' lounge for humanoids was at the end of a pink marble corridor just to the right of the double winding staircase with gold-plated pillars which spiralled to the three upper floors. Several other corridors, all darkened, led away from the hall on this level.

"How beautiful! They certainly do know how to live," Lunzie murmured. Her voice rang in the big empty room. The lights were low, but there was enough illumination at the far end of the corridor for her to see another woman emerging from a swinging door. "Ah. There it is."

Lunzie readjusted her makeup in the mirror once more, straightened the skirt of her dress, and then sat down with a thump on the couch provided under the corner-mounted sconces which illuminated the room. No one else was making use of the facilities, so she was quite alone. There was only so much time she could waste in the ladies' room. It was a shame she didn't know any of the other diplomats present. She hoped that Coromell had nearly finished his negotiations with the Seti.

Well, she couldn't stay hidden in the lounge for the entire evening. She would have to circulate. Sighing, she pushed open the lounge door to return to the party. There, on the other side, was Quinada, massively blocking the hallway. Startled, Lunzie stood aside to let her by, intending to squeeze out and return to Coromell. The heavyworlder female filled the doorway and came on. Lunzie backed a few paces and stepped to the left, angling to pass as soon as the door was clear. Quinada wrapped a burly hand around her upper arm and steered her, protesting, back into the lounge.

"Here you are," she said, bearing the lightweight woman

back into a corner of the room. "I've been waiting for you."

"You have?" Lunzie asked in polite surprise. She braced herself and looked for a way around the heavyworlder's massive frame. "Why?"

Quinada's heavy brow ridges lowered sullenly over her eyes. "My employer wants you disposed of. I must follow his orders. I don't really want to, but I serve him."

Lunzie trembled. So her intuitions hadn't erred. Ienois suspected her. But to order her death on the strength of a recognized word? The heavyworlder pressed her back against the wall and eyed her smugly. Quinada could crush her to death by just bearing down.

Mastering her fear, Lunzie gazed into the other's eyes. "You don't want to kill me?" she asked simply, hoping she didn't sound as if she was begging. That could arouse the sadistic side of the big female's nature. Quinada was the type who would enjoy hurting her. And Lunzie needed just a little more time to muster Discipline. She had already made a tactical mistake, allowing herself to be put at a significant physical disadvantage. Quinada and her master must have been hoping for the opportunity. Quinada had seen her emerging from the FSP complex. Could they possibly know that she was an Adept?

"No, I don't want to kill you," Quinada cooed in a lighter voice, charged with implications which alarmed Lunzie considerably more. "Not if I don't have to. If you weren't my enemy, I wouldn't have to kill you at all."

"I'm not your enemy," Lunzie said soothingly.

"No? You smiled at me."

"I was trying to be friendly," Lunzie replied, disliking the intent and appraising fashion in which Quinada was staring at her.

"I wasn't sure. In this city all the diplomats smile, in deference to the lightweights. Their smiles are phony."

"Well, I'm not a diplomat. When I smile, it's genuine. I'm not paid to practice diplomacy." Lunzie rapidly assessed her chances of talking her way out of this tight spot. If she used Discipline but didn't kill the heavyworlder, her secret would be out. The next attempt on her life wouldn't be face to face. But if she used Discipline to kill, her ability would be revealed when Medical examination would show that a small female's hands had delivered the death blow. And then she'd have an Adept tribunal to face.

"Good," Quinada said, narrowing her eyes to glinting lights under her thick brow ridges, and leaning closer. Lunzie could feel the heat of the big female's skin almost against her own. "That pleases me. I want you to be friendly with me. My employer doesn't like you but if we are friends, I can't treat you like an enemy, can I? That's such a pretty gown." Quinada stroked the fabric covering Lunzie's shoulder with the back of one thick finger. "I saw you when you bought it. It suits you so well, brings out your coloring. You attract me. We don't have to stay at this dull party. Come away with me now. Perhaps we can share warmth."

Lunzie was frightened, but now she had a tremendous urge to laugh. The heavyworlder was offering to trade Lunzie's life for her favors! This scene would have been uproariously funny if it hadn't been in deadly earnest. If she managed to live through it, she could look back on it and laugh.

"Come with me, we'll be friends, and I'll forget my instructions," Quinada offered, purring. Her stare had turned proprietary. Lunzie tried not to squirm with disgust.

Masking her revulsion at Quinada's touch, Lunzie thought that even with the heavyworlder's promised protection, she was likely to wind up dead. Ienois was the sort of man whose orders are followed. How could Quinada fake her death? She had to get away, to warn Coromell. She found herself measuring her words carefully, injecting them with sufficient promise to seem compliant.

"Not now. The Admiral will be waiting for me. I'll give him the slip and meet you later." Lunzie forced herself to give Quinada's arm a soft caress, though her hand felt slimy as she completed the gesture. "It's important to keep up appearances. You know that."

"A secret meeting." Quinada smiled, her lips twisting to one side. "Very well. It adds excitement. When?"

"When the toasting is over," Lunzie promised. "They'll miss me if I'm not there to salute your master. But then I can meet you wherever you say."

"That's true," Quinada agreed, backing away from her. "That is the custom. And your disappearance would be marked."

Lunzie nodded encouragingly and stepped toward the door. Before she had taken a second one, Quinada seized her bare arm and slapped her smartly across the cheek. Lunzie's head snapped back on her neck, and she stared wide-eyed at the heavyworlder, who gripped her with steely fingertips, and then let go. Lunzie staggered back and leaned against the wall to steady herself.

"Where do we meet? You haven't said that. If you are lying, I will kill you." Quinada's voice was caressing and chilled Lunzie to the bone.

"But we meet here," she said as if that had been a foregone conclusion. "It's the safest place. As soon as the toasting is done, I'll come back here and wait for you. That conceited Admiral will think I wish to make myself pretty for him. See you then, Quinada, but I've been gone a long time. I must get back." With a dazzling smile, Lunzie ducked under her arm and out the door.

Whether Quinada would have followed or not became academic, for a group of five chattering humans were coming down the corridor toward the ladies' room, providing a safeguard.

When Lunzie found Coromell and his ambassador, the Seti was expressing his gratitude to Coromell. He bowed to Lunzie as he turned away. Lunzie managed an appropriate response even as she pulled the admiral to one side behind the smoking incense pots.

"I must talk to you," she hissed, casting around to see if Quinada had followed her. To her relief, the heavyworld woman was nowhere in sight.

"Where have you been?" he asked, then clucked his tongue in concern. "What happened? You've bruised your arm. And there's another mark on your cheek."

"Darling Quinada, the Parchandri's aide," Lunzie whispered, letting the revulsion she felt color her words with bitter sarcasm, "followed me to the ladies' lounge and jumped me there." She took some satisfaction in the shock on Coromell's face which he quickly controlled. "She's under his orders to kill me! She didn't only because I tentatively accepted an exchange for my life I have no intention of granting. I'm Fleet now, Coromell. Protect me. Get me out of here! Now!"

PART FOUR

✧ CHAPTER ELEVEN

She went into hiding in a Fleet-owned safe house while Coromell arranged for a shuttle to take her off-planet. Except for the Discipline Master and Admiral Coromell Senior, there was no one to regret her abrupt departure — except perhaps Quinada. But Lunzie did want the Adept to realize that she had been unavoidably called away. That was Discipline courtesy. Her studies in the special course had progressed to a point where she didn't need direct instruction although she had hoped to obtain permission to teach what she had learned. As it was, the powerful new techniques would take her years to perfect.

The next day a shuttle made a rendezvous in space with the Exploration and Evaluation Corps *ARCT-10*, a multi-generation, multi-environmental vessel that carried numerous exploration scouts and shuttlecraft. Lunzie was transferred aboard. Her files were edited so that her enlistment in Fleet Intelligence had been excised and a false employment record with the Tau Ceti medical center inserted. She was an ordinary doctor, joining the complement of the *ARCT-10* to explore and document new planets for colonization.

"There are thousands of beings aboard," Coromell had assured her. "You'll just be one of several hundred human specialists who sign on for three-year stints with the EEC. No one will have any reason to look twice at you. Once you're settled in, you can be another remote sensor on that vessel for me. Keep an ear open."

"You mean, I'm not entirely safe on board?"

"Far safer than on Tau Ceti," he replied encouragingly. "Blend in but don't call attention to yourself. You should be fine. You've got me slightly paranoid for your sake now." He ran restless fingers through his hair and gave her an exasperated look. "Think safe, and you'll be safe! Just be cautious."

"I'm totally reassured!"

Once her shuttle matched velocity with the *ARCT-10*, it circled around the back of the long stern to the docking bay. The ship was built with a series of cylinders arranged in a ring with arcs joining each segment. Along the dorsal edge of the ship, Lunzie could see a partially shaded quartz done which probably contained the hydroponics section. The drives, below and astern of the docking bay, could easily have swallowed the tiny shuttle up with a burp. The five exhaust cones arranged in a ring, rimed with a film of ice crystals, were almost a hundred feet across. The *ARCT-10* was reputed to be 250 years old. It had an air of majestic dignity, instead of creaking old age. It was the oldest of the original EEC generation ships still in space.

There was a Thek waiting in the docking bay as the shuttle doors cracked open. The meter-high specimen waited while Lunzie greeted the deck officer, then neatly blocked her path when she started to leave the deck without acknowledging it.

"I beg your pardon," she said, stopping short, and waited for the translator slung around the Thek's peak to slow her words down enough for it to understand.

"Ttttoooooooooooooorrrrr," it drawled.

Tor. "Your name?" she asked. Talking with a Thek was like playing the child's party game of Twenty Questions, but there was no guarantee she would get twenty answers. Theks did not like to use unnecessary verbiage when a syllable or two would do.

"Yyyyyeeeeessssss." Good, that was short and easy. This must be a relatively young Thek. There was more. Lunzie braced herself to comprehend Tor's voice.

"Lllllluuunnnnnnnn . . . zzzzzzzzzzziiiiiieeeeeeee . . . sssssaaaaaaaffffffeeeee . . . hhhhhhhheeeeeeerrrrrrreeeeee."

Well, bless Coromell. She'd no idea he had Thek confederates aboard the *ARCT-10*. If he'd only thought to mention it, she'd have been more reassured.

"Thank you, Tor," she said. Although come to think on it, she wondered how much help a Thek could provide, flattering though such an offer was from such a source. Even the Thek who had pointed out her escape capsule to Illin Romsey hadn't been able to tow her in on its own. A thought struck her. Theks had no real defining characteristics, but this one was the same size as that Thek. "By any chance, were you the one — no, that's too long — Tor . . . rescued me . . . Descartes?"

A short rumble, sounding like an abbreviated version of his previous "yes," issued from the depths of the silicoid cone. Now this is one for the books, Lunzie thought, much heartened. Then Tor moved aside as an officer entered the landing bay with a hand out for Lunzie and it settled down into anonymous immobility.

"Doctor, welcome aboard," the tall man said. He had the attenuated fingers, limbs and long face that marked him as one of the ship-born, a human who had spent his whole life in space. The lighter gravity frequently allowed humans to grow taller on slenderer, wider-spaced bones than the planet-born. They also proved immune to the calcium attrition that planet-born space travellers experienced on long journeys. As she shook his hand, Lunzie had an uncomfortable feeling of déjà vu. Except for eyes that were green, not brown, the young man fit perfectly the genotype of the banned colony-clones that she'd investigated as a member of the investigative panel on Astris seventy years ago as a medical student. "I'm Lieutenant Sanborn. We had your records just two hours ago. It'll be good to have someone with your trauma specialty on board. Spacebound paranoia is one of the worst things we have to deal with. Walking wounded, you know. You have general training as well?"

"I can sew up wounds and deliver babies, if that's what you mean," Lunzie said drily.

Sanborn threw back his head and laughed. He seemed to be a likable young man. She felt bad about teasing him. "I shouldn't have asked for a two-byte resume. Sorry. Let me show you to the visitors' quarters. You're in luck. There's an individual sleeping cubicle in the visitor's section." He held out a hand for her bags and hoisted them over his shoulder. "This way, please, Lunzie."

Her compartment was tiny and spare, but just big enough to be comfortable. Lunzie put her things away in the drop-down ceiling locker before she followed Sanborn to the common room to get acquainted with her shipmates. The common room doubled as a light-use recreation center.

"The last third of each shift is reserved for conversation only so we don't have to worry about a game of grav-ball bouncing over our heads," Sanborn explained as he introduced Lunzie around. The common rooms in the humanoid oxygen-breathers' section were set with free-form furniture that managed to comfortably accommodate the smallest Weft or the largest heavyworlder.

"Welcome aboard," said the man in blue coveralls who was lounging with his seat tipped backwards against the wall. He had a smooth, dark brown skin and large, mild eyes.

A sallow-faced young man dressed in a pale green lab tunic sat nearby with his elbows braced on the back of his chair and glanced up at her expressionlessly. "I'm Coe. Join us. Do you play chess?" the dark man asked.

"Later perhaps, eh?" Sanborn intervened before she could answer. "I've got to get Lunzie to Orientation."

"Any time," Coe replied, waving.

His companion swept another look and met Lunzie's eyes, and said something to Coe. Lunzie thought she heard her name and the word "ambrosia."

Panic gripped her insides. Oh, no! she thought. Have I left one bad situation for a worse one? I'm trapped aboard this vessel with someone who knows about ambrosia!

"Who's that young man with Coe?" she asked Sanborn, forcing her voice to stay calm.

"Oh, that's Chacal. He's a communications tech. Not much of a conversationalist for a comm tech. Coe is the only one who can stand him. Keeps to himself when he's not on duty."

That would be appropriate if he was an agent for the Parchandri, or the planet pirates. Lunzie wondered to which, if either, Chacal might be attached. She wished she could speak to Coromell, but he was out of reach. Lunzie was on her own, for good or ill. What was the meaning of "ambrosia," anyway? Or was she simply exhibiting symptoms of spacebound paranoia, as Sanborn put it? The *ARCT-10* was so huge that it was easy to forget that she was travelling through space instead of living on a planet. It was designed to be entirely self-sufficient, not needing to make contact with a planet for years. Sanborn took Lunzie to the Administration offices by way of the life support dome where fresh vegetables, fruit, and grain were grown for carbohydrates to feed the synthesizers and to supplement the otherwise boring synth diet as well as refreshing the oxygen in the atmosphere. Lunzie admired the section, which was twice as big as the hydroponics plant aboard the *Destiny Calls*, though by no means stocked with the same exotic varieties.

One section of the ship was the multi-generation hive, where the ship-born and ship-bred lived, apart from the "visitors' habitation." She quickly discovered that there was an unspoken rivalry between the two groups. The ship-born were snobbish about the visitors' difficulty adapting to almost all-synth food and the cramped living conditions on board. The visitors, who were often part of the ship's complement for years on end, couldn't understand why the ship-born were so proud of living under such limited conditions, like laboratory animals who were reduced to minimum needs. It was obvious to each group that its way was better. Mostly the rivalry was good-natured.

Since the visitors on the ship were mission scientists or colonists awaiting transport to FSP-sanctioned colonies, few crossed the boundary to socialize between groups. The matter was temporary, as far as the visitors were concerned. On average, visitors lasted about three years on the *ARCT*. When they could no longer stand the conditions, they quit.

The ship-born felt they could ignore anyone for three years if they wanted to. In the million-light-year vision of the generation ships, that was just an eyeblink. Fortunately for more gregarious souls like Lunzie who joined the EEC, the boundaries were less than a formality.

Several of the major FSP races had groups aboard the *ARCT-10* in both habitations. Heavyworlders occupied specially pressurized units designed to duplicate the gravity and harsh weather conditions of their native worlds. The Ryxi needed more square meters per being than the other groups did. Many visitors were resentful of the seemingly spacious quarters the Ryxi occupied, though the ship-born understood that it was the minimum the Ryxi could stand.

Theks skimmed smoothly through the corridors like mountains receding in the distance with no extraneous movement. They ranged in size from Tor's one meter to a seven-meter specimen who lived in the hydroponics section and who spoke so slowly that it took a week to produce a comprehensible word. A small complement of Brachians worked aboard the ship. Lunzie recognized their long-armed silhouettes immediately in their low-light habitation. A family of the marine race of Ssli occupied their only environment in the ship-born hive. Those Ssli had resolved to devote their entire line to serving the EEC, and the *ARCT-10* was grateful for their expertise in chemistry and energy research.

As on the Descartes mining platform, there was an effort made to draw the inhabitants of the ship together as a community, rather than passengers on a vessel intended only for research and exploration. There was an emphasis on family involvement, in which praise was given not only to the child which got good grades, but for the family which supported and encouraged a child's success. Individual accomplishment was not ignored, but acknowledged in the context of the community. But Lunzie never sensed a heavy administrative hand ensuring that all were equally treated. Departments were given autonomy in their fields. The EEC administration only stepped in when necessary to ease understanding between them. Denizens of the ship were encouraged to sort out matters for themselves. Lunzie admired the system. It fostered achievement in an atmosphere of cooperation.

When she wasn't researching or working an infirmary shift, Lunzie spent time in the common room getting to know her shipmates, and her ship. The *ARCT-10* had been in space two hundred and fifty Earth-Standard years. Some of the ship-born were descended from families who had been aboard since its commissioning. One day, Lunzie became part of a lively discussion group that held court in the middle of the floor, suspending the normal polarization of visitors to one end of the room and ship-born to the other.

"But how can you stand the food?" Varian asked Grabone, rolling over on her free-form cushion to face him. Varian was a tall xenobiologist visitor. "It's been recycled through the pipes, too, for seven generations."

"Not at all," Grabone replied. "We use fresh carbohydrates for food. The recyclate is used for other purposes, such as fertilizer and plas-sheeting. We're completely self-sufficient." The ship-born engineer's shock of red hair helped to express his outrage. "How can you question a system with less than four percent breakdown over a hundred years?"

"But there's something lacking in the aesthetics," Lunzie said, entering the discussion. "I've never been able to stand synthesizer food myself. It's the memory of real food, not the actual stuff."

"If your cooks just didn't make synth food so boring!" Varian said in disgust. "It'd be almost palatable if it had some recognizable taste. I'll bet, Grabone, that you've never *had* real food. Not even the vegetables they grow on the upper deck."

"Why take chances?" demanded Grabone, leaning back defiantly on the floor and crossing his ankles. "You could poison yourself with unhygienically grown foodstuffs. You know the synth food is safe, and nourishing."

"Have you ever even tried naturally grown food?" Varian demanded.

"Can't tell the difference if I have. I've never been off the *ARCT-10*," Grabone admitted. "I'm a drives engineer. There's no reason for me to have to make planetfall on, I might point out, potentially hazardous missions. Risk your own neck. Leave mine alone."

"Life can be hazardous to your health," Lunzie said cheerfully to Varian beside her. She liked the lively, curly-haired girl who was unable to sit still for more than a few minutes. They did Discipline exercises together in the early shift. Lunzie could tell that Varian's training was of the most basic, though it would seem advanced to anyone who was not an Adept. "How are you chosen to go on planetside missions?" she asked Varian. "Do I have to put my name in the duty roster?"

"Oh, no," Varian replied. "Nothing that organized. Each mission requires such different skills that the first person off the queue might not be qualified. Details of a mission's personnel needs are posted days before the actual drop. If you're interested, you inform Comm Center and you're listed as available. A mission leader then picks the complement. Some missions are planned at FSP Center. Some develop out of circumstances. Let me explain. The *ARCT-10*'s job is to keep tabs on all the Exploration and Evaluation vessels in our sector and support them with ground teams when necessary. So you really never know what's or who's going to be needed. The *ARCT* also keeps checking in on message beacons previously set in this sector by initial EEC scouts. They strip off messages whenever we're in line of sight and send reports back to FSP Center. If a recon or an emergency team are needed, *ARCT* supplies it. So really," and Varian shrugged, "you can gain a lot of xeno experience in a three-year stint."

"And that's what you're after?" Lunzie said.

"You bet! That's what'll get me a good dirtside job." Then her vivacious face changed and she lowered her voice. "There may be a very good one coming up. I've a friend in Comm and he said for me to keep my ears open."

"Then you're not at all nervous about the scuttlebutt I've been hearing?"

"Which one?" asked Varian scornfully.

"The one about planting colonists without their permission?"

"That old one." Grabone was openly derisive. "Rumors sometimes start themselves, you know. I'll excuse you this time, Lunzie, since I know you're not long on board. You wouldn't know how many times that one's oozed through the deckplates."

"That's reassuring," Lunzie said. "It seems so unlike an official EEC position."

"It's a lot of space dust," Grabone went on. "You got that from the heavyworlders, didn't you? Their favorite paranoia. They think we'll strand them the first chance we get. Well, it isn't true."

"No, actually, it wasn't the heavyworlders," Lunzie said slowly; she'd kept well away from any of that group. "It was one of the visiting scientists who wants only to finish his duty and go home on time. I gather he's expecting a grandchild."

"For one thing," Grabone went on to prove the rumor fallacious, "*ARCT-10* can't plant anyone. Colonies take years of planning. It's hard enough to find the right mix of people who want to settle on a certain world, and live together in peace, not to say cooperation. You wouldn't believe the filework that has to go out to EEC before a colony is approved."

"Well, planting would be a quicker, if illicit, way to get more colonies started," Varian suggested. "There are some found that don't meet minimum requirements but if people were planted, they'd learn to cope."

"Doesn't anyone planetside practice birth control?" Lunzie asked, with a vivid memory of the crowds on Alpha Centauri. "Having dozens of offspring without a thought for environment or a reasonable standard of living for future citizens."

"Even a mathematical expansion of the population, one child per adult," Varian pointed out, "would soon deplete currently available resources, let alone a geometric increase. Judicious planting could reduce some of the pressure. Not that I advocate it, mind you."

One of the lights on the duty panel flickered. Involuntarily everyone in the room glanced at the blue medical light. Lunzie clambered to her feet. "I can respond."

She flipped on the switch at the panel. "Lunzie."

"Accident at interface A-10. One crew member down, several others injured."

Lunzie mentally plotted the fastest path to the scene of the accident and hit the comm switch again.

"Acknowledged," she said. "I'm on my way." She waved farewell to Grabone and Varian.

The interfaces were one of the most sensitive and carefully watched parts of the multi-environmental system aboard the *ARCT-10*. Whereas normal bulkheads were accustomed to the pressure of a single atmosphere, the interfaces had to stand between two different atmospheric zones, sometimes of vastly different pressure levels which might also vary according to program. A-10 stood between the normal-weight human environment and the heavyworlders' gravity zone. Had this happened in her first few weeks aboard, she'd have become hopelessly lost. Now she knew the scheme which named decks and section by location and personnel, she knew she wasn't far from A-10 and found her way there without trouble.

Dozens of other crew members were on the move through the corridors in the A Section. At the point at which A-10 had been breached, frigid wind of the same temperature as the ambient on Diplo was pouring through into the warmer lightweight zone. Clutching her medical bag to her chest, Lunzie passed through a hastily erected baffle chamber that cut off the icy winds from the rest of the deck and would act as a temporary barrier while the heavy gravity was restored. Beyond the broken wall, heavyworlders who had been in their exercise room were picking up weights and bodybuilding equipment made suddenly light by the drop in gravity. Workers of every configuration hurried in and out of the chambers, clearing away debris, tying down torn circuits and redirecting pipes whose broken ends pumped sewage and water across the floor. Lunzie made a wide circle around two workers who were cutting out the ragged remains of the damaged panel with an arc torch.

"Doctor, quickly!" An officer in the black uniform of environmental sciences motioned urgently where she knelt by the far wall. "Orlig's twitching even if he is unconscious. He was checking the wall when it blew." Lunzie hurried over, ignoring the stench of sewage and the odor of burned flesh. Stretched out on the deck at the woman's side was a gigantic heavy-worlder wearing a jumpsuit and protective goggles. He had been severely gashed by flying metal and a tremendous hematoma colored the side of his face. Though his eyes were closed, he was thrashing wildly and muttering. Lunzie's hands flew to her belt pouch for her bod bird.

"I don't dare give him a sedative until I know if there's neural damage, Truna," Lunzie explained.

"You do what you have to do. Other heavyworlders incurred only heavy bruises when the wall popped and they were blown against the bulkhead toward light gravity. They walked away. No one else was on this side of the wall. Orlig took the full blast. Poor beast." The environmental tech got up and began shouting orders at the mob of workers, leaving Lunzie alone with her patient.

Orlig was one of the largest specimens of his sub-group that Lunzie had ever seen. Her outstretched hand covered only his palm and third phalange of his fingers. She had no idea what she would do if he went out of control.

"Fardling lightweights," he snarled, thrashing. Lunzie jumped back out of range as his swinging arm just missed her and smashed onto the deck. "Set me up to die! I'll kill them!" The arm swept up, fingers curved like claws, ripping at the air, and smashed down again, shaking the deck. "All of them!"

Nervous but equally determined not to let her fear of heavy-worlders keep her from treating one in desperate need of her skills, Lunzie approached to take a bod bird reading. According to that, Orlig was bleeding internally. He had to be sedated and treated before he hemorrhaged to death.

She couldn't fix his arm while he was banging it around like that. The bod bird was inconclusive on the point of neural trauma. She would have to take her chances. She programmed a hefty dose of sedative and applied the hypogun to the nearest fleshy part of the thrashing man. Orlig levered himself up when he felt the injection hiss against his upper arm and snarled bare-toothed at Lunzie. The drug took speedy effect and his arms collapsed under him. He fell to the deck with a bang.

Still shaking, Lunzie began debriding his wounds and slapping patches of synthskin on them. Shards of metal had been driven into his flesh through the heavy fabric of the jumpsuit. The goggles had spared his eyes though the plasglas lens were cracked. What with flying debris and the force of the explosion, the man was lucky to be alive. She tried to think which ship's system could have blown like that.

Unbelievably, Orlig started moving again. How could he move? She'd given him enough sedative to sleep six shifts. Lunzie worked faster. She must unseal the upper half of his jumpsuit to repair his wounds. The fabric was so heavy she got mired in the folds of it. Then in a restless gesture, he jerked his arm and sent Lunzie stumbling across the room.

Lunzie crawled back to him and gathered her equipment together in her lap. She programmed the hypo for another massive dose of sedative and held it to the heavyworlder's arm. Just as she was about to push the button, Orlig's small eyes opened and focussed on hers. His gigantic hand closed around her hand and wrist, immobilizing her but not hurting her.

He'll kill me! Lunzie thought nervously. She drew in a breath to yell for help from the struggling engineers at the broken wall.

"Who are you?" he demanded, bringing the other fist up under her face.

Lunzie kept her voice low out of fear. "My name is Lunzie. I'm a doctor."

Orlig's eyes narrowed, but the fist dropped. "Lunzie? Do you know a Thek?"

He's raving, Lunzie thought. "Orlig, please lie back. You were badly injured. I can't treat you if you keep thrashing about. Let go of my hand." Sometimes a firm no-nonsense voice reassured a nervous patient.

His fist grabbed her up by the neck of her tunic. "Do you know a Thek?"

"Yes. Tor."

Subtly the heavyworlder's attitude altered. He swiveled his head around to glare at the bustling crowd of workers, and technicians, and wrinkled his nose at the sewage, now being mopped up.

"Then get me out of here. Someplace no one would expect to find me." With that he let her go and sagged to the floor.

Lunzie shouted for a gurney and waited by Orlig until it came. She sent an emergency crewman back for a grav lift so that she could manage the gurney herself in spite of Orlig's mass. He snarled when the crewman came a centimeter closer to him than necessary. He had to be in considerable pain with those wounds. She wondered just why he was braving it out. Without any help he somehow rolled his mangled body onto the gurney.

"Get me out of here," he muttered, eyes glittering with pain and an underlying fear that he permitted her to glimpse.

Operating the anti-grav lift, she guided the gurney out of the interface area through one hatch, running along beside her patient and up a freight turbovator.

"Anybody following?" he demanded urgently, gripping her hand in his huge fingers.

"No, no one. Not even a rat."

He grunted. "Hurry it up."

"This was all your idea." But then she saw what she was looking for, one of the small first-aid stations that were located on every deck and section, usually for routine medichecks, contagion isolation quarters, or treatments that didn't require stays in the main infirmary.

Once the door slid shut behind them, Orlig grinned up at her.

"Krims, but you lightweights are easy to scare." He surveyed the room with a searching glance as Lunzie positioned the gurney by the soft-topped examination table which doubled as a hospital bed when the sides were raised. He raised a hand as Lunzie started toward him with the hypo. "No, no more sedatives. I'm practically unconscious now."

Lunzie stared at him. "I thought you must be immune to it."

Orlig grimaced. "I had to use pain to stay awake. Someone rigged that all to fall on me. They want me dead."

With a sigh, Lunzie recognized the classic symptoms of agoraphobic paranoia. She put away the hypospray and held up the flesh-knitter.

"Well, I'm a doctor and as I've never seen you before, I have no urge to kill you." Yet, she thought. "And since you heavyworlders are such big machismo types, I'll sew you into one piece again in front of your eyes. Does that relieve your mind?"

"Coromell didn't say you'd be so dumb, Doctor."

Lunzie nearly dropped the piece of equipment in her hands. "Coromell?" she repeated. "First you want to know my Thek acquaintances, now you're throwing the Admiralty at me. Just who are you?"

"I work for him, too. And I've got some information that he's got to have. This isn't the first attempt on my life. I've been trying to figure out a legitimate reason to contact you. But I had to be careful. Couldn't have suspicion fall on you. . . ."

"Like a wall fell on you?" Lunzie put in.

"Yeah, but it's working out just right, isn't it? I can't risk this information getting lost." He groaned. "I tried to get in touch with Tor. I think that's where I blew it. Us heavyworlders don't generally seek out Theks." He winced. "All right, I think I'll accept a local anesthetic now you're playing tinkertoy with my ribs. It feels like meteors were shot through it. What's it look like?"

Lunzie peered at his chest and ran the bod bird over it. "Like you got meteors shot through it. I might be able to reach Tor without anyone suspecting me. I don't know why, but it likes me."

"Few are as lucky. But you've got to find the right Thek without asking for it by name. That's the hard part. They all look alike at the size they fit on the *ARCT*. Look . . ." Orlig's voice was weaker now as shock began to seep through his formidable physical stamina. He fumbled in his left ear, tilting his head. "Fardles. You got something like tweezers? That wall must've knocked it down inside."

"What am I looking for?"

"A message brick." He turned his head so she had the best angle for the search.

"You might have irreparably damaged your hearing," she said, disapprovingly as she finally retrieved the cube.

"It fit. It was safe," Orlig replied, unpenitent. "If you can't get to Tor, wait until Zebara gets back. You can tell him to check out Aidkisagi VIII, the Seti of Fomalhaut. The cube gives him the rest of the pertinent details."

"The Seti of . . . their head of government?" Lunzie's voice rose in pitch to a surprised squeak.

"Shh! Keep it down!" Orlig hissed. "Whoever rigged that wall to blow may be looking for me now he knows he failed to kill me."

"Who?"

Orlig rolled his eyes at her naivete.

"Sorry."

"Wise up, gal, or you can end up like me. And you couldn't stand a wall falling on you." His voice was now a thin trickle of sound.

She tucked the cube into her soft ship boot. "Tor or Zebara. Count on me. Now, I stop being courier and start being medic."

Just as she finished and had him plas-skinned, his eyes sagged shut. The sedative and shock were finally overwhelming him.

"You're safe now," Lunzie murmured. "I'll pull the food synthesizer within your reach so you don't have to get up if you're hungry or thirsty. I'll lock the room so that no one can get in. And I'll knock if I want to come in."

Orlig nodded sleepily. "Use a password. Say 'ambrosia.' That way I'll know if it's you or someone you sent."

"That particular word keeps getting me in trouble. I'll use 'whisky' instead."

As soon as she sealed the infirmary door, Lunzie immediately went back to her compartment to change out of her bloodstained clothes. She kept the cube in her boot but decided to attach her Fleet ID disk against her skin under her clothes. It was safer to keep it on her person than to risk someone finding it among her possessions. Orlig's "accident" brought a resurgence of her paranoia. Too many odd things happened to couriers of messages to Coromell.

"How's the patient?" Truna called to her as Lunzie returned to the common room. The technician and her assistants were sitting slumped over a table with steaming mugs in their hands.

"As well as can be expected for a man who's been knocked about by a bulkhead blowing out on him," Lunzie answered, programming a cup of coffee for herself. "How'd repairs go?"

"We got the wall temporarily put together again. It's going to take at least a few days to recreate the components needed to replace the damaged systems. Those circuits got truly fried!" Truna said, taking a deep drink from her mug. The woman's eyes were puffy and rimmed with red.

"What caused the explosion?" Lunzie asked, settling down at the table with the others. As soon as she sat, she realized how sore her muscles were from dealing with Orlig and his injuries.

"I was about to ask you. Could Orlig tell what happened?"

"Not really," Lunzie nodded. "He was too shocked to be lucid. Though come to think of it, he rabbited on about the chem lab. Could something have been flushed away that shouldn't be and detonated in the pipe?"

"Well, the waste pipes sure were blown into a black hole," Truna agreed. "I'll check with the biochemistry section on the ninth level. They use that disposal system. Thanks for the suggestion."

"Will Orlig recover?" a crewman asked.

"Oh, I expect so," Lunzie replied offhandedly. "Even heavy-worlder physiques get bent out of shape from time to time. He'll be sore a while."

Lunzie sat with Truna and her crew for a short time, chatting and encouraging them to share their experiences with her. All the time she was apparently listening, she was wondering how she could get to Tor or how long it would be before "someone" discovered that Orlig wasn't in the infirmary. Then her thoughts would revolve back to the astonishing information that a Seti of Fomalhaut was involved in planetary piracy. That news would rock a few foundations. That was what Orlig had implied. Well, Seti were known to take gambles. The stakes would be very high, if the Phoenix affair had been any guide.

In the back of her mind, she ran scenarios on how to track down Tor. First she'd have to find out where the Theks were quartered. She couldn't just list it all on the *ARCT* e-mail channel.

"I must check up on my patient," she told the environment engineers she'd dined with. "I left him alone to sleep, but he's probably stirring again."

"Good idea," Truna said. "Tell him I hope he heals soon."

She took a circuitous route to Orlig but saw no one obviously following her.

"It's Lunzie," she announced in a low voice, tapping on the infirmary door with her knuckles. "Um, oh, whisky."

The door slid back noiselessly on its track. Orlig was behind it, clutching his injured ribs tenderly in one arm. "I wondered how long it was gonna be before you came back. I haven't been able to relax. Even with that sleep-stuff you shot into me I tossed and turned."

Lunzie pushed him into a chair so she could check the pupils of his eyes. "Sorry. That happens sometimes in shock cases. The sedative acts as an upper, instead of a downer. Let me try you on calcium and L-tryptophane. It's an amino acid which the body does not produce for itself. Those should help you sleep. You don't have any sensitivities to mineral supplements, do you?"

"You sure don't know much about heavyworlders, do you? I have to pop mineral supplements all the time to keep my bones from crumbling in your puny gravity." Orlig produced a handful of uncoated vitamin tablets from a singed belt pouch and poured them into her palm.

Lunzie analyzed one with the tracer. "Iron, copper, zinc, calcium, magnesium, boron. Good. And I'll see to it that the amino acid is added to your food for the next few days. It will help you to relax and sleep naturally."

"Look, while you were gone, I thought of something to get the bugger that's after me. You can noise it about that I was critically injured and may not live," Orlig suggested grimly. "Maybe I can trick my assassins into the open. Let them think they have another chance at me while I'm weak."

"That's not only dangerous but plain stupid," Lunzie replied but he gave her such a formidable look, she shrugged in resignation. "You're healing but your injuries were severe. You may think you're smart but right now you've little stamina to get into a fight. Give yourself a chance to regain your strength. Then you can be moved to the infirmary — and at least have assistance near at hand when you try a damfool scheme like that."

"I'll handle this my own way," Orlig said brusquely. "Out. I want to go to sleep." He sat down on the examination bed and swung his legs up, ignoring her.

Irritated by his dismissal, Lunzie left. The door shut behind her, with the double hiss that meant the seals were being put on.

What they both had forgotten was that Lunzie was the medic on record attending that accident. The CMO asked for a report on the status of the victim. Lunzie filled out the requisite forms but asked the CMO to keep it secure.

"The man's suffering from a mild paranoia."

"Don't think I'd blame him with a wall blowing out like that. Those heavyworlder vendettas are costly."

"I've put him in one of the small treatment rooms. He felt safer there, but I'm trying to get him to transfer to the infirmary. He'd be safer from retaliation here."

Her next visit was brief, too. Orlig was improving so much that he had a raging case of cabin fever, and exploded at Lunzie.

"Why haven't you passed that brick on to Tor? What in the comet's tail are you waiting for?"

"I suppose I should just list it on the Bulletin Board that Lunzie Mespil, medic, wishes to speak with Thek Tor?" Lunzie snapped back tartly. "You told me not to draw attention to myself so I'm not."

"I risked my life for that information. You lightweights think you're so smart — well, think up a plausible reason but pass that information on."

"When circumstances permit!"

That began a screaming argument in which, to her surprise, Lunzie managed to hold her own. In retaliation, Orlig threw a few very personal insults at her that questioned her parentage and personal habits, and showed an intimate knowledge of the details of her life. Had Coromell actually given him access to her file? Shocked and offended, she marched out, vowing that it would be a warm and sunny day midspace before she'd go back.

Three more shifts passed. Lunzie felt guilty for having lost her temper with Orlig. He was as much under strain as she was, and it was wrong to indulge in a petty fit of temper at his expense. She returned to the infirmary and tapped on the door.

"Orlig? It's Lunzie. Oh, whisky! Orlig? Let me in."

She tapped at the doorplate and the door swung partly in. It was neither locked nor sealed. Startled, Lunzie leaned cautiously forward to investigate. The chamber was dark inside, reeking with a peculiar, heavy smell. She passed her hand over the panel for lights, and jumped back, gasping at what she saw.

There had been a fight. Most of the furniture was smashed or bent, and there were smears of blood on the walls. The sink had been torn out of the wall and stuffed halfway into the disposer unit. The equipment cabinets were smashed open, with their contents strewn throughout the chamber. Still attached to the wall, the shattered hand dryer sputtered fitfully to itself, dropping hot sparks.

Orlig lay sprawled on the floor. Guiltily Lunzie thought for a moment that internal bleeding had begun again. The cause of death was all too evident. Orlig had been strangled. His face was darkened with extravasated blood, and his eyes bulged. She had seen death before, even violent death. But not ruthless murder.

The marks of opposable digits were livid on the dead man's windpipe. Someone with incredible strength had thrown Orlig all over the room before pressing him to the ground and wringing his neck. Lunzie felt weak.

Only another heavyworlder could have done that to Orlig. And she'd thought that he was the biggest one on the *ARCT-10*. So who? And what did that person know or suspect about her? She checked the door to see how the killer had forced its way. But there was no sign of forced entry. The seals were unsecured. Orlig had let his assailant into the room himself. Had the killer followed her, undetected, and overheard her use the agreed password? Or had Orlig overestimated his own returning strength and cunning? Sometimes being a lightweight was an advantage — you found it easier to recognize physical limitations.

If the murderer should decide to eliminate Orlig's medic on the possibility that the dead man had passed on his knowledge, she was once again in jeopardy from heavyworlders. How long had Orlig been dead? How much more "safety" did she have left?

"I've got to get off this ship. Just finding Tor and passing on that brick are not going to be the answer. But how?"

First she had to report the death to the CMO, who was appalled by the murder but not terribly surprised.

"These guys are temperamental, you know. Strangest things set off personal vendettas." But the CMO could and did slam a security lock on the details.

Since the CMO didn't ask more details from her, Lunzie ventured none. Enough people had seen Orlig manhandle her after the accident so that she would seem an unlikely recipient of any confidences. But she wouldn't rest easy on that assumption. She continued to feel vulnerable. To her own surprise, she felt more anger than fright.

She did take the precaution of attaching her personal alarm to the door of her cubicle at night. She was cautious enough to stay in a group at all times.

"They wanted me to find him, that's clear," Lunzie mused blackly as she went about her duties the next day. "Otherwise they'd have stuffed the body into the disposer and let the recycling systems have it. His absence might even have passed without any notice. Maybe I should grumble about patients who discharge themselves without medic permission." She doubted that would do any good and scanned the updates on mission personnel with an anxious eye. Surely she could wangle the medic's spot on the next one. Even if she had to pull out her FI ID.

✦ CHAPTER TWELVE

"It's Ambrosia," was her greeting from those in the common room the next morning. She recoiled in shock. "It's Ambrosia!" people were chorusing joyfully. "It really is Ambrosia."

Lunzie was stunned to hear the dangerous statement delivered in a chant, taken up by every new arrival.

"What's Ambrosia?" she demanded of Nafti, one of the scientists. He grabbed her hands and danced her around the room in his enthusiasm. She calmed him down long enough to get an explanation.

"Ambrosia's a brand-new colonizable, human-desirable planet," Nafti told her, his homely face wreathed in idiotic delight. "An EEC Team's on its way in. The comm links are oozing news about the most glorious find in decades. The team's called it Ambrosia. Believe it or not, an E-class planet, with a 3-to-1 nitrogen/oxygen atmosphere and .96 Earth gravity."

Everyone was clamoring to hear more details but the captain of the EEC Team was wisely keeping the specifics to himself until the *ARCT-10* labs verified the findings. Rumors ranged to the implausible and unlikely but most accounts agreed that Ambrosia's parameters made it the most Earth-like planet ever discovered by the EEC.

Lunzie wasn't sure of her reaction to the news: relief that "It's Ambrosia" was now public information, or confusion. The phrase that had already cost lives and severely altered hers might have nothing at all to do with the new planet. It could be a ridiculous coincidence. And it could very well mean that the new planet might be the next target for the planetary pirates. Only how could a planet, which was now known to the thousands of folk on board the *ARCT-10*, get pirated out from under the noses of legitimate FSP interests by, if the past was any indication, even the most violent means?

The arrival of the Team meant more than good news to her. Zebara was the captain. A lot easier to find than that one Thek named Tor. She asked one of the communications techs to add her name to the queue to speak to Captain Zebara when he arrived. A moment's private conversation with him and she'd have kept faith with Orlig.

Like most of her plans lately, that one had to be aborted. When Captain Zebara arrived on board, he was all but mobbed by the people on the *ARCT-10* who wanted to be first to learn the details of Ambrosia. Lunzie heard he'd had to be locked in the day officer's wardroom to protect him. Shortly afterward, an announcement was made by the Exec Officer that Zebara would speak to the entire ship from the oxygen-breathers' common room. With a shipwide and translated broadcast, everyone could share Zebara's news.

Lunzie waited with Coe amid a buzzingly eager audience packing the common room. There was a small flurry as the Team Captain entered the room. Lunzie peered around her neighbors, saw a head of fuzzy blond hair, and belatedly realized that the man towered a good foot above most of those in the surrounding crowd.

"He's a heavyworlder," she said, disbelievingly.

"Zebara's an okay guy," Grabone said, hearing the hostility in Lunzie's voice. "He's different. Friendly. Doesn't have the chip on his shoulder that most of the heavyworlders wear."

"He's also not from Diplo," added Coe. "He was raised on one of the heavyworld colonies which had a reasonably normal climate. I'd never thought climate had that much effect on folks, but he's nowhere near as bad as the Diplos."

Lunzie did not voice her doubts but Coe saw her skeptical expression.

"C'mon, Lunzie, he's a fine fellow. I'll introduce you later," Coe offered. "Zebara and I are old buddies."

"Thanks, Coe," Lunzie murmured politely. Zebara had a very catholic selection of friends if both Orlig and Coe were numbered among them.

"Wait, he's starting to speak."

Zebara was a good orator. He had a trick of smiling just before he let go of a piece of particularly encouraging data. His audience soon caught on and was almost holding its breath, waiting for the next grin. For a heavyworlder, whose features tended to be rough, Zebara was the exception, with a narrow face, a beaky, high-bridged nose, and sharp blue eyes.

Lunzie decided that his composure was assumed. He was as excited as his listeners were about his subject.

"Ambrosia! Nectar of the gods! Air you want to drink as well as smell. Only it doesn't smell. It's there, light in the lungs, buoyant about you. This planet is fourth position out from a class-M sun, with a blue sky stretched over six small landmasses that cover only about a third of the surface. The rest is water! Sweet water. Dihydrogen monoxide!" There was a cheer from the assembled as Zebara took a flask from his pouch and held it aloft. "There are of course trace elements," he added, "but nothing toxic in either the mineral content or the oceanic flora. No free cyanides. Two small moons far out and one large one close in, so there are some spectacular tides. There's a certain amount of vulcanism, but that only makes the place interesting. Ambrosia has no indigenous sentient life-forms."

"Are you sure?" one of the heavyworlder men in the audience shouted out.

Sentience was the final test of a planet; the EEC prohibited colonization of a planet which already had an evolving intelligent species. "Brock, we've spent two years there and nothing we tested had an intelligence reading that showed up on any of the sociological scales. One of the insectoids, which we call mason beetles, have a complicated hive society but EVs are more interested in the chemical they secrete while hunting. It can melt solid rock. There's a very friendly species which my xenobiologist calls kittisnakes but they don't even have very much animal intelligence. There're a lot of pretty avians" — a squawk of alarm rose from the Ryxi scattered throughout the crowded chamber — "but no intelligent bird life." The squawks changed to coos. They were jealous of their position as the only sentient avians in the FSP.

Zebara threw the meeting open for questions, and a clamorous chorus of voices attempted to shout one another down.

"Well, this will take hours," Coe sighed. "Let's leave him a message and see him next shift."

"No," Lunzie said. "Let's stay and listen for a while. Then we'll go down and wait for him by the captain's cabin. I'm sure he'll go there next, to give the administrators a private debriefing."

Coe looked at her admiringly. "For someone who hasn't been with the EEC long, you sure figured out the process quickly."

Lunzie grinned. "Bureaucracy works the same way everywhere. Once he's thrown enough to the lower echelons to keep 'em happy, he'll be sequestered with the brass until he satisfies their curiosity."

They timed the approach perfectly, catching the heavyworlder as he emerged from the turbovator near the administrative offices.

"You came back in style from this one, didn't you, Zeb!"

"Coe! Good to see you." Zebara and the brown-skinned man exchanged friendly embraces. The big man reached down to pat the smaller one familiarly on the head. "I've got to talk to the bitty big bosses right now. Wait for me?"

"Sure. Oh, Zebara, this is Doctor Lunzie Mespil. She asked especially to meet you."

"Charmed, citizen." Cold blue eyes turned to her.

Intimidated, Lunzie felt a chill go up her backbone. Nevertheless, she had a promise to keep. She thrust a hand at the heavyworlder who engulfed it in polite reaction. He felt the Fleet ID disk that she had palmed to him.

"Congratulations on your discovery, Captain. I had a patient recently who told me to see you as soon as you got back."

"As soon as the brass finishes with me, Lunzie Mespil," he said, keenly searching her face. "That I promise you. Now if you'll excuse me . . . Lunzie Mespil." He gave her one more long look as he palmed the panel and let himself in.

"Well, he got your name right at least," Coe said, a bit sourly.

"Who can ignore the brass when it calls? I'll catch him later. Thanks for the intro, Coe."

"My pleasure," Coe answered, watching her face in puzzlement.

She left Coe there, right in the passageway, and went back to her cubicle to wait for a response from Zebara. The disk alone was tacit command for a private meeting. Why hadn't she anticipated that he might be a heavyworlder? Because you don't like heavyworlders, stupid, not after that Quinada woman. Maybe she should find Tor. She trusted Theks. Though why she did, she couldn't have said. They weren't even humanoid. Just the nearest thing we have to visible gods, that's all. Well, she was committed now, handshake, cryptic comments, and all.

The passageway along which her space lay was almost empty, unusual for that time of day, but she hardly noticed, except that no eyebrows or feather crests went up when she kicked a wall in frustration.

Both Coe and Grabone spoke well of Zebara, and they hadn't of any of the other heavyworlders. That said something for the man. If he's at all loyal to the EEC — but if he doesn't get back to me as soon as he's finished debriefing, I'm finding me a Thek named Tor.

Then something Zebara had said bobbed up in her thoughts. Zebara had been on Ambrosia for two years. Her first courier job had been less than a year ago, with Ambrosia the important feature. Had Zebara had an informant on his scout ship?

With such uncomfortable thoughts galling her, Lunzie let herself into her room and changed into a uniform tunic for her infirmary shift. She tossed the off-duty tunic into the synthesizer hatch, to be broken down into component fibers and rewoven, without the dirt. The cool, efficient function of the machine made her recall Orlig's body on the infirmary floor. Why had his killer left the body there? What had he expected her to do when she found it? Maybe she ought to have followed her initial impulse and run screaming from the little chamber, alerting everyone in earshot that she had found a murder victim. Maybe that would have been smarter. Maybe she'd outsmarted herself?

The communications panel chimed, breaking into her morbid reflections. It let out a click as an audio pickup was engaged somewhere on the ship.

"Lunzie," said the CMO's voice, "please respond."

She leaned over to slap the panel. "Lunzie here, Carlo."

"Where are you? There's a Brachian in the early stages of labor. She's literally climbing the walls. Someone said you were good with the species."

"Who said that?" Lunzie asked, surprised. She couldn't recall mentioning her gynecological experiences with anyone on the *ARCT-10*.

"I don't know." That didn't surprise her, for the Chief was

notoriously bad at remembering names. "But if you are, I need you asap."

"I'm on my way, sir," she answered, fastening the neck of the tunic. Anyone would be a more capable midwife for a Brachian than the Chief.

Lunzie slipped into the empty corridor. Her quick footsteps echoed loudly back to her in the long empty metal corridor even though she was wearing soft-soled boots. Where was everyone? She had neighbors on both sides who had small children. Probably all were still in the common room, rehashing Zebara's talk. There wasn't a spare sound within earshot, just the *swish-thump swish-thump* of her step. Curious, she altered her pace to hear the difference in the noise she made. There was a T-intersection just ahead. It would pick up the echoes splendidly. Abruptly, she lengthened her stride and the swish grew shorter and faltered. That wasn't an echo of her own step. There was someone behind her, carefully matching her.

She spun to see a human male, half a head taller than she, about ten paces behind her. He was a burly man, with brassy brown hair and a wide, apelike jaw.

"Who are you?" she demanded.

The man only grinned at her and moved to close the distance between them, his hands menacingly outstretched. Lunzie backed away from him, then turned and ran toward the intersecting corridor. Letting out a piercing whistle, the man dashed after her.

He couldn't be Orlig's killer, she thought. He wasn't big enough to have strangled the heavyworlder. But he was big enough to kill her if she wasn't careful. She initiated the Discipline routine, though running was not the recommended starting position. She needed some time. Lunzie thought hard to remember if either corridor ended in a dead end. Yes, the right-hand way led to a thick metal door that housed a supplementary power station. She veered left. As she rounded the corner, a gaudily colored female Ryxi appeared, stalking toward her.

"Help me," Lunzie panted, indicating the man behind her. "He intends me harm."

The Ryxi didn't say anything. Instead, she jumped back against a bulkhead and stuck out a long, skinny leg. Lunzie tried to hurdle it but the Ryxi merely raised her foot. Lunzie fell headlong, skidding on the metal floor into the wall.

Who would have expected the avian to be a human's accomplice? She'd been well and truly ambushed. Her vision swimming from her skid into the hard bulkhead at the end of her spin, she walked her hands up the wall, trying to regain her feet. Before she was fully upright, strong hands grabbed her from behind.

Automatically, Lunzie kicked backwards, but her blow was without real force. She got a rabbit punch in the back of her neck for her pains. Her head swam and her knees sagged momentarily under her. Discipline! Where were all those Adept tricks she'd so carefully practiced?

"Watch it, Birra, she thinks she's tough."

The man's voice was gloating as they turned her around, keeping a tight grip on her upper arms. Dazed, Lunzie struggled. She tried again for Discipline but her head was too fuzzy. The Ryxi was very tall for her species and the muscle masses at the tops of her stalky legs were thick and well corded. She lifted one long-toed foot and wrapped it around Lunzie's leg, picking it up off the ground. Lunzie, leaning her weight on her assailant's arms, kicked at the Ryxi, trying to free herself.

She began to scream loudly, hoping to attract the attention of anyone living on the corridor. Where was everyone?

"Shut up, space dust," the man growled. He hit her in the stomach, knocking the air out of her.

That shut off Lunzie's cries for help but left one of her arms free. She deliberately let herself fall backwards to the deck, twisting out of the Ryxi's grip. She scissored a kick upward at the Ryxi's thin leg and felt her boot jar against its bone. With a squawk of pain, Birra jerked away, clutching her knee. The man dove forward and kicked out at Lunzie's ribs. Clumsily, Lunzie rolled away.

"Kill herrrr," the Ryxi chirred angrily, hopping forward on one foot. "Kill her, Knorrrraadel, she has hurt me."

The man kicked again at Lunzie who found that she had trapped herself against the bulkhead. The Ryxi raked her clawed foot down Lunzie's shoulder and attempted to close the long toes around the human woman's throat. Lunzie curled her knees up close to protect her belly and chest and tried to wrench apart the knobby toes with both hands. It was getting harder to breathe and the talons were as tough as tree roots under her useless fingers. Lunzie felt the bruised patch on the side of her head beginning to throb. A black haze was seeping into her vision from that side. She knew she was about to lose consciousness. The man laughed viciously and kicked her in the side again and brought his boot down against her upraised left arm. The bone snapped audibly in the empty corridor. Lunzie screamed out what little air remained in her lungs.

He raised his foot again — and to her relief and amazement, the surge of adrenaline evoked by fear and pain awoke Discipline.

Ruthlessly ignoring the break in her forearm, she grasped the Ryxi's toes in her hands. With the strength of Discipline she pulled them apart and up, and twisted the leg toward the avian's other limb. Ryxi had notoriously bad knees. They only bent forward and outward, not inward. The Ryxi, caught off balance, opened her claw wide, searching for purchase. The creature fell against the man, knocking him off balance before she collapsed in a heap of swearing, colorful feathers to the deck.

In one smooth move, the human doctor was on her feet, *en garde*, two meters from her would-be assassins. Her mind was alert now as, her chest heaving like a bellow, she coolly summed up her opponents. The Ryxi was more adaptable; she had already proved that by countering Lunzie's moves, but Lunzie knew the avian body's weak point and there wasn't room enough in the corridor for the avian to fly. Though the human was more powerful than Lunzie, he wasn't a methodical fighter.

Lunzie's recovery surprised Knoradel. That gave her her first advantage. She didn't want to kill them unless as a last resort. If she could disable them, knock them unconscious, or lock them up, she could get to safety. Curling her good hand to stiffen the edge, Lunzie feinted forward at the man. Automatically, rather than consciously, his hands balled into fists. He danced backward, one leg forward, and one back. So he'd had some martial arts training — but not the polish of Discipline.

Lunzie had the edge on him. Her left hand, deprived of muscle tension because of the snapped bone, was beginning to curl into a claw. She curved the other hand so it looked as though she had two good ones. She had to get away from her assailants before the adrenaline wore off and she would again feel the pain. As long as it looked as if the broken bone hadn't affected her at all, Knoradel would be disconcerted.

The Ryxi was also on her feet again. Lunzie had to take care of the man before dealing with the wily avian and her long reach. He was sweating. His ambush plan had gone wrong and he hadn't the brains or experience to adapt. Lunzie feinted left, then right, then a double left, which made Knoradel unconsciously step in front of his cohort to counter Lunzie's moves. When he was just far enough in front of the avian to block her attack, Lunzie spun backwards in a swift roundhouse kick. It took the man squarely under the chin and flung him against the wall. His head snapped back, connecting with the metal bulkhead with a hearty *boom!* He slid down to the floor, his eyes rolling back in his head. If Lunzie could dispatch the Ryxi quickly, Knoradel wouldn't be able to chase her.

But Birra stepped swiftly into the fray as soon as her partner was out of her path. She was relying on her clawed feet and the heavy expanse of her wings with their clawed joints as weapons, keeping the delicate three-fingered manipulative extremity at the tips of her wings folded out of danger. Lunzie fought to grab at one of those hands, knowing that Birra would be thrown off guard to protect them.

"You wingless mutant," Birra hissed shrilly, raking at Lunzie's belly with one claw. It tore her tunic from the midriff to the hem as Lunzie jumped back out of the way. She countered immediately with a sweep kick at the avian's bony knees. As the avian moved to guard herself, Lunzie grabbed the fold of a wing that flapped above her head, threw an arm across Birra's body, and flipped her.

Automatically, the wings opened out to save the Ryxi. Birra shrieked as her hands rammed against the walls of the narrow corridors. Her wingspan was too great. Swiftly, she folded her pinions again, with the single deadly claws at their center joints arching over her shoulders at Lunzie. She pecked at the medic with her sharp beak. Lunzie drew up her crossed hands to block the blow and knocked the avian's head up and back.

"Fardles, I really hate to do this to you," she said apologetically. With both hands balled into fists, she smashed them in under Birra's wings against the avian's exposed rib cage. Wincing, she felt the delicate bones snap.

The Ryxi shrieked, her voice carrying into higher and higher registers as she clawed and flapped blindly at Lunzie.

"You're still ambulatory," Lunzie said, moving backward and countering the attack. "If you get to a medic right away he can set those bones so you don't puncture a lung. Let me go, or I'll be forced to keep you here until it's too late."

"Horrible biped! You lie!" Birra cradled one wounded side, then the other. She was gasping, beak open.

"I'm not lying. You know I'm a doctor. You knew that when you were sent to attack me," Lunzie threw back. "Who told you to attack me?"

The Ryxi gasped with fury, and clenched both wings against her midsection. "I die." Her round black eyes were starting to become glassy and she rocked back and forth.

"No!" Lunzie shouted. "You daft bird."

The Ryxi was going into shock. She was no longer a danger to Lunzie but she might put herself into a lethal coma.

Disgusted to be caught by the moral dilemma, Lunzie limped to the nearest communications panel and hit the blue stud.

"Emergency, level 11. Code Urgent. Emergency involving a Ryxi. Rib cage injury, going into shock. Emergency." Lunzie turned away from the panel. "Someone will be here in minutes. I meant to inflict no lasting damage on you but I'm not staying around in case the person who gave you your orders shows up first. You will keep my name out of an investigation, won't you? Good luck."

The Ryxi rocked back and forth rhythmically, ignoring Lunzie as she slipped through the access hatch to the stairs at the end of the corridor.

Impatiently Lunzie tapped out the sequence of the officers' lounge. She couldn't go there, even with an overlarge smock covering the shreds of her bloodstained uniform. But she prayed to all the gods that govern that Zebara was available. The adrenaline of Discipline was wearing off and she would soon be caught by the post-Discipline enervation. She had to hand over the cube asap.

"Officer's lounge." To her infinite relief she recognized Lieutenant Sanborn's bright tenor voice.

"Is Captain Zebara here?" she asked, trying to sound medium and casual. "It's Lunzie Mespil. Something's come up and I need a word with him."

"Yes, he just came in from the brass meeting. Having a drink and he needs it, Lunzie. Is this really urgent?"

"Let him judge. Just tell him I'm standing by, would you, Lieu-tenant?" She wanted to add, "like a good boy and go do as mother asks," but she didn't.

"Right you are," Sanborn replied obligingly.

She fidgeted, blotting blood from the wound on her temple. The flesh was awfully tender: she'd shortly have a massive hema-toma and there weren't many ways to conceal that obvious a bruise. What was taking Sanborn so long? The lounge wasn't that big.

"Zebara." He announced himself in a deep voice that made the intercom rattle. "I'd just placed a call to your quarters. Where are you?"

"Hiding, Captain, and I need to see you as soon as possible." She heard him sigh. Well, he might as well get all the bad news at once. "First they dropped a wall on Orlig, then they strangled him while I had him stashed in a nice out-of-the-way treatment room. I've just had an encounter with a life-seeking duet and I'd like to transfer the incriminating evidence before my demise."

"Where are you?" he repeated.

She gave him the deck, section, and corridor.

"How well do you know this vessel?"

"As well as most. Medics need to get places in a hurry."

"Then I suggest you get yourself to Scout Bay 5 by the best way and wait for me. I certainly have a good reason to return to my ship. Over and out."

His crisp voice steadied her. In the first place it had none of the soggy mushmouth tones that most heavyworlders seemed to project. His suggestion was sensible, keeping her out of the way of anyone likely to see her, and surely the scout ship would be the last place "they" would expect her to go.

She took the emergency shafts down to the flight decks, assisted by the half-G force at which they were kept. She got the wrong bay the first time she emerged into the main access corri-dors, but they were empty so she continued on to Five. He entered from the main turbovator and didn't so much as slow his stride as he caught her by the arm. He pulled out a small comm unit and mumbled into it as he half carried her up the ramp into the not-so-small scout ship.

"You got rightly messed up if your face is any indication," he said, pausing in the airlock to examine her. He twitched away the large coat and his eyebrows rose. "So they got Orlig. What have you got?"

"One of those neat little message bricks which had better go forward to its destination with all possible speed."

"There's usually a phrase to go with a brick?" He arched an eyebrow in query. It gave him a decidedly satanic look.

"I'm paranoid at the moment. I keep thinking people are trying to kill me." Her facetiousness brought a slight smile to his face.

"We'll get your message off and then maybe you'll trust this heavyworlder. Come!"

He took her hand and led her through the narrow corridors of the scout vessel to the command deck. A centimeter less on each side and the ceiling, Lunzie thought, and he wouldn't fit. Then he handed her into a small communications booth, slid the panel shut and went on into the bridge. She sat down dazed while he spoke briefly to the heavyworlder woman on duty. She instantly swung around with a grin to Lunzie and made rapid passes over her comm board.

"This is a secure channel," she said, her voice coming through a speaker in the wall. "Just insert the brick in the appropriate slot in front of you. They're usually constructed to set the coding frequency. I'm shutting down in here." She pulled off her earpiece and held up both hands. For a heavyworlder, she had a very friendly grin.

Lunzie fumbled with the brick but finally got it into the slot which closed over it like some weird alien ingesting sustenance. There was no indication that anything was happening. Abruptly the slot opened, spitting the little brick out. As she watched, the thing dissolved. It didn't steam or smolder or melt. It just dissolved and she was looking at a small pile of black dust.

She sent the Communications Officer the finger-thumb O of completion and sagged back with a deep sigh of relief. Zebara rose from his seat next to the comm tech and came around the doorway into the tiny chamber where Lunzie was seated.

"Mission completed in the usual pile of dust, I see," he said and swept it off onto the floor. Then he took a handful of mineral tablets from his pocket and popped a couple into his mouth.

Lunzie looked up at him limply. "I thank Muhlah!"

"And now we're going to do something about you." He sounded ominous.

Lunzie tensed in a moment of sheer panic which had no basis whatsoever except that Zebara was pounding on the quartz window with one massive palm.

"Flor, tell Bringan to get up here on the double. You look like hell, Lunzie Mespil. Sit tight for the medic."

Lunzie forced herself to relax when she noticed Zebara regarding her with some amusement.

"So what do we do about you?" he asked rhetorically. "Even on a ship as huge as the *ARCT-10*, you can't really be safely hidden. You escaped once but you are unquestionably in jeopardy." She wished he would sit down instead of looming over her. "Did you get a look at your assailants?"

"A Ryxi female named Birra and a human male she called Knoradel." She rattled of physical descriptions. "The Ryxi has a crushed rib cage. I left a few marks on the man."

"They shouldn't be too hard to apprehend," Zebara said and depressed a toggle on the board. She heard him giving the descriptions to the Ship Provost. "You won't object to remaining here until they have been detained? No? Sensible of you." He regarded her for a long moment and then grinned, looking more like a predatory fish than an amused human. "In fact, it would be even more sensible if you didn't go back to the *ARCT-10* at all."

"In deep space there aren't many alternatives," Lunzie remarked, feeling the weakness of post-Discipline seeping through her.

"I can think of one." He looked at her expectantly and, when she didn't respond, gave a disappointed sigh. "You can come back to Ambrosia with us."

"Ambrosia?" Lunzie wasn't certain that the planet appealed to her at all.

"An excellent solution since you're already involved up to your lightweight neck in Ambrosian affairs. Highly appropriate. Assassins won't get another chance at terminating your life on any ship I command. I'll clear your reappointment with the *ARCT-10* authorities."

Lunzie was really surprised. Somehow, she had not expected such positive cooperation and solicitousness from this heavyworlder. "Why?"

"You're in considerable danger. Partly because you gave unstinting assistance to another heavyworlder. I was well acquainted with Orlig. My people are beneficiaries of your risk as much as yours are. Do you have any objections?"

"No," Lunzie decided. "It'll be a great relief to be able to sleep safely again." She was beginning to feel weightless, a sure sign that adrenaline exhaustion was taking hold.

Zebara grinned his shark's-tooth smile again, and crunched another tablet. "If Orlig's murder and the attempt on your life are an indication, and I believe they are, then Ambrosia may be in even more danger than I thought it was. Orlig was keeping his ears open for me on the *ARCT*, which was receiving and transmitting my reports. So we'd already had an indication that this plum would fall into the wrong paws. You confirm that. I came back to ask for military support to meet us there to stave off a possible pirate takeover until a colony can be legitimately installed with the appropriate fanfare. Relax, Lunzie Mespil."

"Thank you," Lunzie called faintly after him, the weight of her own indecision and insecurity sliding off her sagging shoulders now that someone believed her. She let her head roll back against the cushioned chair.

Soon, she became aware that someone was in the tiny cubicle with her.

"Ah, you're awake. Don't move too quickly. I'm setting your arm." A thickset man with red-blond hair cut short knelt at her side. "I'm Doctor Bringan. Normally I'm just the xenobiologist but I'm not averse to using my talents on *known* species. I run the checkups and bandage scratches for the crew. Understand you're signing on as Medical Officer." Very gently, he pulled her wrist and forearm in opposite directions. The curled fingers slowly straightened out. "That'll be a relief," he added with a welcoming smile. "I might just put the wrong bits together and that could prove awkward for someone."

"Um, yes," Lunzie agreed, watching him carefully. Mercifully the arm was numb. He must have given her a nerve block. "Wait, I didn't hear the bones mesh yet."

"I'm just testing to see if any of the ligatures were torn. No. All's well." Bringan waved a small diagnostic unit over her arm. "You were lucky you were wearing a tight sleeve. The swelling would have been much worse left unchecked."

"So I see," Lunzie said, eyeing the reddish wash along the skin of her arm which marked subcutaneous bleeding. It would soon surface as a fading rainbow of colors as the blood dispersed. She poked at the flesh with an experimental finger and, with curious detachment, felt it give.

Bringan put the DU in his belt pouch and gave a deft twist to her arm. Lunzie heard the ulna and the radius grate slightly as they settled into place.

"I'm going to put you in a non-confining brace to hold your bones steady. Won't interfere with movement and you can wash the arm, cautiously. Everything will be tender once the nerve block wears off." He flexed her fingers back and forth. "You should have normal range of motion in a few hours." Then he gave a snort of a chuckle and eyed her. "I should be telling you!"

She managed a weak, but grateful, smile. "Bringan, are we going to Ambrosia?"

The doctor raised surprised blond brows at her. "Oh, yes indeed we are. Myself, I can't wait to get back. Why, I intend to put in to settle here when I retire. I've never seen such a perfect planet."

"I mean, are we going soon?" She stressed the last word.

"That's what I meant." He gave her a searching look. "Zebara has told me nothing about you, or why you arrive looking like the survivor of a corridor war, but he logged you on FTL. So I can enjoy a few shrewd guesses, most of which include planet pirates." He winked at her. "Which gives the most excellent of reasons for burning tubes back there. The FSP needs witnesses on hand. Or maybe that's your role on our roster."

"I'll witness, believe you me, I'll witness," Lunzie said with all the fervor left in her depleted body.

Bringan chuckled as he gathered up his gear. "If we're delayed in any way, by any agency, I think Zebara would probably tank himself up and swim back shipless. He's allergic to the mention of pirates. And bloody piracy's turning epidemic. It seems to me that every time a real plum turns up in the last century, the pirates are there to wrest it away from the legitimate finders. With a sophisticated violence that makes alien creatures seem like housecats."

"Bringan," Lunzie asked again, tentatively, "what's Zebara like?"

"Do you mean, is he your usual prototype heavyworlder chauvinist? No. He's a good leader, and good friend. I've known him for thirty years. You'll appreciate his fair treatment, but watch out for the grin. That means trouble."

Lunzie cocked an eyebrow at Bringan. "You mean the shark-face he puts on? I've already seen it."

"Ho, ho! I hope it wasn't meant for you!" The doctor bunched himself onto his feet. "There, you're in good shape. Come with me, and we'll see about a bunk for you. You need to rest and let those injuries start to heal."

"When do we cast off the *ARCT-10*?" Lunzie asked. She followed Bringan, not too wobbly on her strengthless legs. Had the Ryxi received help before her lungs collapsed?

"As soon as Zebara is back on board."

On the way to that bunk, Lunzie got the briefest of introductions to the rest of the scout crew. Besides Flor, the ship-born communications tech who doubled as historian, and Bringan the xenobiologist, there were seven more. Dondara and Pollili, a mated pair, were heavyworlders from Diplo. Pollili was the telemetry officer, and Dondara was a geologist. Unlike most of their number who served for a few missions and then retired to their cold, bleak homeworlds, Pollili and Dondara had served with Zebara's Explorers Team for eight years, and had every intention of continuing in that posting. They spent one to two months a year in intensive exercise in the heavyworld environment aboard the *ARCT-10* to maintain their muscle tone. The other five EX Team members were human. Scarran, tan-skinned and nearsighted, was a systems technologist. Vir, offshoot of a golden-complected breed with heavily lidded eyes, was an environmental specialist who shared security duties with Dondara. Elessa, charming but not strictly pretty, held the double duties of synthesizer tech and botanist. Timmins was a chemist. Wendell, the pilot, had gone over to the *ARCT-10* with Zebara.

Everyone's specialties overlapped somewhat so that the necessarily small crew of the scout had a measure of redundancy of talent in case of emergency. The little ship was compactly built but amazingly not cramped in its design. Hydroponic racks of edible plants were arrayed anywhere there was space, and the extra light made the rooms seem more cheerful and inviting. Bringan explained the ship was capable of running on its own power indefinitely in sublight, or making a single warp jump between short sprints before recharging.

Ambrosia was a long jump out toward the edge of explored space. The scout could never be certain of finding edible food on any planet it explored and its crew needed to be able to provide their own carbohydrates for the synthesizers.

Lunzie's bunk was in the same alcove as Elessa's. She lay on the padding with her arm strapped across her chest, staring at the bunkshelf above her. Bringan had ordered her to rest but she couldn't close her eyes. She was grateful to be safe but somehow it rankled her that her rescuer should prove to be a heavyworlder. Zebara seemed all right. She couldn't repress the suspicion that he might just be waiting until they got into deep space to toss her out the airlock. That didn't compute — not with a mixed-species crew all of whom were impressively loyal to him.

Abruptly the last adrenaline that had been buttressing her drained away. "Well, I ought to be truly grateful," she chided herself. "And he's got a very good press from his crew. That Quinada! I was getting used to heavyworlders when I had to run into someone like her! I suppose there's a bad chip in every board."

Still vaguely uneasy, Lunzie let herself drift off to sleep.

She awoke with a start to see Zebara staring down at her. It took her a moment to remember where she was.

"We're under way," he announced without preamble. "I've had you made an official member of my crew. No one else tried to pressure the little bosses to get on this cruise, so either your attackers have given up the job or . . . there are nasty plans for all of us."

"You're so comforting," Lunzie remarked drolly, determined to modify her attitude at least toward a heavyworlder named Zebara. "How long have I been asleep?"

The heavyworld captain turned his palms upward. "How'd I know? We've been under way about five hours. Bringan told me to let you rest and I have, but now I need to talk to you. Do you feel strong enough?"

Lunzie tested her muscles and drew herself into a sitting position. Her arm was sore but she could move her fingers now. Bringan's cast held it immobile without putting pressure on the bruised muscles of her forearm. The rest of her body felt battered, but she already felt better for having had some rest.

"Talk? Yes, I'm up to talking."

"Come to my quarters. We can speak privately there."

❖   ❖   ❖

"I was half expecting to be approached on the *ARCT-10*,"
Zebara said, pouring two glasses of Sverulan brandy. His quarters
were close to spacious; that is to say, the room was eight paces
wide by ten, instead of four. Zebara had a computer desk
equipped with a device Lunzie recognized as a private memory
storage. His records would not be accessible to anyone else on
the ship or on the ship's network. "The exact location of Ambrosia
is know only to myself and my crew and, regrettably, the administrators aboard the *ARCT*." He showed his teeth. "I trust my crew.
I suspect there's an unpluggable leak aboard the *ARCT*."

"A leak leading right to the EEC Administration?" Lunzie was
beginning to see the pieces of the minor puzzle which involved
her coming together. The whole was part of a much larger puzzle.

"That's a gamble I have to take. If the pirates beat us back to
Ambrosia, that means the information on Ambrosia's exact location is being transmitted to them right now. I want Fleet
protection, yes, but I'm also interested in luring the pirates out
into the open. They might just catch the spy within the Administration chambers this time." Zebara wrinkled his nose.

"The spy might be too high up in the echelons to find, impossible to trace — above suspicion." As the Seti of Fomalhaut
would assuredly be. Hastily Lunzie took a sip of her drink and felt
the warmth of the liquor in her belly. Zebara had splendid taste in
intoxicants. She said slowly, "In the past the heavyworlders
appear to have been the chief beneficiaries of this sort of piracy.
Is it at all possible that the FSP will believe that YOU let them
know where to find the planet?" Now the feral grin was aimed at
her. Lunzie felt a chill trace the line of her spine. "Mind you," she
added hastily, "I'm acting devil's advocate but if *I* can suspect collusion, others might certainly do so, if only to divert suspicion."

"A possible interpretation, I grant you. Let me say in my own
defense I dislike the idea that my people are beholden in any way
to mass murderers." He drained his glass and poured each of
them a second tot deep enough to bathe in, Lunzie thought. He
must have a truly spectacular tolerance. Nevertheless she took a
deep draught of the brandy, to thaw her spine, of course.

"I feel obliged to explain that I thought for quite a few years
that I had lost my daughter to pirates during the Phoenix incident," she said. "The first thing anyone knew, the legitimate

colony was gone and heavyworlders had moved in. I harbored a very deep resentment that they were living on that bright and shiny new planet while I grieved for my daughter. It's affected my good judgment somewhat ever since." Lunzie swallowed. "I apologize for indulging myself with such a shockingly biased generalization. It's the pirates I should hate, and I do."

Zebara smiled wryly. "I appreciate your candor and your explanation. Biased generalizations are not confined to your subgroup. I resent lightweights as a group for constantly putting my people in subordinate and inferior positions, where we're assigned the worst of the picking, or have to work under lightweights in a mixed group. In my view, there has been no true equality in the distribution of colonizable planets. Many of us, especially groups from Diplo, felt that Phoenix should have been assigned to us in the first place. One of our unassailable skills is mine engineering and production. The gen in my community was that the heavy people who landed on Phoenix had paid significant bribes to a merchant broker who assured them that the planet was virgin and vacant. They were cheated," Zebara added heatedly. "They were promised transuranics, but the planet had been stripped before they got there. It was no more than a place to live, with little a struggling colony could use as barter in the galactic community."

"Then somebody made double profits out of Phoenix. Triple, if you count the goods and machinery that the original settlers brought with them." The brandy had relaxed Lunzie sufficiently so that she had no compunction about refilling her glass. "Do you know the Parchandri?"

Zebara waved a dismissive hand. "Profiteers, every last blinking one of them, and they've a wide family. Weaklings, most of the Parchandri, even by lightweight standards, but they're far too spineless to kill with the ferocity the pirates exhibit."

The Seti could be ruthless but Lunzie couldn't quite cast them in the role which, unfortunately, did fit heavyworlders. "Then who are they? Human renegades? Captain Aelock felt that they were based out of Alpha Centauri."

"Aelock's a canny man but I'd be surprised if the Centauris were actively involved. They've acquired too much veneer, too civilized, too cautious by half." An opinion with which Lunzie privately concurred. "Centauris think only of profit. Every person, every machine, is a cog in the credit machine."

Lunzie took a sip of the warm brown liquor and stared at her reflection in the depths of the glass. "A point well taken. My daughter's descendants all live on that world. I have never met such a pitiful load of stick-in-the-mud, bigoted, shortsighted mules in my life. I was appalled because my daughter herself had plenty of motivation. She's a real achiever. Not afraid to take chances. . . . "

"Like her mother," Zebara added. Lunzie looked up at the heavyworld captain in surprise. He was looking at her kindly, without a trace of sarcasm or condescension.

"Why, thank you, Captain. Only I fret that none of her children, bar one, are unhappy living in a technological slum, polluted and hemmed in by mediocrity and duplication."

"Complacency and ignorance," Zebara suggested, pouring more brandy. "A very good way to keep a large population so tractable the society lacks rebellion."

"But they've no space, mental or physical, to grow in and they don't realize what they're missing. It even grieves me that they're so happy in their ignorance. But I got out of Alpha Centauri as fast as I could, and not just because my life was at risk. Trouble with moving around like that, I keep losing the people I love, one by one." Lunzie halted, appalled by her maundering. "I am sorry. It's this brandy. Or is it sodium pentathol? I certainly didn't intend to download my personal problems on you."

The captain shook his head. "It sounds to me as though you'd had no one to talk to for a long time. Mind you," he went on, musing aloud, "such unquestioning cogs can turn a huge and complex wheel. The pirates are not just one ship, nor even just a full squadron. The vessels have to be ordered, provisioned, staffed with specially trained personnel" — he ignored Lunzie's involuntary shudder at what would constitute training — "and that means considerable administrative ability, not just privileged information."

Lunzie regarded him thoughtfully. He sounded as paranoid as she was, mistrusting everyone and everything. "It all gets so unsortably sordidly convoluted!" Her consonants were suffering from the brandy. "I'm not sure I can cope with all this."

Zebara chuckled. "I think you've been coping extremely well, Citizen Doctor Mespil. You're still alive!"

"A hundred and nine and a half years alive!" Oh, she was feeling the brandy. "But I'm learning. I'm learning. I'm especially learning," and she waggled an admonishing finger at him. "I'm gradually learning to accept each person as an individual, and not as just a representative of their subgroup or species. Each one is individual to his, her, itself and can't be lumped in with his, her or its peer group. My Discipline Master would be proud of me now, I think. I've learned the lesson he was doing his damnedest to impart to me." She took the last swallow of Sverulan brandy and fixed her eyes on his impassive face. "So, Captain, we're on our way to Ambrosia. What do you think we'll find there?"

"All we may find is the kittisnakes chasing each other up trees. We will be ready for any surprises." The captain stood up and extended an arm to Lunzie as she struggled her way out of the deep armchair. "Can you get back to your bunk all right?"

"Captain Zebara, Mespils have been known for centuries to hold their liquor. Dam' fine brandy. Thank you, Captain, for that and the listening ear."

✦ CHAPTER THIRTEEN

The scout ship slowed to sublight speed and came out of its warp at the edge of the disk of a star system. Lunzie was strapped in the fourth seat on the bridge, watching as the stars spread out from a single point before them and filled the sky. Only a single yellow-white star hung directly ahead of the ship.

"There she is, Captain," Pilot Wendell said with deep satisfaction. "Ambrosia's star."

Zebara nodded solemnly and made a few notes in the electronic log. "Any energy traces in range?" the heavyworlder asked.

"No, sir."

"Is Ambrosia itself visible from this position?" Lunzie asked eagerly.

"No, Doctor, not yet. According to system calculations, she's around behind the sun. We'll drop below the plane of the ecliptic and come up on her. There's an asteroid belt we don't like to pass through if we can help it."

"Why do you call Ambrosia she?"

Wendell smiled over his shoulder at her. "Because she's beautiful as a goddess. You'll see."

"Any traces?" Zebara asked again, as they began the upward sweep into the ecliptic toward a blue-white disk.

"No, sir," Wendell repeated.

"Once we drop into atmosphere, we're vulnerable," Zebara reminded him. "Our sensors won't read as clearly. The pirates could get the drop on us."

"I know, Captain." The pilot looked nervous, but he turned up a helpless palm. "I don't have any readings that shouldn't be out there."

"Sir, why are we returning without military backup if you expect pirates to attack?" Lunzie asked, gently, hoping that the question wasn't out of line. "This scout has no defensive armament."

Zebara scowled. "I don't want anyone intruding on Ambrosia. It's our province," he said, waving an arm through the air to indicate the crew. "If we aren't here to back up our claim, someone else — someone who didn't spend years searching — Krims," Zebara said, banging a palm on the console. He passed a hand across his forehead, wiping away imaginary moisture. "I should be enjoying this ride. I suppose I'm too protective of our discovery. See, Lunzie, there's the source of all our pain and pleasure. Ambrosia."

The blue-white disk took on more definition as it swam toward them. Lunzie held her breath. Ambrosia did indeed look like the holos she had seen on Earth. Patterns of water-vapor clouds scudded across the surface. She could pick out four of the six small continents, hazy gray-green in the midst of the shimmering blue seas. A rakishly tilted icecap decorated the south pole of the planet. A swift-moving body separated itself from the cloud layer and disappeared around the planet's edge. The smallest moon, one of three. "The big satellite is behind the planet," Wendell explained. "It's a full moon on nightside this day. Look, there's the second little one, appearing on the left." A tiny jewel, ablaze with the star's light, peeked around Ambrosia's side.

"She is beautiful," Lunzie breathed, taking it all in.

"Prepare for orbit and descent," Zebara ordered. "We'll set down. A ship this small is a sitting target in orbit. Planetside, we'll have a chance to run a few more experiments while we wait for backup."

"Aye, sir."

"Just after midday local time," Wendell had assured them as he set the scout down on a low plateau covered with thick, furry-leaved vegetation. EEC regulations required that an Evaluation Team locate at least five potential landing sites on a planet intended for colonization. The astrogation chart showed no fewer than ten, one in the chief island of a major archipelago in the southern sea, one on each small continent, and more on the larger ones.

As the hatchway opened, Lunzie could hear the scuttling and scurrying of tiny animals fleeing the noisy intrusion. A breeze of fresh, sweet air curled inside invitingly. With force shield belts on, Dondara and Vir did the perimeter search so that no indigenous life would be shut inside the protective shield when it was switched on. They gave the go-ahead and Pollili activated the controls. A loud, shrill humming arose, and dropped almost immediately into a range inaudible to human ears.

If the view from space was lovely, the surface of Ambrosia looked like an artist's rendition of the perfect planet. The air was crisp and fresh, with just a tantalizing scent of exotic flora in the distance. The colors ranged from vivid primaries to delicate pastels and they all looked clean.

Lunzie stepped out of the shuttle into the rich sunlight of dayside. The sky was a pale blue and the cumulus clouds were a pure, soft white. From the hilltop, the scout commanded a panoramic view of an ancient deciduous forest. The treetops were every shade of green imaginable, interspersed every so often with one whose foliage was a brilliant rose pink. Smaller saplings grew on the edge of the plateau, clinging at an absurd angle as if fearful to make the plunge.

Off to the left, an egg-shaped lake glistened in the sun. Lunzie could just pick out the silver ribbons of the two rivers which fed it. One wound down across the breast of the very hill she stood on. Lunzie rested in the sun close to the ship as the other crew members spread out nearby on the slope of the hill and took readings. Under her feet was a thick blue-green grassoid whose stems had a circular cross section.

"More like reeds than grass, but it's the dominant cover plant," Elessa explained. "It doesn't grow to more than six inches in height, which is decent of it. We don't have to slog through thickets of the stuff, unlike other planets I could name. You have to push it over to sit on it or it sticks you full of holes. See that tree with the pink leaves? The fruit is edible, really succulent, but eat only the ones whose rinds have turned entirely brown. We got the tip from the local avians who wait in hordes for the fruit to ripen. The unripe ones give you a fierce bellyache. Oh, look. I don't have a sample of that flower." Carefully, she uprooted a tiny star-shaped flower with a forked tool from among the grassoids and transferred it to a plastic vial. "They have a single deep taproot instead of a spread of small roots, which makes them easy to harvest. It's the stiff stem that keeps them upright, like the grassoid. You could denude this whole hillside with tweezers."

A hovering oval shadow suddenly covered Lunzie and the botanist where they knelt.

"You ought to see more than a single meadow, Doctor," Dondara scolded her from above, appearing from the rear of the ship in a two-man sled. "You're enjoying a rare privilege. Not twelve intelligent life-forms have seen this landscape before. Come on." He beckoned her into the sled. "I've got some readings to take. You can come with me."

Reminding herself of her drink-taken vow to trust individuals of any subgroup, Lunzie levered herself to her feet and climbed in after him. Elessa looked up as she went by and seemed about to say something to her, but changed her mind. Lunzie looked questioningly at the botanist but the girl shot her a "What can I tell you?" expression. Lunzie had confided her distrust to the botanist during the long flight and Elessa only reiterated the statement that Zebara and those on the scout were truly in a class all their own.

The medic wondered as she and Dondara passed through the force-shield and flew over the meadow. The terrain was dramatically different less than half a mile from the grassy landing site. Beyond the breast of the knobby hill which bounded the lake on its other side, the land began to change. The foliage was thinner here, reduced from lush forestry to a thin cover of marsh plants. Water flowed over worn shelves of rock, stained with red-brown iron oxide and tumbled into teeming pools. Nodules of pyrite in the rock faces glittered under the midday sun. Lunzie caught the occasional gleam of a marine creature in the shallow pools near a broad sweep of rapids that swept and foamed around massive boulders. In the distance, more forest covered the bases of rough, bare mountain peaks.

"Quite a division here; this could be another world entirely," Lunzie announced, delighted, twisting around in her seat to get the best view.

Dondara activated his force-belt and signalled to her to do the same as he set the sled down.

"This is a different continental plate from the landing site," Dondara explained, splashing through a pool.

Lunzie skirted it to follow him. He pointed out geological features which supported his theory, including an upthrust face of sedimentary rock that was a rust-streaked gray which contrasted with the sparkling granite of the hilly expanse of the continent. With unexpected courtesy, he helped her up onto a well-worn boulder pocked with small pools.

"This was once a piece with the landmass across the ocean northeast of here, got slid over a spreading center over a few million years. This plate is more brittle. But it's got its own interesting life-forms. Come here." He gestured her over to a tubular hollow in the rock.

Lunzie peered at the hole. It was so smooth that it could have been drilled by a laser. "What's down there?"

"A very shy sort of warm-water crustacean. It'll only come out when the sky is overcast. If you stand over the hole, it'll think it is cloudy." Curious, Lunzie leaned down. "Look closely and be patient."

Dondara moved back and sat down on a dry shelf nearby. "You've got to turn off your force-belt, or it won't come out. The frequency annoys them."

As soon as she had deactivate the belt, she could see movement deep in the hollow. Lunzie knelt closer and spread her shadow over the opening. She heard a soft clattering noise, a distant but distinct rattle of porcelain. Suddenly, she was hit in the face by a fountaining stream of warm water. Lunzie jumped back, sputtering. The water played down the front of her tunic and then ceased.

"What on Earth was that?" she demanded, wiping her face.

Dondara roared with laughter, making the stones ring. He rolled back and forth on his stone perch, banging a hand against the rock in his merriment.

"Just a shy Ambrosian stone crab!" he chortled, enjoying the look on her face. "They do that every time something blocks their lair. Ambrosia has baptized you! You're one of us now, Lunzie!"

Once she recovered from the surprise, Lunzie realized that she had fallen for one of the oldest jokes in the database. She joined in Dondara's laughter.

"How many of the others did you sting with your 'shy rock crustacean'?" she asked suspiciously.

The heavyworlder was pleased. "Everyone but Zebara. He smelled vermin, and refused to come close enough." Dondara grinned. "You're not mad?"

"Why? But you can be sure I won't get caught a second time. Here on Ambrosia or anywhere else," Lunzie promised him. She was obscurely pleased that she had been set up. She'd passed a subtle test. She was also soaking and the air was chilly, weak lightweight that she was. She flicked some of the excess off her hands and shirt.

"You really got a dose. Must have roused the grandaddy. If I don't offend your lightweight sensibilities, you better get yourself back to the scout. Take the sled." She was beginning to feel that such solicitude was only to be expected from one of Zebara's crew. "I've got to take some temperature readings in the hot springs upstream. The exercise will do me good. I've got my communicator." With a hearty wave, the big humanoid waded off upstream.

Lunzie activated the sled's power pack to fly back up the hill to the ship. Just about halfway there, she began to assimilate the full implications of that little encounter. Dondara had treated her to the "baptism" as he had probably done everyone else on the scout . . . enjoying his little joke. She had taken no umbrage and begged no quarter. But he had been considerate without being patronizing, recognizing certain lightweight problems rarely encountered by heavyworlders — like a propensity for catching chills.

"Will such minor wonders never cease?" she said to herself, ruffling her slowly drying hair.

"What happened to you?" Vir called as she came into view.

"Dondara had me baptized Ambrosian style," Lunzie shouted back, holding out the front of her clammy wet tunic with her good hand.

As she came upon Elessa, she saw that the botanist was grinning. "You knew he was going to do that."

"I'm sorry." The girl giggled. "I almost stopped you; he's such an awful practical joker. To make amends, I found you a kittisnake to examine. Aren't they adorable? And so friendly." She held up a small handful of black fur.

"Hang on to it for me," Lunzie called.

She set the sled down behind the scout. Elessa met her halfway and wound the length of animal around her hands.

"This is one of the most plentiful life-forms on Ambrosia," the botanist explained, "oddly enough omnivorous. They're really

Bringan's province but they so love the attention that they're irresistible."

The kittisnake had a small round face, with a round nose and round ears which peered out of its sleek, back-combed fur. It had no limbs, but it was apparent where the thicker body joined the more slender tail. Two bright green eyes with round black pupils opened suddenly and regarded Lunzie expressionlessly. It opened its mouth, revealing two rows of needles, and aspirated a breathy hiss.

"It likes you," Elessa declared, interpreting a response which Lunzie had misjudged. "Pet it. It won't bite you."

It certainly seemed to enjoy the caress, twisting itself into pretzel knots as Lunzie ran her hands down its length. She grinned up at the botanist.

"Responsive, aren't they? Good ambassadors for a flourishing tourist trade on Ambrosia."

While Lunzie was making friends with the kittisnake, a light breeze sprang up. She suddenly decided she needed a warmer tunic over her injured arm. Though the bones had already been knit together by Bringan, the swollen tissue had yet to subside. Lunzie felt her flesh was starting to creep.

"Excuse me, will you?" she asked the botanist.

She squeezed past Zebara, poised in the open hatchway of the scout. He greeted the doctor, raising an eyebrow at her wet hair and clothes.

"Dondara took you to see the snark, huh?"

"A granddaddy snark to judge by the volume of baptismal waters." She grinned up at the heavyworlder.

"Haven't you raised Fleet yet, Flor?" the captain asked, turning back from the hatchway toward the semicircular pilot's compartment. The communications station occupied another quarter arc of the circle facing the rear of the ship between the telemetry station and the corridor.

"Aye, aye, sir," called the communications tech. "I'm just stripping the message from the beacon now. They acknowledge your request and have despatched the *Zaid-Dayan*."

"The who? That's a new designation on me," Zebara growled. Lunzie caught the note of suspicion in his voice.

"Be glad, sir. Brand-new commission, on its maiden voyage," Flor said apologetically. "Heavy cruiser, ZD-43, the Registry says, with lots of new hardware and armament."

"What? I don't want to have to wet-nurse an unintegrated lot of lightweight lubbers . . . " Zebara sighed, pushing back into the communications booth and looking over Flor's shoulder.

Lunzie slipped in behind him. "Isn't telemetry showing a trace?" she said, noticing the blip on the current sweep of the unit.

"Is that the ZD-43 arriving now? Wait, there's an echo. I see two blips." Zebara eased her aside with one huge hand and inserted himself into the telemetry officer's chair. "Oh-oh! Pol-lili!" he roared. His voice echoed out onto the hillside. The broad-faced blond woman appeared on the breast of the slope below the shuttle and hurried up it at double time. "Interpret this trace for me," Zebara ordered. "Is this an FSP vessel of any kind? Specifically a new cruiser?"

Pollili took the seat next to Flor as her captain moved aside. She peered at the controls and toggled a computer analysis. "No way. It's not FSP. Irregular engine trace, overpowered for its size. I'd say it's an intruder."

"A pirate?" Lunzie heard herself ask.

"Two, to be precise." Zebara's expression was ferocious. "They must have been hanging in the asteroid belt or dodging us around the sun. How close are they to making orbit?"

"An hour, maybe more. I get traces of big energy weapons, too," Pollili said, pointing to a readout on her screen. "One of 'em is leaking so much it's as much a danger to the ship carrying it as it is to us. An academic point, to be sure, since we're unarmed."

"Will they land?" Lunzie asked, alarmed.

"I doubt it. If we can see them, they can see us. They know someone is down here, but they don't know who or what," Zebara said.

"Forgive me for pointing out a minor difficulty, sir," Flor said in a remarkably level, even droll tone, "but they can dispose of us from space. The ZD-43 is at least three days behind us," she added, her healthy color beginning to pale. "Once they realize we're alone here, they'll kill us. Is there nothing we can do?"

Zebara smiled, showing all his teeth.

What was it Bringan had said? When he grins like a shark, watch out?

"We bluff. Flor, send another message to the *Zaid-Dayan*. Tell them that we've got two pirates circling Ambrosia. Tell them to take any shortcuts they can. Force multiple jumps. If they don't hurry, we'll be just a scorch mark and crater on the landscape. We're going to stall the inevitable just as long as we can."

"How?" Lunzie demanded, wishing she felt as confident as Zebara sounded.

"That, Doctor, is what we must figure out. Flor, have you sent that? Good. Now get on the general communicator channel and get the crew back here for a conference."

"I want your most positive thinking on how we can keep those pirates offplanet," Zebara began once the crew had assembled in the messroom.

"Those blips couldn't possibly be anything else, could they?" Bringan asked after clearing his throat.

Zebara gave a short bark of laughter. "They haven't answered hails and their profile doesn't match anything in our records. And it's not good neighborliness they're leaking. Think, my friends. Think hard. How do we stall them?"

"No black box, huh?" asked Vir, a thin human with straight black hair and a bleak expression.

Flor shook her head. "Those would be a long time disconnected." No legitimate ship would put out into space without the black box interface between control systems and engines which transmitted automatic identification signals. To disconnect it disabled the drives. Unscrupulous engineers had been know to jury-rig components, but such a ship would never be allowed in an FSP-sanctioned port.

Zebara smashed his fist into a palm. "Stop denying the problem. Think. We've got to stall them long enough to let the *Zaid-Dayan* reach Ambrosian space."

No one spoke for a long moment. No one even exchanged glances in the tense atmosphere of the wardroom.

"What if we take off? Can't we outrun them?" Vir demanded to Wendell, the pilot.

"Not a chance," Wendell said sadly. "My engines don't have the kick to push us far enough out of their range to make a warp jump. They'd catch us halfway there."

"So we're stuck on this planet while the predators line us up in their sights," Dondara growled, scrubbing his dusty hair with his hands. He had taken only thirty minutes to run the distance from the pools after he'd received Flor's mayday recall. Lunzie was full of admiration for the heavyworlder's stamina.

Scarran cleared his throat. His perpetually red-shot brown eyes made him look choleric or sleepy and he had a naturally mild personality.

"What about a violent disease of some sort? We're all dead and dying of it. Highly contagious. Can't find an antidote," he suggested in a self-deprecating voice.

"No, that wouldn't work," Pollili scoffed, drawing her brows together. "Even assuming they're of a species with enough in common with ours to catch it. They'd blow our ship off the face of the planet to wipe out the contagion and then land where they pleased."

"What about natural disaster?" asked Elessa, collecting nods from Flor and Scarran. "Unstable tectonics? An earthquake? A volcano about to blow? They'd have sacrificed scanning potential to some sort of weaponry."

"Possibly," Pollili drawled. "Even the simplest telemetry systems warn you if you're going to put down on a shifting surface. And live volcanoes show up as hot spots on infrared."

"What about hostile life-form?" Lunzie asked, and was generally hooted down by the others.

"What, attack ferrets?" Elessa held up the black-furred kittisnake, which curled around her hands, cooing breathily to show its contentment. "If the pirates are after Ambrosia when FSP has scarcely heard of its existence, they already know what's down here, besides us. Sorry, folks."

"Hold it a moment," Bringan said, raising a hand. "Lunzie has made a positive suggestion that merits discussion. Lunzie . . . "

"I had in mind a free bacterium that gets into your breathing apparatus and caulks it up with goo," Lunzie said, warming to her topic. "Five of our officers are down with it already. Nothing, not even breather masks, seems to keep it out. I feel that it's only a matter of time before they die of oxygen deprivation. The organism didn't appear in our initial reports because it's inert, sluggish during the winter months. It dies off in the cold. Now that the climate's warmed up for summer, the bug reproduces like mad. We're all infected. I've just discovered that it's gotten into the ventilation system, housed in the filters. I doubt we'd ever be able to lift off again, with the ship's air-recycling system fouled.

I'm putting Ambrosia on indefinite quarantine. Only moral, ethical action possible to a medic or any professionality. Contact between ships is likely to doom them both. In fact, it's my professional opinion that the *ARCT-10* is in real danger since Zebara and Wendell were on board to report to Admin. Their lungs were already contaminated and the air they exhaled from their lungs would now be in the *ARCT's* air-recirculation system. Lungs are always warm — until the host is dead."

"What? What are you talking about?" demanded Vir, paling.

"What's this bacterium?" Elessa demanded. "I never observed one here and I prepared all the initial slides!"

"It's called *Pseudococcus pneumonosis*." Lunzie smiled slyly. She was rather pleased with the astonished reaction to her little fable. "I've just discovered it, you see. A nicely non-existent, but highly contagious condition, inevitably and painfully fatal. It might just stall them. It will certainly make them pause a while. If we can be convincing enough." Then she chuckled. "If we get out of this alive, someone better check with the old *ARCT* and see just who scrambled to the infirmary, requiring treatment for a fatal lung disease."

Zebara and Bringan chortled and, when the rest of the crew realized she'd been acting out a scenario, they gave Lunzie a round of applause. Laughter eased the tension and indicated renewed hope.

"That just might work," Bringan agreed after several moments of hard thinking. He gave Lunzie a warm smile. "Would we have trouble with understanding medical lingo?"

Lunzie shrugged. "If I could fool you for a few minutes, I maybe can fool them. You see, Bringan's only a xeno-medic. He diagnosed it as vacation fever: personnel pretending to be sick so they could lounge in the sun. Once we got back here, with me, a human-medically trained person, I began to suspect a serious medical problem. By then it was too late to contain the bacterium. It was widespread. And, for all I know, loose on the *ARCT-10* as well.

"Sorry about this, folks, but I'll make it extremely personal: heavyworlders get it worst." She warded off the violent protests until Zebara bellowed for silence.

"She's got a valid reason to pick on us."

"I said I was sorry, heavyworlders. I'm not disparaging you but it's a fact, piracy has attracted many heavyworlders. Look, I'm not starting an argument . . . "

"And I'm ending it," Zebara said, showing his shark teeth. The muttering subsided immediately. "Lunzie's reasoning is sound. We take the lumps."

"How do you know so much about the planet pirates?" Dondara wanted to know, his eyes narrowed and unfriendly.

"Not my choice, but I do. Sorry about this."

"I'll forgive you if it works," Dondara said, but he gave her a wry twist of a smile.

"I think she's come up with the best chance we've got," the xenobiologist said approvingly. "Unless someone has thought up a better one just recently? Who delivers this deathless message to the pirates?" He looked at Zebara.

"I think I'd better," Zebara replied. "Not to decry Lunzie's dramatic abilities, but because the report of a heavyweight will be more acceptable to them than anything a lightweight could say."

"I hate such an expedient." With a fierce expression, Dondara exploded to his feet. "Do we have to compound the insult to all honorable heavyworlders who abhor the practice of piracy?"

With a sad expression on his face, Zebara shook his head at the geologist. "Don, we both know that some of Diplo's children have been weak enough to go into the service of unscrupulous beings in order to ease the crowding of our homeworlds." Dondara started to protest but Zebara cut him off. "Enough! Such weaklings shame us all and the good carry the disgrace along with them until the real culprits can be exposed. I intend to be part of that exposure. And this is one step in the right direction." He turned to Lunzie. "Brief me, Doctor Mespil!"

The plan, as plans do, underwent considerable revision until a creditable script was finally reached. With the help of the garment synthesizer and Flor's copious history diskfiles, Zebara was tricked out in the uniform of an attaché of Diplo, the heavyworlders' home planet. On a simple disk blue tunic, Flor attached silver shoulder braid and a tight upright collar of silver that fastened with a chain suspended between two buttons. As Zebara was dressed, Lunzie rehearsed him on details.

Meanwhile, Flor and Wendell were tinkering with the scout's black box, trying to mask, shield, electronically alter, or scramble its identification signal. Neither wanted to tamper with the box because that could lead to other problems.

With a prosthetic putty, Bringan sculpted a new nose for Zebara and broadened his cheekbones to enhance his appearance to a more typical heavyworlder cast. Lunzie was stunned by the result. It changed him completely into one of the dull-faced hulks that she remembered from the Mining Platform.

"Zebara, they've achieved parking orbit," Flor called. "The lead ship will be directly overhead in six minutes."

The last touches of his costume in place, the heavyworld captain swaggered into the communications booth and took his place before the video pickup. Out of sight, Lunzie sat next to Flor in the control room and watched as a hail was sent to the two strange ships.

"Attention to orbiting ships," Zebara announced in a rasping monotone. "Arabesk speaking, attaché for His Excellency Lutpostig the Third, the Governor of Diplo. This planet is proscribed by order of His Excellency. Landing is forbidden. Identify yourselves."

On the screen before them, Lunzie and Flor saw a pattern shimmer into coherency. It was not a face but rather an abstract computer-generated graphic.

"So, they can see us, but we can't see them," Flor muttered to Lunzie. "I don't like this," the Communications Officer added miserably.

An electronically altered voice shivered through the audio pickup. Lunzie tried to guess the species of the speaker but it spoke a pure form of Basic with no telltale characteristics. Possibly computer-generated, like the graphic, she guessed.

"We know of no interdiction on this planet. We are landing in accordance with our orders."

Zebara gave a rasping cough which he only half covered with one hand. "The crew of this ship have contracted an airborne bacteria. *Pseudococcus pneumonosis*. This life-form was not, I repeat, NOT, mentioned in the initial landing report."

"Tell me another one, attaché. That report has been circulated."

Zebara's second cough lasted longer and seemed to rake his toes. Lunzie was impressed.

"Of course, but you should also know that the reports were

made during the cold season in this hemisphere. Since the weather has warmed, the bacteria has awoken and multiplied explosively, infiltrating every portion of our ship." For good measure he managed a rasping, gagging cough of gigantic proportion.

The voice became slightly less suspicious. "The effect of this warm season bacteria?"

"It infests the bronchial tubes, in a condition similar to pneumonia. The alveoli become clogged almost immediately. The first symptom is a pernicious cough." Zebara demonstrated, gagging dramatically. "The condition results in painful suffocation leading to death. Five of my crew have died already.

"We heavyworlders appear to be particularly susceptible due to our increased lung capacity," Zebara continued, injecting a note of panic into his voice. "First we tried to filter the bacterium out by using breather masks, but it is smaller than a virus. Nothing keeps it out. It can live anywhere that is warm. It flourished in the ventilation system and the filters are so caulked up that I doubt we will be able to cleanse them sufficiently to take off again. Ironic, for cold slows and kills it. Unfortunately, living pulmonary tissue never becomes cold enough. It even lingers in the lungs of the deceased until the body itself has chilled."

There was a murmuring behind the whirling pattern of colors on the screen, then the audio ceased completely.

"Zebara." Pollili's voice came over the private channel. "I now have readings on their ships. They're big ones. One of them is a fully loaded transport lugger, full of cold bodies. There must be five hundred deepsleepers aboard. It's the smaller one that's leaking energy. An escort, carrying enough firepower to split this planet in two."

"Can you identify the life-forms?" Lunzie asked.

"Negative. They're shielded. I get heat traces of about a hundred bodies, but my equipment's not sensitive enough to identify type, only heat emanations." Pollili's voice trailed off as the pirate spoke again.

"We will consider this information."

"I warn you, in the name of Diplo," Zebara insisted, "do not land on this planet. The bacterium is present throughout the atmosphere. Do not land."

Zebara slumped back into the padded seat and wiped his forehead. Flor hastily cut the connection.

"Bravo! Well done," Lunzie congratulated him, handing him a restorative pepper.

The rest of the crew crowded into the communications station.

"What will they do?" Vir asked nervously.

"What they said. Consider the information." Zebara took a long swig of the pepper. "One thing sure. They're not likely to go away."

"First of all, they'll check their source files to see if there's any mention of the bacterium," Bringan enumerated, ticking off his fingers. "That alone should make it hot for the people who sold them the information and forgot to mention a potentially fatal airborne parasite here. Second, they'll try to get a sample of the bacterium. I think we'll see an unmanned probe scooping the air, looking for samples to analyze."

"Third, they might try to put a volunteer crew down to test the effects of living beings," Elessa offered, bleakly.

"A distinct possibility," Flor said. "I'll just rig a repeater signal to broadcast the Interdict warning over and over again on their frequency. Might make them just a teensy bit more nervous."

Her fingers flew over her console, and then clicked on a button at the far left side. "There. It'll be loud too."

Lunzie grinned. She was becoming more impressed with the imagination and ingenuity of this EEC Team. "I can't imagine that 'volunteers' will be thick in the corridors. But they will figure out all too soon there isn't anything. Shouldn't we grab some rest while we can?"

"Well, I can't," Bringan said. "When they don't find what they're expecting, they'll ask us to identify it, so I better design an organism. Vir, you're a good hack, you can help me."

"I'll help, too," Elessa volunteered. "I wouldn't be able to rest with those vultures circling, just waiting to land on top of us."

"I'll authorize sedatives to anyone who doesn't think he or she can sleep," Lunzie offered, with a look toward Zebara for permission. The captain nodded.

Those who weren't involved in designing the pseudobacteria scattered to their sleeping cubicles and left the others wrangling over mouse-controlled Tri-D graphics program.

Lunzie lay down on her bunk and initiated Discipline technique to soothe herself to sleep. She got a few restful hours before tension roused her. There had been bets as to when another transmission from the pirate vessel would arrive.

After a twenty-four-hour respite, tempers began to fray. The design team had an argument, ending with Elessa storming out of the scout to sit in tears behind a tree, agitatedly soothing her pet kittisnake.

Wendell took a nap, but he was so tense when he awoke that he asked Lunzie for a sedative. "I can't just sit around and wait," the pilot begged, twisting his hands together, "but if there's any chance of us lifting, I also can't be frazzled or fuzzy-minded."

Lunzie gave him a large dose of a mild relaxant, and left him with a complicated construction puzzle to keep his hands busy. Most of the others bore with the tension more stoically. Zebara alternated between popping mineral tablets and drumming on a table with an air of distraction and running the ships' profiles through the computer records. He badgered Flor with frequent updates on the *Zaid-Dayan*'s eta.

The other two heavyworlders paced the common area for all the world like caged exotics; then Dondara irritably excused himself. He left the ship and headed downslope in the sled.

"Where's he going?" Lunzie asked.

"To break rocks," Pollili explained, turning her palms to the sky. "He'll come back when he can hold the frustration in check."

Dondara had been gone for nearly two hours when Flor appeared at the door of the common area. Zebara raised his head. "Well?"

She grimaced. "They've launched an unmanned probe. It's doing the usual loops." Then she really grinned. "I got good news, though." Everyone in the room snapped to. "I just stripped the beacon of a reply from the *Zaid-Dayan*. They say to hold tight. They ought to be here within three hours."

Ragged cheers rose from the crew when suddenly a low-pitched beeping came from the forward section.

"Uh-oh," Flor said. "The upstairs neighbors ahead of schedule!" She turned and ran forward, followed by the rest of the crew. The filtered voice came through the audio monitors.

"Diplomat Arabesk. I wish to speak with Diplomat Arabesk."

Zebara reached for the silver-collared tunic but Lunzie grabbed his sleeve.

"You can't talk to them, Zebara, you're dead. Remember!

Heavyworlders are more susceptible. The bacterial plague has claimed another victim. Pollili, you talk to them."

"Me?" squeaked the telemetry officer. "I can't talk to people like them. They won't believe me."

Flor was wringing her hands with nervousness. "Someone's got to speak to them. Soon. Please."

Lunzie hauled Pollili by the hand into the communications booth. "Poll, this can save all our lives. Will you trust me?"

The heavyworlder female looked at her beseechingly. "What are you going to do?"

"I'm going to convince you that what you are about to say is one hundred percent the truth." Lunzie leaned forward and put a comforting hand, the one in the cast, on the other's arm. "Trust me?"

Pollili shot a desperate look at the beeping console. "Yes."

"Good. Zebara, will you clear everyone else out for a moment?"

Puzzled, the captain complied. "But I'm staying," he announced when everyone had left.

"As you wish." Lunzie resigned herself to his presence. "Flor can't hear us, can she?"

Zebara glanced at the set of indicator lights above the thick quartz glass panel. "No."

"All right. Poll, look at me." Lunzie stared into the heavyworlder's eyes and called upon the Discipline techniques she had learned on Tau Ceti. Keeping the small hypospray out of Flor's line of sight, she showed it to Pollili. "Just something to help you relax. I promise you it's not harmful." Pollili nodded uneasily. Lunzie pressed the head of the hypospray against the big woman's forearm. Pollili sagged back, her eyes heavy and glassy. Flor stared curiously from the other side of the panel and reached for a control. Zebara forestalled her with a gesture and she sat back in her chair, watching.

Lunzie kept her voice low and gentle. "Relax. Concentrate. You are Quinada, servant and aide to Ienois of the Parchandri Merchant Families. You are landed here with a crew of twenty-five. Eight have already died of the bacterial plague, all heavyworlders. Arabesk, the Governor's personal representative, has just succumbed. Nine lightweights, the oldest and weakest ones, are also dead and the clone-types are showing at least the first symptoms of infection. You have a pernicious, deep-lung cough which strikes whenever you get excited. The bacteria is found only within thirty feet of the ground." Lunzie turned to Zebara. "That's too low for a probe to fly safely. With topographical variances, it's more likely to crash into a tree or a rock outcropping." Zebara nodded approval.

Lunzie turned back to programming Pollili. "The bacteria multiplies in direct relation to warmer temperatures. It's 22 degrees Celsius here right now. Optimum breeding time. You, Quinada, have connections with the faction in the Tau Ceti sector. You are something of a bully so you are not easily cowed by the inferior dogsbodies of any pirate vessel." Now Lunzie signalled to Flor to open the channel to the communications booth. "Remember, your name is Quinada, and you don't take guff from anyone, especially the weakling lightweights. You respect only your master, and he is one of those who is ill. You know and trust those of us here in the ship. We are your friends and business associates. When you hear your real name again, you will regain your original memories. I will touch you now and you will reply as circumstances require."

"We seek Diplomat Arabesk," the tinny voice said again. Pollili roused the instant Lunzie touched her arm. The medic leaned out of range of the video pickup and crept from her side.

"Arabesk is dead. Who is this?"

"Who speaks?" the voice demanded, surprised.

"Quinada!" Pollili said with great authority and some annoyance.

"Who is this Quinada?" Zebara asked in a low voice as Pollili's expression assumed a suitably Quinadian scowl.

"Just who I said she is," Lunzie whispered, crossing her fingers as she watched the heavyworlder female lean forward, prepared to dominate. "She works for a merchant who knew about Ambrosia more than two weeks before I left Tau Ceti for the *ARCT-10*. I must now assume that Ienois has direct lines with pirates from here, the *ARCT-10* and Alpha Centauri. Since he's got such a wide family, I'd be willing to bet someone of his kin were involved in setting up the Phoenix double-deal."

"This Quinada must have made quite an impression on you," Zebara replied wryly. "However did you impose her on Poll?"

"A Discipline technique."

"Not one of which I've ever heard. You must be an Adept. Oh, don't worry," Zebara assured her as she began to protest. "I can keep secrets. More than one, if your information on this merchant is true."

"Do I have to repeat everything to you dense-heads? I am Quinada," Pollili said, scowling and pulling her brows together in an excellent imitation of her model. "Servant to Ienois, senior Administrator in the eminent Parchandri Merchant Families. Who are you to challenge me?" There was a long pause during which the audio was cut off.

"We know of your master and we know your name," the voice announced at last, "though not your face. What are you doing on this planet?"

"My master's affairs. My last duty to him," Pollili answered crisply. "No more of that. Arabesk is dead and I speak for those still alive."

"Where is your master?"

"The lung-rotting cough took him yesterday. The puny light-weight stock from which he springs will probably see the end of him before the week is over." Pollili delivered the last with an air of disgust overlaying her evident grief. Lunzie nodded approvingly from her corner. Pollili's own psyche was adding to the pattern Lunzie had impressed on her mind. Fortunately, there weren't the same dangerous leanings in Pollili's makeup that repulsed Lunzie in the original Quinada but the telemetry officer sounded most convincing.

"Quinada" confidently answered the rapid-fire questions that the voice shot to her. To consolidate her position, "Quinada" put up on the screen the genetic detailing of the bacterium which Bringan and the others had created. She explained what she understood of it. As Pollili, she knew a good deal about bacteria but the Quinada overlay wouldn't comprehend that much bioscience.

With her headset clasped to one ear, Flor gestured frantically for Zebra to join her in the soundproof control station. "Sir, I'm receiving live transmission from the *Zaid-Dayan*. They're approaching from behind the sun after making a triple jump! Those must be some fancy new engines. They'll be here within minutes!"

"Keep them talking!" Zebara mouthed through the glass to Pollili.

The woman nodded almost imperceptibly as she ordered the bio-map off the screen.

"It may interest you to know, Citizen Quinada, that we have taken atmospheric samples and find no traces of this organism which you claim has killed five of your colleagues." The voice held a triumphant note.

"Eight," "Quinada" corrected him. "Eight are dead now. The organism hovers within ten meters of the surface. Your probe didn't penetrate far enough."

"Perhaps your entire complement is alive and well, with no cough at all. We have noticed no difference in the number of infrared traces in your group between our first conversation and now."

"Dammit," Bringan groaned. "I knew we forgot something."

"Quinada" had an answer for that. "We have placed some of the sick in cold sleep. You are picking up heat traces from the machinery." "Quinada" coughed pointedly.

"You are not fooling us," the pirate sneered. "Your ship's identification signal is being scrambled. We suspect it is EEC, not Parchandri or Diplo. We have doubts as to your identity, Quinada. Your bio-file will be in our records. If it *is* yours."

Nervous, Zebara began to drum on the door frame. The sound affected Lunzie's nerves. Tension began to knot up her insides. She forced herself to relax, to set an example of calm for the others. In the communications booth, Flor was white-faced with fear. Bringan paced restlessly in the corridor.

Under strain from her interrogator, "Quinada" started coughing. "You dare not accuse me of lying! Not if you were standing here before me. Come down, then, and die!"

"No, *you* will die. We will broil you and your make-believe organism where you lie." The voice became savagely triumphant. "We do not look kindly on those who deceive us. We claim this planet."

The team members looked at one another with dismay.

"Attention, unidentified vessel." Another voice, crisply female and human, broke up the transmission. "This is the Fleet Cruiser *Zaid-Dayan*, Captain Vorenz speaking. Under the authority of the FSP, we call upon you to surrender your vessels and prepare for boarding."

Pollili sat, eyes on the swirling pattern on the screen, without reaction. Scarran dashed for the telemetry station, the others right behind him.

"There is another blip! Phew, but the *Zaid-Dayan* is a big mother," he said.

The light indicating the FSP warship was fast closing with the planet from a sunward direction. On screen, it projected the same intensity as the transport ship but with more powerful emanations. Statistics scrolled beside each blip. The enemy must have been reading the same information on its screens, because the two pirate vessels veered suddenly, breaking orbit and heading in different directions.

Tiny sparks erupted on the edge of the pirate escort facing the FSP cruiser as the transport ship broke for the edge of the Ambrosian system.

"What's that?" asked Lunzie, indicating the flashes.

"Ordnance," Timmins said. "Escort's firing on the ZD so the lugger can escape."

Answering flickers came from the FSP ship as it increased velocity, coming within a finger's width of the pirate.

"They've got to stop the lugger from getting away!" Elessa exclaimed.

"It can't get them both," Vir chided her.

"I'd rather the ZD took out the armed ship, myself. We're not safe and home yet."

"Oh, for a Tri-D tank," Flor complained. "The coordinates say that they're miles apart but you can't get the proper perspective on this obsolete equipment."

The transport zipped off the edge of the screen in seconds. The two remaining blips crossed. For a moment they couldn't tell which was which, until Scarran reached over and touched a control.

"Now they're different colors. Red's the pirate, blue's the *Zaid-Dayan*."

Red vectored away from Blue, firing rapid laser bolts at the larger ship. The blue dot took some hits, not enough to keep it from following neatly on the tail of Red. Now it was Red's turn to be peppered with laser bolts. Then a flash of light issued from the blue dot.

"Missile!" Scarran exclaimed.

A tiny blip joined the larger two on the screen, moving very slowly toward the red light. The pirate vessel began desperate evasive maneuvers which apparently availed nothing against the mechanical intelligence guiding its nemesis. At last, Red had to turn its guns away from Blue long enough to rid itself of the chasing light dogging its movements.

The *Zaid-Dayan* sank a beautiful shot in the pirates' engine section. The red blip yawed from the blow but recovered; the pirate had as much unexpected maneuverability as weaponry. But the FSP cruiser inexorably closed the distance between them.

The speakers crackled again. "Surrender your vessel or we will be forced to destroy you," the calm female voice enjoined the pirate. "Stop now. This is our last warning."

"You will be the one destroyed," the mechanical voice from the pirate replied.

"They're heading into the atmosphere," Flor said, and indeed it seemed that the pirate was making one last throw of the dice, a desperate gamble with death.

"Turn on visual scan," Zebara ordered.

The Communications Officer illuminated another screen which showed nothing but sky. Gradually they could catch the shimmering point of light growing larger and larger in the sky to the north.

"Increase contrast." Flor complied, and the point separated into two lights, one behind the other. "Here they come."

Even at a thousand kilometers the scout team could hear the roar of the ships as they plunged through the atmosphere in controlled dives. On the screen, the two ships resembled hot white comets, arcing from the sky. Laser fire scored red sparks in the blazing white fire of each other's hulls.

"They're coming in nearly on top of us," Flor said in a shriek.

Red fire lanced out of the lead ship on the screen. Instead of pointing backward at the pursuing vessel, it blazed toward the planet's surface. There was a loud hiss and an explosion from outside the scout. Fragments of stone flew past the open hatchway. The force field protected those inside, but it would not hold for long. A smell of molten rock filled the air.

"Bloody pirates!" Zebara roared. "Evacuate ship! Now!" He lunged for the command console, ripping it from its moorings, and made for the exit.

"Well, I expected retaliation," Bringan replied, cradling something against his chest as he followed the captain. "Everybody out!"

The rest of the team didn't wait to secure anything but dove through the hatch. Lunzie was nearly to the ground before she realized Pollili still hadn't moved.

"Come on!" she yelled, urgently. "Hurry! Come on — *Pollili!*"

The woman looked around, dazed and incredulous.

"Lunzie? Where is everyone?"

"Evacuate, Poll. Evacuate!" Lunzie shouted, waving her arm. "Get out now! The pirates are firing on us."

The heavyworlder shot out of the booth like a launched missile. On her way down the ramp, she picked Lunzie up with one muscular arm about her waist and flung them both out of the hatchway. They hit the dirt and rolled down the hillside as another streak of red light destroyed a stand of trees to the left of the ship. The next bolt scored directly on the scout's engines. Lunzie was still rolling down the slope when the explosion dropped the ground a good three feet underneath her. She landed painfully on her arm brace and skidded down into the stream at the bottom of the hill, where she lay, bruised and panting. The only part of her which wasn't abraded was the forearm protected by the arm brace.

Pollili landed beside her. They flipped on their force-screens and covered their heads with their arms. The pirate escort made a screaming dive, coming within sixty feet of the surface. Its engines were covered with lines of blue lightning like St. Elmo's fire. It had sustained quite a lot of damage.

The pirate was followed by a ship so big Lunzie couldn't believe it could avoid crashing.

"The *Zaid-Dayan!*"

The two ships exchanged fire as they changed direction, headed out toward Dondara's rock flats before ascending once more into the sun. Radiant heat from their passage set fire to the trees on the edge of the plateau. The pirate and the cruiser continued to blast away even as they touched the bottom of their parabola and veered upward toward the sky. They were completely out of sight in the upper atmosphere when Lunzie and Pollili felt air sucked away from them and then heard a huge *BOOM!* A tiny fireball erupted in the middle of the sky, spreading out into a gigantic blazing cloud edged with black smoke. The explosion turned into a long rumble which altered to a loud and threatening sibilation.

"Into the water, quickly!" Lunzie gasped.

The two women were just barely under the surface when hot fragments of metal rained down around them, hissing angrily as they struck the water. The fragments were still hot when they touched the edge of their protective force-screen envelopes and passed through harmlessly.

Lunzie's lungs were beginning to ache and her vision was starting to turn black by the time the pieces stopped falling. When she finally crawled up the bank, her legs still in water, she gratefully pulled in deep breaths.

Pollili emerged next to her and flopped on her back, water streaming out of her hair and eyes. There were burns on the fabric of her tunic, and a painful-looking scorch mark on the back of one hand.

"It's over," Lunzie panted, "but who won?"

"I sure hope we did," Pollili breathed, staring up at the sky as the thrum of engines overhead grew louder.

Lunzie rolled over and dared to look up. The FSP warship, its spanking new colors scorched and carbonized and lines etched into its new hull plates by the enemy lasers, hovered majestically over the plateau where the destroyed scout had once rested, and triumphantly descended.

"We sure did." Pollili's voice rang with pride.

"That," declared Lunzie, "is the most beautiful thing I've ever seen. Singed about the edges, scorched a bit, but beautiful!"

The *Zaid-Dayan* carried the scout team to rendezvous with the *ARCT-10*. Zebara's team was lauded as heroes by the Fleet officers for holding off the pirate invasion until help could arrive. Pollili especially was decorated for "performance far beyond the line of duty."

"It should have been for sheer invention," Dondara muttered under his breath.

Pollili was uncomfortable with the praise and asked Lunzie to explain just what she had done which everyone thought was so brilliant.

"I trusted you; now tell me what you trusted me to do," Pollili complained. When Lunzie gave a brief resume, Poll frowned at her, briefly resuming her "Quinada" mode. "Then you should take some of the credit. You thought up the deception."

"Not a bit," Lunzie said. "You did it all. I did nothing but allow you to use latent ingenuity. Chalk it up to the fact that people do extraordinary things when under pressure. In fact, I'd be obliged if you glossed over my part in it to anyone else."

Pollili shook her head at first but Lunzie gave her a soulfully appealing look. "Well, all right, if that's what you wish. Zebara says I can't ask how you did it. Only at least tell me what I said that I don't remember so I can tell Dondara."

Lunzie also reassured Dondara that his mate could not snap back into her "Quinada" role. He'd missed it all since he was returning to the scout just as the ship was blown up. He had been set to wade into the molten wreckage and find some trace of Pollili. He was very proud that his mate was considered hero of the day and constantly groused that the computer record of her stellar performance had been destroyed along with the scout ship. Lunzie was relieved rather than upset and eventually gave Dondara a bowdlerized description of the events.

The other team members had suffered only bruisings and burns in their escape, treated by Fleet medical officers in the Zaid-Dayan's state-of-the-art infirmary. Bringan's hands and feet were scorched and had been wrapped in coldpacks by the medics. In his scramble from the scout ship, he had been so concerned to preserve the records he salvaged that he hadn't turned on his force-belt. He also hadn't realized that he was climbing over melting rock until the soles of his boots began to smoke. He'd had a desperate time trying to pry the boots off with his bare hands.

Zebara had a long burn down his back where a flying piece of metal from the exploding scout had plowed through his flesh. He spent his first eight days aboard the naval cruiser on his belly in an infirmary bed. Lunzie kept him company until he was allowed to get up. She called up musical programs from the well-stocked computer archives or played chess with him. Most of the time, they just talked about everything except pirates. Lunzie found that she had become very fond of the enigmatic heavyworlder.

"I won't be able to give you the protection you'll need once we're back on the ARCT-10," Zebara said one day. "I'd keep you under my protection if I could but I no longer have a ship." He grimaced. Lunzie hastened to check his bandages. The heavy-worlder captain waved her away. "I had a message from the EEC. I have number one priority to take the next available scout off the assembly line but if I break my toys, I can't expect a new one right away." He made a rude noise.

Lunzie laughed. "I wouldn't be surprised if they said just exactly that."

Zebara became serious. "I'd like to keep you on my team. The others like you. You fit in well with us. To reduce your immediate vulnerability, I'd advise that you take the next available mission *ARCT* offers. By the time you come back, I should be able to reclaim you permanently."

"I'd like that too," Lunzie admitted. "I'd have the best of all worlds, variety but with a set of permanent companions. I think I would have enjoyed myself on Ambrosia. But how do I queue-jump past other specialists waiting to get on the next mission?"

Zebara gave her his predatory grin. "They owe us a favor after our luring a pirate gunship to destruction. You'll get a berth in the next exploration available or I'll start cutting a few Administrators down to size." He pounded one massive fist into the other to emphasize his point, if not his methodology.

✧ CHAPTER FOURTEEN

Zebara was right about the level of obligation the EEC felt for the team's actions.

"Policy usually dictates non-stress duty for at least four weeks after a planetary mission, Lunzie," the Chief Missions Officer of the *ARCT-10* told her in a private meeting in his office, "but if you want to go out right away, under the circumstances, you have my blessing. You're lucky. There's a three-month mission due for a combined geological-xenobiological mission on Ireta. I'll put you on the roster for Ireta. With the medical berth filled by you, there are only two more berths to assign. It leaves in two weeks. That's not much turnaround time. . . ."

"Thank you, sir. It relieves my mind greatly," Lunzie said sincerely. She had come straight to him after that talk with Zebara. The scout captain had depressed the right toggles.

Then she had to give the Missions Officer her own report on the Ambrosia incident, with full details. He kept the recorder on through the entire interview, often jotting additional notes. She felt quite exhausted when he finally excused her.

She later learned that he had interviewed each member of the team as well as the *Zaid-Dayan* officers. Apparently the fact that the lugger with its cold sleep would-be invasion force had escaped didn't concern him half as much as he was pleased that the overgunned escort had been destroyed. Most of those *ARCT-10* ship-born felt the same way. "One less of those hyped-up gunships makes space that bit more safe for us."

The rest of Zebara's team was given interim ship assignments until a replacement explorer scout ship was commissioned. Lunzie, waiting out the two weeks before she could depart on the Iretan mission, found herself with one or more of the off-duty team, and usually Zebara himself. To her amusement, a whisper circulated that they were "an item." Neither did anything to dispel the notion. In fact, Lunzie was flattered. Zebara was attractive, intelligent, and honest: three qualities she couldn't help but admire. She was duly informed by "interested" friends that heavyworlder courting, though infrequent, was brutal and exhausting. She wasn't sure she needed to find out firsthand.

During his convalescence, Zebara strained his eyes going through ship records, trying to locate doctored files. The rumor of a bacterium on Ambrosia killing the landing party one by one had indeed made the rounds of the *ARCT-10* before any report had come back from the *Zaid-Dayan*. It was arduously traced back to Chacal, Coe's asocial friend in communications. He was taken in for questioning but died the first night in his cell. Although the official view reported it as a suicide, whisper had it that his injuries couldn't have been self-inflicted. Lunzie felt compassion for Coe, who felt himself compromised by his "friend's" covert activities.

"Which gets us no further than we were before," Bringan remarked at Lunzie's farewell party the night before she embarked on the Iretan mission.

"Somebody's got to do something positive about those fardling pirates," Pollili said, glowering about the room.

Lunzie was beginning to wish that she'd never imposed the Quinada personality on Pollili. Some of it *was* sticking. She devoutly hoped it would have worn off by the time she returned from her three months on Ireta.

At the docking bay while they were waiting for the *ARCT-10* to reach the shuttle's window down to Ireta's surface, she had a moment's anxiety as she saw six heavyworlders filing in. Stop that, she told herself. She'd got on just fine with Zebara's heavyworld crewmen. This lot could be similarly sociable, pleasant and interesting.

She concentrated hard on the activity in the docking area for there were several missions being landed in this system. A party of Theks including the ubiquitous Tor were to be set down on the seventh planet from the sun. A large group of Ryxi were awaiting transport to Arrutan's fifth planet which was to be thoroughly investigated as suitable for colonization by their species. Ireta, the fourth planet of the system's third-generation sun, was a good prospect — some said a textbook example — for transuranic ores since it appeared to have been locked into a Mesozoic age. Xeno-biological surveying would investigate the myriad life-forms sensed by the high-altitude probe, but that search was to take second place to mining assay studies.

The teams would contact one another at prearranged inter-vals, and report to the *ARCT* on a regular basis by means of a satellite beacon set in a fixed orbit perpendicular to the plane of the ecliptic. The *ARCT-10* itself discovered traces of a huge ion storm between the Arrutan system and the next one over. They intended to track and chart its course.

"We'll be back for you before you know it," the Deck Officer assured them on his comm as the Iretan shuttle lifted off and glided out of the landing bay. "Good hunting, my friends."

Ireta was named for the daughter of an FSP councillor who had been consistently supportive in voting funds to the EEC. At first it seemed that the councillor had been paid a significant compliment. Initial probe readouts suggested that Ireta had great potential. There was a hopeful feeling that if Ambrosia was lucky, Ireta would continue the streak. It possessed an oxygen/nitrogen atmosphere, indigenous plant life that ingested CO_2 and spat out oxygen: probe analysis marked significant transuranic ore depos-its and countless interesting life-forms on the part surveyed, none of which seemed to be intelligent.

A base camp was erected on a stony height and the shuttle positioned on a massive shelf of the local granite. A force-screen dome enclosed the entire camp and the veil constantly erupted in tiny blue sparks where Ireta's insect life destroyed itself in clouds on the electrical matrix. Sufficient smaller domes were set up to afford privacy, a larger one for the mess hall-lounge, while the shuttle was turned into a laboratory and specimen storage.

And then there was the extraordinary stench. The air was permeated with hydro-telluride, a fiendish odor like rotting vegetation. One source was a small plant which grew every-where, that smelled like garlic gone berserk. No one could escape it. After one good whiff when the shuttle doors had opened on their home for the next three months, everyone dove for nose filters, by no means the most comfortable appli-ance in a hot, steamy environment. Soiled work clothes were left outside the sleeping quarters. After a while, no amount of cleansing completely removed the stench of Ireta from clothes or boots.

The stink bothered Lunzie far less than the feeling that she was being covertly watched. This began on their third day dirtside when the two co-leaders, Kai on the geological side and her young acquaintance Varian as xeno, passed out assignments.

The remainder of the team was a mixed bag. Lunzie knew no one else well but several of the others by sight. Zebara had personally checked the records of everyone assigned to that mission and she'd been delighted to learn that Kai as well as Varian and a man named Triv were Disciples. She was as surprised as Kai and Varian when the three children had been included for dirtside experience on this mission. Bonnard, an active ten-year-old, was the son of the *ARCT-10*'s third officer. The gen was that she was probably glad to have him out of her hair while the *ARCT* explored the ion storm. Cleiti and Terilla, two girls a year younger than Bonnard, were more docile and proved eager to help.

Kai and Varian had both tried to set the children aside.

"That's an unexplored planet," Kai had protested to the Missions Officer. "This mission could be dangerous. It's no place for children."

Lunzie was not proof against the crushing disappointment in the young faces. There would be a force-shielded camp: there were plenty of adults to supervise their activities. "Oh, why not? Ireta's been benchmarked. No planet is ever completely safe but it shouldn't be too dangerous for a short term."

"If," Kai had emphasized that, holding up a warning finger at the children, "they act responsibly! More important of all, never go outside the camp without an adult."

"We won't!" the youngsters chorused.

"We'll count on that promise," Kai told them, adult to adult. "It isn't uncommon for children to join a mission," he said to the others. "We can use the extra hands if we're to get everything done."

"We'll help, we'll help!" the girls had chorused. "We've never been on a planet before," Bonnard had added wistfully.

The last-minute inclusion of the children was curiously comforting to Lunzie: she'd missed so much of Fiona's childhood that she looked forward to their company. Lunzie preferred making new acquaintances, for strangers wouldn't know any details of her life. The team leaders, of course, knew that she had experienced cold sleep lags, for those were on her file. Varian considered her somewhat mysterious.

Gaber was the team cartographer and endlessly complained about the primitive facilities and noxious conditions. Lunzie usually greeted these outpourings with raised eyebrows. After the scout ship on Ambrosia, their quarters, not to mention the privacy of a separate small dwelling, seemed positively elaborate. However, Lunzie was willing to tolerate Gaber because he had been able to achieve long-term (for an ephemeral) friendships with the oldest Theks on the *ARCT-10* and she would divert his complaints to the relationships which fascinated her. She assisted Kai in making certain that the cartographer remembered to wear his force-belt and other safety equipment. That much was out of pure selfishness on Lunzie's part, for Gaber had to be constantly treated for insect bites and minor lacerations.

Trizein was a xenobiologist whose infectious enthusiasm made him popular with everyone, especially the youngsters, as he would patiently answer their many questions. Trizein applied the same amazing energy to his work though he was absentminded about safety precautions. Lunzie would be assisting him from time to time and had no problem with that duty.

Dimenon and Margit were Kai's senior geologists who would locate Ireta's deposits of useful minerals. They were specifically hoping for transuranics like plutonium which paid the biggest bonuses. Ireta's preliminary scan clearly displayed large deposits of radioactivity. Dimenon's crew was eager to get to work laying detective cores. Triv and Aulia and three of the heavyworlders, Bakkun, Berru, and Tanegli, completed the geologists, while Portegin would set up the core-receiver screen and computer analysis.

Lunzie made no immediate efforts to approach the six heavyworlders. They didn't seem to mix with the lightweighters as easily as Zebara, Dondara, and Pollili. The captain had instilled his team with his own democratic, bootstrapping ideals and, while on the *ARCT-10*, they had not limited their acquaintances to heavyworlders.

Paskutti, the Security Officer, was of the sullen, chip-on-the-shoulder type who would prefer a ghetto in the midst of an otherwise tolerant society. Lunzie wasn't sure if he was just sullen or stupid, but he ruled the female Tardma's every action. Lunzie refused to let him worry her. Her time with Zebara had shown that the attitude problem was theirs, not hers. Fortunately, as time passed, Tanegli and another heavyworlder named Divisti became more sociable though they remained more distant with lightweights than Lunzie's comrades on Zebara's team had been. Bakkun and Berru were a recent pairing and it was understandable if they were much engrossed in each other.

Lunzie could not quite dismiss her lingering anxieties: Orlig's death still haunted her. Chacal, who had proved to be a spy, could never have strangled the heavyworlder. Knoradel and Birra, the Ryxi, when questioned, had both adamantly insisted that Lunzie had insulted Birra and then attacked Knoradel, who had gone to her assistance. Birra had left with the Ryxi settlers and Knoradel transferred off the *ARCT-10*.

Far from being a wonderland, Ireta's landscape became downright depressing after the novelty of it wore off. The purple-green and blue-green growth overhung the camp on every side. What looked like a flat, grassy meadow beckoning to the explorer usually turned out to be a miry swamp. The fauna was far more dangerous than any Lunzie had seen on Ambrosia or on any of the planets she had so far visited. Some of the life-forms were monstrous.

The first sled reconnaissance flights sighted large bodies crashing through the thick green jungle growth but, at first, no images were recorded, just vast shadowy forms. When at last Varian's team saw examples of Ireta's native life, they got quite a shock. The creatures were huge, ranging from a mere four meters to over thirty meters in length. One long-necked, slow-moving swamp herbivore was probably longer, but it hardly ever emerged from the marsh where it fed, so that the length of its tail was still in dispute.

Lunzie watched the xenob files with disbelief. Nothing real could be that big. It could squash a human being in passing, even a heavyworlder, and never notice. Small life there was in plenty, too. Lunzie held morning and evening surgeries to treat insect bites. The worst of them was a stinging insect which left huge welts but the most insidious was a leechlike bloodsucker. Everyone activated their personal force-screens outside the camp compound.

Instead of a second balmy paradise like Ambrosia, Ireta had more nasty surprises and anomalies than Purgatory. Stunners were issued to the geology and xeno teams although Varian made far more use of telltale taggers, marking the native life-forms with paint guns trying to amass population figures. Anyone out on foot wore his lift-belt, to remove himself quickly from scene of trouble.

Lunzie found it curious that there were so many parasites with a taste for red, iron-based blood, when the first specimens of the marine life forms which Varian or Divisti brought in to be examined proved to have a much thinner, watery fluid in their systems. To test the planet for viability, foragers were sent out for specimens of fruits and plants to test and catalog. More than curiosity prompted that for it was always wise to supplement food stocks from indigenous sources in case the EV ship didn't get back on time. In this task, the children were useful, though they were always accompanied by an adult, often Lunzie, frequently Divisti who was a horticulturist. Whenever she thought about the ion storm which the *ARCT-10* was chasing, Lunzie pressed herself to find safe sources of indigenous foodstuffs. Then she chided herself for half believing her "Jonah" reputation. That had been broken by the fortuitous outcome of the Ambrosia incident.

Because her skills did not include mapping or prospecting, Lunzie took up the duties of camp quartermaster. She spent hours experimenting with the local foods when she wasn't overseeing the children's lessons or doing her Discipline exercises. She didn't mind being the camp cook for it was her first opportunity to prepare food by hand since she had left Tee. Making tempting meals out of synth-swill and the malodorous native plants provided her with quite a challenge.

Lunzie and Trizein also combined their skills to create a nutritious green pulp from local vines that filled all the basic daily requirements. On the one hand, the pulp was an extremely healthful meal. On the other, it tasted horrible. Since she had concocted it, Lunzie bravely ate her share but after the first sampling no one else would eat it except the heavyworlders.

"They," Varian declared, "would eat anything."

Lunzie managed a chagrined smile. "My future efforts will be better, I promise. Just getting the hang of it."

"If you could just neutralize the hydro-telluride," Varian said.

"Of course, we can always eat grass like the herbivores. D'you know, it doesn't stink?"

"Humans can't digest that much grass fiber."

On one of their supervised "foragings," the children had spotted a shy, hip-high, brown-furred beast in the ferny peat bogs. All their efforts to capture one of the "cute" animals before an adult could follow the active children, were circumvented by the quadrupeds' native caution. Varian found that odd since there was no reason for the little animals to fear bipeds. Then a wounded herbivore too slow to escape with the others was captured. A pen was constructed outside the camp for Varian to tend and observe the creature. On the next trip, Varian brought back one very small specimen of a furry quadruped breed. It had been orphaned and would have fallen prey to the larger carnivores.

The two creatures proved to compound Ireta's anomalies. Trizein had been dissecting clear-ichored marine creatures, styled fringes because of their shape. The large herbivore, savagely gouged in the flank, was red-blooded. Trizein was amazed that two such diverse species would have evolved on the same planet. Trizein could find no precedents to explain red-blooded, pentadactyl animals and ichor-circulating marine creatures cohabiting. The anomaly didn't fit the genetic blueprint for the planet. He spent hours trying to reconcile the diversities. He requested tissue samples from any big creature Varian's team could catch, both carnivore and herbivore, and he wanted specimens of marine and insect life. He seemed to be constantly in the shuttle lab, except when Lunzie hauled him out to eat his meals. He'd have forgotten that minor human requirement if she'd let him.

Meanwhile, the little creature now named Dandy and the wounded female adult herbivore called Mabel had to be tended and fed: the children assumed the first chore. Lunzie had synthesized a lactose formula for the orphan and put the energetic Bonnard in charge of its feeding, with Cleiti and Terilla to assist.

"Now you kids can't neglect Dandy," Lunzie told them. "I don't mind if you treat it as a pet but once you take responsibility for it, you'd better not forget that obligation. Understand me? Especially you, Bonnard. If you're interested in becoming a planetary surveyor, you must prove to be trustworthy. All this goes down on your file, remember!"

"I will, Lunzie, I will!" And Bonnard began issuing orders to the two girls.

Varian chuckled as she watched him grooming Dandy and fussing over the security of his pen while the girls refilled its water bucket. "He's making progress, isn't he?"

"Considerable. If we could only stop him bellowing like a bosun."

"You should hear his mother," Varian replied, grinning broadly. "I don't blame her for dumping him with us. I wouldn't want him underfoot if I was charting an ion storm."

"How's your Mabel?" Lunzie asked casually although she had another motive for asking.

"Oh, I think we can release her soon. Good clean tissue around the scar once we got rid of all the parasites. I wouldn't want to keep her in a pen much longer or she'll become tame, used to being given food instead of doing her own foraging."

"Mabel? Tame?" Lunzie rolled her eyes, remembering that it had taken all the heavyworlders to rope and secure the beast for the initial surgery.

"Odd, that injury," Varian went on, frowning. "All the adults of her herd had similar bite marks on their haunches. That would suggest that their predator doesn't kill!" Her frown deepened. "And that's rather odd behavior, too."

"You didn't by any chance notice the heavyworlders' reaction?"

Varian regarded Lunzie for a long moment. "I don't think I did but then I was far too busy keeping away from Mabel's tail, legs, and teeth. Why? What did you notice?"

"They had looked . . . " — Lunzie paused, trying to find exactly the right adjective — "hungry!"

"Come on now, Lunzie!"

"I'm not kidding, Varian. They looked hungry at the sight of all that raw red meat. They weren't disgusted. They were fascinated. Tardma was all but salivating." Lunzie felt sick at the memory of the scene.

"There have always been rumors that heavyworlders eat animal flesh on their home planets," Varian said thoughtfully, giving a little squeamish shudder. "But that group have all served with FSP teams. They know the rules."

"It's not a rumor, Varian. They *do* eat animal protein on their homeworlds," Lunzie replied, recalling long serious talks she'd had with Zebara. "This is a very primitive environment, predators hunting constantly. There's something called the 'desert island syndrome.'" She sighed but made eye contact with the young leader. "And ethnic compulsions can cause the most civilized personality to revert, given the stimulus."

"Is that why you keep experimenting to improve the quality of available foodstuffs?" Lunzie nodded. "Keep up the good work, then. Last night's meal was rather savory. I'll keep an eye out for a hint of reversion."

A few days later Lunzie entered the shuttle laboratory to find Trizein combining a mass of vegetable protein with an *ARCT*-grown nut paste. She swiped her finger through the mess and licked thoughtfully.

"We're getting there, but you know, Tri, we're not real explorers yet. I'm sort of disappointed."

Trizein looked up, startled. "I think we've accomplished rather a lot in the limited time with so much to analyze and investigate. We're the first beings on this planet. How much more explorer can we be?"

Lunzie let the grin she'd been hiding show. "We're not considered true explorers until we have made a spirituous beverage from indigenous products."

Trizein blinked, totally baffled.

"Drink, Trizein. Quickal, spirits, booze, liquor, alcohol. What have you analyzed that's non-toxic with a sufficient sugar content to ferment? I think we should have a chemical relaxant. It'd do everyone good."

Trizein peered shortsightedly at her, a grin tugging at his lips. "In point of fact, I have got something. They brought it in from that foraging expedition that was attacked. I ran a sample of it. I think it's very good but I can't get anyone else to try it. We'll need a still."

"Nothing we can't build." Lunzie grinned. "I've been anticipating your cooperation, Tri, and I've got the necessary components out of stores. I rather thought you'd assist in this worthy project for the benefit of team morale."

"Morale's so important," Trizein agreed, exhibiting a droll manner which he'd little occasion to display. "I do miss wine, both for drinking and cooking. Not that anything is likely to improve the pervasive flavor of Iretan food. A little something after supper is a sure specific against insomnia."

"I didn't think anyone suffered that here," Lunzie remarked, and then they set to work to construct a simple distillation system, complete with several filters. "We'll have to remove all traces of the hydro-telluride without cooking off the alcohol."

"A pity acclimatization is taking so long," Trizein said, easing a glass pipe into a joint. "We'll probably get used to the stench the day before the *ARCT* comes for us."

They set the still up, out of the way, in a corner of Lunzie's sleeping dome. With a sense of achievement, they watched the apparatus bubble gently for a time and then left it to do its job.

"It's going to be days before there's enough for the whole team to drink," Trizein said in gentle complaint.

"I'll keep watch on it," she said, her eyes crinkling merrily, "but feel perfectly free to pop in and sample its progress."

"Oh, yes, we should periodically sample it," Trizein replied gravely. "Can't have an inferior product."

They shut the seal on Lunzie's dome just as Kai and Gaber burst excitedly into the camp.

"We've got films of the monster who's been taking bites out of the herbivores," Kai announced, waving the cassette jubilantly above his head.

The lightweights watched the footage of toothy monsters with horrified interest. Varian dubbed the carnivores "fang-faces" for the prominent fangs and rows of sharp teeth. They were terrifyingly powerful specimens, walking upright on huge haunches with a reptilian tail like a third leg that flew behind them when they ran. The much smaller forepaws might look like a humorous afterthought of genetic inadequacy but they were strong enough to hold a victim still while the animal chewed on the living prey. Fortunately the fang-faces on film were not savaging herbivores in this scene. They were greedily eating clumps of a bright green grass, tearing them up by those very useful forelimbs, stuffing them into toothy maws.

"Quite a predator," Lunzie murmured to Varian. She ought to have hauled Trizein away from his beloved electro-microscope. He needed to have the contrast of the macrocosm to round out the pathology of his biological profiles.

"Yes, but this is very uncharacteristic behavior for a carnivore," Varian remarked, watching intently. "It's teeth are suitable for a carnivorous diet. Why is it eating grass like there's no tomorrow?"

As the camera panned past the fang-face, it rested on a golden-furred flying creature, eating grass almost alongside the predator. It had a long sharp beak and wing-hands like the Ryxi but there the resemblance ended.

"We've seen avian nests but they're always near water, preferably large lakes or rivers," Gaber told Lunzie. "That creature is nearly two hundred kilometers from the nearest water. They would have to have deliberately sought out this vegetation."

"They're an interesting species, too," Kai remarked. "They were curious enough to follow our sled and they're capable of fantastic speed."

Varian let out a crow. "I want to be there when we tell that to the Ryxi! They want to be the only intelligent avians in the galaxy even if they have to deny the existence of others by main strength of will."

"Why weren't these species seen on the initial flyby of Ireta?" Divisti asked in her deep slow voice.

"With the dense jungle vegetation a super cover? Not surprising that the report only registered life-forms. Think of all the trouble we've had getting pictures with them scooting into the underbrush."

"I wish the *ARCT* wasn't out of range," Kai remarked, not for the first time. "I'd like to order a galaxy search on EV files. I keep feeling that this planet has to have been surveyed before."

Dimenon, as chief geologist, was of the same opinion. He was getting peculiar echoes from signalling cores all over the continental shield. Kai managed to disinter an old core from the site of one of the echoes. Its discovery proved to the geologists that their equipment was functioning properly but the existence of an unsuspected core also caused consternation.

"This core is not only old, it's ancient," Kai said. "Millions of years old."

"Looks just like the ones you're using," Lunzie remarked, handling the tube-shaped core.

"That's true enough, but it suggests that the planet has been surveyed before, which is why no deposits of transuranics have been found in an area that should be rich with them."

"Then why no report in the EV files?" Dimenon asked.

Kai shrugged, taking the core back from Lunzie. "This is slightly more bulky but otherwise identical."

"Could it be the Others?" Dimenon asked in a hushed voice.

Lunzie shook her head, chuckling at that old childish nightmare.

"Not unless the Others know the Theks," Kai replied. "They make all the cores we use."

"What if the Theks are copying the science of the older technology?" Dimenon argued defensively.

While it was hard to imagine anything older than Theks, Lunzie looked at Kai who knew more about them than she did.

"Then the ancient core has to mean that Ireta was previously surveyed? Only who did it? What do the Theks say?"

"I intend to ask them," Kai replied grimly.

A few days later, Varian sought Lunzie out in her dome. The young leader was shaking and very disturbed. Lunzie made her sit and gave her a mug of pepper.

"What's wrong?"

The girl took a deep sip of the restorative drink before she spoke.

"You were right," Varian said. "The heavyworlders are reverting to savagery. I had two of them out on a survey. Paskutti was flying the sled as we tracked a fang-face. It chased down one of the herbivores and gouged bites out of its flank. It made me sick, but Paskutti and Tardma exhibited a grotesque fascination at the sight. I insisted that we save the poor herbivore before it was killed. Paskutti promptly blasted the fang-face with the sled exhaust, showing his superiority like an alpha animal. He did drive it off but not before wounding it cruelly. Its hide was a mass of char."

Lunzie swallowed her disgust. As surrogate mother-confessor and psychologist for the team, she knew that a confrontation with the heavyworlders was required to discover exactly what was going on in their minds, but she didn't look forward to the experience. Right now she needed to refocus Varian on her mission, to take her mind off the horror.

"The predator just took the animal's flesh," she asked, "leaving a wound like Mabel's? That's interesting. A fang-face has a tremendous appetite. One little chunk of herbivore oughtn't to satisfy it."

"They certainly couldn't sustain themselves just by eating grass. Even though they do eat tons of it in the truce-patch."

Lunzie stroked the back of her neck thoughtfully. "That grass is more likely to provide a nutrient they're missing. We'll analyze anything you bring us."

Varian managed a laugh. "That's a request for samples?"

"Yes, indeed. Trizein is right. There are anomalies here, puzzles left from eons past. I'd like to solve the mystery before we leave Ireta."

"If we leave," Gaber said irritably later that day when Lunzie invited him to share a pot of her brew of synthesized coffee. "I don't intend ever signing up for a planetary mission again. It's my opinion that we've been planted. We're here to provide the core of a planetary population. We'll never get off."

"Nonsense," Lunzie returned sharply, ignoring his basic self-contradiction to concentrate on reducing a new rumor. "The transuranics of this planet alone are enough to supply ten star systems for a century. The FSP is far more desperate for mineral wealth than starting colonies. Now that Dimenon is prospecting beyond the continental shield, he's finding significant deposits of transuranics every day."

"Significant?" Gaber was skeptical.

"Triv is doing assays. We'll have evaluations shortly," Lunzie said in a no-nonsense tone. Gaber responded to firmness. "Add to that, look at all the equipment we have with us. The EEC can't afford to plant such expensive machinery. They need it too badly for ongoing exploration."

"They'd have to make it look like a normal drop, or we all would have opted out." Gaber could be obstinate in his whimsies.

Lunzie was exasperated by the cartographer's paranoia. "But why plant us? We're the wrong age mix and too few in number to provide any viable generations beyond grandchildren."

Gaber sat gloomily over his mug of coffee. "Perhaps they're trying to get rid of us and this was the surest way."

Lunzie was momentarily stunned into silence. Gaber had to be grousing. If there was the least byte of truth to his appalling notion, she was a prime candidate for the tactic. If eighteen people had been put in jeopardy just to remove her, she would never forgive herself. Common sense took hold. Zebara had checked the files on the entire mission personnel: she had been a late

addition to the team and, by the time she was included, it would
have been far to late for even a highly organized pirate network
to have maneuvered a planting!

"Sometimes, Gaber," she said with as light a tone as she could
manage, "you can be totally absurd! The mission planted? Highly
unlikely."

However, when Dimenon returned from the northeast edge
of the shield with his news of a major strike, Lunzie decided that
tonight was a very good occasion to break out the quickal. There
was enough to provide two decent tots for each adult to celebrate
the discovery of the saddle of pitchblende. The upthrust strike
would provide all the geologists with such assay bonuses they
might never have to work again. A percentage was customarily
shared out to other members of an exploratory team. Even the
children.

They had to be content with the riches in their majority, and
fruit juice now in their glasses. However, they were soon merry
enough, for Dimenon brought out the thumb piano he never
travelled without and played while everyone danced.

If the heavyworlders had to be summoned from their quarters
by Kai to join in, they did so with more enthusiasm than Lunzie
would have believed of the dour race. They also appeared to get
drunker on the two servings than anyone else did.

The next day they were surly and clumsy, more of a distraction
to the survey teams than a functioning part. There was physical
evidence that the alcohol had stimulated a mating frenzy. Some
of the males sported bruises, Tardma cradled one arm, and Divisti walked in a measured way that suggested to Lunzie that she
was covering a limp.

Lunzie spent hours over comparative chemical analysis and
called the heavyworlders in one at a time that evening for physical examinations, trying to determine if their mutation was
adversely affected by the native quickal. To be on the safe side,
she added one more filter to the still. Nothing else which could
be construed as harmful was left in the mixture. She took a taste
of the new distillate and made a face. It was potent, but not potent enough to account for the heavyworlder behavior.

Lunzie lay in bed late that night staring up at the top of the
dome and listening to the bubbling of the still.

If, she mused, aware that the quickal had loosened a few inhibitions, Gaber should be correct, I might be planted but I haven't lost anything. I've nothing left of my past except that hologram of Fiona in the bottom of my bag. I started my travels with that: it is proper for it to be with me now.

I wonder how Fiona is, on that remote colony of hers. What would she say if she could see me now, in an equally remote location, escaping yet another life-threatening situation, complete with fanged predators? Lunzie sighed. Why would Fiona care? She knew that when she had escaped from Ireta back to the *ARCT-10*, she'd join Zebara's team, stop running away, and have an interesting life. No big nasty pervert has dumped nineteen people on a substandard planet just to dispose of one time-lagged ex-Jonah medic.

Which brought her right back to the underlying motivation. The planet pirates. They were to blame for everything that had happened to her since her first cold sleep. They had unsettled her life time and again: first by robbing her of her daughter, trying to kill her, and making her live in fear of her life. Somehow, even if it meant turning down a place on Zebara's team, she was going to turn matters around, and start interfering with the pirates, instead of them messing up her life all the time. She'd managed to do a little along those lines already: she just had to improve her efficiency. She grinned to herself. That could be fun now that she had learned to be vigilant. The Ireta mission had a few more weeks to run.

With a sigh, she started the Discipline for putting herself to sleep. In the morning, she kept her mind busy with inventorying the supply dome. As she checked through, small discrepancies began to show up in a variety of items, including some she had had occasion to draw from only the day before. She turned over piles of dome covers, and restacked boxes, but there was no doubt about it. Force-belts, chargers, portable disk reader/writers were missing. Stock had also been moved around, partly to conceal withdrawals. Quickly, she went over the foodstuffs. None of the all-important protein stores were gone, but quantities of the mineral supplements had vanished as well as a lot of vegetable carbohydrates.

The missing items could be quite legitimate, with secondary camps being established for the geology teams. There was no reason they couldn't just help themselves. She would ask one of the leaders later on.

From the hatch of the dome, Lunzie saw Kai coming down the hill from the shuttle and met him at the veil lock. "You look tired."

"Thek contact," Kai said, feigning total exhaustion. "I wish Varian would do some of the contacts but she just hasn't the patience to talk to Theks."

"Gaber likes talking with Theks."

"Gaber wouldn't stick to the subject under discussion."

"Such as the ancient cores?"

"Right."

"What did they say?"

Kai shrugged. "I asked my questions. Now they will consider them. Eventually I'll get answers."

Varian joined them as they walked to the dome. "What word from the Theks?"

"I expect a definite yes or no my next contact. But what in the raking hells could they tell me after all this time? Even Theks don't live as long as those cores have been buried."

"Kai, I've been talking to Gaber." Lunzie took the co-leaders aside. "He's heard a rumor about planting. He swears he has kept his notion to himself, but if he has reached that conclusion on his own, you may assume that others have, too."

"You're smarter than that," Kai snapped. "We haven't been planted."

"You know how Gaber complains, Lunzie," Varian added. "It's more of his usual."

"Then there's nothing wrong in the lack of messages from the ARCT-10, is there?" Lunzie asked bluntly. "There's really been no more news from our wandering ship in several weeks. The kids especially miss word from their parents."

Kai and Varian exchanged worried glances. "There's been nothing on the beacon since they closed with the storm."

"That long?" Lunzie asked, taken aback. "They couldn't have gotten that far out of range since we were dropped off. Had the Theks heard?"

"No, but that doesn't worry me. What does is that our messages haven't been stripped from the beacon since the first week. Look, Lunzie," Kai said when she whistled at that news, "morale will deteriorate if people learn that. It would give credence to that ridiculous notion that we've been planted. I give you my word that the *ARCT-10* means to come back for us. The Ryxi intend to stay on Arrutan-5 but the Theks don't want to remain on the seventh planet forever."

"And even though the Theks wouldn't care if they were left through the next geologic age," Varian said firmly, "this is not the place I intend to spend the rest of my life."

"Nor I," was Lunzie's fervent second.

"Oh, there can't be anything really wrong," Varian went on blithely. "Perhaps the raking storm bollixed up the big receivers or something equally frustrating. Or," and now her eyes twinkled with pure mischief, "maybe the Others got them."

"Not on my first assignment as a leader," Kai said, making a valiant attempt to respond.

"By the way," Lunzie began, "since I've got the two of you at once, did you authorize some fairly hefty withdrawals from stores?"

"No," Varian and Kai chorused. "What's missing?" Kai asked.

"I did an inventory today and we're missing tools, mineral supplements, some light equipment, and a lot of oddments that were there yesterday."

"I'll ask my teams," Kai said and looked at Varian.

She was reviewing the problem. "You know, there have been a few funny things happening with supplies. The power pack in my sled was run down and I recharged it only yesterday morning. I know I haven't used up twelve hours' worth of power already."

"Well, I'll just institute a job for the girls," Lunzie said. "They can do their studies at the stores' dome and check supplies and equipment in and out. All part of their education in planetary management."

"Nice thought," Varian said, grinning.

Dimenon and his crew returned from their explorations with evidence of another notable strike. Gold nuggets glittering in a streambed had led them to a rich vein of ore. The heavy hunks were passed from hand to hand that evening at another celebration. Morale lifted as Ireta once again proved to be a virgin source of mineral wealth.

A lot of the evening was spent in good-natured speculations to the disposition of yet another hefty bonus. Lunzie dispensed copious draughts of fruit ale, keeping a careful eye on the heavy-worlders although she was careful not to stint their portions.

In the morning, everyone seemed normal. In contrast to the drunken incompetence they had displayed the last time, the heavyworlders were in excellent spirits.

A different kind of emergency faced Lunzie as she emerged from her dome.

"I can't take it! I can't take it!" Dimenon cried, clutching first his head and then falling on his knees in front of them.

"What's the matter?" she demanded, alarmed by the distortion of his features. What on Earth sort of disease had he contracted? She fumbled for her bod bird.

"That won't help," Kai said, shaking his head sadly.

"Why not?" she said, her hand closing on the bod bird.

"Nothing can cure him."

"Tell me I'm not a goner, Lunzie. Tell me." He waved his hands so wildly that she couldn't get the bod bird into position.

"He doesn't smell Ireta any more," Kai said, still shaking his head but smiling wryly at his friend's histrionics.

"He what?" Lunzie stopped trying to scope Dimenon and then realized that she hadn't had time to put in her own nose filters. And *she* didn't smell Ireta either. "Krims!" She closed her eyes and gave a long sigh. "It has come to this, huh?"

Dimenon wrapped his arms about her knees. "Oh, Lunzie, I'm so sorry for both of us. Please, my smeller will come back, won't it? Once I'm back in real air again. Oh, don't tell me I'll never be able to smell nothing in the air again. . . ."

"An Ambrosian shadow crab by another name will still get you wet," Lunzie muttered under her breath. Nothing for it but to play out the scene. She picked up Dimenon's wrist and took his pulse, shone the bod bird first in one eye, then the other. "If the acclimatization should just happen to be permanent, you could install an Iretan air-conditioner for your shipboard quarters. The ARCT-10 engineers are very solicitous about special atmospheres for the odd human mutation."

Dimenon looked as if he believed her for a long, woeful moment but the others were laughing so hard that he took it in good part.

Despite the installation of Cleiti and Terilla as requisitions clerks, the depletion of supplies did not cease. More items than those checked out by the girls continued to go missing: some were vital and irreplaceable pieces of equipment.

Coupling that with the increasingly aberrant behavior of the heavyworlders, Lunzie pegged them as the pilferers. At the rate supplies were being raided, they must be getting ready to strike off on their own. They were physically well adapted for the dangers inherent on Ireta. This wasn't, she admitted to herself, the usual way in which heavyworlders usurped a full planet. Perhaps her imagination was going wild. There were only six heavyworlders, not enough to colonize a planet.

But the Theks were still in the system, and the Ryxi. So the system was already opened up in the conventional way. The *ARCT-10* would soon be back to collect them, and if the heavyworlders wished to indulge in their baser instincts until that time, they were no real loss. There were still five qualified geologists and she, Trizein, Portegin, and the kids could help Varian complete her part of the survey.

With Bonnard as Varian's record taper and with the possible alteration of the camp in mind, Lunzie assisted Trizein in his studies of the now-obsessive anomalies of Iretan life-forms.

Today's first task was to lure Dandy into the biologist's lab so he could take measurements of its head and limbs, and samples of hair and skin from the shy little animal. The beast kicked and whistled when Trizein scraped cells from inside its furry ears. Lunzie took it back to its pen and rewarded it with a sweet vegetable. She stayed a moment calming and caressing it before returning to Trizein, who was peering into the eyepiece of a scanner. He gestured her over in excitement.

"There is something very irregular about this planet," he said. "You just compare these two slides: one from the marine fringes and the other fresh from the little herbivore." Obediently Lunzie looked and he was right; the structures represented radically differing biologies. "Judging by the eating and ingesting habits, I have no doubt that the square marine fringes are native to this planet but Dandy and his friends don't belong here.

"I have a theory about the primitive beasts we've been documenting," Trizein went on in a semi-lecturing mode. "It's been plaguing me all along that there was something familiar about the configuration."

"How can that be?" Lunzie asked, racking her brains. "I'll grant you that the Ssli are a tad like the fringes but I've never seen anything like Dandy before."

"That's because Dandy is the primitive form of an animal you're used to in its evolved state: the horse. The Earth horse. The species is not only pentadactyl, it is perissodactyl."

"That's impossible!"

"I'm afraid there's no other explanation though it doesn't explain how the creatures got here — he couldn't have evolved on this planet, but here he is."

"Someone had to have conveyed the stock here," Lunzie mused.

"Precisely," the biologist said. "If I were to ignore the context and study only the data I've been given, first by Bakkun, and now from this little fellow's living tissue, I would have to say that he is a hyracotherium, a life-form which became extinct on old Earth millions of years ago!"

The sound of the sled interrupted them. Lunzie hurried to the shield controls to admit Varian and Bonnard. She informed them that Trizein had news that he wanted to share with them. It was his triumph and he should be allowed to enjoy it by himself. The absentminded biologist was seldom outside his laboratory except to eat or to visit with Lunzie or Kai and had been largely unaware of the other facets of the team.

To the amazement of his small audience, he displayed the disk showing an archival drawing of a hyracotherium from his collection of paleontological files. There was no doubt about it: Dandy was unquestionably a replica of an ancient Earth breed from the Oligocene era.

"Let's see if there's more alike than just the furred beasts," Varian said, leading Trizein to the viewscreen. Varian promptly sat the bemused biologist down to watch her tapes of the golden fliers. Trizein launched into raptures as the graceful creatures performed their aerial acrobatics.

"No way to be certain, of course, without complete analysis, but this unquestionably resembles a pteranodon!"

"Pteranodon?" Bonnard made a face.

"Yes, a pteranodon, a form of dinosaur, misnamed, of course, since patently this creature is warmblooded. . . ." One by one, he identified the genotypes of the beasts Varian and the others had recorded. Each of the Iretan samples could be matched to a holo and description from Trizein's paleontological files. He did point to some minor evolutionary details but they were negligible alterations.

Fang-face was a Tyrannosaurus Rex; Mabel and her breed were crested hadrosaurs; the weed-eating swamp dwellers were stegosauri and brontosauri. The biologist became more and more disturbed. He could not believe that they existed just on the other side of the veil which he himself never crossed. When Varian gave him the survey tapes she'd compiled, he shook an accusatory finger at the screen.

"Those animals were planted here."

"By who?" gasped Bonnard, wide-eyed. "The Others?"

"The Theks planted them, of course," Trizein assured the boy.

"Gaber says we're planted," Bonnard added.

Trizein, in his mild way, was more saddened than disturbed by the suggestion. He looked to Varian.

"We're not planted, Trizein," the young co-leader assured him and gave Bonnard a very intense and disapproving glare.

Kai was urgently summoned back from the edge of the continental shield to hear Trizein's conclusions, leaving Bakkun alone on the ridge. Varian particularly wanted Kai separated from the heavyworlders, for by the time he returned, Trizein had given her even more disturbing news.

Paskutti had asked Trizein to test the toxicity of the fang-flesh and hide, a question which was not mere idle curiosity. Varian now had films of a startling atrocity. That day, Bonnard had led her to Bakkun's "special place." It proved to be a rough campground where five skulls and blackened bones of some of the fang-faces lay among the stones.

Lunzie knew how quickly the parasites of Ireta disposed of carrion. That meant these were very recent. There could be little doubt that the heavyworlders had killed and eaten animal flesh. The situation narrowed down to how well Kai, and Varian, could control the heavyworlders until the *ARCT-10* retrieved them.

✦ CHAPTER FIFTEEN

With a grim expression, Varian began emergency measures. She ordered Bonnard to remove all the sled power packs and hide them in the bushes around the compound. The packs had been depleted at an amazing rate and now she had the answer. Overuse by the heavyworlders. They'd have to have sledded to reach their "secret place," for the ritual slaughter and consumption of the animals.

Kai met them in the shuttle at the top of the hill, puzzled at the unusual urgent summons. He was horrified when he heard Varian's conclusions. Lunzie confirmed the continued drain of supplies which led her to believe that the heavyworlders had reverted to primitivism.

"We're lucky if it isn't mutiny," Varian finished. "Haven't you noticed in the past few days how their attitude toward us has been altering? Subtly, I admit; but they show less respect for our positions than before."

Kai nodded. "Then you think a confrontation is imminent?"

Varian affirmed it: "Our grace period ended last restday."

The heavyworlders could take over. As Lunzie drily pointed out, the mutated humans were far more able to take care of themselves on wild Ireta than the lightweight humans.

"I realize I'm repeating myself," Lunzie added, "but if Gaber felt he had been planted, the heavyworlders must have come to the same conclusion." She paused, hearing the whine of a lift-belt in the distance and listened harder. Who'd be using a lift-belt now?

"Bonnard and I also saw a Tyrannosaurus Rex with a tree-sized spear stuck in his ribs," Varian said, shuddering. "That creature once ruled Old Earth. Nothing could stop him. A heavyworlder did, for fun! Furthermore, by establishing those secondary camps, we have given them additional bases. Where are the heavyworlders right now?"

"I left Bakkun working at the ridge. Presumably when he's finished he'll come back here. He had a lift-belt. . . ."

Lunzie glanced out the shuttle door and saw the whole contingent of heavyworlders coming toward them up the hill. The drawn concentration on their heavy-boned faces was terrifying. They looked dangerous, and they harbored no good intentions for the lightweights in the ship. She shouted a warning to Kai and Varian. She saw the door to the piloting compartment iris shut almost on Paskutti's foot.

As she flattened herself against the bulkhead, she noticed the imperceptible blink that told her the main power supply had been deactivated and the shuttle was now on auxiliaries. Was it too much to hope that one of the leaders had managed to get a message out?

"If you do not open that lock instantly, we will blast," said the hard unemotional voice of Paskutti, blaster in hand.

He was fully kitted out with many items that had so recently gone missing from the stores. Of course, Lunzie told herself; she realized too late that most of that purloined equipment had offensive capability.

"Don't!" Varian's voice sounded sufficiently fearful to keep Paskutti from pulling the release but Lunzie knew the girl was no coward. It did no good for either of them to be fried alive in the compartment.

The hatch opened and massive Paskutti reached through it. He seized Varian by the front of her shipsuit and hauled her out, flinging her against the ceramic side of the shuttle with such force that it broke her arm. Grinning sadistically, Tardma treated Kai the same way.

Lunzie caught Kai and kept him upright, forcing her mind into a Discipline state to calm herself. This was far worse than she could have imagined. How could she have been so naive as to think the heavyworlders would just go quietly?

Then Terilla, Cleiti, and Gaber were unceremoniously herded into the shuttle, the cartographer babbling something about how this was not the way matters should proceed and how dared they treat him with such disrespect.

"Tanegli? Do you have them?" Paskutti asked into his wrist comm unit.

Whom would the heavyworlder botanist have? Lunzie answered her own question — the other lightweights not yet accounted for.

"None of the sleds have power packs," said Divisti, scowling in the lock. "And that boy is missing."

"How did he elude you?" Paskutti frowned in annoyance.

"Confusion. I thought he'd cling to the others." Divisti shrugged.

Good for you, Bonnard, Lunzie thought, seeking far more encouragement from that minor triumph than it really deserved.

"Start dismantling the lab, Divisti, Tardma."

Trizein came out of his confusion. "Now wait a minute. You can't go in there. I've got experiments and analyses going on. Divisti, don't touch that fractional equipment. Have you taken leave of your senses?"

"You'll take leave of yours." With a cool smile of pleasure, Tardma struck Trizein in the face with a blow that lifted the slight man off his feet and sent him rolling down the hard deck to lie motionless at Lunzie's feet.

"Too hard, Tardma," said Paskutti. "I'd thought to take him. He'd be more useful than any of the other lightweights."

Tardma shrugged. "Why bother with him anyway? Tanegli knows as much as he does." She went toward the lab with an insolent swing of her hips.

Lunzie heard the scraping of feet on the rocks and Portegin with a bloody head half carried a groggy Dimenon across the threshold. Bakkun shoved a weeping Aulia and a blank-faced Margit inside. Triv was stretched on the floor when Berru tossed him there, grinning ferociously at his gasps of pain. Inaudible to the heavyworlders, Lunzie could hear Triv begin the measured breathing which led to the trance state of Discipline. At least four of them were preparing for whatever opportunities arose.

"All right, Bakkun," Paskutti ordered, "you and Berru go after our allies. We want to make this look right. That comm unit was still warm when I got here. They must have got a message through to the Theks."

Methodically the heavyworlders continued to strip the shuttle.

Then Tanegli returned. "The storehouse had been cleared and what's useful in the domes."

"No protests, Leader Kai, Leader Varian?" sneered Paskutti.

"Protests wouldn't do us any good, would they?" Varian's level controlled voice annoyed Paskutti. He shot a look at the obviously broken arm and frowned.

"No, no protests, Leader Varian. We've had enough of you lightweights ordering us about, tolerating us because we're useful. Where would we have fit in your plantation? As beasts of burden? Muscles to be ordered here, there, and everywhere, and subdued by pap?" He made a cutting gesture with one huge hand.

Then, before anyone guessed his intention, he grabbed Terilla by the hair, letting her dangle at the end of his hand. When Cleiti jumped up at her friend's terrified shriek and began to pummel his thick muscular thigh, he raised his fist and landed a casual blow on the top of her head. She sank unconscious to the deck.

Gaber erupted and dashed at Paskutti who merely put a hand out to hold the cartographer off while he dangled the shrieking child.

"Tell me, Leader Varian, Leader Kai, to whom did you send that message? And what did you say?"

"We sent a message to the Theks. Mutiny. Heavyworlders." Kai watched as Terilla was swung, her screams diminishing to mere gasps. "That's all."

"Release the child," Gaber shouted. "You'll kill her. You know what you need to know. You promised there'd be no violence."

Paskutti viciously swatted Gaber into silence. His neck smashed into pulp, Gaber hit the deck with a terrible thud and gasped out his dying breaths as Terilla was dropped in a heap on top of Cleiti.

Horrified, Lunzie forced herself to think. Paskutti had to know if a message had been beamed to the beacon. How would that information alter his plans for them? Triv had now completed the preliminaries of Discipline. Lunzie wished for a smidgen of telepathy so that the four of them could coordinate their efforts.

"There isn't a power pack anywhere," Tanegli said, storming into the shuttle. He seized hold of Varian by her broken arm. "Where did you hide them, you tight-assed bitch?"

"Watch it, Tanegli," Paskutti warned him, "these lightweights can't take much."

"Where, Varian? Where?" Tanegli emphasized each syllable with a twist of her arm.

"I didn't hide them. Bonnard did." Tanegli threw Varian's suddenly limp body to the deck.

"Go find him, Tanegli. And the packs, or we'll be humping everything out of here on our backs. Bakkun and Berru have started the drive. Nothing can stop it once it starts."

Lunzie wondered what he meant and whether she dared to go over to Varian and examine her. The heavyworlder leader snarled at Kai.

"Get out of here. All of you. March." Paskutti kicked Triv and Portegin to their feet, gesturing curtly for them to pick up the unconscious Gaber and Trizein, for Aulia and Margit to lift the girls. Lunzie bent to Varian, managing to feel the strong steady pulse and knew the girl was dissembling. "Into the main dome, all of you," he ordered.

The camp was a shambles of wanton destruction from Dandy's broken body to scattered tapes, charts, records, clothing. The search for Bonnard continued, punctuated by curses from Tanegli, Divisti, and Tardma. Paskutti kept glancing from his wrist chrono and then to the plains beyond the force-screen.

With Discipline-heightened senses, Lunzie caught the distant thunder. She spotted the two dots in the sky: Bakkun and Berru, and the black line beneath, a tossing black line, a moving black line, and suddenly with a sinking heart, she knew what the heavyworlders had planned.

The Theks might get the message but they wouldn't reach here in time to save them from a fast approaching stampede. Paskutti was shoving them into the main dome now but he caught Lunzie's glance.

"Ah, I see you understand your fitting end, medic. Trampled by creatures, stupid, foolish vegetarians like yourselves. The only one of you strong enough to stand up to us is a mere boy."

He closed the iris lock and the thud of his fist against the plaswall told them that he had shattered the controls. Lunzie was already checking Trizein over, briefly wondering if "your fitting end, medic" meant this whole hideous mess had been arranged to destroy her.

"He's at the veil," Varian said, peering over the bottom of the far window, her arm dangling at her side.

Trizein groaned, regaining consciousness. Lunzie moved on to Cleiti and Terilla and administered restorative sprays.

"He's opened it," Varian reported. "We ought to have a few moments when the herd tops the last rise when they won't be able to see anything for the dust."

"Triv!" Kai and the geologist jammed Discipline-taut fingers into the fine seam of the plastic skin and ripped the tough fabric apart.

Lunzie got the two girls to their feet. Gaber was dead. She gave the near hysterical Aulia another jolt of spray.

"There are four on lift-belts in the sky now," Varian kept reporting. "The stampede has reached the narrow part of the approach. Get ready."

"Where can we go?" Aulia shrieked. The thunderous approach was making them all nervous.

"Back to the shuttle, stupid," Margit said.

"NOW!" Varian cried.

Stumbling, half crawling, they hurried up the hill. Trizein couldn't walk so Triv slung him over his shoulders. One look at the bobbing heads of crested dinosaurs bearing down on them was sufficient to lend wings to anyone.

The shuttle hatch slammed behind the last human as the forerunners flowed into the compound. The noise and vibration was so overwhelming not even the shuttle's sturdy walls could keep it out. The craft was rattled and banged about in the chaos, death, and destruction outside.

"They outdid themselves with the stampede," Varian said with an absurd chuckle.

"It'll take more than herbivores to dent shuttle ceramic. Don't worry. But I would sit down," Kai added.

"As soon as the stampede has stopped, we'd better make our move," a voice piped up from behind the last row of seats.

"Bonnard!"

Grinning broadly, the dusty, stained boy appeared from the shuttle's lab. "I thought this was the safest place after I saw Paskutti moving you out. But I wasn't sure who had come back in. Am I glad it's you!"

"They'll never find those power packs, Varian. Never," Bonnard said, almost shouting above the noise outside. "When Paskutti smashed the dome controls I didn't see how I could get out in time. So . . . I . . . hid!"

"You did exactly as you should, Bonnard. Even to hiding." Varian reassured him with a firm hug.

Another shift of the shuttle sent everyone rocking.

"It's going to fall," Aulia cried.

"But it won't crack," Kai promised. "We'll survive. By all the things that men hold dear, we'll survive!"

When the stampede finally ended, it took the combined strength of all the men to open the door. The carnage was fearful. They were buried under trampled hadrosaurs. It was full night now. Under the cover of darkness, Bonnard and Kai slipped out and, using lift-belts, managed to bring the power packs back to the shuttle.

"Bonnard was right. We've got to make a move," Kai told them as the survivors huddled together, still shaken and shocked by their ordeal. "Come dawn, the heavyworlders will return to survey their handiwork. They'll assume the shuttle is still here, buried under the stampede. They won't be in any hurry to get to it. Where could it go?"

"I know where," Varian said.

"That cave we found, near the golden fliers?" Bonnard asked, his tired face lighting.

"It's more than big enough to accommodate the shuttle. And dry, with a screen of falling vines to hide the opening."

"Great idea, Varian," Kai agreed, "because even if they used the infrared scan, our heat would register the same as adult giffs."

"And that's the best idea I've heard today," Lunzie said briskly, handing around peppers which had been overlooked by the heavyworlders in the piloting compartment.

It required a lot of skill to ease the shuttle out from under the mountain of flesh but Lunzie knew it had to be done now while Kai and Varian held on to their Disciplined strength. The two managed, with Bonnard assisting in the directions since he'd been outside.

By dawn they had reached the inland sea and maneuvered into the enormous cave, every bit as commodious as Varian and Bonnard had said. Not one of the golden fliers paid attention to the strange white craft that had invaded their area.

"The heavyworlders don't even know this place exists," Varian assured them when they were safely concealed.

Triv and Dimenon used enough of the abundant drooping foliage to synthesize padding to comfort the wounded on the bare plastic deck. Lunzie sent them out again to get enough raw materials to synthesize a hypersaturated tonic to reduce the effects of delayed shock. Then everyone was allowed to sleep.

Lunzie was one of the first awake late the next day. Moving quietly so as not to disturb the exhausted survivors, she cooked up another nutritious broth in the synthesizer, loading it with vitamins and minerals.

"Guaranteed to circulate blood through your abused muscles and restore tissue to normal," she said serving up steaming beakers to Kai and Triv who had awakened. "We've slept around the chrono and half again."

After checking the binding on Kai's arm, she massaged his shoulders to work out some of the stiffness before she ministered in the same way to Triv.

"Thanks. How long before the others rouse?" asked Triv, gratefully working his upper arms in eased circles.

"I'd say we have another clear hour or so before the dead arise," Lunzie answered, holding a beaker of soup to Varian. "I'll need more greenery to fix breakfast for the rest of them."

They filled the synthesizer with vegetation from the hanging vines that curtained the cave's mouth. Weak sunlight, as bright as Ireta ever saw, shone in on the shuttle's tail through the tough creepers. By the time the others awoke, there was food.

"It's not very interesting, but it's nutritious," Lunzie said as she handed around flat brown cakes. "I'd do more with the synthesizer, but how long can we depend upon having the power last? And the heavyworlders might detect its use."

Varian set the children to keep a lookout at the cave opening, warning them not to hang beyond the vines. Bonnard thought that was wasted effort.

"They're not going to look for people they think they've already killed."

"We underestimated them once, Bonnard," Kai remarked. "Let's not make the same mistake twice." Duly thoughtful, the boy took a lookout post.

A very long week went by while the survivors recovered from shock and injury.

"How long do we have to wait for the Theks to come and save

us?" Varian asked the three Disciples when all the others had gone to sleep. "They would have had your message within two hours after you sent it. 'Mutiny' ought to stir their triangles if 'heavyworlder' didn't."

Kai upturned his hands, wincing at the stab of pain in his broken wrist. "The Theks don't rush under any circumstances, I guess. I had hoped they might just this once."

"So, what do we do?" Triv asked. "We can't stay here forever. Or avoid the heavyworlders' search once they realize the shuttle's gone. I know Ireta's a big planet but it's only this part on the equator that's barely habitable. Even if we stay here, we've got to use energy to produce food. We could get caught either way. They've got all the tracers and telltaggers. They have everything, even the stun-guns. What do we do?"

Every instinct in Lunzie shouted "NO" at the obvious answer but she voiced it herself. "There is always cold sleep." Even to herself she sounded defeated.

"That's the sensible last resort," Triv agreed. Lunzie wanted to argue the point but she clamped her lips firmly shut while Kai and Varian nodded solemnly.

"EV is coming back for us, isn't she?" Triv asked with an expressionless face.

Kai and Varian assured him that the *ARCT-10* would not abandon them. The richness of their surveys was on the message beacon to be stripped when the *ARCT* had finished following that storm. The beacon Portegin had rigged outside the cave, camouflaged as a dead branch, would guide the search and rescue team to them.

"With the sort of ion interference a big storm can produce, it's no wonder they haven't been able to make contact with us," Varian said staunchly but none of the others looked as though they quite believed her.

Lunzie kept trying not to think of the word "Jonah."

"Good, then we'll go cold sleep tomorrow once the others have been told," Kai decided briskly.

"Why tell them?" Lunzie asked. She would rather get the whole process over with before she lost her courage.

"They're halfway into cold sleep right now." Varian gestured to the sleeping bodies, startling Kai. "And we'll save ourselves some futile arguments."

"It's a full week now and at the rate carrion eaters work on Ireta, the heavyworlders may have discovered the shuttle is missing," Triv said ominously.

"There's no way the heavyworlders could find a trace of us in cold sleep. And there's a real danger if we remain awake much longer," Varian added.

With the other Disciples in agreement with a course she herself recommended, Lunzie rose slowly to her feet. Unwilling as she was, she went to the cold-sleep locker and tapped in the code that would open it. She really hated to go into cold sleep again. She had wasted so much of her life living in that state. It was almost as bad as death. In a sense, it was a death — of all that was current and pleasant and hopeful in this segment of her life.

But she gathered up the drug and the spraygun, checked dosages and began to administer the medication to those already asleep. Triv, Kai, and Varian moved among them, checking their descent into cold sleep as skins cooled and respirations slowed to the imperceptible.

"You know," Varian began in a hushed but startled tone as she was settling herself, "poor old Gaber was right. We are planted. At least temporarily!"

Lunzie stared at her, then made a grimace. "That's not the comfort I want to take with me into cold sleep."

"Does one dream in cryogenic sleep, Lunzie?" Varian asked as Lunzie handed her a cup of the preservative drug.

"I never have."

Lunzie gave Kai his dose. The young leader smiled as he accepted it.

"Seems a waste of time not to do something," he said.

"The whole concept of cold sleep is to suspend the sense of subjective time," Lunzie pointed out.

"You sleep, you wake. And centuries pass," added Triv, taking his beakerful.

"You're less help than Varian is," Lunzie grumbled.

"It won't be centuries," Kai said emphatically. "Not once EV has those uranium assays. It's too raking rich for them to ignore."

Lunzie arranged the cold-sleep gas tank controls to kick in as soon as its sensors registered the cessation of all life signs. She held her dose in her hand. She wouldn't risk them all if she stayed awake. Her body heat would register as a gift to any heavyworld overflight of the area. She could stay awake.

But if she slept with these, she would, for once, have someone she knew, people she liked and had worked with. She wouldn't be quite so alone when she woke. That was some consolation. Before she could talk herself into some drastic and fatal delay, she tossed the dose down and lay down along one side of the deck, pillowing her head on a pad and settling her arms by her side.

Who knows when they'll come for us, she thought, unable to censor dismal thoughts. She grabbed at another consolation: the heavyworlders didn't get her, or the others. She'd wake again. And there'd be another settlement due her.

The leaden heaviness began to spread out from her stomach, permeating her tissues. The air on her cooling skin felt uncomfortably hot, and grew hotter. Suddenly Lunzie wanted to get up, run away from this place before she was trapped inside herself again. But it was already too late to stop the process. She felt her consciousness sinking fast into another death of sleep. Muhlah!

Book II

SASSINAK

PART ONE

✧ CHAPTER ONE

By the time anyone noticed that the carrier was overdue, no one cared. Celebrations had started two local days before, when the last crawler train came in from Zeebin. Sassinak, along with the rest of her middle school, had met that train, helped offload the canisters of personal-grade cargo, and then wandered through the crowded streets.

Last year she'd been too young — barely — for such freedom. Even now, she flinched a little from the noise and confusion. The City tripled in population for the week or so of celebration when the ore carriers came in. Every farmer, miner, crawler-train tech, or engineer — everyone who possibly could, and some who shouldn't have — came to The City. It almost seemed to deserve the name, with crowds bustling between the rows of one-story prefab buildings that served the young colony as housing, storage, and manufacturing space. Sassinak could pretend she was on the outskirts of a *real* city, and the taller dome and blockhouse of the original settlement, could, with imagination, stand for the great soaring buildings she hoped one day to visit, on the worlds she'd heard about in school.

She caught sight of a school patch ahead of her, and recognized Caris' new (and slightly ridiculous) hairdo. Shoving between two meandering miners, who seemed disposed to slow down at every doorway, Sassinak grabbed her friend's elbow. Caris whirled.

"Don't you —! Oh, Sass, you idiot. I thought you were —"

"A drunken miner. Sure." Arm in arm with Caris, Sassinak felt safer — and slightly more adult. She gave Caris a sidelong look, and Caris smirked back. They broke into a hip-swaying parody of the lead holovid's "Carin Coldae — Adventurer Extraordinary" and sang a snatch of the theme song. Someone hooted, behind them, and they broke into a run. Across the street, a familiar voice yelled, "There go the skeleton twins," and they ran faster.

"Sinder," Caris said a block or so later, when they'd slowed down, "is a planetary snarp."

"Planetary nothing. Stellar snarp." Sassinak glowered at her friend. They were both long and lanky, and they'd heard as much of Sinder's skeleton twin joke as anyone could rightly stand.

"Interstellar." Caris always had to have the last word, Sassinak thought. It might not be right, but it was last.

"We're not going to think about Sinder." Sassinak wormed her fingers through the tangle of things in her jacket pocket and pulled out her credit ring. "We've got money to spend. . . ."

"And you're my friend!" Caris laughed and shoved her gently toward the nearest food booth.

By the next day, the streets were too rowdy for youngsters, Sassinak's parents insisted. She tried to argue that she was no longer a youngster, but got nowhere. She was sure it had something to do with her mother's need for a babysitter, and the adult-only party in the block recreation center. Caris came over, which made it slightly better. Caris got along better with six-year-old Lunzie than Sass did, and that meant Sass could read stories to "the baby": Januk, now just over three. If Januk hadn't managed to spill three months' worth of sugar ration while they were trying to make cookies from scratch, it might have been a fairly good day after all. Caris scooped most of the sugar back into the canister, but Sass was afraid her mother would notice the brown specks in it.

"It's just spice," Caris said firmly.

"Yes, but —" Sassinak wrinkled her nose. "What's that? Oh . . . dear." The cookies were not quite burnt, but she was sure they wouldn't make up for the spilled sugar. No hope that Lunzie wouldn't mention it, either — she was at that age, Sass thought, when having finally figured out the difference between telling a story and telling the truth, she wanted to let everyone know. Lunzie prefaced most talebearing with a loud "I'm telling the truth, now: I really am" which Sass found unbearable. It didn't help to be told that she herself had once, at about age five, scolded the Block Coordinator for using a polite euphemism at the table. "The right word is 'castrated,'" was what everyone said she'd said.

Sass didn't believe it. She would never, in her entire life, no matter how early, have said something like that right out loud at the table. Now she cleaned up the cookcorner, saving what grains of sugar looked fairly clean, and wondered when she could insist that Lunzie and Januk go to bed.

"Eight days." The captain grinned at the pilot. "Eight days should be enough. For most of it anyway. Aren't we lucky that the carrier's late." They both laughed; it was an old joke for them, and a mystery for everyone else, how they could turn up handily when other ships were "late."

"We don't want to leave witnesses."

"No. But we may want to leave evidence . . . of a sort." The captain grinned, and the pilot nodded. Evidence implicating someone else. "Now — if those fools down there aren't drunk out of their wits, anticipating the carrier's arrival, I'm a shifter. We should be able to fake the contact, unless they speak some outlandish gabble. Let's see . . ." He scrolled through the directory information and shook his head. "No problem. Neo-Gaesh, and that's Orlen's birthtongue."

"He's from here?"

"No, the colonists here are from Innish-Ire, and Orlen's from Innish Outer Station. Same difference; same language and dialect. New colony — they won't have diverged that much."

"But the kids — they'll speak Standard?"

"FSP rules: they have to, by age eight. All colonies provided with tapes and cubes for the crèches. We shouldn't have any problem."

Orlen, summoned to the bridge, muttered a string of things the captain hoped was Neo-Gaesh, and opened the communications with the planet's main spaceport. For all the captain could tell, the mishmash of syllables coming back was exactly the same, only longer. Hardly a language at all, he thought, smug in his own heritage of properly crisp and tonal Chinese. He spoke Standard as well, and two other related tongues.

"They say they can't match our ID to the files," Orlen said, this time in Standard, interrupting that chain of thought.

"Tell 'em they're drunk and incompetent," said the captain.

"I did. I told them they had the wrong cube in the lock, an out-of-date directory entry, and no more intelligence than a cabbage, and they've gone to try again. But they won't turn on the grid until we match."

The pilot cleared his throat, not quite an interruption, and the captain looked at him. "We could jam our code into their computer. . . ." he offered.

"Not here. Colony's too new; they've got the internal checks. No, we're going down, but keep talking, Orlen. If we can hold them off just a bit too long, we won't have to worry about their serious defenses. Such as they are."

In the assault capsules, the troops waited. Motley armor, stolen from a dozen different captured ships and minor bases, mixed weaponry of all manufactures, they lacked only the romance once associated with the concept of pirate. These were muggers, gangsters, two steps down from mercenaries and well aware of the price of failure. The Federation of Sentient Planets would not torture, rarely executed . . . but the thought of being whited, mindcleaned, and turned into obedient and useful workers . . . that was torture enough. So they had discipline, of a sort, and loyalty, of a sort, and were obedient, within limits to those who ruled the ship or hired it. On some worlds they passed as Free Trader's Guards.

Orlen's accusations had not been far wrong. When the last crawler train came in, everyone relaxed until the ore carriers arrived. The Spaceport Senior Technician was supposed to stay alert, on watch, but with the new outer beacon to signal and take care of first contact, why bother? It had been a long, long year, 460 days, and what harm in a little nip of something to warm the heart? One nip led to another. When the inner beacon, unanswered, tripped the relays that set every light in the control rooms blinking in disorienting random patterns, his first thought was that he'd simply missed the outer beacon signal. He'd finally found the combination of control buttons that turned the lights on steady, and shushed the excited (and none too sober) little crowd that had come in to see what happened. And having a friendly voice speaking Neo-Gaesh on the other end of the comm link only added to the confusion. He'd tried to say he could speak Standard well enough (not sure if he'd been too drunk to answer a hail in Standard earlier), but it came out tangled. And so on, and so on, and it was only stubbornness that kept him from turning on the grid when the ship's ID scan didn't match the record books. Damned sobersides spacemen, out there in the stars with nothing to do but sneak up on honest men trying to have a little fun — why should he do them a favor? Let 'em match their own ship up, or come in without the grid beacons on, if that's the game they wanted to play. He put the computer on a search loop, and took another little nip.

The computer's override warning buzz woke him again. The ship was much closer, just over the horizon, low, coming in on a landing pattern . . . and it was red-flagged. Pirate! he thought muzzily. It's a pirate. It can't be . . . but the computer, not fooled, and not having been stopped by the override sequence he was too drunk to key in, turned on full alarms, all over the building and the city. And the speech synthesizer, in a warm, friendly, calm female voice, said, "Attention. Attention. Vessel approaching has been identified as dangerous. Attention. Attention . . ."

But by then it was far too late.

Sassinak and Caris had eaten the last of the overbrowned cookies, and were well into the kind of long-after-midnight conversation they preferred. Lunzie grunted and tossed on her pallet; Januk sprawled bonelessly on his, looking, as Caris said, like something tossed up from the sea. "Little kids aren't human," said Sass, winding a strand of dark hair around her finger. "They're all alien, shapechangers like those Wefts you read about, and then turn human at —" She thought for a moment. "Eleven or so."

"Eleven! You were eleven last year; I was. I was human. . . ."

"Ha." Sass grinned, and watched Caris. "I wasn't human. I was special. Different —"

"You've always been different." Caris rolled away from Sass' slap. "Don't hit me; you know it. You like it. You would be alien if you could."

"I would be off this planet if I could," said Sass, serious for a moment. "Eight more years before I can even apply — aggh!"

"To do what?"

"Anything. No, not anything. Something —" Her hands waved, describing arcs and whorls of excitement, adventure, marvels in the vast and mysterious distance of time and space.

"Umm. I'll take biotech training and a lifetime spent figuring out how to insert genes for correctly handed proteins in our native fishlife." Caris wrinkled her nose. "You're not going to leave, Sass. This is the frontier. This is where the excitement is. Right here."

"Eating *fish*? Eating life-forms?"

Caris shrugged. "I'm not devout. Those fins in the ocean aren't sentient, we know that much, and they could give us cheap, easy protein. Personally, I'm tired of gruel and beans, and since we have to fiddle with their genes, too, why not fishlife?"

Sassinak gave her a long look. True, lots of the frontier settlers weren't devout, and didn't find anything but a burdensome rule in the FSP strictures about eating meat. But she herself — she shivered a little, thinking of a finny wriggling in her throat. Something wailed in the distance, and she shivered again. Then the houselights brightened and dimmed abruptly.

"Storm?" asked Caris. The lights blinked, now quickly, now slow. From the terminal in the other room came an odd sort of voice, something Sass had never heard before.

"Attention. Attention . . ."

The girls stared at each other, shocked for an endless instant into complete stillness. Then Caris leaped for the door, and Sass caught her arm.

"Wait — help me get Lunzie and Januk!"

The younger children were hard to wake, and cranky once roused. Januk demanded "my *big* jar" and Lunzie couldn't find her shoes. Sass, mind racing, dared to use the combination her father had once shown her, and opened her parents' sealed closet.

"What are you *doing*?" asked Caris, now by the door again with the other two. Her eyes widened as Sass pulled down the zipped cases: the military-issue projectile weapons issued to each adult colonist, and the lumpy, awkward part of a larger weapon which should — if they had time — mate with those from adjoining apartments to make something more effective.

Lunzie could just carry one of the long, narrow cases; Sass had to use both arms on the big one, and Caris took the other narrow one, along with Januk's hand. "We should stop at my place," Caris said, but when they got outside, they could see the red and blue lines crossing the sky. A white flare, at a distance. "That was the Spaceport offices," said Caris, still calm.

Other shapes moved in the darkness, converging on the Block

Recreation Center; Sass recognized two classmates, both carrying weapons, and one trailing a string of smaller children. They made it to the Block Recreation Center just as adults came boiling out, most unsteady on their feet, and all cursing.

"Sassinak! Bless you — you remembered!" Her father, suddenly looking larger and more dangerous than she had thought for the last year or so, grabbed Lunzie's load and stripped off the green cover. Sass had seen such weapons in class videos; now she watched him strip and load it, hardly aware that her mother had taken the weapon Caris carried. Someone she didn't know yelled for a "PC-8 *base*, dammit!" and Sass' father said, without even looking at her, "Go, Sassy! That's your load!" She carried it across the huge single room of the Center to the cluster of adults assembling some larger weapons, and they snatched it, stripped off the cover, set it down near the door, and began attaching other pieces. An older woman grabbed her arm and demanded, "Class?"

"Six."

"You've had aid class?" When Sass nodded, the woman said, "Good — then get over here." *Here* was on the far side of the Center, out of sight of her family, but with a crowd of middle school children, all busily laying out an infirmary area, just like in the teaching tapes.

The Center stank of whiskey fumes, of smoke, of too many bodies, of fear. Children's shrill voices rose above the adults' talking; babies wailed or shrieked. Sass wondered if the ship was down, that pirate ship. How many pirates would there be? What kind of weapons would they have? What did pirates want, and what did they do? Maybe — for an instant she almost believed this thought — maybe it was just a drill, more realistic than the quarterly drills she had grown up with, but not real. Perhaps a Fleet ship had chosen to frighten them, just to encourage more frequent practice with the weapons, and the first thing they'd see was a Fleet officer.

She felt more than heard the first concussive explosion, and that hope died. Whoever was out there was hostile. Everything the tapes had said or she'd overheard the adults say about pirates ran through her mind. Colonies disappeared, on some worlds, or survived gutted of needed equipment and supplies, with half their population gone to slavers. Ships taken even during FTL travel, when according to theory no one could say where they were.

Waiting there, unarmed, she realized that the thrice-weekly class in self-defense was going to do her no good at all. If the pirates had bigger guns, if they had weapons better than projectiles, she was going to die . . . or be captured.

"Sass." Caris touched her arm; she reached out and gave Caris a quick hug. Around her, the others of her class had gathered in a tight knot. Even in this, Sassinak recognized the familiar. Since she'd started school, the others had looked to her in a crisis. When Berry fell off the crawler train, when Seh Garvis went crazy and attacked the class with an orecutter, everyone expected Sass to know what to do, and do it. Bossy, her mother had called her, more than once, and her father had agreed, but added that bossy plus tact could be very useful indeed. *Tact*, she thought. But what could she say now?

"Who's our triage?" she asked Sinder. He stood back, well away from Sass' friends.

"Gath." He pointed to a youth who had been cleared for off-planet training — medical school, everyone expected. He'd been Senior school medic all four years. "I'm low-code this time."

Sass nodded, gave him a smile he returned uneasily, and checked again on each person's assignment. If they had nothing to do now, they could be sure they knew what to do when things happened.

All at once a voice blared outside — a loudhailer, Sass realized, with the speakers distorting the Neo-Gaesh vowels. From this corner of the building, she could pick out only parts of it, but enough to finish off the last bit of her confidence.

" . . . surrender . . . will blow . . . resistance . . . guns . . ."

The adults responded with a growl of defiance that covered the loudhailer's next statements. But Sass could hear something else, a clattering that sounded much like a crawler train, only different somehow. Then a hole appeared in the wall opposite her, as if someone had drawn it on paper and then ripped the center from the circle. She had never known that walls could be so fragile; she had felt so much safer inside. And now she realized that all together inside this building was the very last place anyone should be. Her shoulders felt hot, as if she'd stood in the summer sunlight too long, and she whirled to see the same kind of mark appearing on the wall behind her.

Later, when she had the training to analyze such situations, she knew that everything would have happened in seconds: from the breaching of the wall to the futile resistance of the adults, pitting third-rate projectile weapons against the pirates' stolen armament and much greater skill, to the final capture of the survivors, groggy from the gas grenades the pirates tossed in the building. But at the time, her mind seemed to race faster than time itself, so that she saw, as in a dream, her father swing his weapon to face the armored assault pod that burst through the wall itself. She saw a line of light touch his arm, and his weapon fell with the severed limb. Her mother caught him as he staggered, and they both charged. So did others. A swarm of adults tried to overwhelm the pod with sheer numbers, even as they died, but not before Sass saw what had halted it: her parents had thrown themselves into the tracks to jam them.

And it was not enough. If all the colonists had been there, maybe. But another assault pod followed the first, and another. Sass, screaming like the rest, charged at it, expecting every instant to be killed. Instead, the pods split open, and the troops rolled out, safe in their body armor from the blows and kicks the children could deliver. Then they tossed the gas grenades, and Sass could not breathe. Choking, she slid to the floor along with the rest.

She woke to a worse nightmare. Daylight, dusty and cold, came through the hole in the wall. She was nauseated and her head ached. When she tried to roll over and retch, something choked her, tightening around her throat. A thin collar around her neck, attached to another on either side by a thin cord of what looked like plastic. Sass gagged, terrified. Someone's boot appeared before her face, and bumped her, hard.

"Quit that."

Sassinak held utterly still. That voice had no softness in it, nothing but contempt, and she knew, without even looking up, what she would see. Around her others stirred; she tried to see, without moving, who they were. Crumpled bodies, all sizes; some moved and some didn't. She heard boots clump on the floor, coming closer, and tried not to shiver.

"Ready?" asked someone.

"These're awake," said someone else. She thought that was the same voice that had told her to quit moving.

"Get'm up, clear this out, and start loading." One set of boots clumped off, the other reappeared in her vision, and a sharp nudge in the ribs made her gasp.

"You eight: get up." Sass tried to move, but found herself stiff and clumsy, and far more impeded by a collar and line than she would have thought. This sort of thing never bothered Carin Coldae, who had once captured a pirate ship by herself. The others in her eight had as much trouble; they staggered into each other, jerking each others' collars helplessly. The pirate, now that she was standing and could see clearly, simply stood there, face invisible behind the body armor's faceplate. She had no idea how big he really was — or even if it might be a woman.

Her gaze wandered. Across the Center, another link of eight struggled up; she saw another already moving under a pirate's direction. A thump in the ribs brought her head around.

"Pay attention! The eight of you are a link; your number is 15. If anyone gives an order for link 15, that's you, and you'd better be sharp about it. You —" the hard black nose of some weapon Sass couldn't name prodded her ribs, already sore. "You're the link leader. Your link gets into trouble, it's your fault. You get punished. Understand?"

Sass nodded. The weapon prodded harder. "You say 'Yessir' when you're asked something!"

She wanted to scream defiance, as Carin Coldae would have done, but heard herself saying "yessir" — in Standard, no less — instead.

Down the line, the boy on the end said, "I'm thirsty." The weapon swung toward him, as the pirate said, "You're a slave now. You're not thirsty until *I* say you're thirsty." Then the pirate swung the weapon back at Sass, a blow she didn't realize was coming until it staggered her. "Your link's disobedient, 15. Your fault." He waited until she caught her breath, then went on with his instructions. Sass heard the smack of a blow, and a wail of pain, across the building, but didn't look around. "You carry the dead out. Pile 'em on the crawler train outside. You work fast enough, hard enough, you might get water later."

They worked fast enough and hard enough, Sass thought later. Her link of eight were all middle-school age, and they all knew her although only one of them was in her class. It was clear that they didn't want to get her into trouble. With her side making every breath painful, she didn't want trouble right then either. But dragging the dead bodies out, over the blood and mess on the floor . . . people she had known, but could recognize now only by the yellow skirt that Cefa always wore, the bronze medallion on Torry's wrist . . . that was worse than anything she'd imagined. Four or five links, by then, were working on the same thing. Later she realized that the pirates had killed the wounded: later yet she would learn that the same thing had happened all over The City, at other Centers.

When the building was clear of dead, her link and two others were loaded on the crawler train as well; pirates drove it, and sat on the piled corpses — as if they'd been pillows, she thought furiously — to guard the children riding behind. Sass knew they would kill them, wondered why they'd waited this long. The crawler train clanked and rumbled along, turning down the lane to the fisheries research station, where Caris had hoped to work. All its windows were broken, the door smashed in. Sass hadn't seen Caris all day, but she hadn't dared look around much, either. Nor had she seen Lunzie or Januk.

The crawler train rumbled to the end of the lane, near the pier. And there the children had to unload the bodies, drag them out on the pier, and throw them in the restless alien ocean. It was hard to maneuver on the pier; the links tended to tangle. The pirate guards hit anyone they could reach, forcing them to hurry, keep moving, keep working.

Sass had shut her mind off, as well as she could, and tried not to see the faces and bodies she handled. She had Lunzie's in her arms, and was halfway to the end of the pier, when she recognized it. A reflexive jerk, a scream tearing itself from her throat, and Lunzie's corpse slipped away, thumped on the edge of the pier, and splashed into the water. Sass stood rigid, unable to move. Something yanked on her collar; she paid it no heed. She heard someone cry out, say, "That was her *sister*!" and then blackness took her away.

❖   ❖   ❖

The rest of her time on Myriad, those few days of desperate work and struggle, she always shoved down below conscious memory. She had been drugged, then worked to exhaustion, then drugged again. They had loaded the choicest of the ores, the rare gemstones which had paid the planet's assessment in the FSP Development Office, the richest of the transuranics. She was barely conscious of her link's concern, the care they tried to take of her, the gentle brush of a hand in the rare rest periods, the way they kept slack in her collar-lead. But the rest was black terror, grief, and rage. On the ship, after that, her link spent its allotted time in Conditioning, and the rest in the tight and smelly confines of the slavehold. For them, no drugs or cold sleep to ease a long voyage: they had to learn what they were, the pirates informed them with cold superiority. They were cargo, saleable anywhere the FSP couldn't control. As with any cargo, they were divided into like kinds: age groups, sexes, trained specialists. As with any slaves, they soon learned ways to pass information among themselves. So Sass found that Caris was still alive, part of link 18. Januk had been left behind, alive but doomed, since no adults or older children remained to help those too young to travel. Most of The City's adults had died trying to defend it against the pirates; some survived, but none of the children knew how many.

Conditioning was almost welcome, to ease the boredom and misery of the slavehold. Sass knew — at least at first — that this was intentional. But as time passed, she and her link both had trouble remembering what free life had been like. Conditioning also meant a bath of sorts, because the pirate trainers couldn't stand the stench of the slavehold. For that alone it was welcome. The link stood, sat, reached, squatted, turned, all as one, on command. They learned assembly-line work, putting together meaningless combinations some other link had taken apart in a previous session. They learned Harish, a variant of Neo-Gaesh that some of the pirates spoke, and they were introduced to Chinese.

The end of the voyage came unannounced — for, as Sass now expected, slaves had no need for knowledge of the future. The landing was rough, bruisingly rough, but they had learned that complaint brought only more pain. Link by link the pirates — now unarmored — marched them off the ship, and along a wide gray street toward a line of buildings. Sass shivered; they'd been hosed down before leaving the ship, and the wind chilled her. The gravity was too light, as well. The planet smelled strange: dusty and sharp, nothing like Myriad's rich salt smell. She looked up, and realized that they were inside — a dome? A dome big enough to cover a spaceport and a city?

All the city she could see, in the next months, was slavehold. Block after block of barracks, workshops, factories, five stories high and stretching in all directions. No trees, no grass, nothing living but the human slaves and human masters. Some were huge, far taller than Sass' parents had been, heavily muscled like the thugs that Carin Coldae had overcome in *The Ice-World Dilemma*.

They broke up the links, sending each slave to a testing facility to see what skills might be saleable. Then each was assigned to new links, for work or training or both, clipped and unclipped from one link after another as the masters desired. After all that had happened, Sass was surprised to find that she remembered her studies. As the problems scrolled onto the screen, she could think, immerse herself in the math or chemistry or biology. For days she spent a shift at the test center, and a shift at menial work in the barracks, sweeping floors that were too bare to need sweeping, and cleaning the communal toilets and kitchens. Then a shift at assembly work, which made no more sense to her than it ever had, and a bare six hours of sleep, into which she fell as into a well, eager to drown.

She had no way to keep track of the days, and no reason to. No way to find her old friends, or trace their movements. New friends she made easily, but the constant shifting from link to link made it hard for such friendships to grow. Then, long after her testing was finished, and she was working three full shifts a day, she was unclipped and taken to a building she'd not yet seen. Here, clipped into a long line of slaves, she heard the sibilant chant of an auctioneer and realized she was about to be sold.

By the time she reached the display stand, she had heard the spiel often enough to deaden her mind to the impact. Human female, Gilson stage II physical development, intellectual equivalent grade eight general, grade nine mathematics, height so much, massing so much, planet of origin, genetic stock of origin, native and acquired languages, specific skills ratings, all the rest.

She expected the jolt of pain that revealed to the buyers how sensitive she was, how excitable, and managed to do no more than flinch. She had already learned that the buyers rarely looked for beauty — that was easy enough to breed, or surgically sculpt. But talents and skills were chancy, and combined with physical vigor, chancier yet. Hence the reason for taking slaves from relatively young colonies.

The bidding went on, in a currency she didn't know and couldn't guess the value of. Someone finally quit bidding, and someone else pressed a heavy thumb to the terminal ID screen, and someone else — another slave, this time, by the collar — led her away down empty corridors and finally clipped her lead to a ring by a doorway. Through all this Sass managed not to tremble visibly, or cry, although she could feel the screams tearing at her from inside.

"What's your name?" asked the other slave, now stacking boxes beside the door. Sass stared at him. He was much older, a stocky, graying man with scars seaming one arm, and a groove in his skull where no hair grew. He looked at her when she didn't answer, and smiled a gap-toothed smile. "It's all right — you can answer me if you want, or not."

"Sassinak!" She got it out all at once, fast and almost too loud. Her name! She had a name again.

"Easy," he said. "Sassinak, eh? Where from?"

"M-myriad." Her voice trembled, now, and tears sprang to her eyes.

"Speak Neo-Gaesh?" he asked, in that tongue. Sass nodded, too close to tears to speak.

"Take it easy," he said. "You can make it." She took a long breath, shuddering, and then another, more quietly. He nodded his approval. "You've got possibilities, girl. Sassinak. By your scores, you're more than smart. By your bearing, you've got guts to go with it. No tears, no screams. You did jump too much, though."

That criticism, coming on top of the kindness, was too much; her temper flared. "I didn't so much as say ouch!"

He nodded. "I know. But you jumped. You can do better." Still angry, she stared, as he grinned at her. "Sassinak from Myriad, listen to me. Untrained, you didn't let out a squeak . . . what do you think you could do with training?"

Despite herself, she was caught. "Training? You mean . . . ?"

But down the corridor came the sound of approaching voices. He shook his head at her, and stood passively beside the stacked cartons, at her side.

"What's *your* name?" she asked very quietly, and very quietly he answered:

"Abervest. They call me Abe." And then so low she could hardly hear it, "I'm Fleet."

✧ CHAPTER TWO

Fleet. Sassinak held to that thought through the journey that followed, crammed as she was into a cargo hauler's front locker with two other newly purchased slaves. She found out afterwards that that had not been punishment, but necessity; the hauler went out of the dome and across the barren, airless surface of the little planet that served as a slave depot. Outside the insulated, pressurized locker — or the control cab, where Abe drove in relative comfort — she would have died.

Their destination was another slave barracks, this one much smaller. Sassinak expected the same sort of routine as before, but instead she was assigned to a training facility. Six hours a day before a terminal, learning to use the math she already knew in mapping, navigation, geology. Learning to perfect her accent in Harish and learning to understand (but never speak) Chinese. Another shift in manual labor, working at whatever jobs needed doing, according to the shift supervisor. She had no regular duties, nothing she could depend on.

One of the most oppressive things was the simple feeling that she could not even *see* out. She had always been able to run outdoors and look at the sky, wander into the hills for an afternoon with friends. Now . . . now some blank ugliness stopped her gaze, as if by physical force, everywhere she looked. Most buildings had no windows: there was nothing outside to see but the wall of another prefab hulk nearby. Trudging the narrow streets from one assignment to another, she learned that looking up brought a quick scolding, or a blow. Besides, she couldn't see anything above but the grayish haze of the dome. She could not tell how large the moon or planet was, how far she'd been taken from the original landing site, even how many buildings formed the complex in which she

was trained. Day after day, nothing but the walls of these prefabs, indoors and out, always the same neutral gritty gray. She
quit trying to look up, learned to contain herself within herself
and hated herself for making that adjustment.

But one shift a day, amazingly, was free. She could spend it in
the language labs, working at the terminal, reading . . . or, as most
often, with Abe.

Fleet, she soon learned, was his history and his dream. He had
been Fleet, had enlisted as a boy just qualified, and worked his
way rating by rating, sometimes slipping back when a good brawl
intruded on common sense, but mostly rising steadily through
the ranks as a good spacer could. Clever, but without the intellect
that would have won him a place at the Academy; strong, but not
brutal with it; brave without the brashness of the boy he had
been, he had clenched himself around the virtues of the Service
as a drowning man might cling to a limb hanging in the water.
Slave he might be, in all ways, but yet he was Fleet.

"They're tough," he said to her, soon after they arrived. "Tough
as anything but the slavers, and maybe even more. They'll break
you if they can, but if they can't . . ." His voice trailed away, and
she glanced over to see his eyes glistening. He blinked. "Fleet
never forgets," he said. "Never. They may come late, they may
come later, but they come. And if it's later, never mind. Your
name's on the rolls, it'll be in Fleet's memory, forever."

Over the months that followed, Sassinak began to think of
Fleet as something other than the capricious and arrogant arm of
power that her parents had told her about. Solid, Abe said.
Dependable. The same on one ship as on any; the ranks the
same, the ratings the same, the specialties the same, barring the
difference in a ship's size or weaponry.

He would not say how long he had been a slave, or what had
happened, but his faith in the Fleet, in the Fleet's long arm and
longer memory, sank into her mind, bit by bit. Her supervisors
varied: some quick to anger, some lax. Abe smiled, and pointed
out that good commanders were consistent, and good services
had good commanders. When she came to their meetings
bruised and sore from an undeserved punishment, he told her to
remember that: someday she would have power, and she could
do better.

She could do better even then, he said one evening, reminding her of their first meeting. "You're ready now," he said. "I've something to show you."

"What?"

"Physical discipline, something you do for yourself. It'll make it easier on you when things get tough, here or anywhere. You don't have to feel the pain, or the hunger —"

"I can't do that!"

"Nonsense. You worked for six hours straight at the terminal today — didn't even break for the noonmeal. You were hungry, but you weren't thinking about it. You can learn not to think about it unless you want to."

Sass grinned at him. "I can't do calculus all the time!"

"No, you can't. But you can reach that same core of yourself, no matter what you think of. Now sit straight, and breath from down here —" He poked her belly.

It was both harder and easier than she'd expected. Easier to slip into a trancelike state of concentration *on* something — a technique she'd learned at home, she thought, studying while Lunzie and Januk played. Harder to withdraw from the world without that specific focus.

"It's in *you*," Abe insisted. "Down inside yourself, that's where you focus. If it's something outside, math or whatever, they can tear it away. But not what's inside." Sass spent one frustrating session after another feeling around inside her head for something — anything — that felt like what Abe described. "It's not in your head," he kept insisting. "Reach deeper. It's way down." She began to think of it as a center of gravity, and Abe nodded when she told him. "That's closer — use that, if it helps."

When she had that part learned, the next was harder. A simple trance wasn't enough, because all she could do was endure passively. She would need, Abe explained, to be able to exert all her strength at will, even the reserves most people never touched. For a long time she made no progress at all, would gladly have quit, but Abe wouldn't let her.

"You're learning too much in your tech classes," he said soberly. "You're almost an apprentice pilot now — and that's very saleable." Sass stared at him, shocked. She had never thought she might be sold again — sent somewhere else, away from Abe. She had almost begun to feel safe. Abe touched her arm gently. "You see, Sass, why you need this, and need it now. You aren't safe:

none of us is. I could be sold tomorrow — would have been before now, if I weren't so useful in several tech specialties. They may keep you until you're a fully qualified pilot, but likely not. There's a good market for young pilot apprentices, in the irregular trade." She knew he meant pirates, and shuddered at the thought of being back on a pirate ship. "Besides," he went on, "there's something more you need to know, that I can't tell you until you can do this right. So get back to work."

When she finally achieved something he called adequate, it wasn't much more than her normal strength, and she exhausted it quickly. But Abe nodded his approval, and had her practice almost daily. Along with that practice came the other information he'd promised.

"There's a kind of network," he said, "of pirate victims. Remembering where they came from, who did it, who lived, and how the others died. We keep thinking that if we can ever put it all together, everything we know, we'll find out who's behind all this piracy. It's not just independents — although I heard that the ship that took Myriad was an independent, or on the outs with its sponsor. There's evidence of some kind of conspiracy at FSP itself. I don't know what, or I'd kill myself to get that to Fleet somehow, but I know there's evidence. And I couldn't put you in touch with them until you could shield your reactions."

"But who —"

"They call themselves Samizdat — an old word, some language I never heard of, supposed to mean underground or something. Maybe it does, maybe not. That doesn't matter. But the name does, and your keeping it quiet does."

Study, work, practice with Abe. When she thought about it — which she did rarely — it was sort of a parody of the life she'd expected at home on Myriad. School, household chores, the tight companionship of her friends. But flunking a test at home had meant a scolding; here it meant a beating. Let Januk spill precious rationed food — her eyes filled, remembering the sugar that last night — and her mother would expostulate bitterly. But if she spilled a keg of seeds, hauling it to the growing frames, her supervisor would cuff her sharply, and probably dock her a meal. And instead of friends her own age, to gossip about schoolmates and families, to share the jokes and dreams, she had Abe. Time passed, time she could not measure save by the subtle changes in her own body: a little taller, she thought. A little wider of hip, more roundness, even though the slave diet kept her lean.

It finally occurred to her to wonder why they were allowed such freedom, when she realized that other slave friendships were broken up intentionally, by the supervisors. Abe grinned mischievously. "I'm valuable; I told you that. And they think I need a lovely young plaything now and then —"

Sass reddened. Here girls younger than she were taught arts of love; but on Myriad, in her family's religion, only those old enough to start a separate family were supposed to know how. Although they'd all complained mildly, life on a pioneer planet kept them too busy to regret. Abe went on.

"I told 'em I'd instruct you myself. Didn't want any of their teachings getting in my way." Sass stared at the floor, furious with him and his amusement. "Don't fluff feathers at me, girl," he said firmly. "I saved you a lot of trouble. You'd never have been assigned that full-time, smart as you are, and saleable as tech-slaves are, but still . . ."

"All right." It came out in a sulky mutter, and she cleared her throat loudly. "All right. I understand —"

"You don't really, but you will later." His hand touched her cheek, and turned her face towards his. "Sass, when you're free — and I do believe you'll be free someday — you'll understand what I did and why. Reputation doesn't mean anything here. The truth always does. You're going to be a beauty, my girl, and I hope you enjoy your body in all ways. Which means *you* deciding when and how."

She didn't feel comfortable with him for some time after that. Some days later, he met her with terrifying news.

"You're going to be sold," he said, looking away from her. "Tomorrow, the next day — that soon. This is our last meeting. They only told me because they offered me another —"

"But, Abe —" She finally found her voice, faint and trembling as it was.

"No, Sass." He shook his head. "I can't stop it."

Tears burst from her eyes. "But — but it can't be —"

"Sass, *think!*" His tone commanded her; the tears dried on her cheeks. "Is this what I've taught you, to cry like any silly spoiled brat of a girl when trouble comes?"

Sass stared at him, and then reached for the physical discipline he'd taught her. Breathing slowed, steadied; she quit trembling. Her mind cleared of its first blank terror.

"That's better. Now listen —" Abe talked rapidly, softly, the rhythm of his speech at first strange and then compelling. When he stopped, Sass could hardly recall what he'd said, only that it was important, and she would remember it later. Then he hugged her, for the first time, his strength heartening. She still had her head on his shoulder when the supervisor arrived to take her away.

She passed through the sale barn without really noticing much; this time the buyer had her taken back to the port, to a scarred ship with no visible registration numbers. Inside, her escort handed her collar thong to a lean man with scarlet and gold collar tabs. Sass recalled the rank — senior pilot — from a far-distant shipping consortium. He looked her over, then shook his head.

"Another beginner. Bright stars, you'd think they'd realize I need something more than a pilot apprentice. And a dumb naked girl who probably doesn't even speak the same language." He turned away and poked the bulkhead. With a click and hiss, a locker opened; he rummaged inside and pulled out rumpled tunic and pants, much-mended. "Here. Clothes. You understand?" He mimed dressing, and Sass took the garments, putting them on as he watched. Then he led her along one corridor, then into a pop-tube that shot them to the pilot's "house" — a small cramped compartment lined with vidscreens and control panels. To Sass' relief, her training made sense of the chaos of buttons and toggles and flickering lights. That must be the insystem computer, and that the FTL toggle, with its own shielded computer flickering, now, in not-quite-normal space. The ship had two insystem drives, one suitable for atmospheric landings. The pilot tweaked her thong and grinned when she looked at him.

"I can tell you recognize most of this. Have you ever been off-station?" He seemed to have forgotten that she might not speak his language. Luckily, she could.

"No . . . not since I came."

"Your ratings are high — let's see how you do with this. . . ." He pointed to one of the three seats, and Sass settled down in front of a terminal much like that in training — even the same manufacturer's logo on the rim. He leaned over her, his breath warm on her ear, and entered a problem she remembered working.

"I've done that one before," she said.

"Well, then, do it again." Her fingers flew over the board: codes for origin and destination, equations to calculate the most efficient combination of travel time, fuel cost of Insystem drive, probability flux of FTL . . . and, finally, the transform equations that set up the FTL path. He nodded when she was done.

"Good enough. Now maximize for travel time, using the maximum allowable FTL flux."

She did that, and glanced back. He was scowling.

"You'd travel a .35 flux path? Where'd you get that max from?" Sass blushed; she'd misplaced a decimal. She placed the errant zero, and accepted the cuff on her head with equanimity. "That's better, girl," he said. "You youngers haven't seen what a high flux means — be careful, or you'll have us spread halfway across some solar system, and you won't be nothin' but a smear of random noise in somebody's radio system. Now — what's your name?"

She blinked at him. Only Abe had used her name. But he stared back, impudent and insistent, and ready to give her a clout. "Sass," she said. He grinned again, and shrugged.

"Suits you," he said. Then he swung into one of the other seats, and cleared her screen. "Now, girl, we go to work."

Life as an indentured apprentice pilot — the senior pilot made it clear they didn't like the word "slave" — was considerably more lax than her training had been. She wore the same collar, but the thong was gone. No one would tell her what the ship's allegiance was — if any — or any more than its immediate next destination, but aside from that she was treated as a crew member, if a junior one. Besides senior pilot Krewe, two junior pilots were aboard: a heavy-set woman named Fersi, and a long, angular man named Zoras. Three at a time worked in the pilothouse when maneuvering from one drive system to another, or when using insystem drives. Sass worked a standard six-hour shift as third pilot under the others. When they were off, one or the other of the pilots gave her instruction daily — ship's day, that is. Aside from that, she had only to keep her own tiny cubicle tidy, and run such minor errands as they found for her. The rest of the time she listened and watched as they talked, argued, and gambled.

"Pilots don't mingle," Fersi warned her, when she would have sought more interaction with the ship's crew. "Captain's due respect, but the rest of 'em are no more spacers than a rock is a miner. They'd do the same work groundside; fight or clean or cook or run machinery or whatever. Pilots are the old guild, the first spacers; you're lucky they trained you to that."

History, from the point of view of the pilots, was nothing like she'd learned back on Myriad. No grand pattern of human exploration, meetings with alien races, the formation of alliances and then the Federation of Sentient Planets. Instead, she heard a litany of names that ran back to Old Terra, stories with all the details worn away by time. Lindbergh, the Red Baron, Bader, Gunn — names from before spaceflight, they said, all warriors of the sky in some ancient battle, from which none returned. Heinlein and Clarke and Glenn and Aldridge, from the early days in space . . . all the way up to Ankwir, who had just opened a new route halfway across the galaxy, cutting the flux margin below .001.

If she had not missed Abe so much, she might almost have been happy. Ship food that the others complained about she found ample and delicious. She had plenty to learn, and teachers eager to instruct. The pilots had long ago told each other their timeworn stories. But long before she forgot Abe and the slave depot, the raid came.

She was asleep in her webbing when the alarm sounded. The ship trembled around her; beneath her bare feet the deck had the odd uncertain feel that came with transition from one major drive to another.

"Sass! Get in here!" That was Krewe, loud enough to be heard over the racket of the alarm. Sass staggered a little, working her way around to her usual seat. Fersi was already there, intent on the screen. Krewe saw her and pointed to the number two position. "It's not gonna do any good, but we might as well try. . . ."

Sass flicked the screen to life, and tried to make sense of the display. Something had snatched them out of FTL space, and dumped them into a blank between solar systems. And something with considerable more mass was far too close behind.

"Fleet heavy cruiser," said Krewe shortly. "Picked us up awhile back, and set a trap —"

"What?" Sass had had no idea that anything could find, let alone capture, a ship in FTL.

He shrugged, hands busy on his board. "Fleet has some new tricks, I guess. And we're about out. Here —" He tossed a strip of embossed plastic over to her. "Stick that in your board, there on the side, when I say."

Sass looked at it curiously: about a finger long, and half that wide, it looked like no data storage device she'd seen. She found the slot it would fit, and waited. Suddenly the captain's voice came over the intercom.

"Krewe — got anything for me? They're demanding to board —"

"Maybe. Hang on." Krewe nodded at Sass, and slid an identical strip into the slot on his board. Sass did the same, as did Fersi. The ship seemed to lurch, as if it had tripped over something, and the lights dimmed. Abruptly Sass realized that she was being pressed into the back of her seat — and as abruptly, the pressure shifted to one side, then the other. Then something made a horrendous noise, all the lights went out, and in the sudden cold dark she heard Krewe cursing steadily.

She woke in a clean bunk in a brightly lit compartment full of quiet bustle. Almost at once she missed a familiar pressure on her neck, and lifted her hand. The slave collar was gone. She glanced around warily.

"Ah . . . you're awake." A man in a clean white uniform, sleeves striped to the elbow with black and gold, came to her. "And I'll bet you wonder where you are, and what happened, and — do you know what language I'm speaking?"

Sass nodded, too amazed to speak. Fleet. It had to be Fleet. She tried to remember what Abe had told her about stripes on the sleeves; these were wing-shaped, which meant something different from the straight ones.

"Good, then." The man nodded. "You were a slave, right? Taken in the past few years, I daresay, from your age —"

"How do you know my —"

He grinned. He had a nice grin, warm and friendly. "Teeth, among other things. General development." At this point Sass realized that she had on something clean and soft, a single garment that certainly was not the patched tunic and pants she'd worn on the other ship. "Now — do you remember where you came from?"

"My . . . my home?" When he nodded, she said, "Myriad." At his blank look, she gave the standard designation she'd been taught in school, so long ago. He nodded again, and she went on to tell him what had happened to the colony.

"And then?" She told of the original transport, the training she'd received as a slave, and then her work on the ship. He sighed. "I suppose you haven't the faintest idea where that depot planet is, do you?"

"No. I —" Her eyes fixed suddenly on the insignia he wore on his left breast. It meant something. It meant . . . Abe's face came to her suddenly, very earnest, speaking swiftly and in an odd broken rhythm, something she had never quite remembered, but didn't worry about because someday — And now was someday, and she found herself reciting whatever he had said, just as quickly and accurately. The man stared at her.

"You —! You're too young; you couldn't —!" But now that it was back out, she knew . . . knew what knowledge Abe had planted in her (and how many others, she suddenly wondered, who had been sold away?), hoping that someday, somehow she might catch sight of that insignia (and how had he kept his, hidden it from his owners?) and have the memory wakened. She knew where that planet was, and the FTL course, and the codewords that would get a Fleet vessel past the outer sentinel satellites . . . all the tidbits of knowledge that Abe had gleaned in years of slavery, while he pretended obedience.

Her information set off a whirlwind of activity. She herself was bundled into a litter and carried along spotless gleaming corridors, to be set down at last, with utmost gentleness, in a cabin bunk. A luxurious cabin, its tile floor gentled with a brilliant geometric carpet, several comfortable-looking chairs grouped around a low round table. She heard bells in the distance, the scurry of many feet . . . and then the door to the cabin closed, and she heard nothing but the faint hiss of air from the ventilators.

In that silence, she fell asleep again, to be wakened by a gentle cough. This time, the white uniform was decorated with gold stripes on the sleeves, straight ones that went all the way around. *Rings*, she thought vaguely. Four of them. And six little somethings on the shoulders, little silvery blobs. "Stars are tops," Abe had said. "Stars are admirals. But *anything* on the shoulders means officer."

"The Medical Officer says you're well enough," said the person with all that gold and silver. "Can you tell me more about what you remember?" He was tall, thin, gray-haired, and Sass might have been frightened into silence if he hadn't smiled at her, a fatherly sort of smile.

She nodded, and repeated it all again, this time in a more normal tone.

"And who told you this?" he asked.

"Abe. He . . . he was Fleet, he said."

"He must be." The man nodded. "Well, now. The question is, what do we do with you?"

"This — this *is* a Fleet ship, isn't it?"

The man nodded again. "The *Baghir*, a heavy cruiser. Let me brief you a little. The ship you were on — know anything about it?" Sass shook her head. "No — they just stuck you in the pilot-house, I'll bet, and put you to work. Well, it was an independent cargo carrier. Doubles as a slave ship some runs; this time it had maybe twenty young, prime tech-trained slaves and a load of entertainment cubes — if you call that kind of thing entertainment." He didn't explain further, and Sass didn't ask.

"We'd heard a shipment might be coming into a neighboring system, so we had a fluxnet in place. You don't need to know how that works, only it can jerk a ship out of hyperspace when it works right. When it works wrong, there's nothing to pick up. Anyway, it worked, and there your ship was, and there we were, ready to trail and take it. Which we did. The other slaves — and there's two from Myriad, by the way — are being sent back to Sector HQ, where they'll go through Fleet questioning and court procedures to reestablish their identities. They're innocent parties; all we do is make sure they haven't been planted with dangerous hidden personalities. That's happened before with freed slaves; one of them had been trained as an assassin while under drugs. Freed, and back at school, he went berserk and killed fourteen people before he could be subdued." He shook his head, then turned to her.

"You, though. You're our clue to what's really happened, and you know where the slave depot is. You've told us what you know — or what you think you know — but I'm not sure your Fleet friend put all he had to say in one implanted message. If you were willing to come along when we go —"

Sass pushed herself upright. "You're going *there*? Now?"

"Well, not this instant. But soon — in a few shipdays, at the most. The thing is, you're a civilian, and you're underage. I have no right to ask you, and no right to take you. But it would be a help."

Tears filled her eyes; it was too much too soon. She struggled to regain the discipline Abe had taught her, slowing her breathing, and steadying against the strain. The officer watched her, his expression shifting from concern through puzzlement to something she could not define. "I . . . I want to go," she said. "If . . . if Abe —"

"If Abe is still alive, we'll find him. Never fear. And now you, young lady, need more sleep."

There had been another implanted message, one that came out under the expert probing of the ship's medical team. This one, Sass realized, gave details of the inner defenses, descriptions of the little planet's surface, and the name of the trading combines which dealt in the slaves . . . including the one which had purchased and trained her. She came from that session shaken and pale, regaining her normal energy only after another long sleep and two solid meals. For the rest of the journey, she had nothing to but wait, a waiting made more bearable by the friendly crewwomen who showered her with attention and minor luxuries — real enough for someone who'd been a slave for years. Although the captain would not let her join the landing party, when the cruiser had cleared the skies and sent the marines down, she was on hand when Abe returned to the Fleet. Scarred and battered as he was, wearing the ragged slave tunic, and carrying nothing but his pride, he marched from the shuttle into the docking bay as if on parade. The captain had come to the docking bay himself. Sass hung back, breathless with awe and delight, as they went through the old ritual. When it was over, and Abe came to her, she was suddenly shy of him, half-afraid to touch him. But he hugged her close.

"I'm so *proud* of you, Sass!" He pushed her away, then hugged her again.

"I didn't do much," she began, but he snorted.

"Didn't do much! Well, if that's the way you want to tell the story, it's not mine. Come on, girl — soon's I've changed into decent clothes —" He looked around, to meet the grins of the others in the bay . . . kind grins, Sass noticed.

One of the men beckoned to him, and he followed. Sass stared after him. He belonged here; she could tell that. Where would she belong? She thought of the captain's comments on the other freed slaves . . . Fleet questioning and court procedures . . . hardly an inviting prospect.

"Don't worry," one of the men said to her. "There's enough wealth here to give every one of you a new start — and you most of all, being as you found the place."

Still she worried, waiting for Abe to reappear, and when he did, clad in the crisp uniform and stripes of his rank, she was even more worried. A new start, somewhere else, with strangers . . . she knew, without asking for details, that none of her family were left.

"Don't worry." He echoed the other man's comment. "You're not going to be lost in the system somewhere. You're my girl, and I'm Fleet, and it's going to be fine."

✧ CHAPTER THREE

By the time Sassinak arrived at Regg with Abe, she was as ready as he to praise the Fleet, and glad to think of herself as almost a Fleet dependent. The only thing better than that was to be Fleet herself. Which, she soon found, was exactly what Abe planned for her.

"You've got the brains," he said soberly, "to make the Academy list and be a Fleet officer. And more than the brains, the guts. You weren't the first I tried to help, Sass, but you were one of only three who didn't fall apart when the time came to leave. And both of those were killed."

"But how?" Sass wanted nothing more than to enter the gleaming white arches of the Academy gates . . . but that required recommendations from FSP representatives. How would an orphan from a plundered colony convince someone to recommend her?

"First there's the Fleet prep school. If I formally adopt you, then you're eligible, as the daughter of a Fleet veteran — and no, it doesn't matter than I'm not an officer. Fleet's Fleet."

"But you're —" Sass reddened. Abe had been retired, over his protests; his gimpy arm was past treatment, and wouldn't pass the Medical Board. He had argued, pled, and finally come back to their assigned quarters grim as she'd never seen him before.

"Retired, but still Fleet. Oh, Cousins take it, I knew they'd do it. I knew when the arm didn't heal straight — after six months or so, it's too late. But I thought maybe I could Kipling them into it."

"Kipling?"

"Kipling. Wrote half the songs the Fleet sings, and probably most of the rest. Service slang is, if you're sweet-talking someone into something, 'specially if it's sort of sentimental, that's Kipling. Where you came from, they probably said 'Irish them into it,' and

I'll bet you don't know where that came from. But don't worry —
I can't be active duty, but disabled vets —" His expression made
it clear that he refused to think of himself as disabled. "— we old
crips can usually get work in one of the bureaus." Sass asked
again about the prep school.

"Three or four years there, 'til you pass the exams — and I
don't doubt you will. Don't worry about the letters you need. You
impressed the captain more than a little, and he's related to half
the FSP reps in this sector."

From there, things went smoothly: the adoption, the entry
into the prep school. Although the other students were her age,
none had her experience, and they were still young enough to
show their awe. Sass found herself ahead of schedule in her math
classes, thanks to the slave tech training, while Abe's lessons in
physical discipline and concentration helped her regain lost
ground in the social sciences. She felt out of place at first in the
social life of school — she could not regain the carefree camaraderie of younger years — but she looked forward to the Academy
with such single-minded ambition that everyone soon considered
her another Academy-bound grind.

Abe's apartment, in a large block of such buildings, was unlike
any place Sass had ever lived. Her parents' apartment on Myriad
had been a standard prefab, the same floor plan as every other
apartment in the colony. Large families had had two or three as
needed, with doors knocked through adjoining walls. None of the
living quarters were more than one story high, and few of the
other buildings. At the slaver depot, all the buildings were even
cheaper prefabs, big ugly buildings designed to hold the maximum cubage. There she had slept in a windowless barracks, in a
rack of bunks.

Abe had a second-floor corner apartment, with a bedroom for
each of them, a living room, study, and small kitchen. From her
room, Sass looked into a central courtyard planted with flowers
and one small tree with drooping leaves. From the living room
she could see across a wide street to a similar building across
from them. It felt amazingly spacious and light; she spent hours,
at first, watching people in the street below, or looking out across
the city. For their apartment, like most, stood on one of the low
hills that faced the harbor.

Regg itself was a terraformed planet, settled first by the usual colonists, in their case agricultural specialists, and then chosen as Fleet Headquarters because of its position in human-dominated space. Here in its central city, Fleet was the dominant force. Abe took Sassinak touring: to the big blocky buildings of Headquarters itself, all sheathed in white marble, to the riverside parks that ended in the great natural harbor, a wide almost circular bay of deep blue water edged in gray cliffs on the east and west, opening past a small rocky island to the greater sea beyond. By careful design, the river mouth itself had been left clear, but Sass saw both the Fleet and civilian ports set back on either side. Although FSP regulations forbade the eating of meat, fishing was still done on many human-settled worlds, whose adherence to the code was less than perfect. Ostensibly the excuse was that the code should apply only to warmbloods and *intelligent* (not just sentient) aquatic coldbloods such as the Wefts or Ssli. Sass knew that many of the civilian locals ate fish, though it was never served openly in even the worst dockside joints. The fish, originally of Old Earth origin, had been stocked in Regg's ocean centuries before.

Besides the formal Headquarters complex, there were the associated office buildings, computer centers, technology and research centers . . . each in a landscaped setting, for Regg was still, after all these years, uncrowded.

"Fleet people do retire here," Abe said, "but they mostly homestead inland, upriver. Maybe someday we can do a river cruise during your holidays, see some of the estates. I've got friends up in the mountains, too."

But the city was exciting enough for a girl reared in a small mining colony town. She realized how silly it had been for the Myriadians to call their one-story collection of prefabs The City. Here government buildings soared ten or twelve stories, offering stunning views of the surrounding country from their windswept observation platforms atop. Busy shops crowded with merchandise from all over the known worlds, streets bustling from dawn until long after dark. Festivals to celebrate seasons and historical figures, theater and music and art. . . . Sass felt drunk on it, for weeks. This was the real world she had dreamed of, on Myriad: this colorful crowded city connected by Fleet to everywhere else, ships coming and going every day. Although the spaceport was behind the nearest range of hills, protecting the city from the noise, Sass loved to watch the shuttles lifting above forested slopes into an open sky.

In the meantime, she'd had a chance to meet some of the other survivors of Myriad's raid. Caris, now grim and wary, all the playfulness Sass remembered worn away by her captivity. She had found no one like Abe to give her help and hope, and in those years aged into a bitter older woman.

"I just want a chance to work," she said. "They say I can go to school." Her voice was flat, barely above a whisper, the voice of a slave afraid of discovery.

"You could come here," said Sass, half-hoping Caris would agree. Much as she loved Abe, she missed having a close girl-friend, and her room was big enough for two. And Caris had known her all her life. They could talk about anything; they always had. Her own warmth could bring Caris back to girlhood, rekindle her hopes. But Caris pulled back, refusing Sass' touch.

"No. I don't — Sass, we were friends, and we were happy, and someday maybe I can stand to remember that. Right now I look at you and see —" Her voice broke and she turned away.

"Caris, please!" Sass grabbed her shoulders, but Caris flinched and pulled back.

"It's all over, Sass! I can't — I can't be anyone's friend now. There's nothing left . . . if I can just have a place to work in peace, alone. . . ."

Sass was crying then, too. "Caris, you're all I have —"

"You don't have me. I'm not here." And with that she ran out of the room. Sass learned later that she'd gone back into the hospital, for more treatment. Later, she went offplanet without even telling Sass, letting her find out from the hospital records that her friend had left forever. For this grief, Abe insisted that work was the only cure — and revenge, someday, against whatever interests lay behind the slave trade. Sass threw herself into her classwork . . . and by the time the Academy Open Examinations came around, she'd worked off the visible remnants of her grief. She passed those in the top five percent, to Abe's delight. His scarred face creased into a grin as he took her to buy the required gear.

"I knew you could do it, Sass. I knew all along. You just remember what I told you, and in a few years I'll be cheering when you graduate."

But he would not walk her to the great arch that guarded the Academy entrance. He went off to work that morning, as he did every day (she never knew which of the semi-military bureaucracies had found a place for him; he never volunteered the information), leaving her to stare nervously into the mirror, twitching one errant strand of hair into place, until she had to walk fast or risk being late. She made her entrance appointment with time to spare, only to run into a marauding senior on her first trip through the Front Quad. She had carefully memorized the little booklet she'd been sent, and started to answer his challenge in the way it had instructed.

"Sir, Cadet Sassinak, reporting —" Her voice faltered. The cadet officer she had saluted had crossed his eyes and put his tongue out; he had his hands fanned out by his ears. As quickly, his face returned to normal, and his hands to his sides, but the smile on that face was grim.

"Rockhead, didn't anyone ever teach you how to report to a senior?" His voice attempted the cold arrogance of the pirate raiders, and came remarkably close. Sass realized she'd been tricked, fought down the responsive anger, and managed an equable tone in return. Abe hadn't told her they called the entering cadets "rockhead."

"Sir, yes, sir."

"Well, then . . . get on with it."

"Sir, Cadet Sassinak, reporting . . ." This time both eyes slewed outward, his mouth puckered as if he'd bitten a gari fruit, and he scratched vigorously at both armpits. But she wasn't fooled twice, and managed to get through the formal procedure without changing tone or expression, ending with a crisp " . . . sir!"

"Sloppy, slow, and entirely too smug," was the senior cadet's comment. "You're that petty officer's orphan tagalong, aren't you?"

Sass felt her ears burning, started to nod with clenched teeth, and then remembered that she had to answer aloud. "Sir, yes, sir."

"Hmph. Sorry sort of recommendation, letting himself get captured and slaved all those years. Not much like Fleet —" He stopped as Sass opened her mouth, and cocked his head. "Something to say, rockhead? Someone give you permission to speak?"

She didn't wait. "Sir, Abe is worth four of you, *sir*!"

"That's not the point, rockhead. The point is that you —" He tapped her shoulder. "You have to learn how to behave, and I don't think anything in your background's taught you how." Sass stared at him, back in control, furious with herself for taking the bait. "On the other hand, you're loyal. That's something. Not much, but something." He dismissed her, and she set off to find her assigned quarters, careful not to gawk around.

For reasons known only to the architects, the main buildings at the Academy had been constructed in a mix of antique styles, great gray blocks of stone that looked like pictures of ancient buildings on Old Earth. Towers, arches, covered walkways, intricate carvings of ships and battles and sea monsters around windows and doorways, enclosed courtyards paved in smooth slabs of stone. Six of these patriarchal buildings surrounded the Main Quad Parade: Themistocles, Drake, Nelson, Farragut, Velasquez, and the Chapel. Here, where the boldest street urchins could peer through the entrance gates to watch, cadets formed up many times a day to march to class, to mess, to almost every activity. Sass soon learned that the darker gray paving stones which marked out open squares against a pale background were slippery in the rain. She learned just where a slash of reflected sunlight from an open window might blind a cadet long enough to blunder into someone else. That meant a mark off, and she wanted no marks off.

Through the great arching salleyport of Velasquez, wide enough for a cadet platoon, were the cadet barracks, these named for the famous dead of Fleet battles. Varrin Hall, Benis, Tarrant, Suige. By the time they had been there a half-year, cadets knew those stories, and many others. Sass, on the third deck of Suige Hall, could recite from memory the entire passage in the history.

Other cadets complained (quietly) about their quarters, but Sass had spent years as Abe's ward. She had never been encouraged to spread her personality around her quarters, "to acquire bad habits" as Abe put it, although he admitted that Fleet officers, once they were up in rank, could and did decorate and personalize their space. But the regulation bunk with its prescribed covers folded just so, the narrow locker for the required uniforms (and nothing else), the single flat box for personal items, the single desk with its computer terminal and straight-backed chair — that was enough for her. She didn't mind sharing, or taking the top bunk, which made her popular with a series of roomies. She felt the neat, clean little cubicles were perfect for someone whose main interest lay elsewhere, and willingly did her share of the floor-polishing and dusting that daily inspections required.

She had actually expected neutral or monotone interiors, but the passages were tinted to copy the color-code used on all Fleet vessels. By the time the cadets graduated, this system would be natural, and they would never have to wonder which deck, or which end of a deck, they were on. Main or Command Deck, anywhere, had white above gray, for instance, and Troop Deck was always green.

Most classes went on in the "front quad" or in the double row of simplest stone-faced buildings that lay uphill from it. History — from Fleet's perspective, which included knowing the history of "important" old Earth navies, all the way back to ships rowed or sailed. Sass could not figure out why they needed to know what different ranks had been called a thousand years ago, but she tucked the information away dutifully, in case it was needed for anything but the quarterly exams. She did wonder why "captain" had ever been both a rank and a position, given the confusion that caused, and was glad someone had finally straightened it out logically. Anyone commanding a ship was a captain, and the rank structure didn't use the term at all. "You think it's logical," the instructor pointed out, "but there was almost a mutiny when the first Fleet officer had to use the rank 'major' and lieutenant commanders and commanders got pushed up a notch." Sass enjoyed far more the analysis of the various navies' tactics, including a tart examination of the effect of politics on warfare, using an ancient text by someone called Tuchman.

Cadets ate together, in a vaulted mess hall that would have been lovely if it hadn't been for the rows and rows of tables, each seating eight stiff cadets. Looking around — up at the carvings on the ceiling, for instance — was another way to get marks taken off. Sassinak, with the others, learned to eat quickly and neatly while sitting on the edge of her chair. Students in their last two years supervised each table, insisting on perfect etiquette from the rockheads. At least, thought Sass, the food was adequate.

The Academy was not quite what she'd expected, even with

the supposedly inside information she'd had before. From Abe's attitude towards Fleet officers, she'd gotten the idea that the Academy was some sort of semi-mystical place which magically imbued the cadets with honor, justice, and tactical brilliance. He had told her about his own Basic Training, which he described succinctly as four months of unmitigated hell, but that was not the same, he'd often said, as officer training. Sass had found, more or less by accident, a worn copy of an etiquette manual, which had prepared her for elaborate formalities and the fine points of military courtesy — but not for the Academy's approach to freshman cadets.

"We don't have hazing," the cadet commander had announced that first day. "But we do have discipline." The distinction, Sass decided quickly, was a matter of words only. And she quickly realized that she was a likely target for it, whatever it was called: the orphan ward of a retired petty officer, an ex-slave, and far too smart for her own good.

She wished she could consult Abe, but for the first half-year the new cadets were allowed no visitors and no visits home. She had to figure it out for herself. His precepts stood like markers in her mind: never complain, never argue, never start a fight, never boast. Could that be enough?

With the physical and mental discipline he'd taught her, she found, it could. She drew that around her like a tough cloak. Cadet officers who could reduce half the newcomers to red rage or impotent tears found her smooth but unthreatening equanimity boring after a few weeks. There was nothing defiant in that calmness, no challenge to be met, just a quiet, earnest determination to do whatever it was better than anyone else. Pile punishment details on her, and she simply did them, doggedly and well. Scream insults at her, and she stood there listening, able to repeat them on command in a calm voice that made them sound almost as silly as they were.

Abe had been right; they pushed her as hard as the slavers had, and the cadet officers had — she sensed — some of the same capacity for cruelty, but she never lost sight of the goal. *This* struggle would make her stronger, and once she was a Fleet officer, she could pursue the pirates who had destroyed her family and the colony.

That calm reticence might have made her an outcast among

her classmates, except that she found herself warming to them. She would be working with them the rest of her life — and she wanted friends — and before the first half-year was over, she found herself once more the center of a circle.

"You know, Sass, we really ought to do something about Dungar's lectures." Pardis, an elegant sprout of the sector aristocracy sprawled inelegantly on the floor of the freshman wardroom, dodged a feinted kick from Genris, another of her friends.

"We have to memorize them; that's enough." Sass made a face, and drained her mug of tea. Dungar managed to make the required study of alien legal systems incredibly dull, and his delivery — in a monotone barely above a whisper — made the class even worse. He would not permit recorders, either; they had to strain to hear every boring word.

"They're so . . . so predictable. My brother told me about them, you know, and I'll swear he hasn't changed a word in the past twenty years." Pardis finished that sentence in a copy of Dungar's whisper, and the others chuckled.

"Just what did you have in mind?" Sass grinned down at Pardis. "And you'd better get up, before one of the senior monitors shows up and tags you for unofficerlike posture."

"It's too early for them to be snooping around. I was thinking of something like . . . oh . . . slipping a little something lively into his notes."

"Dungar's notes? The ones he's read so many times he doesn't really need them?"

"We must show respect for our instructors," said Tadmur. As bulky as most heavyworlders, he took up more than his share of the wardroom, and sat stiffly erect. The others groaned, as they usually did. Sass wondered if he could really be that serious all the time.

"I show respect," said Pardis, rolling his green eyes wickedly. "Just the same as you, every day —"

"You make fun of him for his consistency." Tadmur's Vrelan accent gave his voice even more bite. "Consistency is good."

"Consistency is dull. Consistently wrong is stupid —" Pardis broke off suddenly and sprang to his feet as the door swung open without warning, and the senior monitor's grim face appeared around it. This weekend, the duty monitor was another heavyworlder, from Tadmur's home planet.

"You were lounging on the deck again, Mr. Pardis, weren't you?" The monitor didn't wait for the reply and went on: "The usual for you, and one for each of these for not reminding you of your duty." He scowled at Tadmur. "I'm surprised at *you* most of all."

Tadmur flushed, but said nothing more than the muttered "Sir, yes, sir" that regulations required.

Sassinak even made some progress with Tadmur and Seglawin, the two heavyworlders in her unit. When they finally opened up to her, she began to realize that the heavyworlders felt deep grievances against the other human groups in FSP.

"They want us for our strength," Tadmur said. "They want us to fetch and carry. You look at the records — the transcripts of the Seress expedition, for instance. How often do you think the med staff is assigned heavy duty, eh? But Parrih, not only a physician but a specialist, a surgeon, was expected to do the heavy unloading and loading in addition to her regular medical work."

"They like to think we're stupid and slow." Seglawin took up the complaint. Although not quite as large as Tadmur, she was far from the current standard of beauty, and with her broad forehead drawn down into a scowl looked menacing enough. Sass realized suddenly that she had beautiful hair, a rich wavy brown mass that no one noticed because of the heavy features below it. "Pinheads, they call us, and muscle-bound. I know our heads look little, compared to our bodies, but that's illusion. Look how surprised the Commandant was when I won the freshmen history prize: 'Amazingly sensitive interpretation for someone of your background.' I know what that means. They think we're just big dumb brutes, and we're not."

Sass looked at them, and wondered. Certainly the heavyworlders in the slave center had been sold as cheap heavy labor, and none had been in any of her tech classes. She'd assumed they weren't suited for it, just as everyone said. But in the Academy, perhaps five percent of the cadets were heavyworlders, and they did well enough in classwork. The two heavyworlders looked at each other, and then back at Sass. Seglawin shrugged.

"At least she's listening and not laughing."

"I don't —" Sass began, but Tad interrupted her.

"You do, because you've been taught that. Sass, you're fair-minded, and you've tried to be friendly. But you're a lightweight, and reasonably pretty enough, to your race's standard. You can't know what it's like to be treated as a — a thing, an animal, good for nothing but the work you can do."

It was reasonable, but Sass heard the whine of self-pity under the words and was suddenly enraged. "Oh, yes, I do," she heard herself say. Their faces went blank, the smug blankness that so many associated with heavyworlder arrogance, but she didn't stop to think about it. "I was a slave," she said crisply, biting off the words like so many chunks of steel. "I know *exactly* how it feels to be treated as a thing: I was sold, more than once, and valued on the block for the work I could do."

Seglawin reacted first, blankness then a surging blush. "Sass! I didn't —"

"You didn't know, because I don't want to talk about it." Rage still sang in her veins, lifting her above herself.

"I'm sorry," said Tad, his voice less hard than she'd ever heard it. "But maybe you do understand."

"You weren't slaves," Sass said. "*You* don't understand. They killed my family: my parents, my baby sister. My friends and their parents. And I will *get* them," Sass continued finally. "I will end that piracy, that slavery, every chance I get. Whether it's lights or heavies or whoever else. Nothing's worse than that. Nothing." She met their eyes, one and then the other. "And I won't talk about it again. I'm sorry."

To her surprise, they both rose, and gave a little bow and odd gesture with their hands.

"No, it's our fault." Seglawin's voice had a burr in it now, her accent stronger. "We did not know, and we agree: nothing's worse than that. Our people have suffered, but not that. We fear that they might, and that is the source of our anger. You understand: you will be fair, whatever happens." She smiled, as she offered to shake hands, the smile transforming her features into someone Sass hoped very much to have as a friend.

Other times, more relaxed times, followed. Sass learned much about the heavyworlders' beliefs. Some reacted to the initial genetic transformations that made heavyworld adaption possible with pride, and considered that all heavyworlders should spend as much time as possible on high-gravity planets. Others felt it a degradation, and sought normal-G worlds where they hoped to breed back to normal human standards. All felt estranged from their lighter-boned distant relations, blamed the lightweights — at least in part — for that estrangement, and resented any suggestion that their larger and heavier build implied less sensitivity or intelligence.

Cadet leave, at the end of that first session, brought her home to Abe's apartment in uniform, shy of his reaction and stiff with pride. He gave her a crisp salute and then a bear hug.

"You're making it fine," he said, not waiting for her to speak. Already, she recognized in herself and in his reactions the relationship they would have later.

"I hope so." She loosened the collar of the uniform and stretched out on the low divan. He took her cap and set it carefully on a shelf.

"Making friends, too?"

"Some." His nod encouraged her, and she told him about the heavyworlders. Abe frowned.

"You want to watch them; they can be devious."

"I know. But —"

"But they're also right. Most normals *do* think of them as big stupid musclemen, and treat them that way. Poor sods. The smart ones resent it, and if they're smart enough they can be real trouble. What you want to do, Sass, is convince 'em you're fair, without giving them a weak point to push on. Their training makes 'em value strength and endurance over anything else."

"But they're not all alike." Sass told him all she'd learned, about the heavyworld cultures, "— and I wonder myself if the heavyworlders are being used by the same bunch who are behind the pirates and slavers," she finished.

Abe had been setting out a cold meal as she talked. Now he stopped, and leaned on the table. "I dunno. Could be. But at least some of the heavyworlders are probably pirates themselves. You be careful." Sass didn't argue; she didn't like the thought that Abe might have his limitations; she needed him to be all-knowing, for a long time yet. On the other hand, she sensed, in her heavyworld friends, the capacity for honesty and loyalty, and in herself an unusual ability to make friends with people of all backgrounds.

❖　❖　❖

By her third year, she was recognized as a promising young cadet officer, and resistance to her background had nearly disappeared. Colonial stock, yes: but colonial stock included plenty of "good" families, younger sons and daughters who had sought adventure rather than a safe seat in the family corporation. That she never claimed such a connection spoke well of her; others claimed it in her name.

Her own researches into her family were discreet. The psychs had passed her as safely adjusted to the loss of her family. She wasn't sure how they'd react if they found her rummaging through the colonial databases, so she masked her queries carefully. She didn't want anyone to question her fitness for Fleet. When she'd entered everything she could remember, she waited for the computer to spit out the rest.

The first surprise was a living relative (or "supposed alive" the computer had it) some three generations back. Sass blinked at the screen. A great-great-great-grandmother (or aunt: she wasn't quite sure of the code symbols) now on Exploration Service. Lunzie . . . so *that* was the famous ancestor her little sister had been named for. Her mother had said no more than that — may not have known more than that, Sass realized. Even as a cadet, she herself had access to more information than most colonists, already. She thought of contacting her distant family members someday . . . someday when she was a successful Fleet officer. Not any time soon, though. Fleet would be her family, and Abe was her father now.

He took his responsibility seriously in more ways than one, she discovered at their next meeting.

"Take the five-year implant, and don't worry about it. You're not going to be a mother anytime soon. Should have had it before now, probably."

"I don't want to be a sopping romantic, either," said Sass, growling.

Abe grinned at her. "Sass, I'm not telling you to fall in love. I'm telling you that you're grown, and your body knows it. You don't have to do anything you don't want to do, but you're about to want to."

"I am *not*." Sass glared at him.

"You haven't noticed anything?"

Sass opened her mouth to deny it, only to realize that she

couldn't. He'd seen her with the others, and he, more than any-one, knew every nuance of her body.

"Take the implant. Do what you want afterwards."

"You're not telling me to be careful," she said, almost petu-lantly.

"Stars, girl, I only adopted you. I'm not really your father, and even if I were I wouldn't tell you to be careful. Not you, of all people."

"My . . . my real father . . ."

"Was a dirtball colonist. I'm Fleet. You're Fleet now. You don't believe all that stuff you were taught. You're the last woman to stay virginal all your life, Sass, and that's the truth of it. Learn what you need, and see that you get it."

Sass shivered. "Sounds very mechanical, that way."

"Not really." Abe smiled at her, wistful and tender. "Sass, it's a great pleasure, and a great relaxation. For some people, long-term pairing is part of it. Your parents may have been that way. But you aren't that sort. I've watched you now for what? Eight years, is it, or ten? You're an adventurer by nature; you always were, and what happened to you brought it out even stronger. You're passionate, but you don't want to be bothered with long-term relationships."

The five-year implant she requested at Medical raised no eye-brows. When the doctor discovered it was her first, she insisted that Sass read a folder about it. ". . . So you'll know nothing's wrong when that patch on your arm changes color. Just come in for another one. It'll be in your records, of course, but sometimes your records aren't with you."

Once she had the implant, she couldn't seem to stop thinking about it. Who would it be? Who would be *first*, she scolded her-self, accepting with no more argument Abe's estimate of her character. She watched the other cadets covertly. Bronze-haired Liami, who bounced in and out of beds with the same verve as she gobbled dessert treats on holidays. Cal and Deri, who could have starred in any of the romantic serial tragedies, always in one crisis of emotion or another. How they passed their courses was a constant topic of low-voiced wonder. Suave Abrek, who assumed that any woman he fancied would promptly swoon into his arms — despite frequent rebuffs and snide remarks from all the women cadets.

She wasn't even sure what she wanted. She and Caris, in the old days, watching Carin Coldae reruns, had planned extravagant sexual adventures: all the handsome men in the galaxy, in all the exotic places, in the midst of saving planets or colonies or catching slavers. Was handsome really better? Liami seemed to have just as much fun with the plain as the handsome. And Abrek, undeniably handsome, but all too aware of it, was no fun at all. What kind of attraction was *that* kind, and not just the ordinary sort that made some people a natural choice for an evening of study or workouts in the gym? Or was the ordinary sort enough?

In the midst of this confusion of mind, she noticed that she was choosing to spend quite a bit of time with Marik Delgaesson, a senior cadet from somewhere on the far side of known space. She hadn't realized that human colonies spread that far, but he looked a lot more human than the heavyworlders. Brown eyes, wavy dark hair, a slightly crooked face that gave his grin a certain off-center appeal. Not really handsome, but good enough. And a superior gymnast, in both freeform and team competitions.

Sass thought about it. He might do. When their festival rotations came up on the same shift, and he asked her to partner him to the open theater production, she decided to ask him. It was hard to get started on the question, so they were halfway back to the Academy, threading their way between brightly decorated foodstalls, when she brought it up. He gave her a startled look and led her into a dark alley behind one of the government buildings.

"Now. What did you say?" In the near dark, she could hardly see his expression.

Her mouth was dry. "I . . . I wondered if you'd . . . you'd like to spend the night with me."

He shook his head. "Sass, you don't want that with me."

"I don't?" Reading and conversation had not prepared her for *this* reaction to a proposal. She wasn't sure whether she felt insulted or hurt.

"I'm not . . . what I seem." He drew his heavy brows down, then lifted them in a gesture that puzzled Sass. People did both, but rarely like that.

"Can you explain that?"

"Well . . . I hate to disillusion you, but —" And suddenly he wasn't there: the tall, almost-handsome, definitely charming cadet senior she'd known for the past two years. Nothing was there — or rather, a peculiar arrangement of visual oddities that had her wondering what he'd spiked her mug with. Stringy bits of this and that, nothing making any sense, until he reassembled suddenly as a very alien shape on the wall. Clinging to the wall.

Sass fought her diaphragm and got her voice back. "You're — you're a Weft!" She felt cold all over: she had wanted to embrace *that*?

Another visual tangle, this time with some parts recognizable as they shifted towards human, and he stood before her, his face already wistful. "Yes. We . . . we usually stay in human form around humans. They prefer it. Though most don't prefer the forms we choose quite as distinctly as you did."

Her training brought her breathing back under full control. "It wasn't your form, exactly."

"No?" He smiled, the crooked smile she'd dreamed about the past nights. "You don't like my other one."

"I liked *you*," Sass said, almost angrily. "Your — your personality —"

"You liked what you thought I was — my human act." Now he sounded angry, too, and for some reason that amused her.

"Well, your human act is better than some who were born that way. Don't blame me because you did a good job."

"You aren't scared of me?"

Sass considered, and he waited in silence. "Not scared, exactly. I was startled, yes: your human act is damn good. I don't think you could do that if you didn't have some of the same characteristics in your own form. I'm not — I don't —"

"You don't want to be kinky and sleep with an alien?"

"No. But I don't want to insult an alien either, not without cause. Which I don't have."

"Mmm. Perceptive and courteous, as usual. If I were a human, Sass, I'd want *you*."

"If you were human, you'd probably get what you wanted."

"Luckily, my human shape has no human emotions attached; I can enjoy you as a person, Sass, but not wish to couple with you. We mate very differently, and in an act far more . . . mmm . . . *biological* . . . than human mating has become."

Sass shivered; this was entirely too clinical.

"But we do — though rarely — make friends, in the human sense, with humans. I'd like that."

All those books gave her the next line. "I thought I was supposed to say that — no thanks, but can't we just be friends?"

He laughed, seemingly a real laugh. "You only get to say that if you don't make the proposal in the first place."

"Fine." Sass put out her hands. "I have to touch you, Marik; I'm sorry if that upsets you, but I have to. Otherwise I'll never get over being afraid."

"Thank you." They clasped hands for a long moment: his warm, dry hands felt entirely human. She felt the pulse throbbing in his wrist. She saw it in his throat. He shook his head at her. "Don't try to figure it out, Sass. Our own investigators — they're not really much like human scientists — don't understand it either."

"A Weft. I had to fall in love with a damned Weft!" Sass gave him a wicked grin. "And I can't even brag about it!"

"You're not in love with me. You're a young human female with a nearly new five-year implant and a large dose of curiosity."

"Dammit, Marik! How old are you, anyway? You talk like an older brother!"

"Our years are different." And with that she had to be content, for the moment. Later he was willing to say more, a little more, and introduce her to the other Wefts at the Academy. By then she'd spotted two of them, sensitive to some signal she couldn't define. Like Marik, they were all superb gymnasts and very good at unarmed combat. This last, she found, they accomplished by minute shifts of form.

"Say you grab my shoulder," said Marik, and Sass obligingly grabbed his shoulder. Suddenly it wasn't *there*, in her grasp, and yet he'd not shifted to his natural form. He was still right in front of her, only his hand gripped her forearm.

"What did you do?"

"The beginning of the shift changes the surface location and density — and that's what the enemy has hold of, right? We're not where we're supposed to be, and we're not all there, so to speak. In combat, serious combat, we'd have no reason to hold too tightly to the human form anyway."

"Does it . . . uh . . . hurt, to stay in human form? Are you more comfortable in your own?"

Marik shrugged. "It's like a tight uniform: not painful, but we like to get out of it now and then." He shifted then and there, and Sass stared, fascinated as always.

"It doesn't bother you?" asked Silui, one of the other Wefts.

"Not any more. I wish I knew how you do it!"

"So do we." Silui shifted, and placed herself beside Marik. <Can you tell us apart?> The question echoed in Sass' head. Of course. In their own form they hadn't the apparatus for human speech. But telepathy? She pushed that thought aside and watched as Silui and Marik crawled over and around each other. No more brown eyes and green, although something glittered that might be eyes of another sort. Shapes hard to define, because they were so outlandish . . . fivefold symmetry? She finally shook her head.

"Not by looking, I can't. Can you?"

"Oh yes." That was Gabril, the Weft who had not shifted. "Silui's got more graceful *sarfin*, and Marik *immles* better."

"That might help if I knew what *sarfin* and *immles* were," said Sass grumpily. Gabril laughed, and pointed out the angled stalk-like appendages, and had Marik demonstrate an *immle*.

"Do you ever take heavyworlder shapes?" asked Sass.

"Not often. It's hard enough with you; the whole way of moving is so different. They're too strong; we can make holes in the walls accidentally."

"Can you take *any* shape?"

Silui and Marik reshifted to human, and joined the discussion aloud. "That's an argument we have all the time. Humans, yes, even heavyworlders, though we don't enjoy that. Ryxi is easier than humans, although the biochemistry causes problems. Our natural attention span is even longer than yours, but their brain chemistry interferes. Thek —" Marik looked at the others, as if asking a question.

"Might as well," said Silui. "One of us that we know of shifted to Thek form. A child. He'd meant to shift to a rock, which any of us can do briefly, but a Thek was there, and he took the pattern. He never came back. The Thek wouldn't comment."

"Typical." Sass digested that. "So . . . you can take different shapes. How do you decide what kind of human to be? Are you even bisexual, as we are?"

"Video media, for the most part," said Gabril. "All those tapes and disks and cubes of books, plays, holodramas, whatever. We're taught never to choose a star, or anyone well-known, and preferably someone dead a century or so. And then we can make minor changes, of course, within the limits of human variation. I chose a minor character in a primitive adventure film, something about wild tribesmen on Old Earth. At first I wanted blue hair, but my teachers convinced me it wouldn't do. Not for an Academy prospect."

Silui grinned. "I wanted to be Carin Coldae — did you ever see her shows?"

Sass nodded.

"But they said no major performers, so I made my hair yellow and did the teeth different." She bared her perfect teeth, and Sass remembered that Carin Coldae had had a little gap in front. She also noticed that none of them had answered her questions about Weft sexuality, and decided to look it up herself. When she did, she realized why they hadn't tried to explain: *four* sexes, and mating required a rocky seacoast at full tide with an entire colony of Wefts. It reproduced freeswimming larvae, who returned (the lucky few) to moult into a smaller size of the adult form. Wefts were exquisitely sensitive to certain kinds of radiation, and Wefts who left their homeworlds would never join the mating colony. No wonder Marik wouldn't discuss sex — and had that combination of wistfulness and amused superiority towards eager young humans.

By this time, some of her other friends had realized which cadets were Wefts, and Sass found herself getting sidelong looks from those who disapproved of "messing around with aliens." It was this which led to her worst row in the Academy.

She had never been part of the society crowd, not with her background, but she knew exactly which cadets were. Randolph Neil Paraden, a senior that year, lorded it over all with any social pretensions at all. Teeli Pardis, of her own class, wasn't in the same league with a Paraden, and once tried to explain to Sass how important it was to stay on the right side of that most eminent young man.

"He's a snob," Sass had said, in her first year, when Paraden, then a second-year, had held forth at some length on the ridiculousness of letting the children of non-officers into the Academy. "It's not just me — take Issi. So her father's not commissioned: so

what? She's got more Fleet in her little finger than a rich fop like
Paraden has in his whole —"

"That's not the point, Sass," Pardis had said. "The point is that
you don't cross Paraden Family. No one does, for long. Please . . .
I like you, and I want to be friends, but if you get sour with Neil,
I'm — I just *can't*, that's all."

By maintaining a cool courtesy towards everyone that turned
his barbs aside, Sass had managed not to involve herself in a row
with the Paraden Family's representative — until her friendship
with Wefts made it necessary. It began with a series of petty
thefts. The first victim was a girl who'd refused to sleep with
Paraden, although that didn't come out until later. She thought
she'd lost her dress insignia herself, and accepted the rating she
got philosophically. Then her best friend's heirloom silver earrings disappeared, and two more thefts on the same corridor (a
liu-silk scarf and two entertainment cubes) began to heighten
tension unbearably in the last weeks before midterm exams.

Sass, in the next corridor, heard first about the missing cubes.
Two days later, Paraden began to spread rumors that the Wefts
were responsible. "They can change shape," he said. "Take any
shape they want — so of course they could *look* just like the
room's proper occupant. You'd never notice."

Issi told Sass about this, mimicking Paraden's accent perfectly.
Then she dropped back into her own. "That stinker — he'll do
anything to advance himself. Claims he can prove it's Wefts —"

"It's not!" Sass straightened up from the dress boots she'd been
polishing. "They won't take the shape of someone alive: it's
against their rules."

Issi wrinkled her brow at Sass. "I suppose *you'd* know — and
no, I don't hate you for having them as friends. But it's not going
to help you now, Sass, not if Randy Paraden has everyone suspecting them."

Worse was to come. Paraden himself called Sass in, claiming
that he had been given permission to investigate the thefts. From
the way his eyes roamed over her, she decided that theft wasn't all
he wanted to investigate. He had the kind of handsome face that
is used to being admired, and not only for its money. But he
began with compliments for her performance, and patently false
praise for her "amazing" ability to fit in despite a deprived childhood.

"I just wish you'd tell me what you know about the Wefts," he said bringing his gaze back to hers. "Come on — sit down here, and fill me in. You're supposed to be our resident expert, and I hear you're convinced they're not guilty. Explain it to me — maybe I just don't know enough about them. . . ."

Her instinct told her he had no interest whatever in Wefts, but she had to be fair. Didn't she? Reluctantly, she sat and began explaining what she understood of Weft philosophy. He nodded, his lids drooping over brilliant hazel eyes, his perfectly groomed hands relaxed on his knees.

"So you see," she finished, "no Weft would consider taking the form of someone with whom it might be confused: they don't take the forms of famous or living persons."

A smile quirked his mouth, and his eyes opened fully. His voice was still smooth as honey. "They really convinced you, didn't they? I wouldn't have thought you'd be so gullible. Of course, you haven't had a *normal* upbringing — there are so many things beyond your experience. . . ."

Rage swamped her, interfering with coherent speech, and his smile widened to a predatory grin. "You're gorgeous when you're mad, Cadet Sassinak . . . but I suppose you know that. You're tempting me, you really are . . . d'you know what happens to girls who tempt me? I'll bet you're good in bed —" Suddenly his hands were no longer relaxed on his knees; he had moved even as he spoke, and the expensive scent he wore (surely that's not regulation! Sass' mind said, focussing on the trivial) was right there in her nose. "Don't fight me, little slave," he said in her ear. "You'll never win, and you'll wish you hadn't . . . OUCH!"

Despite the ensuing trouble, which went all the way to the Academy Commandant (and probably further than that, considering the Paraden Family) Sass had no happier memory for years than the moment in which she disabled Randolph Neil Paraden with three quick blows and left him grunting in pain on the deck. There was something so satisfying about the *crunch* transmitted up her arm, that it almost frightened her, and she never considered telling Abe, lest he find a reason she should repent. Nor did she confess that part to the Academy staff, though she left Paraden's office and went straight to the Commandant's office to turn herself in.

Paraden's attempt to explain himself, and put the blame for

theft on the Wefts, did not work . . . although Sass wondered if it
would have, given more time, or if she had not testified so
strongly against him. When the first theft victim found that
Paraden was involved, she realized that her "missing" dress insignia might have been stolen instead, and her testimony put the
final seal on the case. Paraden had no chance to threaten Sass in
person after that, but she was sure she'd earned an important enemy for the future. At least he wouldn't be *in* the Fleet. Paraden's
clique, subject to intense scrutiny by the authorities after his dismissal, avoided Sass strictly. Even if one of them had wanted to
be friendly, they'd not have risked more trouble.

Sass came out of it with a muted commendation. "You'll not
say anything of this to your fellow cadets," the Commandant said
severely. "But you showed good judgment. It's too bad you had to
resort to physical force — you were justified, I'm not arguing
that, but it's always better to think ahead and avoid the need to hit
someone, if you can. Other than that, though, you did exactly the
right things at the right time, and I'm pleased. The others will be
wary of you awhile, and I would be most unhappy to find you
using that to your advantage . . . you understand?"

"Yes, sir." She did, indeed, understand. It had been a narrow
scrape, and could have gone badly. What she really wanted was a
chance to get back to work and succeed the way Abe would want
her to: honestly, on her own merits, without favoritism.

"We may seem to be leaning on you a bit, in the next week or
so: don't worry too much."

"Yes, sir."

No one had to lean; she seemed sufficiently subdued, and
eager to return to normal, as much as Academy life was ever normal. Her instructors were not surprised, and she would not know
for years of the glowing comments in her record.

✧ CHAPTER FOUR

Graduation: Sassinak, scoring high on all the exam postings, came into graduation week in the kind of euphoria she had once dreamed of. Honor graduate, with the gold braid and tassels. Cadet commandant: and the two did not often go together. She felt on fire with it, crackling alive a centimeter beyond her fingertips, and from the way the others treated her, that's exactly how she looked. At the final fitting for graduation, she stared into the tailor's mirror and wondered. Was she really *that* perfect, that vision of white and gold? Not a wrinkle, not a rumple, a shape that — she now admitted — was nothing short of terrific, what with all the gymnastics practice. The uniform clung to it, but invested it with dignity, all at once. Nowhere in the mirror could she see a trace of the careless colonial girl, or the ragged slave, or even the rumpled trainee. She looked the way she'd always wanted to look. The mischievous brown eyes in the mirror crinkled . . . except that she'd never intended to be smug. She hated smug. Laughter fought with youthful dignity, as she struggled to hold perfectly still for the tailor's last stitches. Dare she breathe, in that uniform? She had to.

Abe would be so proud, she thought, leading the formation into the Honor Square for the last time. He was there, but she didn't even think of glancing around to find him. He would see what he had made, what he had saved . . . for a moment her mood went grim, thinking of the latest bad news, another colony plundered. Every time such news came in, she thought of girls like her, children like Lunzie and Janek, people, real people, murdered and enslaved. But the crisp commands brought her back to the moment. Her own voice rang out in answer, brisk and impersonal.

The ceremony itself, inherited from a dozen military academies

in the human tradition, and borrowing bits from all of them and
the nonhumans as well, lasted far too long. The planetary governor
welcomed everyone, the senior FSP official responded.
Ambassadors from all the worlds and races that sent cadets to the
Academy had each his or her or its speech to make. Each time the
band had the appropriate anthem to play, and the Honor Guard
had the appropriate flag to raise, with due care, on the pole beside
the FSP banner. Sassinak did not fidget, but without moving a
muscle could see that the civilians and guests did exactly that, and
more than once. A child wailed, briefly, and was removed. Sunlight
glinted suddenly from one of the Marine honor guard's
decorations: he'd taken a deep breath of disgust at something a
politician had said. Sass watched a cloud shadow cross the Yard and
splay across Gunnery Hall. Awards: distinguished teaching award,
distinguished research into Fleet history, distinguished (she
thought) balderdash. Academic departments had awards, athletic
departments had theirs.

Then the diplomas, given one by one, and then — at last —
the commissioning, when they all gave their oaths together. And
then the cheers, and the hats flying high, and the roar from the
watching crowd.

"So — you're going to be on a cruiser, are you?" Abe held up a
card, and a waiter came quickly to serve them.

"That's what it said." Sass wished she could be three people: one
here with Abe, one out celebrating with her friends, and one
already sneaking aboard the cruiser, to find out all about it.
Everyone wanted to start on a cruiser, not some tinpot little escort
vessel or clumsy Fleet supply ship. Sure, you had to serve on
almost everything at least once, but starting on a cruiser meant
being, in however a junior way, *real* Fleet. Cruisers were where the
action was, real action.

They were having dinner in an expensive place, and Abe had
already insisted she order the best. Sass could not imagine what
the colorful swirls on her plate had been originally, but the meal
was as tasty as it was expensive. The thin slice of jelly to one side
she *did* know: crel, the fruiting body of a fungus that grew only
on Regg, the world's single most important export . . . besides
Fleet officers. She raised a glass of wine to Abe, and winked at
him.

He had aged, in the four years she'd been a cadet. He was almost bald now, and she hadn't missed the wince when he folded himself into the chair across from her. His knuckles had swollen a little, his wrinkles deepened, but the wicked sparkle in his eye was the same.

"Ah, girl, you do make my heart proud. Not 'girl,' now: you're a woman grown, and a lady at that. Elegant. I knew you were bright, and gutsy, but I didn't know you'd shape into elegant."

"Elegant?" Sass raised an eyebrow, a trick she'd been practicing in front of her mirror, and he copied her.

"Elegant. Don't fight it; it suits you. Smart, sexy, and elegant besides. By the way, how's the nightlife this last term?"

Sass grimaced and shook her head. "Not much, with all we had to do." Her affair with Harmon hadn't lasted past midyear exams, but she looked forward to better on commissioning leave. And surely on a cruiser she'd find more than one likely partner. "You told me the Academy would be tough, but I thought the worst would be over after the first year. I don't see how being a real officer can be harder than being a cadet commander."

"You will." Abe drained his wine, and picked up a roll. "You never had to send those kids out to die."

"Commander Kerif said that's old-fashioned: you don't send people out to die, you send them out to win."

Abe set the roll back on his plate with a little thump. "He does, does he? What kind of 'win' is it when your ship loses a pod in the grid, and you have to send out a repair party? You listen to me, Sass: you don't want to be one of those wet-eared young pups the troops never trust. It's not a game any more, any more than being hauled off by slavers was a game. You're back in the real world now. Real weapons, real wounds, real death. I'm damned proud of you, and that won't change: it's not every girl that could make it like you have. But if you think the Academy was tough, you think back to Sedon-VI and the slave barracks. I daresay you haven't really forgotten, whatever polish they've put on your manners."

"No. I haven't forgotten." Sass stuffed a roll in her mouth before she said too much. He didn't need to know about the Paraden whelp, and all that mess. A shiver ran across her shoulderblades. He must know she hadn't changed that much . . . but he sure seemed nervous about something. As soon as they'd finished eating, he was ready to go, and she knew something more was coming. Outside in the moist fragrant early-summer night, Sass wished again she could be two or three people. She'd had her invitation, to the graduation frolic up in the parked hills behind the Academy square. It was just the night for it, too . . . soft grass, sweet breeze. Mosquito bites where you can't scratch, she reminded herself, and wondered why the geniuses who'd managed to leave the cockroaches back on Old Terra hadn't managed the same thing with mosquitoes.

Abe led her across town, to one of his favorite bars. Sass sighed inwardly. She knew why he came here: senior Fleet NCOs liked the place, and he wanted to show her off to his friends. But it was noisy, and crowded, and smelled, after the cool open air, like the cheap fat they fried their snacks in. She saw a few other graduates, and waved. Donnet: his uncle was a retired mech from a heavy cruiser. Issi, her family's pride: the first officer in seven generations of a huge Fleet family, all noisily telling her how wonderful it was. She shook hands with those Abe introduced: mostly the older ones, tough men and women with the deft precise movements of those used to working in a confined space.

It took them awhile to find a table, in that crowd. Civilian spacers liked the place, too, and Academy graduation brought everyone out to raise a glass for the graduates. Even the hoods, Sass noted, spotting the garish matching jackets of a street gang huddled near the back door. She was surprised they came here, to a Fleet and spacer bar, but a second, smaller gang followed the first in.

"Go get our drinks, Sass," said Abe, once he was down. "I'll just have a word with the Giustins." Issi's family . . . Sass grinned at him. He knew everyone. She took the credit chip he held out and found her way to the bar.

She was halfway back to him with the drinks when it happened. She missed the beginning, never knew who threw the first blow, but suddenly a row of tables erupted into violence. Fists, chains, the flash of blades. Sass dropped the tray and leaped forward, already yelling Abe's name. She couldn't see him, couldn't see anything but a tangled mass of Fleet cadet uniforms, gang jackets, and spacer gray. Her shout brought order to the cadets, or seemed to. At her command they coalesced, becoming a unit; with her they started to clear that end of the room, in a flurry of feints and blows and sudden clutches. From the corner of one eye, as she ducked under someone's knife and then disarmed him with a kick, she saw a move she recognized from one of their opponents. For an instant, she almost recognized that combination of size, shape, and motion.

She had no time to analyze it; there were too many drunken spacers who reacted to any brawl with enthusiasm, too many greenjacketed, masked hoodlums. The fight involved the whole place now, an incredible crashing screaming mass of struggling bodies. She rolled under a table, came up to strike precise blows at a greenjacket about to knife a spacer, ducked the spacer's wild punch, kicked out at someone who clutched her leg. Something raked her arm; the lights went out, then came on in a dazzle of flickering blue. Sirens, whistles, the overloud blare of a bullhorn. Sass managed a glance back toward the entrance, and saw masked Fleet MPs with riot canisters.

"DOWN . . ." the bullhorn blared. Sass dropped, as all the cadets did, knowing what was coming. Most of the spacers made it down before the MPs fired, but the hoods tried to run for it. A billowing cloud of blue gas filled the room; a thrown canister burst against the back door and felled the hoods who'd headed that way. Sass held her breath. One potato, two potato. Her hand reached automatically to her belt, and her fingernail found the slit for release. Three potato, four potato. She flicked the membrane mask open, and covered her face with it. Five potato, six potato. Now she had the tube of detox, and smeared it over the nose and mouth portions of the mask. Seven, eight, nine, ten . . . a cautious breath, smelling of nutmeg from the detox, but no nausea, no pain, and no unconsciousness. Beside her, a spacer already snored heavily. She looked up, eyes protected by the mask. Already the gas had dissipated to a blue haze, still potent enough to knock out anyone without a mask, but barely obscuring vision.

The MPs spread around the room, checking IDs. Several other cadets were clambering to their feet, protected by their masks. Sass pushed herself up, looking for Abe. She wondered if he carried a Fleet emergency mask.

"ID!" It was a big MP in riot gear; Sass didn't argue but pulled out her new Fleet ID and handed it over. He slipped it into his beltcomp, and returned it. "You start this?" he asked. "Or see it start?"

Sass shook her head. "It started over here, though. I was coming across the room —"

"Why didn't you get out and call help?"

"My father — my guardian was over here."

"Name?"

Sass gave Abe's name and ID numbers; the MP waved her out to search. She veered around two fallen tables . . . was it this one, or that? Three limp bodies lay in an untidy pile. Sass shifted the top one; the MP helped. The next wore spacer gray, a long scrawny man with vomit drooling from the corner of his mouth. And there at the bottom lay Abe. Sass nodded at the MP, and he took a charged reviver from his belt and handed it to her; she put it over Abe's gaping mouth. He looked so . . . so *dead*, that way, with his mouth slack. The MP had dragged away the tall spacer, and now helped her roll Abe onto his back.

They saw the neat black hole in his chest the same moment. Sass didn't recognize it at first, reached down to brush off the smudge on the front of his jacket. He'd hate that, dirt on the new jacket he'd bought for her graduation. But the MP caught her wrist. She looked at him.

"He's dead," the MP said. "Someone had a needler."

Even as the room hazed around her, she thought "Shock. That's what's happening." She couldn't think about Abe being dead . . . he wasn't dead. This was another exercise, another test, like the one in the training vessel, when half the students had been made up to look like wounded victims. She remembered the realistic glisten of the fake gut wound, trailing a tangle of intestines across the deck plating. Easier to think about that, about the equally faked amputation, than that silly little black hole in Abe's jacket.

Later she heard, through an open doorway in the station, that she'd acted normally, not drugged, drunk, or irrational. She was sitting on a gray plastic chair, across a cluttered desk from someone who was busy at a computer. The floor had a pattern of random speckles, like every floor she'd seen for the past four years. She turned her head to look out the door, and an MP with his riot headgear under his arm gave her a neutral glance. She was Fleet, she hadn't started it, she hadn't had hysterics when they found Abe's body. Good enough.

It didn't feel good enough. Her mind raced back and forth

over that minute or so the fight lasted, playing back minute fragments very slowly, looking for something she couldn't yet guess. Where had it started? Who? She had been carrying the drinks: Abe's square squatty bottle of Prium brandy, and the footed glass for it, and a special treat for herself: Caprian liqueur. She'd been afraid the tiny cup of silver-washed crystal — the only proper receptacle for Caprian liqueur — would bounce off the tray if someone bumped her, so she hadn't been looking more than one body ahead when the fight started. She'd looked up when . . . was it a sound, or had she seen something, without really recognizing it? She couldn't place it, and went on. She'd dropped the tray, and in her mind it fell in slow motion, emptying its contents over the shoulders of someone in spacer gray at the table she'd been passing.

Suddenly she had something, or a hint of it. In the midst of that fight, someone to her right had blocked a kick with a move that had to come from Academy training . . . a move that almost had to be learned in low-grav tumbling, although you could use it in normal-G. Only it hadn't been one of the graduates, nor . . . her mind focussed on the anomaly . . . nor one of the spacers. It had been someone in purple and orange, with blue sleeves . . . a gang jacket. She'd tried to take a fast look, but like all the second gang, the fighter's face had been painted in geometric patterns that made identification nearly impossible. Eyes . . . darkish. Skin color . . . from the way it took the paint, neither very light nor very dark.

"Ensign." Sass looked up, ready to curse at the interruption until she saw the rank insignia. Not local police; Fleet. And not just any Fleet, but the Academy Vice-Commandant, Commander Derran.

"Sir." She stood, and wished she'd had time to change uniforms. But they hadn't run the scan over all the spots yet, and they'd told her to wait.

"I'm sorry, Ensign," the commander was saying. "He was a good man, Fleet to the core. And on your graduation night, too."

"Thank you, sir." That much was correct; she couldn't manage much more through a tight throat.

"You're his only listed kin," Derran went on. "I assume you'll want a military funeral?" Sass nodded. "Burial in the Academy grounds, or —"

She had only half-listened when he'd told her, years ago, how he wanted it. "I don't hold with spending Fleet money to send scrap into a star," he'd said. "Space burial's for those who die there. They earned it. But I'm no landsman, either, to be stuck under a bit of marble on a hillside; I hold by the old code. My life was with Fleet, I had no homeland. Burial at sea, if you can manage it, Sass. The Fleet does it the right way."

"At sea," she said now. "He wanted it that way."

"Ashes, or —?"

"Burial, sir, he said, if it was possible."

"Very well. The superintendent's told me they'll release the body tomorrow; we'll schedule it for —" He pulled out his hand-comp and studied the display. "Two days . . . is that satisfactory? Takes that long to get the arrangements made."

"Yes, sir." She felt stupid, stiff, frozen. This could not be Abe's funeral they discussed: time had to stop, and let her sort things out. But time did not stop. The commander spoke to the police officer behind the desk, and suddenly they were ready for her in the lab. A long-snouted machine took samples from every stain on her uniform; the technician explained about the analysis of blood and fiber and skin cells to identify those she'd fought.

When she came out of the lab, she found a Lt. Commander Barrin waiting for her, with a change of clothes brought from her quarters, and the same officer escorted her back to Abe's apartment. There, another Fleet officer had already opened the apartment, set up a file to receive and organize visits and notes that required acknowledgment. Already dozens of notes were racked for her notice, and two of her class waited to see her before leaving for their new assignments.

Sass began to realize what kind of support she could draw on. They knew what papers she needed to find, recognized them in Abe's files when she opened the case. They knew what she should pack, and what formalities would face her in the morning and after. Would he be buried from the Academy, or the nearby Fleet base? Would the circumstances qualify him for a formal military service, or some variant? Sass found one or the other knowledgeable about every question that came up. Someone provided meals, sat her in front of a filled plate at intervals, and saw to it that she ate. Someone answered the door, the comm, weeded out those she didn't want to see, and made sure she had a few minutes alone with special friends. Someone reminded her to apply for a short delay in joining her new assignment: she would have to stay on Regg for another week or so of investigation. Her rumpled, stained uniform disappeared, returned spotless and mended. Someone forwarded all required uniforms to her assignment, leaving her only a small bit of packing to do. And all this was handled smoothly, calmly, as if she were someone of infinite importance, not a mere ensign just out of school.

She could never be alone without help, as long as she had Fleet: Abe had said that, drummed it into her, and she'd seen Fleet's help. But now it all came together. No enemy could kill them all. She would lose friends, friends as close as family, but she could not lose Fleet.

Yet this feeling of security could not make Abe's funeral easier. The police had offered her the chance to be alone with his body, a chance she refused, concealing the horror she felt. (Touch the body of someone she had loved? For an instant the face of her little sister Lunzie, carried in her arms to the dock, swam before her.) Wrapped in a dark blue shroud, it was taken by Fleet Marines to the Academy mortuary. Sass had no desire to know how a body was prepared for burial; she signed the forms she was handed, and skimmed quickly over the information given.

The body of an NCO, retired or active, could remain on view for one day. That she agreed to: Abe had had many friends who would want to pay their respects. His flag-draped coffin rested on the ritual gun-cradle in a side chapel. A line of men and women, most in uniform, came to shake hands with Sass and walk past it, one by one. Some, she noticed, laid a hand on the flag, patted it a little. Two were Wefts, which surprised her. . . . Abe had never told her about Weft friends.

The funeral itself, the ancient ritual to honor a fellow warrior, required of Sass only the contained reticence and control that Abe had taught her. She, the bereaved, had only that simple role, and yet it was almost too heavy a burden for her. Others carried his coffin; she carried her gratitude. Others had lost a friend; she had lost all connection to her past. Again she had to start over, and for this period even Fleet could not comfort her.

But she would not disgrace him. The acceptable tears slid down her cheeks, the acceptable responses came from her mouth. And the old cadences of the funeral service, rhythms old before ever the first human went into space, comforted where no living person could.

"Out of the deep have I called unto thee, O Lord —" The chaplain's voice rang through the chapel, breaking the silence that had followed the entrance hymn, and the congregation answered.

"Lord, hear my voice."

Whatever the original beliefs had been, which brought such words to such occasions, no one in Fleet much cared — but the bond of faith in something beyond individual lives, individual struggles, a bond of faith in love and honesty and loyalty . . . that they all shared. And phrase by phrase the old ritual continued.

"O let thine ears consider well —"

"The voice of my complaint." Sass thought of the murderer, and for a few moments vengeance routed grief in her heart. Someday — *someday*, she would find out who, and why, and — she stumbled over a phrase about redemption following mercy, having in mind neither.

Readings followed, and a hymn Abe had requested, its mighty refrain "Lest we forget — lest we forget" ringing in her ears through another psalm and reading. Sass sat, stood, knelt, with the others, aware of those who watched her. It seemed a long time before the chaplain reached the commendation; her mind hung on the words "dust to dust . . ." long after he had gone on, and blessed the congregation. And now the music began again, this time the Fleet Hymn. Sass followed the casket out through the massed voices, determined not to cry.

"Eternal Father, strong to save . . ." Her throat closed; she could not even mouth the words that had brought tears to her eyes even from the first.

Across the wide paved forecourt of the Academy, the flags in front of the buildings all lowered, a passing squad of junior middies held motionless as the funeral procession went on its way. Out the great arched gates to the broad avenue, where Fleet Marines held the street traffic back, and the archaic hearse, hitched to a team of black horses, waited. Sass concentrated on the horses, the buckles of their harness, the brasses stamped with the Fleet seal . . . surely it was ludicrous that a spacegoing service would maintain a horsedrawn hearse for its funerals.

But as they followed on foot, from the Academy gates to the

dock below the town, it did not seem ludicrous. Every step of a human foot, every clopping hoofbeat of the horses, felt right. This was respect, to take the time in a bustling, modern setting to do things the old way. As Abe's only listed kin, Sass walked alone behind the hearse; behind her came Abe's friends still in Fleet, enlisted, then officer.

At the quay, the escort commander called the band to march, and they began playing, music Sass had never heard but found instantly appropriate. Strong, severe, yet not dismal, it enforced its own mood on the procession. On all the ships moored nearby, troops and officers stood to attention; ensigns all at half-mast. The *Carly Pierce*, sleek and graceful, Fleet's only fighting ship (a veteran of two battles with river pirates in the early days of Regg's history, before it became the Fleet Headquarters planet). The procession halted; from her position behind the hearse, Sass could barely see the pallbearers forming an aisle up the gangway. Exchange of salutes, exchange of honors: the band gave a warning rattle of drumsticks, and the body bearers slid the casket from the hearse. Sass followed them toward the gangway. Such a little way to go; such a long distance to return. . . .

And now they were all on the deck, the body bearers placing the casket on a frame set ready, lifting off the flag, holding it steady despite a brisk sea breeze. Sass stared past it at the water, ruffled into little arcs of silver and blue. She hardly noticed when the ship cast off and slid almost soundlessly through the waves, across the bay and around the jagged island in it. There, in the lee of the island, facing the great cliffs, the ship rested as the chaplain spoke the final words.

"— Rest eternal grant to him, O Lord —" And the other voices joined his. "And let light perpetual shine upon him."

The chaplain stepped aside; the escort commander brought the escort to attention and three loud volleys racketed in ragged echoes from island and cliffs beyond. Birds rose screaming from the cliffs, white wings tangled in the light. Sass clenched her jaw: now it was coming. She tried not to see the tilting frame, the slow inexorable movement of the casket to the waiting sea.

As if from the arc of the sky, a single bugle tolled the notes out, one by one, gently and inexorably. Taps. Sass shivered despite herself. It had ended her days for the past four years — and now it was ending his. It had meant sunset, lights out,

368 THE PLANET PIRATES

another day survived — and now it meant only endings. Her throat closed again; tears burned her eyes. No one had played taps for her parents, for her sister and brother and the others killed or left to die on Myriad. No one had played taps for the slaves who died. She was cold all the way through, realizing, as she had not ever allowed herself to realize, that she might easily have been another dead body on Myriad, or in the slaver's barracks, unknown, unmourned.

All those deaths . . . the last note floated out across the bay, serene despite her pain, pulling it out of her. Here, at least, the dead could find peace, knowing someone noticed, someone mourned. She took a deep unsteady breath. Abe was safe here, "from rock and tempest, fire and foe," safe in whatever safety death offered, completing his service as he had wished.

She took the flag, when it was boxed and presented, with the dignity Abe deserved.

PART TWO

✧ CHAPTER FIVE

"Ensign Sassinak requests permission to come aboard, sir." Coming aboard meant crossing a painted stripe on the deck of the station, but the ritual was the same as ever.

"Permission granted." The Officer of the Deck, a young man whose reddish skin and ice-blue eyes indicated a Brinanish origin, had one wide gold ring and a narrow one on his sleeve. He returned her salute, and Sass stepped across the stripe. Slung on her shoulder was the pack containing everything she was permitted to take aboard. Her uniforms (mess dress, working dress, seasonal working, and so on) were already aboard, sent ahead from her quarters before her final interview with the Academy Commandant after Abe's funeral.

Her quarters were minimal: one of two female ensigns (there were five ensigns in all), she had one fold-down bunk in their tiny cubicle, one narrow locker for dress uniforms, three drawers, and a storage bin. Sass knew Mira Witsel only slightly; she had been one of Randolph Neil Paraden's set, a short blonde just over the height limit. Sass hoped she wasn't as arrogant as the others, but counted on her graduation rank to take care of any problems. With the other ensigns, they shared a small study/lounge (three terminals, a round table, five chairs). Quickly, she stowed her gear and took a glance at herself in the mirror strip next to the door. First impressions . . . reporting to the captain . . . she grinned at her reflection. Clean and sharp and probably all too eager . . . but it was going to be a good voyage . . . she was sure of it.

"Come in!" Through the open hatch, the captain's voice sounded stuffy, like someone not quite easy with protocol. Fargeon. Commander Fargeon — she'd practiced that softened g, typical of his homeworld (a French-influenced version of Neo-Gaesh). Sass took a deep breath, and stepped in.

He answered her formal greeting in the same slightly stuffy voice: not hostile, but standoffish. Tall, angular, he leaned across his cluttered desk to shake her hand as if his back hurt him a little. "Sit down, Ensign," he said, folding himself into his own chair behind his desk, and flicking keys on his desk terminal. "Ah . . . your record precedes you. Honor graduate." He looked at her, eyes sharp. "You can't expect to start on the top here, Ensign."

"No, sir." Sassinak sat perfectly still, and he finally nodded.

"Good. That's a problem with some top graduates, but if you don't have a swelled head, I don't see why you should run into difficulties. Let me see —" He peered at his terminal screen. "Yes. You are the first ensign aboard, good. I'm putting you on third watch now, but that's not permanent, and it doesn't mean what it does in the Academy. Starting an honor cadet on the third watch just ensures that everyone gets a fair start."

And you don't have to listen to complaints of favoritism, Sassinak thought to herself. She said nothing, just nodded.

"Your first training rotation will be Engineering," Fargeon went on. "The Exec, Lieutenant Dass, will set up the duty roster. Any questions?"

Sass knew the correct answer was no, but her mind teemed with questions. She forced it back and said, "No, sir."

The captain nodded, and sent her out to meet Lieutenant Dass. Dass, in contrast to his captain, was a wiry compact man whose dark, fine-featured face was made even more memorable by light green eyes.

"Ensign Sassinak," he drawled, in a tone that reminded her painfully of the senior cadets at the Academy when she'd been a rockhead. "Honor cadet . . ."

Sassinak met his green gaze, and discovered a glint of mischief in it. "Sir —" she began, but he interrupted.

"Never mind, Ensign. I've seen your record, and I know you can be polite in all circumstances, and probably work quads in your head at the same time. The captain wanted you in engineering first, because we've installed a new environmental Homeostasis system and it's still being tested. You'll be in charge of that, once you've had time to look over the system documentation." He grinned at her expression. "Don't look surprised, Ensign: you're not a cadet in school any more. You're a Fleet officer. We don't have room for deadweights; we have to know right away if you can perform for us. Now. It's probably going to take you all your off-watch time for several days to work your way through the manuals. Feel free to ask the Engineering Chief anything you need to know, or give me a holler. On watch, you'll have the usual standing duties, but you can spend part of most watches with the engineering crew."

"Yes, sir." Sass' mind whirled. She was going to be in charge of testing the new system? A system which could kill them all if she made a serious mistake? This time the flash of memory that brought Abe to mind had no pain. He'd told her Fleet would test her limits.

"Your record says you get along with allies?"

Allies was the Fleet term for allied aliens; Sassinak had never heard it used so openly. "Yes, sir."

"Good. We have a Weft Jig, and several Weft battle crew, and that Weft ensign: I suppose you knew him at the Academy?" Sassinak nodded. "Oh, and have you ever seen an adult Ssli?"

"No, sir."

"We're Ssli-equipped, of course: all medium and heavy cruisers have been for the past two years." He glanced at the timer. "Come along; we've time enough to show you."

The Ssli habitat was a narrow oval in cross-section: ten meters on the long axis, aligned with the ship's long axis, and only two meters wide. It extended "upward" from the heavily braced keel through five levels: almost twenty meters. The plumbing that maintained its marine environment took up almost the same cubage.

At the moment, the Ssli had grown only some three meters in diameter from its holdfast, and its fan was still almost circular. Two viewing ports allowed visual inspection of the Ssli's environment. The Executive Officer's stubby fingers danced on the keyboard of the terminal outside one viewing port.

"Basic courtesy — always ask before turning on the lights in there."

Sassinak peered over his shoulder. The screen came up, and displayed both question and answer, the latter affirmative. Dass flipped a toggle, and light glowed in the water inside, illuminating a stunning magenta fan flecked with yellow and white. Sassinak stared. It seemed incredible that this huge, motionless, intricate object could be not only alive, but sentient . . . sentient

enough to pass the FSP entry levels. She could hardly believe
that the larval forms she had seen in the Academy tanks had anything to do with this . . . this thing.

Somehow the reality was much stranger than just seeing
tapes of it. I wonder what it feels like, she thought. How it
thinks, and —

"How did they ever figure out . . . ?" she said, before she
thought.

"I don't know, really. Thek discovered them, of course, and
maybe they're more likely to suspect intelligence in something
that looks more mineral than we are." Dass looked at her closely.
"It bothers some people a lot — how about you?"

"No." Sassinak shook her head, still staring through the viewing port. "It's beautiful, but hard to realize it's sentient. But why
not, after all? How do you communicate with it?"

"The usual. Biocomp interface . . . look, there's the leads." He
pointed, and Sassinak could see the carefully shielded wires that
linked the Ssli to the computer terminal. "Want an introduction?"

When she nodded, he tapped in her ID code, asked her favorite name-form, and then officer crew: general access.

"That gives it access to the general information in your file.
Nothing classified, just what any other officer would be able to
find out about you. Age, class rank, sex, general appearance,
planet of origin, that kind of thing. If you want to share more, you
can offer additional access, either by giving it the information
directly, or by opening segments of your file. Now you come up
here, and be ready to answer."

On the screen before her, a greeting already topped the space.
"Welcome, Ensign Sassinak; my name in Fleet is Hssrho. Have
been installed here thirty standard months; you will not remember, but you met me in larval stage in your second year at the
Academy."

Sassinak remembered her first introduction to larval Ssli, in
the alien communications lab, but she'd never expected to meet
the same individual in sessile form. And she hadn't remembered
that name. Quickly she tapped in a greeting, and apologies for
her forgetfulness.

"Never mind . . . we take new names when we unite with a
ship. You could not know. But I remember the cadet who apologized for bumping into my tank."

From the Ssli, Lieutenant Dass led her through a tangle of passages into the Engineering section. Sassinak tried to pay attention to the route, but had to keep ducking under this, and stepping over that. She began to wonder if he was taking a round-about and difficult way on purpose.

"In case you think I'm leading you by the back alleys," he said over his shoulder, "all this junk is the redundancy we get from having two environmental systems, not just one. As soon as you've got the new one tuned up to Erling's satisfaction — he's the Engineering Chief — we can start dismantling some of this. Most of it's testing gear anyway."

Even after the study of ship types at the Academy, Sass found it took awhile to learn the geography of the big ship. Cruiser architecture was determined by the requirement that the ships not only mount large weapons for battles in space or against planets, but also carry troops and their support equipment, and be able to land them. Cruisers often operated alone, and thus needed a greater variety of weaponry and equipment than any one ship in a battle group. But to retain the ability to land on planet in many situations, and maneuver (if somewhat clumsily) in atmosphere, cruiser design had settled on a basic ovoid shape. Thanks to the invention of efficient internal artificial gravity, the ships no longer had to spin to produce a pseudo-gravity. The "egg" could be sliced longitudinally into decks much easier to use and build.

In their first few days, all the new ensigns took a required tour of each deck, from the narrow silent passages of Data Deck, where there was little to see but arrays of computer components, to the organized confusion of Flight Two, with the orbital shuttles, drone and manned space fighters, aircraft, and their attendant equipment, all the way down to the lowest level of Environmental, where the great plumbing systems that kept the ship functioning murmured to themselves between throbbing pump stations. Main Deck, with the bridge, nearly centered the ship, as the bridge sector centered Main Deck. Aft of the bridge was Officers' Country, with the higher ranking officers nearer the bridge (and in larger quarters), and the ensigns tucked into their niches near the aft cargo lift that ran vertically through all decks. Lest they think this a handy arrangement, they were reminded that regulations forbade the use of the cargo lift for personnel only: they were supposed to keep fit by running up and down the ladders between decks. Main Deck also held all the administrative offices needed. Between Data Deck and Environmental was Crew, or Troop Deck, which had, in addition to crew quarters, recreation facilities, and mess, the sick bay and medical laboratory. When the ship landed onplanet, a ramp opening from Troop Deck offered access to the planet's surface.

Yet nothing, they were warned, was excess: nothing was mere decoration. Every pipe, every fitting, every electrical line, had its function, and the interruption of a single function could mean the life of the ship in a crisis. So, too, all the petty regulations: the timing of shower privileges, the spacing of the exercise machines in the gyms. It was hard for Sass to believe, but with the stern eye of a senior officer on them all, she nodded with the rest.

Shipboard duty had none of the exotic feel the ensigns had hoped for, once they knew their way around the ship. Mira, away from the social climbers at the Academy, turned out to be a warm, enthusiastic girl, willing to be friends with anyone. Her father, a wealthy merchant captain, had set her sights on a career in space. She frankly admired Sassinak for being "really strong." To Sassinak's surprise when it came to working out in the gym, Mira was a lot tougher than she seemed.

"We weren't supposed to show it off," said Mira when Sassinak commented on this. "Mother wanted us to be ladies, not just spacer girls — she said we'd have a lot more fun that way. And then in Neil's bunch at the Academy . . ." She looked sideways at Sassinak who suddenly realized that Mira really did want to be friends. "They always said there's no use exceeding requirements, 'cause the Wefts'll get all the medals anyway. And Neil — Mother sent me a whole long tape about it when she found out he was in the same class. She'd have eaten me alive if I'd made an enemy of him without cause." She patted Sassinak on the shoulder, as if she weren't a decimeter shorter. "Sorry, but you weren't cause enough, and it was clear you could deck Neil any time you wanted to."

"You're —" Sass couldn't think of a good term, and shook her head. Mira grinned. "I'm a typical ambitious, underbred and overfed merchanter brat, who'll never make admiral but plans to spend a long and pleasurable career in Fleet. Incidentally serving FSP quite loyally, since I really do believe it does a lot of good, but not ever rising to flag rank and not really wanting it. Deficient in ambition, that's what they'd grade me."

"Not deficient in anything else," said Sassinak. She caught the wink that Mira tipped her and grinned back. "You devious little stinker — I'll bet you're a good friend, at that."

"I try to be." Mira's voice was suddenly demure, almost dripping honey. "When I have the chance. And when I like someone."

Sassinak thought better of asking, but Mira volunteered.

"I like you, Sass . . . now. You were pretty stiff in the Academy, and yes, I know you had reasons. But I'd like to be friends, if you would, and I mean friends like my people mean it: fair dealing, back-to-back in a row with outsiders, but if I think you're wrong I'll say it to your face."

"Whoosh. You can speak plain." Sassinak smiled and held out her hand. "Yes, Mira; I'd like that. 'Slong as I get to tell you."

And after that she enjoyed the little free time she had to share impressions with Mira. Meals in the officers' mess were not as formal as those in the Academy, but they knew better than to put themselves forward.

For the first month, Sassinak was on third shift rotation, which meant that she ate with other third shift officers; the captain usually kept a first-shift schedule. From what Mira told her, she wasn't missing much. When she rotated to first-shift watch, and Communications as her primary duty, she found that Mira was right.

Instead of a lively discussion of the latest political scandal from Escalon or Contaigne, with encouragement to join in, the ensigns sat quietly as Captain Fargeon delivered brief, unemotional critiques of the ship's performance. Sassinak grew to dread his quiet "There's a little matter in Engineering . . ." or whatever section he was about to shred.

The shift to Communications Section gave her some sense of contact with the outside world. Fleet vessels, unlike civilian ships, often stayed in deepspace for a standard year or more. None of the cadets had ever experienced that odd combination of isolation and confinement. Sassinak, remembering the slave barracks and the pirate vessel, found the huge, clean cruiser full of potential friends and allies an easy thing to take, but some did not.

❖   ❖   ❖

Corfin, the ensign who slipped gradually into depression and then paranoia, had not been a particular friend of hers in the Academy, but when she recognized his withdrawal, she did her best to cheer him up. Nothing worked; finally his supervisor reported to the Medical Officer, and when treatment slowed, but didn't stop, the progression, he was sedated, put in cold sleep, and stored for the duration, to be discharged as medically unfit for shipboard duty when they reached a Fleet facility.

"But why can't they predict that?" asked Sassinak, in the group therapy session the Medical Officer insisted on. "Why can't they pick them out, clear back in the first year, or before —"

Because Corfin had been in the Academy prep school, and had a Fleet medical record going back ten years or more.

"He was told of the possibility," she was told, "it's in his chart. But his father was career Fleet, died in a pod repair accident: the boy wanted to try, and the Board agreed to give him a chance. And it's not wasted time, his or ours either. We have his record, to judge another by, and he'll qualify for a downside Fleet job if he wants it."

Sassinak couldn't imagine anyone wanting it. To be stuck on one planet, or shipped from one to another by cold sleep cabinet? Horrible. Glad she had no such problems herself, she went back to her work eagerly.

It was, in fact, a prized assignment. The communications "shack" was a good-sized room that opened directly onto the bridge. Sassinak could look out and see the bridge crew: the officer of the deck in the command module — or, more often, standing behind it, overlooking the others from the narrow eminence that protruded into the bridge like a low stage. Of course she could not see it all; her own workstation cut off the view of the main screens and the weapons section. But she felt very much at the nerve-center of the cruiser's life. Communications in the newly refitted heavy cruiser were a far sight from anything she'd been taught in the Academy.

Instead of the simple old dual system of sublight radio and the FTL link, both useful only when the ship itself was in sublight space, they had five separate systems, each for use in a particular combination of events. Close-comm, used within thirty LM of the receiver, was essentially the same old sublight microwave relay that virtually all technical races developed early on.

Low-link, a low-power FTL link for use when they themselves were not on FTL drive, brought near-instantaneous communications within a single solar system, and short-lag comm to nearby star systems. Two new systems gave the capability for transmissions while in FTL flight: a sublight emergency channel, SOLEC, which allowed a computer-generated message to contact certain mapped nodes, and the high-power FTL link which transmitted to mapped stations. Even newer, still experimental and very secret, was the computer-enhanced FTL link to other Fleet vessels in FTL flight.

For each system, a separate set of protocols and codes determined which messages might be sent where, and by whom . . . and who could or should receive messages.

"One thing is, we don't want the others to know what we've got," said the Communications Chief. "So far, all the commercials in human space are using the old stuff: electromagnetic, light-speed — radio and stuff like that — and FTL link — really a low-link. Arbetronics is about to come out with a commercial version of the FTL sublight transmitter, but Fleet's got a total lock on the high-link. Our people developed it; all that research was funded in house, and unless someone squeaks, it's our baby. And the Fleet IFTL link even more so. You can see why."

Sassinak certainly could. Until now, Fleet vessels had had to drop into sublight to pick up incoming messages — usually at mapped nodes, which made them entirely too predictable. Her instructors at the Academy had suspected that Fleet messages were being routinely stripped from the holding computers by both Company and unattached pirates. The IFTL link would make them independent of the nodes altogether. "Information," the Comm Chief said. "That's the power out here — who knows what? Now, ordinarily, in any disputed or unsecured sector, all crew messages are held for batch transmission, ordinary sublight radio, to the nearest mail facility. Anything serious — death, discharge, that kind of thing — can be put on the low-link with clearance from the Communications Officer, who may require the captain to sign off on it. The initiating officer's code goes on each transmission. That means whoever authorized it, not who actually punched the button — right now you're not booked to initiate any signals. The actual operator's code also goes on it; whoever logs onto that system transmitter automatically gets hooked to the transmission. Incoming's always accepted, and automatically dumped in a protected file unless its own security status requires even more. Accepting officer's code — and that's you, if you're on duty right then — goes on it in the file. If it's the usual mail-call batch, check with 'Tenant Cardon; if he says it's clear, then let the computer route it to individuals' e-mail files."

"What about other incoming?"

"Well, if it's not a batch file message, if it's a singleton for one person, you have to get authorization to move it to that individual's file. If it's a low-link message, those are always Fleet official business, and that means route to the captain first, but into his desk file, not his private e-mail file. We don't get any incoming on highlink or SOLEC, so you don't have to worry about them. Now if it's something on the IFTL, that's routed directly to the captain's desk file. Pipe the captain, wherever he is, and no copies at all. Nothing in main computer. Clear?"

"Yes, sir. But do I still patch on my ID code, on an IFTL message?"

"Yes, of course. That's always done."

Some days later, Sassinak came into Communications just as the beeper rang off on the end of an incoming message burst. Cavery, who had already discovered the new ensign could do his job almost as well as he could, pointed at the big display. Sassinak scanned the grid and nodded.

"I'll put it down," she said.

"I've already keyed my code to it. Just the mail run from Stenus, nothing fancy."

Sass flicked a few keys and watched the display. The computer broke each message batch into its component messages, and routed them automatically. The screen flickered far faster than she could read it. She liked the surreal geometries of the display anyway. It hovered on the edge of making sense, like math a little beyond her capability.

Suddenly something tugged at her mind, hard, and she jammed a finger on the controls. The display froze, halfway between signals, showing only the originating codes.

"Whatsit?" asked Cavery, looking over to see why the flickering had stopped.

"I don't know. Something funny."

"Funny! You've been here over six Standard months and you're surprised to find something funny?"

"No . . . not really." Her voice softened as she peered at the screen. Then she saw it. Out of eighteen message fragments on the screen, two had the same originator codes, reduplicated four times each. That had made odd blocks of light on the screen, repeating blocks where she'd expected randomness. She looked over at Cavery. "What's a quad duplication of originating blocks for?"

"A quad? Never saw one. Let's take a look —" He called up the reference system on his own screen. "What's the code?"

Sassinak read it off, waited while he punched it in. He whistled. "Code itself is Fleet IG's office . . . who the dickens is getting mail from the IG, I wonder. And quad duplication. That's . . ."

She heard his fingers on the keys, a soft clicking, and then another whistle. "I dunno, Ensign. Some kind of internal code, I'd guess, but it's not in the book. Who're they to?"

Sassinak read off the codes, and he looked them up.

"Huh. 'Tenant Achael and Weapons Systems Officer . . . and that's 'Tenant Achael. Tell you what, Ensign, someone sure wants to have Achael get that signal, whatever it is." He gave her a strange, challenging look. "Want me to put a tag on it?"

"Mmm? No," she said. Then more firmly, as he continued to look at her. "No, just the receiving code tag. It's none of our business, anyway."

Still, she couldn't quite put it out of her mind. It wasn't unknown for the IG to pull a surprise inspection — and not unheard of for a junior officer to be tipped off by a friend ahead of time. Or someone — presumably 'Tenant Achael — might have made a complaint directly to the IG. That also happened. But she couldn't leave it at that. She was responsible, whenever she was on duty, for spotting anything irregular in the Communications Section. Two messages from the IG's office — two messages sent to the same person by different routes, and with an initiating code that wasn't in the book. That was definitely irregular.

"Come in, Ensign," said Commander Fargeon, seated as usual behind his desk. She wished it had been some other officer. "What is it?" he asked.

"An irregularity in incoming signals, sir." Sassinak laid the hardcopy prints on his desk. "This came in with a regular mail batchfile. Two identical strips for Lieutenant Achael, one direct to his e-mail slot, and one to Weapons Officer. The same originating code, in the IG's office, but repeated four times. And it's in code . . ." She let her voice trail off, seeing that Fargeon's attention was caught. He picked up the prints and looked closely at them.

"Hmm. Did you decode it?"

"No, sir." Sass managed not to sound aggrieved: he knew she knew that was strictly against regulations. She hadn't done anything yet to make him think she was likely to break regs.

"Well." Fargeon sat back, still staring at the prints. "It's probably nothing, Ensign — a friend in the IG's office, wanting to make sure he'd get the message — but you were quite right to bring it to my attention. Quite right." By his tone, he didn't think so — he sounded bored and irritable. Sassinak waited a moment. "And if anything of a similar nature should happen again, you should certainly tell me about it. Dismissed."

Sassinak left his office unsatisfied. Something pricked her mind; she couldn't quite figure it out, but it worried her constantly. Surely Fargeon, the most rigid of captains, couldn't be involved in anything underhanded. And was it underhanded to be receiving messages from the IG? Not really.

She mentioned her inability to feel comfortable with Fargeon's attitude to the Weft ensign, Jrain.

"No, we don't think he's bent," was Jrain's response. "He doesn't like Wefts, but then he doesn't like much of anyone he didn't know in childhood. They're pretty inbred, there on Bretagne. A bit like the Seti, in a way: they have very rigid ideas of right and wrong."

"I thought the Seti were pretty loose," said Sass. "Vandals and hellraisers, always willing to start a fight or gamble it all on one throw."

"They are, but that doesn't mean they don't have their own rules. Did you know Seti won't do any gene engineering?"

"I thought they were primitive in that field."

"They are, but it's because they want to be. They think it's wrong to load the dice — genetic or otherwise. But that's beside the point: what matters is that Fargeon is straight, so far as Wefts can tell. Even though he doesn't like us, Wefts choose to serve on his ship, because he is fair."

✧   ✧   ✧

Only a few shipdays later, they had their first break in routine since leaving Base. The cruiser had orders to inspect a planet in the system which had generated conflicting reports: an EEC classification of "habitable; possibly suitable for limited colonization" and a more recent free scout's comment of "dead — no hope."

From orbit, the remote survey crews backed up the free scout's report. No life, and no possibility of it without major terraforming. But Fleet apparently wanted a closer investigation, some idea of who had done it — the *Others*, or what? Commander Fargeon himself chose the landing team: Sassinak went as Communications Officer, along with ten specialists and ten armed guards.

It was her first time since the training cruise at the Academy in full protective gear. This time, a sergeant checked her seals and tanks, instead of an instructor. The air tasted "tanky" as they put it, and she had to remind herself where all the switches were. Carefully, very aware that this was no training exercise, she checked out the main and backup radios she'd be using on the surface, made sure that the recording taps were all open, the computer channels cleared for input.

She didn't see the planet until the shuttle cleared the cruiser's hull. It looked exactly like the teaching tapes of dead planets. Sassinak ignored it after a glance and ran another set of checks on her equipment. Although the planet had once had a breathable oxygen atmosphere, sustained by its biosphere, it had already skewed towards the reducing atmosphere common to unlivable worlds.

Besides, whatever had been used to kill its living component might still be active. They would be on tanks the entire time. She had hardly cleared the shuttle ramp on the surface, and felt the alien grit rasping along her bootsoles, when the landing team commander called a warning.

At first Sassinak could not judge the size or distance of the pyramidal objects that seemed to grow, like the targets in a computer simulation game, from nothing in the upper air. Certainly they didn't follow the trajectories required by normal insystem drives, nor did they slow for the careful landing the shuttle pilot had made. Instead they hovered briefly overhead, then sank apparently straight down to rest firmly on the bare rock.

Sassinak reported this, hardly aware of doing it, so fascinated was she by the display. Half a dozen of the pyramids now sat, or lay, in an irregular array near the shuttle. Theks, the landing party commander had said; apart from teaching tapes, she had never seen a Thek and now she saw many in person, if such designation was accurate for those entities.

Another member of the landing party beeped the LPC and asked, "What do we do about them, sir?"

The LPC snorted, a splatter of sound in the suit comm units. "It's more what are they going to do about us. For future reference, this looks to me like the beginnings of a Thek conference. Meanwhile, look your fill. Not many of us ephemerals get a chance to see one forming."

His suit helmet tilted; Sassinak looked up, too. More of the pyramids appeared, sank, and landed nearby.

"If that's what they're doing," the LPC said after a brief silence, "we might as well go back in the shuttle and have something to eat. This is going to take longer than we'd planned. Inform the captain, Ensign."

More and more pyramids arrived . . . and then, without sound or warning, the ones already landed rose and joined the others to form a large, interlocking structure of complex geometry.

"That," said the LPC, sounding impressed, "is a Thek cathedral. It's big enough inside for this whole shuttle, and it lasts until they're through. The Xenos think they're linking minds. Humans who have been *in* one don't talk about what happened."

"Humans get drawn into one of those things?" someone asked, clearly unsettled by the notion.

"If a Thek calls, you come," replied the LPC.

"How would you know a Thek wanted you?"

"Oh, there's evidence that the Thek recognize individual humans from time to time. . . ."

"Their time?" a wise guy quipped.

"It does look a lot like the Academy Chapel right now," said Sassinak softly. She didn't think this was a time to be clever but people reacted differently to something they couldn't quite understand.

"Most people think that. You're lucky to see one, you know. Just try to keep out of one, if you've got the option. No one says 'no' to one Thek, let alone a whole flotilla."

"Does anyone know more about them than the Academy tapes?"

"Did you take Advanced Alien Cultures? No? Well, it's not that much help anyway. An allied alien race, co-founders of the Federation, we think. Wefts are one of their client races, although I don't know why. They're mineral, and they communicate very . . . very . . . slowly . . . with humans, if at all." Although they were back in the shuttle now, the LPC kept his voice low. "Have a taste for transuranics, and they're supposed to remember everything that ever happened to them, or a distant ancestor. Live a long time, but before they dissolve or harden, or whatever it is they do that corresponds with death, they transmit all their memories somehow. Maybe they're telepathic with each other. For humans they use a computer interface or modulate sound waves. Without, as you can see, any mouth. Don't ask me how; it's not my field, and this is only the second time I've seen a Thek."

Hours later, the Theks abruptly disassembled themselves and flew — or whatever it was — back into the darkening sky. The landing party, now thoroughly bored and stiff, grumbled back into action.

Sass followed them to the outcrop that had been chosen for primary sampling. They set to work as she relayed their results and comments back to the ship. Worklights glared, forming haloes at the edge of her vision as the dust rose, almost like smokehaze in a bar, she thought, watching suited figures shift back and forth. Suddenly she stiffened, wholly alert, her heart racing. One of them — one of the helmeted blurs — she had seen before. Somewhere. Somewhere in a fight.

It came to her: the night of Abe's murder, the night of the brawl in the bar. That same bold geometric pattern on the helmet had then been on the jacket of one of the street gang. That same flicking movement of the arm had — she closed her eyes a moment, now recognizing something she'd never quite put together — had aimed something at Abe.

Rage blurred her vision and thought. She opened her mouth to scream into the comm unit, but managed to clamp her teeth on the scream. Abe's murderer here? In a Fleet uniform? She didn't know all the landing party, but she could certainly find out whose helmet that was. And somehow, some way, she'd get her revenge.

Through the rest of the time on planet, she worked grimly, determined to hide her reactions until she found out just who that was, and why Abe had been killed. She wondered again about the mysterious duplicated message to 'Tenant Achael. Could that be part of the same problem?

Back on the ship, Sass made no sudden moves. She had had time to think about her options. Going to Fargeon with a complaint that someone on the ship had murdered her guardian would get her a quick trip to the Medical Section for sedation. Querying the personnel files was against regulations, and even if she could get past the computer's security systems, she risked leaving a trace of her search. Whoever it was would know that she was aware of something wrong. Even asking about the helmet's assigned user might be risky, but she felt it was the least risky . . . and she had an idea.

Partly because of the Thek arrival and conference, the LPC had permitted more chatter on the circuits than usual, and Sass had already found it hard to tag each transmission with the correct originating code, as required. She had reason, therefore, to ask the rating in charge of the helmets for a list of occupants, "just to check on some of this stuff, and be sure I get the right words with the right person."

The helmet she cared most about belonged to 'Tenant Achael. Gotcha, thought Sass, but kept a bright friendly smile on her face when she called him on the ship's intercom. "Sorry to bother you, sir," she began, "but I needed to check some of these transmissions. . . ."

"Couldn't you have done that at the time?" he asked. He sounded gruff, and slightly wary. Sass tried to project innocent enthusiasm, and pushed all thought of Abe aside.

"Sorry, sir, but I was having trouble with the coded data link while the Theks were there." This was in fact true, and she'd mentioned it to the LPC at the time, which meant she was covered if Achael checked. "The commander said that was more important. . . ."

"Very well, then. What is it?"

"At 1630, ship's time, a conversation on the geo-chemical sulfur cycle and its relation to the fourth stage of re-seeding . . . was it you, sir, or Specialist Nervin, who said, 'But that's only if you consider the contribution of the bacterial substrate to be nominal.'

That's just where the originating codes began to get tangled." Just as she spoke, Sass pushed the capture button on her console, diverting Achael's response into a sealed file she'd prepared. Highly illegal, but she would have need of it. And if the shielded tap she'd put together didn't work, he'd hear the warning buzz on her speech first. He should react to it.

"Oh —" He sounded less tense. "That was Nervin — he was telling me about the latest research from Zamroni. Apparently there's some new evidence that shows a much greater contribution from the bacterial substrate in fourth stage. Have you read it?"

"No, sir."

"Really. You were involved in installing the new environmental system, though, weren't you? I'd gotten the idea that biosystems was your field."

"No, sir," said Sassinak firmly, guessing where he wanted to go with this. "I took command course: just general knowledge in the specialty fields. Frankly, sir, I found most of that environmental system over my head, and if it hadn't been for Chief Erling —"

"I see. Well, does that give you enough to go on, or do you need something else?"

Sassinak asked two more questions, each quite reasonable since it involved a period with multiple transmissions at a time when her attention might have been on data relay. He answered freely, seemingly completely relaxed now, and Sassinak kept her own voice easy. He was still willing to chat. Then she cut him off, making herself sound reluctant. Did she want to meet for a drink in the mess next shift indeed!

I'll drink at your funeral, she thought to herself, *and dance on your grave, you murdering blackheart.*

✧ CHAPTER SIX

Sassinak wondered how she could get into the personnel files without being detected. And could she find out anything useful if she did? Certainly Achael wouldn't have "murderer" filling in some blank (secondary specialty?), and since she had no idea who or what had marked Abe for death, she wasn't sure she could recognize anything she found anyway. Still, she had to do something.

"Sassinak, can I ask you something?" Surbar, fellow ensign, was a shy, quiet young man, who nonetheless used his wide dark eyes to good advantage. Sassinak had heard, through Mira, that he was enjoying his recreational hours with a Jig in Weapons Control. Nonetheless, he'd given her some intense looks, and she'd considered responding.

"Sure." Sassinak leaned back, in the relaxed atmosphere of the second watch mess, and ran her hands through her hair. In one corner of her mind, she considered that it was getting a bit too long, and she really ought to go get it trimmed again. Tousled was one thing, but a tangled mass — which is what her hair did every chance it got — was another. The difference between sexy and blowsy.

"D'you know anything about 'Tenant Achael?"

Sassinak barely controlled her reaction. "Achael? Not really — he was on the landing party, but I was too busy with all my stuff to talk to him. Why?"

"Well." Surbar frowned and scratched his nose. "He's been asking about you. Lia wanted to know why, and he said you were too good looking to be running around loose. Thought you might be related to somebody he'd known."

Sassinak made herself chuckle casually. Apparently it worked because Surbar didn't seem to notice anything. "He's one of those, is he? After every new female on the ship?"

Surbar shrugged. "Lia said he made eyes at her, but backed off when she said no. Then he started asking about you — so I guess maybe he is that kind."

"Mmm. Well, then, I'll be sure to stay out of airlocks and closets and other closed spaces if Mr. Lieutenant Achael is around."

"Meaning you're not interested?" Surbar gave her his most melting look.

"Not in *him*," said Sassinak, glancing at the overhead and then letting her glance slide sideways to meet Surbar's. "On the other hand . . ."

"Lia's coming to play gunna tonight," said Surbar quickly. "Maybe another time?"

Sassinak shrugged. "Give me a call. Thanks, anyway, for the warning about Achael." On her way back to her compartment, she thought about it. Achael had enough seniority to cause her trouble, and as Weapons Officer he had high enough clearance to access most communications files. If he wanted to. If he thought he needed to. She wanted him dead, if he was Abe's killer, or in league with Abe's killer, but she didn't want to ruin herself in the process.

The next shift, Sassinak had her first IFTL message to process. Muttering her way through the protocol, she logged it, stripped the outer codes, and got it into the captain's eyes-only file without help. Cavery nodded. "Good job — you're doing well at that."

"Wonder what it's about."

"Ours not to know — they say your eyes turn to purple jelly and your brain rots if you peek at those things."

Sassinak chuckled; Cavery had turned out to have quite a sense of humor. "I thought ensigns didn't have brains, just vast pools of prediluvian slime — isn't that what I heard you tell Pickett, yesterday?"

"Comes from trying to decode IFTL messages, that's what I just said. Keep your mind, such as it is, on your work. You can't afford to lose more." His grin took all the sting out of it, and Sassinak went on logging in routine communications for the rest of the shift.

That night Fargeon announced in the wardroom that they were to intercept an EEC craft and pick up reports for forwarding. He spent a long time droning on about the delicate handling necessary to rendezvous in deep space, and Sassinak let her attention wander. Not so far as some, though, for Fargeon's rebuke fell on a Jig from Engineering, who had been doodling idly on her napkin. For some reason, Fargeon chose to interpret this as carelessness with classified information, and by the time he'd finished reaming her out, everyone in the room felt edgy. Of course deep-space rendezvous were tricky, everyone knew that, and of course the EEC pilot couldn't be depended on to arrive at a precise location, as the cruiser would do, but this was no different from any other time, surely. If the EEC ship fouled up badly enough, and they all made a fireworks display that wouldn't be seen anywhere for fifty years or so, too bad.

Since everyone came out of dinner disgruntled, Sassinak didn't pay much attention to her own mood. But the next morning she found that Lieutenant Achael had the bridge: Fargeon, Dass, and Lieutenant Commander Slachek were, he said, in conference. Sassinak glanced around the bridge, and ducked into the communications cubby. It was empty. A scrawled note on the console said that Perry had gone to Sickbay: Achael had cleared it. Sassinak frowned, wondering if that's why Cavery was late — perhaps he'd gone with Perry to Sickbay. But communications hadn't been uncovered long; the incoming telltales showed nothing in the queue in any system. Odd — they'd been getting regular bursts last shift, relayed position checks on the EEC ship. Sassinak pulled up the last entries in the incoming file, to check the log-in times — if they hadn't had anything coming in for awhile, it might mean trouble with the systems.

She was so intent on the idea of a systems failure that she almost didn't recognize her own initiation code when it flashed on the screen. What? Her nose wrinkled in concentration. She'd just gotten there, and yet her code was time-linked to a file query five minutes before. It couldn't be — unless someone had entered her code by mistake . . . or for some other reason.

"Hey — sorry I'm late." Cavery slid into his seat, took a look at the display, and recoiled. "I thought I told you not to go poking around in the incoming message files."

"You did. I didn't. Somebody used my code."

"What!" After that first explosive word, his voice lowered. "Don't *say* that, Sassinak. Probably every comm posting in the universe has snooped one time or another, but lying doesn't make it better."

"I'm not lying." Sassinak laid her hand over his on the console. "Listen to me. I wasn't here at the time that was logged; I came in right on time, not early as usual. Someone logged my code five minutes before I was here."

"What'd Perry say?"

"He's in Sickbay. Nobody was here when I got here, just a note —" She handed it over. Cavery frowned.

"Hardcopy, not on the computer. That's odd. Who's got duty —?" He craned to see around the angle, and snorted. "Oh, great. Achael. Where's Fargeon?"

"In conference, Achael said. But, Cavery, the thing is —"

"The thing is, your code's on there, telling the whole world you were snooping in the IFTL files, and if you say you're not either you're a liar, which is one problem, or someone else is, which is another. Damn! All we needed, with the captain the way he is right now, is a Security glitch."

"But I didn't —"

Cavery looked at her, hard, then his mouth relaxed. "No, I don't think you would. But with your code on the file, and what the dickens is *that*?" He pointed to the realtime display, which was filling with the outgoing batch message for SOLEC transmission. "I don't suppose you put your code on that one either?"

Sassinak looked and saw the other anomaly that Cavery had missed. "Or that quad code for the Inspector General's office, either — it's the same thing we had before, only outgoing, and using my code as originator."

"That one, I will strip." Cavery froze the display, keyed in the ranking codes, and displayed the message itself, along with its initiating and destination sequences. Sassinak noticed that he was copying all this into another file, sealed with his own code. He sat back, clearly baffled by the message.

"Subject unaware; no suspicious activity. Assignment coincidental. Will continue observation."

Cavery looked over at her, brows raised. "Well, Ensign, are you keeping someone under surveillance?"

"I — don't know." *Achael*, she thought. *It has to be Achael, but why? And who's behind it?*

"Well, I know one thing, and that's where all this is going: straight to the captain."

"But —" Sassinak stopped herself; if she protested, he'd have reason to think she knew more. Yet she wasn't near ready to accuse Achael of involvement with Abe's death . . . how could she? No matter how it came out, she'd lose: ensigns don't get anywhere accusing lieutenants of murder months back and somewhere else.

Cavery waited, his expression clearly daring her to object.

"I know," she said finally, "that Captain Fargeon has to be informed. But he's not on the bridge, and I don't . . . really . . . want to involve any more officers than necessary."

"I remember whose number was on those quad-coded messages, Ensign Sassinak —" Cavery nodded toward the main bridge area. "You needn't try to be obscure."

"Sorry, sir. I wasn't trying to be obscure, I was just —" She paused, as near to waving her hands in confusion as she'd ever been. Then inspiration hit. She saw by Cavery's expression that her own had changed with her idea. "Sir, *if* all this ties together, right now is a bad time to go charging out of here to the captain, isn't it? And if it doesn't, it would still . . . confuse things, wouldn't it?"

Cavery leaned back fractionally, considering. "You have a point." He sighed, and cleared the display. "I can't see that it would hurt to wait until midwatch break, anyway, and maybe later. Depends on the captain's schedule."

Sassinak said nothing more, but settled to her work. Thank whatever gods there were she hadn't meddled with the Personnel files or the message banks: Achael didn't know she suspected anything. Assignment coincidence? What else could it be, when she had no powerful family to pull strings for her . . . or had that been Abe's secret, perhaps? More than ever, she needed to see Achael's file, but how was she going to do that?

The shattering clamor of the emergency alarm brought her upright. Fast as she was, Cavery's hand almost covered hers as they shut the console down for normal use and flicked on the emergency systems. After the first blast of noise, the siren warbled up, down, up twice: evacuation drill.

"Stupidest damn drill in the book," grumbled Cavery as he fished under the console for the emergency masks. "Here — put this on. Nobody ever evacuates a cruiser; as long as it takes to get everyone in the shuttles and evac pods, whatever it is will have blown the whole place up. Now remember, Ensign, you close the board when you leave, and that's not until the duty officer clears the bridge." His voice was muffled, now, through the foil and plex hood and mask. Sassinak found that hers cut off all vision to the side and rear. As she fastened the tabs to the shoulders of her uniform, Cavery grunted. "Ah, good: Fargeon's taken the bridge. Soon as this damn drill's over, we can get this other taken care of —" His voice sharpened. "Yes, sir; communications secured, sir."

Although Cavery's acid comments implied that pirates could have boarded the ship and flown it to the far side of the galaxy before their turn came, Sassinak thought it wasn't long at all before she was jogging forward along the main portside corridor from the bridge to the transport bays where the shuttles and evac pods were docked. A stream of hooded figures jogged her way, and another jogged back; once you were logged into your assigned evacuation slot, you had to return to your duty post. It did seem illogical. She looked again at the strip of plastic giving her assigned pod: E-40-A. Here, along a side corridor, through a narrow passage she'd never explored. Bay E: someone in full EVA gear glanced at her assignment strip and waved her to the right; section 40 was the last one at the end. Someone else, also suited up, pointed out Pod A, one of a row of hatches still dogged shut. Sassinak struggled with the hatch lock, checked to see that the telltales were all green, and pulled the heavy lid open. Inside the little brightly lit compartment, she could see the shape of an acceleration couch, shiny fittings, a bank of switches and lights.

She ducked her head to clear the hatch opening. Suddenly a sharp pain jabbed her arm, and when she tried to turn it felt like the weight of the whole cruiser landed on her head. She could do nothing but fall forward into darkness.

Commander Fargeon in a rage was no pleasant sight. His officers, ranged around his desk at attention, had no doubt of his mood. "What I want to know," he said icily, "is *who* dumped that pod. Who sent it out there, and what's that ensign doing in it, and why isn't the beacon functioning, and what's all this nonsense about communications security leaks."

Eyes slid sideways; no one volunteered. Fargeon barked, "Cavery!"

"Sir, Ensign Sassinak had reported an incident of duplicate transmissions with unusual initiation codes —"

394 THE PLANET PIRATES

"I know about *that*. That's got nothing to do with this, has it?"

Cavery wasn't sure how far to go, yet. "I don't know, sir: I was just starting at the beginning." He took a breath, waited for Fargeon's nod, and went on. "Today she reported that someone had used her initiation code to attempt access to a restricted file —"

"Ensign Sassinak? When?"

"Apparently it happened about five minutes before she came on duty. She reported it to me when I arrived —" Cavery went on to explain what had happened up until the drill alarm went. Fargeon listened without further comment, his face expressionless. Then he turned to another officer.

"Well, Captain Palise: what did you see in E-bay?"

"Sir, we logged Ensign Sassinak into E-bay at 1826.40; she logged off the bridge on evac at 1824.10, and that's just time to go directly to E-bay. As you know, sir, in an evac drill we have personnel constantly shifting about; once someone's logged into the bay, there's no way to keep watch on them until they're into their assigned shuttle or pod. When the hatches are dogged, then they're logged as onboard evac craft, and they're supposed to return to duty as quickly as possible. Within two minutes of Ensign Sassinak's bay log-in, we show fifty-three individuals logging into the same bay — about what you'd expect. Eight of them were in the wrong bay — and that's about average, too. We had two recording officers in E-bay, but they didn't notice anything until Pod 40-A fired."

"Very well, Captain Palise. Now, Engineering —"

"The pod was live, sir, as they always are for drill. We can't be shutting down the whole system just because somebody might make a mistake —"

"I know that." It had been Fargeon's own policy, in fact, and the Engineering Section had warned more than once that having evac drills with live pods and shuttles while in FTL travel was just asking for trouble. Fargeon glared at his senior engineer, and Erling glared back. Everyone knew that Erling had taken to Sassinak in her first assignment. Whatever had happened, Erling was going to pick Sassinak's side, if he knew which it was.

"Well, sir, activation would be the same as always. If the hatch is properly dogged, inside and out, and the sequence keyed in —"

"From inside?"

"Either. The shuttles have to be operated from inside, but the whole reason behind the pods was safe evacuation of wounded or disabled individuals. Someone in the bay can close it up and send it off just as easy as the occupant."

"I don't think we need to worry about *that*," said Fargeon repressively. "My interest now is in determining if Ensign Sassinak hit the wrong button out of stupidity, or did she intend to desert the ship?"

Into the silence that followed this remark, Lieutenant Achael's words fell with the precision of an artisan's hammer.

"Perhaps I can shed some light on that, sir. But I would prefer to do so in private."

"On the contrary. You will tell me now."

"Sir, it is a matter of some delicacy. . . ."

"It is a matter of some urgency, Lieutenant, and I expect a complete report at once."

Achael bowed slightly, a thin smile tightening his lips. "Sir, as you know I have a cousin in the Inspector General's office. As Weapons Officer, I have particular interest in classified document control, and when that directive came out two months ago, I decided to set up such a test on this ship. You remember that you gave your permission —?" He waited for Commander Fargeon's nod before going on. "Well, I had three hardcopies of apparently classified documentation on the new Witherspoon ship-to-ship beam, and — as the directive suggested — I made an opportunity to let all the newly assigned officers know that they existed and where they were."

"Get to the point, Lieutenant."

"The point, sir, is that one of them disappeared, then reappeared one shift later. I determined that three of the ensigns, and two Jigs, had the opportunity to take the copy. I handled the copy with tongs, and put it in the protective sleeve the directive had included, for examination later at a forensic lab. And I reported this, in code, to my cousin, in case anything — ah — happened to me."

"And you have reason to believe that Ensign Sassinak was the person who took the document?"

"She had the opportunity, along with several others. Forensic examination should show whether she handled it. Or rather, it would have."

"Would have?"

"Yes, sir. The document in question, in its protective sleeve, is missing from my personal safe. We have not only a missing pod, and a missing ensign, but a missing document which might have identified someone who had broken security regulations. And a nonfunctioning beacon on the pod. I scarcely think this can be coincidence."

"Not Sassinak!" That was Cavery, furious suddenly. He had had his doubts, but not after the pod ejected. If Sassinak had wanted to escape, she wouldn't have called herself to his attention that very morning.

"As for the outgoing message with her initiation code, I believe she may have been reporting to whomever she — er — worked with."

"The destination code was in the IG's office," said Cavery. "The same code as your incoming message."

"You're sure? Of course, she might have done that to incriminate me —"

"NO!" Erling and Cavery shouted it together.

"Gentlemen." Fargeon's voice was icy, his expression forbidding. "This is a matter too serious for personalities. Ensign Sassinak may have been ejected accidentally. Or, despite her high ratings in the Academy, she may have been less than loyal. There is her background to consider. Of course, Lieutenant Achael, it's one you share."

Achael stiffened. "Sir, I was a prisoner. She was a slave. The difference —"

"Is immaterial. She didn't volunteer for slavery, I'm sure. However, her captors would have had ample time to implant deep conditioning — not really her responsibility. At any rate, Lieutenant, your information only adds to the urgency and confusion of this situation." He took a long breath, but before he could begin the long speech they all knew was coming, Makin, the Weft Jig, spoke up.

"Begging the captain's pardon, but what about retrieval?"

Fargeon became even stiffer, if possible. "Retrieval? Mr. Makin, the pod was ejected during FTL flight, and we are en route to a scheduled rendezvous with an EEC vessel. Either of those conditions alone would make retrieval impossible —"

"Sir, not impossible. Difficult, but —"

"Impossible. The pod was ejected into a probability flux —

recall your elementary physics class, Mr. Makin — and would have dropped into sublight velocity at a location describable in cubic light-minutes. With a vector of motion impossible to calculate. Now if the beacon had functioned — which Engineering assures me it did not — we would be getting some sort of distorted signal from it. We might spend the next few weeks tracking it down, if we didn't have this rendezvous to make. But we have no beacon to trace, and we have a rendezvous to make. My question now is what report to make to Fleet Headquarters, and what we should recommend be done about that ensign."

When Fargeon dismissed them, he announced no decision; outside his office, the buzzing conversations began.

"I don't care what that sneak says." Cavery was beyond caution. "I will not believe Sassinak took anything — so much as a leftover muffin — and if she did she'd be standing here saying so."

"I don't know, Cavery." Bullis, of Admin, might not have cared: he argued for the sheer joy of it. "She was intelligent and hard-working, I'll grant you that, but too sharp for her own good. If you follow me."

"Not into that, I won't. I —" He paused, and looked around at Makin, the Weft Jig, who had tapped his arm.

"If I could speak to you a moment, sir?"

Cavery looked at Bullis and shrugged, then followed Makin down the corridor. "Well?"

"Sir, is there any way to convince the captain that we *can* locate that pod, even without a beacon on it?"

"You can? Who? And how?"

"We can because Ensign Sassinak is on it — Wefts, I mean, sir. With Ssli help."

Cavery cocked his head. "*Ssli* help? Wait a minute — you mean the Ssli could locate that little pod, even in normal space, while we're —"

"Together, we could, sir." Cavery had the feeling that the Weft meant something more than he'd said, but excitement overrode his curiosity for the moment.

"But I don't know what I can do about the captain," he murmured, lowering his voice as Achael strolled nearer. "I'm not going to get anywhere arguing."

"Cavery." Achael broke into their conversation. "I know you

liked the girl, and she *is* attractive. I'd have spent a night or so with her gladly." Cavery reddened at that insinuation. "But the circumstances are suggestive, even suspicious."

"I suppose you'd suspect any orphan ex-slave?" Cavery meant it to bite, and Achael stiffened.

"I'm not the one who brought up her ancestry," he pointed out.

"No, but you have to admit, if it's a matter of access, you were in the same place at the same time. Maybe someone twisted your mind. Curious you never saw her, hmm?"

Achael glared at him. "You've never been anyone's prisoner, have you? I spent my entire time on that miserable rock locked in a stinking cell with five other members of the *Caleb's* crew. One of them died, of untreated wounds, and my best friend went permanently insane from the interrogation drugs. I hardly had the leisure to go wandering about the slaveholds looking for little girls, as she must have been then."

"I — I'm sorry," said Cavery, embarrassed. "I didn't know."

"I don't talk about it." Achael had turned away, hiding his face. Now he spun about, pinning Cavery suddenly with a stiffened forefinger. "And I don't expect you, Cavery, to tell everyone in the mess about it, either."

"Of course not." Cavery watched the other man stalk away, and wished he'd never opened his mouth.

"You notice he never answered your question," Makin said. At Cavery's blank look, he went on. "You're right, sir, that during that captivity an enemy had a chance to deep-program Lieutenant Achael . . . and nothing he said makes that less likely. A friend who went insane from interrogation drugs . . . perhaps Achael did not."

"I don't — like to accuse anyone who went through — through something like that —"

"Of course not. But that's what they may have counted on, to cover any lapses. Now, about the pod and Ensign Sassinak —"

Sassinak's supporters barely crammed into Cavery's quarters. Wefts, other ensigns, Erling from Engineering. After the first chaos, when everyone assured everyone else that she couldn't have done any of it, they concentrated on ways and means.

"We have to do it soon, because those damn pods don't carry

much air. If she's conscious, she'll put herself in cold sleep — and amateurs trying to put themselves in are all too likely to make a fatal mistake."

"Worse than that," said Makin, "we can't track her if she's in cold sleep — it'll be like death. We've got to get her before she does that, or before she dies."

"Which is how long, Erling?" Everyone craned to see the engineer's face. It offered no great amount of hope. He spread his hands.

"Depends on her. If she takes the risk of holding out on the existing air supply as long as she can, or if she opts to go into cold sleep while she's alert. And we don't even know if the person who ejected the pod sabotaged the airtanks or the cold sleep module, as well as the beacon. At an outside, maximum, if she pushes it, hundred-ten to hundred-twenty hours from ejection." Before anyone could ask, he glanced at a clock readout on the wall and went on. "And it's been eight point two. And the captain's determined to make the rendezvous with the EEC ship tomorrow, which eats up another twenty-four to thirty." His glare was a challenge. The Weft ensign Jrain took it up.

"Suppose we can't convince the captain to break the rendezvous — what about going back afterwards? He might be in a more reasonable frame of mind then."

Erling snorted. "He might — and then again he might be hot to go straight to sector command. To go back — hell, how would I know? You tell me you can find her, you and the Ssli, but I sure couldn't calculate a course or transit time. Even if we hit the same drop-point as the ejection — if that's not a ridiculous statement in talking of paralight space — we'd have no guarantee we'd come out with the same vector. They found that out when they tried dropping combat modules out of FTL in the Gerimi System. Scattered to hell all over the place, and it took months to clean up the mess. But again, assume we can use you as guides, we still have to maneuver the ship. Maybe we can, maybe we can't."

"We have to *try*." Mira rumpled her blonde hair as if she wanted to uproot it. "Sassinak isn't guilty, and I'm not going to have her take the blame. She helped others at the Academy —"

"Not *your* bunch," Jrain pointed out.

"So I grew up," Mira retorted. "My mother pushed me into

that friendship; I didn't know better until later. Sassinak is my friend, and she's not going to be left drifting around in a dinky little pod for god knows how long. . . ."

"Well, but what are we going to *do* about it?"

"I think Jrain had a good idea. Let Fargeon get this rendezvous out of his head, and then try him again. And if he doesn't agree . . ." Cavery scowled. No one wanted to say mutiny out loud.

✦ CHAPTER SEVEN

When Sassinak woke up, to the dim gray light of the evacuation pod, she had a lump on her forehead, another on the back of her head, and the vague feeling that too much time had passed. She couldn't see much and finally realized that something covered her head. When she reached for it, her arm twinged, and she rubbed a sore place. It felt like an injection site, but . . . Slowly, clumsily, she pawed the foil hood from her head and looked around. She lay crumpled against the acceleration couch of a standard evac pod; without the hood's interference, she could see everything in the pod. Beneath the cushions of the couch was the tank for cold sleep, if things went wrong. She had the feeling that perhaps things had gone wrong, but she couldn't quite remember.

Slowly, trying to keep her churning stomach from outwitting her, she pushed herself up. It would do no good to panic. Either she was in a functioning pod inside a ship, or she was in a functioning pod in flight: either way, the pod had taken care of her so far, or she wouldn't have wakened. The air smelled normal . . . but if she'd been there long enough, her nose would have adapted. She tried to look around, to the control console, and her stomach rebelled. She grabbed at the nearest protruding knob, and a steel basin slid from its recess at one end of the couch. Just in time.

She retched until nothing came but clear green bile, then wiped her mouth on her sleeve. What a stink! Her mouth quirked. What a thing to think about at a time like this. She felt cold and shaky, but a little more solid. Aches and twinges began to assert themselves. She pushed the basin back into its recess, looked for and found the button that should empty and sterilize it (she didn't really want to think about the pod's recycling system, but her mind produced the specs anyway), and turned over, leaning against the couch.

Over the hatch, a digital readout informed her that the pod had been launched eight hours and forty-two minutes before. Launched! She forced herself to look at the rest of the information. Air supply on full; estimated time of exhaustion ninety-two hours, fourteen minutes. Water and food supplies: maximum load; estimated exhaustion undetermined. Of course, she hadn't used any yet, and the onboard comp had no data on her consumption. She tried to get onto the couch and almost passed out again. How could she be that weak if she'd only been here eight hours? And besides that, what had happened? Evac pods were intended primarily for the evacuation of injured or otherwise incapable crew. Had there been an emergency; had she been unconscious on a ship or something?

The second try got her onto the bench, with a bank of control switches ready to her hand. She fumbled for the sipwand, and took two long swallows of water. (The recycling couldn't be working *yet*, she told her stomach.) A touch of the finger, and she cut the airflow down to fifteen percent. She might not tolerate that, but if she did it would give her more time. Another swallow of water. The taste in her mouth had been worse than terrible. She felt in her uniform pocket for the mints she liked to carry, and at that moment the memory came back.

The drill . . . E-bay . . . ducking to enter her assigned pod . . . and *something* had jabbed her arm, and landing on her head. She rolled up her sleeve, frowning. Sure enough, a little red weal, slightly itchy and sore. She'd been drugged, and slugged, and dumped in a pod and sent off — As suddenly as that first memory, the situation on the cruiser came to her. Mysterious messages, someone using *her* comm code, and her belief that Achael had had something to do with Abe's murder. If she'd had any doubts, they vanished.

With the wave of anger, her mind seemed to clear. Perhaps Achael or his accomplice had thought she'd die of the drug — or maybe they meant to force her into taking cold sleep, and intended the pod to be picked up by confederates.

You have such cheerful thoughts, she told herself, and looked around for distraction.

There, on the control console an arm's length away, a large

gray envelope with bright orange stripes across it. *Fleet Security. Classified. Do Not Open Without Proper Authorization.* The pressure seal hadn't quite taken; the opening gaped. Sassinak started to reach for it, then stopped her hand in midair. Whoever had dumped her in here must have left that little gift . . . which meant she wanted no part of it.

It might even become evidence. She grinned to herself. A proper Carin Coldae setup this was, and no mistake. Now what would Carin do? Figure out a way to catch the villain, without ruffling one hair of her head. Sassinak rumpled her own hair and remembered that she'd been planning to cut it.

Moment by moment she felt better. She'd suspected that something was going on, and she'd been right. And now she was helplessly locked into an evac pod, which was headed who knows where, and even with the beacon on no one was likely to find her until she'd run out of air . . . and she was happy. Ridiculous, but she was. A little voice of caution murmured that it might be the drug, and she shouldn't be overconfident. She told the little voice to shut up. But just in case . . . she found the med kit, and figured out how to lay her arm in the cradle for a venous tap. Take a blood sample, that should do it. If she had been drugged, and the drug proved traceable . . . the sting of the needle interrupted that thought for a moment. Beacon. She needed to check the beacon.

But as she had already begun to suspect, the beacon wasn't functioning. She looked thoughtfully at the control console. The quickest way to disable the beacon, and the simplest, required a screwdriver and three or four minutes with that console. Lift the top, giving access to the switches and their attached wiring. Then, depending on how obvious you wanted to be, clip or crosswire or remove this and that. She was not surprised to see a screwdriver loose on the "deck" of the pod.

And her first impulse would normally have been to check out the beacon, using that screwdriver to free the console top. After she'd picked up the envelope with *Classified* all over it. Her fingerprints, her body oils, would have been on the tool, the envelope, the console, even the switches underneath, obscuring the work of the person who'd put her here.

Sassinak took another long swallow of water, and rummaged in the med kit for a stimulant tab. This was no time to miss anything.

❖   ❖   ❖

In the end, the med kit provided most of what she needed. Forceps, with which to lift the screwdriver and put it into a packet that had held headache pills. It occurred to her that while she was unconscious, her assailant might have pressed her fingers against the envelope, or the screwdriver, but she couldn't do anything about that. She found the little pocket scanner that was supposed to be in every evac module, and shot a clip of the envelope as it lay on the console. When she had all the evidence secured, she suddenly wondered how that would help if she were in cold sleep when she was found. Suppose her assailant had confederates, who were supposed to pick her up? They could destroy her careful work, incriminate her even more. That gave her the jitters for awhile, and then she remembered Abe's patient voice saying, "What you can't change, don't cry over: put your energy where it works, Sass."

Right now it had to go into prolonging her time before cold sleep.

Which meant, she remembered unhappily, no eating. Digestion used energy, which used oxygen. No exercise, for the same reason. Lie still, breathe slow, think peaceful thoughts. You might as well spend the time in cold sleep, she grumbled to herself, as try to act as if you *were* in cold sleep. But she took the time to clean herself up as well as she could, using the tiny mirror in the med kit. The slightly overlong hair could be tied back neatly, the stains wiped from her uniform. Then she lay down on the couch, pulled up the coverlet, and tried to relax.

She had not been hungry like this since her slave days. Her empty stomach growled, gurgled, and finally settled for sharp nagging pains. She chivvied her mind away from the food fantasies it wanted to indulge in, steering it into mathematics instead. Squares and square roots, cubes and cube roots, visualizing curves from equations, and imagining how, with a shift in values, the curve would shift . . . as a loop of hose shifts with water pressure. Finally she slipped into a doze.

She woke in a foul mood, but more clearheaded than before. Elapsed time since ejection was now twenty-five hours, sixteen minutes. Clearly the cruiser hadn't stopped to look for her, or hadn't been able to find her. She wondered if the Ssli could sense such a small distortion in the fields they touched. Or could the

Wefts detect her, as a living being they'd known? But that was idle speculation. She gave her arm to the med kit's blood sampler again; she remembered being told that each drug had a characteristic breakdown profile, and that serial blood tests could provide the best information on an unknown drug.

For a moment, the pod seemed to contract around her, crushing her to the couch. Had some unsuspected drive come on, to flatten her with acceleration? But no: the pods had the same artificial gravity as the cruiser itself, to protect injured occupants. She knew that; she knew the walls weren't really closing in . . . but she suddenly understood just how Ensign Corfin might have felt. She couldn't see out; she had no idea where she was or where she was going; she was trapped in a tiny box with no way *out*. Her breath came fast: too fast. She fought to slow it. So, this was claustrophobia. How interesting. It didn't feel interesting; it felt terrible.

She had to do something. Squares and square roots seemed singularly impractical this time. Could she figure out a way to ensure that the evidence couldn't be faked against her? Any worse than it already was, she reminded herself. That brought another chilling thought: maybe the cruiser hadn't come looking for her because Commander Fargeon was already convinced she was an enemy agent and had absconded with the pod.

Her stomach growled again; she set herself to enter the first stages of control Abe had taught her. Hunger was just hunger; in this case nothing to worry about. But she did need to worry about her career.

In the long, lonely, silent hours that followed, Sassinak spent much of her time in a near-trance, dozing. The rest she spent doing what she could to make tampering with the evidence as hard as possible. If the pod were picked up by enemies, with plenty of time at their disposal, none of her ploys would work . . . but if a Fleet vessel, her cruiser or another, came along, it would take more than a few minutes to undo what she'd done and rework it to incriminate her.

When the lapsed-time monitor read one hundred hours, and the time to exhaustion of her air supply was less than five hours, she pulled out the instruction manual for the cold sleep cabinet. Evac pods had an automated system, but she didn't trust it: what if the same person who had sabotaged the beacon had fiddled with the medications? She pushed aside the thought that sabotaging the entire cold sleep cabinet wouldn't have been that hard. If it didn't work, she'd never wake up, and that was that. But she had to try it, or die of oxygen starvation . . . and the films they'd been shown at the Academy had made it clear that oxygen starvation was not a pleasant way to go.

She filled the syringes carefully, checking and rechecking labels and dosages. With the mattress off the acceleration couch, she looked the cabinet over as well as she could. Ordinarily, cold sleep required only enclosed space; she could go into it using the whole pod as the container. But for extra protection in the pods, the reinforced cabinet had been designed, and was strongly recommended. She looked into that blank, shiny interior, and shuddered.

First, the protocol said, program the automatic dispenser, and then have it start an IV. But she wasn't doing that. Her way would mean getting into the cabinet, with the syringes in hand, giving herself the injections, pulling down the lid, turning the cylinder controls, and then . . . then, she hoped, just sleeping away whatever time it took before someone found her.

Nor could she wait until the last moment. Oxygen starvation would make her clumsy and slow, and she might make fatal mistakes. She set the medication alarm in the medkit for one hour before the deadline. The last minutes crept by. Sassinak looked around the pod interior, fighting to stay calm. She dared not put herself in trance, yet there was nothing to do to ease her tension. There was the tape she'd made, her log of this unplanned journey with all her surmises about cause and criminal. In the acceleration couch mattress was a handwritten log, in the hope that redundancy might help.

When the alarm sounded, she snatched the syringe and reached for the alarm release. But it didn't work. Great, she thought, I'll go into cold sleep with that horrible noise in my ears and have nightmares for years. Then she realized it wasn't the same buzzer at all — in fact, it wasn't time for the medalarm — she had fifteen more minutes. She looked wildly around the pod, trying to figure it out, before her mind dredged up the right memory. Proximity alarm: some kind of large mass was nearby, and it might be a ship, and they might even have compatible communications gear.

Only she had carefully set up the console to trap additional evidence while she was in cold sleep, and if she touched it now she'd be confusing her own system.

And what if it wasn't a Fleet vessel? What if it was an ally of her assailant? Or worse, suppose it wasn't a ship at all, and the pod was falling into a star?

In that case, she told herself firmly, you still don't have to worry; you can't stop it, and it'll all be over very quickly. She found the override switch for the proximity alarm, and cut it off. Now it was a matter of deciding whether to ride it out blind, or try to communicate. She decided to save her careful work, and then realized this meant she wouldn't know if whatever it was could rendezvous before her air ran out. It wouldn't take much error, on either side: ten minutes without oxygen would do as well as four days.

Ten minutes left. Five. She had left herself that safe buffer: dare she use it now? Zero. Sassinak looked at the syringe, but didn't pick it up. She'd feel silly if she lost consciousness just as someone came through the door. She'd be flat stupid if she died because she cut it too close. But she could — and did, quickly — tape an addition to her log.

Now she was using her safe margin. Minute by minute went by with no clue from without, of what was happening. She had just picked up the syringe, with a grimace, when something clunked, hard, against the pod. Another thump; a loud clang. Sassinak put the syringe down, lowered the lid of the cold sleep cabinet, and sat on it. She could not — *could not* — miss whatever was going to happen.

What happened first was total silence as the blower in her oxygen system went out. She had a moment to think how stupid she'd been, and then it cut in again; the readout flickered, and shifted to green. "Exterior source," it said now. "Unlimited. Tanks charging." It smelled better, too. Sassinak took a second long breath, and unclenched her fingers from the edge of the cabinet. Other lights flickered on the control console. "Exterior pressure equalized," said one. She didn't trust it enough to open the hatch . . . not yet. "Exterior power source confirmed," said another.

Finally she heard various clicks and bangs from the hatch, and braced herself, not sure what she would do if she found enemies when it opened. But the first face she saw was familiar.

"Ensign Sassinak." Familiar, but not particularly welcoming. The captain himself had chosen to greet her, and behind him she saw both friendly and scowling faces. And a squad of marines, armed. Sassinak stood, saluted, and nearly fell as the hours of inactivity and fasting caught up with her all at once. "Are you hurt?" Fargeon asked when she staggered.

"Just a knock on the head," she said. "Excuse me, sir, but I must warn you —"

"You, Ensign, are the one to be warned," he said stiffly, that momentary warmth gone as if it had never happened. "Charges have been made against you, serious charges, and it is my duty to warn you that anything you say may be used in evidence against you."

Sassinak stared at him, momentarily speechless. Had he really believed Achael's (it must have been Achael's) accusations? Wasn't he going to give her a chance? She caught herself, shook her head, and went on. "Captain, please — it's very important that this pod be sealed, and all contents handled by forensic specialists."

That got his attention. "What? What are you talking about?"

Sassinak waved her hand at the pod's interior. "Sir, I've done my best to secure it, but I really don't know how. Someone knocked me out during evac drill, dumped me in this pod, jettisoned it, and planted it full of items I was supposed to handle, to incriminate myself. I believe those same items may carry traces of the perpetrator —" She nearly stumbled over the word, catching sight of Lieutenant Achael in the group behind the captain. His face was frozen in an expression of distaste. Then it changed to eagerness, and he leaned forward.

"That's exactly what she *would* say, sir. That someone tried to frame her —"

"I can see that for myself, Mr. Achael." Fargeon's expression soured even more.

"I could hardly have planted someone else's fingerprints on the interior of the console while disabling the beacon," Sassinak said crisply. Achael paled; she saw his eyes glance sideways.

"You disabled the beacon?" asked Fargeon, missing the point.

"No, sir. I realized the beacon was disabled, and also realized that if I made an attempt to repair it, I would destroy evidence pointing to the person who *did* disable it. That evidence is intact."

She looked straight at Achael as she spoke. He flinched from her gaze, took a step backward.

Fargeon's head tilted minutely; she had surprised him with some of that. "There's a document missing," he said.

Sassinak nodded. "There's a classified document envelope, not quite sealed, in this pod. I found it when I woke —"

"Likely story," said Achael. This time the captain's response was clearly irritated, a quick flip of the hand for silence.

"And did you handle it?" asked the captain.

"No, sir, I did not. Although it's possible that whoever dumped me in there put my fingers on it while I was unconscious."

"I see." The captain pulled himself up. "Well. This is . . . unexpected. Very well; I'll see to it that the pod is sealed, and the contents examined for evidence of what actually happened. As for you, Ensign, you'll report to Sickbay, and then to your quarters. I'll want a full report —"

"Sir, I taped a report while in the pod. May I bring that tape?"

"You did?" Again this threw him off his stride. "Very good thinking, Ensign. By all means, let me have it now."

Sassinak picked up the tape, and started forward. Her vision blurred, and she nearly hit her head on the hatch rim. A hand came forward, steadied her arm. She ducked under the hatch, and came out into the chilly air of E-bay. It smelled decidedly fresher than the pod. Fargeon peered at her.

"You're very pale — are you sure you're not ill?"

"It's just not eating." The bulkheads seemed to shimmer, then steadied. She was conscious of having to concentrate firmly on the here and now.

"You — but surely there were emergency rations in the pod?"

"Yes, but — to make the air last —" She fought to stay upright, with a soft blackness folding itself around her. "I didn't — trust the cold sleep cabinet — if the same person had tampered with it —"

"Gods!" That was Cavery, she realized as she looked towards the voice. But the blackness rose around her, inescapable, and she felt herself curling into it.

"Don't forget the blood samples," she heard herself say, and then everything disappeared.

The medician's face hung over hers, suspended in nothingness.

Sassinak blinked, yawned, and found the rest of the compartment in focus again. Sickbay, clearly. An IV ran from her left hand to a bag; wires trailed across her chest.

"I'm fine," she said helpfully.

"You're lucky," said the medician, pinching back a smile. "You came close to the edge — you can't use Discipline like that and not eat."

"Huh?"

"Don't try to tell me you weren't using it, either — nothing but a crash from it would have sent you that far down. Here — have a mug of this." A flick of the hand, and Sass' couch lifted her so that she could take the mug of thick broth the medician offered.

"What did the blood samples show?" asked Sassinak between sips. She could practically feel the strength flowing back into her.

"You're lucky," the medician said again. "It was a cold sleep prep dose. If you'd hit the tank controls by mistake, you might have been in cold sleep immediately . . . or if you'd chosen to enter cold sleep early, the residual in your blood could have killed you. It didn't completely clear until the third day."

"The cabinet?" She remembered her fear of that featureless interior.

"Nothing: it was normal." The medician looked at her curiously. "You're in remarkably good shape, all things considered. That lump on the back of your head may still hurt, but there's no damage. You're not showing any signs of excessive anxiety —"

Sassinak slurped the last bit of broth and grinned. "I'm safe now. And not hungry. When can I get up?"

Before the medician could answer, a voice from the corridor said, "That's Sass, all right! I can tell from here."

"Not yet," said the medician to Sass. Then, "Do you want visitors? I can easily tell them to let you rest."

But Sassinak could hardly wait to find out what had happened so far. Mira, all trace of fashionable reserve gone, and Jrain, almost visibly shimmering into another shape in his excitement, were only too glad to tell her.

"I knew," Mira began, "that it couldn't have been your fault. You aren't ever careless like that; you wouldn't have hit the wrong button or anything. And of course you, of all people, wouldn't cooperate with slavers or pirates."

"But how did you find me without the beacon?"

Mira nodded at Jrain. "Your Weft friends did it. I don't know if Jrain can explain it — he couldn't to me — but they tracked you, somehow —"

"It was really the Ssli interface," Jrain said. "You know how they can sense other vessels in FTL space —"

"Yes, but I wasn't in FTL space after the pod went off, was I?"

"No, but it turns out they can reach beyond it, somehow. Doesn't make any sense to me, and what Hssrho calls the relevant equations I call gibberish. The pod is really too small to sense — like something small too far away to see — but we knew exactly when you'd been dumped, and the Ssli was able to — to do whatever it does in whatever direction that was. Then we Wefts sort of rode that probe, feeling our way toward you."

"But you said —"

"Because you're alive, and we know you. We had to go in our own shapes, of course —" He frowned, and Sassinak tried to imagine the effect on Fargeon of all the crew's Wefts in their own shape, clinging, no doubt, to the bulkheads of the Ssli contact chamber. Or on the bridge? She asked.

"He wasn't pleased with us," said Jrain, a reminiscent smile on his face. "We don't usually clump on him, you know: he doesn't like aliens much, though he tries to be fair. But when it came to risking the loss of your pod, or giving in to Achael's insinuations —"

"Kirtin *changed* right there in front of the captain," put in Mira. "I thought he was going to choke. Then Basli and Jrain —"

"Ptak first: I was the last one," Jrain put in.

"Whatever." Mira shrugged away the correction and went on. "Can you imagine — this was in the big wardroom, and there they were all over the walls! I'd never seen more than one Weft changed at a time —" She quirked an eyebrow at Sass.

"I have. It's impressive, isn't it?"

"Impressive! It's crowded, is what it is, with these big spiky *things* all over the walls and ceiling." Mira wrinkled her nose at Jrain, who grinned at her. "Not to mention all those eyes glittering out at you. And you never told me," she said to Jrain, "that you're telepaths in that shape. I thought you'd use a biolink to the computer or something."

"There wasn't time," said Jrain.

"But what about the rendezvous with the EEC ship? Did we miss that?"

"No. What we decided — I mean —" Mira looked sideways. "What the *Wefts* decided, was to let that go on, and then pick you up afterwards. It seemed risky to me — the further we went, the further away you were, the harder to find. It was a real gamble —"

"No," said Jrain firmly and loudly. Mira stared at him, and Sassinak blinked. He took a long breath, and said more quietly, "We don't gamble. We don't ever gamble."

"I didn't mean like a poker game," said Mira sharply. "But it was risky —"

"No." As they looked at him, his form wavered, then steadied again. "I can't explain. But you must not think —" an earnest look at Sassinak "— you must not think we gamble with your life, Sassinak. Never."

"I — oh, all right, Jrain. You don't gamble. But if one of you doesn't get all this in order and tell me *what happened,* and where we are, and where Achael is, I'm going to crawl out of this bed and stuff *you* in a pod."

Jrain, calmer now, sat on the end of her bed. "Achael is dead. That evidence you spoke to the captain about — remember?" Sassinak nodded. "Well, the captain had it put under guard. The pod, and the items removed, like the blood samples. Achael tried to get at it. He did get into the med lab, and destroyed one test printout before he was discovered. Then he broke for the docking bays — I think to steal a pod himself. When the guards spotted him, and he knew he was trapped, he killed himself. Had a poison capsule, apparently. The captain won't *tell* us, not all the details, but we've had our ears open." He patted Sass' foot under the blanket. "At first the captain wanted to think that you and Achael were co-conspirators, but he couldn't ignore the evidence . . . you know, Sass, you really did *cram* that pod with evidence. You did such a good job it was almost suspicious that way."

"Fleet Intelligence is going to get the whole load dumped on them when we get back to Sector HQ," Mira put in. "I heard Fargeon won't even trust the IFTL link."

"We'd better go," said Jrain, suddenly looking nervous. "I think — I think the captain would rather you heard some of this from him. . . ." He grabbed Mira's arm and steered her away. Sassinak caught his unspoken thought. . . . *And he's had quite enough to put up with from Wefts already this week.*

"Ensign Sassinak." Captain Fargeon's severe face was set in

slightly friendlier lines, Sassinak thought. She was, however, immediately conscious of every wrinkle of the bedclothes. Then he smiled. "You had a very narrow escape, Ensign, in more than one way. I understand you've been told about the drug that showed up in the blood samples?" Sassinak nodded, and he went on. "It was very good thinking to take those serial samples. Although normally — mmm — there's nothing to commend in a young officer who manages to get sandbagged and shanghaied, in this case you seem to have acted with unusual intelligence once you woke up. You have nothing to reproach yourself for. I know Lieutenant Cavery looks forward to your return to duty in Communications Section. Good day."

Following that somewhat confusing speech, Sassinak lay quietly, wondering what Fargeon *did* think of her. She had been expecting praise, but realized that to the ship's captain her entire escapade was one big headache. He'd had to leave his intended course to go looking for her, even if the guidance of Wefts and Ssli made that easier than usual. He'd had to worry about her motives, and the presence of unknown saboteurs in his ship; he'd had to assign someone else to cover her work; when they got back to Sector HQ, he was going to have to fill out a lot of forms, and spend a lot of time talking to Fleet Intelligence . . . all in all, she'd caused a lot of trouble by not being quicker in the evacuation drill. If she'd managed to turn and drop Achael with a bit of fancy hand-to-hand, she'd have saved everyone a lot of trouble. She shook her head at her own juvenile imagination. No more Carin Coldae: no more playing games. She'd done a good job with a bad situation, but she hadn't managed to avoid the bad situation. She'd have to do better.

So it was that Fargeon's annual Fitness Report, which he showed her before filing it, startled her.

"Clearheaded, resourceful, good initiative, outstanding self-discipline: this young officer requires only seasoning to develop into an excellent addition to any Fleet operation. Unlike many who rest on past achievements, this officer does not let success go to her head, and can be counted on for continued effort. Recommended for earliest promotion eligibility." Sassinak looked up from this to find Fargeon's face relaxed in a broad smile for the first time in her memory.

"Just as I said the first day, Ensign Sassinak: if you realize that you can't ever start at the top, and if you continue to show your willingness to work, you'll do very well indeed. I'd be glad to have you in my command again, any time."

"Thank you, sir." Sassinak wondered whether to strain this approval by telling him what she suspected about Achael and Abe's death. "Sir, about Lieutenant Achael —"

"All information will go to Fleet Security — do you have something which you did not put in your tape?"

She had included her suspicion that Achael had murdered Abe, but would anyone take it seriously? "It's in there, sir, but — about my guardian, who was killed —"

"Abe, you mean." The captain permitted himself a tight smile. "A good man, Fleet to the bone. Well, this is not for discussion, Ensign, but I would agree with your surmise. Achael was a prisoner on the same slaver base where you and Abe were; the most logical supposition is that Abe knew something about his conduct or treatment there which would have been dangerous to Achael. Perhaps he was deep-conditioned, or something. He killed Abe to keep his secret, and suspected that Abe might have told you something."

"But what might be behind Achael?" asked Sass. But with this question, she had gone too far. The captain's face closed again, although he did not seem angry.

"That's for Security to determine, when they have all the evidence. Myself, I suspect that he was merely protecting himself. Suppose Abe knew he had stolen from other prisoners — that would ruin his Fleet career. I would be willing to wager that the final report will conclude that Achael was acting on his own behalf when he killed Abe and attempted to incriminate you."

Sassinak was not convinced, but knew better than to argue. As Fargeon predicted, Fleet Security agreed with his surmise, and closed the file on the murder. Achael's attacks on Sassinak, and his suicide made a clear pattern with his years as a prisoner: too clear, Sassinak thought, too simple. When she was older, when she had rank, she promised herself, she'd find out who was *really* responsible for Abe's death, who had set Achael on his trail. For now, she'd honor his memory with her own success.

PART THREE

✧ CHAPTER EIGHT

The striking, elegant woman in the mirror, Sassinak thought, had come a long way from the young ensign she had been. She had been lucky; she had been born with the good bones, the talent, the innate toughness to survive. She had had more luck along the way. But . . . she winked at herself, then grinned at the egotism. But she had cooperated with her luck, given it all the help she could. Tonight — tonight it was time for celebration. She had made it to Commander, past the dangerous doldrum ranks where the unwanted lodged sullenly until retirement age. She was about to have her own ship again, and this one a cruiser.

She eyed the new gown critically. Once she'd learned that good clothes fully repaid the investment, she'd spent some concentrated time learning what colors and styles suited her best. And then, one by one, she'd accumulated a small but elegant wardrobe. This now . . . her favorite rich colors glowed, jewellike reds and deep blues and purples, a quilted bodice shaped above a flowing, full skirt of deepest midnight, all in soft silui that caressed her skin with every movement. She slipped her feet into soft black boots, glad that the ridiculous fashion for high heels had once again died out. She was tall enough as it was.

Her comm signal went off as she was putting on the last touches, the silver earrings and simple necklace with its cut crystal star.

"Just because you got the promotion and the cruiser doesn't mean you can make us late," said the voice in her ear, the Lieutenant Commander who'd arranged the party. He'd been her assistant when she was working for Admiral Pael. "Tobaldi's doesn't hold reservations past the hour —"

"I know; I'm coming." With a last look at the mirror, she picked up her wrap and went out. As she'd half-expected, two

more of her friends waited in the corridor outside, with flowers
and a small wrapped box.

"You put this on *now*," said Mira. Her gold curly hair had
faded a little, but not the bright eyes or quick mind. Sassinak took
the gift, and untied the silver ribbon carefully.

"I suppose you figured out what I'd be wearing," she said
laughing. Then she had the box open, and caught her breath.
When she looked at Mira, the other woman was smug.

"I bought it years ago, that time we were shopping, remember? I saw the way you looked at it, and knew the time would
come. Of course, I could have waited until you made admiral —"
She ducked Sass' playful blow. "You will, Sass. It's a given. I'll
retire in a couple of years, and go back to Dad's shipping company — at least he's agreed to let me take over instead of that
bratty cousin. . . . Anyway, let me fasten it."

Sassinak picked up the intricate silver necklace, a design that
combined boldness and grace (and, she recalled, an outrageous
price — at least for a junior lieutenant, which she had been then)
and let Mira close the fastening. Her star went into the box — for
tonight, at least — and the box went back in her room. Whatever
she might have said to Mira was forestalled by the arrival of the
others, and the six of them were deep into reminiscences by the
time they got to Tobaldi's.

Mira — the only one who had been there — had to tell the
others all about Sass' first cruise. "They've heard that already,"
Sassinak kept protesting. Mira shushed her firmly.

"You wouldn't have told them the good parts," she said, and
proceeded to give her version of the good parts. Sassinak retali-
ated with the story of Mira's adventures on — or mostly off —
horseback, one leave they'd taken together on Mira's homeworld.
"I'm a spacer's brat, not a horsebreeder's daughter," complained
Mira.

"You're the one who said we ought to take that horsepacking
trip," said Sass. The others laughed, and brought up their own
tales.

Sassinak looked around the group — which now numbered
fourteen, since others had arrived to join them. Was there really
someone from *every* ship she'd been on? Four were from the
Padalyan Reef, the cruiser on which she'd been the exec until a
month ago. That was touching; they had given her a farewell

party then, and she had not expected to see them tonight. But the two young lieutenants, stiffly correct among the higher ranks, would not have missed it — she could see that in their eyes. The other two, off on long home leave between assignments, had probably dropped in just because they enjoyed a party.

Her glance moved on, checking an invisible list. All but the prize she'd been given command of, she thought — and wished for a moment that Ford, wherever he was, could be there, too. Forrest had known her, true, but he'd missed that terrifying interlude, staying on the patrol ship with its original crew. Carew, whom she'd known as a waspish major when she was a lieutenant, on shore duty with Commodore . . . what had her name been? Narros, that was it. . . . Carew was now a balding senior commander, whose memory had lost its sting. Sassinak almost wondered if he'd ever been difficult, then saw a very junior officer across the room flinch away from his gaze. She shrugged mentally — at least he wasn't causing *her* trouble any more.

Her exec from her first command was there, now a lieutenant commander and just as steady as ever, though with gray streaking his thick dark hair. Sassinak blessed the genes that had saved her from premature silver . . . she wanted to wear her silver by choice, not necessity. She didn't need gray hair to lend her authority, she thought to herself. Even back on the *Sunrose*. . . . But he was making a small speech, reminding her — and the others — of the unorthodox solution she had found for a light patrol craft in a particular tactical situation. Her friends enjoyed the story, but she remembered very well that some of the senior officers had not liked her solution at all. Her brows lowered and Mira poked her in the ribs.

"Wake up, Sass, the battle's over. You don't need to glare at *us* like that."

"Sorry . . . I was remembering Admiral Kurin's comments."

"Well . . . we all know what happened to *him*." And that was true enough. A stickler for the rulebook, he had fallen prey to a foe who was not. But Sassinak knew that his opinion of her had gone on file before that, to influence other seniors. She had seen the doubtful looks, and been subject to careful warnings.

Now, however, two men approached the table with the absolute assurance that comes only from a lifetime of command, and high rank at the end of it. Bilisics, the specialist in military law from Command and Staff, and Admiral Vannoy, Sector Commandant.

"Commander Sassinak — congratulations." Bilisics had been one of her favorite instructors, anywhere. She had even gone to him for advice on a most private and delicate matter — and so far as she could tell, he had maintained absolute secrecy. His grin to her acknowledged all that. "I must always congratulate an officer who steers a safe course through the dangerous waters of a tour of Fleet Headquarters, who avoids the reefs of political or social ambition, the treacherous tides of intimacy in high places . . ." He practically winked: they both knew what *that* was about. The others clearly thought it was one of Bilisics' usual mannered pleasantries. As far as she knew, no one had ever suspected her near-engagement to the ambassador from Arion.

"Yes: congratulations, Commander, and welcome to the Sector. You'll like the *Zaid-Dayan*, and I'm sure you'll do well with it." She had worked with Admiral Vannoy before, but not for several years. His newer responsibilities had not aged him; he gave, as always, the impression of energy under firm control.

"Would you join us?" Sassinak asked. But, as she expected, they had other plans, and after a few more minutes drifted off to join a table of very senior officers at the far end of the room.

It hardly needed Tobaldi's excellent dinner, the rare live orchestra playing hauntingly lovely old waltzes, or the wines they ordered lavishly, to make that evening special. She could have had any of several partners to end it with, but chose instead a scandalously early return to her quarters — not long after midnight.

"And I'll wager if we had a spycam in there, we'd find her looking back over the specs on her cruiser," said Mira, walking back to a popular dance pavilion with the others. "Fleet to the bone, that's what she is, more than most of us. It's her only family, has been since before the Academy."

Sass, unaware of Mira's shrewd guess, would not have been upset by it — since she was, at that moment, calling up the crew list on her terminal. She would have agreed with all that statement, although she felt an occasional twinge of guilt for her failure to contact any of her remaining biological kin. Yet . . . what did an orphan, an ex-slave, have in common with ordinary, respectable citizens? Too many people still considered slavery a disgrace to the victim; she didn't want to see that rejection on the faces of her own relatives. Easier to stay away, to stay with the family that had rescued her and still supported her. And that night, warmed by the fellowship and celebration, intent on her new command, she felt nothing but eagerness for the future.

Sassinak always felt that Fleet had lost something in the transition from the days when a captain approached a ship lying at dockside, visible to the naked eye, with a veritable gangplank and the welcoming crew topside, and flags flying in the open air. Now, the new captain of, say, a cruiser, simply walked down one corridor after another of a typical space station, and entered the ship's space by crossing a line on the deck planking. The ceremony of taking command had not changed that much, but the circumstances made such ceremony far less impressive. Yet she could not entirely conceal her delight, that after some twenty years as a Fleet officer, she was now to command her own cruiser.

"Commander Kerif will be sorry to have missed you, Commander Sassinak," said Lieutenant Commander Huron, her Executive Officer, leading the way to her new quarters. "But under the circumstances —"

"Of course," said Sassinak. If your son, graduating from the Academy, is going to marry the heiress of one of the wealthiest mercantile families, you may ask for, and be granted, extra leave: even if it means that the change of command of your cruiser is not quite by the book. She had done her homework, skimming the files on her way over from Sector HQ. Huron, for instance, had not impressed his captain overmuch, by his latest Fitness Report. But considering the secret orders she carried, Sassinak had doubts about all the Fitness Reports on that ship. The man seemed intelligent and capable — not to mention fit and reasonably good-looking. He'd have a fair chance with her.

"He asked me to extend you his warmest congratulations, and his best wishes for your success with the ship. I can assure you that your officers are eager to make this mission a success."

"Mission? What do you know about it?" Supposedly her orders were secret: but then, one of the points made was that Security breaches were getting worse, much worse.

Huron's forehead wrinkled. "Well . . . we've been out on

patrol, just kind of scouting around the sector. Figured we'd do more of the same."

"Pretty much. I'll brief the senior officers once we're in route; we have two more days of refitting, right?"

"Yes, Commander." He gave her a quizzical look. "With all due respect, ma'am, I guess what they say about you is true."

Sassinak smiled; she knew what they said, and she knew why. "Lieutenant Commander Huron, I'm sure you wouldn't listen to idle gossip . . . any more than I would listen to gossip about you and your passion for groundcar racing."

It was good to be back on a ship again, good to have the command she'd always wanted. Sassinak glanced down at the four gold rings on her immaculate white sleeve, and on to the gold ring on her finger that gave her Academy class and carried the tiny diamond of the top-ranking graduate. Not bad for an orphan, an ex-slave . . . not bad at all. Some of her classmates thought she was lucky; some of them, no doubt, thought her ambitions stopped here, with the command of a cruiser in an active sector.

But her dreams went beyond even this. She wanted a star on her shoulder, maybe even two: sector command, command of a battle group. This ship was her beginning.

Already she knew more about the 218 *Zaid-Dayan* than her officers realized. Not merely the plans of the class of vessel, which any officer of her rank would be expected to have seen, but the detailed plans of the particular cruiser, and the records of all its refittings. You cannot know too much, Abe had said. Whatever you know is your wealth.

Hers lay here. Better than gold or jewels, she told herself, was the knowledge that won respect of her officers and crew . . . something that could not be bought with unlimited credits. Although credits had their uses. She ran her hand lightly along the edge of the desk she'd installed in her office. Real wood, rare, beautifully carved. She'd discovered in herself a taste for quality, beauty, and indulged it as her pay allowed. A custom desk, a few good pieces of crystal and sculpture, clothes that showed off the beauty she'd grown into. She still thought of all that as luxury, as frills, but no longer felt guilty for enjoying them in moderation.

While the cruiser lay at the refitting dock, Sassinak explored her new command, meeting and talking with every member of the crew. About half of them had leave; she met them as they returned. But the onboard crew, a dozen officers and fifty or so enlisted, she made a point of chatting up.

The *Zaid-Dayan* wore the outward shape of most heavy cruisers, a slightly flattened ovoid hull with clusters of drive pods both port and starboard, aft of the largest diameter. Sassinak never saw it from outside, of course; only the refitting crews did that. What she saw were the human accessible spaces, the "living decks" as they were called, and the crawlways that let a lean service tech into the bowels of the ship's plumbing and electrical circuitry. For the most part, it was much the same as the *Padalyan Reef*, the cruiser she'd just left, with Environmental at the bottom, then Troop Deck, then Data, then Main, then the two Flight Decks atop. But not quite.

In this ship, the standard layouts in Environmental had been modified by the addition of the stealth equipment; Sassinak walked every inch of the system to be sure she understood what pipes now ran where. The crowding below had required rearranging some of the storage areas, so that only Data Deck was exactly the same as standard. Sassinak paid particular attention to the two levels of storage for the many pieces of heavy equipment the *Zaid-Dayan* carried: the shuttles, the pinnace, the light fighter craft, the marines' tracked assault vehicles. Again, she made certain that she knew exactly which craft was stowed in each location, knew without having to check the computers.

Her own quarters were just aft of the bridge, opening onto the port passage, a stateroom large enough for modest entertaining — a low table and several chairs, as well as workstation, sleeping area, and private facilities. Slightly aft and across the passage was the officers' wardroom. Her position as cruiser captain required the capacity to entertain formal visitors, so she also had a large office, forward of the bridge and across the same passage. This she could decorate as she pleased — at least, within the limits of Fleet regulations and her own resources. She chose midnight-blue carpeting to show off the striking grain of her desk; the table was Fleet issue, but refinished to gleaming black. Guest seating, low couches along the walls, was in white synthi-leather. Against the pale-gray bulkheads, this produced a room of simple elegance that suited her perfectly.

Huron, she realized quickly, was an asset in more ways than one. Colony-bred himself, he had more than the usual interest in their safety. Too many Fleet officers considered the newer colonies more trouble than they were worth. As the days passed, she found that Huron's assessment of the junior officers was both fair and leavened by humor. She began to wonder why his previous commander had had so little confidence in him.

That story came out over a game of sho, one evening some days into their patrol. Sassinak had begun delicately probing, to see if he had a grievance of any sort. After the second or third ambiguous question, Huron looked up from the playing board with a smile that sent a sudden jolt through her heart.

"You're wondering if I know why Commander Kerif gave me such a lukewarm report last period?"

Sass, caught off guard as she rarely was, smiled back. "You're quite right — and you don't need to answer. But you've been too knowledgeable and competent since I came to have given habitually poor performance."

Huron's smile widened. "Commander Sassinak, your predecessor was a fine officer and I admire him. However, he had very strong ideas about the dignity of some . . . ah . . . prominent, old-line, merchant families. He never felt that I had sufficient respect for them, and he attributed a bit of doggerel he heard to me."

"Doggerel?"

Huron actually reddened. "A . . . uh . . . song. Sort of a song. About his son and that girl he's marrying. I didn't write it, Commander, although I did think it was funny when I heard it. But, you see, I'd quoted some verse in his presence before, and he was sure . . ."

Sassinak thought about it. "And do you have proper respect for wealthy merchants?"

Huron pursed his lips. "Proper? I think so. But I am a colony brat."

Sassinak shook her head, smiling. "So am I, as you must already know. Poor Kerif . . . I suppose it was a very *bad* song." She caught the look in Huron's eye, and chuckled. "If that's the worst you ever did, we'll have no problems at all."

"I don't want any," said Huron, in a tone that conveyed more than one meaning.

Years before, as a cadet, Sassinak had wondered how anyone could combine relationships both private and professional without being unfair to one or the other. Over the years, she had established her own ground rules, and had become a good judge of those likely to share her values and attitudes. Except for that one almost-disastrous (and, in retrospect, funny) engagement to a brilliant and handsome older diplomat, she had never risked anything she could not afford to lose. Now, secure in her own identity, she expected to go on enjoying life with those of her officers who were willing and stable enough not to be threatened — and honest enough not to take advantages she had no intention of releasing.

Huron, she thought to herself, was a distinct possibility. From the glint in his eyes, he thought the same way about her: the first prerequisite.

But her duty came first, and the present circumstances often drove any thought of pleasure from her mind. In the twenty years since her first voyage, Fleet had not been able to assure the safety of the younger and more remote colonies; as well, planets cleared for colonization by one group were too often found to have someone else — legally now the owners — in place when the colonists arrived. Although human slavery was technically illegal, colonies were being raided for slaves — and that meant a market somewhere. "Normal" humans blamed the heavyworlders; heavyworlders blamed the "lightweights" as they called them, and the wealthy mercantile families of the inner worlds complained bitterly about the cost of supporting an ever-growing Fleet which didn't seem to save either lives or property.

Their orders, which Sassinak discussed only in part with her officers, required them to make use of a new, supposedly secret, technology for identifying and trailing newer deep-space civilian vessels. It augmented, rather than replaced, the standard IFF devices which had been in use since before Sassinak joined the Fleet. A sealed beacon, installed in the ship's architecture as it was built, could be triggered by Fleet surveillance scans. While passive to detectors in its normal mode, it nonetheless stored information on the ship's movements. The original idea had been to strip these beacons whenever a ship came to port, and thus keep records on its actual travel — as opposed to the log records presented to the portmaster. But still newer technology allowed specially equipped Fleet cruisers to enable such beacons while still in deepspace, even FTL flight — and then to follow with much less chance of detection. Now the plan was for cruisers

such as the *Zaid-Dayan* to patrol slowly, in areas away from the
normal corridors, and select suspicious "merchants" to follow.

So far as the junior officers were concerned, the cruiser
patrolled in the old way; because of warnings from Fleet about
security leaks, Sassinak told only four of her senior crew, who had
to know to operate the scan. Other modifications to the *Zaid-
Dayan*, intended to give it limited stealth capability, were
explained as being useful in normal operations.

As the days passed, Sassinak considered the Fleet warnings.
"Assume subversives on each ship." Fine, but with no more guidance than that, how was she supposed to find one? Subversives
didn't advertise themselves with loud talk of overturning FSP
conventions. Besides, it was all guessing. She might have one
subversive on her ship, or a dozen, or none at all. She had to admit that if she were planting agents, she'd certainly put them on
cruisers, as the most effective and most widespread of the active
vessels. But nothing showed in the personnel records she'd run a
preliminary screen on — and supposedly Security had checked
them all out before.

She knew that many commanders would think first of the
heavyworlders on board, but while some of them were certainly
involved in subversive organizations, the majority were not. However difficult heavyworlders might be — and some of them, she'd
found, had earned their reputation for prickly sullenness — Sassinak had never forgotten the insights gained from her friends at
the Academy. She tried to see behind the heavy-boned stolid
faces, the overmuscular bodies, to the human person within —
and most of the time she felt she had succeeded. A few real
friendships had come out of this, and many more amiable working relationships . . . and she found that her reputation as an
officer fair to heavyworlders had spread among the officer corps.

Wefts, as aliens, irritated many human commanders, but
again Sassinak had the advantage of early friendships. She
knew that Wefts had no desire for the worlds humans preferred — in fact, the Wefts who chose space travel were sterile,
having given up their chance at procreation for an opportunity
to travel and adventure. Nor were they the perfect mental
spies so many feared: their telepathic powers were quite limited; they found the average human mind a chaotic mess of
emotion and illogic, impossible to follow unless the individual

tried hard to convey a message. Sass, with her early training in Discipline, could converse easily with Wefts in their native form, but she knew she was an exception. Besides, if any of the Wefts on board had identified a subversive, she'd already have been told.

After several weeks, she felt completely comfortable with her crew, and could tell that they were settling well together. Huron had proved as inventive a partner as he was a versifier — after hearing a few of his livelier creations in the wardroom one night, she could hardly believe he *hadn't* written the one about the captain's son and the merchant's daughter. He still insisted he was innocent of that one. The Weapons Officer, a woman only one year behind her at the Academy, turned out to be a regional sho champion — and was clearly delighted to demonstrate by beating Sassinak five games out of seven. It was good for morale, and besides, Sassinak had never minded learning from an expert. One of the cooks was a natural genius — so good that Sassinak caught herself thinking about putting him on her duty shift permanently. She didn't, but her taste buds argued with her, and more than once she found an excuse to "inspect" the kitchens when he was baking. He always had something for the captain. All this was routine — even finding a homesick and miserable junior engineering tech, just out of training, sobbing hopelessly in a storage locker. But so was the patrol routine . . . nothing, day after day, but the various lumps of matter that had been mapped in their assigned volume of space. Not so much as a pleasure yacht out for adventure.

She was half-dozing in her cabin, early in third watch, when the bridge comm chimed.

"Captain — we've got a ship. Merchant, maybe CR-class for mass, no details yet. Trigger the scan?"

"Wait — I'm coming." She elbowed Huron, who'd already fallen asleep, until he grunted and opened an eye, then whisked into her uniform. When he grunted again and asked what it was, she said, "We've got a ship." At that, both eyes came open, and he sat up. She laughed, and went out; by the time she got to the bridge, he was only a few steps behind her, fully dressed.

"Gotcha!" Huron, leaning over the scanner screen was as eager as the technician handling the controls. "Look at that. . . ." His fingers flew on his own keyboard, and the ship's data came up

on an adjoining screen. "Hu Veron Shipways, forty percent
owned by Allied Geochemical, which is wholly owned by the
Paraden family. Well, well . . . previous owner Jakob Iris, no previous criminal record but went into bankruptcy after . . . hmm . . .
a wager on a horse race. What's that?"

"Horse race," said Sassinak, watching the screen just as intently. "Four-legged mammal, big enough to carry humans. Old
Earth origin, imported to four new systems, but they mostly die."

"Kipling's corns, Captain, how *do* you know all that?"

"Kipling indeed, Huron. Our schools had a Kipling story about
a horse in the required elementary reading list. With a picture.
And the Academy kept a team for funerals, and I have seen a tape
of a horse race. In fact, I've actually ridden a horse." Her mouth
quirked, as she thought of Mira's homeworld and that ill-fated
pack trip.

"You would have," said Huron almost vaguely. His attention
was already back to his screen. "Look at that — Iris was betting
against Luisa Paraden Scofeld. Isn't that the one who was married to a zero-G hockey star, and then to an ambassador to Ryxi?"

"Yes, and while he was there she ran off with the landscape ar-
chitect. But the point is —"

"The point is that the Paradens have laid their hands on that
ship *twice!*"

"That we know of." Sassinak straightened up and regarded the
back of Huron's head thoughtfully. "I think we'll trail this one,
Commander Huron. There are just a few too many coincidences. . . ."

Even as she gave the necessary orders, Sassinak was conscious
of fulfilling an old dream — to be in command of her own ship, on
the bridge, with a possible pirate in view. She looked around with
satisfaction at what might have been any large control room,
anything from a reactor station to a manufacturing plant. The
physical remnant of millennia of naval history was under her feet,
the raised dais that gave her a clear view of everyone and
everything in the room. She could sit in the command chair, with
her own screens and computer linkages at hand, or stand and
observe the horseshoe arrangement of workstations, each with its
trio of screens, its banks of toggles and buttons, its quietly
competent operator. Angled above were the big screens, and
directly below the end of the dais was the remnant of a now

outmoded technology that most captains still used to impress visitors: the three-D tank.

Trailing a ship through FTL space was, Sassinak thought, like following a groundcar through thick forest at night without using headlights. The unsuspecting merchant left a disturbed swath of space which the Ssli could follow, but it could not simultaneously sense structural (if that was the word) variations in the space-time fabric . . . so that they were constantly in danger of jouncing through celestial chugholes or running into unseen gravitational stumps. They had to go fast, to keep the quarry in range of detection, but fast blind travel through an unfamiliar sector was an excellent way to get swallowed by the odd wormhole.

When the quarry dropped out of FTL into normal space, the cruiser followed — or, more properly, anticipated. The computer brought up the local navigation points.

"That's interesting," said Huron, pointing. It was more than interesting. A small star system, with one twenty-year-old colony (in the prime range for a raid) sited over a rich vein of platinum. Despite Fleet's urging, FSP bureaucrats had declined to approve effective planetary defense weaponry for small colonies . . . and the catalog of this colony's defenses was particularly meager.

"Brotherhood of Metals," said Sass. "That's the colony sponsor; they hold the paper on it. I'm beginning to wonder who *their* stockholders are."

"New contact!" The technician's voice rose. "Excuse me, Captain, but I've got a Churi-class vessel out there: could be extremely dangerous —"

"Specs." Sassinak glanced around the bridge, pleased with the alert but unfrantic attitudes she saw. They were already on full stealth routine; upgrading to battle status would cost her stealth. Her Weapons Officer raised a querying finger; Sassinak shook her head, and he relaxed.

"Old-style IFF — no beacon. Built forty years ago in the Zendi yards, commissioned by the —" He stopped, lowered his voice. "The governor of Diplo, Captain."

Oh great, thought Sass. *Just what we needed, a little heavy-worlder suspicion to complete our confusion.*

"Bring up the scan and input," she said, without commenting on the heavyworlder connection. One display filled with a computer analysis of the IFF output. Sassinak frowned at it. "That's not right. Look at that carrier wave —"

"Got it." The technician had keyed in a comparison command, and the display broke into colored bands, blue for the correspondence between the standard signal and the one received, and bright pink for the unmatched portions.

"They've diddled with their IFF," said Sass. "We don't know *what* that is, or what it carries —"

"Our passive array says it's about the size of a patrol craft —" offered Huron.

"Which means it could carry all sorts of nice things," said Sass, thinking of them. An illicitly armed patrol craft was not a match for the *Zaid-Dayan*, but it could do them damage. If it noticed them.

Huron was frowning at the displays. "Now . . . is this a rendezvous, or an ambush?"

"Rendezvous," said Sassinak quickly. His brows rose.

"You're sure?"

"It's the worse possibility for us: it gives us two ships to follow or engage if they notice us. Besides, little colonies like this don't get visits from unscheduled merchants."

Judging by the passive scans, which produced data hours old, the two ships matched trajectories and traveled toward the colony world together — certainly close enough to use a tight-beam communication band. The *Zaid-Dayan* hung in the system's outer debris, watching with every scanning mode it had. Hour by hour, it became clearer that the destination must be the colony. *They're raiders*, Sassinak thought, and Huron said it aloud, adding, "We ought to blow them out of the system!" For an instant, Sassinak let the old fury rise almost out of control, but she forced the memory of her own childhood back. If they blew these two away, they would know nothing about the powers who hired them, protected them, supplied them. She would not let herself wonder if another Fleet commander had made the same decision about her homeworld's raid.

She shook her head. "We're on surveillance patrol; you know that."

"But, Captain — our data's a couple of hours old. If they *are* raiders, they could be hitting that colony any time . . . we have to warn them. We can't let them —" Huron paled, and she saw a terrible doubt in his eyes.

"Orders." She turned away, not trusting herself to meet his gaze. She had exorcised many demons from her past, in the years since her commissioning: she could dine with admirals and high government officials, make polite conversation with aliens, keep her temper and her wits in nearly all circumstances . . . but deep in her mind she carried the vision of her parents dying, her sister's body sliding into the water, her best friend changed to a shivering, depressed wreck of the lively girl she'd been. She shook her head, forced herself to concentrate on the scan. Her voice came out clipped and cold; she could see by their reactions that the bridge crew recognized the strain on her. "We *must* find the source of this — we must. If we destroy these vermin, and never find their master, it will go on and on, and more will suffer. We have to watch, and follow —"

"But they never meant us to let a colony be raided! We're — we're supposed to *protect* them — it's in the Charter!" Huron circled until he faced her again. "You've got discretion, in any situation where FSP citizens are directly threatened —"

"Discretion!" Sassinak clamped her jaw on the rest of that, and glared at him. It must have been a strong glare, for he backed a step. In a lower voice, she went on. "Discretion, Huron, is not questioning your commanding officer's orders on the bridge when you don't know what in flaming gas clouds is going on. Discretion is learning to think before you blow your stack —"

"Did you ever think," said Huron, white-lipped and angrier than Sassinak had ever seen him, "that someone might have made this decision when *you* were down there?" He jerked his chin toward the navigation display. She waited a long moment, until the others had decided it would be wise to pay active attention to their own work, and the rigidity went out of Huron's expression.

"Yes," she said very quietly. "Yes, I have. I imagine it haunts that person, if someone actually was there, as this is going to haunt me." At that his face relaxed slightly, the color rising to his cheeks. Before he could speak, Sassinak went on. "You think I don't care? You think I haven't imagined myself — some child the age I was, some innocent girl or boy who's thinking of tomorrow's test in school? You think I don't *remember*, Huron?" She glanced around, seeing that everyone was at least pretending to give them privacy. "You've seen my nightmares, Huron; you know I haven't forgotten."

His face was as red as it had been pale. "I know. I know that, but how *can* you —"

"I want them all." It came out flat, emotionless, but with the power of an impending avalanche . . . as yet no sound, no excitement . . . but inexorable movement accelerating to some dread ending. "I want them all, Huron: the ones who do it because it's fun, the ones who do it because it's profitable, the ones who do it because it's easier than hiring honest labor . . . and above all the ones who do it without thinking about why . . . who just do it because that's how it's done. I want them *all*." She turned to him with a smile that just missed pleasantry to become the toothy grin of the striking predator. "And there's only one way to get them all, and to *that* I commit this ship, and my command, and any other resource . . . including, with all regret, those colonists who will die before we can rescue them —"

"But we're going to try —?"

"Try, hell. I'm going to do it." The silence on the bridge was eloquent; this time when she turned away from Huron he did not follow.

The scans told the pitiable story of the next hours. The colonists, more alert than Myriad's, managed to set off their obsolete missiles, which the illicit patrol craft promptly detonated at a safe distance.

"Now we know they've got an LDs14, or equivalent," said Huron without emphasis. Sassinak glanced at him but made no comment. They had not met, as usual after dinner, to talk over the day's work. Huron had explained stiffly that he wanted to review for his next promotion exam, and Sassinak let him go. The ugly thought ran through her mind that a subversive would be just as happy to have the evidence blown to bits. But surely not Huron — from a small colony himself, surely he'd have more sympathy with them . . . and besides, she was sure she knew him better than any psych profile. Just as he knew her.

Meanwhile, having exhausted the planetary defenses, the two raiders dropped shuttles to the surface. Sassinak shivered, remembering the tough, disciplined (if irregular) troops the raiders had landed on her world. The colonists wouldn't stand a chance. She found she was breathing faster, and looked up to find Huron watching her. So were the others, though less obviously; she caught more than one quick sideways glance.

Yet she had to wait. Through the agonizing hours, she stayed on the bridge, pushing aside the food and drink that someone handed her. She had to wait, but she could not relax, eat, drink, even talk, while those innocent people were being killed . . . and captured . . . and tied into links (did *all* slavers use links of eight? she wondered suddenly). The two ships orbited the planet, and when this orbit took them out of LOS, the *Zaid-Dayan* eased closer, its advanced technology allowing minute hops of FTL flight with minimal disturbance to the fields.

Their scan delay was less than a half hour, and the raiders had shown no sign of noticing their presence in the system. Now they could track the shuttles rising — all to the transport, Sassinak noted — and then descending and rising again. Once more, and then the raiders boosted away from the planet, on a course that brought them within easy range of the *Zaid-Dayan*. Huron only looked at Sass; she shook her head, and caught her Weapons Officer's eye as well. Hold on, she told the self she imagined lying helpless in the transport's belly. We're here: we're going to come after you. But she knew her thoughts did those children no good at all — and nothing could wipe out the harm already done.

◆ CHAPTER NINE

All too quickly the transport and its escort showed that they were preparing to leave the system. Powerful boosters shoved them up through the planet's gravity well — a system cheap and certain, if inelegant. Sassinak wondered if the transport that had carried her had had an escort — or if Fleet activities in the past twenty years had had that much effect. Considering the cost of each ship, crew, weaponry . . . if Fleet had made escorts necessary . . . then either the profit margin of slavers should be much narrower, or the slave trade brought even more money than anyone had guessed. And why?

"Commander Sassinak —" This mode of address, perfectly correct but slightly more formal than usual to a ship's captain on board, made it clear to her just how upset her bridge crew were. She glanced at Arly, Senior Weapons Officer, who was pointing at her own display. "We finally got a good readout on their weapons system . . . that's one more hot ship."

Sassinak welcomed the diversion, and leaned over the display. Since the escort vessel had tampered with its own IFF transmission, they had had to use other detection methods to figure out its class and armament . . . methods which were supposed to be indetectible, although they'd not yet been tested against any but Fleet vessels. Now she had to find out — in the fabric of her own ship if the designers were wrong — just how accurate and indetectible they were.

"Patrol class: way too big and hot for anyone but Fleet to have legally," Arly went on, pointing out the obvious. "Probably modified and refitted from a legal insystem escort or patrol vessel . . . although it might be a pirated hull from something consigned to scrap."

"I hope not," said Sass. "If there's a hole in our scrap and recycling operation, we could find ourselves facing a pirated battle platform —"

"Best fit of hull and structure is to a Vannoy Combine insystem escort. Then if they retrofitted an FTL drive component —" The Weapons Officer's fingers danced over the controls, and the display split, one vertical half showing a schematic with the changes she proposed. "— and beefed up the interior a good bit — they'd lose crew space, but gain the reinforcement they need to mount *these*." A final flick of the finger, and the armament that the *Zaid-Dayan*'s detectors and computer had come up with came up as a list.

"On *that*?" Sassinak stared at it. A vessel only one third the mass of her own was carrying nearly identical weaponry, with a nice mix of projectile, beam, and explosives.

"Just as well we didn't sail in to take an easy kill," said the Weapons Officer quietly. Her expression was completely neutral. "Could have been messy."

"It's going to be messy," said Sassinak, just as quietly. "When we catch them."

"We *are* following —" It was not quite a question.

"Oh, yes. And as soon as we have their destination coordinates, we'll be calling in the whole bloody Fleet."

But it was not that easy. The two ships moved away from the planet they'd raided, boosting toward a safe range for FTL flight. Sassinak would like to have checked the planet itself for survivors (unlikely though she knew that to be) and evidence, but she could not risk losing the ships when they left normal space. She waited as the ships built speed, until their own scans must be nearly blind as they approached their insertion velocity. The Ssli had queried twice when she finally gave the order to shift position and pursue. Just before they entered FTL flight, she had a burst sent to Sector HQ by lowlink, explaining what happened to the colony and her plan of pursuit.

Then it was the same blind chase as they had had following the transport in the first place. Sassinak could only imagine how it must seem to the Ssli on whose ability to sense the trace they all depended. Their lives were hostage to the realities of such travel . . . the Ssli concentrated so on the traces of their quarry that it could not warn them of potentially fatal anomalies in their path.

With the Ssli controlling the ship's movement through its computer link, the crew had all too little to do. Sassinak spent some time on the bridge each shift, and much of the rest prowling the ship wondering how she was going to find her subversives — without driving the perfectly loyal and honorable crew up the walls in the process. Dhrossh, their link to their quarry, would not initiate an IFTL link without her direct command, but someone still might loose a message by SOLEC or highlink, not to warn the raiders, but their allies. That would require knowing the coordinates of either a mapped Fleet node or receiving station, but an agent might. She considered sending regular reports to Fleet by the same means, and decided against it. Better to have some conclusion to report, after that disaster at the colony.

Sassinak worked out a duty schedule that involved keeping a Weft on the bridge constantly — at least they could contact her, instantly, if something happened, and they were exceptionally able in reading the minute behaviors of humans. She had to hope that her human crew would not guess her reasons.

She was acutely aware of the crew's reaction to her decision not to engage the raiders before they attacked the colony, or during the attack. She imagined their comments. . . . "Is the captain losing it? Has someone bought her off?" Volume 8 of the massive *Rules of Engagement* managed to be lying around the senior officers' wardroom more than once, although she never caught anyone reading the critical article. Some of the crew sided with her, and she heard some of that. "Pretty sharp, figuring out we were outgunned before we'd come in close-scan range," one of the biotechs was saying one day as Sassinak passed quietly along on a routine inspection of the environmental system. "I wouldn't have guessed that the initial readouts were wrong . . . whoever heard of someone fooling with an IFF?" Sassinak smiled grimly: that wasn't a new trick, and bridge crew all knew it. But it was nice to have credit somewhere. Too bad that she discovered a minor leak in the detox input filter line, and had to file a report on the very tech who'd been defending her.

The environmental system was, in fact, a nagging worry. Among the modifications made on station, a rerouting of most of the main lines had meant shifting them into cramped, hard-to-inspect compartments rather than out in the open where inspection was easy. Sassinak remembered her first cruise, and the awkwardness of it. Supposedly the equipment now mounted in midline was worth it, in the protection it gave from enemy surveillance, but if the environmental system failed, they would have a miserable trip back — if they survived. Sassinak glared at the big gray cylinders that lay in recesses originally meant for pipelines. They'd *better* work. In the meantime, either because of the less efficient layout, with its more variable line pressures, or because the line was harder to inspect, minor leaks repeatedly developed in one or another subsystem.

Of course, it could be sabotage. That's why she walked the lines herself, struggling to relearn the details of the system so that she knew what she was looking for. But in any complicated system of tubing and pumps, a thousand opportunities exist for subtle acts of sabotage, and she didn't expect to find anything obvious. She was right.

As the ship's days passed in pursuit, with the Ssli certain that it had a lock on the ships ahead, Huron finally came around. Literally, as he appeared at her cabin door with a peace offering: wine and pastries. Sassinak had not realized how much she'd missed his support until she saw the old grin on his face.

"Peace offering," he said. Typically, he wasn't trying to pretend they'd had no quarrel. Sassinak nodded, and waved him in. He set the basket of hot, sugary treats on her desk, and opened the wine. They settled down in comfortable chairs, one on either side of the pastry basket, and munched in harmony for a few minutes.

"I was afraid they'd split up, or we'd lose them," he said with a sideways glance. "And then when we got the final scan on the escort — that it might have been fatal to take it on — I knew you were right, but I just couldn't —"

"Never mind." Sassinak leaned back against the padded chair. Just to have someone to talk with, to relax with — it wasn't over, and it was going to get worse before it got better, but if Huron could accept her decision . . .

"I wish we knew *where* they're going!" He bit into his pastry so hard that flaky bits showered across his lap. He muttered a curse through the mouthful of food, and Sassinak chuckled. Problems and all, life was more fun with Huron in her cabin some nights.

"Huh. Don't we all! And I don't dare send anything back to Sector HQ in case something intercepts it. . . ."

"Remember when Ssli and the IFTL system were new, and we

were *sure* no one else had them?" He was still swiping crumbs from his lap, and looked up at her with the mischievous lift of eyebrow she'd come to love.

"Sure do." Sassinak ran her hands through her dark hair, and flipped the ends towards him. His eyes widened, then narrowed again.

"One track mind." He shook his head at her.

"You're any different?" Sassinak pointed to the now-empty pastry basket and the bottle of wine. "Think I can't recognize bait when I see it?"

"Brains with your beauty — and a few other things. . . ." His eyes finished what she had started, and they were more than half-way undressed when Sassinak remembered to switch the intercom to alert-only. The bridge crew knew what that meant, she thought with satisfaction, before dragging the big brilliantly rainbowed comforter over the pair of them.

"And what I still don't understand," said Huron, far more awake than usual for 0200, "is how they could mount all that on a hull that size. Are they crewing it with midgets, or what?"

Sassinak had taken a short nap, and wakened to find Huron tracing elaborate curlicues on her back while he stared at the readout on the overhead display. She yawned, pushed back a thick tangle of hair, and reached up to switch the display off. "Later . . ."

He switched it back on. "No, seriously —"

"Seriously, I'm sleepy. Turn it off, or go look at it somewhere else."

He glowered at her. "Some Fleet captain *you* are, lazing around like someone's lapcat after a dish of cream."

Sassinak purred loudly, yawned again, and realized she was going to wake all the way up, like it or not. "Big weapons, small hull. Reminds me of something." Huron blushed, extensively, and Sassinak snapped her teeth at him. "Call your captain a cat, and you deserve to get bit, chum. If we're going to go back to work, I'm getting dressed." She felt a lot better, relaxed and alert all at once.

Now that she was awake, she realized that she had not fol-lowed through on the analysis of the escort vessel as carefully as she could have. She'd been thinking too much about her main decision and its implications. Together she and Huron ran the figures several times, and then adjourned to the main wardroom. She called in both Arly and Hollister. They arrived blinking and yawning: as mainshift crew, they were normally asleep at this hour. After a cup of stimulant and food, they came fully awake.

"The question is, are we sure of our data, even that last? Is that thing built on a patrol-class hull, and if so does it really carry all those weapons, and if so what's their crew size and how are they staying alive?" Sassinak took the last spiced bun off the platter the night cook had brought in.

Hollister shrugged. "That new detection system isn't really my specialty, but if that's the size we think — dimensional and mass — then it'll depend on weaponry. With up-to-date environmental, guidance, and drive systems, they'd need a crew of fifty to work normal shifts — plus weapons specialists. Say, sixty to seventy altogether. If they work long shifts, maybe fifty altogether, but they'd chance fatigue errors —"

"But they don't expect to need top efficiency for long," Sassinak said. "They come in, rout a colony, escort the transport to their base, wherever that is . . . and most times they never see trouble."

"Fifty, then. That means . . . mmm . . ." He ran some figures into the nearest terminal. "'Bout what I thought. Look —" A ship schematic came up on the main screen at the end of the table. "Fifty crew, here's the calories and water needs . . . best guess at system efficiency . . . and that means they'll need eight standard filtration units, eight sets of re-op converters, plus the UV trays —" As he talked, the schematic filled with green lines and blocks, the standard representation of environmental system units. "This is assuming their FTL route doesn't take more than twenty-five standard days, and they've got the same kind of oxygen recharge system we do. Most surveyed routes come in under twenty days, as you know. Now if we add the probable drives: we know they have insystem chem boosters as well as insystem mains, and FTL —" The drive components came up in blue. "And minimum crew space: access and living —" That was yellow. "Weapons?"

Arly took over, and the schematic suddenly bled with red weapons symbols. "This is what we got off the scans, Captain. Their IFF was a real nutcase: no sense at all. But the passives showed two distinct patterns of radiation leakage: here, and there. And we saw how they knocked out those ground-space missiles . . . they do have optical weapons."

"And it doesn't fit," said Huron, sounding entirely too smug. "Look." Sure enough, the display had a blinking symbol in one corner: excess volume specified.

Arly looked stubborn. "I could not ignore the scan data —"

"Of course not." Sassinak held up her hand for silence when both mouths opened. "Look, Huron, both the scans and this schematic come in part from assumptions we made about those criminals. *If* they crew their ship to a level we think safe, *if* they aren't stressing their environmental system, *if* a few extra particles means they've got a neutron bomb . . . all if."

"We have to make some assumptions!"

"Yes. I do. I'm assuming they sacrifice everything else to speed and firepower. They want no witnesses: they want to be sure they can blow anything — up to a battle platform, let's say — into nothing, before it can call in help. They want to be able to escape any pursuit. They're not out on patrol as long as we normally are: they sacrifice comfort, and some levels of efficiency. I will bet you that they're undercrewed and carry every scrap of armament our scans found."

"Less crew means they could have a smaller environmental system," said Hollister.

"And with any luck less crew means they're a little less alert to a tail."

"I wish I knew how good their fire-control systems were," said Arly, running a finger along the edge of the console. "If they've got anything like the Gamma system, we could be in trouble with them."

"Are you advising me not to engage?" asked Sass. Arly's face darkened a little. A Senior Weapons Officer could give such advice, but under all the circumstances, it meant taking sides in the earlier argument: something Arly had refused to do.

"Not precisely . . . no. But they've got almost as much as we have, on a smaller hull with different movement capability. Normally I don't have to worry about something that size — with all its mobility, it still can't take us. But this —" She tapped the display. "This *could* breach us, if they got lucky . . . and their speed and mobility increase the danger. Call it even odds, or a shade to their favor. I'd be glad to engage them, Captain, but you need to be aware of all the factors."

"I am." Sassinak stretched, then shook the tension out of her hands. "And you'll no doubt have a chance to test our ideas before long. If they're short-crewed and short on environmental supplies, surely they'll have a short FTL route picked out . . . it's been eighteen days now."

"Speaking of environmental systems," said Hollister gruffly. "That number nine scrubber's leaking again. I could take it down and repack it, but that'd mean tying up a whole shift crew —"

Sassinak glanced at Huron. "Nav got any guesses on their destination?"

"Not a clue. Dhrossh is downright testy about queries, and about half the equation solutions don't fit anything in the books."

"Just keep an eye on the scrubber, then. We don't want Engineering tied up if we're suddenly on insystem drive with combat coming up."

Another Standard day passed, and another. None of the crew did anything but what she expected. No saboteur or subversive stood up to expound a doctrine of slavery and planet piracy. At least her relationship with Huron was better, and the other hotheads in the crew seemed to follow his lead. She was squatting on her heels beside the number nine scrubber, with Hollister, looking at a thin line of greasy liquid that had trickled down the outer casing, when the ship lurched slightly as the Ssli-controlled drive computers dropped them out of FTL.

✦ CHAPTER TEN

By the time Sassinak reached the bridge, Huron had their location on the big display.

"Unmapped," said Sassinak sourly.

"Officially unmapped," agreed Huron. "Sector margins — you can see that both the nearest surveys don't quite meet."

"By a whole lot of useful distance," said Sassinak. Five stars over *that* way, the Fleet survey codes were pink. Eight stars on the other, the Fleet survey codes were light green. And nothing showed in the other vectors.

"Diverging cones don't fill space," said Huron. She glowered at him; she'd hit her head on the input connector of the scrubber when the call came in, and besides, she'd wanted to be on the bridge when they came into normal space.

"They could have, if those survey crews had been paying attention. This is one *large* survey anomaly out here." Then it came to her. "I wonder, Huron, if this was *missed*, or left out on purpose." He looked blank, and she went on. "By the same people who found it so handy to have an uncharted system to hide out in."

"Who assigns survey sectors?" asked Arly.

"I don't know, but I intend to find out." Huron had already put the cruiser on full stealth mode; Sassinak now tapped her own board into the Ssli biolink. Two more screens of data came up in front of her, highlighted for easy recognition. "But after we deal with this — and without getting killed. I have the feeling that their detection systems out here will be very, very good."

The ships they pursued had dropped out of FTL in the borders of a small star system: only five planets. The star itself was a nondescript little blip on the classification screen: small, dim, and, as Huron said, "as little there as a star can be." In that first few minutes, their instruments revealed three large clusters of mass on "this" side of the star — presumably planets or planet-systems towards one of which their quarry moved.

They were still days from any of them. Sassinak insisted that their first concern had to be the detection systems the slavers used. "They wouldn't assume anything: they'll have some way to detect ships that happen to blunder in here."

Huron frowned thoughtfully at the main display screen, now a shifting pattern of pale blues and greens as the *Zaid-Dayan's* passive scans searched for any signs of data transmission. "We can't hang around out here forever hunting for it —"

"No, we're going in. But I want to surprise them." Suddenly she grinned. "I think I know — did you ever live on a free-water world, Huron? Skip stones on water?"

"Yes, but —"

"Everyone sees the splash of the skips — and then the rock sinks, and disappears. We'll make sure they see us — and then they don't — and if we're lucky it'll look like someone in transit with a malfunctioning FTL drive, blipping in and out of normal space."

"They'll see *that* —"

"Yes. But with our special capabilities, they're unlikely to spot us when we're drifting. Suppose we get in really close to whatever planet they're using —"

"It'd help if it had a moon, and if we knew which it was." As the hours passed, and their tracking computers reworked the incoming data, it became clear where the others were going. A planet somewhat larger than Old Earth Standard, with several small moons and a ringbelt.

"The gods are with us this time," said Sass. "Bless the luck of a complicated universe — that's as unlikely a combination as I've seen, but perfect for creating unmappable chunks of debris. . . ."

"Into which we can crunch," pointed out Huron.

"Getting cautious in your old age, Lieutenant Commander?" Her question had a little bite to it, and he reddened.

"No, Captain — but I'd prefer to take them with us."

"I'd prefer to take them, and come home whole. That's what we have Ssli assistance for."

After careful calculation, Sassinak's plan took them "through" the outer reaches of the system in a series of minute FTL skips, a route that taxed both the computers and the Ssli. With a last gut-wrenching hop, the *Zaid-Dayan* came to apparent rest, drifting within a few kilometers of a large chunk of debris in the ring, its velocity not quite matched, as would be true of most chunks. Their scans began to pick up transmissions from the surface, apparently intended for the incoming slaver ships. At first, some kind of alarm message, about the skip-traces noted . . . but as the hours passed, it became clear that the surface base had not detected them, and had decided precisely what Sassinak had hoped: something had come through the system with a bad FTL drive, and was now somewhere else. In the meantime, the alarm message had activated beacons and outer defenses: Sassinak now knew exactly where the enemy's watchers watched.

One of the moons had a small base, on the side that faced away from the planet, and a repeated station placed to relay communications to and from the surface. A single communications satellite circling the planet indicated that all settlement was confined to one hemisphere — and by the scans, to one small region.

"A *big* base," was Arly's comment, as scans also picked up weapon emplacements on the surface. "Their surface-to-space missiles we can handle. But those little ships are going to cause us trouble; they've got only one or two optical weapons each, but —"

"Estimated time to launch and engagement?" Sassinak looked at Hollister.

"If they're really battle-ready, they can launch in an hour, maybe two. Nobody keeps those babies really ready-to-launch: you boil off too much propellant. Most of the time they like to fight from a high orbit, or satellite transit path, in systems like this with moons. I'd say a minimum of ninety Standard minutes, from the alarm . . . but will we pick up their signals?"

"We'd better. What about larger ships?"

"There's something like the slaver escort, but it's cold . . . no signs of activity at all. More than two hours to launch — at least five, I'd say. But it's still twenty-three Standard hours before the incoming ships arrive, if they hold their same trajectory and use the most economical deceleration schedule. We may see more activity as they get closer."

But except for brief transmissions every four hours, between the incoming ships and the base, little happened that they could detect from space. Sassinak insisted on regular shift changes, and rest for those off-duty. She followed her own orders to the extent of taking a couple of four-hour naps.

Then the ships neared. For the first time, they drifted apart; the escort, Sassinak realized, was taking up an orbit around the outermost moon, alert for anything following them or entering the system. The slave-carrying trader began braking in a long descending spiral.

Taking the chance that the attention of the base below would be fixed on the incoming slaver, and the attention of the escort ship above on anything "behind" them, Sassinak ordered the *Zaid-Dayan's* insystem drive into action: they would ease out of the ring-belt, and intercept the slaver on the blind side of the planet, out of sight/detection of the escort.

All stations were manned with backup crews standing by. Sassinak glanced around the bridge, seeing the same determination on every face.

One of the lights on Arly's panel suddenly flashed red, and a shrill piping overrode conversation. She slammed a fist down on the panel, and shot a furious glance around her section, then to Sass.

"It's a missile — Captain, I didn't launch that!"

"Then who —?" But the faces that stared back at her, now taut and pale, had no answer. *Yes, we do have a saboteur on board,* Sassinak thought, then automatically gave the orders that responded to this new threat. All firing systems locked into bridge control, automatic partitioning of the ship, computer control of all access to bridge . . . and the fastest maneuver possible, to remove them from the backtrail of that missile.

"They know something's here, and they know it's armed — so if we want to save those kids on the slaver, we'd better do it *fast.*"

Red lights winked on displays around the bridge, scans picking up enemy activity, from communications to missile launch.

"Oh, brillig! Of course they saw it, and just what we need!" Huron gave her an uneasy glance, and she grinned at him. "But life is risky, eh? If we go for their armed ships, we'll lose the kids for sure, and if that slaver has any sense and a peashooter, it could plug us in the rear. So —" The *Zaid-Dayan* surged, suddenly freed of its stealth constraints, and closed on the slaver. They were just over the limb, out of line-of-sight from both the escort and the base below, although the missiles launched would be a

factor in a few minutes. The slaver vessel, cut off from radio communication with its base, could have chosen to boost away from
the planet, or try a faster descent . . . but whether in confusion or
resignation did neither. Nor did it fire on them.

"Huron!" He looked up from his own console, when Sassinak
called. "You take the boarding party — get that ship out of here,
safely into the next sector. I'll give you Parrsit: he's good in a row,
and Currald's sending half our ground contingent —" She quickly
named the other boarding party members. Huron frowned when
she named the two Wefts.

"Captain —"

"Don't argue now, Huron. Wait 'til they've shown you — you
need both the heavyworld muscle *and* Weft ability. Get ready —"
Huron saluted, and left the bridge. Sassinak waited for the boarding party's report: the marines had already donned their battle
armor, but the crew that would take the trader on had to get into
EVA suits and armor. Seconds passed; the ships closed. When the
forward docking bay signalled green, Sassinak nodded to the
helmsman. "Screens open to code, tractor field on —" Now the
screen showed a computer-enhanced visual of the fat-bellied
trader vessel, within easy EVA range. It attempted a belated
burn, but the shields absorbed the energy, and the tractor field
held it, dragged it nearer. The boarding party, clustered in assault
pods whose nav codes overrode the tractor, blew an airlock and
started in.

The fight for the slaver was short and bitter: once inside the
lock, the boarding party found well-armed and desperate slavers
who fought hand-to-hand in the passages, between the decks,
and finally on the bridge. The marines lost five, when a passage
they thought they'd cleared erupted behind them in a last desperate flurry of fighting. Sassinak followed the marine officer's
comments on her headset, wincing at the losses. Slavers were
dangerous: they knew they faced mindwipe if they were taken
alive. You had to check *every* hole and corner. But she could do
nothing from the *Zaid-Dayan*, and she could not leave her ship.
The last thing the marines needed was her scolding them over
the radio. Deck by deck the marines reported the ship safe; in the
background Sassinak could hear hysterical screams which she
assumed must be the prisoners.

Finally a very out-of-breath Huron called to report success, and admitted that the Wefts were "more than impressive." The trader had, he said, adequate fuel, air, and supplies for a shortest route journey to the nearest plotted station, but he wouldn't be able to use the ship's maximum insystem capabilities because of the captives, some seven to eight hundred of them.

"They're not in good shape, and they're half-wild with panic and excitement. They don't know a thing about ship discipline; there aren't any acceleration barriers, and this thing doesn't have a zero-inertia converter. I'd pile 'em all up along the bulkheads like fruit in a dropped crate —"

"All right. We'll shield you. Just get out as quick as you can, and if you *do* jink, be sure we know ahead of time."

"I can't jink in this junk," said Huron, quick-tongued as ever, even in a crisis. "I'll be lucky to jump in it. And the nav computer is a joke."

"That we can help," she said. "What's your cleanest comm link?" When he told her, she had her communications specialist patch a direct line from the *Zaid-Dayan's* navigation computer to the slaver's. Now Huron could keep track of the various incoming threats, and have a chance to evade them.

"Take care," she said. She wished she'd said it before he left; she wished they'd had time for a real farewell. His face in the vid-screen already looked different, the face of a fellow captain . . . she saw him turn as one of his crew — no longer hers — asked a question.

"You, too," he said, his expression showing that his thoughts ran with hers, as they did so often. She wanted to touch his hand, his shoulder, wanted a last feel of his body against hers. But it was too late: he was captain of a very vulnerable ship, and she was captain of a Fleet cruiser — and even if they met again, it would be a different meeting.

Sassinak looked around the bridge at a very sober crew. Fighting off a single enemy was one problem — keeping several enemies from blowing an unarmed transport with limited maneuvering capability was another. They all realized that the pirates would be perfectly happy to lose that ship — the evidence of their crimes. Now that lost ship would include loss of Fleet personnel as well — their own friends and shipmates.

But there was little time to think about it. Already the missiles from the surface were within range, homing (as Sassinak had suspected they might) on the transport. Arly took out this first assault easily, dumping the data generated by their explosion into a primary bank for analysis later. If there was a later. For the escort vessel, boosting at its maximum acceleration, would all too soon round the planet's limb on their trail. Already Huron had boosted the transport into an outward trajectory; Sassinak let the *Zaid-Dayan* fall behind and inward, where she could more easily intercept the surface-launched missiles. Behind them, she knew, would be the manned craft: the little one-man killerships, and the larger escort. Their only chance to protect the transport, and save themselves, lay in using every scrap of cover the complex system offered.

The main display screen now showed a moire pattern of red, yellow, and green: safe zones, when both transport and cruiser were hidden from all known enemy bases and ships, zones when one or the other were exposed, and maximum danger zones when both were exposed. On this pattern their current and extrapolated courses showed in two shades of blue — and the display shifted every time another factor came into play.

"If that tub had any performance capabilities at all," Sassinak muttered angrily, punching buttons, "Huron could use that inner moon as a swingpoint, and head back out picking up another swing from the middle one — and that'd take him safely over the ring, too. But I'll bet that thing won't take it —" Sure enough the return from Huron's ship showed unacceptable acceleration that way. But she had performance to spare, plenty of it, if she guessed right about how the slaver escort would choose to come in.

"Swingpoint off the second moon gives 'em the best angle," said Arly, hands busy on her console as she checked out the systems again.

"No — fastest is the deep slot, using the planet itself. They'll come by like blown smoke — maybe get a lucky shot, and for sure see what they're up against. They can use the maneuver Huron can't — it's a high-G trick, but they'll save fuel, really, and it gives them a reverse run in less than two hours."

"So?"

"So we go up and meet them. Outside."

The *Zaid-Dayan* barely vibrated as the most versatile insystem drive known lifted her poleward and away from the planet.

Sassinak held to the edge of their own green zone, making sure that they could blow any missile sent after the transport with their LOS optical weaponry. Ahead, the transport lumbered along, slow and graceless. Sassinak tried not to think of the children on board, and hoped that Huron had enough sedative packs along.

"Captain — got a ripple." The faint disturbance ahead of the escort's high speed movement showed on one screen. Sassinak tapped her own console, while nodding a commendation to the Helm tech. "Good eyes, good handling. Yes — here she comes. Arly, see what you can do —"

Arly chose an EM beam, lethal to unshielded ships, and temporarily blinding to the sensors of most others. Sassinak followed the green line of its path on the monitor; the beam itself was invisible. Something flared out there, and Arly grunted. "Thought they'd have shields. But it may have glared out their scan." In the meantime, a flick of pale blue sparkled into brilliant rainbows: the escort had fired back, but their own shields held easily. Sassinak watched another line score with bright orange the yellow zone near them on the monitor — a clear miss, but remarkably good aim for a ship that had just been lashed by an EM beam. The *Zaid-Dayan* shifted in one of the computer-controlled jinks, covering the transport's stern just as the escort vessel fired at it. Again the cruiser's shields held.

The escort, on the course Sassinak had predicted, was now in rapid transit between them and the planet. Arly lay a barrage of missiles near its expected path. At the same time, the scans showed the telltale white blips of missiles boosting from the escort.

"Those are targeted to the transport," Arly said. "They've got all its signature." Even as she spoke, she had their own optical weapons locking on. But although two of the missiles burst suddenly into silent clouds of light, another had jinked wildly and continued. Arly swore, and reset her system. "If that sucker gets too close to Huron, I can't use these —" Again the missile seemed to buck in its course, and continued, now clearly aiming up the transport's stern.

Sassinak opened the channel to Huron on the transport. "Huron — dump the bucket!" The only defenses they'd been able to give him had all been passive, and this one depended on a fairly stupid self-guidance system.

The "bucket" was a small container of metal foil strips, armed with explosive to disperse them and make a hot spot of itself. It could be launched from a docking bay or airlock. If heat, light, and a cloud of metal fragments could confuse it, they'd be safe. If not, Sassinak would have to try to "grab" the missile with the cruiser's tractor field, a technique dismissed in the *Fleet Ordinance Manual* as "unnecessarily risky."

She watched tensely as the monitor showed the "bucket" being launched on a course that fell behind and below the transport. When it exploded, the missile shifted course, and headed for that bait. So — they had stupid missiles. Now if Huron had enough buckets . . .

But in the meantime, the escort passing "beneath" them had gained on the transport, improving its firing angle. It had detonated or avoided the missiles Arly had sent to its expected position. Helm countered with a shift that again brought the cruiser between the worst threat and the helpless transport. The cruiser's shields sparkled as unseen beam weapons lashed at her. Arly's return attack met adequate shielding; the deflected beams glowed eerily as they met the planet's atmosphere below.

Unfortunately, the best solution was narrowing rapidly, as all three vessels were approaching the termination. Beyond that, too quickly, the base's own missiles and scoutships would be rising to join the fray. Sassinak could not keep the cruiser between the transport and everything else. There are no easy answers, she thought, and opened the channel to Huron again.

"If your ship will take it, get on out of here," she said. "I know you'll have casualties, but we can't hold them off for long."

"I know," he said. "We can't afford another close transit — I've done what I can for 'em." She saw by the monitor that the transport had increased its acceleration, climbing more steeply now.

"Can you make the swingpoint for that inner moon?" she asked.

"Not . . . quite. Here's the solution —" And her right-hand screen came up with it: far from the ideal trajectory, but much better than before. It would lengthen the attack interval from below and the manned moonlet would be on the far side of the planet when they passed its orbit. Best of all, surface-launched missiles wouldn't have the fuel to catch it. Only the escort already engaged was a serious threat. And that, committed as it was to its own high-speed path, could not maneuver fast enough to follow, after the next few minutes. Not without going into FTL — *if* it had the capability to do that so near a large mass.

"Good luck, then." She would not think of the children crushed in the slaveholds, the terrified ones who found themselves pressed flat on the deck, or against a bulkhead, unable to scream or move. They would be no better off if a missile got them, or one of the optical beams.

The configuration of the three ships had now changed radically. The *Zaid-Dayan* had fallen below the transport, keeping between it and the escort, which was now approaching its turnover if it was intending to use the inner moon as a swingpoint. Its course so far made that likely. All she had to do, Sassinak thought, was keep it from blowing the transport before the transport was out of LOS around the planet's limb.

She had just opened her mouth to explain her plan to Arly when the lights darkened, and the *Zaid-Dayan* seemed to stumble on something, as if space itself had turned solid. Red lights flared around the bridge: power outage. Before anyone could react, a flare of light burned out the port exterior visuals, and a gravity flux turned Sass' stomach. A simple grab for the console turned into a wild flailing of arms, and then a thump as normal-G returned. Someone hit the floor, hard, and stifled a cry; voices burst into a wild gabble of alarm.

Sassinak took a deep breath and bellowed through the noise. Silence returned. The lights flickered, then steadied. An ominous block of red telltales glowed from Helm's console, red lights blinked on others. The main screen was down, blank and dark, but to one side a starboard exterior visual showed some kind of beam weapon flickering harmlessly against the shields.

"Report," said Sass, more calmly than she expected. Her mind raced: another act of sabotage? But what, and how, and why hadn't the ship blown? She couldn't tell anything by the expressions of those around her. They all looked shaken and unnatural.

"Ssli . . ." came the speech synthesizer, from the Ssli's biolink. Sassinak frowned. The Ssli usually communicated by screen or console, not by speech. For one frantic instant she feared the Ssli might be her unknown saboteur — and the cruiser depended, absolutely, on its Ssli — but its words reassured her. "Pardon, Captain, for that unwarned maneuver. The enemy ship went into

FTL, to catch the transport — no time to explain. Used full power to extend tractor, and grab enemy. This lost power to the shields, and enemy shot blew the portside pods." From relief she fell into instant rage: how *dared* the Ssli act without orders, or warning, and put her ship in danger. She fought that down, and managed a tight-lipped question.

"The transport?"

"Safe for now."

"The escort?" This time, instead of speech, the graphics came up on her monitor: the escort had decelerated, braking away from its original course to attempt to match their course. Well — she'd wanted the transport safe, and she'd hoped to get the escort into a one-to-one with the *Zaid-Dayan*. However unorthodox its means, the Ssli had accomplished that . . . and she was hardly the person to complain of unorthodoxy in tactical matters. If it worked. Her temper passed as quickly as it had risen. Sassinak glanced up at the worried faces on the bridge, and grinned. "Shirty devils . . . they think they can take us hand-to-hand!" An uncertain chuckle followed that. "Never mind: they won't. Thanks to our Ssli, they didn't get the transport, and they aren't going to get us, either. Now, let's hear the rest: report."

Section by section, the report came in. Portside pods out — probably repairable, but it could take days. Most of their stealth systems were still operative — fortunate, since they couldn't get into FTL flight without at least half the portside pods. Internal damage was minimal: minor injuries from the gravity flux, and loss of the portside visual monitors. All their weapons systems were functional, but detection and tracking units mounted on the pods were blown.

And where, Sassinak wondered, do I find a nice, quiet little place to sit tight and do repairs? She listened to the final reports with half her mind, the other half busy on the larger problem. Then it came to her. Unorthodox, yes, and even outrageous, but it would certainly keep all the enemy occupied, their minds off that transport.

Everyone looked startled when she gave the orders, but as she explained further, they started grinning. With a click and a buzz, the main monitor warmed again and showed where they were going — boosting toward the course Sassinak had originally plotted for the escort.

The *Zaid-Dayan* had lost considerable maneuvering ability with the portside pods, but Sassinak had insisted that they make her disability look worse than it was. Having lost the transport, surely the escort would go after the "crippled" cruiser — and what a prize, could it only capture one! As if the cruiser could not detect the escort, now nearly in its path, it wallowed on. Such damage would have blinded any ship without a Ssli on board . . . and apparently the escort didn't suspect anything. Sassinak watched as the escort corrected its own course, adjusting to the cruiser's new one. They would think she was trying to hide behind the moonlet . . . and they would be right, but not completely.

Comm picked up transmissions from the escort to the planet's single communications satellite, and routed them to her station. Sassinak didn't know the language, but she could guess the content. "Come on up and help us capture a cruiser!" they'd be saying.

If they were smart, they'd go for the crippled side: try to blow the portside docking bay. So far they'd been smart enough; she hoped they'd find the approach just obvious enough. Would they know that was normally a troophold bay? Probably not, although it shouldn't matter if they did. Handy for the marines, thought Sass.

"ETA twenty-four point six minutes," said Bures, Navigation Chief. Sassinak nodded.

"Everyone into armor," she said. That made it official, and obvious. Bridge crew never wore EVA and armor, except during drills — but this was no drill. The enemy would be on their ship — on board the cruiser itself — and might penetrate this far. If they were unlucky. If they were extremely unlucky. The marines, already clustering near the troop docking bay below, were of course already in battle armor, and had been for hours. Sassinak clambered into her own white plasmesh suit, hooking up its various tubes and wires. Once the helmet was locked, her crew would know her by the suit itself — the only all-white suit, the four yellow rings on each arm. But for now, she laid the helmet aside, having checked that all the electronic links to communications and computers worked.

The one advantage of suits was that you didn't have to find a closet when you needed one; the suit could handle that, and much more. She saw by the relaxation on several faces that hers hadn't been the only full bladder. Minutes lurched past in uneven procession — time seemed to crawl, then leap, then crawl again. From the Ssli's input, they knew that the escort was sliding in on their supposedly blind side. If it had external visuals, Sassinak thought, it probably had a good view of the damage — and blown pods would look impressively damaged. She'd seen one once, like the seedpod of some plant that expels its seeds with a wrenching destruction of the once-protective covering.

Closer it came, and closer. Sassinak had given all the necessary orders: now there was nothing to do but wait. The Ssli reported contact an instant before Sassinak felt a very faint jar in her boot-soles. She nodded to Arly, who poured all remaining power to their tractor field. Whatever happened now, the escort and cruiser were not coming apart until one of them was overpow-ered. With any luck the escort wouldn't notice the tractor field, since it wasn't trying to escape right now anyway.

Interior visuals showed the docking bay where she expected the attack to come. Sure enough, the exterior bay lock blew in, a cloud of fragments obscuring the view for a moment, and then clearing as the vacuum outside sucked them free. A tracked as-sault pod straight out of her childhood nightmare bounced crazily from the escort's docking bay and its artificial gravity, to the cruiser's, landing so hard that Sassinak winced in sympathy with its contents, enemies though they were.

"Bad grav match," said Helm thoughtfully. "That'll shake 'em up."

"More coming," Arly pointed out. She was hunched over her console, clearly itching to do *something*, although none of her weaponry functioned inside the ship. Sassinak watched as two more assault pods came out of the escort to jounce heavily on the cruiser's docking bay deck. How many more? She wanted them all, but the docking bay was getting crowded: they'd have to move on soon. A thin voice — someone's suit radio — came over the intercom at her ear.

"— Can see another two pods, at least, Sarge. Plus some guys in suits —"

That clicked off, to be replaced by Major Currald, the marines' commanding officer. "Captain — you heard that?" Sassinak acknowledged, and he went on. "We think they'll stack the pods in here, and then blow their way in. We've bled the whole quadrant, and everyone's in position; if they can fit all the pods in here we'll take them then, and if they can't we'll wait until they unload the last one."

"As you will; fire when ready." Sassinak looked around the bridge again, meeting no happy faces. Letting an enemy blow open your docking bay doors was not standard Fleet procedure, and if she got out of this alive, she might be facing a court-martial. At the very least she could be accused of allowing ruinous damage to Fleet property, and risking the capture of a major hull. That, at least was false: the *Zaid-Dayan* would not be captured; she had had the explosives planted to prevent that, by Wefts she knew were trustworthy.

Two more pods came into the docking bay: now six of them waited to crawl like poisonous vermin through her ship. Sassinak shuddered, and fought it down. She saw on the screen an enemy in grayish suit armor walk up to the inner lock controls and attach something, then back away. A blown door control was easier to fix than a blown door. The white flare of a small explosion, and the inner lock doors slid apart. One pod clanked forward, its tracks making a palpable rumbling on the deck, steel grating on steel.

"Three more waiting, Captain," said the voice in her ear.

"Snarks in a *bucket*," said someone on the bridge. Sassinak paid no attention. One by one the assault pods entered the ship, now picked up on the corridor monitors. Here the corridor was wide, offering easy access for the marines' own assault vehicles when these were being loaded.

"They can do one *hell* of a lot of damage," said Arly, breathing fast as she watched.

"They're going to take one hell of a lot of damage," said Sass. The first pod came to a corner, and split open, disgorging a dozen armored troops who flattened themselves to the bulkhead on either side. Now the escort's last pods were entering the docking bay. "And any time now they'll start wondering why no one seems to have noticed —"

A wild clangor drowned out her words, until Communications damped it. The enemy should take it that the damaged sensors were finally reacting, and that the *Zaid-Dayan*'s unsuspecting crew were only now realizing the invasion. On the monitor, the first assault pod, its troop hatch now shut, trundled around the corner and loosed a shot down the corridor to the right. That shot reflected from the barrage mirrors placed for such occasion, and shattered the pod's turret. Its tracks kept moving, but as they passed over a mark on the deck a hatch opened from below and a shaped explosive charge blew a hole in its belly. Sassinak could see, on the screen, its troop hatch come partway open, and a tangle of armored limbs as the remaining men inside fought to get free. One by one they were picked off by marine snipers shooting from loopholes into the corridor. By now the second and third pods were open, unloading some of their troops. The second one then lumbered to the corner, and around to the left.

"Stupid," commented Arly, looking a little less pale. "They ought to realize we'd cover both ends."

"Not that stupid." Sassinak pointed. The enemy assault pod, moving at higher speed and without firing, was making a run for the end of the corridor. With enough momentum, it might trigger several traps, and open a path for those behind. Sure enough, the first shaped charge slowed, but did not stop it, and even after the second blew off one track, it still crabbed slowly down the passage toward the barrage mirror. This slid aside to reveal one of the marines' own assault vehicles which blew the turret off the invader before it could react to the mirror's disappearance. Another shot smashed it nearly flat.

"That's the last time I'll complain about the extra mass on Troop Deck," said the Helm Officer. "I always thought it was a stupid waste, but then I never thought we'd have a shooting war inside."

"It's not over yet," said Sass, who'd been watching the monitor covering the docking bay itself. Three more assault pods had entered, and now the foremost started toward the inner hatch. "We're going to lose some tonnage before this is done." Even as she spoke, high access ports in the docking bay bulkheads slid aside to reveal the batteries that provided fire support in hostile landings. The weapons had been hastily remounted to fire down into the docking bay, with charges calculated to blow the docking bay contents — but not that quadrant of the cruiser. Even so, they could all feel the shocks through their bootsoles, as the big guns chewed the attackers' pods to bits. None of the troops in five of the pods escaped, but the foremost one managed to unload some into the corridor beyond, where they joined the remnants from the first three pods.

With frightening speed, that group split into teams and disappeared from the monitor's view. Sassinak flicked through the quadrant monitors, picking up stray visuals: gray battle armor jogging here, flashes from weapons there, Fleet marine green armor sprawled gracelessly across a hatchway — she noted the location, and keyed it to the marine commander.

The computer, faster than any human, displayed a red tag for each invader, moving through the schematics of the cruiser. Marines were green tags, forming up a cordon around the docking bay, and a backup cordon of ship's crew, blue tags, closed off the quadrant.

Almost. Someone — Sassinak had no time then to think what someone — had left a cargo lift open on Troop Deck. Five red tags went in . . . and the computer abruptly offered a split screen image, half of Troop Deck, and half of the schematic of the cargo lift destination. The lift paused, airing up as it passed from the vacuum of the evacuated section to the pressurized levels. But it was headed for Main!

In one fluid motion, Sassinak slammed her helmet on and locked it, scooped her weapons off the console, and ran out the door. She tongued the biolink into place just under her right back molar, and felt/saw/heard the five who followed her: two Wefts and three humans. Fury and exultation boiled in her veins.

The cargo lift opened onto the outer corridor, aft of the bridge and behind the galleys that served the officers' mess. Instead of going forward to the cross corridor, and then aft, Sassinak led her party through the wardroom, and the galley behind it. Through the exterior pickup, she could hear the invaders clomping noisily out of the lift, and in her helmet radio she could hear the marine commander even more noisily cursing the boneheaded son of a Ryxi egglayer who left the lift down and unlocked. Forward, the nearest guardpost on Main was in the angle near the forward docking bay. Aft, the same. Main Deck had not been built to be defended; it was never supposed to be subject to attack.

They heard the invaders heading aft; Sass' computer link said all five were together. Cautiously, she eased the hatch open, and a flash of fire nearly took it apart and her hand with it. They were all together, but some of them were facing each way. Too late for surprise — and the standing guard might walk into this in a moment. Sassinak dove out the door and across the corridor, trusting her armor; she came to rest in the cargo lift itself, with a hotspot on her shoulder, but no real damage — and a good firing position. Behind her, the two Wefts went high, grabbing the overhead and skittering towards the enemy like giant crabs. The other humans stayed low.

Everyone fired: bolts of light and stunner buzzes and old fashioned projectiles that tore chunks from the bulkheads and deck. That was one of the enemy, and whatever it was fired rapidly, if none too accurately, knocking one of the Wefts off the bulkhead in pieces, and smashing a human into a bloody pulp. The other was wounded, huddled in the scant cover of the galley hatch. His weapon had been hit by projectiles, and the bent metal had skidded five meters or so down the corridor. One of the enemy went down, headless, but another one apparently recognized Sassinak by her white armor.

"That's the captain," she heard on the exterior speaker of her helmet. "Get him, and we've got the ship."

You've got the wrong sex, Sassinak thought to herself, and you're not about to get me or my ship. She braced her wrist and fired carefully. A smoking hole appeared in one gray-armored chest.

"He's armed," said a surprised voice. "Captains don't carry —" This time she checked her computer link first, and her needler burned a hole in the speaker's helmet. Three down — and where was that Weft?

He was flattened to the overhead, trying to position a Security riot net over the two remaining, but they edged away aft, firing almost random shots at Sassinak and the Weft.

"Forget capture," Sassinak said into her helmet intercom. "Just get 'em."

The Weft made a sound no human could, and *shifted*, impossibly fast, onto one of the enemy. Sassinak heard the terrified shriek over her speakers, but concentrated on shooting the last one. She lay there a moment, breathless, then hauled herself up and locked the cargo lift's controls to a voice-only, bridge-crew only command. The forward guard peeked cautiously around the curve of the corridor, weapon ready. Sassinak waved, and spoke on the intercom.

"Got this bunch — you take over; I'm going back to the bridge." The Weft clinging to the dead enemy let go — reluctantly, Sassinak thought — and *shifted* back to human form. Inside his armor — a neat trick.

"I'll call Med," he said. On the way back through the galley and wardroom, Sassinak queried the situation below. No other group had broken out; in fact, none had reached the outer cordon, and the marines had lost only five to the twenty-nine enemy dead. Two of the enemy had thrown plasma grenades, damaging the inner hull slightly, but Engineering was on it. The marine assault team was about to enter the escort, and someone on it had signalled a desire to surrender. "And I trust that like I'd trust a gambler's dice," the marine commander said grimly.

Sassinak came back onto the bridge to find everyone helmeted and armed and as much in cover as the bridge allowed. She nodded, popped her helmet, and grinned at them, suddenly elated and ready to take on anything. Other helmets came off, the faces behind them smiling, too, but some still uncertain. Most of the consoles had red lights somewhere, blinking or steady . . . too many steady.

"Report," she said, and the reports began. With portable visual scanners, Engineering had finally gotten a view of the portside pod cluster.

"Not much left to work with," was the gruff comment. "We'll have to use the replacement stores, and we may still be one or two short."

"But we can shift again?"

"Oh, aye, if that's all you want. I wouldn't go on another chase in FTL, though, not if you want to live to see your star. It'll get us home, that's about it. And that's assuming you find us a quiet place to work. From what I hear, they're in short supply. We'll need three to five days, and that's for the pods alone. What you did to the portside docking bay is something else."

Sassinak shook her head. Engineering always thought the ship counted for more than anything else. "I didn't blow that hole," she said, well aware that a court-martial might think she'd been responsible anyway.

Fire Control was next, reporting that their external shields were still operative: to normal levels except in the damaged quadrant, where they would hold off minor weapons and offer partial protection from larger ones. Their own distance weapons were in good shape, although the detection and ranging systems on the port side were not. "Soon as we can get someone outside, we can rig something on the midship vanes, and link it to the portside battle computers — except the one that got holed, of course."

Nav reported that they were almost out of LOS of the oncoming ships from the planet. "They only had a two-minute window, and apparently were afraid of hitting their own ship: they didn't fire, and they won't be in position for the next five hours." Sassinak grimaced. Five hours wasn't enough for any of the repairs, except — maybe — rigging the detector lines. And she still didn't know how the fight for the escort was coming.

Just then the marine commander came on line, overriding another report. "Got it," he said. "And they didn't get word off, either: we had to blow a hole in the bow, and they're all dead — nobody to question —" Sassinak didn't really care about that, not now. She didn't want to worry about prisoners on board. "You wouldn't believe this ship," he went on. "Damn thing's stuffed with weaponry and assault gear: like a miniature battle platform. Most of the crew travels in cold sleep: that's how they did it."

"Anything we need?" she asked, interrupting his recital. "Never mind — I'll patch you to Engineering and Damage Control: if they've got components we can use, take 'em . . . then clear the ship. Twenty minutes."

"Aye, Captain." Med was next: eighteen wounded, including the man who'd been with Sass, and the Weft she'd thought was dead. Its central ring and one limb were still together, and Med announced smugly that Wefts could regenerate from that. Minor ring damage, but they'd sewn it up and put the whole thing in the freezer. Sassinak shivered, and glanced around to see if the other Weft had come back in yet. No. She looked at the bridge chronometer, and stared in disbelief. All that in less than fifteen minutes?

❖ CHAPTER ELEVEN

By the grace of whatever gods ruled this section of space they had a brief respite, and Sassinak intended to make the most of it. She had the grain of an idea that might work to buy them still more time. Now, however, her crew labored to dismantle the escort's docking bay hatch — although not as large as their own, it could form part of the repair far more quickly than Engineering could fabricate a complete replacement. Another working party picked its way along the *Zaid-Dayan's* outer hull, rigging detector wires and dishes to replace the damaged portside detectors. Inside the cruiser, the marines hauled away the battered remains of the enemy assault pods, and stacked the corpses near the docking bay. That entire quadrant remained in vacuum.

Red lights began to wink off on consoles in the bridge. A spare targeting computer came online to replace the one destroyed by a chance shot, a minor leak in Environmental Systems was repaired without incident, and Engineering even found that a single portside pod could deliver power — it had merely lost its electrical connection when the others blew. One pod wasn't enough to do much with, but everyone felt better nonetheless.

One hour into the safe period, Sassinak confirmed that the escort vessel had been stripped of everything Engineering thought they might need, and was empty, held to the cruiser by their tractor field.

"This is what I want to do," she explained to her senior officers.

"It'll stretch our maneuvering capability," said Hollister, frowning. "Especially with that hole in the hull —"

"The moon's airless — there's not going to be any pressure problem," said Sass. "What I want to know is, have we got the power to decelerate, and has anyone seen a good place to go in?"

Bures, the Senior Navigation Officer, shrugged. "If you wanted a rugged little moon to hide on, this one's ideal. Getting away again without being spotted is going to be a chore — it's open to surveillance from the ground and that other moon — but as long as we don't move, and our stealth gear works?" Sassinak glanced at Hollister.

"*That's* all right — and it's the first time I've been happy with where it is."

"— Then I can offer any patch of it," said Bures. "— the only thing regular about it is how irregular it is. And yes, before you ask, our surface systems are all functional."

The next half hour or so was frantic, as working parties moved the enemy corpses and attack pods into the escort — along with escape modules from the cruiser, a Fleet distress beacon and every bit of spare junk they had time to shift. Not all would fit back in, and cursing crewmen lashed nets of stuff to the escort's hull. Deep in the escort's hull and among the wreckage in its docking bay, they placed powerful explosive charges. Last, and most important, the fuses, over whose timing and placement Arly fussed busily. Finally it was all done, and the cruiser's tractor field turned off. The *Zaid-Dayan's* insystem drive caught hold again, easing the cruiser away from the other ship, now a floating bomb continuing on the trajectory both ships had shared. The cruiser decelerated still more, pushing its margin of safety to get to the moonlet's surface before any of the pursuit could come in sight.

It was only then that Sassinak remembered that Huron's navigational computer, on the transport, was still slaved to the *Zaid-Dayan's*. She dared not contact him — had no way to warn him that the violent explosion about to occur was not the mutual destruction of two warships. The Fleet beacon would convince him — and he was not equipped to detect that the *Zaid-Dayan's* tiny IFF was not in the wreckage — only a Fleet ship could enable that. She looked at the navigational display — there, still boosting safely away, was the transport. She tapped the Nav code, and said, "Break Huron's link."

A startled face looked back at her. "Omigod. I forgot." Bures' thumb went down on the console and the coded tag for Huron's ship went from Fleet blue to black neutral.

"I know. So did I — and he's going to think the worst, unless it occurs to him that the link went quite a while first."

On the main screen, the situation plot showed the cruiser's rapid descent to the moon's surface. Navigation were all busy, muttering cryptic comments to one another and the computer; Helm stared silently at the steering display, with Engineering codes popping up along its edges: yellow, orange, and occasionally red. Sassinak called up a visual, and swallowed hard. She'd wanted broken ground, and that's exactly what she saw. At least the radar data said it was solid, and the IR scan said it had no internal heat sources.

They were down, squeezed tight as a tick between two jagged slabs on the floor of a small crater, within eight seconds of Nav's first estimate. Given the irregularity of the moon, this was remarkable, and Sassinak gave Nav a grin and thumbs-up. Ten seconds later, the escort blew, a vast pulse of EM, explosion of light, fountains of debris of every sort. And on the outward track, the Fleet distress beacon, screaming for help in every wavelength the designers could cram into it.

"That had me worried," Hollister admitted, grinning, as he watched it. "If that damn thing had blown this way, they might have decided to come get it and shut it off. I had it wired to the far side, but still —"

"The gods love us," said Sass. She looked around, meeting all their eyes. "All right, people, we've done it so far: now we'll be hiding out *silently* for awhile, until they're convinced. Then repairs. Then I suppose we'd better explain to Fleet that we weren't actually blown away." They looked good, on the whole, she thought: still tense, but not too stressed, and confident. "Full stealth," she said, and they moved to comply, switching off nonessential systems, and powering up the big gray canisters amidships to do whatever they did however they did it.

There was still the matter of the person who caused the first disturbance, and Sassinak wondered why more trouble hadn't surfaced during the fight. Surely that would have been the perfect time . . . unless she'd sent the subversive off with Huron, part of the boarding party. Her heart contracted. If she had — if he didn't know, if he were killed because — she shook her head. No time for that. Huron had his own ship; he'd deal with it. She had to believe he could do it — and besides, she hadn't any choice. Here, though — what about that cargo lift?

She called Major Currald, the marine commander, and asked who had been assigned to secure the cargo lift when they cordoned the area.

"Captain, it's my fault. I didn't give specific orders —"

She looked at his broad face in the monitor. Subversive? Saboteur? She couldn't believe it, not with his record and the way he'd handled the rest of the engagement. If he'd slipped much, the enemy would have won. "Very well," she said finally. "I'm holding a briefing in my quarters after the overpass — probably about four hours — we're going to need your input, too."

So. The cargo lift could be pure accident, or "Once is accident, twice is coincidence, and three times is enemy action." That reminded her to take it off bridge voice command, now that the fight was over. Once could be enemy action, too.

Sassinak had taken what precautions she could to ensure that only a few senior officers had access to controls for exterior systems. If her bridge crew wanted to sabotage her, there was really no way to prevent it. Now, with the ship on full stealth routine, all they could do was wait as the enemy's ships appeared, and see if they accepted the evidence of a fierce and fatal struggle. Every kind of debris they might expect to find was there, and surely none of them had any idea what, precisely, the *Zaid-Dayan* was. They would not know what total mass to expect. Besides, that Fleet beacon screeching its electronic head off was not the sort of thing a live captain wanted reporting on his or her actions. She winced, thinking of what would happen when its signal finally reached a Fleet relay station, if she hadn't managed to get word through on a sublight link earlier. She had better have a whole ship, and a live crew, and a good story to tell.

In the meantime, they had another hour and a bit to wait until the first of the enemy ships came into scan. Miserable as it was, they should stay in their protective gear until it was obvious that the enemy had accepted the scam. Not that a suit would really keep anyone alive long on that moonlet, but —

"Coffee, Captain?" Sassinak glanced around, and smiled at the steward with a tray of mugs. She was, she realized, feeling the letdown after battle. She waved him toward the rest of the bridge crew. They could all use something. But she had something better than coffee . . . a private vice, as Abe had called her leftover sweet tooth. She always kept some in her emergency gear, and this was just the time for it . . . chocolate, rare and expensive. And addictive, the medical teams said, but no worse than coffee. She left her mug cooling on the edge of her console as the thin brown wedge went into her mouth. Much better. As they waited, the crew settled again to routine tasks, and Sassinak assessed their mood. They had gained confidence — she liked the calm but determined expressions, the clear eyes and steady voices. Most of the bridge crew made an excuse to speak to her; she sensed their approval and trust.

The first enemy vessel appeared on scan, high and fast, a streak across their narrow wedge of vision. It continued with no visible sign of burn or course change; the computer confirmed. Another, lower, from the other side, followed within an hour. This one flooded the moonlet with targeting radar impulses . . . which the *Zaid-Dayan* passively absorbed, analyzed, and reflected as if it were just another big rock. Over the next couple of hours, three more of the small ships crossed their scan; none of them changed course or showed any interest in the moon.

"I don't expect any of them carrying the fuel to hang around and search," said Hollister. "If they were going to, they'd have to get into a stable orbit — which this thing doesn't encourage."

"And I'm glad of it." Sassinak stretched. "Gah! I can't believe I'm stiff after that little bit of running —"

"And getting shot at. Did you know your back armor's nearly melted through?"

So that had been the hotspot she'd felt. "Is it? And I thought they'd missed. Now — do you suppose that other escort is going to show up — and if it is, do they have it crammed with as much armament?"

"Yes, and yes, but probably not for another couple of hours. The little ships will have told them about the explosion. Wish we could pick up their transmissions."

"Me, too. Unfortunately, they don't all speak Standard, or anything close to it."

Finally, the steward came again to pick up the dirty mugs, and gave Sassinak a worried look. "Anything wrong, Captain?"

"No — thanks for the thought. I just indulged my taste for chocolate instead. Tell you what — I'm briefing the senior officers in my office in —" she looked at the chronometer, "— about fifteen minutes. Why don't you bring a pot of coffee in there, and something to eat, too. We'll be there awhile." The steward nodded and left. Sassinak turned to the others. "Bridge crew, you can get out of armor, if you want: have your reliefs stand by in case. Terrell —" This to her new Executive Officer, a round-faced young man.

"Yes, Captain?"

"Take the bridge, and tell the cooks to serve the crew coffee or some other stimulant at their duty stations. As soon as we're sure that cruiser isn't onto us, we'll stand down and give everyone a rest, but not quite yet. I'll be in my office, but I'm going to the cabin first." Sassinak went aft to her cabin, got out of the armored suit, and saw that the beam had charred a streak across her uniform under it. Grimacing, she worked it off her shoulder, and peered at the damage in her mirror. A red streak, maybe a couple of blisters; she'd peel a little, that was all. It didn't hurt, really, although it was stiffening up. She grinned at her reflection: not bad for forty-six, not bad at all. Not a silver strand in that night-dark hair, no wrinkles around the eyes — or anywhere else, for that matter. Not for the first time she shook her head at her own vanity, ducked into the stall, and let the fine spray wash away sweat and fatigue. A clean, unmarked uniform, a quick brush to her curly hair, and she was ready to face the officers again.

In her office, her senior officers waited; she saw by their faces that they appreciated this effort: nothing could be too wrong if the captain appeared freshly groomed and serenely elegant. Two stewards had brought a large pot of coffee and tray of food: pastries and sandwiches. Sassinak dismissed the stewards, with thanks, and left the food on the warmer.

"Well, now," she said, slipping into her chair behind the broad fonwood desk, "we've solved several problems today —"

"Created a few, too. Who let off that firecracker, d'you know?"

"No, I don't. That's a problem, and it's part of another one I'll mention later. First, though, I want to commend all of you: you and your people."

"Sorry about that cargo lift —" began Major Currald.

"And I'm sorry about your casualties, Major. Those here and those on the transport both. But we wouldn't have had much chance without you. I want to thank you, in particular, for recommending that we split the marines between us as we did. What I really want to do, though, is let you all in on a classified portion of our mission." She tapped the desk console to seal the room to intrusive devices, and nodded as eyebrows went up around the room. "Yes, it's important, and yes, it has a bearing on what happened today. Fleet advised me — has advised all captains, I understand — of something we've all known or suspected for some time. Security's compromised, and Fleet no longer considers its personnel background screening reliable. We were told that we should expect at least one hostile agent on each ship — to look for them, neutralize their activities, if we could, and *not* report them back through normal channels." She let that sink in a moment. When Hollister lifted his hand she nodded.

"Did you get any kind of guidance at all, Captain? Were they suspecting enlisted? Officers?" His eyes travelled on to Currald, whose bulk dwarfed the rest of them, but he didn't say it.

Sassinak shook her head. "None. We were to suspect everyone — any personnel file might have been tampered with, and any apparent political group might be involved. They specifically stated that Fleet Security believes most heavyworlders in the Fleet are loyal, that Wefts have never shown any hint of disloyalty, and that religious minorities, apart from political movements, are considered unlikely candidates. But aside from that, everyone from the sailor swabbing a latrine to my Executive Officer."

"But you're telling us," said Arly, head cocked.

"Yes. I'm telling you because, first of all, I trust you. We just came through a fairly stiff engagement; we all know it could have ended another way. I believe you're all loyal to Fleet, and through Fleet to the FSP. Besides, if my bridge crew and senior officers are, singly or together, disloyal, then I'm unlikely to be able to counter it. You have too much autonomy; you *have* to have it. And there we were, right where you could have sabotaged me and the whole mission, and instead you performed brilliantly: I'm not going to distrust that. We need to trust each other, and I'm starting here."

"Do you have any ideas?" asked Danyan, one of the Wefts who had been in the firing party. "Any clues at all?"

"Not yet. Today we had two incidents: the firing of an unauthorized missile which gave away our position, and the cargo lift being left unlocked in an area which could easily be penetrated. The first I must assume was intentional: in twenty years as a Fleet officer, I have never known anyone to fire a missile accidentally once out of training. The second could have been accidental or intentional. Major Currald takes responsibility for it, and thinks it was an accident; I'll accept that for now. But the first . . . Arly, who could have fired that thing?"

The younger woman frowned thoughtfully. "I've been trying to think, but haven't really had time — things kept happening —"

"Try now."

"Well — I could, but I didn't. My two techs on the bridge could have, but I think I'd have seen them do it — I can't swear to that, but I'm used to their movements, and it'd take five or six strokes. At that time, the quadrant weaponry was on local control — at least partly. Ordinarily, in stealth mode, I have a tech at each station. That's partly to keep crew away, so that accidents won't happen. That went out of quad three, and there were two techs on station. Adis and Veron, both advanced-second. Beyond that, though, someone could have activated an individual missile with any of several control panels, if they'd had previous access to it, to change its response frequency."

"What would they know about the status of any engagement?" asked Sass.

"What I'd said today, was that we were insystem with those slavers, trying to lie low and trap them. Keep a low profile, but be ready to respond instantly if the captain needed us, because we probably would get in a row, and it would happen fast. I'd have expected them to be onstation, but not prepped: several key-strokes from a launch, though not more than a five-second delay."

"The whole crew knew we were trailing slavers, Captain," said Nav. "I expect the marines, too —?" The marine commander nodded. "So they'd know when we came out of FTL that we were reasonably close. Full-stealth mode's a shipwide an-nouncement . . . easy enough for an agent to realize that's just when you don't want a missile launched."

"Arly, I'll need the names of those on duty, the likeliest to have access." She had already keyed in Adis and Veron, and their per-sonnel records were up on her left-hand screen. Nothing obvious — but she'd already been over all the records looking for some-thing obvious. "And, when you've time, a complete report on alternate access methods: if an exterior device was used, what it would look like, and so on." Sassinak turned to Major Currald. "I know you consider that cargo lift your fault, but in ordinary circumstances, who would have locked it off?"

"Oh . . . Sergeant Pardy, most likely. He had Troop Deck watch, and when the galley's secured, he usually does it. But I'd snagged him to supervise the mounting of those barrage mirrors, because Carston was already working on the artillery. That would have left . . . let's see . . . Corporal Turner, but she went with the boarding party, because we needed to send two people with extra medical training. I really think, Captain, that it was a simple accident, and my responsibility. I didn't stop to realize that Pardy's usual team had been split, when the boarding party left, and that left no one particular assigned to it."

Sassinak nodded. From what he said, she thought herself that it was most likely an accident — almost a fatal one, but not intentional. And even if it had been — even if one of the marines now dead had told another to do it, in all that confusion she would find no proof.

"What I'm planning to do now," she told them all, "is sit here quietly until the fuss clears, then do our repairs as best we can, and then continue our quiet surveillance until something else happens. If the slavers decide to evacuate that base, I'd like to know where they go. Even if they don't leave, we can log traffic in and out of the system. Huron's taking that transport to the nearest station — a minimum of several weeks. If something happens to him, our beacon is . . . mmm . . . telling the world just where the *Zaid-Dayan was*. It'll be years before anyone picks it up, probably, but they will. If we see something interesting enough to tail, we will; otherwise, we'll wait to see if Huron brings a flotilla in after us."

"Won't he think we're destroyed?" asked Arly.

"He might. Then again, he might think of the trick we used — we both read about a similar trick used in water-world navies, long ago. Either way, though, he knows the base is here, and I'm sure he'll report it." Sassinak paused, her throat dry. "Anyone for coffee? Food?" Several of them nodded. Nav and Helm rose to serve it. Sassinak took two of her favorite pastries, and sipped from her full mug. Her nose wrinkled involuntarily. Coffee wasn't her favorite drink, but this had a strange undertaste. Major Currald, who'd taken a big gulp of his, grimaced.

"Somebody didn't scrub the pot," he said. He took another swallow, frowning. The others sniffed theirs, and put them down. Nav sipped, and shook his head. Helm shrugged, and went to fill the water pitcher at the corner sink.

Sassinak had taken a bit of pastry to cover the unpleasant taste when Currald gagged, and turned an unlovely shade of bluish gray. His eyes rolled up under slack lids. Hollister, beside him, quickly rolled him out of the seat onto the floor, where the commander sprawled heavily, his breathing harsh and uneven. "Heart attack," he said. "Probably the stress today —" But as he reached for the emergency kit stowed along the wall, Sassinak felt an odd numbness spread across her own tongue, and saw the frightened expression of those who had taken a sip of coffee.

"Poison," she managed to say. Her tongue felt huge in her mouth, clumsy. "Don't drink —" Her vision blurred, and her stomach roiled. Suddenly she doubled up, helplessly spewing out the little she'd had. So was Bures, and now Currald, apparently unconscious, vomited copiously, gagging on it. Someone was up, calling for Med on the intercom. Someone's arm reached into her line of sight, wiping up the mess, and then her face. She nodded, acknowledging the help but still not able to speak.

When she looked again, Hollister was trying to keep the commander's airway open, and Bures was still hunched over, wild-eyed and miserable. She expected she herself didn't look much better. A last violent cramp seized her and bent her around clenched arms. Then it eased. Her vision was clearer: she could see that Arly was trying to open the door for Med, and realized that it was still on voice-only lock. She cleared her throat, and managed an audible command. The door slid aside. While the med team went to work, she put the room ventilation on high to get rid of the terrible stench, and rinsed her mouth with water from the little sink. This was not what she'd had in mind when she'd insisted on running a water line into this office, but it was certainly handy. The med team had Currald tubed and on oxygen before they spoke to her, and then they wanted her to come straight back to Sickbay.

"Not now." She was able to speak clearly now, though she suspected the poison was still affecting her. "I'm fine now —"

"Captain, with all due respect, if it's a multiple poison there may be delayed effects."

"I know that. But later. You can take Bures, keep an eye on him. Now listen: we think it's the coffee, in here —" She pointed to the pot. "I don't want panic, and I don't want the whole ship knowing that someone tried to poison the officers: clear?"

"Clear, Captain, but —"

"But you have to find out. I know that. If we're the only victims, that's one thing, but you'll want to protect the others — I recommend the sudden discovery that those invaders may have put something in the galley up here, and you need to see if they contaminated the galley on Troop Deck."

"Right away, Captain."

"Lieutenant Gelory will help you." Gelory, a Weft, smiled quietly; she was the assistant quartermaster, so this was a logical choice.

The movement of a litter with an unconscious Major Currald aboard couldn't be concealed. Sassinak quickly elaborated her cover story about the invaders having somehow contaminated the galley for the officers' mess. The bridge crew were angry and worried — so was she — but she had to leave them briefly to get out of her stinking uniform. Her face in the mirror seemed almost ten years older, but after another shower her color had come back, and she felt almost normal — just hungry.

Bures and the others who had sipped the coffee were also better, and had taken the opportunity to get into clean uniforms. That was good: if they cared about appearance, they were going to be fine. She settled into her seat and thought about it. Poisoning, an open cargo lift through the cordons, and a missile launch . . . ? Three times enemy action; that was the old rule, and a lot better than most old rules. But it didn't feel right. It didn't feel like the same *kind* of enemy. If someone wanted the ship to reveal itself to the slavers — and that was the only reason for a missile launch — what was the poison supposed to do? If they all died of it, retching their guts out on the decks, the whole crew together wouldn't make enough noise to be noticed. So the subversive could take over the ship? No one person could: a cruiser was too complicated for any one individual to launch. Was it pique because the earlier sabotage hadn't done its work? Then why not put poison in something where it couldn't be tasted? The poison was, in fact, a stupid person's plot — she leaned forward to put Medical on a private line and picked up her headset.

"Yes?"

"Yes, poison in the coffee: a very dangerous alkaloid. Yes, more cases, although so far only one is dead." Dr. Mayerd's usually businesslike tone had an extra bite in it.

Dead. Tears stung her eyes. Bad enough to lose them in combat, bad enough to have her ship blown open . . . but for someone *in* the crew to poison fellow crew! "Go on," she said.

"Major Currald's alive, and we think he'll make it, though he's pretty bad. He'll be out for at least three days. Two more have had their stomachs pumped; those who just sipped it heaved it all up again, as you did. So far everyone's buying the idea of the invaders having dumped poison in the nearest canister in the galleys — that would almost fit, because the coffee tins were sitting out, ready to brew. Apparently it wasn't in all the coffee — or didn't you drink that first batch sent to the bridge?"

"I didn't, but some others did, with no effect. What else?"

"The concentration was wildly different in the different containers we found — as if someone had just scooped a measure or so, carelessly, into the big kettles, and not all of those. Altogether we've had eleven report in here, and reports of another nine or ten who didn't feel bad enough to come in once they quit vomiting — I'm tracking those. More important: Captain, if you experience any color change in your vision — if things start looking strange — report here at once. Some people have a late reaction to this; it has to do with the way some people's livers break down the original poison. Some of the metabolites undergo secondary degradation and lose the hydroxy —"

Sassinak interrupted what was about to be an enthusiastic description of the biochemistry of the poison, with, "Right — if things change color, I'll come down. Talk to you later." She found herself smiling at the slightly miffed snort that came down the line before she clicked it off. Mayerd would get over it; she should have known the captain wouldn't want a lecture on biochemical pathways.

So someone had tried to poison not only the more senior officers, but also the crew — or some of the crew. She wondered just how random the poisoning had been . . . had the kettles which hadn't been poisoned been chosen to save friends? Poisoning still made little sense in terms of helping the slavers. Unless this person planned to kill everyone, and somehow rig a message to them . . . but only one of the Communications specialists would be likely to have the skills for that. Sassinak was careful not to turn and look suspiciously at the Comm cubicle. Morale was going to be bad enough.

Her intercom beeped, and she put the headset back on. "Sassinak here."

It was the Med Officer again. "Captain, it's not only an alkaloid, it's an alkaloid from a plant native to Diplo."

She opened her mouth to say "So?" and then realized what that meant. "Diplo. Oh . . . dear." A heavyworld system. As far as some were concerned, the most troublesome heavyworld political unit, outspoken to the point of rudeness about the duties of the lightweights to their stronger cousins. "Are you sure?"

"Very." Mayerd sounded almost smug, and deserved to be. "Captain, this is one of the reference poisons in our databank — because it's rare, and its structure can be used to deduce others, when we run them through the machines. It is precisely that one — and I know you don't want to hear the name, because you didn't even want to hear about the hydroxy-group cleavage —" Sassinak winced at her sarcasm, but let it pass. "— And I can confirm that it did *not* come from medical stores: someone brought it aboard as private duffel." A longish pause, and then, "Someone from Diplo, I would think. Or with friends there."

"Currald nearly died," said Sass, remembering that the Med Officer had had more than one sharp thing to say about heavyworlders and their medical demands on her resources.

"And might still. I'm not accusing Currald; I know that not every heavyworlder is a boneheaded fanatic. But it is a poison from a plant native to an aggressively heavyworlder planet, and that's a fact you can't ignore. Excuse me, they're calling me." And with the age-old arrogance of the surgeon, she clicked off her intercom and left Sassinak sitting there.

A heavyworlder poison. To the Med officer, that clearly meant a heavyworlder poisoner. But was that too easy? Sassinak thought of Currald's hard, almost sullen face, the resigned tone in which he claimed responsibility for the open cargo lift. He'd expected to be blamed; he'd been ready for trouble. She knew her attitude had surprised him — and his congratulations on her own success in the battle had also been a bit surprised. A lightweight, a woman, and the captain — had put on armor, dived across a corridor, exchanged fire with the enemy? She wished he were conscious, able to talk . . . for of all the heavyworlders on the ship, she trusted him most.

If not a heavyworlder, her thoughts ran on, then who? Who wanted to foment strife between the types of humans? Who would gain by it? A *medical reference poison*, she reminded herself . . . and the medical staff had their own unique opportunities for access to food supplies.

"Captain?" That was her new Exec, to her eye far too young and timid to be what she needed. She certainly couldn't get any comfort from him. She nodded coolly, and he went on. "That other escort's coming across."

Sassinak looked at the main screen, now giving a computer-enhanced version of the passive scans. This vessel's motion was relatively slower; its course would take it through the thickest part of the expanding debris cloud.

"Its specs are pretty close to the other one," he offered, eyeing her with a nervous expression that made her irritable. She did not, after all, have horns and a spiked tail.

"Any communications we can pick up?"

"No, Captain. Not so far. It's probably beaming them to that relay satellite —" He paused as the Communications Watch Officer raised a hand and waved it. Sassinak nodded to her.

"Speaks atrocious Neo-Gaesh," the Comm Officer said. "I can barely follow it."

"Put it on my set," said Sass. "It's my native tongue — or was." She had kept up practice in Neo-Gaesh, over the years, just in case. If they had even the simplest code, though, she'd be unlikely to follow it.

They didn't. In plain, if accented, Neo-Gaesh, the individual on the escort vessel was reporting their observation of the debris "— And a steel waste disposal unit, definitely not ours. A . . . a cube reader, I think, and a cube file. Stenciled with Fleet insignia and some numbers." Sassinak could not hear whatever reply had come, but in a few seconds the first speaker said, "Take too long. We've already picked up Fleet items you can check. I'll tag it, though." Another long pause, and then, "Couldn't have been too big — one of their heavily armed scouts, the new ones. They're supposed to be damned near invisible to everything, until they attack, and almost as heavily armed as a cruiser." Another pause, then, "Yes: verified Fleet casualties, some in evac pods, and some in ship clothes, uniforms." That had been hardest, convincing herself to sacrifice their dead with scant honor, their bodies as well as their lives given to the enemy, to make a convincing display of destruction.

When the escort passed from detection range, Sassinak relaxed. They'd done it, so far. The slavers didn't know they were there, alive. Huron and his pitiful cargo were safely away. One lot of slavers were dead — and she didn't regret the death of any of them.

But in the long night watch that followed, when she thought of the Fleet dead snagged by an enemy's robot arm to be "verified" as a casualty, she regretted very much that Huron had gone with the trader, and she had no one to comfort her.

✧ CHAPTER TWELVE

Repairs, as always, ran overtime. Sassinak didn't mind that much: they had time, right then, more than enough of it. Engineers, in her experience, were never satisfied to replace a malfunctioning part: they always wanted to redesign it. So mounting replacement pods involved rebuilding the pod mounts, and changing the conformation of them, all to reconcile the portside pod cluster with the other portside repairs. Hollister quoted centers of mass and acceleration, filling her screen with math that she normally found interesting . . . but at the moment it was a tangle of symbols that would not make sense. Neither did the greater problem of ship sabotage. If someone hadn't blown their cover, they might have gotten away without that great gaping hole in the side of her ship, or the fouled pods. Or the deaths. This was not, by any means, the first time she'd been in combat, or seen death . . . but Abe had been right, all those years ago: it was different when it was her command that sent them, not a command transmitted from above.

Finally they were done, the engineers and their working parties, and as the pressure came up in the damaged sector, and the little leaks whistled until they were patched, Sassinak could see that the ship itself was sound. It needed time in the refitting yards, but it was sound. Marine troops moved back into their quarters when the pressure stabilized, to the great relief of the Fleet crew who'd been double-bunking, and not liking it. Seven days, not three or four or five, but it was done, and they were back to normal.

Currald was out of Sick Bay, just barely in time to move his troops back into their own territory. Sassinak had visited him daily once he regained consciousness, but he'd been too sick for much talk. He'd lost nearly ten kilos, and looked haggard.

She was in the gym, working out with Gelory in unarmed combat, when Currald came in for the first time. His eyes widened when he saw the shiny pink streak across her shoulder.

"When did that —?"

"One of the pirates nearly got me — the five that got up to Main." She answered without pausing, dodging one of Gelory's standing kicks, and throwing a punch she blocked easily.

"I didn't know you'd been hurt." His expression flickered through surprise, concern, and settled into his normal impassivity. Sassinak handsigned Gelory to break for a moment.

"It wasn't bad," she said. "Are you supposed to be working out yet?"

He reddened. "I'm supposed to be taking it easy, but you know the problem —"

"Yeah, your calcium shifts too readily in low-grav. I could have Engineering rig your quarters for high-grav. . . ."

His brows raised; Sassinak gave herself a point for having gotten through his mask again. "You'd do that? It takes power, and we're on stealth —"

"I'd do that rather than have you blow an artery working out here before you're ready. I know you're tough, Major, but poisoning doesn't favor your kind of strength."

"They said I could use the treadmill, but not the weight harness yet." That was an admission; the treadmill wasn't even in the gym proper. Currald gave her the most human look she'd had yet, and finally grinned. "I guess you aren't going to think I'm a weakling even when I look like one. . . ."

"Weaklings don't survive that kind of poisoning, and weaklings aren't majors in the marines." She delivered that crisply, almost barked it, and was glad to see the respectful glint in his eye. "Now — if you and Med think that a high-grav environment would help you get back to normal, tell me. We can't take the power to do more than your quarters, without risking exposure, but we can do that much. I have no idea if that's enough to do any good. In the meantime, I'd appreciate it if you'd follow Med's advice — you don't want them telling you how to handle troops, and they know a bit more about poisoning then either of us."

"Yes, Captain," he said. This time with neither resentment, defensiveness, nor guilt.

"I'll expect you for the staff conference at 1500," Sassinak went on. "Now, I've got another fifteen minutes of Gelory's expertise to absorb."

"May I watch?"

"If you want to see your captain dumped on the gym floor a dozen times, certainly." She nodded to Gelory, who instantly attacked, a move so fast she was sure it must have been half shapechange. Something that felt almost boneless at first stiffened into a leg over which she was flipped — but she coiled in midair, managed to hang onto a wrist, and flipped Gelory in her turn. But this was the only change that Gelory pulled on her for the rest of the session. Instead they sparred as near-equals, and she hit the floor only once. She could not ask, in front of Currald, but suspected the Weft of making her look good in front of the heavyworlder.

Staff meeting that day found almost the same group in her office as on the day of the poisoning. Sassinak noted with amusement that suddenly no one went near the coffee service — although until Currald's return, the coffee fiends had been drinking at their normal rate.

"I'm fairly sure *this* coffee is safe," she said, and watched their faces as they realized their unconscious behaviors. When everyone was settled, and had taken the first cautious sips, she brought Currald up to date, outlining the repairs, the few changes necessary for the marines on Troop Deck, and the discreet hunt for the poisoner. The Chief Medical Officer had already told him the poison was from Diplo, she knew, and she outlined what they had discovered since.

"It's obvious that any saboteur, as we discussed before, would want to foment trouble between factions. My first thought was that having a heavyworld poison pointed to someone who wanted to put heavyworlders in a bind, and knew that I had a reputation for trusting them. But we had to take a look at the possibility that a heavyworlder had, in fact, done the poisoning. It had to be someone with access to the galleys — preferably both, although it's just barely possible that some of the coffee from Main made it down to Troop Deck. Since we were serving all over the ship, it's hard to trace the source of everyone's drink . . . particularly if one or more of the stewards was involved."

"You no longer believe that the intruders poisoned open canisters?"

"No. There'd have been no reason for them to do so: they thought they were taking the ship. They'd have used our supplies. And remember, we have that other sabotage to consider, the missile."

"Have you figured it out, Captain?"

"No. Frankly, Major, I wanted you well before we went further. I do have a list of suspects . . . and one of them is a young woman from an ambiguous background." She paused; no one said anything, and Sassinak went on. "She was a medical evacuee from Diplo — an unadapted infant who did not respond to treatment. Reared on Palun —"

"That's an intermediate world," said Currald slowly. Sassinak nodded.

"Right. She lived there until she was thirteen, with a heavy-worlder family related to her birth family. Applied for light-G transfer on her own, as soon as she could, and joined Fleet as a recruit after finishing school."

"But you're not sure —"

"No, if I were sure she'd be in the brig. She had access, but so did at least four other stewards and the cooks. Thing is, she's the only one with a close link to Diplo — not just any heavyworld planet, but Diplo. She's actually visited twice, as an adult, in protective gear. We don't know anything about it, of course. And anyone who wanted to incriminate a heavyworlder could hardly have found a better way than to use a Diplo poison."

"Could she have popped the missile?" Currald glanced at Arly, who quickly shook her head.

"No — we checked that, of course, right away. Particularly when both my techs in that quadrant came up sick. But they were well when the missile went off, and unless they're in it together they clear each other. I think myself it was a handheld pulse shot, probably from a service hatch down the corridor, that triggered the missile."

"You remember that Fleet Intelligence warned each captain to expect at least one agent . . . they didn't say *only* one," said Sass. "I think the character of the missile launch and the poisoning are so different as to point to two different individuals with two different goals. But what I can't figure out for sure is what someone hoped to gain by random poisoning. Unless the poisoner had a group of supporters to take over the ship. . . ."

Currald sighed, and laced his fingers together. Even gaunt from his illness, he outweighed everyone else at the table, and his somber face looked dangerous. "Captain, you have a reputation of being fair. . . ." He stopped clearly unhappy with that beginning and started over. "Look: I'm just the marine commander, I don't mingle with your ship's crew that much. But I know you all believe heavyworlders clump together, and to some extent that's true. I think I'd know if you had any sort of conspiracy among them on your side of the ship, and I hope you'll believe that I'd have told you."

Sassinak smiled at his attempt to avoid the usual heavyworlder paranoia, but gave him a serious response. "I told you before, Major, that I trust you completely. I don't think there was a conspiracy, because nothing happened while the poisonings were being discovered. But I am concerned that *if* this steward is the source, and *if* I arrest her, you and other heavyworlders will see that as a hasty and unthinking response to the Diplo poison. And I'd be very interested in what you thought such a person could hope to gain by it. What I know of heavyworlder politics and religion doesn't suggest that poisoning would be the usual approach."

"No, it's not." Currald sighed again. "Though if I had to guess, I'd bet her birth family — and her relations on Palun — were strict Separationists. She couldn't be, because she couldn't handle the physical strain. Some of those Separationists are pretty harsh on throwback babies. A few even kill them outright — unfit, they say." He ignored the sharp intakes of breath, the sidelong glances, and went on. "If she's been unable to adjust to being a lightweight, or if she thinks she has to make up for being unadapted, she might do something rash just to make the point." He glanced around, then looked back at Sass. "You don't have any heavyworlder officers, then?"

"I did, but I sent them with Huron on the prize ship." At his sharp look, Sassinak shrugged. "It just worked out that way: they had the right skills, and the seniority."

Something in that had pleased him for he relaxed a little. "So you might like a heavyworlder officer to have a few words with this young woman?"

"If you think you might find out whether she did it, and why."

"And you do trust me for that." It was not a question, but a statement tinged with surprise. "All right, Captain; I'll see what I can do."

The rest of the meeting involved the results of their surveillance. For the first few days after the landing, they'd recorded no traffic in the system except for a shuttle from the planet to the occupied moon. But only a few hours before, a fast ship had lifted, headed outsystem by its trajectory.

"Going to tell the boss what happened," said Bures.

"So why'd they wait this long?" asked Sass. She could think of several reasons, none of them pleasant. No one answered her; she hadn't expected them to. She wondered how long it would be before the big transports came, to dismantle the base and move it. The enemy would know the specs on the ship Huron had taken; they'd know how long they had before Fleet could return. A more dangerous possibility involved the enemy attempting to defend the base, trapping a skimpy Fleet expedition with more overweaponed ships like the little escort she had fought.

"So what we can do," she summed up for them at the end of the meeting, "is trail one of the ships that leaves and hope we're following one that goes somewhere informative, *or* sit where we are and monitor everything that goes on, to report it to Fleet later, *or* try to disrupt the evacuation once it starts. I wish we knew where that scumbucket was headed."

Two hours later, Currald called and asked for a conference. Sassinak agreed, and although he'd said nothing over the intercom, she was not surprised to see the steward under suspicion precede him into her office.

The story was much as Currald had suggested. Seles, born without the heavyworlder's adaptations to high-G, had nearly died in the first month of life. Her grandfather, she said, had told her mother to kill her, but her mother had lost two children in a habitat accident, and wanted to give her a chance. The medical postbirth treatments hadn't worked, and she'd been evacuated as a two-month-old infant, sent to her mother's younger sister on Palun. Even there, she had been the weakling, teased by her cousins when she broke an ankle falling from a tree, when she couldn't climb and run as well as they could. At ten, on her only childhood visit to Diplo, she had needed the adaptive suits that lightweights wore . . . and she had had to listen to her grandfa-ther's ranting. She had ruined them, he said: not only the cost of her treatment, and her travel to Palun, but the simple fact that a throwback had been born in their family. They had lost honor; it would have been better if she had died at birth. Her father had glanced past her and refused to speak; her mother now had two "normal" children, husky boys who knocked her down and sat on the chest of her pressure suit until her mother had called them away — clearly annoyed that Seles was such a problem.

In school on Palun, she had been taught by several active Separationists, who used her weakness as an example of why the heavyworlders should avoid contact with lightweights and the FSP. One of them, though, had told her of the only way in which throwbacks could justify their existence . . . by proving them-selves true to heavyworlder interests, and serving as a spy within the dominant lightweight culture.

In that hope she had requested medical evacuation to a nor-mal-G world, a request quickly granted. She'd been declared a ward of the state, and put into boarding school on Casey's World.

Sassinak realized that Seles must have gone to that strange boarding school at about the same age she herself had come to the Fleet prep school — within a year or so anyway. But Seles had had no Abe, no mentor to guide her. Bigger than average, stronger than usual (though weak to heavyworlders), she already believed she was an outcast. Had anyone tried to befriend her? Sassinak couldn't tell; certainly Seles would not have noticed. Even now her slightly heavy-featured face was not ugly — it was her expression, the fixed, stolid, slightly sullen expression made her look more the heavyworlder, and more stupid, than she was. She had been in trouble once or twice for fighting, she admitted, but it wasn't her fault. People picked on her; they hated heavy-worlders and they hadn't trusted her. Sassinak heard the self-pitying whine in her voice and mentally shook her head, though she made no answer. No one likes the whiner, no one trusts the sullen.

So Seles had come from school still convinced that the world was unfair, and still burning to justify herself to her heavyworld relatives. In that mood, she had joined Fleet — and in her first leave after basic training, had gone back to Diplo. Her family had been contemptuous, refused to believe that she really meant to be an agent for the heavyworlders. If she'd had any ability, they told her, she'd have been recruited by one of the regular intelligence services. What could she do alone? Useless weakling, her grandfather stormed, and this time even her mother nodded, as her younger brothers smirked. Prove yourself first, he said, and then come asking favors.

On her way back to the spaceport, she had bought a kilo of poison — since its use on Diplo was unregulated, she had assumed that the heavyworlders were immune to it. She was going to kill all the lightweight crew of whatever ship she was on, turn the whole thing over to heavyworlders, and that would prove —"

"Exactly *nothing!*" snapped Major Currald, who had held his tongue with difficulty through this emotional recitation. "Did you *want* the lightweights to think we're all stupid or crazy? Didn't it occur to you that some of us *know* our best hope is alongside the lightweights?"

The girl's face was red, and her hands shook as she laid a rumpled, much-folded piece of paper on Sass' desk. "I — I know how it is. I know you're going to kill me. But — but I want to be buried on Diplo — or at least my ashes — and it says in regulations you have to do that — and send this message."

It was as pitiful and incoherent as the rest of her story. "In the Name of Justice and Our Righteous Cause —" it began and wandered around through bits of bad history (the Gelway riots had not been caused by prejudice against heavyworlders — the heavyworlders hadn't been involved at all, except for one squad of riot police) and dubious theology (at least Sassinak had never heard of Darwin's God before) to justify the poisoning of the innocent, including other heavyworlders as "an Act of Pure Defiance that shall light a Beacon across the Galaxy." It ended with a plea that her family permit the burial of her remains on their land, that "even this Weak and Hopeless Relic of a Great Race can give something back to the Land which nurtured her."

Sassinak looked at Currald, who at the moment looked the very personification of heavyworlder brutality. She had the distinct feeling that he'd like to pound Seles into mush. She herself had the same desires toward Seles' family. Perhaps the girl wasn't too bright, but she could have done well if they hadn't convinced her that she was a hopeless blot on the family name. She picked up the paper, refolded it, and laid it in the folder that held the notes of the investigation. Then she looked back at Seles. Could anything good come out of this? Well, she could try.

Briskly, holding Seles' gaze with hers, she said, "You're quite right, that a captain operating in a state of emergency has the right to execute any person on board who is deemed to represent a threat to the security of the vessel. Yes, I could kill you, here and now, with no further discussion. But I'm not going to." Seles' mouth fell open, and her hands shook even more. Currald's face had hardened into disgust. "You don't deserve a quick death and this —" she slapped the folder, "sort of thing, these *spurious* heroics. The Fleet's spent a lot of money training you — considerably more than your family did treating you and shipping you around and yelling at you. You owe us that, and you owe your shipmates an apology for damn near killing them. Including Major Currald."

"I — I didn't *know* it would hurt heavyworlders —" pleaded Seles.

"Be quiet." Currald's tone shut her mouth with a snap; Sassinak hoped he'd never speak to *her* like that, although she was sure she could survive it. "You didn't think to try it on yourself, did you?"

"But I'm not pure —"

"Nor holy," said Sass, breaking into that before Currald went too far. "That's the point, Seles. You had a bad childhood: so did lots of us. People were mean to you: same with lots of us. That's no reason to go around poisoning people who haven't done you any harm. If you really want to poison someone, why not your family? They're the ones who hurt you."

"But I'm — but they're —"

"Your birth family, yes. And Fleet has tried to be — and could have been — your *life* family. Now you've done something we can't ignore; you've *killed* someone, Seles, and not bravely, in a fight, but sneakily. Court-martial, when we get back, maybe psychiatric evaluation —"

"I'm not crazy!"

"No? You try to please those who hurt you, and poison those who befriend you; that sounds crazy to me. And you *are* guilty, but if I punish you then other heavyworlders may think I did so because of your genes, not your deeds."

"Heavyworlders should get out of FSP, and take care of themselves," muttered Seles stubbornly. "It never helped *us*."

Sassinak looked at Currald, whose mask of contempt and disgust had softened a little. She nodded slightly. "I think, Major Currald, that we have a combined medical and legal problem here. Under the circumstances, we don't have the best situation for psychiatric intervention . . . and I don't want to convene a court on this young lady until there's been a full evaluation."

"You think it's enough for —"

"For mitigation, and perhaps a full plea of incompetence. But that's outside my sphere; my concern now is to minimize the damage she's done, in all areas, and preserve the evidence."

Seles looked back and forth between them, clearly puzzled and frightened. "But I — I demand —!"

Sassinak shook her head. "Seles, if a court-martial later calls for your execution, I will see that your statement is returned to your family. But at the moment, I see no alternative to protective confinement." She opened a channel to Sickbay, and spoke briefly to the Medical Officer. "Major Currald, I can have Security take her down, or —"

"I'll do it," he said. Sassinak could sense that pity had finally replaced disgust.

"Thank you. I think she'll be calmer with you." For several reasons, Sassinak thought to herself. Currald had the size and confident bearing of a full-adapted heavyworlder, trained for battle . . . Seles would not be likely to try to escape, and under his gaze would be unwilling to have hysterics.

Less than an hour later, the Medical Officer called back, to report that he considered Seles at serious risk of suicide or other violent action. "She's hanging on by a thread," she said. "That note — that's the sort of thing the Gelway terrorists used. She could go any minute, and locked in the brig she'd be likely to do it sooner rather than later. I want to put her under, medical necessity."

"Fine with me. Send it up for my seal, when you've done the paperwork, and let's be very careful that nothing happens to *that* cold sleep tank. I don't want any suspicions whatever about our proceedings."

Now that was settled. Sassinak leaned back in her seat, wondering why she felt such sympathy for this girl. She'd never

liked whiners herself, the girl had killed one of her crew — but
the bewildered pain in those eyes, the shaky alliance of courage
and stark fear — that got to her. Currald said much the same
thing, when he got back up to Main Deck.

"I'm an Inclusionist," he said, "but I've always believed we
should test our youngsters on high-G worlds. We've got something worth preserving, something *extra*, not just something
missing. I've even supported those who want to withhold special treatment from newborn throwbacks. There's enough
lightweights in the universe, I've said, breeding fast enough:
why spend money and time raising another weakling? At first
glance, this kid is just the point of my argument. Her family
spent all that money and worry and time, FSP spent all that
money on her boarding school, Fleet spent money and time on
her in training, and all they got out of it was an incompetent,
fairly stupid poisoner. But — I don't know — I want to stomp
her into the ground, and at the same time I'm sorry for her.
She's not good for anything, but she *could* have been." He gave
Sassinak another, far more human, glance. "I hate to admit it,
but the very things I believe in probably turned her into that
wet mess."

"I hope something can be salvaged." Sassinak pushed a filled
mug across her desk, and he took it. "But what I told her is perfectly true: many of us have had difficult childhoods, many of
us have been hurt one way or another. I expect you've faced
prejudice on account of your background —" He nodded, and
she went on. "— But you didn't decide to poison the innocent
to get back at those who hurt you." Sassinak took a long swallow from her own mug — not coffee, but broth. "Thing is,
humans of all sorts are under pressure. There've been questions asked in Council about the supposed human domination
of Fleet."

"What!" Clearly he hadn't heard that before.

"It's not general knowledge, but a couple of races are pushing
for mandatory quotas at the Academy. Even the Ryxi —"

"Those featherdusters!"

"I know. But you're Fleet, Currald: you know humans need to
stick together. Heavyworlders have a useful adaption, but they
couldn't take on the rest of FSP alone." He nodded, somber
again. Sassinak wondered what went on behind those opaque

brown eyes. Yet he was trustworthy: had to be, after the past week. Anything less, and they'd not have survived.

Her next visitor was Hollister, with a report on the extended repairs and probable performance limits of the ship until it went in for refitting. Even though the portside pods had not been as badly damaged as they'd originally thought, he insisted that the ship would not stand another long FTL chase. "One hop, two — a clear course to Sector — that we can manage. But the kind of maneuvering that the Ssli has to call for in a chase, no. You've no idea what load that puts on the pods —"

Sassinak scowled. "That means we can't find out where they go when they leave?"

"Right. We'd be as likely to end up here as there, and most likely to be spread in between. I'd have to log a protest."

"Which would hardly be read if we did splatter. No, never mind. I won't do that. But there must be something more than sitting here. If only we could tag their ships, somehow. . . ."

"Well, now, that's another story." He'd been prepared to argue harder, Sassinak realized, as he sat back, brow furrowed. "Let's see . . . you're assuming that someone'll come along to evacuate, and you'd like to know where it goes, and we can't follow, so . . ." His voice trailed off; Sassinak waited a moment, but he said nothing. Finally he shook himself, and handed her another data cube. "I'll think about it, but in the meantime, we've got another problem. Remember the trouble we were having with the scrubbers in Environmental?"

"Yes." Sassinak inserted the cube, wondering why he'd brought a hardcopy up here instead of just switching an output to her terminal. Then she focussed on the display and bit back an oath. When she glanced at him, he nodded.

"It's worse." It was much worse. Day by day, the recycling efficiency had dropped, and the contaminant fraction had risen. Figures that she'd skimmed over earlier came back to her now: reaction equilibrium constants, rates of algal growth. "One thing that went wrong," Hollister went on, pointing to the supporting data, "is that somehow an overflow valve stuck, and we back-flushed from the 'ponics into the supply lines. We've got green crud growing all along here —" He pointed to the schematic. "Cleaned it out of the crosslines by yesterday, but that's nutrient-rich flow, and the stuff loves it. We can't kill it off without killing off the main 'ponics tanks, and that would mean going on backup oxygen, and we lost twenty percent of our backup oxygen in that row with that ship."

Sassinak winced. She'd forgotten about the oxygen spares damaged or blown in that fight.

"Ordinarily," Hollister went on, "it'd help that we have a smaller crew, with the prize crew gone. But because we weren't sure of the biosystems on that transport, I'm short of biosystems crew. Very short. What we need to do is flush the whole system, and replant — but it'd be a lot safer to do that somewhere we could get aired up. In the meantime, we're going to be working twice as hard to get somewhat less output, and that's if nothing else goes wrong."

"Could it be sabotage?" asked Sass.

Hollister shrugged. "Could be. Of course it could be. But it could just as easily be ordinary glitches."

✧ CHAPTER THIRTEEN

Day by day the biosystems monitors showed continued system failure. Sassinak forced herself to outward calmness, though she raged inwardly: to be so close, to have found a slaver base, and perhaps a line to its supporters, and then — not to be able to pursue. Hollister's daily reports reinforced the data on her screens: they had no reserves for pursuit, and they could not hold station much longer.

She hung on, nonetheless, hoping for another few ships to show up, anything to give her something to show for this expedition. Or, if Huron's relief expedition arrived, they could take over surveillance. She spent sometime each day digging through the personnel files, checking each person who should have been in the quadrant from which the missile came, and who might have had access to a signalling device. There were forty or fifty of them, and she worked her way from Aariefa to Kelly, hoping to be interrupted by insystem traffic. Finally a single ship appeared at the edge of her scanning range, just entering the system. Its IFF signal appeared to be undamaged, giving its mass/volume characteristics straightforwardly.

"Hmm." Sassinak frowned over the display. "If that's right, it should have the new beacon system installed."

"Can we trip it?"

"We can try." The new system functioned as planned, revealing that the ship in question had come from Courcy-DeLan: before that it had hauled "mixed liquids" on the Valri-Palin-Terehalt circuit for eighteen months. "Mixed liquids" came in ten-liter carboys, whatever that meant. Fuels? Drugs? Chemicals for some kind of synthetic process? It could be anything from concentrated acids to vitamin supplements for the slaves' diet. Not that it was important right then, but Sassinak wished she could get a look at the ship's manifest.

Two more transports entered the system, and cautiously made their way down to the planet surface. The *Zaid-Dayan's* sensitive detectors were able to pinpoint the ships' locations on the surface, confirming that they had both settled onto the original contact site. Then a huge ship appeared, this one clearly unable to land on-planet. A Hall-Kir hull, designed for orbital station docking, settled into a low orbit. Now Sassinak was sure they were going to evacuate the base. A Hall-Kir could handle an enormous load of machinery and equipment. But the ship was at least twelve years old, and lacked the new beacon; nor could Sassinak figure out a way to tag it for future surveillance. Its IFF revealed only that it was leased from General Systems Freight Lines, a firm that had nothing on its records. Since the IFF reported only serial owners, Sassinak could not tell who had it under lease, or if it had been leased to doubtful clients before.

"Fleet signal!" Sassinak woke from her restless doze at the squawk in her ear, and thumbed down the intercom volume control.

"What is it?"

"Fleet signal — inbound light attack group, Commodore Verstan commanding. It's on a tight beam, coded — but they're sure to have noticed —"

"I'm on my way." Sassinak shook her head, wondering if the slight headache was an artifact of worry, or really a problem with the air quality. Into the shower, fresh uniform, then onto the bridge, where alertness replaced the slightly jaded look of the past few days.

"It was aimed for this planet's local system," said the Comm Officer. "They must know we're —"

Sassinak shook her head. "They're hoping — they don't know for sure."

"Well, aren't you going to send a return signal?"

"What's our window?"

"Oh. That's right." Shoulders sagged. "We just barely picked it up, and now that miserable planet's in the way."

"And their moon station should have intercepted it, right?"

"Yes, but —"

"So we lie low a little longer," said Sass. "Give me a plot to the nearest Fleet position, and your best guess at its course."

That came up in light blue on the system graphics. Sassinak tried to think what she'd heard about Commodore Verstan. Would he ease cautiously into the system on the slower but very accurate insystem drives, or would he take FTL chunks across, as she had? How many were in his battle group — would he send a scoutship or escort vessel ahead? Surely Huron would have warned him about the falsified IFF signals, and he'd be ready for trouble . . . but some flag officers tended to downplay the warnings of juniors.

She called Hollister up to the bridge, to ask about their capabilities. It would be lovely if they could spring a trap on the pirates — although how to arrange that without revealing their existence was a bit tricky.

Far sooner than she expected, they intercepted another Fleet signal — evidently the commodore *had* elected to come in fast, leapfrogging his smaller vessels ahead of the cruisers. The *Scratch*, an escort-class ship, was now sunward of them, scanning the entire "back" side of the planet system for any activity. Sassinak put a single coded message burst onto the tightest focus she could manage, and then waited. With any luck, the pirates wouldn't have anything around to notice that transmission.

Within seconds, she had a reply, and then a relayed link to Commodore Verstan. He wanted a rendezvous, and insisted that she move the *Zaid-Dayan* from its hidden location. Her suggestion that they arrange a trap, in which her concealed ship could suddenly intercept ships fleeing from his more obvious attack force, was denied.

There was nothing to do but comply. The outside crew retrieved the sensors and nets it had deployed on nearby chunks of rock, and when they were all back inside, Hollister gave the various drive components a last check. Then they waited over two hours, to clear the pirate surveillance.

"I may have to give up a good observation post," said Sass, "but I'm not about to jump out in front of them and say 'Boo.' We might be able to sneak away without their knowing we existed."

Carefully, delicately, the pilots extricated the *Zaid-Dayan* from the rocky cleft in which it had been hidden, and boosted away from the moonlet. Once free of it, Sassinak took a deep breath. Although it had given them safety at a critical time, a moon's surface was not her ship's natural home, and she felt irrationally safer

492 THE PLANET PIRATES

in free flight. Besides, they could now "see" all around them, no longer confined to the narrowed angle of vision imposed by the moon and its rugged surface.

As the ship came up to speed, all systems functioned perfectly — no red lights flared on the bridge to warn of imminent disaster. If she had not known about the damaged pods, and the patched hole in the portside docking bay, Sassinak would have thought the ship in perfect condition.

Navigating through the planet's cluttered space required all her concentration for the next few hours. By the time they were outside all the satellites and rings, the Fleet attack force was only a couple of light minutes away. She elected not to hop it, but continued on the insystem main drives, spending the hours of approach to ensure that her ship and its crew were ready for inspection. A couple of minutes with the personnel files had reminded her that Commodore Verstan had a reputation for being finicky. She had a feeling he would have plenty to say about the appearance of her ship.

Meanwhile, she noted that his approach to the pirate base followed precisely the recommendations of the *Rules of Engagement*. Two escort-class vessels, *Scratch* and *Darkwatch*, were positioned sunward of the planet, no doubt "to catch strays." The command cruiser, *Seb Harr*, and the two light cruisers formed a wedge; three patrol craft were positioned one on either flank and one trailing. They held these positions as the *Zaid-Dayan* approached, rather than closing with the planet system.

Sassinak brought the *Zaid-Dayan* neatly into place behind the *Seb Harr*, and opened the tightly shielded link to Commodore Verstan. He looked just like his holo in the Flag Officer directory, a lean, pink-faced man with thick gray hair and bright blue eyes. Behind him, she could see Huron watching the screen anxiously.

"Commander Sassinak," said Verstan, formally. "We received signals from a Fleet distress beacon."

Sassinak's heart sank. If he was going to take *that* approach . . .

"But I see that was some kind of . . . misunderstanding." She started to speak but he was going on without waiting. "Lieutenant Commander Huron had suggested the possibility that the apparent explosion of your ship was *staged* somehow, though I believe . . . uh . . . tradition favors disabling the beacon if this is done. . . ."

"Sir, in this instance the beacon's signal was necessary to fool the pirates —"

"Ah, yes. The pirates. And how many armed ships were you facing, Commander?"

Sassinak gritted her teeth. There would be a court of inquiry; there was always a court of inquiry in circumstances like these, and *that* was the place for these questions.

"The first armed ship," she said, "was escorting the slaver transport. We didn't know at that time if the slaver was armed —"

"But it wasn't. You had the IFF signal —"

"We knew the IFF of the escort had been falsified, and weren't sure of the transport. Some of them are: you will recall the *Cles Prel* loss, when a supposedly unarmed transport blew a light cruiser away —" That was a low blow, she knew: the captain of the *Cles Prel* had been Verstan's classmate at the Academy. His face stiffened, then she saw dawning respect in his eyes: he was a stickler for protocol, but he liked people with gumption.

"You said 'the first armed ship,' " he went on. "Was there another?"

Sassinak explained about the well-defended base, and the ships that had boosted off to join the battle. She knew Huron would have told him about the weaponry on the first ship — if he'd listened. Then, before he could ask details of the battle, she told him about the traffic in the system since.

"They've had three Gourney-class transports land in the past few days, and there's a Hall-Kir in low orbit. One of the Gourney-class is definitely from a heavyworlder system, and it's made unclassified trips before. I think they're planning to evacuate the base; we monitored considerable shuttle activity up to the orbital ship."

"Any idea how big this base is?"

"Not really. We were on the back side of that moonlet, with only a small sensor net deployed for line of sight to the planet. The thermal profile is consistent with anything from one thousand to fifteen thousand, depending on associated activities. If we knew for sure what they were doing, we could come closer to a figure. I can dump the data for you —"

"Please do."

Sassinak matched channels, and sent the data. "If their turnaround is typical, Commodore, they could be loaded and ready to lift in another couple of days."

"I see. Do you think they'll do it with our force here?"

"Probably — they won't gain anything by waiting for you to put them under siege. Oh — that outer moon — did Huron tell you about their detection profile?"

"Yes. I know they know we've entered the system — we also stripped their outer warning beacon. But that's exactly what I'm hoping for. Three medium transports, one Hall-Kir hull . . . we should be able to trail several of them, if we can tag them. If we wait another week, we may have more in the net when we attack. How about you?"

She wanted to join the hunt more than anything in years, but Hollister was shaking his head at her. "Sir, my environmental system is overloaded, and my portside pods sustained considerable damage . . . the engineers tell me we can't do another long chase."

"Hmmph. Can you give us a visual? Maybe we have something you can use for repairs?"

Apparently one of the other cruisers had a visual on them, for before Sassinak could reply, she saw a picture come up on the screen behind Commodore Verstan. One of his bridge officers pointed it out to him, and he turned — then swung back to face Sassinak with a startled expression.

"What the devil happened to you? It looks like your portside loading bay —"

"Was breached. Yes, but it's tight now. Looks pretty bad, I know —"

"And you're short at least two portside pods . . . you're either lucky or crazy, Commander, and I'm not sure which."

"Lucky, I hope," said Sassinak, not displeased with his reaction. "By the way, is Lieutenant Commander Huron attached to your command, now, or are you bringing him back to me?"

Verstan smiled, and waved Huron forward. "We weren't sure you were here, after all — but if you're in need I'm sure he'll be willing to transfer over."

Huron had aged in those few weeks, a stern expression replacing the amiable (but competent) one he had usually worn. Sassinak wondered if he felt the same about her — would he even want to come back? She shook herself mentally — he was telling her about his trip with the slaver transport, the horrible conditions they'd found, the impossibility of comforting all those helpless children, orphaned and torn from their homes. Her eyes filled with tears, as much anger and frustration at not having been able to stop it as grief from her own past. His ship had been short of rations — since it had been inbound, at the end of a planned voyage — and to the other miseries of the passengers hunger and thirst had been added. Now he wanted to be in the assault team; as he had no regular assignment on the flagship, he had requested permission to land with the marines.

"I'll come back, of course, if you need me," he said, not quite meeting her eyes. Sassinak sighed. Clearly his experience haunted him; he would not be content until he'd had slavers in his gunsight . . . or gotten himself killed, she thought irritably. He wasn't a marine; he wasn't trained in ground assault; he ought to have more sense. In the long run he'd be better off if she ordered him back to the *Zaid-Dayan*, and kept him safe.

"Huron —" She stopped when he looked straight at her. Captain to captain, that gaze went — he was no longer the compliant lover, the competent Executive Officer whose loyalty was first to her. She could order him back, and he would come — but without the self-respect, the pride, that she had learned to love. She could order him to her bed, no doubt, and he would come — but it would not be the Huron she wanted. He would have to fight his own battles awhile first, and later — if they had a later — they could discover each other again. She felt an almost physical pain in her chest, a wave of longing and apprehension combined. If something happened to him — if he were killed — she would have to bear the knowledge that she *could* have kept him out of it. But if she forced him to safety now, she'd have to bear the knowledge that he resented her.

"Be careful," she said at last. "And get some of the bastards for me."

His eyes brightened, and he gave her a genuine smile. "Thank you, Commander Sassinak. I'm glad you understand."

Whatever she did, the battle would be over by the time she got back to Fleet Sector Headquarters for refitting. Sassinak hoped her answering smile was as open and honest as his: she felt none of his elation.

In fact, the trip back to Sector Headquarters was one of the most depressing of her life. She, like Huron, had itched to blow away some pirates and slavers . . . and yet she'd had to run along home, like an incompetent civilian. She found herself grumbling at Hollister — and it wasn't *his* fault.

Her new Executive Officer seemed even less capable after that short conversation with Huron . . . she knew she criticized him too sharply, but she couldn't help it. She kept seeing Huron's face, kept imagining how it would have been to have him there. For distraction, such as it was, she kept digging at the personnel records looking over every single one which could possibly have had access to the right area of the ship when the missile was fired. After Kelly came Kelland, and from there she plowed through another dozen, all the way to Prosser. Prosser's ID in his records had an expression she didn't like, a thin-lipped, self-righteous sort of smirk, and she found herself glaring at it. Too much of this, and she'd come to hate every member of her crew. They couldn't all be guilty. Prosser didn't look that bad in person (she made a reason to check casually); it was just the general depression she felt. And she knew she'd face a Board of Inquiry, if not a court-martial, back at Sector.

Sector Headquarters meant long sessions with administrative officers who wanted to know *exactly* how each bit of damage to the ship had occurred, exactly why she had chosen to do each thing she'd done, why she hadn't done something else instead. As the senior engineers shook their heads and tut-tutted over the damage, critiquing Hollister's emergency repairs, Sassinak found herself increasingly tart with her inquisitors. She had, after all, come back with a whole ship and relatively few casualties, *and* rescued a shipload of youngsters, when she might have been blown into fragments if she'd followed a rigid interpretation of the *Rules of Engagement*. But the desk-bound investigators could not believe that a cruiser like the *Zaid-Dayan* might be out-gunned by a "tacky little pirate ship" as one of them put it. Sassinak handed over the data cubes detailing the escorts profile, and they sniffed and put them aside. Was she *sure* that the data were accurate?

Furthermore, there was the matter of practically *inviting* a hostile force to breach her ship and board. "Absolutely irrespon-sible!" sniffed one commander, whom Sassinak knew from the Directory hadn't been on a ship in years, and never on one in combat. "Could have been disastrous," said another. Only one of the Board, a one-legged commander who'd been marooned in cold sleep in a survival pod on his first voyage, asked the kinds of questions Sassinak herself would have asked. The chair of the Board of Inquiry, a two-star admiral, said nothing one way or the other, merely taking notes.

She came out of one session ready to feed them all to the recycling bins, and found Arly waiting for her.

"Now what?" asked Sass.

Arly took her arm. "You need a drink — I can tell. Let's go to Gino's before the evening rush."

"I feel trouble in the air," said Sass, giving her a hard look. "If you've got more bad news, just tell me."

"Not here — those paperhangers don't deserve to hear things first. Come on."

Sassinak followed her, frowning. Arly was rarely pushy, and as far as Sassinak knew avoided dockside bars. Whatever had come unstuck had bothered her, too.

Gino's was a favorite casual place for senior ship officers that season. For a moment, Sassinak considered the change in her taste in bar decor. Ensigns liked tough exotic places that let them feel adventurous and mature; Jigs and 'Tenants were much the same, although some of them preferred a touch of elegance, a preference that increased with rank. Until, Sassinak had discovered, the senior Lieutenant Commanders and Commanders felt secure enough in their rank to choose more casual, even shabby, places to meet. Such as Gino's, which had the worn but scrubbed look of the traditional diner. Gino's also had live, human help to bring drinks and food to the tables, and rumor suggested a live, human cook in the kitchen.

Arly led her to a corner table in the back. Sassinak settled herself with a sigh, and prodded the service pad until its light came on. After they'd ordered, she gave Arly a sidelong look.

"Well?"

"An IFTL message. For you." Arly handed her the hardcopy slip. Sassinak knew instantly, before she opened it, what it had to be. An IFTL for a captain in refitting? That could only be an official death notice, and she knew only one person who might . . . she unfolded the slip, and glanced at it, trying to read it without really looking at it, as if this magic might protect her from the pain. Official language left the facts bald and clear: Huron was dead, killed "in the line of duty" while assaulting the pirate base. She blinked back the tears that came to her eyes and gave Arly another look.

"You knew." It wasn't a question.

"I . . . guessed. An IFTL message, after all . . . why else?"

"Well. He's dead, I suppose you guessed that, too. Damn *fool!*" Rage and grief choked her, contending hopelessly in her heart and mind. If only he hadn't — if only she had — if only some miserable pirate had had a shaky hand. . . .

"I'm sorry, Sass. Commander." Arly stumbled over her name, uncertain. Sassinak dragged herself back to the present.

"He was . . . a good man." It was not enough; it was the worst trite stupid remark, but it was also true. He had been a good man, and being a good man had gotten himself killed, probably unnecessarily, probably very bravely, and she would never see him again. "He wanted to go," she said, as much to herself as to Arly.

"He was headed for that before you ever got the *Zaid-Dayan*," said Arly, surprisingly. Sassinak stared at her, surprised to be surprised. Arly gulped half her own drink and went on. "I know you . . . he . . . you two were close, Commander, and that's fine, but you never did know him before. I served with him six years, and he was good . . . you're right. He was also wild — a lot wilder before you came aboard, but still wild."

"Huron?" It was all she could think of to say, to keep Arly talking so that she could slowly come to grips with her own feelings.

Arly nodded. "It's not in his record, because he was careful, too, in his own way, but he used to get in fights — people would say things, you know, about colonials, and he'd react. Political stuff, a lot of it. He wouldn't ever have gotten his own ship — he told me that, one time, when he'd been in a row. He'd said too many things about the big families, in the wrong places, for someone with no more backing than he had."

"But he was a good exec. . . ." She had trouble thinking of Huron as a hothead causing trouble.

"Oh, he was. He liked you, too, and that helped, although he was pretty upset when you didn't go in and fight for that colony."

"Yeah . . . he was." Sassinak let herself remember their painful arguments, his chilly withdrawal.

"I — I thought you ought to know," said Arly, tracing some

design with her finger on the tabletop. "He really did like you, and he'd have wanted you to know . . . it's nothing you did, to make him insist on going in. He'd have managed, some way, to get into more and more rows until he died. No captain could have been bold enough for him."

Despite Arly's well-meant talk, Sassinak found that her grief lasted longer than anyone would approve. She had lost other lovers, casual relationships that had blossomed and withered leaving only a faint perfume . . . and when the lover disappeared, or died, a year or so later, she had felt grief . . . but not like this grief. She could not shake it off; she could not just go on as if Huron had been another casual affair.

She was not even sure why Huron had meant so much. He had been no more handsome or skilled in love, no more intelligent or sensitive than many men she'd shared her time with. When more details of the raid came in, she found that Arly's guess had been right: Huron had insisted on joining the landing party, had thrown himself into danger in blatant disregard of basic precautions, and been blown away, instantly and messily, in the assault on the pirate's headquarters complex. Sassinak overheard what her own crew were too thoughtful to tell her: the troops he'd gone with considered him half-crazy or a gloryhound, they weren't sure which. But the more official reports were that he'd distinguished himself with "extreme bravery" and his posthumous rating was "outstanding." Still, this evidence of his instability didn't make her feel any better. She *should* have been able to influence him, in their months together, should have seen something like this coming and headed it off — it was such a waste of talent. She argued with herself, in the long nights, and carefully did not take a consoling drink.

Meanwhile the ship's repairs neared completion. The environmental system had had to be completely dismantled and refitted, filling the two lower decks with a terrible stench for several days. Apparently the sulfur bacteria had overgrown the backflow sludge, and coupled with the fungal contamination from the downstream scrubbers created a disgusting mix of smells. Worse than that, the insides of the main lines had become slightly pitted, providing a vast surface for the contaminants to grow on. So every meter of piping had to be replaced, as well as all valves, pumps, scrubbers, and filters.

Hollister still could not tell whether the problems were inherent in the new layout, or had resulted from deliberate sabotage. Attempts to model the failures on computer, and backtrack to a cause, led to six or seven different possible routes to trouble. Two of them would have involved a single component failure very early in the voyage — highly unlikely to be tampering, in Hollister's opinion. The others required multiple failures, and one clearly favored sabotage, with eight or ten minor misadjustments in remote compartments. But which of these was the *real* sequence of events, no one could now determine. In trying to correct the problems once they developed, Hollister and his most trusted technicians had handled virtually every exposed millimeter of the system.

Sassinak grimaced at Hollister's presentation. "So you can't tell me anything solid?"

"No, Captain. I think myself sabotage was involved — things could have gone a lot worse, as the simulations show, and someone wanted to save his or her own life — but I can't prove it. Worse than that, I can't prevent it happening next time, either. If I request entirely new personnel, who's to say *they're* all loyal? And it needn't be an engineering specialist, although that's a good guess. Everyone knows some of the basics of environmental systems: they have to, in case of disaster. An agent could have been provided specialist knowledge, if it comes to that — Fleet's environmental systems use the same standard components as everyone else's."

"What about the other repairs?" Hollister nodded, and brought her up to date on those. The structural damage had required more dismantling of the portside than Sassinak expected; Hollister explained that was nearly always true. But repairs on that were complete, and on the portside pods as well. To his personal satisfaction, mounting the newest issue of pods there meant replacing half the starboard pods to match them . . . he had been worried, he confided, that their prolonged FTL flight on unbalanced pods, with the starboard pods taking the strain, might have caused hidden damage in them. None of the stealth gear had taken damage, and all the computer sections out of service had been replaced. It was just the environmental systems holding them up, and he calculated it would be another two weeks before it was done.

Sassinak began to wonder if the *Zaid-Dayan* would still be in refitting when Verstan's battle group returned with Huron's body. By now everyone had seen reports of the successful assault on the pirate base, holos of shattered domes and blasted prefab buildings. Sassinak stared at them, wondering if the base where she'd lived for her years as a slave had looked anything like this. At least her action had saved those children from being imprisoned in those domes. She visited the hospital once or twice, chatting with youngsters who were now orphans, as she had been. They were less damaged psychologically, if "less" meant anything. Looking at some of them, mute anguished survivors of inexplicable disaster, she almost cursed herself for not intervening before the colony was raided. But some had already bounced back, and some had relatives already coming to take them into known families.

The Board of Inquiry wound down, and turned in a preliminary report — subject to further analysis, the chair explained to her. She was commended for saving the children from the colony, and mildly scolded for not having saved the colony itself — although a dissenting comment argued that any such attempt would have been an unnecessary and reckless risk to her ship. She was commended for the outcome of the battle, but not for the methods she'd chosen. Entirely too risky, and not a good example for other commanders — but effective, and perhaps justified by circumstances. The structural damage to the *Zaid-Dayan* certainly resulted from her decision to allow the enemy too close, but the environmental system damage might well have been sabotage, or simply bad engineering in the first place. They approved of her handling of the suspected poisoner: "a deft manipulation of a politically explosive situation." Sassinak thought of the girl, now in the hands of the psychiatric ward of the Sector military hospital — could she ever be rehabilitated? Could she ever find a way to respect herself? Fleet wouldn't take another chance on her, that was certain. On the whole, the Board chair said, recapturing her full attention, they found that she had acted in the best interests of the service, although they could not give an unqualified approval.

Under the circumstances, that was the best she could hope for. Admiral Vannoy, Sector Commandant, would make his own decision about how this Board report would affect her future. She had worked with him several years before, and expected better from him than from the Board. He liked officers with initiative and boldness. Sure enough, when he called her in, he waved the report at her, then slapped it on his desk.

"The vultures gathered, eh?"

Sassinak cocked her head a little. "I think they were fair," she said.

"Within their limits, I hear under your words. So they were — some Boards would have landed on you a lot harder for coming in with damage like that. And for having a Fleet distress beacon telling the universe that a Fleet cruiser had bumped its nose on something painful. Bad for our reputation. But I'm satisfied: you got back a load of kids — frightened out of their wits, some of them hurt, but still alive and free. And you defeated one of their little surprise packages — which, by the way, have caused more than one cruiser to come to grief. You're the first survivor to come out with a good profile of them and the specifics of their faked IFF signals: that's worth all the rest, to my mind. And then you managed to stick tight, undiscovered, and pick up quite a bit of useful information. Now we know how well the stealth technologies work in real life. All in all, I'm pleased, Commander, as you probably expected. After all — you know my prejudices. We're going to put you back out on the same kind of patrol, in another part of the sector, and hope you catch another odd fish."

"Sir, there is one thing —"

"Yes?"

"I'd like to have more options free in case of another encounter."

"Such as?"

"Last time my orders specified that surveillance was my primary mission — and on that basis, I did nothing when the colony was attacked. My crew and I both had problems with that . . . and I'd like to be free to act if we should face another such situation."

The admiral's eyes fell. "Commander, you have an excellent record, but isn't it possible that in this case your own experience is affecting your judgment? We've tried direct, immediate confrontation before, and repeatedly the perpetrators, or some of them, have been able to escape, and strike again. Tracking them to their source must be more important —"

"In the long term, yes, sir. But for the people who die, who are orphaned or enslaved — have you been to the hospital, sir, and talked to any of the kids Huron brought in?"

"Well, no . . . no, I haven't."

"All they want to know is why Fleet couldn't prevent the attack — why their parents died — and what's going to happen to them now. And it's not just my own feeling, sir. Lieutenant Commander Huron, my Exec, was very upset about my decision not to intervene — and, as you know, he insisted on joining the attack force, and then the landing party, and he died. Other officers and crew have expressed the same feelings —"

"Openly? To you?" Sassinak could tell he did not entirely approve of such openness.

She nodded. "Some of them. Others in conversations I overheard. They don't like to think of themselves — of Fleet — as standing by idly, in safety, while helpless civilians get killed and captured."

"I see. Hmm. I still feel, Commander, that surveillance must be your primary mission, but under the circumstances . . . and considering your crew's most recent experience . . . yes, if you find it absolutely necessary to engage a hostile force, to save innocent lives . . . yes. And I'll amend your orders to make that discretion explicit." He looked closely at her. "But I'm not going to take kindly to any shoot-'em-up action you get into that's not absolutely necessary, is that clear? You've damn near bankrupted our sector repair budget for the next eighteen standard months, with that bucket of bent bolts you brought into the yard, so take better care of it. And call for help if you need it — don't wait until you're shot to pieces."

"Yes, sir!" She left his office with a lighter heart. No, she would not get into an unnecessary fight — but she wouldn't have to go through the misery of standing by while others suffered, either.

In the meantime, she would be busy checking additional crew. Some were those who had been assigned to the prize vessel, but had not gone back with the battle group. Others were newly assigned to replace casualties or transfers out.

PART FOUR

✦ CHAPTER FOURTEEN

"Commander Sassinak . . ." The voice was vaguely familiar; Sassinak pulled her attention out of an engineering report and glanced up. Incredulous joy engulfed her.

"Ford!" She could hardly believe it, and then wondered why she hadn't already known. Surely the name would have been on the roster of incoming officers —

"Lieutenant Commander Hakrar broke a leg and two ribs in a waterboat race . . . and they offered it to me, so —" His broad grin was the same as ever, but now he subdued it. "Lieutenant Commander Fordeliton reporting for duty, Captain." He held out his order chip, and she took it, feeding it into the reader. Her side screen came up with a list.

"There're just a few chores waiting for you, as you can see —"

"Mmm. Maybe I should have stopped for a drink before I reported aboard." He leaned over to take a look at the screen, and feigned shock. "Good grief, Commander, hasn't anyone done any work on this ship since you docked?"

Sassinak found herself grinning. "Did you see the holos of the damage we came in with?"

"No — but I heard rumors of a Board of Inquiry. Bad fight?"

"Fairly stiff. I'll tell you later. For now —" She looked him up and down. The same dark bronze face, the same lean body that could slouch carelessly in a dockside bar or dance elegantly at a diplomatic reception, the same tone of voice, wordlessly offering support without challenge. If she had had her pick of all the possible Executive Officers, he would have been the one. And yet — she wasn't ready for anything more, not yet. Would he understand? "Just get yourself settled, and we'll have a briefing at 1500. Need any help?"

"No, Commander, thank you. I met your Weapons Officer on

the way to the dock, and she's helped me find my way around."

Sassinak leaned back, after he'd gone, and let herself remember the crazy trip as prize crew on a captured illicit trader, something more than ten years before. She'd been exec on a patrol-class vessel, *Lily of Serai*, and they'd caught a trader carrying illegal and unmarked cargo. So her captain had put her and five others aboard, as a prize crew to bring the trader to Sector HQ; she'd had command, and Fordeliton, then a Jig, had been her Exec. She'd hardly known him before, but it was the kind of trip that made solid relationships. For the trader crew had tried to take the ship back, and they'd killed two of the marines — and almost killed Ford, but she had led the other two in a desperate hand-to-hand fight through the main deck corridors. If Huron had seen *that*, she told herself, he'd never have doubted her will to fight. In the end they'd won — though they'd had to space most of the trader's original crew — and she had brought the ship in whole. When Ford recovered from his injuries, they'd become lovers — and in the years since, whenever they chanced to meet, they had enjoyed each other's company. Nothing intense, nothing painful — but she could count on his quiet, generous support.

Another incoming officer brought her much less content. Fleet Security, apparently impressed by her conviction that she had yet another agent on board, decided to assign a Security Officer to the ship. Sassinak frowned over his dossier: a lieutenant commander (in Security, a very high rank) from Bretagne. All she'd wanted was a deeper scrutiny of her personnel records, and instead she got this . . . she looked at his holo. Slim, dark hair and eyes, somehow conveying even in that official pose a certain dapper quality.

In person, when he reported for duty, he lived up to his holo: suave, courteous, almost elegant. His voice had the little lilt she remembered from Bretagne natives, and he used it to compliment her on her ship, her office decor, her reputation. Sassinak considered biting his head off, but it was never wise to alienate Security. She gave him courtesy for courtesy, alluding to her first ship service under a Bretagnan captain, and he became even sleeker, if possible. When he'd gone to his quarters, Sassinak took a long breath and blew it out. Security! Why couldn't they do the job right in the first place, and prevent hostiles from getting into

Fleet, instead of sending people like this to harass honest officers and interfere with their work?

But Dupaynil turned out better than his first impression. He got along well with the other officers, and had a strong technical background that made him useful in both Engineering and Weaponry. His witty conversation, which skirted but never quite slid into malicious gossip about the prominent and wealthy among whom he'd worked, livened their meals. And he was more than a quick wit, Sassinak found out, when they discussed the matter of planet piracy and slave trading.

"You haven't been at Headquarters for several years," he said. "I'm sure you remember that speculation about certain families had begun even ten years ago. . . ."

"Yes, of course."

"Our problem has been not in finding out who, but in proving how — with persons of such rank, we cannot simply accuse them of complicity. And they've been very, very clever in covering their tracks, and making their accounts clean for inspection. That ship you captured, for instance —"

"I was thinking Paraden," said Sass.

"Precisely. But you noted, I'm sure, that although there were apparent links to Paraden Family enterprises, there was no direct, traceable proof. . . ."

"No. I'd hoped the traces on those transports coming into the pirate base would be helpful."

"Oh, they were. Commodore Verstan forwarded all available data — and we're now sure of some kind of complicity between the Paradens and at least one group of political activists from Diplo."

"That's what I don't understand," said Sass. "The Paradens I've met were all prejudiced against any of the human variants — I'd think they'd be the last people to consort with heavyworlders."

"The Paraden family stronghold maintains a body of heavyworlder troops. That's not widely known, but we have — had, I should say — an agent that had infiltrated them just so far. It would be within their philosophy to use the heavyworlders that way — to gain exclusive access to chosen worlds."

"That young woman who went crazy and tried to poison us all was born on Diplo. But I thought she was too irrational to be anyone's agent —"

"You're undoubtedly right. No, if you have a saboteur on your ship, Commander, it's someone more subtle than that. And quite possibly not a heavyworlder. There's a growing sentiment that Fleet demands too much and delivers too little protection . . . that it's used to keep colony planets subdued, or to prevent the opening of suitable worlds for colonies. Exploration has shifted a lot of blame to Fleet, over the past decade or so — and that concerns us, too. Why are we blamed when Exploration chooses to classify a world as unsuited for colonization? Why is Fleet responsible when the alien vote in the FSP puts a system off-limits for humans? Because we enforce the edicts, apparently . . . but who is emphasizing that, and why?"

"And you have no idea if any of this crew is such an agent?"

Dupaynil shook his head. "No — the records all seem clear, and that's what you'd expect from a professional. They're not going to do anything stupid, like use a faked name or background. We can check too easily on that sort of thing these days — the Genetic Index gives us the references for each planet-of-origin. If I said I was from Grantly-IV, for instance, you could look it up in the Index and find out that I should be blue-eyed and a foot taller."

"But surely most planets have a variety of genomes —"

"A variety, yes, but not the entire range of human possibilities. Much of the time it doesn't tell us precisely where someone is from — although with tissue samples for analysis it does much better — but it certainly tells me what questions to ask, and what to look for. Anyone from Bretagne, my homeworld, has experienced double moonlight, and knows about the Imperial Rose Gardens. You're from Myriad — you lived in its one city — and so I know you experienced a seacoast with mountains inland, and you must have seen at least one gorbnari."

Sassinak had an instant memory of the gorbnari, the wide-winged flyers of Myriad, who preyed on its native sealife. Not birds, not fishes — exactly — but gorbnari swooping down for krissi.

"So if I asked you," Dupaynil went on, "whether gorbnari were gray or brown, you'd know —"

"That they were pale yellow on top and white underneath, with a red crest on the males. . . . I see what you mean."

"Since the Myriad colony was wiped out, and not replanted,

the references to native wildlife are pretty vague. In fact, the only comment on gorbnari gives their color as 'mid-to-light brown, lighter below' because it's taken from the first scoutship report — and that ship sampled on the other continent, where they *are* that color."

"So you're going to mingle with the crew, and check that sort of thing, stuff that doesn't come up in the records at all?"

"Right. And of course, I'll fill you in on whatever I find."

Dupaynil was the last incoming crewman — when Sassinak thought about it, the perfect arrangement, since anyone transferring out so late would be noticed. The orders came through for them to leave, and soon they were on their way to their assigned position. Sassinak wasn't sure whether to be glad or sorry that she had no chance to attend Huron's funeral. Soon she was far too busy to brood about it.

For one thing, she had to supervise the continuing education of five newly "hatched" ensigns, fresh from the Academy, and eager to prove themselves capable young officers. Fordeliton handled their assignment slots, but she had an interview with each one, and chaired the regular evaluation sessions. It was a very mixed group. Claas, one of the largest heavyworlder women Sassinak had ever seen, came with a special recommendation from Sass' old friend Seglawin at the Academy. ("I can trust you," she'd written, "to perceive the sensitivity and generosity of this ensign — she's bright, of course, and reasonably aggressive, but still too easily hurt. Toughen her, if you can, without sending her straight into the Separationists.") Sassinak looked up — and up — at the broad face with its heavy brow and cheekbones, and mentally shook her head. If this girl was still oversensitive, after four years in the Academy, she had small chance of curing it.

Timran, stocky and just above the minimum height, had a low rank in the graduating class, and an air of suppressed glee. Clearly he was thrilled (surprised, even?) to have made it through commissioning, and equally delighted to have such a good assignment — and such a commanding officer. Sassinak was used to male appreciation, but his wide-eyed admiration almost embarrassed her. She wondered if she'd really been that callow herself. His only redeeming characteristic, according to the file, was "luck." As his pilot instructor said, "Under normal circumstances this cadet is adequate at best, and too often careless or rash. But in emergencies, everything seems to come together, and he will do five wrong things that add up to the best combination. If he continues to show this flair in active duty, he may be worth training as a scoutship pilot, or a junior gunnery officer."

Gori, on the other hand, was a quiet studious, almost prim young man who had ranked high in academics and sports, but only average in initiative. "The born supply officer," his report said. "Meticulous, precise, will do exactly what he is told, but does not react well in chaotic situations. He should do well in a large crew, and ultimately onstation in a noncombat capacity. Note that this is not lack of courage; he does not panic in danger — but he does not exceed his orders even when this is desirable."

Kayli and Perran were more "average," in that their abilities seemed to be all on one level. Physically they were something else. Kayli was a stunning diminutive brunette, who could have had a new partner every night if she'd wanted it. What she wanted, apparently, was Gori. Sassinak was not surprised to find that they were already engaged, and planned to marry at the end of their first cruise. What did surprise her was Kayli's continuing disinterest in the other men — very few people were exclusive in their relationships. But despite all suggestions, Kayli spent her off-duty time with Gori, much of it in the junior officers' mess with books spread all over the table. Perran, not at all as overtly attractive, turned out to be the vamp of the group. She had an insatiable interest in electronics . . . and men. Ford's description of her stalk of the senior communications tech gave Sassinak her first relaxed laugh in weeks.

As the trip progressed, Claas seemed content enough, if quiet, and Sassinak noted that she seemed to spend some free time with Perran. It seemed like an odd combination, but Sassinak knew better than to interfere with what worked. Timran got into one scrape after another, always apologetic but undaunted as he discovered the inexorable laws of nature all over again. Sassinak wondered if he'd ever grow up — it didn't seem likely at this point. Only her experience with other such youngsters, who surprisingly grew into competent adults if given the chance and a few years, reassured her. Gori and Kayli occupied each other, and Perran, having caught her first man, soon started looking for another. Sassinak felt a twinge of sympathy for the unlucky quarry; Perran was none too gentle in her disposal of the former lover.

Dupaynil turned up evidence of several anomalies in the crew. He said quite frankly that most of them were probably innocent errors — data entered wrong in the computer, or misunderstandings of one sort or another. But sorting them out meant hours of painstaking work, correlating all the data and holding more interviews to recheck vital facts.

"I had no idea that the personnel files were this sloppy," grumbled Sass. "Surely most of these must mean *something*." They were back to Prosser, and Sassinak was careful to say nothing about her earlier reaction to his holo in the files. His eyes weren't quite as close together as she'd thought earlier. Dupaynil passed over the file with a shrug — nothing wrong with it at all.

"Have you ever really looked at your own file?" asked Dupaynil with a sly smile.

"Well, no — not carefully." She had never wanted to brood over the truncated past it would have revealed.

"Look." He called up her file onscreen, and ran it through his expanded database backups. "According to this, you had two different grades in advanced analytic geometry in prep school . . . and you never turned in your final project in social history . . . and you were involved in a subversive organization back on Myriad —"

"What!" Sassinak peered at it. "I wasn't in anything —"

"A club called *Ironmaids*?" Dupaynil grinned.

"Oh." She had forgotten completely about *Ironmaids*, the local Carin Coldae fan club that she and Caris had founded in their last year of elementary school. She and Caris and — who was that other girl? Glya? — had chosen the name, and written to the address on the bottom of the Carin Coldae posters. And almost a year later a packet had come for them: a club charter, replica Carin Coldae pocket lasers, and eight copies of the newest poster. Her parents wouldn't let her put it up where anyone could see it, so she'd had it on the inside of her closet door. "But it wasn't *subversive*," she said to Dupaynil. "It was just a kid's club, a fan club."

"Affiliated with the Carin Coldae cult, right?"

"Cult? We weren't a cult." Even her parents, conservative as they were, had not objected to the club . . . although they'd insisted that a life-size poster of Carin Coldae, in snug silver bodysuit with a blazing laser in each hand, was not the perfect living room decoration.

Dupaynil laughed aloud. "You see, Captain, how easy it is for someone to be caught up in something without realizing it? I suppose you didn't know that Carin Coldae's vast earnings went into the foundation and maintenance of a terrorist organization?"

"They did?"

"Oh, yes. All you little girls — and boys, too, I must admit — who sent in your bits of change and proofs of purchase were actually funding the Sector XI resurgents, as nasty a bunch of racist bullies as you could hope to find. The Iron Chain, they called themselves. Carin herself, I understand, found them romantic — or one of them, anyway. She was convinced they were misunderstood freedom fighters, and of course they encouraged that view. So your little *Ironmaids* club, in which I presume you all felt brave and grownup, was a front for terrorists . . . and you had your brush with subversive activity."

Sassinak thought back to their six months of meetings, before they got tired of the routine. The little charter and handbook, which had them elect officers and discuss "old business" and "new business" according to strict rules. The cookies they'd made and served from a Carin Coldae plate, and the fruit juice they'd drunk from special glasses. If that was subversive activity, how did anyone keep doing it without suffering terminal boredom? She remembered the day they'd disbanded — not to quit watching Carin Coldae films, of course, but because the club itself bored them stiff. They'd gone back to climbing in the nearby hills, where they could pretend that villains were hiding behind the rocks.

"I think the most subversive thing we did," she said finally, "was decide that our school principal looked exactly like the villain in *White Rims*. I still have trouble believing —"

Dupaynil shrugged. "It doesn't really matter. Security knows that nearly all the kids in those clubs were innocent. But some of them went on to another level of membership, and a few of those ended up joining the Iron Chain . . . and *those* have been a continuing problem."

"I remember . . . maybe a year after we quit holding meetings, we got another mailout, suggesting that we form a senior club.

But we'd lost interest, and anyway that was just before the colony was taken."

"Right. Now — can you explain the two grades in analytic geometry? Or the uncompleted social history project?"

Sassinak frowned, trying to remember. "As far as I know, I always got top grades in math . . . what are those? Oh . . . sure . . . they were trying a pass/fail system, and gave all us of dual grades in math that semester. It's not two grades, really; it's the same grade expressed two ways. As for social history — I can't remember anything."

"You see? Three little things, and you can't clear up all of them. And yet it's not important. If we had a pattern — if you seemed to have incompletes in all your social science classes — it might matter. But this is nothing, and most of the odd things in your crew's records are nothing. Still, we must look into all of it, even so silly a thing as a child's fan club."

Among the odd bits Dupaynil turned up in the next week were a young man who'd chosen to use his matrilineal name rather than his far more prominent patrilineal title, and yet another person of heavyworlder genetic background posing as a normal human. Sassinak came in on the interviews of both these, but neither had the unstable personality of the poisoner. The young man insisted that he'd joined Fleet to get away from his father's influence — he'd been pushed to enter the diplomatic service, but preferred to work with his hands. The heavyworlder said frankly that heavyworlders looked down on him, but that he had found acceptance and even friendships among the lightweights. "If they know I'm from a heavyworld family, they're afraid of my strength — I can tell by the way they hold back. But I can pass as a strong normal, and that suits me just fine. No, I wouldn't help heavyworlders expand their influence — why should I? They're snobs — they teased me and threw me out for being a weakling, as if they really were superior. They're not. Let 'em stay on their worlds, and let me go where I fit in."

Dupaynil, Sassinak noticed, seemed far more sympathetic to the young man escaping a pushy father than to the heavyworlder. She herself found both convincing.

They had been on-station a month when their detectors picked up a ship off the normal FTL paths. Its IFF and passive beam gave its ownership as General Freight (again! thought Sass), but from the passive beam they could strip its origin code . . . and that was a heavyworld system.

Once more the *Zaid-Dayan* took up the chase, guided by its Ssli perception of the quarry's disturbance of space. And once more it soon became clear that the quarry was headed for some-place unusual.

✧ CHAPTER FIFTEEN

"And just what is *this*?" No one answered the Navigation Officer's murmur; Sassinak leaned over to see what identification data were coming up on the screen. Nav went on. "Mapped . . . hmm . . . on the EEC survey, Ryxi on the fifth planet, which is on this side of the system, and a human team dropped to do some exploration on the fourth, called Ireta. Wonder why it's got a name, if it doesn't have a colony and this was the first exploration team. Something about mesozoic fauna, whatever *that* means."

"New contact: ship on insystem drive boosting out of the fifth planet's system —" That went up on the main screen, where they could all see it. "No leech beacon — d'you want to try its IFF, Captain?"

"No — if they're what I think, another pirate escort, they'll notice that," said Sass. "But . . . Ryxi?"

"Dropped here some forty years ago — colonial permit —"

"No one's *ever* suggested Ryxi were involved in this kind of thing," said Dupaynil, looking as confused as Sassinak felt. "Certainly not in anything with heavyworlders. They hate them worse than they do normal humans."

The *Zaid-Dayan* crept cautiously after the other two ships, which now seemed to be making for Ireta, a journey of some days on insystem drive. Sassinak wondered what someone might be planning — another "accidental" missile release? Some other dangerous accident? Dupaynil had come up with nothing definite, and although she had moved both the most likely suspects away from their usual duties, that didn't make her feel any safer. She made sure that none of the same people were assigned duty in the quadrant missile rooms, that the stewards' duties were rotated differently. What else could she do? Nothing, really.

Day by day the two target ships arced towards the distant fifth planet. Sassinak had time to look it up in the Index for herself, and check out the reference to "mesozoic." One of her new Jigs, a biology enthusiast, rattled on to everyone about the possibilities. Huge reptilian beasts from prehuman history on old Terra, superficially similar to some races of reptiloid aliens, but really quite stupid. . . . Sassinak grinned to herself. Had she ever had that kind of enthusiasm, and been so unaware of everyone else's lack of interest? She thought not, but indulged him when he showed her his favorite slides from his files.

Fordeliton happened into the middle of this, and turned out to be another enthusiast, though more restrained. "Dinosaurs!" he said. "Old Terran, or near enough —"

"Pirates," said Sassinak firmly. "Dangerous, or near enough."

By the time they were close enough to be sure the quarry was intending to land, Sassinak had to worry what the other ship was doing. This could not be a colony raid, as on Myriad — there was no colony to raid. The ship that had come up from the Ryxi world was not holding a particularly good position for an escort — in fact, it almost seemed to be unaware of the transport. Could it be accidental? A ship on regular movement between planets?

The transport began to decelerate, dropping toward the planet. Behind, the second vessel seemed to be heading for a stable orbit. So far neither had detected the *Zaid-Dayan* in its stealth mode. But she could not take the cruiser to the surface leaving a possible enemy up in orbit . . . yet she wanted to be sure just what the transport was up to. She needed two ships . . . and there was a way. . . .

"Take a shuttle down, and see where they're going. This world doesn't have a landing grid, that we know of — hard to believe they're actually going to land, but what else could they be doing? Stay in their dead zone, until they're committed to a site, and then if you can possibly get away unseen, do it. Stay below and behind, until their landing pattern —"

"What about a landing party?" Timran's dark eyes flashed.

"Ensign, I just said I wanted you to observe and return without alarming them — you don't *need* a landing party. Just stay behind 'em, low and fast, and once they're down get back here. If I give you a troop of marines, you'll try to find a use for 'em."

Ford shook his head as they watched the ensigns clamber into the shuttle hatch. "You know Timran would try to take on that entire transport by himself —"

"Yes, that's why I wanted Gori with him. Gori's got sense, besides being a good shuttle pilot. I just hope they follow orders."

"Oh, they will. You've got 'em scared proper." The docking bay alarm hooted, and the load crew scurried for airlocks. The docking hatch opened, flowerlike, and the shuttle elevator lifted it level with the ship's outer hull. Sassinak watched the flight deck officer signal the shuttle to start engines, and then boost away from the *Zaid-Dayan*.

The shuttle made an uneventful approach to the transport, and on their screens appeared to be snugged into the transport's blind spot. From high orbit, the *Zaid-Dayan's* technicians observed the next few descending circuits of the planet. Nothing indicated that the transport had realized it had a tail. Nor did any signal come from the ground. Then Comm picked up a landing beacon, and radio signals from below.

"There's a grid . . . weird . . . it's on the edge of that plateau."

"City? Town?"

"Nothing. Well . . . some infrared indication of cleared fields, plantings . . . but nothing big enough to put in a grid like that."

"We can take *that* out easily enough," said Arly. "One lousy transport and landing grid —"

"But what are they after? There's no colony to raid for slaves, nothing to raid for minerals or other goods. Why's there a grid here, and what are they doing here?"

"Wait a minute — that's got to be artificial —" Onto the main screen went a shot of something that looked like a working open-pit mine. "I haven't seen anything like that without someone nearby. A mine? Iron? Copper?"

Sassinak looked at the puzzled faces around her, and grinned. It had to be important. And this time she had a degree of freedom to act. "A landing grid, a beacon, an open pit mine, and no city — on a world supposedly not open for colonization. I think it's time we stripped our friend's IFF."

"Right, Captain." The Comm Officer flipped a switch, and then came back on line, sounding puzzled. "Captain, it's a colony supply hauler, on contract to that Ryxi colony."

"And I'm a rich ambassador's wife. Try again." A screen came up at her right hand as the Comm Officer insisted. "Nothing wrong with the IFF signal, Captain. I'd swear it. Look."

It looked clean. *Mazer Star*, captained by one Argemon Godheir, owned by Kirman, Vini & Godheir, Ltd., registration numbers, crew size, mass cargo and volume . . . every detail crisp and unmistakable. Comm had already queried the database: *Mazer Star* was a thirty-seven-year-old hull from a respectable shipyard, refitted twice at the normal intervals, ownership as given, and no mysterious disappearances or changes in use.

"So what is it doing *here*?" asked Sass, voicing everyone's confusion. She looked back at the Comm Section, as the Comm watch all shrugged. "Well. They're acting as if we don't exist, so let's see how close we can get."

Whatever *Mazer Star* was doing, it was not looking for a cruiser in its area; Sassinak began to feel a wholly irrational glee at how close they were able to come. Either their stealth gear was better than even she had supposed, or the stubby little insystem trader had virtually no detection gear (or the most incompetent radar operator in seven systems). Finally they were within tractor distance, and Sassinak ordered the shields full on and stealth gear off. And a transmission by tight-beam radio, although she felt she could almost have shouted across the space between ships. Certainly could have, in an atmosphere.

"*Mazer Star, Mazer Star!* FSP Cruiser *Zaid-Dayan* to *Mazer Star* —"

"What the — who the formative novations are *you*! Get off our tail or we'll —" That voice was quickly replaced by another, and a screen image of a stocky man in a captain's uniform.

"*Mazer Star*, Godheir commanding, to Federation ship *Zaid-Dayan* . . . where did you come from? Did you receive the same distress message?"

Distress message? What was he talking about? Sassinak took over from the Comm Officer, and spoke to him herself.

"Captain Godheir, this is Commander Sassinak of the *Zaid-Dayan*. We're tracking pirates, Captain. What do you mean, distress beacon? Can you explain your presence in company with a heavyworlder transport?"

"Heavyworlder transport? Where?" On the screen, his face looked both ways as if he expected one to come bursting through his bulkheads.

"Below — it's going in to land. Now what's this about a distress beacon? And what kind of range and detection gear do you have?"

His answers, if a bit disorganized, quickly made sense out of the past several days. On long-term contract to supply the Ryxi colony, he'd recently returned to the system from a Ryxi relay-point. "You know they prefer to hire human crews," he said with a twinkle. "Routine flying's too boring for them, or something like that. We'd picked up some incoming specialists, and the supplies. Unloaded over there —" He waved in a way that Sassinak interpreted as meaning the planet in question. "Then we heard about some kind of problem here, a human exploration team that needed help, maybe a mutiny situation. So we came over — we can land without a grid, you see — But if you're here instead, then I guess we're not needed. You certainly gave us a start, Commander, that you did —"

"You may be needed yet," said Sass. "How were you supposed to find this missing team?" Godheir gave her the reference numbers, and said he'd detected a faint beacon signal from near the coast. While they were talking, Comm suddenly waved wildly.

Timran, piloting the number one shuttle of the *Zaid-Dayan*, felt for the first time since coming on active duty like a *real* Fleet officer. On the track of slavers or pirates or something, in command of his own ship, however small. Actually it was better small — more of an adventure. Gori, hunched in the copilot's seat, was actually pale.

"This is really it," Timran said, with another quick sideways glance. He had said it before.

"Don't look at me, Tim — keep an eye on your sensors."

"We're doing just fine." In his mind's eye, he saw himself reporting back to Commander Sassinak, telling her exactly what she needed to know, saw her smiling at him, praising him. . . .

"Tim! You're sliding up on him!"

"It's all right." It wasn't, quite, but he eased back on the power, and settled the shuttle in the center of the transport's blind cone, where turbulence from its drive prevented its sensors from detecting them. It was harder than he'd thought, keeping the shuttle in the safe zone. But he could do it, and he'd follow it down to the bottom of the sea, if he had to. Too bad he didn't have enough armament to take it himself. He toyed with the idea of enabling the little tractor beam that the shuttles used around space stations, what the engineering chief called the "parking brake," but realized it wouldn't have much effect on something the mass of that transport.

"This is what I thought about during finals," he said, hoping to get some kind of reaction from Gori.

"Huh. No wonder you came in only twelfth from the bottom."

"Somebody has to be on the bottom. If they didn't think I could do the work, they wouldn't have let me graduate. And the captain gave me this job —"

"To get you out of her hair while she deals with that escort or whatever it is. Krims, Tim, you spend too much time daydreaming about glory, and not enough — look *out!*"

Reflexively, Tim yanked on the controls, and the shuttle skimmed over a jagged peak, its drive whining at the sudden load. "She said stay low," he said, but Gori snorted.

"You could let me fly. I can keep my mind on my work."

"She gave it to me!" In that brief interval, the transport had pulled ahead. "And I've got better ratings as a shuttle pilot."

Gori said nothing more, which suited Timran fine right then. He *had* cut it a little close — although he was certainly low enough for fine-detail on the tapes. Now he concentrated on the landscape ahead, wild and rough as it was, and tried to anticipate where the transport would land. There — that plateau. "Look at that," he breathed. "A landing grid. A monster —" The transport sank towards it, seeming even larger now that it was leaving its own element and coming to rest.

He barely saw the movement — something small, but clearly *made*, not natural — when a bolt of colored light from the transport reached out to it. "Look out!" he yelled at Gori, and slammed his hand on the tractor beam control. The shuttle lurched, as the badly aimed beam grabbed for anything in its way. Tim's hands raced over the controls, bringing the shuttle to a near hover, and catching the distant falling object in the tractor beam just before it hit a low cliff.

"An *airsled!*" breathed Gori. "Oh gods, Tim, what have you *done!*"

"Did you see those murderers?" His teeth were clenched as he worked the beam to set the airsled down as gently as possible. "Those dirty, rotten, slimy —"

"Tim! That's not the point! We're supposed to be invisible!"

All the latent romanticism burst free. "We're Fleet! We just saved lives, that's what we're supposed to do."

"That's not what the captain *ordered* us to do. Tim, you just told everyone, from the transport to whoever they're meeting, that we're here. That *Fleet's* here."

"So . . . so we'll just . . . mmm . . . we'll just tell them they're under arrest, for . . . uh . . . attempting to . . . uh . . ."

"Illegal use of proscribed weaponry in a proscribed system is one charge you're looking for." Gori was punching buttons on his console. "Kipling's copper corns! The captain's going to be furious, and I've heard about her being furious. She's going to eat us alive, buddy, and it's all your fault."

"She'd want us to save lives. . . ." Tim didn't sound quite so certain now. For one thing, that transport had lifted, and then settled itself firmly on the grid. He sent the shuttle forward again, slowly, and wondered whether to stand guard over the airsled or threaten the transport, or what. It had seemed so simple at the time. . . .

The voice in his earplug left him in no doubt. "I told you," the captain's crisp voice said, "to follow that transport down *cautiously*, with particular care not to be noticed. Did you understand that order?"

"Yes, ma'am, but —"

"Yet I find that you have engaged a possibly hostile vessel, making sure that you would be noticed; you may have damaged Federation citizens —" That wasn't fair at all; it was the crash that damaged them, and he hadn't caused the crash . . . at least, he hadn't shot the airsled, although his handling of the tractor beam had been less than deft. "Moreover, you've made it necessary for me to act — or abandon *you*, and if you were alone that would be a distinct temptation!" Gori smirked at this, he was getting the same tirade in his own earplug. "Now that you've started a riot, young man, you'd better stay in control of things until I get there."

"But how —?" Tim began, but the comm cut off. He was breathing fast, and felt cold. He looked over at Gori, no longer smirking. "What do we do now?"

Gori, predictably, had a reference. "Fleet Landing Force Directives, Chapter 17, paragraph 34.2 —"

"I don't care where it *is* — what does it say?"

Gori went on, pale but determined, with his quotation. "It says if the landing party — which is us — is outnumbered or outgunned, and Fleet personnel are in danger of capture or injury —"

"They're civilians," said Timran. As he said it he wondered — but surely anyone on the planet had to be civilians, or they would have known Fleet was down here..

"Really? Those look like Fleet duty uniforms to me." Gori had a magnifier to his eye. "Shipboard working . . . Anyway, when personnel are in danger of capture or injury, and the landing party is outnumbered, then the decision to withdraw must be made by the commander of the orbiting ship, unless such ship —"

"She told us to stay here and stay in charge —"

"So that's paragraph 34.3: In cases where rescue or protection of the Fleet personnel is deemed possible or of paramount importance, the pilot of the landing party shuttle will remain with the craft at all times, and the copilot will lead the rescue party —"

"That's backwards!" said Tim, thinking of Gori's character.

"That's regulations," said Gori. "Besides, if we just hover here we can keep anyone from bothering them. By the way, d'you have the shields up?"

He hadn't thought of it, and thumbed the control just as the transport's single turret angled their way. Gori was watching the plateau now, and commented on the people clumped near the ship. "Native? This planet's not supposed to be inhabited at all, but —"

"They might shoot, Gori," Tim pointed out. He was glad to hear that his voice was steady, though his hands trembled slightly. He'd never expected that the mere sight of a blast cannon muzzle aimed his way would be so disturbing. Were shuttle shields strong enough, at this distance, to hold against a blast cannon?

Time passed. Down below still figures slumped in an airsled crumpled against the rocky face of the plateau. Above, the transport's blast cannon continued to point directly at them. With only two of them aboard, Tim couldn't see asking Gori to go out and check on the injured (dead? He hoped not) sled passengers. Should he hail the transport? Command them to send medical aid? What if they didn't? What if they fired? Gori maintained a prudent silence, broken only by observations on activity around the transport. It felt like years before the comm unit burped, and put the Navigation Senior Officer on the line. "Not long," Bures said. "We've got a fix on you and the transport. How's it going?"

Tim swallowed hard. "Oh . . . nothing much. We're just hovering above the sled —"

"Don't move," Bures advised. "We're coming in *very* fast, and if you move we could run right over you."

"Where are you going to land?" But no one answered that question; the line had cut off. Gori and Tim exchanged anxious glances before settling to their watch again. Tim let his eyes stray to the clock — surely it had been longer than *that*.

Even through the shields they heard and felt the shock waves of the *Zaid-Dayan's* precipitous descent. "Krims!" said Gori. "She's using the emergency insystem —" Another powerful blast of wind and noise, and the great cruiser hung above the plateau, its Fleet and Federation insignia defining the bow. Clouds of dust roiled away from it, temporarily blinding Tim even in the shuttle; when it cleared, Tim could see the transport shudder at its berth. "— drive," finished Gori, paler than before. Tim, for once, said nothing.

"The only good thing about all this," said Sassinak, when they were back aboard, "is that I know you can't be a saboteur, because you weren't on board when the sabotage occurred, and it would have required immediate access. Of course you might be in collusion. . . ."

Tim tried to swallow, unsuccessfully. It wasn't that she bellowed, or turned red, the way some of his instructors had when he had been particularly difficult. She looked perfectly calm, if you didn't notice the pale rim around her mouth, or the muscles bunched along her jaw. Her voice was no louder than usual. But he had the feeling that his bones were exposed to her gaze, not to mention the daydreams in his skull . . . and they seemed a lot less glamorous right then. Even, as she said, stupid, shortsighted, rash, and unjustified. She had left them hovering where they were until the locals (whoever they were) had extricated the injured and moved them into the cruiser. Then the cruiser's own tractor beam had flicked out and towed them in as if the shuttle were powerless and pilotless. Once in the shuttle bay, they'd been ordered to their quarters until "the captain's ready for you." Gori had said nothing while they waited, and Tim had imagined himself cashiered and stranded on this malodorous lump of unsteady rock.

"I'll expect you to recite the relevant sections of regulations, Ensign, the next time you see me. I'm sure your cohort can give you the references." That was her only dig at Gori, who had after all been innocent. "You may return to your quarters, and report for duty at shift-change." He didn't ask where: it would be posted in his file. He and Gori saluted, and retired without tripping over anything — at that point Tim was mildly surprised to find out his body worked as usual.

Curiosity returned on the way to their quarters. He looked sideways at Gori. No help there. But who were the husky, skin-clad indigenes? They had to be human, unless everything he'd been told about evolution was wrong. Why had someone built a landing grid on an uncharted planet? Who were the people in the Fleet uniforms, if they weren't from this ship?

Alone with Gori in their quarters, he had no one to ask. Gori said nothing, simply called up the *Fleet Regulations: XXIII Edition* on screen, and highlighted the passages the captain had mentioned. The computer spat out a hardcopy, and Gori handed it to Tim. Duties, obligations, penalties . . . he tried not to let it sink in, but it got past his defenses anyway. Disobeying a captain's direct order in the presence of a hostile (or presumed hostile) force was grounds for anything the captain chose to do about it, including summary execution. She *could* have left him there, left both of them there, including innocent Gori, if she'd wanted to, and no one in Fleet would have had a quibble.

For the first time, Tim thought about the stories he'd heard . . . *why* the ship was so long in the repair yard, what kind of engagement that had been. A colony plundered, while Sassi-nak did nothing, in hopes of catching more pirates later. More than two or three people had died there; she had let them die, to save others. He didn't like that a bit. Did she? The ones who'd talked about it said not, but . . . if she really cared, how could she? Men and women, children, people of all sorts — rich, poor, in be-tween — had died because she didn't do what he had done — she didn't come tearing in to save them.

Gradually, in the hollow silence between his bunk and

Gori's, Tim began to build a new vision of what the Fleet really was, and what his captain had intended. What he had messed up, with his romantic and gallant nonsense. Those people in the colony had died, so that Sassinak could trace their attackers to powers behind them. Some of her crew had died, trying to save the children, and then destroy a pirate base. This very voyage probably had something to do with the same kind of trouble, and saving two lives just didn't mean that much. If he himself had been killed before his rash act — and for the first time he really faced that chilling possibility of not-being — it would have done Fleet no harm, and possibly his captain some good.

When the chime rang for duty, Tim set off for his new job (cleaning sludge from the filters) with an entirely new attitude. He fully intended to become the reformed young officer the Fleet so needed, and for several hours worked diligently. No more jokes, no more wild notions: sober reality. He recited the regulations under his breath, just in case the captain should appear in this smelly little hole.

In this mood of determined obedience to nature and nature's god in the person of his captain, he didn't even smile when Jig Turner, partner in several earlier escapades, appeared in the hatchway.

"I guess you know," said Turner.

"I know if I don't finish these filters, we'll be breathing this stink."

"This isn't bad — you should smell the planet's atmosphere." Turner lounged against the bulkhead, patently idle, with the air of someone who desperately wants to tell a secret.

"You've been out?" Despite himself, Tim couldn't fail to ask that.

"Well, no. Not *out* exactly, but we all smelled it when they brought the injuries in. Worse than this . . . like organic lab." Turner leaned closer. "Listen, Tim — did you really fire on that transport?"

"No! I put a tractor on the airsled, that's all."

"I wish you *had* blown it."

"I didn't have anything to blow it with. But why? The captain's mad enough that I caught the sled."

"D'you know what that transport was?" Of course he didn't,

and he shook his head. Turner went on, lowering her voice. "Heavyworlders."

"So?"

"So *think*, Tim. Heavyworlders, meatheads, in a transport — tried to tell the captain they were answering a distress beacon, but it scans like a colony ship. To a proscribed planet . . . which has heavyworlders on it *already*."

"Huh?" He couldn't follow this. "The ones in the airsled?"

"No. The ones on the ground . . . near the transport, and getting the victims out . . . you *must* have been watching, Tim, even you."

"I saw them, but they didn't look like heavyworlders . . . exactly." Now he came to think of it, they had been big and well-muscled.

"It's a heavyworlder *plot*," Turner went on quickly. "They wanted the planet — there was a mutiny, I heard, in a scouting expedition, and the heavyworlders started eating raw meat, and killed the others and ate them —"

"I don't believe it!" But he would, if he let himself think about it. Eating one sentient being had to be the same as eating another: that's why the prohibition. He'd had an aunt who wouldn't eat anything synthesized from perennial plants, on the grounds that shrubs and trees might be sentient.

"The thing is, if one heavyworlder can mutiny, why not all? There's already this bunch of them living free out there, eating meat and wearing skins — what's to stop the ones on this ship from going crazy, too? Maybe it's the smell in the air, or something. But a lot of us think the captain should put 'em all under guard. Think of the heavyworld marines . . . we wouldn't stand a chance if they mutinied."

Tim thought about it a moment, while screwing the access port back on the filter he'd just cleaned, and shook his head. "No — I can't see anyone from this ship turning on the captain —"

"But they could. They could be planning something right now, and if we don't warn her —"

Tim grinned. "I don't think, Turner, that the captain needs our warning to know where danger is."

"You mean you won't sign the petition? Or come with us to talk to her?"

"No. And frankly I think you're nuts to bother her with this."

"I'm glad you think so." Commander Sassinak, Tim saw, looked as immaculate as usual, though she must have gone through the same narrow passages that had smudged his uniform. She gave him a frosty smile, which vanished as she met Turner's eyes. "Tell me, Lieutenant Turner, did you ever happen to read the regulations on shipboard conspiracy?"

"No, Captain, but —"

"No. Nor were you serving on this ship when heavyworlder marines — the very ones you're so afraid of — saved the ship and my life. Had they been inclined to mutiny, Lieutenant, they'd have had more than one opportunity. You exhibit a regrettable prejudice, and an even more regrettable tendency to faulty logic. The actions of heavyworlders on an exploration team more than four decades ago say nothing about the loyalty of my crew. I trust them a long sight more than I trust you — they've given me reason. I don't want to hear any more of this, or that you've been spreading such rumors. Is that clear?"

"Yes, Captain." At Sass' nod, Turner hurried away. Tim stood at attention, entirely too aware of his smelly, stained hands and messy uniform. The captain's lips quirked: not a smile, but something that required control not to be.

"Learned anything, Ensign Timran?"

"Yes, Captain. I . . . uh . . . memorized the regulations —"

"About time. As it happens, and I don't want you getting a swelled head about this, things have worked out very well. From this point on, consider that you acted under orders at all times: is that clear?"

It wasn't clear at all, but he tried to conceal his confusion. His captain sighed, obviously noticing the signs, and explained. "The other ship, Tim, the one that appeared from the Ryxi planet, was not a pirate: it was a legal transport, on contract to supply the Ryxi, replying to a distress signal."

"Yes, Captain." That was always safe, even though the rest of it made no sense at all.

"For political reasons, which you will no doubt hear discussed later, your rash intervention has turned out to benefit Fleet and the FSP. It is necessary that those outside this ship believe your actions were on my orders. Therefore, you are not to mention, ever, to anyone, at any time, in any place, that your actions in the shuttle were your own bright idea. You did what I told you to do — is that clear now?"

Slightly clearer, and from the tone in her voice he had better understand, with no more questions.

"I've also told Gori, and all previous comments in the files have been wiped." Which meant it was *serious* . . . but also that he wasn't going to have that around his neck forever. Dawning hope must have shown on his face, for hers softened slightly. "Timran, listen to me, and pay attention. You've got natural good luck, and it's priceless . . . but *don't* depend on it. It takes more than good luck to make admiral."

"Yes, Captain. Uh — if I may — are the people all right? The ones in the airsled?"

"Yes. They're quite well, and you may even meet them someday. Just remember what I said."

"*Yes*, Captain,"

"And clean up before mess." With that she was gone, a vision of grace and authority that haunted his life for years.

CHAPTER SIXTEEN

Sassinak returned to the bridge by way of Troop Deck, as she wanted to manage a casual encounter with the marine commander. She had already realized that the combination of events might alarm some of the crew, and inflame suspicion of heavyworlders.

She found Major Currald inspecting a rack of weapons; he gave her a somewhat abstracted nod. "Captain — if you've a moment, there's something —"

"Certainly, Major." He led the way to his office, and Sass noticed that he had seating for both heavyworlders and smaller frames. She chose neither, instead turning to look at the holos on the wall across from his desk. A team of futbal players in clean uniforms posed in neat rows, action shots of the same players splattered with mud, a much younger Currald rappelling down a cliff, two young marine officers (one of them Currald? She couldn't tell) in camouflage facepaint and assault rifles. A promotion ceremony; Currald getting his "tracks." Someone not Currald, the holo in a black frame.

"My best friend," said Currald, as her eyes fixed on that one. She turned to face him; he was looking at the holo himself. "He was killed at Jerma, in the first wave, while I was still on a down shuttle. He'd named his son after me." He cleared his throat, a bass rasp. "That wasn't what I asked to speak to you about, Captain. I hesitated to come up to Main Deck and bother you, but —" He cleared his throat again. "I'm sorry to say I expect some trouble."

Sass nodded. "So do I, and I wanted to tell you first what I'm going to do." His face stiffened, the traditional heavyworlder response to any threat. "Major Currald, I know you're a loyal officer; if you'd wanted to advance heavyworlder interests at my expense, you'd have done it long before. We've discussed politics before, you know where I stand. Your troops have earned my trust, earned it in battle, where it counts. Whoever that saboteur is, I'm convinced it's not one of your people, and I'm not about to let anyone pressure me into thinking so."

He was surprised; she was a little annoyed that he had not trusted her trust. "But I know a lot of the crew think —"

"A lot of the crew *don't* think," she interrupted crisply. "They worry, or they react, but they don't think. Kipling's bunions! The heavyworlder mutiny here was forty-three years ago: before you were born, and I was only a toddler on Myriad. None of your marines are old enough to have had anything to do with that. Those greedyguts would-be colonists set out months ago — probably while we were chasing that first ship. But scared people put two and two together and get the Annual Revised Budget Request —" At that he actually grinned, and began to chuckle. Sass grinned back at him. "I trust you, Major, and I trust you to know if your troops are loyal. You'll hear, I'm sure, that people have asked me to 'do something' — throw you all in the brig or something equally ridiculous — and I want you to know right now, before the rumors take off, that I'm not even thinking about that. Clear?"

"Very clear, Captain. And thank you. I thought . . . I thought perhaps you'd feel you had to make some concession. And I'd talked to my troops, the heavyworlders, and we'd agreed to cooperate with any request."

Sass felt tears sting her eyes . . . and there were some who thought heavyworlders were always selfish, never able to think of the greater good. How many of *them* would have made such an offer, had they been innocent suspects? "You tell your troops, Major, that I am deeply moved by that offer — I respect you, and them, and appreciate your concern. But if no other good comes out of this, the rest of this crew is going to learn that we're *all* Fleet: light, heavy, and in-between. And thank you."

"Thank *you*, Captain."

Sassinak found the expected delegation waiting outside the bridge when she got back to the main deck. Their spokesman, 'Tenant Varhes, supervised the enlisted mess, she recalled. Their concern, he explained in a reedy tenor, was for the welfare of the ship. After all, a heavyworlder had already poisoned officers and crew. . . .

"A mentally imbalanced person," said Sassinak coldly, "who happened to also be a heavyworlder, poisoned officers — including the marine commander, who happens to be a heavyworlder — and crew, including some heavyworlders. Or have you forgotten that?"

"But if they should mutiny. The heavyworlders on this planet mutinied —"

"Over forty years ago, when your father was a toddler, and Major Currald hadn't been born. Are you suggesting that heavyworlders have telepathic links to unborn heavyworlders?" That wasn't logical, but neither were they, and she enjoyed the puzzlement on their faces as they worked their way through it. Before Varhes could start up again, she tried a tone of reasonableness, and saw it affect most of them. "Look here: the heavyworlders on this ship are *Fleet* — not renegades, like those who mutinied here, or those who want to colonize a closed world. They're our companions, they've fought beside us, saved our lives. They could have killed us many times over, if that's what they had in mind. You think they're involved in sabotage on the ship — I'm quite sure they're not. But even so, we're taking precautions against sabotage. If it should be a heavyworlder, that individual will be charged and tried and punished. But that doesn't make the others guilty. Suppose it's someone from Gian-IV —" a hit at Varhes, whose homeworld it was, "would that make Varhes guilty?"

"But it's not the same," came a voice from the back of the group. "Everybody knows heavyworlders are planet pirates, and now we've found them in action —"

"*Some* planet pirates are heavyworlders, we suspect, and some are not — some are even Ryxi." That got a nervous laugh. "Or consider the Seti." A louder laugh. Sassinak let her voice harden. "But this is enough of this. I don't want to hear any more unfounded charges against loyal members of Fleet, people who've put their lives on the line more than once. I've already told one ensign to review the regulations on conspiracy, and I commend them to each of you. We have real hostiles out there, people: real would-be planet pirates, who may have allies behind them. We can't afford fingerpointing and petty prejudices among ourselves. Is that quite clear?" It was; the little group melted away, most of them shamefaced and clearly regretting their impetuous actions. Sass hoped they'd continue to feel that way.

Back on the bridge, Sass reviewed the status of the various parties involved. The heavyworld transport's captain had entered a formal protest against her action in "interfering with the attempt to respond to a distress beacon." Her eyebrows rose. The only distress beacon in the story so far had been at the Ryxi planet, the beacon that had sent *Mazer Star* on its way here. The heavyworlder transport had run past there like a grass fire in a windstorm. Now what kind of story could he have concocted, and what kind of faked evidence would be brought out to support it? She grinned to herself; this was becoming even more interesting than before.

The "native" heavyworlders, descendants of the original survey and exploration team . . . or at least of the mutineers of that team . . . were mulling over the situation but keeping their distance from the cruiser. The transport's captain had kept in contact with them by radio, however.

The *Mazer Star*, supply ship for the Ryxi colony, had managed to contact the survivors who'd been in cold sleep. So far their statements confirmed everything on the distress beacon, with plenty of supporting detail. A mixed exploration team, set down to survey geological and biological resources — including children from the EEC survey vessel, the *ARCT-10*, that had carried them, highly unusual. Reversion of the heavyworlder team members to carnivory — their subsequent mutiny — murder, torture of adults and children — their attempt to kill all the lightweights by stampeding wildlife into the camp. The lightweights' successful escape in a lifeboat to a seacliff cave, and their decision to go into cold sleep and await the *ARCT-10*'s return.

Sass ran through the computer file Captain Godheir had transferred, explaining everything from the original mixup that had led the Ryxi to think the human team had been picked up by the *ARCT-10*, to the *Mazer Star*'s own involvement, after a Thek intrusion. Thek! Sass shook her head over that. This had been complicated enough before; Thek were a major complication in themselves. Godheir's story, unlike that of the heavyworlder Captain Cruss, made perfect (if ironic) sense, and his records checked out clean with her on-board databanks. *Mazer Star* was in fact listed as one of three shuttle-supply ships on contract to a

Ryxi colony in this system. She frowned at the personnel list God-heir had transferred, of the expedition members stranded after the mutiny. Lunzie? It couldn't be, she thought — and yet it wasn't a common name. She'd never run into another Lunzie. Medic, age 36 elapsed — and what did *that* mean? Then she saw the date of birth, and her breath quickened. By date of birth this woman was ancient — impossibly old — and yet — Sass fed the ID data into the computer, and told Comm to ready a lowlink to Fleet Sector Headquarters. About time the admiral knew what had happened, and she was going to need a *lot* of information. Starting with this.

"Captain?" That was Borander, on the pinnace, with a report of the airsled victims' condition.

"Go ahead."

"The woman is conscious now; the medics have cleared her for transport. The man is still out, and they want to package him first."

"Have you had a contact from their base?"

"No, Captain."

"You may find them confused, remember, and not just by a knock on the head. Don't argue with them; try to keep them calm until you get a call from their base, or our medical crew gets to them." The message relayed from Godheir was that both crew were barriered by an Adept, and thought they were members of a Fleet cruiser's crew. They'd be more than a little surprised to find themselves in a different cruiser, Sass thought, particularly if the barriers had been set with any skill.

And one of these was the team co-leader — essentially the civilian authority of the entire planet. Governor? Sass wondered what she was like, and decided she'd better be set up for a formal interview just in case. Some of these scientist types didn't think highly of Fleet. She signalled for an escort, then went to her office and brought up all the screens. One showed the pinnace just landing, and when she plugged in her earpiece, Borander told her that a message had just come from the survivor's base for the woman. Sass approved a transfer, and watched on the screen as Borander and his pilot emerged to give their passenger privacy. She presumed that the unconscious man was in the rear compartment, with a medic.

When the woman — Varian, Sass reminded herself — came

out, she seemed to be a vigorous, competent sort. She was certainly used to having her own way, for she took one look around and began to argue with Borander about something. Sass wished she'd insisted on an open channel between them, but she hadn't expected that anything much would happen. Now she watched as the argument progressed, with handwaving and headshaking and — by the expressions — raised voices. She pressed a button, linking her to the bridge, and said, "Comm, get me an audio of channel three."

"— Nothing to do with Aygar and anyone in his generation or even his parents'." The woman's voice would have been rich and melodic if she hadn't been angry — or stressed by the crash, Sass reminded herself. She followed the argument with interest. Borander let himself be overwhelmed — first by the woman's vehemence, and then by her claim of precedence as planetary governor. Not, Sass was sorry to notice, by her chain of logic, which was quite reasonable. She shook her head at the screen, disappointed; she'd thought Borander had more backbone. Of course the woman was right: the descendants of mutineers were not themselves guilty, and he should have seen that for himself. He should also have foreseen her claim of authority, and avoided the direct confrontation with it. Most of all, Fleet officers shouldn't be so visibly nervous about their captains' opinion — acting that way in a bar, as an excuse not to get into a row, was one thing, but here it made him look weak — never a good idea. How could she help him learn that, without losing all his confidence — because he didn't seem to have much.

So, Co-leader Varian wanted to bring both those young heavyworlders into her office and argue their case right away, did she? She was no doubt primed for an argument with a boneheaded Fleet battleaxe. . . . Sass grinned to herself. Varian might be a planetary governor, of sorts, but she didn't know much about tactics. Not that she planned to be an enemy.

She followed their progress up the ramp and through the ship, but by the time they appeared outside her office, she was waiting to greet them. As she stood and shook hands with Varian, she saw the younger woman's eyes widen slightly. Whatever she'd thought a cruiser captain was like, this was clearly not it. . . . Not the old battleaxe you expected, hmm? thought Sass. Nor the office you expected? For Varian's eyes had lingered on the crystal sculpture, the oiled wood desk with its stunning pattern of dark red and black graining, the rich blue carpet and white seating. Sass gave the two young heavyworlders a polite greeting. One of them — Winral? — seemed almost dazed by his surroundings, very much the country cousin lost in a world of high technology. The other, poised between hostility and intelligent curiosity, was a very different order of being indeed. If there were wild humans, Sass thought, as there are wild and domestic kinds of some animals, this would be a wild one. All the intelligence, but untamed. On top of that, he was handsome, in a rough-cut way.

She continued with pleasantries, offering a little information, feeling out the three of them. Varian relaxed quickly once she realized Sassinak intended no harm to the innocent descendants of the mutineers. Clearly she felt at home in civilized surroundings and had not gone native. Varian wanted to know the location of the *ARCT-10*, of course.

"That's another good question to which I have no answer," Sass told her, and explained that she'd initiated a query. It hadn't been listed as destroyed, and no distress beacon had shown up, but it might take days to figure out what might have happened. Then she turned to Aygar, and asked for his personal identification — which he gave as a pedigree. Typical, she thought, for the planet-born: you are who your parents were. Fleet personnel gave ship and service history; scientists, she'd heard, gave university affiliation and publications. Winral's pedigree, when he gave it, contained some of the same names . . . and after all the mutineers had been few. They'd probably worked to avoid inbreeding, especially if they weren't sure how long it would be before a colony ship joined them. Or if one would come at all.

When she began to review the legal status of the younger heavyworlders, Varian interrupted to insist that the planet did, indeed, have a developing sentient species. Sass let her face show surprise, but what she really felt was consternation. Things had been complicated enough before, with the contending claims of mutiny, mining rights, developmental rights derived from successful settlement — and the Theks' intervention. But all rules changed when a planet had a sentient or developing sentient native species. She was well-read in space law — all senior officers were — but this was more than a minor complication — and one she could not ignore.

Avian, too, Varian told her. Sass thought of the Ryxi, volatile
and vain, and decided to keep all mention of Varian's flyers off the
common communication links. At least the Ryxi weren't as curious as they were touchy — they wouldn't come winging by just to
see what the excitement was all about.

Aygar, meanwhile, wanted to insist that the heavyworlders at
the settlement owned the entire planet — and could grant parts
of it to the colonists in that transport if they wanted to. Sassinak
found herself enjoying his resistance, though she made it clear
that under Federation law his people could not claim anything
but what they had developed: the mine, the fields, the landing
grid. And she strongly advised him to have nothing more to do
with the heavyworlder transport, if he wanted to avoid suspicion
of a conspiracy.

When she offered him her hand, at the conclusion of the interview, she wondered if he'd try to overwhelm her. If he was as
smart as he looked — as he must be to have accomplished what
the reports said — he would restrain himself. And so he did. His
grip on her hand was only slightly stronger than hers on his, and
he released her hand without attempting a throw. She smiled at
him, well-pleased by his manner, and made a mental note to try
recruiting him for Fleet duty. He'd make a terrific marine, if he
could discipline himself like that. She explained that she'd be
sending over data cubes on FSP law, standard rights and responsibilities of citizenship, the sections on colony law, and so on, and
that she'd supply certain items from the ship's stores under the
shipwreck statutes. Then the two heavyworlders were gone, with
an escort back to the outside, and she turned her attention back
to Varian.

Varian would clearly rather have left with the heavyworlders,
and Sass wondered about that. Why was she being so protective?
Most people in her position would, Sass thought, have been more
ready to see all the heavyworlders in irons. Had she formed some
kind of attachment? She watched the younger woman's face as
she settled into one of the chairs. "A rather remarkable specimen,
that Aygar. Are there more like him?" She let her voice carry
more than a hint of sensuality, and watched a flush spread across
Varian's cheek. So . . . did she really think older women had no
such interests, or was it jealousy?

"I've only encountered a few of his generation —"

"Yes, generation." Sassinak decided to probe a little deeper. "You're now forty-three years behind your own. Will you need counseling? For yourself or the others?" She knew they would, but saw Varian push that possibility away. Did she not realize the truth, or was she unwilling to show weakness in front of a stranger?

"I'll know when I get back to them," Varian was saying. "The phenomenon hasn't caught up with me yet."

Sassinak thought it had, at least in part, but admired the woman for denying it. And what was this going to do to Lunzie? Somehow she wasn't nearly as worried about *her*. Varian asked again about the *ARCT-10*, as if Sassinak would have lied in the first place. A civilian response, Sass thought: she never lied without a good reason, and usually managed without needing to. Someone came in to report that Varian's sled had been repaired, and Sass brought the interview to a close. Supplies — of course, a planetary governor could requisition anything she required — just contact Ford. Sass knew he would be glad for a chance to get off the plateau and see some of the exotic wildlife. But now . . .

"Your medic's name *is* Lunzie, isn't it?" she asked. Varian, slightly puzzled, nodded. Sass let her grin widen, enjoying the bombshell she was about to drop. "I suppose it was inevitable that one of us would encounter her. A celebration is in order. Will you convey my deepest respects to Lunzie?" Varian's expression now almost made her burst out laughing: total confusion and disbelief. "I cannot miss the chance to meet Lunzie," Sass finished up. "It isn't often one gets the chance to entertain one's great-great-great grandmother." Varian's mouth hung slightly open, and her eyes were glazed. Gotcha, thought Sass wickedly, and in the gentlest possible tones asked one of the junior officers to escort Varian to her sled.

Nothing wrong with that young woman that seasoning wouldn't cure, *but* — Sass chuckled to herself — it was fun to outwit a planetary governor. Even one who'd had a concussion. She followed Varian's progress through the ship, and was pleased to note that shock or not, she remembered to check on her crewmate. When Med queried, with a discreet push of buttons, Sass acknowledged and approved his leaving with Varian. Varian, she suspected, never considered that he might have been held.

Ford appeared, and shook his head at her expression. "Captain, you look entirely too pleased about something."

"I may be. But compared to the last cruise, things are going extremely well, complications and all. Of course we don't know why the Thek are here, or what they're going to do, or if that heavyworlder transport has allies following after —"

Ford shook his head. "I doubt that. A hull that size could carry colony seedstock, machinery and all —"

"True. That's what I'm hoping — but you notice I put a relay satellite in orbit, and left a streaker net out. Just in case. Oh, yes — you're interested in the sort of wildlife they've got here, aren't you?"

"Sure — it was kind of a hobby of mine, and when I was on the staff at Sector III, they had this big museum just down the hill —"

"Good. Are you willing to take on a fairly dangerous outside job? And do some acting in the meantime?"

"Of course." He blanked all the expression off his face and faked a Diplo accent. "I could pretend to be a heavyworlder if you want, but I'm afraid they'd notice something. . . ."

Sass shook her head at him. "Be serious. I need to know more about this world — direct data, not interpreted by those survivors, no matter how expert they are in their fields. Varian, the co-leader who came today, is entirely too eager to claim sentient status for an avian species. It may be justified, or it may not, but I want independent data. There's something odd about her reactions to the Iretan-born heavyworlders, too. She ought to be furious, still — she's less than a tenday out of cold sleep; she witnessed a murder; the initial indictment filed with Godheir spoke of intentional injury to both co-leaders. That's all fresh in her mind, or should be. Her reasoning's correct: the grandchildren of mutineers are not responsible. But it's just not normal for her to think that clearly when her friends and colleagues have suffered. I've seen this kind of idealism backfire — this determination to save every living thing can be carried too far. She's very dedicated, and very spirited, but I'm not sure how stable she is. With a tribunal coming up to determine the fate of this planet and those people, I need something solid."

"I see your point, Captain, but what do you want me to do?"

"Well — I'd guess she'd fall for unconditional enthusiasm. Boyish gush, if you can manage it — and I know you can." She let her eyes caress him, and he laughed aloud. "Yes — exactly that. Be dinosaur-crazy, act as if you'd do anything for a mere glimpse of them — you're so lucky to have the chance, and so on. You can start by being skeptical — are they really dinosaurs? Are they *sure*? Let's pick a survey team today, and brief them — you can introduce them as fellow hobbyists tomorrow. They'll probably accept two or three, and if they go for that maybe another two or three later. How's that sound?"

"Right. Makes sense." Ford, faced with a problem, tackled it wholly, absorbed and alert at once. She watched as he scrolled through the personnel files, with a search on secondary specialties. "We'll have to pick those who *do* have a real interest — they'd catch on to something faked, and I can't teach someone all about dinosaurs in one night —" He stopped, and fed an entry to screen. "How about Borander? He's taken twelve hours of paleontology."

"No, not Borander. Did you see how he interacted with Varian?"

"No, I was with Currald then."

"Well, take a look at the tape later. Young trout let her dominate him. Admittedly, she's a Disciple, and she's declared herself planetary governor, but I don't like my officers buckling that easily. He needs a bit of seasoning. Who else?"

"Segendi — no, he's a heavyworlder and I doubt you want to complicate things that way —"

"Right."

"What about Maxnil, in supply? His secondary specialty is cartography, and he's listed as having an associate degree in xenobio." Sass nodded, and Ford went on, quickly turning up a short list of three crew members who could be considered "dinosaur buffs." It was even easier to come up with a list of those who knew a reasonable amount of geology, although harder to cut the list to three. All had excellent records, and all had worked with non-Fleet personnel.

Sass nodded, at last. "Good selection. You brief them, Ford, and be sure they understand that they did *not* know dinosaurs were here until tomorrow. We didn't see anything on the way down: we came in too fast. I had seen the information stripped from the beacon, but no one else had. Once you see the beasts, I imagine you won't have to fake your reactions. But keep in mind that I need information on more than large, noisy, dangerous reptiloids."

Ford nodded. "Do you still want to speak to Major Currald before lunch?"

"If he feels he has things well in hand with the transport.

What's the captain's name — Cruss? Foul-mouthed creature, that one. I want Wefts and heavyworlders, round the clock —"

"Here's the roster." As usual, Ford had anticipated her request. She thought again how lucky she was to have Ford this time, and not Huron. In a situation like this, Huron's initiative and drive could have been disastrous. She could trust Ford to back her tactics, not go off and do something harebrained on his own.

She glanced at the roster of Fleet personnel stationed inside the transport to ensure that personnel in cold sleep were not revived. She didn't want to face a thousand or more heavyworlders: the *Zaid-Dayan* would have no trouble killing them all, but Fleet commanders were supposed to avoid the necessity of a massacre. Each shift combined Wefts and heavyworlders: she trusted her heavyworlders, but with Wefts to witness, no one could later claim that they'd betrayed her trust. "Get Currald on the line, would you."

A few moments later, Currald's face filled one of the screens, and he confirmed that the situation remained stable.

"I've told the native-born survivors that I'll supply some of their needs, too," Sassinak told him. "I don't want them to think that all good comes from Diplo. I've got some things on order, that'll be delivered to the perimeter. But if you can turn surveillance and supervision over to someone, I'd appreciate your company at lunch."

"You're not giving them weapons —"

"No, certainly not."

"Give me about half an hour, if you can, Captain; I'm still arranging the flank coverage."

"That's fine. I'll order a meal for half an hour from now — and if you're held up along the way, just give me a call." She cleared the circuit, and turned to Ford. "See if Mayerd can meet with us, too — and you, of course, after you've notified your short lists that you'll brief them this afternoon. I'll be on the bridge, but we'll eat in here."

On the bridge, she told the duty officer to carry on, and came up behind Arly. Although most of the ship had been released from battle stations, the weapons systems were powered up and fully operational. It would be disastrous if someone erred at this range — no doubt the transport would be destroyed (with great loss of life she'd have to account for) but the resultant backlash could endanger the *Zaid-Dayan*. Arly acknowledged her without taking her gaze from the screens.

"I'm just running a test on quadrant two —" she said over her shoulder. "Interlock systems — making sure no one can pull the same trick again —"

Sass had more sense than to bother her at that moment, and waited, watching the screens closely, although she could not interpret some of the scanning traces. Finally Arly sighed, and locked her board down.

"Safe. I hope." She smiled a bit wearily. *"Are* you going to explain, or is this a great security mystery?"

"Both," said Sass. "How about lunch in my office?"

Arly's eyes slid back to her screens. "I should stay —"

"You've got a perfectly competent second officer, and it's my considered opinion that nothing's going to break loose right now. That Cruss may be up to something, but we've interrupted his plans, and this is our safe period. Relax — or at least get out of that seat and eat something."

Currald brought the stench of the Iretan atmosphere back into Sassinak's office, just as the filters had finally cleared it out after the morning's visit. He apologized profusely, but she waved his apology aside.

"We're going to be here awhile, and we might as well adapt. Or learn to wear noseplugs."

Arly was trying not to wrinkle her nose, but positioned herself a seat away from Currald. "It's not you," she said to him, "but I simply can't handle the sulfur smell. Not with a meal on the table. It makes everything taste terrible."

Currald actually chuckled, a sign of unusual trust. "Maybe that's what drove the mutineers to eating meat — I've heard it ruins the sense of smell."

"Meat?" Mayerd looked up sharply from a sheaf of lab reports. "It makes the person who eats it stink of sulfur derivatives, but it doesn't confuse the eater's own nose."

"I don't know. . . ." Sass paused with a hump of standard green vegetable in white sauce halfway to her mouth. "If things taste different in a sulfurous atmosphere — and they do —" She eyed the lump of green with distaste. "Then maybe meat would taste good."

"I never thought of that." Mayerd's brow wrinkled. Ford grinned at the table generally.

"Here comes another scientific paper . . . 'The Effect of Ireta's Atmosphere on the Perception of Protein Flavorings' . . . 'Sulfur and the Taste of Blood.' "

"Don't say that in front of Co-leader Varian," Sass warned. "She seems to be very sensitive where the prohibition is concerned. She wouldn't think it was funny."

"It's *not* funny," Mayerd said thoughtfully. "It's an idea. . . . I never thought of it before, but perhaps an atmospheric stench would affect the kinds of foods people would prefer, and if someone were already tempted to consider the flesh of living being an acceptable food, the smell might increase the probability —" The others groaned loudly, in discordant tones, and Mayerd glared at them. Before she could retort, Sassinak brought them to order, and explained why she'd wanted them to meet.

"Co-leader Varian is perfectly correct that the Iretans are not responsible for the mutiny or its effects. At the same time, it's in the interests of FSP to see that this planet is not opened to exploitation, and that the Iretans assimilate into the Federation with as little friction as possible. They've been told a pack of lies, as near as we can tell: they think that the original team was made up of heavyworlders, and abandoned unfairly. They expected help from heavyworlders only, and apparently think heavyworlders and lightweights cannot cooperate.

"We have the chance to show them that heavyworlders *are* assimilated, and welcome, in our society. We all know about the problems — Major Currald has had to put up with harassment, as have most if not all heavyworlders in Fleet — but he and the others in Fleet believe that the two types of humans are more alike than different. If we can drive a friendly wedge between those young people and that heavyworlder colony ship — if we can make it clear that they have a chance to belong to a larger universe — perhaps they'll agree to compensation for their claims on Ireta, and withdraw. That would be a peaceful solution, quite possible for such a small group, and with compensation they could gain the education they'd need to live well elsewhere. Even if they don't give up all their claims, they might be more willing to live within the limits a tribunal is almost certain to impose . . . especially if Varian is right, and there's a sentient native species."

Currald said, "Do you want active recruitment? The ones I've seen would probably pass the interim tests."

Sass nodded. "If you find some you want for the marine contingent, let me know. I'd approve a few, but we'd have to be sure we could contain them. I don't believe any have been groomed as agents, but that's a danger I can't ignore."

Mayerd frowned, tapping the lab reports on the table beside her tray. "These kids were brought up on natural foods, not to mention meat. Do you think they could adjust to shipboard diets right away?"

"I'm not sure, and that's why I want you in on this from the beginning. We're going to need to know everything about their physiology. They're apparently heavyworlder-bred, but growing up on a normal-G planet hasn't brought out the full adaptation. Major Currald may have some insights into the differences, or perhaps they'd be willing to talk to other heavyworlders more freely. But you're the research expert on the medical staff: you figure out what you need to know and how to find out. Keep me informed on what you need."

"I've always thought," said Mayerd, with a sidelong glance at Currald, "that it's possible heavyworlders *do* require a blend of nutrients delivered most efficiently in meat. Particularly those on cold worlds. But you can't do research on that in the Federation — it's simply unmentionable. Not fair, really. Scientific research shouldn't be hampered by religious notions."

A tiny smile had twitched Currald's lips. "Research has been done, clandestinely of course, on two heavy-G worlds I know of. It's not just flesh, Doctor, but certain kinds, and yes, it's the most efficient source of the special requirements we have. But I don't think you want to hear this at table."

"Another consideration," said Sassinak into the silence that followed, "is that of crew solidarity. It will do the heavyworlder critics in our crew good to see what heavyworlder genes look like when not stressed by high-G: with all respect, Currald, the Iretans look like normals more than heavyworlders." He nodded, sober but apparently not insulted. "But as you know, we've had trouble with a saboteur before. If anything happened now, to heighten tensions between heavyworlders and lightweights —" She paused, and glanced at every face. They all nodded, clearly understanding the implications. "Arly, I know you've made every possible safety check of the weapons systems, but it's going to be hard to keep your crews fully alert in the coming days. Yet you must: we must not have any accidental weapons discharges."

"Speaking of that," said Hollister. "I presume we're screened . . . ?" Sass pressed the controls and nodded. "I hadn't had a chance to tell you, and since the crisis appeared to be over —" He pulled a small gray box from his pocket and laid it on the table. "I found *this* in the number two power center just as we landed. Disabled it, of course, but I think it was intended to interfere with the tractor controls."

Sass picked up the featureless box and turned it over in her hands. "Induction control?"

"Right. It could be used for all sorts of things, including setting off weapons —"

"Where, precisely, did you find it?"

"Next to a box of circuit breakers, where it looked like it might be part of that assembly — some boxes have another switchbox wired in next to them. Same shade of gray, same type of coating. But I've been looking everyday for anything new, anything different — that's how I spotted it. At first I wasn't even sure, but when I touched it, it came off clean — no wires. Nela cracked it and read the chips for me; that's how I know it was intended to mess up the tractor beam."

"Dupaynil?" She looked down the table at him. His expression was neutral.

"I'd wish to have seen it in place, yet clearly it had to be disabled in that situation, with the possibility of hostile fire. Did you consider physical traces?"

Hollister nodded. "Of course. I held it with gloves, and Nela dusted it, but we didn't find any prints. Med or you, sir, might find other traces."

"The point is," said Sassinak, "that we've finally found physical evidence of our saboteur. Still aboard, since I'm sure Hollister can say that wasn't in place yesterday, and still active."

"If we find a suspect," Dupaynil said, "we might look inside this for traces of the person who programmed it."

"If we find a suspect," said Sassinak. "And we'd better." On that note, the meeting adjourned.

✧ CHAPTER SEVENTEEN

Sassinak had made extensive preparations for her meeting the next morning with Captain Cruss. Unless he had illegal Fleet-manufactured detectors, he could not know that a full audio-video hook-up linked her office to Ford's quarters and the bridge. Currald had furnished his most impressive heavyworld marines for an escort through the ship, although Sassinak had chosen Weft guards for her personal safety. She wanted to see if Cruss would overreach himself.

When Curald signalled that Cruss was on his way, she watched on the monitor. The five men and women that sauntered across the grid between ships were unpleasant-looking, even for heavyworlders. They had not bothered to put on clean uniforms, Sassinak noticed; even Cruss looked rumpled and smudged. She glanced briefly at her white upholstered chairs, and muttered a brief curse to rudeness . . . no doubt they would do their best to soil her things, and smirk to themselves about it. She knew too many fastidious heavyworlders to believe that they were innately dirty.

By the time they reached Main Deck, Sassinak had heard comments from observers she'd stationed along their path. They had argued about leaving their hand weapons with the guards; Captain Cruss carried a small, roughly globular object which he insisted he must hand-carry to Sassinak himself. She signalled an assent. They had made snide remarks to Currald and the heavy-worlder escort, and pointedly turned away from the Wefts. They had lounged insolently on the grabbar in the cargo lift, and commented on the grooming of ship's crew in terms that had the reporting ensign red-faced. And of course they were late . . . a studied discourtesy which Sassinak met with her own. When Gelory ushered them in with cool precision, Sassinak glanced up from a desk covered with datacards.

"Oh! Dear me, I lost track of time." She could see, behind the heavyworlders, Currald's flick of a grin: she *never* lost track of time. But she went on, smoothly and sweetly. "I'm so sorry, Captain Cruss — if you'll just take a seat — anywhere will do — and give me a moment to clear this." She turned back to her work, quickly organizing the apparent disarray, and tapping the screen before her with a control wand. Arly, by prearrangement, appeared in the doorway with a hardcopy file, and apologized profusely for interrupting.

"It's all right, Commander," said Sass. Arly's eyes widened at this sudden promotion in rank, but she had the good sense to ride with it. "Are those the current status reports? Good — if you'll relay these to Comm, and tell them to use the Blue codebook — and then ask the Chief Engineer to clear these variations, that will be all." She handed Arly a stack of datacards and the hardcopy that had just spit from her console. With a quick glance at the file Arly had handed her, she thumbed a control that opened a desk drawer, deposited it therein, and returned her attention to Cruss and his crew. "There, now. We've had so much message traffic, it's taken me this long to sort things out. Captain, I've spoken to you — and this is your crew —?"

Cruss introduced his crew with none of the overused, but filthy, epithets of the day before. They glowered, uniformly, and stank of more than Ireta. Sassinak wondered if their ship were really that short of sanitary facilities, or if they preferred to smell bad.

"May I see your ship's papers —" It was not really a request, not with the *Zaid-Dayan's* weaponry trained on the transport, and her marines on board. Cruss took a crumpled, stained folder out of the chest pocket of his shipsuit, and tossed it across the room. One of the marines turned to glare at him, and then glanced to Sassinak for guidance, but she did not react, merely picking up the distasteful object and opening it to read. "I'll also need your personal identification papers," she said. "Crew ratings — union memberships — if you'll hand those to Gelory —" They knew Gelory was a Weft; she could tell by the subtle withdrawal, as if they were afraid a Weft could harm them by skin touch. Sassinak went on reading.

According to the much-smudged (and probably faked) papers, transport and crew were on lease to Newholme, one of the shabbier commercial companies licensed by the Federation Colonial Service to set up colonies. Stamps from a dozen systems blotched the pages. Entry and exit from Sorrell-III, entry and exit from Bay Hill, entry and exit from Cabachon, Drissa, Zaduc, Pross . . . and Diplo. Destination a heavyworld colony two systems away, which Sassinak thought she recalled had reached its startup quota.

With hardly a sound, Gelory deposited the crew's individual papers on Sass' desk, murmuring "Captain," and drifting back to her place. Sassinak made no comment, and turned to these next, ignoring the squeaks and grunts of her furniture as the heavy-worlders shifted in bored insolence, as well as their sighs and muttered curses. With the heavyworlders safely installed in her office, Ford should soon have Varian and Kai — the co-leader she hadn't met — in his quarters nearby, where they could see the interview without being seen. Until then, she intended to pore over these papers as if they were rare gems.

Luckily they were about as she'd expected, justifying a long examination. Captain Cruss, it turned out, had no master's license — just a temporary permit from Diplo. He had been a master mate (and what kind of rank was *that*, Sassinak won-dered . . . she'd not seen that before) on an ore-hauler for eight years, and second mate on an asteroid-mining shuttle before that. Newholme had granted a temporary waiver of its usual requirements on the basis of Diplo's permit — that looked like a bribe.

First mate, senior pilot Zansa, on the other hand, had had a master's license and once worked for Cobai Chemicals — which implied that her master's license had been legitimate. But it was stamped "rescinded" in the odd orange ink that nothing could eradicate completely — and with a notation that Zansa had become addicted to bellefleur, a particularly dangerous drug for a ship captain. Sassinak looked up and found Zansa, who bore the characteristic facial scars of a bellefleur addict, though they were all pale and dry.

"I'm clean," the woman growled. "Been clean for five years, and next year I can retake the exams —"

"Shut *up*," said Cruss, savagely, and Zansa shrugged, clearly not intimidated. Sassinak went back to the papers. So . . . Zansa was the expert, and Cruss the cover — though she wondered why they hadn't found a legitimate master. Surely they could have done better than a recovering bellefleur addict.

Second pilot Hargit had had a checkered career, with rescinded visa stamps all over his records: charges and some convictions for petty theft, assault and battery, and "disturbance." That was from Charade, which usually had a pretty tolerant attitude towards disturbances. For the past five years, he'd piloted a cargo hauler between two heavyworlder planets, apparently without incident.

Lifesystems engineer Po was the largest of the five, a gross mass of flesh that escaped his shipsuit where the fastenings had strained from the cloth. He had a toothy grin that made Sassinak want to reach for a stunner — the kind of grin she remembered too well from her days as a slave. He had also been cashiered from the Diplo insystem space militia. She wondered how many of the hopeful colonists in cold sleep on the transport would have a chance to wake up with this . . . person . . . watching over their safety. He'd given up the fight to maintain traditional heavy-worlder fitness on shipboard, but Sassinak did not doubt his strength.

And last was the "helper," Roella. Her papers listed a variety of occupations, in space and on planet, including "entertainer" — which, for someone of her appearance, meant only one thing. She'd also been jailed twice, for "disrespect" — but that was on Courance, where unlike Charade they were very picky indeed.

Plenty of questions to ask, but nothing she wanted to pursue too far, not now. A light came up on her console; she ignored it, and went on reading, rolling the control wand in her fingers. If they were clever, these heavyworlders, they would realize what it was — a stun-wand, as well as a link to her computers. With their backgrounds, they'd all had intimate experience with a stun-wand, somewhere. She finished turning through Roella's ID packet, and sighed, as if deeply pained by all this. Then she looked up at the tense, angry faces across from her.

"Yes, yes, Captain Cruss," she said, pouring all the smoothness she could into her voice. "Your papers do seem to be in order, and one cannot fault your chivalry in diverting to investigate a distress call. . . ." What distress call? For they'd have had to receive it many light years away, the way they'd come. Of course they didn't know they'd been followed.

But Cruss was explaining, or trying to, that it had not been a normal distress call. Sassinak pushed her own thoughts aside to listen. A homing capsule, intended for the EEC compound ship which had dropped both the Ryxi colony and the exploration team. It had gone astray, somehow been damaged, and been found just beyond the orbit of the outermost planet of this system.

Not bloody likely, Sassinak thought grimly . . . it would be like someone in an aircraft happening to notice a single small bead on the end of the runway as they landed. Nothing that size could be detected in FTL flight, and it was more than a little unlikely that they'd come out of FTL on top of it by accident. She was surprised when Cruss stood up, and deposited the battered hunk of metal on her desk with insolent precision. So — that was his surprise — and he *had* a homing capsule, or part of it. Stripped of its propulsion unit and power pack, it was hardly recognizable. She refrained from touching it, noting only that engraved ID numbers were just visible along one pitted side.

She was not convinced of his story, even when he generously offered to let her extract the capsule's message from his computer, but she had no intention of arguing with him at this point. She doubted he knew that the Fleet computers had their own way with such capsules — and could extract more than a faked message implanted therein. But all that would come out at the trial. Now she smiled, graciously, and explained her reasons for confining them all to their ship, but with permission to trade for fresh foodstuffs with the locals. Cruss surged to his feet with another stale curse, and his companions followed. Sassinak sat quietly, relaxed: behind them the two Wefts had shifted to their own form, and clung to the angle of bulkhead and overhead. The marine escort was poised, hands hovering over weapons.

"I hope your water supplies are adequate," she said in the same conversational tone. "The local water is foul-tasting and smells." Cruss actually growled, a rumble of furious denial that he needed *anything* from her or anyone else. "Very well, then," she went on. "I'm positive you'll wish to continue on your way as soon as we have received clearance for you. The indigenes will have all the help we can give them. You may be sure of that." She stood, tapping the wand against her left palm, to watch them leave. Cruss made a motion towards the capsule, but Sassinak lowered the wand to forestall him.

"I think that had better remain," she said calmly. "Sector will wish to examine it —" His eyes shifted angrily. Guilty, she thought. What had they done to that thing? And where had it been sent? Surely not all the way to Diplo — at the sublight speed a capsule traveled, that would take years. His muscles bunched; Sassinak flicked a finger signal and the Wefts reassembled themselves beside him. He flinched, his expression shifting from barely controlled fury and contempt to alarm.

"Good day, Captain," she said easily, despite a mouth suddenly dry as the crisis passed. Of the others, only Zansa looked longingly toward the pile of personal documents on her desk — Sassinak avoided her eyes until she'd turned to leave.

As soon as the door slid shut, Sassinak relaxed back into her chair and turned it to face the video pickup. Ford quickly hooked their video into her screen, so that she could see them. Varian looked much better today: a vividly alive young woman who reminded Sassinak of herself, with those thick dark curls. But Varian's eyes were a clear gray, today untinged by the pain or stress that had clouded them the day before. Kai, on the other hand, looked nothing like an expedition leader. Slumped in his seat, pale, a padded suit protecting vulnerable skin . . . and his voice, when he spoke, revealed the strain even this much activity placed on him. He seemed harried, nervous — in a way more normal than Varian, for someone who'd been through a mutiny and forty-three years of cold sleep. Plus whatever had attacked him. She chatted with them, trying to assess Kai's condition and Varian's wits. Neither of them had any idea what the Thek presence meant although Kai told her about the existing cores, found before the mutiny. She was still digesting that when Kai turned formal, and asked if she considered her presence to be the relief of the expeditionary team.

"How could it?" she asked, meanwhile wondering why he'd give her such an opening. Did he *want* to be removed from command? Did he distrust his co-leader? Varian seemed as surprised by his question as Sassinak. Sassinak filled out her quick answer, explaining her understanding of their entirely legitimate position, and reminding them again of her willingness to give them any assistance. Varian accepted this happily, but Kai still seemed constrained. Either he was very sick still, from all that had happened, or something else was wrong. After she'd turned them over to

Ford, who would take Kai down to Sickbay for Mayerd's diagnostic unit to work on, and Varian to supply, she sat for awhile, frowning thoughtfully at the screen that had held their image.

She put the ID papers of both transport and crew in a sealed pouch, and stored it safely away for later examination. Dupaynil came in, with two Comm specialists, to take the homing capsule away. He asked if she wanted to watch them extract the message, but she shook her head. At the moment, she'd take a break from the day's craziness, and discuss the evening's menu with her favorite cook.

When the call came in from the survivors' geologist, one Dimenon, relayed through Comm, she collected the Iretan heavyworlders and the expedition co-leaders. Mayerd shepherded Kai, clearly unwilling to let such an interesting case out of her sight, and Ford brought Varian. Dimenon had had a good reason for contacting the cruiser — not only a video of twenty-three small Thek, but an interaction between them and the creature that had attacked Kai. Sassinak had already viewed the tape once, and now in the rerun watched Kai's reaction to these odd creatures — fringes, they called them. The man was positively terror struck as the fringes advanced on the Thek, his breathing labored and his skin color poor. He had not moved well, coming into her office, but she thought if a fringe appeared in real life he would somehow manage to run. Pity and disgust contended in her mind. Had he always been like this, or had events overcome him? What did Varian think? Sassinak glanced at her, and realized that she, too, was covertly watching him, her expression guarded.

Sassinak distracted Varian with a question about the fringes, and Mayerd, bless her perception, kept the conversation going thereafter . . . although Kai's answers, when he spoke, tended to cause a sudden rift. Then the Iretans began to ask their own questions, about the Thek, and their place in the Federation. Sass' opinion of Aygar's intelligence climbed another notch. He could think — and, it seemed in the next exchange, he even had a sense of humor. For when Sassinak asked him what weapon his people used against the fringes, he said, "We run," in a tone of rich irony.

A slight easing of tension, and the conversation continued:

fringes and their habits, the aquatic fringes the expedition had observed before the mutiny. Aygar was surprised by that . . . and Sassinak was just wondering how she could shift the conversation to the reptiloids when Varian, answering a question, mentioned the word. Dinosaurs. Fordeliton leaped on it with such eagerness that Sassinak half-expected Varian to recoil suspiciously. But apparently she thought it was natural for a grown man, a Fleet cruiser Executive Officer, to leap into an argument about whether anything resembling a true Old Earth dinosaur could have evolved in such a different world. Varian reeled off a string of names, Ford gaped, and then brought Aygar into it.

Sassinak let the excited exchange continue a minute or so, then put a halt to it with such pointed lack of interest for anything but the political situation that she knew they'd erupt again when her back was turned. So much the better. By the time she ushered the Iretans out, Varian and Kai had practically adopted Ford. She had no trouble persuading them to take all six of the short-listed specialists. . . . Varian, in fact, was openly gleeful.

She wondered if Mayerd had found out anything useful from Kai, besides the nature of his injuries and illness, but the medic had spent all her time on physical symptoms.

"It's no use asking why he's depressed and nervous until he's no longer in pain, feverish, and numb in places."

"I should think numbness preferable to pain," said Sassinak tartly. "How can he be both?"

Mayerd gave her a look which reminded her she hadn't eaten on time, and suggested they take a short break. "Eat a bit of that chocolate you keep hidden around here," she said. "And I'll have a cup of tea, and we'll all keep from biting our heads off, shall we?"

"Don't mother me, Mayerd. I'm not old and decrepit."

"No," said Mayerd shrewdly, "but you're about to meet a fourth generation ancestor who's years younger than you are, and for all you know a raving beauty who'll steal Ford's heart away and leave you withering in the blast of dead passions."

Sassinak whooped, and her tension dissolved in an instant. "You — That's ridiculous!"

"True, O Captain. So are some other people. Done grieving for Huron yet, or are you still feeling so guilty you can't enjoy your many admirers?"

"You're making me blush. None of your business, I'd say, except it is, since you're my physician. Well, yes, I have enjoyed normal — or at least pleasurable — involvement in the last few weeks."

"Good. About time. That boy Tim's in awe of you, by the way, so I hope you're going to let him back into your good graces sometime."

"Already done, fairy godmother, so let me be."

"Back to Kai, then. The toxin destroyed nerve tissue, so he's got sensory deprivation on some areas of skin — nasty, because he doesn't know when he's hurt himself. Where the tissue's not destroyed, it's stimulated — just like pain, but the brain can't register constant stimulus like that, so he just gets these odd stabs and twinges, and a general feeling of something very wrong, very deep. His blood count's off, which probably causes the exhaustion you noticed, and he's not sleeping well, which doesn't help. I offered to slap him in one of the big tanks, and let him sleep it off until we got him to Sector, but he refused. Which, in this case, took considerable guts, despite that display while you ran the tape."

"Umm. It bothered me, particularly in someone in his position."

"That Varian's got enough bounce for two," said Mayerd; Sassinak could detect the faintest trace of distaste, and knew that Mayerd would always prefer a patient to a patient's healthy friend. With that in mind, she suggested that Mayerd visit the survivors that afternoon, when the diagnostic unit had finished meditating over Kai's condition.

"I'd already thought of that. They'll need clothes . . . you *were* planning a formal dinner, weren't you?"

"To show off, yes." Sassinak chuckled. "You mindreader: people will think you're a Weft if you keep that up. Raid my closet, if you need anything I've got — there's a red dress that might suit Varian."

"I've got a green that will be perfect for Lunzie," said Mayerd smugly. "And all Kai's measurements, so I've already located something for him."

By the time Mayerd stopped by to show Sassinak what she'd chosen, on her way to the sled, the stewards were giving Sassinak sideways looks that meant they'd like her to clear out so they could set up for dinner. She had elected to serve in her office, a more intimate setting than the officers' mess.

"I'm going, I'm going," she said, grinning at the cook as he came to survey the room's layout, with an eye to planning service. She stopped by the bridge, where everything seemed to be under control, and discovered that most of them knew about her ancestress . . . after all, she hadn't told Ford or the others to keep it a secret. She worked through the day's reports, noting replies to some queries back to Sector, and some pending — she'd hoped to have more information for Kai and Varian tonight, but apparently not. Something might come in any time, of course. Finally Arly caught her attention and pointed to the clock. Time to be getting ready — but she'd cleared most of her work, and would start the morrow only slightly behind.

As she went to her cabin to clean up, she found she could not quite analyze her emotions. Lunzie . . . another Lunzie. No, not another Lunzie, but *the* Lunzie. That hardly seemed fair to her little sister — but then nothing had been. She wouldn't think about that, she told herself, and poured another dollop of shampoo on her hair. Thank the gods that the cruiser didn't have to use Iretan water!

But what would she be like? What *could* she be like? More like someone her elapsed age, or more like an old lady . . . a very, *very* old lady? She had the file holo . . . but that told her little. Her own file holo, the still one, didn't tell a viewer that much. Movement was so much of a person — she thought of this, wringing out her hair, and flipping it into a towel with easy practiced gestures. No two people even bathed alike, dried themselves alike . . . and what if her ancestress turned out to be prudish about sex? That thought brought a blush to her cheeks. She looked at herself in the mirror, thinking of Mayerd's teasing remarks. What if she *wasn't* . . . what if she had Sass' own casual attitude . . . and after all Ford *was* very good looking. No. Ridiculous. Here she hadn't even met her, and already she was thinking of *that* kind of rivalry with her great-great-great-grandmother?

Besides, Mayerd would be back before then, and could tell her — if she would, because doctors did stick together — and would it be worse, Sassinak asked herself suddenly, to lose a family because of long cold sleep, as Lunzie had certainly done, or gain one because someone down the line was alive when you awoke? She eased into the long black slip that fit under her formal evening dress uniform, and began assembling it: the black gown, skirt glittering with tiny stars, and the formal honors winking on the left breast of the bodice. Somehow the formals, jeweled as they were, seemed more remote from the events that earned them than the full-sized medals that jingled softly on a white-dress suit. This was the first time she'd pinned the formal rank jewels of commander on the shoulders; the last time she'd worn this outfit, she'd been a lieutenant commander at Sector Headquarters, on duty at a diplomatic ball. The long, close-fitting black sleeves were ringed with gold: the captain of the ship, even in evening dress.

A last look — the merest touch of color on her lips — and she was ready. The proper twenty minutes before the guests would arrive, and there was Mayerd, also ready, and Ford. They grinned at each other, and Sassinak resisted the temptation to check on her office. Ford would have done it. She congratulated Ford on the increased "coverage" of his chest . . . he had picked up more than a few impressive medals, in the years since she'd seen him last. Mayerd wore her Science Union badge, and the little gold pin that meant honor graduate of the best medical school in the human worlds. They chatted idly, waiting at the head of the ramp, and Sassinak was very aware that both were watching her closely, to catch her reaction to Lunzie. They'd said nothing except that her relative would "suit" her.

"There it is —" Ford gestured, and Sassinak caught a moving gleam in the darkness. Hard to see which was which, with so many bits of light shifting around, but Ford, as usual, was right. A four-seater airsled settled gently near the foot of the ramp, and the honor guard jogged out into place. Sassinak wondered, suddenly, if she should have gone quite this far without warning them . . . civilians, after all . . . but they seemed to understand what the shrill piping whistle meant. And the crisp ruffle of drums.

Varian and Lunzie, long skirts swirling in the wind, led the way up the ramp and past a rigid honor guard. Sassinak could tell they were impressed, though she had trouble keeping her eyes off Lunzie's face: she hadn't wanted to stare like that since she was a first-year cadet. Instead, she pulled herself up and saluted: appropriate to the planetary governor and her staff, but they'd all know it was for Lunzie. Varian gave a quick dip of the head, like a nervous bird, but Lunzie drawled a response to her greeting and offered a firm handshake.

For a long moment they stood almost motionless, then Lunzie retrieved her hand, and Sassinak felt a bubble of delight overcoming the last bit of concern. She would have liked this woman even if she hadn't been a triple great-grandmother — and she'd *have* to find an easier way to say all that. They had too much to say to each other! She grinned, cocking her head, and Lunzie's response was too quick to be an attempt to mimic — it was *her* natural gesture, too.

From there, the evening went quickly from delight to legend. Whatever chemistry went into the food, the drink, and the companionship combined into a heady brew that had Lunzie making puns, and Sassinak reciting long sequences of Kipling's verse. She noticed, as she finished a rousing version of "L'Envoi" that Lunzie had a speculative expression, almost wary. On reflection, perhaps she shouldn't have accented "They travel fastest who travel *alone*" quite so heavily, not when meeting the only member of her family she'd seen since Myriad. She grinned at Lunzie, and raised her glass.

"It's kind of a Fleet motto," she said. "Convince the youngsters that they have to cut free from home if they want to wander the stars. . . ."

Lunzie's answering smile didn't cover the sadness in her eyes. "And your family, Sassinak? Where were you brought up?"

It had never occurred to her that Lunzie wouldn't know the story. She felt rather than saw Ford's sudden stiffness, Mayerd's abrupt pause in lifting a forkful to her mouth. No one had asked in years, now: Fleet knew, and Fleet was her family. Sassinak regained control of her breathing, but Lunzie had noticed; the eyes showed it.

"My family were killed," she said, in as neutral a voice as she could manage. "In a slaver raid. I . . . was captured."

Varian opened her mouth, but Kai laid a hand on hers and she said nothing. Lunzie nodded without breaking their gaze.

"They'd be proud of you," she said, in a voice with no edges. "I am."

Sassinak almost lost control again . . . the audacity of it, the gall . . . and then the love that shone so steadfastly from those quiet eyes.

"Thank you, great-great-great-grandmother," she said. A pause followed, then Ford leaped in with an outrageous story about Sassinak as a young officer on the prize vessel. The others followed with their own wild tales, obviously intent on covering up the awkwardness while Sassinak regained her equanimity. Mayerd and Lunzie knew the same hilarious dirty rhyme from medical school, and rendered it in a nasal accent that had them all in stitches. Varian brought up incidents from veterinary school, equally raunchy, and Kai let them know that geologists had their own brand of humor.

As they lingered over their liqueurs, the talk turned to the reports Kai and Varian had filed on the mutiny. Sassinak noticed that Kai had not only moved better, coming up the ramp, but seemed much less tense, much more capable, during dinner. Now he described the details of the mutiny in crisp, concise sentences. Mayerd had said she'd begun a specific treatment for him, but had it really worked this fast? Or had something else happened to restore his confidence?

They were interrupted by Lieutenant Borander, who was still, to Sass' eyes, far too nervous in the presence of high rank. But his news was riveting: the heavyworlder transport had tried to open communications with the Iretan settlement, and had not received an answer. Sassinak's party mood evaporated faster than alcohol in sunlight, and she noticed that the others were as sober-faced as she was. Lunzie pointed out that they had nothing to answer with — no comm units could last forty-three years in the open in this climate. But Aygar, Ford said, had not asked for communications equipment. Yet, when they all thought about it, the Iretans had been in contact with the transport before it landed. How?

"On what frequency was Cruss broadcasting?" asked Kai. Sassinak looked at him: whatever had happened, he was clearheaded and alert now. Borander answered him and Kai gave a wicked grin. "That was our frequency, Commander Sassinak . . . the one we used before the mutiny."

"Interesting. How could he have learned that from the supposed message in the damaged homing capsule? It doesn't mention any frequencies. He's well and truly used enough rope. . . ." She called in Dupaynil, after a little more discussion, and the party broke up. Sassinak wished they'd had just a little longer to enjoy the festive occasion. But the time for long dresses and fancy honors was over — an hour later she was back in working uniform.

✧ CHAPTER EIGHTEEN

The next morning, after several hours in conference with her supply officers, she began allocating spares and replacement supplies to the Iretans and the expedition survivors. Surely Sector would order them back to report, rather than expecting them to finish the usual cruise — and that meant they could spare all this. She put her code on the requisitions, and went back to lean on Comm again. Better than brooding about Lunzie — the more she thought about that, the more unsettled she felt. The woman was younger, not older — apparently a fine doctor, certainly an interesting dinner companion, but she could not feel the awe she wanted to feel. Lunzie might have been one of her younger officers, someone she could tease gently. And yet this "youngster" had a right to ask things that Sassinak didn't want to recall. She knew, by the look in Lunzie's eyes, that she would ask: she would want to know about Sassinak's childhood, what had happened.

She saw a crewman flinch from her expression, and realized her thoughts had control of her face again. This would never do. She wondered if Lunzie felt the same tangle of feelings. If she thought her ancestress should somehow be older, in experience, perhaps Lunzie felt that Sassinak should be younger. And yet she'd had that jolt of sympathy, that instant feeling of recognition, of kinship. They'd be able to work their way through the tangle somehow. They had to. For the first time since her capture, Sassinak felt a longing for something outside Fleet. Perhaps she shouldn't have avoided her family all these years. It might not have been so bad, and certainly Lunzie wasn't the stuff of nightmares.

She caught herself grinning as she remembered Mayerd's tart comments. No, Lunzie wasn't a raving beauty — though she wasn't exactly plain either, at least not in that green dress, and she had the warm personality which could draw attention when she wanted it. And Lunzie approved of her, at least so far. It will work out, she thought again, fiercely. I'm not going to lose her without at least trying. Trying what, she could hardly have said.

From this musing, the alarm roused her to instant alertness. Now what? Now, it seemed, the Thek were appearing, and demanding that the expedition leaders be brought to the landing site.

"Ford, take the pinnace," said Sassinak, ignoring Timran's eager upward glance. She had finally let him take an airsled on one of the supply runs, and he'd managed to drop one crate on its corner and spew the contents all over the landing area. One disk-reader landed on an Iretan's foot, creating another diplomatic crisis (fortunately brief: they were barely willing to acknowledge pain, which made it hard to claim injury), and Tim was grounded again.

While the pinnace was on its way, she tried to guess what the Thek were up to this time. They'd been acting like ephemerals, in the past few days, whizzing from place to place, digging up cores, and, unusual for Thek, chattering with humans. Then the Thek appeared above the landing grid.

"Large targets," said Arly, her fingers nervously flicking the edges of her control panel. They were, in fact, the largest Thek Sassinak had ever seen.

"They're friendly," she said, wishing she was entirely sure of that. She had enough to explain to the admiral now, without a Thek/human row.

"Are they coming to see us, or that co-leader fellow?"

"Or them?" Sassinak pointed to the main screen, showing two of the largest Thek descending near the heavyworlder transport. "Umm. Let's treat it as diplomatic: Major Currald, let's have a formal reception out there, and," she turned, quickly pointing at officers with the most experience in working with aliens, "you and you, and — yes, you. We'll assume a delegation's coming, and since we represent FSP here, they'll come to us."

By the time she reached Troop Deck and the landing ramp, two of the smallest Thek had planted themselves on the grid nearby. Around the bulge of the *Zaid-Dayan*, she could see a section of the pinnace as Ford landed it.

But the Thek appeared to be far more interested in Kai than in the cruiser's welcoming committee. One of them actually greeted him, in recognizable if strained speech. Sassinak motioned her officers to silence and did not interrupt. Whatever was going on, she'd find out more by going along with the Thek plan.

The Thek offered a core to Kai for examination; he gave the coordinates of its original location. Thunder rumbled underfoot: Sassinak noticed nothing in the sky. Theks talking to Theks? Sassinak glanced at each of them in turn: the immense ones and a medium-huge one near the heavyworlder colony ship, the medium-large and relatively smaller ones nearby. After a moment's silence, Sassinak leaned forward.

"Kai, ask if this planet is claimed by Thek." Although she spoke as softly as she could, the Thek answered instantly.

"Verifying." Then, a moment later, "Dismiss. Will contact."

Kai turned to Sassinak, a look between respect, frustration, and annoyance. Well, she had intruded on his private conversation. She shrugged, and tried to lighten the mood.

"Dismissed, are we?"

Apparently that worked, for she could see his lips twitching with controlled laughter. Ford gave her a fast wink, then smoothed his face into utter blandness as Kai looked at him. What had Ford been up to with the co-leader? The wink told her only that he'd have a good story to tell later . . . and she'd have to wait to hear it. In the meantime, she dismissed the honor guard, who departed cursing quietly at having been put into the tight-collared formal uniform in this heat if it wasn't really necessary, and invited Kai up for a visit.

He certainly looked better today, far more the sort of vigorous, outgoing young geologist who had been chosen co-leader with Varian. For a moment she wondered if he and Varian had ever paired up — and if so, why they weren't paired now.

But the real question was what the Thek were doing on Ireta. So many Thek on one supposedly unclaimed planet was as great a mystery as anything else. Kai ventured hardly any explanation, beyond saying that perhaps the Thek were "worried." Sassinak wondered if that was really all he thought, or all he thought he should say. She had no reason to hide her chain of logic from him, and went on to explain, watching closely for his reaction.

"A convocation of such size surely suggests a high degree of interest, Kai. And that old core — that was the same core which brought Tor?" He nodded, and she went on. "All those little Thek sucking up old cores — when they weren't frying fringes . . . you see my point, surely. Your EEC ship's records, and Fleet records, both list Ireta as unexplored. Yet you found Thek relics and the first Thek on scene appeared surprised at them. Doesn't that suggest a missing link in the famous Thek chain of information? Something happened, here on Ireta, to one or more Theks, which somehow did not transmit to the others?"

Kai followed her argument but his expression settled on anxiety rather than relief. "The old core is of Thek manufacture," he said almost reluctantly. "Unquestionably it's generated Thek interest. But I can't see why. . . ."

Sassinak felt a moment's impatience. The scientists always wanted to know why, before they halfway understood exactly what had happened. Or so it seemed to her. She was glad enough to put events in order, sure she had all the relevant parts, before worrying about why and what if. She let Kai and her officers go on talking, wandering their own logical or illogical paths through Thek behavior, the geology of Ireta, and the probable age of the core in question.

A light flashed on her console: message from the bridge. She thumbed the control on her earplug. "Sir, all those little Thek have landed near the original expedition campsite. . . ."

With two key punches, she had that up on one of the screens and the scene stopped Kai in mid-sentence.

"Every fringe on Ireta is homing in on our campsite," he said, his expression anxious.

It took her a moment to realize what he meant: the heat exuded by so many Thek would inevitably attract fringes, just as one Thek had attracted the fringe that had attacked Kai. Before she could think of something to reassure him, the screen showed new Thek activity as a score or more spun away crazily into the sky and offscreen. Now what were they doing? Kai looked as confused as she felt.

By this time, Sassinak felt the need of refreshment and, noticing that Kai looked a little wan, she invited him into the officers' mess. A few deft comments from her and Kai, and Anstel and Pendelman were into a lively discussion of Iretan geology with excursions into evolutionary biology. Sassinak listened politely enough, but with the internal feeling of the adult listening to eight-year-olds discussing the merits of competing toys. At least they were busy and happy, and if they stayed out of trouble, she might get some work done.

Varian's arrival added another bit of fizz to the meeting, so that Sassinak had no need to keep up any corner of the conversation. Relaxed, she let herself think about the Thek from a Fleet perspective. If the data relays had all worked correctly — and she knew whose heads would roll if they hadn't — they'd gathered more information about Thek in flight and landing today than Fleet had anywhere in its files.

Her technical specialists, now busily talking hyracotheriums and golden fliers with Varian, had already taken discreet samples of the landing grid and the plateau face. Those data, along with the observations of the large Thek sinking into the landing grid, should reveal more about the way Thek handled heat dispersion.

Varian broke into her musings with the kind of question a planetary governor ought to ask, Sassinak noted. Were the Thek known to be interested in planet piracy? Were they indeed? She wished she knew.

The meeting broke up shortly after that, with Anstel now in the role of one of the "science officers" accompanying Varian and Kai. The rest of that day, Sassinak spent composing messages for Sector Headquarters, and poring over the first, incomplete replies to her queries. Fleet had to be informed that the Thek were there, and rather than be bombarded by stupid questions when she was likely to be busy, better that they be supplied with some sort of explanation . . . but the admiral would want all the data. In order.

Her original signals, asking for clarification of *Mazer Star's* status, the Ryxi colony's status, and so on, had of necessity been brief. The incoming stack in her official file had its own priorities. Only one item surprised her, and that was "predominant owner" of the company holding title to the heavyworlder transport: Paraden.

She thought of the pale-eyed, red-headed young man who had tried to get her in such trouble in the Academy, and of Luisa Paraden's connection (of sorts) to the slaver she and Huron had captured. This time it was Arisia Paraden Styles-Hobart, holding fifty-three percent, and not on the board of directors at all . . . but Fleet had been able to discover that she was active in the company . . . or at least A. P. Hobart, whose ID for tax purposes was the same, was the "Assistant Director of Employee Assignment." Handy, if you wanted to hire a crooked man to captain your crooked ship.

She wondered where Randolph Neil Paraden had ended up: somewhere in Newholme? The treasurer or something? Surely not; Fleet would have noticed that, too. The good news was that *ARCT-10* had shown up — or at least its message to Sector HQ had arrived. Severe damage from a cosmic storm (Sassinak quirked her lips: "investigating a cosmic storm" was a stupid sort of civilian idea. Space had enough hazards when you tried to play it safe), some (unlisted) casualties, but "no great loss of life." Whatever that meant to a ship the size of most moons, with a normal shipboard population in the thousands in a variety of races.

They'd lost their FTL capability, and most of their communications, and spent nearly all the elapsed time hobbling toward a nearby system at well below lightspeed. No real hardship for those who lived their lifetimes on board anyway, but it must have been tough on the "temporary" specialists who'd expected to be home in six months.

And, of course, for the ones left behind on Ireta. Sassinak's hand hesitated on the console. Should she call Kai now, or wait until tomorrow? She glanced at the time, and decided to wait. They'd be getting ready for that gathering she'd heard about, and perhaps by morning she'd have a list of casualties so that he could quit worrying (or start mourning) his family. And those children — their parents on the ship would be old, or dead, by now. She could and did call up *Mazer Star* to confirm that she'd received Fleet clearance for them.

"And you should receive some kind of official recognition," she told Godheir. "There's a category for civilian assistance. Depending on the tribunal outcome, it might even mean a cash bonus for you and your crew; certainly I'll recommend it."

"Ye don't have to do that, Commander Sassinak. . . ." Captain Godheir's screen image looked appropriately embarrassed.

"No, but you deserve it. Not just for your quick response, although it's in everyone's interest to encourage honest citizens to respond to mayday calls, but for your continued willingness to help the expedition. I know you aren't designed to deal with youngsters recovering from that kind of trauma. And I know you and your crew have spent a lot of hours with them."

"Well, they're good kids, after all, and it's not their fault. And no family with them."

"Yes, well, I expect, with the Thek here, this will wrap up shortly, and you'll be free to go. But you have my gratitude for your help."

"I'm just glad you weren't the pirate I thought you at first," said Godheir, rubbing his head. "When you hailed us, that's all I could think of."

Sassinak grinned at him; she could imagine that having something like the *Zaid-Dayan* suddenly pop up behind him could have startled a peaceful transport captain. "I was just as glad to find that you weren't an armed slaver escort. Oh, by the way, do you have as many dinosaur buffs as I seem to have brought along?"

"A few, yes. They're convening at the main camp tonight, along with some of yours, I think."

"That's what I thought."

His expression asked if she had a problem with that, and she didn't, except to wonder if fanning the flames of the dinosaur enthusiasts had been such a good idea.

"I don't expect any trouble from Captain Cruss, with the Thek nearby, but still —"

"I'm taking precautions, Commander," he said quickly, not quite offended at her presumption. Sassinak nodded, glad he'd taken the hint, and willing to have him a little huffy with her. Better that than trouble in the night.

"I assumed you had, Captain Godheir," she said. "But so many things aren't going according to Regulations already. . . ." He smiled, again relaxed.

"Right you are, and we'll be buttoned up tight. I'll tell my crew not to overdo the hospitality juice, whatever it is and wherever it comes from."

Dupaynil was waving at her from the corridor; Sassinak signed off, and turned to him.

"Captain, we got the homing capsule stripped," he said happily. "And a fine bit of imaginative writing that was, let me tell you. Imaginative wiring, too. We're still doing forensics on it. We've got surface deposit/erosion scans going, another seven hours on that, and there's a new technique for analyzing bio-chemical residues, but basically we've got Cruss and Co. in a locked cell right now."

"In order?" suggested Sassinak. Dupaynil nodded, and laid it all out for her.

"A fake, of course: a clever one, but a fake. First the homing capsule itself, which clearly shows the pitting and scarring one would expect from some four decades of space travel. Except where the propulsion unit and so on were removed — not by natural causes, either, but by tools available to any civilized world. Then roughed up to a pretense of the distressed natural surface."

"Which tells you that the homing capsule went somewhere, then was broken apart, and returned —"

"Probably with Cruss in his ship, although not certainly. It might have been placed for him to find. Now the message . . . the message was clever, very clever. Ostensibly, it's the message Cruss told you, the one he let us 'copy' from his computer. It's not a long message, and it repeats six times."

Dupaynil cocked his head, giving Sassinak the clear impression that he wanted her to guess what followed. "And then another message?" she prompted. "On the loop behind those?"

"Precisely. I was sure the Commander would anticipate. Yes, after six boring repetitions, which any ordinary rescuer must have assumed would go on until the end, we found a sixty-second delay — presumably the number of repetitions coded the length of the following delay — and then the real message. The location of Ireta; the genetic data of the surviving heavyworlders, includ-ing the planned breedings for several generations; a brief account of the local biology and geology; a list of special supplies needed; a recommendation for founding colony size. There are, as you would expect, no destination codes remaining. We cannot prove, from the message alone, who were its intended recipients. For that we await the physical evidence of the shell; it is just possible that its travels are, in a way, etched on its surface. But what they sent was an open invitation: this is who we are, where we are, and what we have. Come join us."

Sassinak could think of no adequate comment. Proof indeed that the mutineers were intentional planet pirates. She took a long breath and let it out. Then: "Are you sure they intended it for heavyworlders exclusively?"

"Oh, yes. The genetic types they asked for all code that way. Besides, I've now got the old Security data on the mutineers. Look, Separationists, but not Purists. All of them, at one time or another, were in one of two political or religious movements."

"And no one spotted this beforehand?" She felt a rumble of anger that no one had noticed, and therefore people had died, and others had lost over forty years of their lives.

Dupaynil shrugged eloquently. "Exploration ships do not welcome Security, especially not Fleet Security. They insist that their specialists must have the freedom to investigate, to think for themselves. Of course I am not against that, but it makes it very hard to prevent the 'chance' connivance of those whose associations cause trouble."

"Umm. I expect that Kai and Varian will visit again tomorrow, Dupaynil, and I would prefer to withhold this until we have the physical data — or until something else happens. At the rate things are going wild, something else may indeed make disclosure necessary."

"I understand. When you're ready for me to arrive with the discovery, just let me know." He gave her a very Gallic wink, and withdrew to continue his investigations.

The next morning, Sassinak was glad that she had made it to bed at a reasonable hour: the Thek abruptly summoned her, Kai, Varian, and, to her surprise, the Iretans and Captain Cruss. She sent Ford with the pinnace to pick up the governors and Lunzie and recall any crew from the campsite.

Meanwhile, the outside pickups revealed that the Thek which had been positioned near cruiser and transport were now grouped at the far end of the landing grid. Sassinak studied the screen for a few moments, and turned away, baffled. What were they doing?

She ate breakfast and changed into a dress uniform without expressing any such confusion to the crew, though their bafflement was apparent to her. Halfway through a glass of porssfruit juice, something tickled her memory about Thek.

She'd seen something like this . . . it came back in a rush. The dead world, the time she had gone down with a landing party, and the Thek had come. First a few had clustered like that, and then others had come and clumped into some kind of structure.

She'd forgotten about it for years, because of that mess with Achael, but . . . "cathedral" was what someone had termed it, the special conference mode of the Thek. To which she was bidden.

Despite herself, Sassinak shivered, remembering that folk involved in a Thek conference often found themselves extremely obedient servants of its determinations. She promptly initiated a Discipline procedure so that she would remember *all* that transpired during that unique experience. Then grinned to herself. This could make a riveting recital the next time she needed something to enliven a dull evening at the Sector HQ Officers' Club.

While she and most of the other "invited" guests went willingly through the one opening left by Theks fitting themselves into the immense structure, Captain Cruss did not. His boots dug grooves in the ground to show his unwillingness but inexorably he was brought into the cathedral and the last Thek clunked into place. Oddly enough, a curious ambient light provided illumination. Sassinak caught Aygar's contemptuous look and turned away, only then noticing the collection of porous shards, a dull dark charcoal gray rather than the usual Thek obsidian, but patently a nearly disassembled Thek.

"Your core evidently bore strange fruit," she said to Kai, keeping her voice low. "And if that is indeed a very ancient Thek, we ephemerals will have to revise some favorite theories . . . and some good jokes."

"Commander," Cruss cried, his heavy voice reverberating so loudly the others winced, "I demand an explanation of the outrageous treatment to which I have been subjected."

"Don't be stupid, Cruss," Sassinak said, pivoting to him. "You know perfectly well the Thek are a law unto themselves. And you are now subject to that law, and about to sample its justice."

"We have verified." The words, intoned in a nondirectional voice, opened the conference. "Ireta is for Thek as it has been for hundreds of millions of years. It will remain Thek. For these reasons . . ."

With no apparent passage of time, Sassinak found herself leaning against Aygar. She needed to: she felt every second of her age in the steamy Iretan midday with its blazing sun beating down on them. Aygar clung to her for a moment more, obviously experiencing a similar disorientation. In the touch of his strong hands, she sensed that his earlier contempt for her had lessened. When he came out of his current shock, she expected he'd be a much more pleasant fellow.

Someone groaned. Sassinak blinked her eyes clear and saw Varian holding Kai upright. Cruss crouched on the ground in such an attitude of dejection that she could almost pity him. Almost, not quite.

In the meantime, she had had her orders. She had to get her marines, Weft and human, off that transport before Cruss woke up and lifted it offworld. Innocent or not, anyone on board at lift-off would have only one destination. That, the Thek had made quite clear. Trying to shake off the aftereffects of that extraordinary experience and access the Discipline-retained memories, she let Ford and Lunzie shepherd them into the pinnace for the short hop back to the cruiser. But she couldn't organize her thoughts beyond responding to the implanted instructions.

Once in her quarters she gave the necessary orders and then paused to catch her breath. The Thek had somehow compressed the very air inside their cathedral, enervating to the humans, and what she'd really have liked was a long quiet stretch of solitary meditation, to regain her own sense of space.

Half-bemused, and half-annoyed, she noticed that Lunzie was not so patient. Her great-great-great prodded Ford into finding her liquor cabinet, poured drinks for everyone, and offered a toast "To the survivors!"

Sassinak drank, thinking to herself that Lunzie must have enjoyed that Sverulan brandy as much as it deserved, to be so eager to find more. Prior to the conference, Lunzie had buffered Kai and Varian and now she snapped them out of it. They burst into speech, and stopped as their voices clashed.

Sassinak chuckled. "Cruss took quite a beating." Gingerly she touched her temples where a massive headache was gathering. "We all did."

"Despite our clear consciences and pure hearts," Varian added with a sly grin at Lunzie.

Sassinak depressed the comm unit button. "Pendelman, request Lieutenant Commander Dupaynil to join us. And didn't we just get exactly the information we needed. Cruss spilled his guts. Not that I blame him."

"Then you know who's behind the piracy?" Lunzie asked, excited.

"Oh, yes. I'll wait until Dupaynil gets here. Kai and Varian have been covered with glory, too. Which is only fair."

Kai took up the narrative then, explaining that they had rescued a Thek who had been trapped for eons and buried so deeply it had been unable to summon help. Originally Ireta had been earmarked as a feeding ground with its rich transuranics so satisfying to Thek appetites, hence the cores. The Thek Ger had been guardian, to make certain young Thek did not strip the planet of its riches and leave it a barren husk.

"The Thek are the *Others*," Lunzie gasped.

"That is the inescapable conclusion," Sassinak agreed. "Thek are nothing if not logical. We were also exposed to quite a hunk of Thek history. I'll joggle the rest out of my head later. The relevant fact is that it became apparent to the Thek after a millennium of gorging that, if they couldn't curtail their appetites, they ran the risk of eating themselves out of the galaxy."

"No wonder they had an affinity for dinosaurs," Fordeliton exclaimed with a whoop of laughter.

"We get to preserve them now," Varian said, rather proudly.

Kai grinned shyly. "Ireta is restricted, of course, as far as transuranics go but I, and my 'ilk,' as they put it, have the right to mine anything up to the transuranics for . . . is it as long as 'we' live? I'm not sure if the limit is just for *my* lifetime."

"No," said Lunzie. "By ilk, the Thek probably mean the ARCT-10, for as long as it survives. You deserve it, Kai. You really do."

"Curiously enough," Sassinak said into the respectful pause that followed, "the Thek did appreciate the fact that you all have lost irreplaceable time. Thek justice is unusual."

Thek had lumped all humans — the timelagged, the survivors, and the descendants — in one group as survivors. They could remain or leave as they chose.

"I wonder if some of the Iretans might consider enlisting in the Fleet," Sassinak mused, thinking of Aygar. "Wefts are excellent guards but Ireta produced some superb physical types. Ford, do see if we can recruit a few."

"And the surviving member of the original heavyworlder contingent?" Lunzie asked.

"Mutiny cannot be excused, or the mutineer exonerated," Sassinak answered, her expression stern. "He is to be taken back to Sector Headquarters to stand trial. The Thek were as adamant on that score as I am."

"And Cruss is being sent back?" Ford asked.

Sassinak steepled her fingers, permitting herself a satisfied smile. "Not only sent back but earthed for good. Neither he, his crew, nor any of the passengers will ever leave their planet. Nor will that transport lift again."

"The Thek do nothing by halves, do they?"

"They have been exercised, if you can imagine a Thek agitated," Sassinak went on, getting to the real meat of the cathedral's findings, "about the planetary piracies and patiently waiting for *us* to do something constructive about the problem. The intended rape of Ireta has forced them, with deep regret, to interfere." Just then, Dupaynil entered. "On cue, for I have good news for you, Commander. Names, only one of which was familiar to me." She beckoned the Intelligence Officer to take a seat as she leaned forward to type information on the terminal. "Parchandri is so conveniently placed for this sort of operation. . . ."

"Inspector General Parchandri?" Fordeliton exclaimed shocked.

"The same."

Lunzie chuckled cynically. "It makes sense to have a conspirator placed high in Exploratory, Evaluation, and Colonization. He'd know exactly which planetary plums were ready to be plucked."

Kai and Varian regarded her with stunned expressions.

"Who else, Sassinak?" Lunzie asked.

She looked up from the visual display with a smug smile. "The Sek of Formalhaut, Aidkisaga IX, is a Federation Councillor of Internal Affairs." She noticed Lunzie's startled reaction but went on when she saw Lunzie close her lips tightly. "One now understands just how his private fortune was accrued. Lutpostig appears to be the Governor of Diplo, a heavyworlder planet. How convenient! Paraden, it will not surprise you to discover, owns the company which supplied the grounded transport ship."

"We could never have counted on uncovering duplicity at that level, Commander," was Dupaynil's quiet assessment. He frowned slightly. "It strikes me as highly unusual for a man at Cruss' level to know such names."

"He didn't," Sassinak replied equably. "He was only vaguely aware that Commissioner Paraden was involved. The Thek extrapolated from what he could tell them of recruitment procedures, suppliers, and what they evidently extracted from the transport's data banks."

"But how can we use the information they obtained?" Dupaynil asked.

"With great caution, equal duplicity and superior cunning, Commander, and undoubtedly some long and ardent discussions with the Sector Intelligence Bureau. Fortunately, for my hypersuspicious nature, I've known Admiral Coromell for years and trust him implicitly. . . ."

"*You* know Admiral Coromell?" Lunzie asked, amazed.

"We are in the same Fleet, dear ancestress. And knowing where to look for one's culprits is more than half the battle, even those so highly placed." Sassinak saw her thoughtful look and went on briskly. "I have been given sailing orders, too. So, Fordeliton, brush up on your eloquence and see whom you can recruit from among the Iretans. Kai, Varian, Lunzie, I'll have Borander return you to your camp with any supplies you might need to tide you over until the *ARCT-10* arrives. Just one more thing . . ." and she swiveled her chair about, turning to the rank of cabinets behind her and opening one with a thumblock. She heard Lunzie's sigh of satisfaction as the squatty little brandy bottles came into view.

"Clean glasses, Ford — I've a toast to propose." And when all stood with their glasses ready, she expanded Lunzie's brief presentation: "To the brave, ingenious, and honored survivors of this planet . . . including the dinosaurs."

That got a smile from all of them, and a chuckle as the smooth brandy slid down. Revived by the brandy's kick, Kai and Varian rose, eager to get back to their camp. The Thek decision had given them both a lot to look forward to, and plenty of work.

"Kai, Varian, you go on without me," Lunzie said, surprising the co-leaders but not Sassinak. "I'd like a little while longer with this relative of mine." She turned to Sassinak, a bit shy and stiff suddenly.

In the flurry of parting, Sassinak rather hoped she knew what might be coming. After all, Varian would have her animals to study; Kai would have his minerals to mine . . . what would Lunzie have? Nothing. She'd be picked up by the *ARCT-10*; she'd try to find a recertification course to bring her up to date in medicine, and then she'd hire out for something else. Not the sort of life Sassinak would want. Even if she'd been a doctor.

"Let's eat here," she said, as Kai and Varian, escorted by Ford, went off down the corridor. "It's an awkward time for them in the messhall, right between shifts."

"Oh. Fine." Lunzie wandered around the office as Sassinak ordered the meal, looking at the pictures and the crystal fish.

"That's my favorite," said Sassinak of the fish. "After the desk. This thing is my great hunk of self-indulgence."

"Doesn't seem to have hurt you much," said Lunzie, with a bite to it.

Sassinak laughed. "I saw it fifteen years ago, saved for seven years. The place makes them one at a time and won't start one on credit. They spent two years building it, and then for five years it sat in storage until I had a place to put it."

"Umm." Lunzie's eyes slid across hers, then came back.

"As near as I can make it, that Thek conference lasted four and a half hours," Sassinak said, running her finger around her damp collar. She'd loosen it once lunch had been served. Right now she had to loosen up Lunzie. She held up the bottle. "Wouldn't you recommend another shot, Doctor Mespil? Purely medicinal, of course."

"If this old fool can prescribe a similar dose for herself?" Lunzie's smile was a little more natural as Sassinak filled both their glasses with a generous tot.

"Thanks."

Before they'd finished savoring the brandy, two stewards brought trays heaped with food: thinly sliced sandwiches, two bowls of soup, bowls of fried delicacies, fresh fruit obviously bartered from the Iretans.

Lunzie shook her head. "You Fleet people! And I always thought a military life in space was austere!"

"It can be." Sassinak tasted her soup and nodded. Another one of her favorite cook's creative successes. The stewards smiled and withdrew. Now Sassinak loosened her tunic. "There are certain . . . mmm . . . perks that come with rank and age."

"Mostly rank, I'd guess. I'm happy for you, Sass, you seem to have earned a lot of respect, and you're clearly suited to your life."

For some reason this made Sassinak vaguely uneasy.

"Well . . . I like it. Always have. It's not all this pleasant, of course."

"No? Have you seen combat often?"

"Often enough. Cruise before this one, we were boarded. Someone even took a potshot at me."

That caught Lunzie with her spoon stopped halfway to her mouth, and she put it down safely in the soup before asking more.

"Boarded? I didn't know that happened in . . . I mean, a Fleet cruiser?"

"That's exactly the reaction of the Board of Inquiry. It seemed like a good idea at the time, though, Lunzie." Far from being upset by her great-great-great as a listener, Sassinak discovered a certain catharsis easing tension, almost as beneficial as medication. And just the thread of a new thought, bearing on the information the Thek had extracted. "My Exec had a shipload of slaves to get out of that system asap." She told Lunzie the whole story, backing and filling as necessary.

"And you'd been a slave . . . you knew . . ." Lunzie murmured softly.

There was more understanding in that tone than Sassinak could well stand; she changed the subject again, surprised to find herself mentioning another problem.

"Yes, and as for crew loyalty, by and large you're right. But not entirely. For instance," and Sassinak leaned back in her chair, regarding her guest with a measuring glance, "right now, I'm fairly sure that we have an informer aboard: someone in the pay of any one of those prestigious names we've been made privy to. Dupaynil and I have scanned and dissected the records of everyone on board and it hasn't done us a bit of good. We can't find tampering or inconsistencies or service lapses. But we have got a saboteur. My crew're all starting to suspect each other. You can imagine what that does to morale!" Lunzie nodded, eyes sharpening. "The timid ones come to me, wanting me, of all things, to arrest our heavyworlders. As if heavyworlders were the Jonahs."

She noticed Lunzie's startled expression. "And the next thing will be some political movement or other. There has to be a way to find the rotter, but I confess I'm stymied. And I particularly want the bugger found before any hint of what we've discovered here on Ireta can possibly leak."

Lunzie began peeling a fruit, letting the rind curl below her fingers. "Would you like me to look through the files — the unclassified stuff, I mean? Maybe an outside eye? Sort of singing for my lunch, as it were?"

"Singing for your lunch?"

"Never mind. If you don't trust an outsider . . ."

"Oh, I trust you — gods below, my own great-great-great grandmother." Sassinak caught herself on the rim of a hiccup, and decided that she was the least bit cozy from the brandy. "You could look through my bottom drawers if you wanted. But what can you find that Dupaynil and I haven't found?"

"I dunno. But being older ought to do some good, if being younger can't."

At this, they locked glances and giggled. Fresh eyes, Lunzie's eyes, made no sense, and very good sense, and they were both more relaxed than necessary. Two hours later, poring over the personnel files, they had sobered but were no nearer solving Sassinak's problem.

"I didn't think you needed this many people to run a cruiser," said Lunzie severely. "It would be easier to check a smaller crew."

"Part of that great life I have as a cruiser captain."

"Right. One more engineer technician, grade E-4, and I'm going to . . ." Suddenly she paused, and frowned. "Hold it! Who's this?"

Sassinak called up the same record on her own screen. "Prosser, V. Tagin. He's all right; I've checked him out, and so has Dupaynil." She glanced again at the now-familiar file. Planet of origin: Colony Makstein-VII, somatotype: height range 1.7-2 meters, weight range 60-100 kg, eye color blue/gray, skin: red/yellow/black ratio 1:1:1, type fair, hair type: straight, fine, light-brown to yellow to gray. Longheaded, narrow pelvis, eighty percent chance missing upper outer incisors. She screened Prosser's holo and saw a 1.9 meter, 75-kilogram male with gray eyes in a longish pale face under fine, fair hair. By his dental chart, he was missing the upper outer incisors, and his blood type matched. "There's nothing off in his file, and he's well within the genetic index description. His eyes are too close together, but that's not a breach of Security. What's wrong with him?"

"He's impossible, that's what."

"Why?"

Lunzie looked across at her, a completely serious look. "Did you ever hear of clone colonies?"

"Clone colonies?" Sassinak stared at her blankly. She had neither heard of such a thing nor seen a reference to it. "What's a clone colony?"

"What databases do you have onboard? Medical, I mean? I want to check something." Lunzie had gone tense suddenly, alert, almost vibrating with what she wouldn't explain — yet.

"Medical? Ask Mayerd. If that's not enough, I can even get you access to Fleet HQ by FTL link."

"I'll ask Mayerd. They were talking about covering it up, and if they did —" Lunzie didn't go on; Sassinak didn't push her. Time enough.

Lunzie was on the internal comm, talking to Mayerd about medical databases, literature searches, and specific medical journals, in a slang Sassinak could hardly follow. "What do you mean, *Essentials of Cell Reference* isn't publishing? Oh — well, that's a stupid reason to change titles. . . . Well, try *Bioethics Quarterly*, out of Amperan University Press, probably volume 73 to 77 . . . nothing? Ceiver and Petruss were the authors. . . . Old Mackelsey was the editor then, a real demon on stuff like this. Of course I'm sure of my reference: as far as I'm concerned it was maybe two years ago." Finally she clicked off and looked at Sass, a combination of smugness and concern. "You've got a big problem, great-great-great-granddaughter, bigger than you thought."

"Oh, I need any more?"

"Worse than one saboteur. Someone's been wiping files. Not just your files. All files."

"What exactly do you mean?" It was the first time she'd used her command voice in Lunzie's presence and she was glad to see that it was effective. It didn't, she noticed, scare Lunzie, but it did get a straight answer out of her.

"You never heard of clone colonies, nor has Mayerd who ought to have. I was a student on an Ethics Board concerning such a colony." Lunzie paused just a moment before continuing. "Some bright researchers had decided that it would be a possibility to have an entire colony sharing one genome: one colony made up exclusively of clones."

"But that can't work," Sassinak said, recalling what she knew of human genetics. "They'd inbreed, and besides you need different abilities, mixtures . . ."

Lunzie nodded. "Humans are generalists. Early human societies had no specialization except sexual. You can't build a large, complicated society that way, but a specialized colony, maybe. They thought they could. Anyway, in terms of the genetic engineering needed for certain environments, it would be a lot cheaper to engineer one, and then clone, even given the expense of cloning. And once they'd cleared the generation-limit problem, and figured out how to insert the other sex without changing *anything* else, it would be stable. If you know there are no dangerous recessives, then inbreeding won't cause trouble. Inbreeding merely raises the probability that, if such harmful genes exist, they will combine. If they don't exist, they can't combine."

"I see. But I'm not sure I believe."

"Wise. The Ethics team didn't either. Because I'd been around, so to speak, when that first colony was set up and because I'd worked in occupational fields, I had the chance to give an opinion on the ethical and practical implications. One of a panel of two hundred or so. We saw the clones, well, holos of them, and the research reports. I thought the project was dangerous, to both the clones and to everyone else. For one thing, in the kind of environment the clones were designed for, I thought random mutations would be far more frequent than the project suggested. Others thought the clones should be protected: the project had a fierce security rating anyway, but apparently it went a step further and all references were wiped."

"What does that have to do with Prosser, V. Tagin?"

Lunzie looked almost disgusted, then relented. "Sassinak, that colony was on Makstein-VII. Everyone in it — *everyone* had the same genome and the same appearance. Exactly the same appearance. I saw holos of members of that colony. Your Mr. Prosser is *not* one of the clones, though he's been given the somatypes."

"Given?"

"The index entries were written to cover the appearance of the clones should any of them travel, while indicating a range of values as if they were from a limited but normal gene pool. His somatype has been faked, Sassinak. That's why you didn't catch it. No one would, who didn't know about clone colonies in general and Makstein-VII in particular. And you couldn't find out because it's not in the files anymore."

"But someone knows," said Sassinak, hardly breathing for the thought of it. "Someone knew to fake his ID that way. . . ."

"I wonder if your clever Lieutenant Commander Dupaynil could ask Mr. Prosser where he actually does come from?" Lunzie said in a drawl as she examined her fingertips, a mannerism which made Sassinak blink for it was much her own.

She keyed in Dupaynil's office and when he acknowledged, she sent him the spurious ID they'd uncovered. "Detain," was all she said but she knew Dupaynil would understand. "Great-great-great-grandmother," she said silkily, well pleased, "you're far too smart to stay in civilian medicine."

"Are you offering me a job?" The tone was meek, but the sharp glance belied it.

"Not a job exactly," Sassinak began. "A new career, a mid-life change, just right for fresh eyes that see with old knowledge that has somehow got lost for us who need it." Lunzie raised an inquiring eyebrow but her expression was alert, not skeptical. Sassinak went on with mounting enthusiasm, building on that little inkling she'd had before lunch. "Listen up, great-great. Do you realize what you have, to replace what you think you've lost? Files in your head, accessible facts that weren't wiped . . . and who knows how many more than just references to a prohibited colony!"

"The old clone colony trick works only once, great-great."

"Let's not put arbitrary limits to what you have in your skull, revered ancestress. The old clone colony trick may not be all you've *saved* behind your fresh old eyes. You've got an immediate access to things forty-three and even a hundred and five years old which to me are either lost in datafiles or completely unknown. And this planetary piracy's been going on a long, long time by either of our standards." She saw the leap of interest in Lunzie's eyes and then the filming of old, sadder memories before the new hope replaced them. "I'm not offering a job, old dear, I'm declaring you a team member, a refined intelligence that those planet-hungry moneygrubbing ratguts could never expect to have ranged against them. How could they? A family team with almost the same time-in-service of say, the Paradens. . . ."

"Yes, the Paradens," and Lunzie sounded very grim. Then her thin lips curved into a smile that lit up her eyes. "A team? A planet pirate breaking team. I probably do know more than one useful thing. You're a commander, with a ship at your disposal. . . ."

"Which is supposed to be hunting these planet pirates. . . ."

"You're Fleet and you can ask certain questions and get certain information. But I'm," and Lunzie swelled with self-pride, "a nobody, no big family, no fortune, no connections — bar my present elegant company — and they don't need to know that. Yes, esteemed descendant, I accept your offer of a team action."

Sassinak had just picked up the brandy bottle to charge their glasses when a loud thump on the bulkhead and raised voices indicated some disturbance. Sassinak rolled her eyes at Lunzie and went to see what it was.

Aygar was poised on the balls of his feet just outside her office, with two marines denying him entry.

"Sorry about the noise, Captain," said one of them. "He wants to speak to you and we told him . . ."

"You said," Aygar burst out to Sassinak, "that as members of FSP, we had privileges. . . ."

"Interrupting my work isn't one of them," said Sassinak crisply. She felt a discreet tug on her sleeve. "However, I've a few moments to spare right now," and she dismissed the marines.

Aygar came into her office with slightly less swagger than usual. If he ever dropped that half-sulk of his, Sassinak thought he'd be extremely presentable. He didn't have the gross heavyworlder appearance. He could, in fact if he mended his attitude, be taken as just a very well-developed normal human type. He'd fill out a marine uniform very well indeed. And fill in other places.

"Did Major Currald recruit you?"

"He's trying," and that unexpected humor of Aygar flashed through again.

"I thought you intended to remain on Ireta, to protect all your hard work," Lunzie said in the mild sort of voice that Sassinak would use to elicit information. But she had a gleam in her eye as she regarded the handsome young Iretan that Sassinak also instantly recognized. It surprised her for a moment.

"I . . . I thought I wanted to stay," he said slowly, "if Ireta was going to remain our world. But it's not. And there are hundreds of worlds out there. . . ."

"Which you could certainly visit as a marine." Sassinak sweetened her tone and added a smile. Two could play this game and she wasn't about to let her great-great-great-grandmother outmaneuver her in her own office.

Aygar regarded her through narrowed eyes. "I've also had an earful of the sort of prejudice heavyworlders face."

"My friend, if you act friendly and well behaved, people will like a young man as well favored as you," Sassinak said, ignoring Lunzie. "Life on Ireta and out of high-G environment has done you a favor. You look normal, although I'd wager that you'd withstand high-G stress better than most. Act friendly and most people will accept you with no qualms. Swagger around threatening them with your strength or size and people will react with fear and hatred." Sassinak shrugged. "You're smart enough to catch on to that. You'd make an admirable marine."

Aygar cocked an eyebrow in challenge. "I think I can do better than that, Commander. I'm not about to settle for second best. Not again. I want the chance to learn. That's a privilege in the FSP, too, I understand. I want to learn what they didn't and wouldn't teach us. They consistently lied to us." Anger flashed in his eyes, a carefully contained anger that fascinated Sassinak for she hadn't expected such depths to this young man. "And they kept us ignorant!" That rankled the deepest. Sassinak could almost bless the cautious, paranoid mutineers for that blunder. "Because we," and when Aygar jabbed his thumb into his chest he meant all of his generations, "were not meant to have a part of this planet at all!"

"No," Sassinak said, suddenly recalling another snippet of information gleaned from the cathedral's Thekian homily, "you weren't."

"In fact," Lunzie began, in a voice as sweet as her descendant's, "you've a score to settle with the planet pirates, too. With the heavyworlders who sent Cruss and that transport ship."

Aygar shot the medic such a keen look that Sassinak damned

her own lapse — that'd teach her to look at the exterior of a man and forget what made him tick.

"You might say I do at that," he replied in much too mild a tone.

"In that case," Sassinak said, glancing for approval at Lunzie, "I think we could actually take you on as a . . . mmm . . . special advisor?"

"I've just signed on in a similar capacity," Lunzie said when she saw Aygar hesitate. "Special duties. Special training."

"Not in the usual chain of command." Sassinak gave him a look that had melted scores of junior officers.

"And who do I have to take orders from?" he asked, looking from Sassinak to Lunzie with the blandest of expressions on his handsome face.

"I'm still the captain," Sassinak said firmly, with a glare for her great-great-great-grandmother, who only grinned.

"You may be a lightweight, Captain, but I think I can endure it," he said in a drawl, holding her gaze with his twinkling eyes.

"Welcome aboard, specialist Aygar!" Sassinak extended her hand to take his in a firm shake of commitment.

Lunzie chuckled wickedly. "I think this is going to be a most . . ." her pause was pregnant " . . . instructive voyage, granddaughter. Shall we toss for it?"

Just for a moment, Aygar looked from one to the other, with the expression of someone who suspects he hasn't quite caught a hidden meaning.

"We specialists should stick together," she added, offering him a glass of the amber brandy. "You'll drink to that, won't you, Commander?"

"That, and other things! Like 'down with planet piracy!'" She pinned Lunzie with a meaningful stare, wondering just what she'd got herself in for this trip.

"Hear, hear!" Lunzie lustily agreed.

Book III

GENERATION WARRIORS

✧ CHAPTER ONE

On the FSP Fleet heavy cruiser Zaid-Dayan

"We have resources they don't know about," Sassinak said, and not for the first time. It did not reassure her.

The convivial mood in which Sassinak and Lunzie had first made their plans to combine forces against the planet pirates had long since evaporated. They had been carried by the euphoria following the incredible Thek cathedral which had dispensed right justice to Captain Cruss who had illegally landed a heavy-worlder colony transport ship on the planet Ireta, right under the bows of Sassinak's pursuing cruiser. The Thek conference had elicited considerable fascinating information about the captain's superiors. Apart from sorting out the problem of which race "owned" Ireta, the Thek had departed without reference to bringing the perpetrators of planet pirating to a similar justice.

Neither Sassinak nor Lunzie felt they would be lucky enough to obtain more support from the Theks, even if that long-lived race were the oldest of the space-faring species. Theks rarely interfered with members of the various ephemeral species that they had discovered over the centuries. Only when, as on Ireta, some ancient plan of their own might be jeopardized would they intervene. As a rule, Thek permitted all their client races, from the lizardlike Seti, the shape-changing Wefts, the marine Ssli down to humans, to "dree their ain weirds." No sooner than the Thek had resolved the matter of Ireta than they had departed, leaving Sassinak and Lunzie with an irresistible challenge: to seek out and destroy those who indulged in the most daring sort of piracy — the rape and pillage of entire planets and the mass enslavement of their legally resident populations. The problems were immense. Sassinak was too experienced a commander to ignore real problems, and Lunzie had seen too many good plans go wrong herself. Lunzie, sprawled comfortably on the white leather cushions in Sassinak's office, watched her distant offspring with amusement. She was so young to be so old.

"So are you," Sassinak retorted.

Lunzie felt herself reddening.

"There's no such thing as telepathy," she said. "It's never been demonstrated under controlled conditions."

"Twins do it," Sassinak said. "I read that somewhere. And other close relatives, sometimes. As for you and me . . . nobody knows what that many deepfreezes have done to your brain, and what my life's done to me. You were thinking I'm young to be so old, and I was thinking the same thing about you. You're *younger* than I am. . . ."

"Which doesn't give you the right to play boss," said Lunzie. Then she wished she hadn't. Sassinak's face had hardened . . . and of course to her, she did have the right. She was the captain of her ship, one step below her first star, and she had ten more years of actual, awake, living-experience age.

"I'm sorry," Lunzie said quickly. "You *are* older, and you *are* the boss . . . I'm just still adjusting."

Sassinak's quick smile almost reassured her. "Same here. But I do have to be the boss on this ship. Even if you are my great-great-great, you don't know which pipes hold what."

"Right. Point taken. I will be the good little civilian." And try, she thought to herself, to adjust to having a distant offspring not only older than herself but quite a bit tougher. She leaned forward, setting her mug down on the table. "What are you thinking of doing?"

"What we need," said Sass, frowning at nothing, "is a lot more information. The kind of proof we can bring before the Council meeting, for instance. Take the Diplo problem. Who's been contacting whom, and whose money paid for that heavyworlder seedship? Which factions of heavyworlders are involved, and do they all know what they're doing? Then there's the Paraden family. I have my own reasons to think they're guilty, root and branch, but no proof. If we could get someone into position, some social connection . . ."

Lunzie picked up her mug, gulped down the last of her drink, and tried to ignore the hollow in her belly. Was she about to do something stupid, or brave, or both?

"I . . . might be able to help with the Diplo bit."

"You? How?"

Sassinak had been thinking of her own heavyworlder friends, but she hated to use any of them that way. It would be too risky for them if some agent within Fleet caught on.

"They don't let many lightweights visit Diplo, but because of their continuing medical problems, genetic and adaptive, medical researchers and advisers are welcome. As welcome as lightweights ever are. I'd need a refresher course with a Master Adept . . ."

Sassinak pursed her lips. "Hmmm. That's reasonable, the refresher part. If anyone were watching you, they'd expect you to. You've gone a stage or so beyond your rating, haven't you? And you people go back fairly regularly, once you're in the Adept rating, so I've heard. . . ."

She let that trail away, in case Lunzie wanted to offer more information, but wasn't surprised when Lunzie simply nodded and went on to talk about Diplo.

"Doctors are expected to ask questions. If I were on a research team, perhaps statistical survey of birth defects, something like that, I'd have a chance to talk to lots of people as part of my job."

Sassinak cocked her head to one side; Lunzie barely stopped herself from making the same gesture.

"Are you sure you're not doing this just to exorcise your own heavyworld demons? From what you've said . . ."

Lunzie didn't want to go into that again. "I know. I have reason to hate and fear them. Some of them. But I've also known good ones; I told you about Zebara." Sassinak nodded, but looked unconvinced. Lunzie went on. "Besides, I'll have time to talk to the Master Adept renewing my training. You know enough about Discipline to know that's as good as any psych software. If a Master says I'm not stable enough to go, I'll let you know."

"You'll discuss it with him?" By Sassinak's tone, she wasn't entirely happy with that.

Lunzie sighed internally. "Not everything, no. But my going to Diplo, certainly. There are certain special skills which can make it easier on a lightweight."

"Just be sure a Master passes you. This is too important to risk on an emotional storm, and with the trouble you've had . . ."

"I can handle it." Lunzie let her voice convey the Discipline behind it, and Sassinak subsided. Not really impressed, Lunzie noticed, as most people would be, but convinced for the time being.

"That's Diplo, then." Sassinak gave a final minute shrug, and went on to the other problems. "You're going off. And you don't know how long that will take, either, do you? I thought not. You're going off for a refresher course and a visit to Diplo, and that leaves us with digging to be done among the suspect commercial combines, the Seti, and the inner workings of EEC, Fleet, and the Council. It would be handy if we had our own private counterintelligence network, but . . ."

Lunzie interrupted, feeling smug. "You know Admiral Coromell, don't you?"

Sassinak's jaw did not drop because she would not let it, but Lunzie could tell she was surprised. "Do *you* know Admiral Coromell?"

"Quite well, yes." Lunzie watched Sassinak struggle with the obvious implications, and decided not to ask. Or perhaps the implications weren't obvious to her. By now Coromell would be as old as his father had been; Sassinak would have known him as an old man. Lunzie fought off yet another pang of sorrow, and concentrated on the present moment. "Coromell actually recruited me, temporarily, back before the Ambrosia thing."

"Recruited you!" Was that approval or resentment? Lunzie did not ask, but gave as brief a synopsis as possible of the circumstances of that recruitment, and what followed. Sassinak listened without interrupting, her eyes focussed on some distant vision, and shook her head slightly when Lunzie finished.

"My dear, I have the feeling we could talk for weeks and you'd still surprise me." There was nothing in the tone to indicate whether this most recent surprise had been pleasant or not; Lunzie suspected that respect for Coromell's stars might be part of Sassinak's reticence. To underscore that reticence, Sassinak pushed away from her desk. "I feel like stretching my legs, and you haven't really seen the ship yet. Want a tour?"

"Of course." Lunzie was as glad to take a break from their intense conversation. She followed Sassinak out into the passage that led nearly the length of Main Deck.

"It's so different," Lunzie said, as Sass led her down the aft ladder to Troop Deck. She wondered why the walls — bulkheads, she reminded herself — were green here, and gray above.

"Different?"

"I hadn't had time to mention it, but when we were rescued from Ambrosia that time, the Fleet cruiser that came was this one. The *Zaid-Dayan*. I never saw the captain, but it was a woman. That's why I used the name in the cover I gave Varian and the others back on Ireta. It was a déjà vu situation, you and this ship . . ."

Sassinak grunted. "Couldn't have been *this* ship. Wasn't the Ambrosia rescue before Ireta and your cold sleep? Forty years or so back? That must have been the '43 version . . . that ship was lost in combat the year I graduated from the Academy." She nodded to the squad of marines that had flattened themselves along the bulkhead to let her by, and waited for Lunzie to catch up.

Lunzie felt cold all over. Another reminder that she had not grown *naturally* older, when she would know things, but had simply skipped decades. "Are you sure? When I heard this was the *Zaid-Dayan*, with a woman captain, I thought maybe . . ." Sassinak shook her head. "I'm not that much older than you. No — the Ambrosia rescue — we were taught that battle, in TacSim II. That was Graciela Vinish-Martinez, her first command and a new ship. She caught hell from a Board of Inquiry at first, bringing it back needing repairs like that, but someone on Ambrosia, some scout captain or something . . ."

"Zebara," said Lunzie, hardly breathing.

"Whoever it was wrote a report that got the Board off her neck. I thought of that when I had to go before a Board. I saw her." Sassinak's expression was strange, almost bemused. She punched a button on the bulkhead, and a hatch slid open: a lift. They entered, and Sassinak pushed another button inside before she said more. Lunzie waited. "She gave us — the female cadets — a lecture on command presence for women officers. We all thought that was a stupid topic. We were muttering about it, going in; the room was empty except for this little old lady in the corner, looked like the kind of retirement-age warrant officers that swarmed all around the Academy, doing various jobs no one ever explained. I hardly glanced at her. She had an old-fashioned clipboard and a marker. We sat down, wondering how late

Admiral Vinish-Martinez was going to be. We knew better than to chatter, but I have to admit there was a lot of quiet murmuring going on, and some of it was mine." Sassinak grinned reminiscently. "Then this little old lady gets up. Nobody saw that; we figured she was taking roll. Walks around to the front, and we thought maybe she was going to tell us the Admiral was late or not coming. And then — I swear, Lunzie, not one of us saw her stars until she wanted us to, when she *changed* right there in front of us without moving a muscle. Didn't say a word. Didn't have to. We were out of our seats and saluting before we realized what happened."

"And then?" Lunzie couldn't help asking; she was fascinated.

"And then she gave us a big bright smile, and said, 'That, ladies, was a demonstration of command presence.' And then she walked out, while we were still breathless."

"Mullah!"

"Right. The whole lecture in one demonstration. We never forgot that one, I can tell you, and we spent hours trying it on each other to see if we'd learned anything yet. She said it all: it's not your size or your looks or your strength or how loud you can yell — it's something *else*, inside, and if you don't have that, no amount of size, strength, beauty, or bellowing will do instead." The lift opened onto a tiny space surrounded by differently colored pipes that gurgled and hissed. A sign said, "ENVIRONMENTAL LEVEL ONE."

"Adept Discipline?" asked Lunzie, curious to know what Sass thought.

"Maybe. For some. You know we have basic classes in it in Fleet. But there has to be a certain potential or something has to happen later. Certainly the element of focus is the same . . ." Sassinak's voice trailed away; her brow furrowed.

"You have it," said Lunzie. She had seen the crew's response to Sassinak, and felt her own — an almost automatic respect and desire to please her.

"Oh . . . well, yes. Some, at least; I can put the fear of reality into wild young ensigns. But not like that." She laughed, putting the memory aside. "For years I wanted to do that . . . to be that . . ."

"Was she your childhood idol, then? Were you dreaming about Fleet even before you were captured?" Was that what had kept her sane?

"Oh, no. I wanted to be Carin Coldae." Lunzie must have looked as blank as she felt, for Sassinak said, "I'm sorry — I didn't realize. Forty-three years — she must not have been a vid star when you were last — I mean . . ."

"Don't worry." Another example of what she'd missed. She hadn't been one to follow the popularity of vid stars at any time, but the way Sassinak had said the name, Coldae must have been a household word.

"Just an adventure star," Sassinak was explaining. "Had fan clubs, posters, all that. My best friend and I dreamed of having adventures all over the galaxy, men at our feet . . ."

"Well, *you* seem to have made it," said Lunzie dryly. "Or so your crew let me know."

Sassinak actually blushed; the effect was startling. "It's not much like the daydreams, though. Carin never got a scratch on her, only a few artistically placed streaks of soot. Sometimes that soot was all she had on, but mostly it was silver or gold snugsuits, open halfway down her perfect front. She could toss twenty pirates over her head with one hand, gun down another ten villains with the other, and belt out her theme song without missing a beat. When I was a child, it never dawned on me that someone supposedly being starved and beaten in a thorium mine shouldn't have all those luscious curves. Or that climbing naked up a volcanic cliff does bad things to long scarlet fingernails."

"Mmm. Is she still popular?"

"Not so much. Reruns will go on forever, at least the classics like *Dark of the Moon* and *The Iron Chain*. She's doing straight dramas now, and politics." Sassinak grimaced, remembering Dupaynil's revelations about her former idol. "I've been told she's behind some subversive groups, has been for years." Then she sighed, and said, "And I dragged you through Troop Deck without showing you much . . . well. This is Environmental, that keeps us alive."

"I saw the sign," said Lunzie. She could hear the distant rhythmic throbbing of pumps. Sassinak patted a plump beige pipe with surprising affection.

"This was my first assignment out of Academy. Installing a new environmental system on a cruiser."

"I thought you'd have specialists —"

"We do. But officers in the command track have to be generalists. In theory, a captain should know every pipe and wire, every chip in every computer, every bit of equipment and scrap of supplies . . . where it is, how it works, who should be taking care of it. So we all start in one of the main ships' specialties and rotate through them in our first two tours."

"Do you know?" She couldn't, Lunzie was sure, but did she know she didn't know, or did she think she did?

"Not all of them, not quite. But more than I did. This one," and she patted it again, "this one carries carbon dioxide to the buffer tanks; the oxygen pipes, like all the flammables, are red. And no, you won't see them in this compartment, because some idiot coming off the lift could have a flame, or the lift could spark. Since you're a doctor, I thought you'd like to see some of this. . . ."

"Oh, yes."

Luckily she knew enough not to feel like a complete idiot. Sassinak led her along low-ceilinged tunnels with pipes hissing and gurgling on either hand, pointing out access parts to still other plumbing, the squatty cylindrical scrubbers, the gauges and meters and status lights that indicated exactly what was where, and whether it should be.

"All new," Sassinak said, as they headed into the 'ponics section. "We had major trouble last time out, not just the damage, but apparently some sabotage of Environmental. Ended up with stinking sludge growing all along the pipes where it shouldn't, and there's no way to clean that out, once the sulfur bacteria start pitting the pipe linings."

Hydroponics on a Fleet cruiser looked much like hydroponics anywhere else to Lunzie, who recognized the basic configuration of tanks and feeder lines and bleedoff valves, but nothing special. Sassinak finally took her back to the lift and they ascended to Main again.

"How long does it take a newcomer to find everything?"

Sassinak pursed her lips. "Well . . . if you mean new crew or ensigns, usually a week or so. We start 'em off with errands in every direction, let 'em get good and lost, and they soon figure out how to use a terminal and a shipchip to stay found. You noticed that every deck's a different color, and the striping width indicates bow and stern; there's no reason to stay lost once you've caught on to that." She led the way into her office, where a light blinked on her board. "I've got to go to the bridge. Would you like to stay here, or go back to your cabin?"

Lunzie had hoped to be invited onto the bridge, but nothing in Sassinak's expression made that possible. "I'll stay here, if that's convenient."

"Fine. Let me give you a line out." Sassinak touched her terminal's controls. "There! A list of access codes for you. I won't be long."

Lunzie wondered what that actually meant in terms of hours, and settled down with the terminal. She had hardly decided what to access when she heard heavy steps coming down the passage. Aygar appeared in the opening, scowling.

"Where's Sassinak?"

"On the bridge." Lunzie wondered what had upset him this time. The Weft marine corporal behind him looked more amused than concerned. "Want to wait here for her?"

"I don't want to wait." He came in, nonetheless, and sat down on the white-cushioned chair as if determined to stay forever. "I want to know how much longer it will be." At Lunzie's patient look, he went on. "When we will arrive at . . . at this Sector Headquarters, whatever that is. When Tanegli's mutiny trial will be. When I can speak for my . . . my peers." He hesitated over that; "peer" was a new word to him, and Lunzie wondered where he'd found it.

"I don't know," she said mildly. "She hasn't told me, either. I'm not sure she knows." She glanced at the door, where the Weft stood relaxed, projecting no threat but obviously capable. "Does it bother you to be followed?"

Aygar nodded, and leaned closer to her. "I don't understand these Wefts. How can they be something else, and then humans? How does anyone know who is human and who isn't? And they tell me of other aliens, not only Wefts and Thek that I have seen, but Ryxi who are like birds, and Bronthin, and . . ."

"You saw plenty of strange animals on Ireta."

"Yes, but . . ." His brow furrowed. "I suppose. I grew up with them. But that so many are spacefaring races."

"'Many are the world's wonders,'" Lunzie found herself quoting, "'but none more wonderful than man . . .' Or at least, that's the way we humans think of it."

From his expression, he'd never heard the quotation — but she didn't think the heavyworlder rebels had been students of ancient literature. A Kipling rhyme broke into her mind and she wondered if Aygar's East would ever meet civilization's West, or if they were doomed to be enemies. She dragged her wandering mind back to the present (no quotes, she told herself) and found Aygar watching her with a curious expression.

"You're younger than she is," he said. No doubt at all of who "she" was. "But she calls you her great-great-great grand-mother . . . why?"

"Remember we told you about cold sleep? How the light-weight members of the expedition survived? That isn't the only time I've been in cold sleep; my elapsed age is . . . older than you'd expect." She was not sure why she was reluctant to tell him precisely what it was. "Commander Sassinak is my descendant, just as you're descended from people who were young when I went into cold sleep on Ireta, people who are old now."

He looked more interested than horrified. "And you don't age at all, in cold sleep?"

"No. That's the point of it."

"Can you learn at the same time? I've been reading about the sleep-learning methods . . . would that work in cold sleep as well?"

"And let us wake up stuffed with knowledge and still young?" Lunzie shook her head. "No, it won't work, though it's a nice idea. If there were a way to feed in information that the person's miss-ing, waking up forty or fifty years later wouldn't be so bad."

"Do you *feel* old?"

Aygar's question was lowest on Lunzie's list of things to think about. She was sure Sassinak had the same back-and-forth tug faced with someone that many generations removed, an uncer-tainty about what "age" really meant.

Lunzie put a touch of Discipline in her voice again. "Not old and feeble, if that's what you mean. Old enough to know my mind, and young enough to . . ." Now how was she going to finish that? "To . . . to do what I must," she finished lamely.

But Aygar subsided, asking no more in that difficult area. What he did ask about — and what Lunzie was prepared to answer cheerfully — was the psychological testing procedure that Major Currald, the marine commander, had recommended to him.

"It's a good idea," Lunzie said, nodding. "My field at one time was occupational rehab. With my experience, they felt I understood troubled spaceworkers better than most. And quite often the root of the problem is that someone's stuck in a job for which they're not suited. They feel trapped — and if they're on a spaceship or station, in a way they *are* trapped — and that makes for trouble when anything else goes wrong."

Aygar frowned thoughtfully. "But we were taught that we should not be too narrow — that we should learn to do many things, have many skills. That part of the trouble between heavyworlders and lightweights came from too much specialization."

"Yes, that can be true. Humans are generalists, and are healthier when they have varied activities. But their primary occupation should draw on innate abilities, should not require them to do what is hardest for them. Some individuals are naturally better at sit-down jobs, or with very definite routines to follow. Others can learn new things easily, but quickly become bored with routines. That's not the person you want running the 'ponics system, which needs the same routine servicing shift after shift."

"But what about me?" Aygar thumped his chest. "Will I fit in, or be a freak? I'm big and strong, but not as strong as Currald. I'm smart enough, you said, but I don't have the educational background, and I don't have any idea what's available."

Lunzie tried to project soothing confidence. "Aygar, with your background, both genetic and experiential, I'm sure you'll find — or make — a good niche for yourself. When we get to Sector Headquarters, you'll have direct access to various library databases, as well as testing and counseling services of FSP. I'll be glad to advise you, if you want . . ." She paused, assessing his expression.

His slow smile made her wonder if this was her idea or his. "I would like that. I will hope you are right." He stood up, still smiling down at her.

"Are you leaving? I thought you wanted to talk to the captain."

"Another time. If you are my ally, I will not worry about her."

With that he was gone. Lunzie stared after him. Ally? She was not at all sure she wanted Aygar for an ally, in whatever sense he meant it. He might be more trouble that way.

Sassinak returned shortly from the bridge, listened to Lunzie's report on Aygar's visit, and nodded.

"You put exactly the bee in his ear that I wanted. Good for

you."

"But he said *ally*. . . ."

"And I say fine. Better for us, better for what we want to do. Look, Lunzie, he's got the best possible reason for stirring around in the databases: he's entitled. His curiosity is natural. We said that." Sassinak put in a call to the galley for a snack, and started to say more, but her comm buzzed. She turned to it. "Sassinak here."

"Ford. May I come in? I've had an idea."

"Come ahead."

Sassinak punched the door control and it slid aside. Ford gave Lunzie the same charming smile and nod as always, and lifted an eyebrow.

"You know you can speak in front of her," Sassinak told him. "She's my relative, and she's on the team."

"Did I ever tell you about Auntie Q?"

Sassinak frowned. "Not that I remember. Was that the one who paints birds on tiles?"

"No, that's Auntie Louise, my mother's sister. This is Auntie Quesada, who is actually, in her right name, Quesada Mira Louisa Darrell Santon-Paraden."

"Paraden!"

Sassinak and Lunzie tied on that one, and Sassinak glared at her Executive Officer in a way Lunzie hoped would never be directed at her.

"You never told me you were related to the Paradens," she said severely.

"I'm not. Auntie Q is my father's uncle's wife's sister, who married a Paraden the second time around, after her first husband died of — well, my *mother* always said it was an overdose of Auntie Q, administered daily in large amounts. My father always said it was gamboling debts, and I mean gambol," he said, accenting the last syllable.

"Go on," said Sassinak, a smile beginning to twitch in the corner of her mouth.

Ford settled one hip on her desk. "Auntie Q was considered a catch, even for a Paraden, because her first husband's older brother was Felix Ibarra-Jimenez Santon. Yes, *those* Santons. Auntie Q inherited about half a planet of spicefields and a gold mine: literal gold mine. With an electronics manufacturing plant on top. Then in her own right, she was a Darrell of the Westwitch Darrells, who prefer to call their source of income 'sanitary engineering products' rather than soap, so she wouldn't have starved if she'd run off with a mishi dancer."

"So what about this Paraden?"

"Minor branch of the family, sent out to find an alliance worth the trouble; supposedly he met her at an ambassadorial function, ran her through the computer, and the family said yes, by all means. Auntie Q was tired of playing merry widow and looking for another escort so they linked. She gave him a child by decree — it was in the contract — but he was already looking for more excitement or freedom or whatever, and ran off with her dressmaker. So she claimed breach of contract, dumped the child on the Paradens, kept the name and half his stocks and such, and spends her time cruising from one social event to another. And sending the family messages."

"Aha," said Sassinak. "Now we come to it. She's contacted you?"

"Well, no. Not recently. But she's always sending messages, complaining about her health, and begging someone to visit her. My father warned me years ago not to go near her; said she's like a black hole, just sucks you in and you're never seen alive again. He had been taken to meet her once. Apparently she cooed over him, rumpled his hair, hugged him to her ample bosom, and talked him out of the chocolates in his pocket, all in about twenty seconds. But what I was thinking was that I could visit her. She knows all the gossip, all the socialites, and yet she's not quite in the thick where they'd be watching her."

Sassinak thought about that. Wouldn't an efficient enemy know that Sassinak's Exec was related to an apparently harmless old rich lady? But she herself hadn't. They couldn't know everything.

"I'd planned to have you do the database searches at Sector HQ," she said slowly. "You're good at that, and less conspicuous than I am. . . ."

Ford shook his head. "Not inconspicuous enough, not after this caper. But I know who can . . . either Lunzie here, or young Aygar."

"Aygar?"

Ford ticked off reasons on his fingers. "One, he's got the perfect reason to be running the bases: he's new to the culture, and needs to learn as much as he can as fast as he can. Two, no one's ever done a profile on him, so no one can say if any particular query is out of character. In that way, he's better than Lunzie; anyone looking for trouble would notice if she ran queries outside her field or the events of her own life. Three, even an attempt at a profile would cover exactly those fields we want him to be working on anyway."

"But is he trustworthy?" Lunzie asked it of Ford, as she had been about to ask it of Sassinak. Ford shrugged.

"What if he's not? He needs us to get access, and keep it; he's bright but he's not experienced, and you know how long it took any of us to learn to navigate through one of the big databases. And we can put a tag on him; it'll be natural that we do. We shouldn't seem to trust him."

Sassinak laughed. "I do like a second in command who thinks like I do. See, Lunzie? Two against one; both of us see why Aygar is ideal for that job."

"But he's expecting something more from us — from me, at least. If he doesn't get it . . ."

"Lunzie!" That was the command voice, the tone that made Sassinak no longer a distant relative but the captain of a Fleet cruiser on which Lunzie was merely a passenger. It softened slightly with the next words, but Lunzie could feel the steel underneath. "We aren't going to do anything to hurt Aygar. We know he's not involved in the plotting . . . of all the citizens of the Federation, he's one of the few who *couldn't* be involved. So he's not our enemy, not in any way whatever. Stopping the piracy will help everyone, including Aygar's friends and relatives back on Ireta. Including Aygar. We are on his side, in that way, and by my judgment — which I must remind you is ten years more experienced than yours — by my judgment that is enough. We can handle Aygar; we have dangerous enemies facing all of us."

Lunzie's gaze wavered, falling away from Sassinak's to see Ford as another of the same type. Calm, competent, certain of himself, and not about to change his mind a hairsbreadth for anything she said.

✦ CHAPTER TWO

Lunzie carried her small kit off the *Zaid-Dayan*, nodded to the parting salute of the officer on watch at the portside gangway, and did not look back as she crossed the line that marked ship's territory on the Station decking. It was so damnably hard to leave family again, even such distant family. She had liked Sassinak, and the ship, and . . . she did not look back.

Ahead were none of the barriers she'd have faced coming in on a civilian ship. She had Sassinak's personal authorization, giving her the temporary rank and access of a Fleet major, so exiting the Fleet segment required nothing but flashing the pass at the guard and walking on through. No questions to answer, no interviews with intrusive media.

Sassinak had made reservations for her on the first available shuttle to Liaka. Lunzie followed the directions she'd been given, in two rings and right one sector, and found herself in front of the ticketing office of Nilokis InLine. Lunzie's name and Sassinak's reservation together meant instant service. Before she realized it, Lunzie was settled in a quiet room with video-relay views of the Station and a mug of something hot and fragrant on the table beside her. A few meters away, another favored passenger barely glanced up from his portable computer before continuing his work. The padded chair curved around her like warm hands; her feet rested on deeply cushioned carpet.

She tried to relax. She had not lost Sassinak forever, she told herself firmly. She was not going to have a disaster on every spaceflight for the rest of her life, and if she did she would just survive it, the way she'd survived everything else. Her steaming mug drew her attention, and she remembered choosing *erit* from the list of beverages. One sip, then another, quieted her nerves and settled her stomach. Four hours to departure and nothing to

do. She thought of going back out into the Station but it was easier to sit here and relax. That's why she'd asked for *erit*. She
closed her eyes, and let the steam clear her head. After all, if
something happened this time, she'd know who'd come after her
and with what vigor. Sassinak was not one to let someone muck
about with her family, not now. Lunzie felt her mouth curving
into a grin. Quite a girl, that Sassinak, even at her age.

She forced herself to concentrate, to think of the days she'd
spent studying with Mayerd. With Sassinak's authority behind
her, she'd been able to catch up a lot of the lost ground in her
field. She knew which journals were current, what to read first,
which areas would require formal instruction. (She was not about
to try the new methods of altering brain chemistry from a cook-
book — not until she had seen a demonstration, at least.) Her
mind wandered to the time she had available for gathering information and she pulled out her calculator to check elapsed and
Standard times. If Sassinak was right about the probable trial
date, in the Winter Assizes (and *that* was an archaic term, she
thought), then she had to complete her refresher course in Discipline, whatever medical refreshers were required for
recertification, get to Diplo, and back to Sassinak (or the information back to Sassinak) in a mere eight months.

Another passenger came into the lounge, and then a pair,
absorbed in each other. Lunzie finished her drink and eyed them
benignly. They all looked normal, business and professional travellers (except the couple, who looked like two junior executives
off on vacation). The shuttle flew a three-cornered route, to Liaka
first and then Bearnaise and then back here; Lunzie tried to
guess who was going where, and how many less favored passengers were waiting in the common lounge (orange plastic benches
along the walls, and a single drinking fountain).

Even with the *erit*, and her own Discipline, Lunzie spent the
short hop to Liaka in miserable anxiety. Every change in sound,
every minute shift of the ship's gravity field, every new smell,
brought her alert, ready for trouble. She slept lightly and woke
unrested. On such short trips, less than five days, experienced
passengers tended to keep to themselves. She was spared the
need to pretend friendliness. She ate her standard packaged
meals, nodded politely, and spent most of the time in her tiny
cabin, claustrophobic as it was. Better that than the lounge,

where the couple (definitely junior executives, and not likely to be promoted unless they grew up) displayed their affection as if it were a prizewinning performance, worth everyone's attention.

When the shuttle docked, Lunzie had been waiting, ready to leave, for hours. She took her place in the line of debarking passengers, checking out her guesses about which were going where (the lovers were going to Bearnaise, of course), and shifting her weight from foot to foot. Over the bobbing heads she could see the Main Concourse, and tried to remember the quickest route to the Mountain.

"Ah . . . Lunzie Mespil." The customs officer glanced at the screen in front of her, where Lunzie's picture, palm-print, and retinal scan should be displayed. "There's a message for you, ma'am. MedOps, Main Concourse, Blue Bay. Do you need a guide?"

"Not that far," said Lunzie, smiling, and swung her bag over her shoulder. MedOps had a message? Just how old was that message, she wondered.

Main Concourse split incoming traffic into many diverging streams. Blue was fourth on the right, after two black (to Lunzie) and one violet section. The blacks were ultraviolet, distinguishable by alien races who could see in those spectra, and led to services those might require. Blue Bay opened off the concourse, all medical training services of one sort or another; MedOps centered the bay.

"Ah . . . Lunzie." The tone was much the same, bemused discovery. Lunzie leaned on the counter and stared at the glossy-haired girl at the computer. "A message, ma'am. Will you take hardcopy, or would you prefer a P-booth?"

The girl's eyes, when she looked up, were brown and guileless. Lunzie thought a moment. The option of a P-booth meant the message had come in as a voice or video, not info-only.

"P-booth," she said, and the girl pointed to the row of cylinders along one side of the room. Lunzie went into the first, slid its translucent door shut, punched the controls for privacy, and then entered her ID codes. The screen blinked twice, lit, and displayed a face she knew and had not seen for over forty years.

"Welcome back, Adept Lunzie." His voice, as always, was low, controlled, compelling. His black eyes seemed to twinkle at her; his face, seamed with age when she first met him, had not

changed. Was this a recording from the past? Or could he still be
here, alive?

"Venerable Master." She took a long, controlling breath, and
bent her head in formal greeting.

"You age well," he said. The twinkle was definite now, and the
slight curve to his mouth. His humor was rare and precious as the
millennia-old porcelain from which he sipped tea. It was not a recording. It could not be a recording, if he noticed she had not
aged. She took another deliberate breath, slowing her racing
heart, and wondering what he had heard, what he knew.

"Venerable Master, it is necessary . . ."

"For you to renew your training," he said.

Interruptions were as rare as humor; part of Discipline was
courtesy, learning to wait for others without hurrying them, or
feeling the strain. Had that changed, along with the rest of her
world? *Never hurry; never wait* had been one of the first things
she'd memorized. It had always seemed odd, since doctors faced
so many situations when they must hurry to save a life, or wait to
see what happened. His face was grave, now, remote as a stone
that neither waits nor hurries but simply exists where it is.

"The moment arrives," he said. Part of another saying, which
she had no time to recite, for he went on. "Fourth level, begin
with the Cleansing of the Stone."

And the screen blanked, leaving her confused but oddly reassured. Back to the MedOps desk, to see if Liaka's corridor plans
had changed in the intervening years.

They had; she received a mapbug which chirped at her when
she came to turns and crossings, and guided her into and out of
droptubes. A few things looked familiar: the cool green doors that
led to SurgOps, the red stripe that meant Quarantine. White-
coated or green-gowned doctors still roamed the corridors in
little groups, talking shop. She glanced after them, wondering if
she'd ever feel at home with her colleagues again. Terminals for
access to the medical databases filled niches along every wall. She
thought of stopping to see if all the clone colony data had really
been excised, then thought better of it. Later, when she felt
calmer, would be soon enough.

Fourth level. She came out of the last droptube a little breathless, as always, facing a simple wood door, broad apricot-colored
planks pegged together with a lighter wood. The wood glowed, as

unmistakably real as Sassinak's desk. Lunzie took a deep breath, letting herself settle into herself, feeling that settling. She bowed to the door, and it swung open across a snowy white stone sill. A novice in brown bowed to her, stepped back to let her pass, and swung the door shut behind her. Then, bowing again, the novice took Lunzie's bag, and moved silently along the path toward the sleeping huts.

Here was a place unlike any other in this Station, or any Station. Ahead, on the left, a waist-high stone like a miniature mountain reared from a path artfully designed to lead the eye toward a pavilion. Lunzie stood where she was, looking at that stone, and the small, irregular pool behind it.

"Cleansing the Stone" was an elementary exercise, but the foundation on which more striking ones were built. Empty the mind of all concerns, see the stone as it is . . . cleansed of associations, wishes, dreams, fantasies, fears. The word *stone* resonated in her mind, became all the hard things that had hurt her, became the mysterious Thek who confounded everyone's attempt to understand them. She stood quietly, relaxed, letting all these thoughts spill out, and then wiped them away. Again they came, and again, and once more she cleared them away from the stone before her. It had a certain beauty of its own, a history, a future, a *now*. She let her eyes wander over that irregular surface, not bothering to remember the glitter of mica, the glint of quartz . . . she did not need to remember, the stone was here and now, as solid as she, and as worthy of knowing.

When she had looked, she let her hand touch it, lightly, delicately, learning again (but not remembering) its irregular lumpy shape. She bent slowly to smell it, the curious and indescribable scent of stone, with behind it the smell of water, and other stones. Something more sweet also scented the air, now that she was attending to smell, but she rested her attention on the stone.

When she was quite still, unhurried and unaware of waiting, he was there, in the pavilion. Venerable Master Adept, who had a name that no one spoke in this place, where names meant nothing and essence was all. When she became consciously aware of him, she realized he had been there for a time. What time she did not know, and it did not matter. What mattered was her mind's control of itself, its ability to engage or withdraw at her will. He would be ready when she was ready; she would be ready when he was ready. She heard a drop of water fall, and realized that the fountain was on. She bowed to the rock, her mind completely easy for the first time in too many years (for even in cold sleep she had been willing to worry, if not capable of it), and moved slowly along the path. Thoughts moved in her mind, like the carp in the pool. She let them move, let some rise almost to the surface, their scaled beauty clear, while others hung motionless, mere shapes below the surface.

This was the center of the world — of her world — of the world of every Adept, this place that was, in a physical sense, not the center of anything. Embarrassment had no place with the Master Adept. She knelt across the little table from him, no longer aware that her worn workclothes from Ireta (however cleaned and smartened up by Sassinak's crew) were different from his immaculate white robe. His sash this day was aswirl with greens and blues and purples . . . a single thread of sulfur yellow. Her eye followed that thread, and then returned to his hands, as they gently touched petal-thin cups and saucers. He offered one, and she took it. Even in the subdued light within the pavilion, the cup seemed to glow. She could feel the warmth of the tea through it; that fragrance soothed.

After a time, he raised his cup, and sipped, and she did the same. They said nothing, for nothing needed to be said at this time. They shared the silence, the tea, the small pool where water fell tinkling from a fountain and carp dimpled the water from underneath.

Lunzie might have thought how very different this was, from the world she had just left, but such thoughts were unnecessary. What was necessary was recognition, appreciation, of the beauty before her. As she watched the carp, sipping her tea at intervals, a novice came silently to the pool and threw a handful of crumbs. The carp rose in a flurry of fins; a tiny splash broke the random song of the fountain. The novice retired.

The Master Adept spoke, his voice hardly louder than that splash. "It is what we identify as *lost* which brings us into concern, Adept Lunzie. When one knows that one owns nothing, nothing can be lost, and nothing mourned."

Her mind shied from that as from hot metal: instant rejection. He had never had a child, and they had had this discussion before.

"I am not speaking of your child," he said. "A mother's instinct is beyond training . . . so it must be. But the years you have lost, that you call yours: no one owns time, no one can claim even an instant."

Her heart steadied again. She could feel the heat in her face; it would have betrayed her. That shame made her blush again.

"Venerable Master . . . what I feel . . . is confusion."

It was safest to say what one felt, not what one thought. More than one tradition had gone into the concept of Discipline, and the Venerable Master had a Socratic ability to pursue a lame thought to its lair and finish it off. She dared to look at him; he was watching her with those bright black eyes in which no amusement twinkled. Not now.

"Confused? Do you perhaps believe that you *can* claim time as your own?"

"No, Venerable Master. But . . ."

She tried to sort out her thoughts. She had not seen him for so long . . . what would he know, and not know, about what had happened to her? How could he help if she did not explain everything? Part of her early training as a novice had been in organizing and relating memories and events. She called this up, and found herself reciting the long years' adventures calmly, softly, as if they had been written by someone else about a stranger's life.

He listened, not interrupting even by a shift of expression that might have affected her ability to recall and report what had happened. When she was through, he nodded once.

"So. I can understand your confusion, Adept Lunzie. You have been stretched and bent past the limits of your training. Yet you remained the supple reed; you did not break."

That was acceptance, and even praise. This time the warmth that rushed over her brought comfort to cramped limbs and to spaces of her mind still sore despite Cleansing the Stone. She had been sure he would say she had failed, that she was unfit to be an Adept.

"Our training," he was saying, "did not consider the peculiar strains of those with repeated temporal displacements, even though you brought the original problem to our attention. We should have foreseen the need, but . . ." He shrugged. "We are not gods, to know all we have not yet seen. Again, you have much to teach us, as we help you regain your balance."

"I live to learn, Venerable Master," said Lunzie, bowing her head.

"We learn by living; we live by learning."

She felt his hand on her head, the rare touch of approval, affirmation. When she looked up again, he was gone and she was alone in the pavilion with her thoughts.

Retraining, after that, was both more and less stressful than she had feared. Her pallet in the sleeping hut was comfortable enough after Ireta and she had never minded plain food. But it had been a long time since she'd actually done all the physical exercises; she spent the first days constantly sore and weary.

All the Instructors were perfectionists; there was only one right way (they reminded her) to make each block, each feint, each strike. Only one right way to sit, to kneel, to keep the inner center balanced. She had never been as good with the martial skills of Discipline; she had always thought them less fitting for a physician. But she had never been this bad. Finally one of them put her at rest and folded herself down nearby.

"I sense either unwillingness or great resistance of the body, Lunzie. Can you explain?"

"Both, I think," Lunzie began slowly, letting her breathing slow. "As a healer, I'm committed to preserving health; this side of Discipline always seems a failure to me . . . something we haven't done right, that let things come to conflict. And then some physician — perhaps me, perhaps another — will have to work to heal what we break."

"That is the unwillingness," said the instructor. "What is the body's difficulty? Only that?"

"I'm not sure." Lunzie started to slump, and reminded herself to balance her spine properly. "I would like to think it is the many times in cold sleep — the long times, when I spent years in one position. Supposedly there's no aging, but there's such stiffness on waking. Perhaps it does something, some residual loss of flexibility."

The instructor said nothing for a long moment, her eyes half-closed. Lunzie relaxed, letting her sore muscles take the most comfortable length.

"For the unwillingness, you must speak to the Venerable Master," said the instructor finally. "For the body's resistance, you may be right — it may be the repeated cold sleep. We will try another approach on that, for a few days, and see what comes of it."

Another approach meant hours in hot and cold pools, swimming against artificial currents. Lunzie could feel her body stretching, loosening, then re-knitting itself into the confident, capable body she remembered, almost as if it had been a broken bone. Her conditioning included gymnastics, running, climbing, music, and finally — after long conferences with the Venerable Master — renewed work with unarmed combat.

She would never be a figure of the Warrior, he had told her, but each aspect of Discipline had its place in every Adept, and she must accept the need to cause injury and even death, when failure meant the deaths of others.

But her dislike of conflict was not all they discussed. He had lived the years she had spent exiled in cold sleep; he remembered both her as she had been, and all she had missed of those years. He let her talk at length of her distress at the estrangements in her family, the guilt she felt for disliking some of her descendants and resenting their attitudes. About the pain of losing a lover, the fear that no relationship could ever be sustained. She told him about meeting Sassinak, and about the strains between them. "She's the older one, really — she even said so —" Her voice broke for an instant, and he insisted on hearing the whole conversation, every detail.

"That hurt you," he said afterwards. "You are older, you feel, and you want the respect naturally due to elders. . . ." He let that trail away in a neutral tone.

"But I don't feel like an elder, either," Lunzie said, consciously relaxing her hands, which wanted to clamp into fists. "I feel . . . I don't know what I feel. I can't be young, it seems, *or* old: I'm suspended in life now just as much as when I was in cold sleep. I don't even know *which* child she is — did I see her and forget her? Is she one they never mentioned?"

"The leaf torn from the branch by wind," he said softly, smiling a little.

"Exactly."

"You must come to believe that the branch was no more yours than the wind is; you must come to see that we are each, in each moment, in the right place, the place from which all action and reflection come, and to which they go." He cocked his head, much like a bird. "What will you do if you must enter cold sleep again?"

THE PLANET PIRATES

She had not let herself think of that, forcing away the panic it brought with all the Discipline she could bring to bear. How had he known that she woke sweating some nights, sure that the terrifying numbness was once more spreading through her?

"I — I can't." She held her breath, stiff in every muscle, looking down and away from him. She heard the faintest sigh of breath.

"You cannot know that it will never happen." His voice was neutral.

"Not *again* —" It was as much plea as promise to herself; all the days of retraining might have been nothing for the rush of that emotion.

"I had hoped this would heal of itself," his voice said, musing. "But since it has not, we must confront it." A pause so long she almost looked up, and then he snapped, "Adept Lunzie!" and her eyes met his. "This is not beyond your strength or ability: this you will conquer. We cannot send you out still subject to such fears."

She wanted to protest, but knew it would do no good. The next several days tested her strength of will and body both: intense sessions of counseling, hours spent in a variety of cubicles resembling cold-sleep tanks of various types, even a couple of cold-sleep inductions, with the preliminary drugs taking her briefly into unconsciousness.

She thought at first she would simply go crazy, but the Venerable Master had been right: she could endure it, and come out sane. Valuable knowledge if she needed it, though she hoped she would not.

By the time her other instructors approved her skills, her mind had found a new balance. She could see her past uncertainties, her flurries of worry, her bouts with envy and guilt, as the struggles of a creature growing from one form to another. Most people had some emotional turmoil in their thirties; at least some of hers was probably just that: growing out of one stage of life. She had been that person; now she was someone else, someone who no longer envied Sassinak's power or Aygar's physical strength. Her life made sense to her, not as a tragic series of losses, but as challenges met, changes endured and even enjoyed.

The memory of her stuffier descendants no longer irritated her — poor darlings, she thought, they don't even know what fun they're missing — and Sassinak's potential for violence now seemed the appropriate foil for her own more pacific abilities. She could cherish Sassinak as a descendant, and respect her as an elder, at one and the same time, with a ruffle of amusement for the odd circumstance that made her both.

Her last sight of the Mountain was of that same quiet pool, that same boulder, the door opening now in the hands of another novice. She knew her own face expressed nothing but calm; inside she could feel her heart smiling, feel the excitement of another chance at life with all its difficulties.

Now the medical personnel in the corridors looked more like potential colleagues, and less like fortunate strangers who would never accept her. Lunzie checked into the Transient Physicians' Hostel at the first open terminal, and then entered the callcode the Venerable Master Adept had given her. The screen flashed briefly, then steadied as a line scrolled across it.

"Lunzie . . . good news. Level seven, Concourse B, 1300 tomorrow." And that was that, and she was on her way.

The Hostel, when she arrived at its door, gave her the clip to a single room with cube reader and datalink. She put her duffel on the single bed and touched the keypad. A menu of services available filled the wallscreen. She could find a partner for chess or sleep, purchase goods or information (to be included, with a service charge, in her hostel total), or roam the medical databases, all without leaving the room.

She was tempted to send a message to Sassinak; Fleetcom, the public access mail system for all Fleet personnel, would forward it. But that might bring attention they didn't want. Safer to wait. She had almost a full Standard day before meeting someone (the Venerable Master had not said who) the next day at 1300. She would use that time to make predictable inquiries, things anyone would expect her to want to know.

She treated herself to a good meal at a cafe that occupied the space where, years before, she'd known a bar. The music now had a different sound, lots of chiming bells and some low woodwind behind a female trio. Back in her room, she fell asleep easily and woke without concern.

Level seven of Concourse B still sported the apricot-striped walls that made Lunzie feel she had fallen into a layered dessert. Various names had been tried for this section, from Exotic

Epidemiology to Nonstandard Colonial Medical Assistance. None had stuck; everyone called it (and still called it, she'd found out) the Oddball Corps. Its official designation, at the moment, was Variant Medical Concerns Analysis Division . . . not that anyone used it.

Lunzie presented her credentials at the front desk. Instead of the directions she expected, she heard a cheerful voice yelling down the corridor a moment later.

"Lunzie! The legendary Lunzie!" A big bearded man grinned as he advanced, his hands outstretched. She searched her memory and came up with nothing. Who was this? He went on. "We heard you were coming. Forty-three years, in this last cold sleep? And that makes how much altogether? We've got a lot of research we can do on you." His face fell slightly and he peered more closely at her. "You *do* remember me, don't you?"

She was about to say no, when a flicker of memory gave her the face of an enthusiastic teenager touring a hospital with a class. Now where had that been? She couldn't quite say . . . but he had been the most persistently curious in his group, asking questions long after his companions (and even his instructors) were bored. He had been pried loose only by the fifth reminder that their transport was leaving . . . *now*. She had no idea what his name was.

"You were younger," she slowly, giving herself time to think. "I don't remember that beard."

His hands touched it. "Oh . . . yes. It does make a difference, I suppose. And it's been over forty years for you, even if most of that wasn't real time. I mean wake time. I was just so glad to see your name come up on the boards. I suppose you never knew that it was that hospital tour that got me into medicine, and beyond that into the Oddballs —"

"I'm glad," she said. What *was* his name? He had worn a big square nameplate that day; she could remember that it was green with black lettering, but not what the name was.

"Jerik," he said now, relieving her of that anxiety. "Doctor Jerik now, but Jerik to you, of course. I'm an epidemiologist, currently stranded in Admin because my boss is on leave."

He had the collar pin of an honor graduate and the second tiny chip of diamond which meant he was also an Adept. It was not something to speak of, but it meant he was not just out here blathering away for nothing. His pose of idle chatter and innocent enthusiasm was just that — a pose.

"You'll be wondering," he said, "why you were dragged into the Oddballs when you deserve a good long rest and chance to catch up on your education."

"Rather," said Lunzie. He must think the area was under surveillance, and it probably was. Only the Mountain would be certainly beyond anyone's ability to spy on.

"There are some interesting things going on — and you, with your experience of cold sleep, may be just the person we need. Of course, you will have to recertify . . ."

Lunzie grimaced. "I hate fast-tapes."

He was all sympathy. "I know. I hate them, too — it's like eating three meals in five minutes; your brain feels stuffed. But it's the only way, and unless you have two or three years to spare . . ."

"No. You're right. What will I need?"

What she would need, after 43 years out of date, was far more than Mayerd on Sassinak's ship had been able to give her. And she'd refused Mayerd's offer of fast-tape equipment. New surgical procedures, using new equipment: that meant not only fast-tape time, but actual in-the-OR work on "slushes," the gruesomely realistic androids used for surgical practice. New drugs, with all the attendant information on dosages, side effects, contraindications, and drug interferences. New theories of cognition that related to the cold sleep experience.

One of the neat things about her hop-skip-and-jump experiences, Lunzie realized partway through this retraining, was that it gave her an unusual overview of medical progress . . . and regress. She solved one diagnostic problem on the fourth day, pointing out that a mere 45 years ago, and two sectors away, that cluster of symptoms was called Galles Disease. It had been wiped out by a clever genetic patch, and had now reoccurred ("Probably random mutation," said the senior investigator with a sigh. "I should have thought of that") in an area where everyone had forgotten about it.

Differences between sectors, and between cultures within a sector, meant that what she learned might not be new in one place — or available in twenty others. Access to the best medical technology was at least as uneven as on Old Earth. Lunzie spent all her time in the fast-tape booths, or practicing procedures and taking the preliminary recertification exams. Basic and advanced life support, basic and advanced trauma first response, basic and advanced contagious disease techniques . . . her head would have spun if it could.

In her brief time "off," she tried to catch up with current research in her area, flicking through the computerized journal abstracts.

"What we really need is another team member for a trip to Diplo." Someone groaned, in the back of the room, and someone else shushed the groaner.

"Come on," the speaker said, half-angrily. "It's only a short tour, thirty days max."

"Because that's the medical limit," came a mutter.

"This comes up every year," the speaker said. "We have a contract pending; we have an obligation; whatever your personal views, the heavyworlders on Diplo have significant medical problems which are still being researched."

"Not until you give us an allowance for G-damage."

Lunzie thought that was the same mutterer, someone a few seats to her left and behind.

"Pay and allowances are adjusted for local conditions," the speaker went on, staring fixedly at his notes. "This year's special topic is the effect of prolonged cold sleep on heavyworlder biochemistry, particularly the accumulation of calcium affecting cardiac function." He paused. Lunzie wondered when that topic had been assigned. Everyone would know, from her qualifications posted in the files, that she had special knowledge relevant to the research. But it would not do to show eagerness. The speaker went on. "We've already got a molecular biologist, and a cardiac physiologist —"

The names came up on the main room screen, along with their most recent publications. Very impressive, Lunzie thought to herself. Both Bias, the biologist, and Tailler, the cardiac physiologist, had published lead articles in good journals.

"Rehab medicine?" asked someone in back.

The speaker nodded. "If your Boards include a subspecialty rating in heavyworlder rehab, certainly. Clearly relevant to this year's special problem."

Another name went up on the screen, presumably the rehab

specialist who'd spoken: Conigan, age 42, had published a text-book on heavyworlder rehabilitation after prolonged work undersea. Lunzie decided she'd waited long enough. What if someone else qualified for "her" slot?

"I've got a background in prolonged cold sleep, and some heavyworlder experience." Heads turned to look at her; Discipline kept her from flushing under that scrutiny. The speaker peered at what she assumed was her file on his podium screen. "Ah . . . Lunzie. Yes. I see you haven't yet taken your Boards re-certification exam?"

"It's scheduled for three days from now." It had been scheduled for six months from now but Jerik had arranged for her to take the exam singly, ahead of time. "All the prelims are on file."

"Yes, they are. It's amazing you've caught up so fast, and your skills are well suited to this mission. Contingent on your passing your Boards, you're accepted for this assignment." He looked up, scanning the room for the next possible applicant.

The woman next to Lunzie nudged her.

"Are you sure you want to go to Diplo? I heard your last cold sleep was because heavyworlders went primitive."

Lunzie managed not to glare. She had not heard the rumors herself, but she'd known they would be flying around the medical and scientific community.

"I can't talk about it," she said, not untruthfully. "The case won't be tried for months, and until then —"

"Oh, I quite understand. I'm not prying, Doctor. It's just that *if* it was heavyworlders, I'm surprised you're signing up for Diplo."

Lunzie chuckled. "Well, there's this glitch in my pay records —"

The woman snorted. "There would be. Of course; I see. You'd think they could realize the last thing you need is worry about money, but the Feds have acute formitis."

"A bad case," Lunzie agreed.

With the others, she craned her head to see the last responder, a dark man whose specialty was heavyworlder genetics. From the heft of his shoulders, he might have heavyworlder genes of his own, she thought.

So it proved when the whole team met for briefing. Jarl was the smaller (and nonadapted) of twins born to a heavyworlder couple; he was fascinated by the unusual inheritance patterns of adaptation, and by the equally unusual inheritance patterns of tolerance or intolerance to cold sleep. Aside from his heavy-worlder genes, he seemed quite normal, and Lunzie felt no uneasiness around him.

Bias, the volatile molecular biologist, was far more upsetting; he seemed ready to fly into pieces at any moment. Lunzie wondered how he would take the heavy gravity; he didn't look particularly athletic. Tailler, the cardiac physiologist, impressed Lunzie as a good team leader: stable, steady, but energetic, he would be easy to work with. She already knew, from a short bio at the foot of one of his papers, that he climbed mountains for recreation: the physical effort should be within his ability. Conigan, the rehab specialist, was a slender redheaded woman who reminded Lunzie of an older (but no less enthusiastic) Varian.

She was aware that she herself was the subject of just such curiosity and scrutiny. They would know little about her besides her file info: she had no friends or past associates they could question covertly. She wondered what they saw in her face, what they expected or worried about or hoped for. At least she had passed her Boards, and by a respectable margin, so Jerik had told her. She wondered, but did not ask, how he had gotten the actual raw scores, which supposedly no one ever saw.

And all the while, Bias outlined the project in excited phrases, pausing with his pointer aloft to see if they'd understood the last point. Lunzie made herself pay attention. Whatever information she could get for Sassinak and the trial aside, her team members deserved her best work.

By the time their ship came to the orbital station serving Diplo, they were all working easily together. Lunzie thought past the next few months, and Tanegli's trial, to hope that she would find such professional camaraderie again. There were things you could not say to a cruiser captain, however dear to your heart she was, jokes she would never get, ideas beyond her scope. And here Lunzie had that kind of ease.

✧ CHAPTER THREE

"I did not need this." Sassinak waved the hardcopy of the Security-striped message at Dupaynil and Ford. "I've got things to do. We *all* have. And the last thing we need to do is waste time playing nursemaid to a senile conspirator." Things had gone too smoothly, she thought, when she'd sent Lunzie off. She should have expected some hitch to her plans.

Dupaynil had the suave expression she most disliked. "I beg your pardon, Commander?"

He could not be that suave unless he knew what was in the message: Ford, who clearly did not, looked worried.

"Orders," Sassinak said crisply. "New orders, sent with all applicable coding on the IFTL link. We are to transport the accused conspirator Tanegli and the alleged native-born Iretan Aygar to . . ." She paused, and watched them. Dupaynil merely waited, lips pursed; Ford spoke up.

"Sector HQ? Fleet HQ on Regg?"

"No. *Federation* Headquarters. For a full trial before and in the presence of the Federation High Council. We are responsible," and she glanced down at the message to check the precise wording, "responsible for the transportation and safe arrival of said prisoner, who shall be released to the custody of Council security forces only. The trial date has already been set, for a local date that translates to about eight standard months from now. Winter Assizes, as we were told before. Prisoner's counsel is given as Klepsin, Vigal, and Tollwin. And you know what that means."

"Pinky Vigal, Defender of the Innocent," said Dupaynil, almost chuckling. "That ought to make an exciting trial. You know, Commander, he can probably make you look like a planet pirate yourself, a villainous sort masquerading as a Fleet officer.

Hmmm . . . you stole the uniform from Tanegli, bribed everyone else to testify against him."

"It's not funny," said Sassinak, glowering. She had never been one to follow the escapades of fashionable lawyers, but anyone in human space had heard of Pinky Vigal. It was another of the failings of civilian law, Sassinak thought, that someone everyone knew had done something could not be punished if a honeytongued defense counsel could convince even one member of a trial jury that some minute error had been made in procedure. Fleet had better methods.

"So," Ford broke in, clearly intending a distraction. "We're responsible for Tanegli until we get to Federation Central . . . and for Aygar as well? Why Aygar?"

"Witness for both sides, I suppose," Dupaynil said with a flourish of his hand. "Friendly to one, hostile to the other, but indispensable to both."

"*And* registered copies of all the testimony we took and depositions from all bridge officers, and any other crew members having contact with the said Tanegli and Aygar," Sassinak continued to read. "Kipling's bunions! By now that's half the crew, the way Aygar's been roaming around. If I'd known . . ."

She knew from Ford's expression that she must look almost as angry as she felt. They would spend weeks getting in and out of the required transfer points for Federation Central, and then weeks being interviewed — *deposed*, she reminded herself — and no doubt Fleet Security would have its own band of interrogators there. In the meantime, the *Zaid-Dayan* would be sitting idle while the enemy continued its work. She would no doubt have umpteen thousand forms to fill out and sign: in multiple copies which had to be processed individually, rather than on computer, for security reasons.

She noticed that Dupaynil was watching her with alert interest. So he *had* read the message even before she'd seen it — which meant he had a tap on the IFTL link, or had somehow coerced one of her Communications Officers into peeling a copy to his quarters. What else did he know, or had he been told? She decided not to ask; he wouldn't tell her, and she'd just be angry when he refused.

"Dupaynil." The change in her tone surprised him; his smugness disappeared. "I want you to start finding out which crew Aygar has been in contact with. Marines, Wefts, officers, enlisted, everyone. You can have a clerk if you need one —"

"No . . . I can manage . . ." His voice was bemused; she felt a surge of glee that she was making him think.

"I suspect it's too late to restrict his contacts. And after all, we want him friendly to FSP policies. But if the crew know that they'll have to go through paperwork and interviews because they talk to him, some may pull back."

"Good idea . . . and I'd best get started." Dupaynil sketched a salute — to more than her rank, she was sure — and left.

Sassinak said nothing for a moment, engaging her own (surely still undiscovered?) privacy systems. Then she grinned at Ford.

"That *sneak*: he knew already."

"I thought so, too. But how?"

"He's Naval Intelligence — but I'm never sure with those types if he's Intelligence for someone else, or someones else, as well. The fact that he's planted his own devices — and too cleverly to reassure me of his ultimate aims — is distinctly unsettling because there's no telling *why* he's doing it. *I'm*" — and Sassinak pushed her thumb into her chest, grinning — "allowed to be that clever, but not my subordinates.

"At the moment, that's not the issue. Getting you away to find your dear great-aunt or whatever *is* the issue, because I don't want you tied up for the time this is going to take. We need information before that trial date." Sassinak pushed the orders over to Ford who noted the date and its conversion to Fleet Standard notation on his personal handcomp. "If you can't find anything by then, be sure you're back to say so."

"But how can I leave when all —"

Sassinak hushed him with a gesture. "There are more tricks in that comm shack than Dupaynil knows about. So far, he's the only one who knows that you were present when these orders arrived. And *he's* got priority orders he doesn't know about yet. But he soon will. Just follow my lead."

The bridge crew came to attention when Sassinak arrived, but she gave the helm to Ford and entered the communications alcove.

"Captain's orders," she said crisply to the officer on watch. "You received an IFTL a short time ago?"

"Yes, ma'am, to the captain's address with encryption."

Sassinak could not tell if the Comm Officer's tension was normal or not. "The contents of that message require me to sit comm watch myself for two hours." This was unusual, but not unheard of: sometimes extremely sensitive information was sent this way. "I expect incoming IFTL signals, encrypted, and by these orders," and she waved the paper, "only the ship's captain can receive them."

"Yes, ma'am. Will the captain need any assistance?"

Sassinak let herself glare, and the Comm Officer vanished onto the bridge. What she was going to do was both illegal and dangerous . . . but so was what Dupaynil had done, and what the enemy had done. She logged onto the board and engaged her private comm link to the Ssli interface.

So far, normal procedure. But now . . . her fingers danced on the board, calling up the file of the original encrypted message. And there it was, the quadruple header code she had never forgotten, not in all the years. Idiots, she thought; they should have changed that long since, as she had changed from a naive ensign standing communications watch to an experienced and powerful ship captain.

With the right header code, it was easy to prepare an incoming message Dupaynil would have to believe was genuine. The other "incoming" message would be in regular Fleet fashion, Ford's detachment on "family compassionate leave" . . . but it would not arrive until Dupaynil was gone.

Where to send Dupaynil? Where would he be safely out of her way, and also, in his own mind, doing something reasonable? She wished she could send him to a Thek, preferably a large, old, very slow one . . . but that wouldn't work. Fleet Security had nothing to do with the pacifist Bronthins, or the Mrouxt.

Suddenly it came to her, and she fought back a broad grin which anyone glancing into the alcove might notice (why would the captain be grinning to herself in the comm shack?): Ford would dig up dirt on the Paraden family's dealings, and Lunzie would find what she could on Diplo . . . and that, according to what they'd found on Ireta, left the alien Setis without an investigator. *That* would be Dupaynil's chore.

He had done a lot of diplomatic work, he'd said. He had bragged after dinner, once, about his ability to get along with any of the alien members of the Federation, and even said the Seti weren't as bad as everyone thought.

So, quickly, carefully, Sassinak wrote the orders. The Ssli had always shown her special considerations, above and beyond their usual shipboard duties. She owed her life to the sessile Ssli Communications Officer on her first tour of duty when Hssrho had located her in deep space after she'd had a "misadventure" in an evac pod. In gratitude she had always taken care to cultivate the Ssli Communications Officers on every other posting. Now she consulted the resident Ssli. She could not simply pretend that an IFTL had come in; the computer records would show it had not and Dupaynil probably had subverted computer security to some degree. But Dupaynil's actual shipboard experience was limited and Sassinak knew that he had never bothered to introduce himself to Dhrossh. Her favorite Wefts, such as Galory, had mentioned in passing that Dupaynil's mind was not the right sort for direct contact. Whatever they meant by that.

The Ssli thought her scheme was delightful . . . an odd choice of adjective, Sassinak thought, and wondered if the speech synthesizer software was working correctly. She had never suspected the Ssli of any remotely human emotions. Ssli syntax tended toward the mathematical. But she entered her encrypted message, and the Ssli initiated IFTL communication with another Ssli on another Fleet vessel. Which one she would never know.

The Ssli, her own had informed her, felt no compunction about concealing such communications from human crew. Her own message bounced back, and appeared as a true incoming message on the computer and the board. Sassinak routed it to the decryption computer, peeled a copy for Dupaynil's file, and leaned out to call to the Comm Watch Officer, who had taken a seat on the bridge.

"Get me Dupaynil," she said, letting herself glower a bit.

Ford glanced at her but did not even let his brows rise. Dupaynil arrived in a suspiciously short time; this time Sassinak's glower was not faked at all.

"You," she said, pointing a finger at him. The rest of the bridge crew became very busy at their own boards. "You have an incoming IFTL, which not only required decryption and states that I do not have access, but in addition to *that*, it carries initiation codes I remember all too well!"

He would have to know that, or he could find out — and perhaps her flare of anger would distract him from the unlikeliness of his own orders. At the moment, he looked confused, as well he might.

"This!" Sassinak pointed to the display she'd frozen onscreen. "The last time I saw that initiation code, that very one, in quad like that, someone smacked me over the head and dumped me in an evac pod. If you think you're going to do something like that, *Major* — take me out and take over my ship — you are very much mistaken!" She could hear the anger in her own voice, and the bridge was utterly silent.

"I . . . Commander Sassinak, I'm sorry, but I don't know what you're talking about. That code is known to me, yes — it's from the IG's office. But . . ."

"I don't like secrets on my ship, Dupaynil! I don't like junior officers receiving IFTL messages to which the captain is forbidden access. And encrypted messages at that. I don't like people going over my head to the IG's office. What's your gripe, eh?"

Dupaynil, she was sure, was not as upset as he looked. He was too smart by half. But he was responding to her obvious anger and had lost some of his gloss. "Commander, the IG's office might have reason to contact me about the Security work I've done here — if nothing else, about that — you know . . ." His voice lowered. Sassinak let herself calm down.

"I still don't like it," she grumbled, but softly. Someone smothered a cough, over in Weapons, and nearly choked from the effort. "All right. I see what you mean, and from what Lunzie said that whole thing was classified. Maybe there is a reason. But I don't like secrets. Not like this, at a time when we're all . . ." She let her voice trail away. Dupaynil's lids drooped slightly. Was he convinced? "Take your damned message, and unless you *like* causing me grief, tell me what's so important I can't even read it."

Dupaynil moved to the decryption computer and entered his password.

Sassinak turned to the Communications Watch Officer, and said, "Take over. And make sure I know about any incoming or outgoing messages. From anyone." This last with a sidelong glance at Dupaynil.

The Security Officer was staring at the screen as if it had grown tentacles; Sassinak controlled an impulse to laugh at him. He glanced at her, a shrewd, calculating look, and she spoke immediately.

"Well? Are you supposed to clap me in irons, or what?" He shook his head, and sighed.

"No, Commander, it's nothing like that. It is . . . odd . . . that is all. May we speak in your office? Privately?"

Sassinak nodded shortly and left the bridge with a final glower for everyone. She could feel the support of her crew — her *own* crew — like a warm blanket around her shoulders. In her office, she put her formal desk between herself and Dupaynil. His brows rose, recognizing that for what it was, and he sighed again.

"Captain, I swear to you . . ."

"Don't bother." Sassinak turned away, briefly, to glance at the hardcopy he offered her, then met his dark eyes squarely. "If you don't know what I'm talking about, then you don't — but I cannot ignore anything like that. It nearly cost me my life twenty years ago."

"I'm sorry. Truly sorry. But just as you received unwelcome orders a short while ago, I have now received unwelcome orders to leave this ship — unwelcome and even stranger than yours."

"Oh? And were are you supposed to go?" She saw Dupaynil, wince at the unbending ice in that tone. She could care less, as long as she rid herself of a potential traitor.

"To the Seti — to the Sek of Fomalhaut, in fact. One of my past sins come to haunt me, I suppose. Apparently there's some kind of diplomatic problem with the new human ambassador to the High Court, and I'm supposed to know someone who might be of assistance."

"But you can't," Sassinak said sharply. "You can't leave: we're all under orders to proceed to Federation Central, you most of all. You were in on all of it; your testimony . . ."

"Can be recorded, and will have to be. I'm sorry. Truly sorry, as I said, but these orders take precedence. Have to." His finger tapped the authorizing seals and codes; in the labyrinthine regulations of Fleet and FSP, the IG's signature outweighed even the Judge Advocate General's. "Besides, I might still be of use to you. The Thek hinted that the Seti were involved, but they had no solid data, or none they passed to us. That's something I can look into, with my contacts in the Seti diplomatic subculture. They estimate the assignment proper will take me only about six Standard months; I can be back in time to share what I've learned, and testify if called."

Sassinak heaved a dramatic sigh. "Well. I suppose, if you have to, you have to. And maybe you *can* find something useful, although the Seti are the least likable bunch of bullies I've ever met."

"They do require careful handling," Dupaynil murmured, almost demurely.

Sassinak wondered what he was up to now. She did not trust him one hairsbreadth. "Very well. Where are we supposed to drop you off?"

"It says your orders will be in shortly and I'm to leave at the next transfer point. Wherever that is."

"Somebody's entirely too clever," Sassinak growled. She hoped she hadn't been clever enough to trip herself with this — but so far Dupaynil seemed convinced.

Just then the Junior Comm Officer tapped timidly on her door, and offered a hardcopy of her second faked IFTL message, the one telling her to drop out of FTL drive, and proceed to the nearest Fleet station. The nearest Fleet station was a resupply center with only monthly tanker traffic and the occasional escort or patrol craft dropping by. She remembered it well, from her one previous visit fifteen years before. She showed Dupaynil the orders.

"Supply Center 64: says there's an escort in dock. You'll take that, I imagine?" At his nod, she said, "I'll expect you back at 1500, to give your deposition; we'll have the equipment set up by then, and an ETA for the supply center."

The rest of that day Sassinak hardly dared look at Ford; she would have burst out laughing. Dupaynil came back, gave his testimony while she asked every question she could think of before she sent him off to pack his gear.

They popped out of FTL space within a few hours of the supply center. Sassinak had already dispatched messages to it and the escort vessel (whose pilot had been planning an unauthorized three-day party with the supply center's crew). Escorts, not large enough to house a Ssli, were out of the IFTL links. Once aboard, Dupaynil would have only sublight ways of checking up on his orders.

Docking the *Zaid-Dayan* at the supply station was simple: the station had equipment to handle large transports of all shapes, and the small escort took up only a minute space at the far end of the station. Sassinak indulged herself, as she rarely could any-more, and brought the cruiser in herself, easing it to the gantry so gently that no one detected contact until the status lights changed color.

"Nice job!" said the station Dockmaster, a Weft. "We'll have air up in the tubes in a few minutes. Is your passenger ready to trans-fer?"

"Ready when you are."

Dupaynil would leave by one of the small hatches, an airlock on the second flight deck. Even with a Fleet facility, Sassinak didn't like opening up real interior space to a possible pressure loss. She glanced at Dupaynil, visible on one of the side screens, and flicked a switch to put him on-channel.

"They're airing up the tube. Sure you don't want a pressure suit?"

"No, thank you."

He had already explained how he felt about pressure suits. Sassinak was tempted to teach him a lesson about that, but under the circumstances she wanted their parting to be as friendly as possible.

"Fine . . . we're standing by for your departure signal." She could see, in the monitor, the light above the hatch come on, flick twice, and steady to green.

"On my way," said Dupaynil. Then he paused, and faced the monitor-cam squarely. "Commander? I did *not* intend to cause you trouble and I have no idea what that initiation code means to you. You may not believe me, but I have no desire to see you hurt."

And I have a great desire to see your back going off my ship, thought Sassinak, but she smiled for his benefit. "I'd like to believe you, and if that's true, I hope we serve together again someday. Have a good trip. Don't let those Seti use you for nest padding."

When the status lights confirmed that Dupaynil was safely off the ship and into the station, Sassinak breathed a sigh of relief. *Now* she could tell Ford what she was up to — or enough for him to help her with the last of Dupaynil's maneuver. That involved a bit of straight talking to the escort captain, on the need for immediate departure, and the importance of keeping his mouth firmly shut. Sassinak kept the *Zaid-Dayan* linked to the station until the escort broke away.

❖   ❖   ❖

"And just how did you manage *that*?" Ford had waited just long enough for her to engage her office's privacy circuits. Sassinak grinned at him. "And don't bother to look innocent," he went on. "I don't know how you did it, but you must have."

"Let's just say that someone who's spent her career on ships knows a bit more about them than a Security office rat."

"And you're not going to explain, eh?"

"Not entirely. Would you trust Dupaynil to have unclipped whatever bugs he's set out on this ship?"

"Mmm. I see."

"And you are smart enough to figure out everything you need to know. You can think about it while looking up your remarkable relative."

"But what about the depositions? I can't leave now!" His face changed expression suddenly. "Oh. The only one who knew about those orders is . . . Gods above, Captain, what did you *do*?"

"Used the resources available to make appropriate dispositions of personnel in a situation of extreme delicacy," said Sassinak crisply. "And that's all I'm going to say about it. Your assignment is to uncover whatever links you can between the suspect merchant families and planet piracy and the slave trade. On my orders, by my assessment that this need overrides any other orders you may have heard about."

"Ummm . . . yes, ma'am."

"Good. Dupaynil, meanwhile, is supposed to be investigating the Seti and their connection with all this nastiness. I have heard, from time to time, that the Seti expressed sympathy with the heavyworlders for having been the victims of genetic engineering. You remember that they believe all such activity is wrong and refuse any kind of bioengineering on their own behalf. They're also known to hate Wefts, although no one seems to know why, and the Wefts won't comment."

"I've never understood why the Seti came into the Federation at all," Ford said. He seemed glad enough of a detour.

"Let Dupaynil worry about that," Sassinak said. "Now d'you think a direct call to your family will locate your great aunt?"

"No, probably not. Let me think. The family hears at least once a Standard year at Homefaring, but that's five months away. And she travels, you know; she's supposed to have one of the most luxurious yachts in space. We might find her in one of the society papers."

"*Society* papers!"

Ford flushed. "She's that kind; I told you. Minor aristocracy, but considers herself well up there. Once we locate her, I can fake — I mean arrange — a message from the family to justify a visit."

Sassinak did not even know the names of the papers called up on their next shift down into normal space. She glanced at the sheets as he passed them over: even in flat copy, the photographs fairly glittered with wealth. Women in jewels and glistening gowns, men in formal Court dress, ribbons streaming from one knee. The sumptuous interiors of "gracious homes" as they were called, homes that existed merely to show off their owners' wealth. Sassinak could not imagine actually sleeping in one of the beds shown, a "sculpted masterpiece" with a stream of moving water actually running through it. She could feel her lip curling.

"Ah! Here she is." Ford had his finger on the place. "Among the notable guests at the wedding — would you look at that so-called bride! — is my very own noble relative. Will travel on to participate in the Season at the usual Rainbow Arc events . . . which means she's somewhere between Zalaive and the Rainbow Arc. Permission to initiate search?"

"Go ahead." Sassinak was deep in a discussion of the reasons why cuulinda was destined to replace folsath as the newest sporting rage among the nobility. She hadn't heard of either, and the article didn't mention whether they were played with teams, animals, or computers. Ford busied himself at the terminal, checking Fleet's comprehensive database on vessel ownership and movement on the lowlink.

"Ah! She's en route to Colles, ETA two weeks, and there's a . . . Oh snarks!"

"A what?" asked Sassinak, looking up at his tone.

"Well. I can get to her by her next planetfall, but it means hitching a ride on a tanker-transport."

Sassinak grinned at him. Tankers had a reputation as bare-bones transportation, and they played out that game on visitors.

"It'll make the contrast all the greater." She looked at the route he'd found. "I'll cut your orders, get you on that patrol-class. Don't forget to arrange that family message somehow."

"I won't."

His routing didn't give them much time, but, with Lunzie and Dupaynil both out of the way, they enjoyed a last festive evening in Sassinak's cabin. Then he was gone, and Sassinak had the final planning to do as they approached the crowded inner sector of the Federation.

She wondered how Aygar would react to the publicity and culture shock of FedCentral. He had been using the data banks on the *Zaid-Dayan* several hours a day. Ford kept a record of his access. He talked to both Marines and Fleet enlisted personnel and word of that trickled back to Sassinak by channels she doubted Aygar knew about. He had asked to take some of the basic achievement tests, to gauge for himself where he stood educationally. Sassinak had given permission, even though Dr. Mayerd thought "the boy," as she called him, should have professional advice.

The test results lay in the computer files. Sassinak had not accessed them, out of respect for the little privacy Aygar had, but from his demeanor he seemed well pleased with himself. She was less certain.

He was a striking young man, attractive if you liked muscles and regular features, and she admitted to herself that she did. But except for that subtle sense of rivalry with Lunzie, she would not have been drawn to him. She liked men of experience, men with whom she could share her broad background. Fleet officers of her own rank, or near it. It was all very well to impress youngsters like that ensign Timran. No woman minded starry-eyed boys as long as they stayed respectful. But Aygar did not fit that category, or any other.

"Commander? Central docks wants a word."

That brought her out of her reverie, and across the passage onto the bridge. She had never brought a ship into Federation Central's Docking Station before. Few did; Fleet protected the center of Federation government services, but was not entirely welcome here in force. Some races, and some humans, feared military rebellion and takeover. Hence the slow approach, dropping to sublight drive well outside the system, zigging and zagging (at high cost in fuel and time) to make unhandy checkpoints where defense satellites scrutinized their appearance and orders.

"Commander Sassinak, FSP cruiser *Zaid-Dayan*," said Sassinak.

"Ah . . . Commander . . . ah . . . procedures for securing armament, as required by the Federation for all incoming warships, must be complete before your vessel passes the outer shell."

Sassinak frowned, catching Arly's eye. The *Zaid-Dayan* could, in fact, take on most planetary defenses; she could understand why the more nervous members of the Federation would not want a human-crewed, fully armed heavy cruiser over their heads. But her trust in Federation Security right now was severely limited. She did not want her ship vulnerable.

"Securing," she said, with a nod to Arly.

Arly was scowling, but more with concentration than discontent. They had already discussed what to do; it remained to see if it would work. As a technical problem, Sassinak thought, watching Arly's hands rove over her control board, it was interesting.

The Federation had only one telepathic race, the Wefts. Since the Wefts usually got along with humans, and had nothing to gain by disarming Fleet ships, any Wefts were unlikely to complain. The Seti would certainly complain of anything they recognized, and the pacifist members of the Federation, the Bronthin, would drop their foals if they knew. But would they know? Would they consider weaponry the same way Sassinak and Arly did?

The more obvious armament, items specified in the ship's Fleet classification, had to be secured. In this context, that meant control circuits patched out, projectile weapons unloaded and projectiles secured in locked compartments, power detached from EM projectors and opticals. A FedCentral Insystem Security team would be aboard, guarding access to those areas, to prevent anyone from launching a missile, or frying something with a laser.

But the *Zaid-Dayan's* power did not reside only in its named armaments. The most dangerous weapon you will ever control, one of her instructors had said back in the Academy, is right here: between your ears. The weapons you can see, or hold in your hand, are only chunks of metal and plastic.

Arly and Sassinak together had worked out ways of bypassing the patchouts, producing readouts that looked clean, while the systems involved still functioned. Not the projectiles. Someone could look and actually see whether or not a launcher had anything in the tube. But the EM and opticals, and the locks on the missile and ammunitions storage bins, could appear to be locked.

"Admiral Coromell's office," said Sassinak, facing the ident screen squarely. She had no idea where on this planet the admiral would be, but the comm comp would take care of that. Surely there was only one Admiral Coromell at this time.

"Admiral Coromell's office, Lieutenant Commander Dallish speaking." Dallish looked like most lieutenant commanders stuck with shore duty: slightly bored but wary. When he'd had a moment to take in Sassinak's rank, his eyes brightened. "Commander Sassinak! A pleasure, ma'am. We've heard about your exciting tour!"

Sassinak let herself smile. She should have realized that, of course, rumor would have spread so far. Fleet kept no secrets from itself. "Not entirely my idea. Is the admiral available?"

Dallish looked genuinely disappointed. "No, Commander, he's not. He's gone rhuch hunting over on Six and won't be back for several weeks Standard. You could go and —"

Sassinak shook her head. "No, worse luck. Orders say to deliver my prisoner and stand by for pre-trial depositions and hearings."

"Kipling's copper corns! Sorry, Commander. That's too bad. This is no port for a cruiser."

"Don't I know it! Look, is there anywhere I can give leave to the crew who aren't involved? Someplace they can have a good time and not get into too much trouble?" She did not miss the change in Dallish's expression, a sudden cool wariness. Had she caused it, or something in his office outside the scan area?

"Commander, perhaps I'd better come aboard, and you can give me your message for Admiral Coromell in person."

Perfectly correct, perfectly formal, and completely wrong: she had said nothing yet about any message. Sassinak's experienced hackles rose. "Fine," she said. "What time shall we expect you?"

"Oh . . . sixteen hundred Fleet Standard; that's twenty-three fifty local."

Late, in other words. Late enough Fleet time that he wouldn't be going back to the admiral's office afterwards; very late in local time.

"Very well. Fleet shuttle, or . . ."

"Federation Insystem Security shuttle, Commander. Fleet has no dedicated planetary shuttles."

Oho, Sassinak thought. So Fleet personnel onplanet are isolated unless Security lets them fly? She asked for, and got, an identification profile, and signed off. When she looked around, her bridge crew had clearly been listening.

"I don't like that," she said to Arly. "If — when — I go downside, I'll want one of our shuttles available, just in case."

Arly nodded, eyes twinkling. Sassinak knew she was thinking of the last shuttle expedition. And young Timran's unexpectedly lucky rashness.

"Weapons systems lockdown is supposed to include shuttle lockdown," Arly reminded her.

Sassinak did not bother to answer; Arly had had her orders. They understood each other. She hoped an unauthorized shuttle flight would not be necessary. But if it was, she trusted that Arly would arrange it somehow.

Lieutenant Commander Dallish, when he appeared in her office shortly after debarking from the Security shuttle, apologized for his earlier circumlocutions.

"The admiral told me he considers you in a unique position to provide evidence against the planet pirates," he said. "For that reason, he warned me to take every precaution if you contacted his office. I don't really think that anyone there is a traitor, but with that much traffic . . . and one of them a Council bureaucrat . . . I decided not to take chances."

"Very wise," said Sassinak.

In person he looked just as he had on the screen: perhaps five years younger than she, professional without being stuffy, obviously intelligent.

"You asked about liberty for your crew. Frankly, you could not be in a worse place, particularly right now. You know the Grand Council's in session this year?"

Sassinak hated to admit that she had only the vaguest idea how the Federation Grand Council actually scheduled its work, and gave a noncommittal response. Dallish went on as if she'd said something intelligent.

"All the work gets done in the preliminary Section meetings, of course: the Grand Council's mostly a formality. But it does overlap the Winter Assizes; a convenience for delegates when a major intercultural case is on the schedule. As it is now. And that means the hotels are already filling up — yes, months early — with delegations from every member. Support staff arriving early. Your crew, since they've been involved in the case, will, of course, have to be debriefed by Fleet Intelligence *and* Federation Security. And if they go onplanet after that, they'll be harassed by the news media."

Sassinak frowned. "Well, they can't stay locked up in the ship the entire time. We're not going anywhere and there's not enough to do." In the back of her mind, she was running over all the miserable long-hour chores that she could assign, but with the weapons systems locked, and flight decks supposedly off limits, nothing but cleaning the whole environmental system with toothbrushes would keep everyone busy.

"My advice, Captain, would be to see if those who've been deposed, and whose testimony is at best minor, couldn't be released to go on long liberty over on Six. That's a recreational reserve: hunting, fishing, sailing, a few good casinos. Fleet has a lodge in the mountains, too. They'd have to go by civilian carrier, but at least they'd be out of your hair."

"I don't like splitting my crew." Without calling up the figures, she couldn't be sure just how far away Six was: days of travel, anyway, on a civilian insystem ferry, perhaps more. If something did happen . . . She shut that line of thought down. Better to clean the whole environmental system with toothbrushes. Preparedness, she'd noticed, tended to keep trouble from happening. And there were worse problems than boredom.

✧ CHAPTER FOUR

"Darling boy!" Auntie Q, Ford thought, was the archetypal spoiled rich widow. She had sparkling jewels on every exposed inch of flesh: rings, bracelets, armlets, necklaces, earrings, and even a ruby implanted between her eyes. He hoped it was a ruby, and not a Blindeye, a medjewel. "You can't know how I've longed to meet you!" Auntie Q also had the voice his father had warned him about. Already he could feel his spine softening into an ingratiating curve.

"I'm so glad, too," he managed.

He hoped it sounded sincere. It had better. He'd spent a lot of time and money tracking Auntie Q down. Most of his immediate family had intentionally lost her address and her solicitors were not about to give her yacht's private comcode to a mere great-nephew by marriage serving on a Fleet cruiser. He had finally had to go through Cousin Chalbert, a harrowing inquisition which had started with an innocent enough question, "But *why* do you want to see her? Are you short of funds, or anything like that?" and ended up with him confessing every venial and mortal sin he had ever committed.

Then he'd had to endure that ride on a tank-hauler, whose bridge crew seemed delighted to make things tough for someone off a cruiser. They seemed to think that cruiser crews lived in obscene luxury and had all the glory as well. Ford was willing to admit that hauling supplies was less thrilling than chasing pirates, but by the third day he was tired of being dumped on for the luxuries he'd never actually enjoyed.

Auntie Q gave him a glance that suggested she had all oars in the water, and turned to speak into a grill. "Sam, my great-nephew arrived after all. So we'll be three for dinner and I want your very best."

"Yes, ma'am," came the reply.

Ford wished he had a way out, and knew he hadn't. The tank-hauler's crew had insisted he share their mess and his stomach was still rebelling.

"You did bring dress things, didn't you?" asked Auntie Q, giving Ford another sharp look.

But he'd been warned. Some of his outlay had been for the clothes which Auntie Q expected any gentleman to have at hand.

"Of course . . . although they may be a little out of date. . . ."

She beamed at him. "Not at all, dear. Men's clothes don't go out of date like that. All this nonsense of which leg to tie the ribbons on. That's ridiculous. Black tie, dear, since no one's visiting."

Auntie Q's favorite era of male dress had been thirty years back: a revival of 19th century Old Earth European. Ford thought it was ridiculous, but then all dress clothes were, and were probably intended to be. Fleet taught you to wear anything and get the job done. He thought of that, checking himself in the mirror of his vast stateroom. It was as big as Sassinak's *Zaid-Dayan* stateroom and office combined, full of furniture as costly as her desk. His black tie, crisply correct, fitted between stiffly white collar points. Studs held the stiff front panels of his shirt together (buttons were pedestrian, daytime wear) and cufflinks held his cuffs. It was utterly ridiculous and he could not keep from grinning at himself. He shrugged on the close-fitting dinner jacket. Like his dress uniform, it showed off broad shoulders and a lean waist (if you had them) or an expanse of white shirt, if you did not. He already wore the slim black trousers, the patent-leather shoes. He looked, to himself, like a caricature of a Victorian dandy.

A face appeared in the mirror behind him: haughty, willful, her graying hair piled high in elaborate puffs and curls, a diamond choker around her wattled neck. Her gown, draped artfully to suggest what she no longer had to display, was a shimmering mass of black shot with silver-gray. From the top of her hairdo three great quills stuck up, quivering in shades of green and silver. Ford blinked. Surely they weren't *really* . . . ?

She winked at him, and he had to grin back. "Yes they are, dearie," she said. "Ryxi tailfeathers, every one, and you shall hear how I came by them."

Impossibly, this visit was going to be fun. No wonder his father had been overwhelmed; no male under thirty-five would stand a chance. Ford swept her a bow, which she received as her due, and offered his arm. Her hand on his was light but firm; she guided him unobtrusively to her dining room.

Three for dinner meant Ford himself, Auntie Q, and her "companion," introduced as Madame Flaubert. Ford's excellent education reminded him of all possible associations, and his Fleet-honed suspicions quivered. Madame Flaubert had excruciatingly red hair, a bosom even more ample than Auntie Q, and an ornate brooch large enough to conceal a small missile launcher. The two women exchanged raised eyebrows and significant nods and shrugs while Ford attempted to pretend he didn't notice. Then Madame Flaubert leaned over and laid her hand on Ford's. He managed not to flinch.

"You are Lady Quesada's great-great-nephew?" Her voice was husky, with a resonance that suggested she might have been trained as a singer.

"Only by courtesy," said Ford smoothly, with a smiling nod to Auntie Q. "The relationship is by marriage, not by blood, on my father's side."

"I told you that, Seraphine," his aunt said, almost sharply.

"I'm sorry, but you know my mind wanders." Ford could not decide if the menace that weighted those words was intentional or accidental. But his aunt sat up straighter; she knew something about it. Madame Flaubert smiled at Ford, an obviously contrived smile. "Your aunt will not have told you, perhaps, that I am her spiritual advisor."

Despite himself, his eyes widened and shifted to his aunt's face. Two spots of color had come out on her cheeks. They faded slowly as he watched. Madame Flaubert pressed his hand again to get his attention, and he forced himself to meet her gaze.

"You do not believe in spirit guides? No. I see you are a *practical* young man, and I suppose your . . . Fleet . . . does not encourage a spiritual nature."

Ford tried to think of something innocuous to say. Of all the things he had thought about coming to meet his notorious Auntie Q, spiritualism had not entered his mind. Madame Flaubert finally patted his hand, as one would pat a child who had just proven a disappointment, and smiled sadly.

"Whether you believe or not, my dear, is of little consequence as long as your heart is filled with purity. But for you, a man who makes his living by war, I see trouble ahead for you, if you do not seek a higher road." Her hand fell from his heavily, with a little thump on the table, and she lay back in her chair, eyes closed. Ford glanced at his aunt, who was sitting bolt upright, her lips folded tightly. She said nothing, staring past him down the table, until Madame Flaubert moaned, sat up, and (as Ford by this time expected) said, "Oh! Did I say something?"

"Later, Seraphine." Auntie Q lifted the crystal bell and, in response to its delicate ring, a uniformed servant entered with a tray of food.

Whatever else Auntie Q had, Ford thought later that evening, she had a miracle of a cook. He was sure it was not just contrast with the supply hauler's mess. He had eaten well enough on the *Zaid-Dayan*, and at plenty of elegant restaurants in several Sectors. No, this was special, a level of cuisine he had never even imagined. Nothing looked like what it was, or tasted the way he thought it would, and it all made "good" or "delicious" into inadequate words. If only his unsteady stomach had not suffered through the tanker crew's cookery, he'd have been in culinary heaven.

Conversation, on the other hand, was limited. Madame Flaubert kept giving Ford meaningful looks, but said nothing except to ask for the return of certain dishes. Spiritual advising was evidently hungry work; she ate twice as much as Auntie Q, and even more than Ford. Auntie Q asked Ford perfunctory questions about his family, and was satisfied with the barest outline of answers. He had the feeling that normally she'd want to know what color stockings his sister's bridesmaids had worn at her wedding, and who had given what gift, but something was distracting her. Suddenly, while Madame Flaubert still had a mouthful of food, Auntie Q pushed back her chair.

"We shall retire," she said, "while you enjoy your port."

Madame Flaubert flushed, swallowed gracelessly but without choking, and stood. Ford was already on his feet, and bowed them out. Port? After clearing away, the servant had returned, carrying a tray with bottle, glass, and a box of cigars. Ford eyed them. He did not smoke, and everything he'd read about cigars warned him not to start now. The port was something else. Would it settle his stomach or make things worse? And how long was he supposed to wait before joining the ladies? For that matter, what *did* the ladies do while waiting for the gentleman to finish his port?

He took a cautious sip, and smiled in spite of himself. Wherever Auntie Q had found this, it was grand stuff for a stomachache, warming all the way down. He stretched his legs beneath the table and tried to imagine himself lord of all he surveyed. With the exception of Auntie Q, who would rule whatever domain she happened to be in.

After a time, the same servant appeared to take away the tray, and direct Ford to "Madame's drawing room." Originally a *withdrawing* room, Ford recalled, to which the ladies withdrew while the menfolk made noise and rude smells with their cigars.

His aunt's drawing room was furnished with more restraint than Ford would have expected. A small instrument with black and white keys, reversed from the usual, and too small for a piano. Ford wondered what it was, but did not ask. Several elegant but sturdy chairs, each different. A low table of some remarkable wood, sawn across knots and knurls to show the intricate graining. A single tall cabinet, its polished doors closed, and two graceful etchings on the walls but none of the cluttered knickknacks her other mannerisms had suggested.

Madame Flaubert lounged in a brocaded armchair, a pose he suspected of concealing more tension than she would admit. She fondled a furry shape he gradually recognized as a dog of some sort. Its coat had been brushed into fanciful whirls, and it had a jeweled collar around its tiny neck. Two bright black eyes glittered at him, and it gave one minute yip before subsiding into Madame Flaubert's ample lap. His aunt, on the contrary, sat upright before a tapestry frame.

"I remember your father," Auntie Q said. "Hardly more than a boy, he was then. Seemed afraid of me, for some reason. Very stiff."

Ford gave her the smile that had worked with other women. "If I'd been a boy, you'd have frightened me."

"I doubt that." She snipped the needle free and threaded a length of blue. "I know what your side of the family thinks of me. Too rich to be reasonable, too old to know what she's doing, troublesome. Isn't that right?" Her eye on him was as sharp as her needle's point.

Ford grinned and shrugged. "Spoiled, overbearing, arrogant, and tiresome, actually. As you, without doubt, already know."

She flashed a smile at him. "Thank you, my dear. Honesty's best between relatives, even when, as so often, it is inconvenient elsewhere. Now we know where we stand, don't we? You didn't come to see a spoiled, overbearing, arrogant, tiresome old lady for the fun of it."

"Not for the fun of it, no." Ford let himself frown. "It was actually curiosity."

"Oh?"

"To see if you were as bad as they said. To see if you were as sick and miserable as *you* said. To see what kind of woman could have married into both Santon and Paraden and then gotten free of them."

"And now?"

"To see what kind of woman would wear Ryxi tailfeathers to dinner. How could anyone resist *that*?"

"I can't tell you what you want to know," she said, somber for an instant. "I can't tell you why. But never mind, I can tell you about the Ryxi."

Ford was not surprised to notice that Madame Flaubert was back in the room, cooing to her dog, which had spent the interim curled on her chair.

"Even the Ryxi are fellow beings searching for the light," said Madame Flaubert. "Ridicule damages the scoffer. . . ."

"I'm not scoffing," said Auntie Q tartly. "I'm merely telling Ford where I got these feathers."

She plunged into the tale without looking at Madame Flaubert again; her voice trembled at first, then steadied. Ford listened, amused by the story. He could have predicted it, what a high-spirited rich young wife might do at one of the fancy balls when her "incorrigibly stuffy" husband tried to insist that she be discreet. Discretion, quite clearly, had never been one of Auntie Q's strong points. He could almost see her younger (no doubt beautiful) self, capering in mock courtship with a Ryxi in diplomatic service . . . a Ryxi who had let himself get overexcited, who had plucked the jeweled pin from her turban, and crowed (as Ryxi sometimes did, when they forgot themselves).

He could imagine her shock, her desire to do something outrageous in return. When the Ryxi had gone into the final whirling spin of the mating dance, she had yanked hard on his tailfeathers. By the time the whirling Ryxi could stop, screeching with mingled pain and humiliation, she had run away, safely hidden by her own wild crowd. Ford glanced at Madame Flaubert, whose mouth was pinched into a moue of disgust. He could almost hear her mental comment: *vulgar*. Ford himself agreed, but not with any intensity.

Most of what he knew about the wealthy and powerful he considered vulgar, but it didn't bother him. He certainly didn't bother about the degrees of vulgarity they might assign to one another's actions. Tenuous as the family connection might be, he would pick Auntie Q over Madame Flaubert anytime. His aunt had finished her story, with a challenging, almost defiant lift of her chin. He could imagine her as a spoiled child, when she would have had dimples beside her mouth. He grinned as much at the memory as at her story.

"Didn't he file a protest?" asked Ford.

His aunt bridled. "Of course he did. But I had filed a protest, too. Because he still had my jewel and he'd made a public nuisance of himself by losing control and going into the mating sequence. It's quite unmistakable even if you've never seen it."

"I have." Ford fought to keep his voice under control. It must have been the spectacle of the year, he thought to himself.

"So there was a lot of buzzing around. My husband's attorneys got involved and eventually everyone withdrew charges. The Ryxi ambassador himself sent a note of apology. Everyone insisted I do the same. But both of us kept our trophies. I had to agree not to display them *then* — not in public, you know — but that was years back, and this is my own private yacht."

It sounded as if she expected an argument; another glance at Madame Flaubert suggested with whom. Ford felt protective, but realized that Auntie Q expected (and trained) her menfolk to feel protective.

"It's a wonderful story," he said, quite honestly. "I wish I'd been there to see it." He meant that, too. Formal diplomatic functions with multiple races were usually painfully dull, kept so by everyone's attempts not to break another culture's rules of etiquette. Fleet officers stuck with attendance expected to spend long hours standing politely listening to civilian complaints while all the good-looking persons of opposite sex enjoyed themselves across a crowded dance floor. He remembered Sassinak telling him about a little excitement once, but that was all.

His aunt leaned over and touched his cheek. "You'd have enjoyed it, I can tell. You might even have helped me."

"Of course I would."

His stomach rumbled, loudly and insistently, and he felt himself flush. His aunt ignored the unmentionable noise, turning instead to Madame Flaubert, who was staring at Ford's midsection as if she could see into it.

"Seraphine, perhaps you could find the cube with the news stories from that event?" Her tone made it more command than request; Madame Flaubert almost jumped, but nodded quickly and set her lapdog back down.

"Of course."

But even as she rose to comply, Ford's stomach clenched, and he realized he was about to be sick. He felt cold, clammy, and his vision narrowed.

"Excuse me, please," he said, between gritted teeth.

Auntie Q glanced at him politely, then stiffened. "You've gone quite green," she said. "Are you ill?"

Another pain twisted him, and he barely whispered, "Something I ate on the tanker, perhaps."

"Of course. I'll have Sam find you some medicine." She rose, as imperious as he had been after dinner. "Come, Seraphine."

They swept out as Ford groped his way to the door. He was perversely irritated that she had seen him lose control, and at the same time that she had left him to find his own way back to his stateroom. He didn't want to throw up on her elegant silver and rose carpet, but if he had to wander far . . .

He had hardly taken a few steps down the corridor when a strongly built man in chef's whites (another uniform unchanged through the centuries) grasped him under the arm and helped him swiftly back to his quarters.

He had been very thoroughly sick in the bathroom, losing with regret that delicious dinner, hardly noticing the silent, efficient help of the cook. When he regained his sense of balance, he was tucked into bed, his dress clothes draped across a chair, and the cold clamminess had passed into a burning fever and aching joints. What a beginning to a social inquiry, he thought, and then lapsed into unrestful sleep.

❖   ❖   ❖

He woke to a foul taste in his mouth, the sour smell of sickness, and the suspicion that something was very wrong indeed. He had had bad dreams, full of dire symbolism (a *black* Ryxi dancing around his aunt's casket waving her two stolen plumes in macabre triumph? Commander Sassinak handing him a shining medal that turned into a smoking fuse when he pinned it to his uniform? A scaly, clawed hand tossing a handful of Fleet vessels, including the *Zaid-Dayan*, like dice onto a playing board whose pieces were planets and suns?).

He was quite sure that Madame Flaubert could "explain" them all, in ways that would make him responsible if he didn't reform, but he felt too weak to reform. Even to get up. Someone tapped on his door, and he croaked a weak answer.

"Sorry, sir, to be so late with breakfast."

It was the man in white, the cook. Sam, he remembered. He had not expected anyone, but if he'd thought, he'd have expected the servant who served dinner. Sam carried a covered tray; Ford thought it probably smelled delicious, but whatever it was he didn't want it. He shook his head, but Sam brought it nearer anyway, and set it on a folding table he had had in his other hand.

"You're still not well. I can see that." Off came the tray cover, revealing a small plate with crisp slices of toast, small glasses of fruit juice and water, and a tiny cut-glass pillbox. "This may not sit well, but at least it'll give me an idea what to try next. . . ."

"I don't want anything." That came out in a hoarse voice he hardly recognized for his own. "Something on the tanker . . ."

"Well, I didn't think it came out of *my* kitchen." That barely missed smugness, the certainty of a master craftsman. "Did you get a look in that tanker's galley?" Sam held out the glass of water, and Ford sipped it, hoping to lose the taste in his mouth. It eased the dryness in his throat, at least.

"They told me, boasted in fact, that they didn't have a galley. Cooked their own food, mostly just heated up whatever came out of the synthesizer."

"And didn't clean the synthesizer coils often enough, I daresay. It's not easy to make great meals from basic synth, but it doesn't have to be sickening, either." As he spoke, Sam offered the toast, but Ford shook his head again.

"Just the water, thanks. Sorry to cause you any inconvenience."

Which was a mild way of apologizing for the night before, when he had done more than cause inconvenience. And what was he going to do now? In Auntie Q's circle, he was sure that one did not inflict one's illnesses on hosts. But he had no place to go. The *Zaid-Dayan* was on her way to FedCentral; the nearest Fleet facility was at least a month's travel away, even if the yacht was headed that direction, which it wasn't.

"Not at all, sir." Sam had tidied away the toast replacing the tray's cover, while leaving the cold water on his bedside table. Ford wished he would go away soon. He no longer felt nauseated, but he could tell he was far from well. "Bowers will be in later, to help you with your bath. I will inform Madame that you are still indisposed; she inquired, of course."

"Of course," Ford murmured.

"She regrets that her personal physician is presently on vacation, but when we reach our destination, she will be able to obtain professional assistance for you from the local community."

"I shall hope not to need it by then." That had a double meaning, he realized after it came out. The cook — not quite what he would have expected from Auntie Q's cook, barring the expertise — smiled at him.

"Taking that the best way, sir, I hope not, too. We do have a fair assortment of medicines, if you're prone to self-medicate?"

"No, thanks. I'll wait it out. These things never last long."

At last the cook was standing, tray in hand, giving a last smile as he went out the door. Ford sagged back against his pillows. What a bad start to his investigation! He was sure that Auntie Q liked him . . . that she would have told him all about her connection to the Paradens . . . but she would not be the sort to waste her time nursing a nastily sick invalid. He hoped the virus or whatever it was would be as brief as most such illnesses. Leaving aside his mission, he wanted to try more of Sam's marvelous cooking.

Two days later, after surviving a light breakfast with no aftershocks, he made his way to the dining room, once more clad in the formal daytime dress of a nineteenth century European. (He thought it was European — something Old Earth, and the Europeans had been dominant that century.) Auntie Q had sent him a couple of ancient books (real books, with paper leaves) for amusement, had inquired twice daily about his welfare, but otherwise left him alone. He had to admit it was better than having someone hovering, whose feelings he would have had to respect.

Auntie Q greeted him with restrained affection; Madame Flaubert inquired volubly about his symptoms until Auntie Q raised a commanding hand.

"Really, Seraphine! I'm sure dear Ford doesn't wish to discuss his shaky inner organs, and frankly I have no interest in them. Certainly not before a meal." Madam Flaubert subsided, more or less, but commented that Ford's aura seemed streaky.

Luncheon, despite this, was another culinary masterpiece. Ford savored every bite, aware that Sam had done a great deal with color and texture, while keeping the contents easy on a healing stomach. Auntie Q led the conversation to curiosities of collecting, something Ford knew nothing about. He let her wrangle amiably with Madame Flaubert over the likelihood that a certain urn in the collection of the Tsing Family was a genuine Wedgwood, from Old Earth, or whether it was (Madame Flaubert's contention) one of the excellent reproductions made on Gaehshin, in the first century of that colony.

They came up for air with dessert, as Madame Flaubert passed Ford a tray of pastries and said, "But surely we're boring you . . . unless this touches your fancy?"

Ford took the pastry nearest him, hoping from the leak of rich purple that it might be filled with dilberries, his favorite. Madame Flaubert retrieved the plate, and set it aside; his aunt, he noticed, was dipping into a bowl of something yellow. He bit into the flaky pastry, finding his hope fulfilled, and swallowed before he answered.

"I'm never bored hearing about new things, although I confess you lost me back where you were arguing about pressed or carved ornament."

As he had half-hoped, his aunt broke in with a quick lecture on the difference and why it was relevant to their argument. When she wanted, she could be concise, direct, and remarkably shrewd. No fool, and no spoiled idler, he thought to himself. If she appears that way, it's because she wants to — because it works for her. Except for the two hours that Auntie Q spent lying down "restoring my youth," they spent the afternoon in the kind of family gossip they'd missed the first night. Auntie Q had kept up with all the far-flung twigs of her family tree, many of them unknown to Ford, including the careers and marriages of Ford's own sibs and first cousins. She thought his brother Asmel was an idiot for leaving a good job at Prime Labs to try his fortune raising liesel fur; Ford agreed. She insisted that his sister Tara had been right to marry that bank clerk, although Ford felt she should have finished graduate school first.

"You don't understand," Auntie Q said for the third time, and this time explained in detail. "That young man is the collateral cousin of Maurice Quen Chang; he was a bank clerk when Tara married him but he won't be one in ten years. Maurice is by far the shrewdest investor in that family. He will end with control of two key industries in the Cordade Cluster. Didn't your sister explain?"

"I didn't see her; I got this in the mails, from Mother."

"Ah yes. Your mother is a dear person; my old friend Arielle knew her as a girl, you know. Before she married your father. Very upright, Arielle said, and not at all inclined to play social games, but charming in a quiet way." Ford thought that was a fair description of his mother, although it left out her intelligence, her wit, and her considerable personal beauty. He had inherited her smooth bronze skin, and the bones that let him pass in any level of society. True enough, even if his mother had known that the bank clerk was someone's cousin, she would not have approved of such calculation in one of her daughters. Auntie Q went on. "I'm sure, though, that any daughter of your mother's would have had a genuine affection for the young man, no matter what his connections."

"Mother said so." Interesting, too, that Mother had never mentioned knowing a friend of Auntie Q's, all those times his father had talked about her. Had she known that Arielle was Auntie Q's friend? Or not cared? He tried to puzzle it out, aware of a growing fuzziness in his head. He blinked to clear his vision, and realized that Auntie Q was peering at him, her mouth pursed.

"You're felling ill again." It was not a question. Nor did he question it: he was feeling ill again. This time the onset was slower, more in the head than the stomach, a feeling of swooping and drifting, of being smothered in pale flowers.

"Sorry," he said. He could see in her eyes that he was being tiresome. Visiting relatives were supposed to be entertaining.

They were supposed to listen to her stories and provide the material for new ones she could tell elsewhere. They were not supposed to collapse ungracefully in her exquisitely furnished rooms, fouling the air with bad smells.

He realized he had fallen sideways off his chair onto the floor. A disgrace. She did not say it aloud and he did not need her to say it. He knew it. He lay there remembering to breathe, wishing desperately that he were back on the *Zaid-Dayan*, where someone would have whisked him to Sickbay, where the diagnostic unit would have figured out what was wrong, and what to do, in a few minutes, and a brusque but effective crew of Fleet medics would have supervised the treatment. And Sassinak, more vivid in her own way than Auntie Q at her wildest, would have come to see him, not walked out of the room in a huff. He remembered, with the mad clarity of illness, the jeweled rosettes on the toes of Auntie Q's shoes as she pushed herself from her chair, pivoted, and walked away.

This time he came to himself back in bed, but with the feeling that some catastrophic conflict was happening overhead. He felt bruised all over, his skin flinching from the touch of the bedclothes. The space between his ears, where his mind should have been ticking along quietly, seemed to be full of a quiet crackling, a sensation he remembered from five years before, when he'd had a bout of Plahr fever.

"I assure you, Sam, that Madame's nephew is in need of my healing powers." That syrupy voice could only be Madame Flaubert.

Ford tried to open his eyes, but lacked the strength. He heard something creak and the rustle of layers of clothes.

"His aura reveals the nature of his illness: it is seated in the spiritual house of his darkest sin. Through study and prayer, I am equipped to deal with this. I will need quiet, peace, and absolutely no interference. You may go."

Ford struggled again to open his eyes, to speak, but could not even twitch. Had he been hypnotized somehow? Given a paralytic drug? Panic surged through him, but even that did not unlock his muscles. For the first time, he realized that he might actually *die* here, in a luxurious stateroom in a private yacht, surrounded by rich old women and their servants. He could not imagine a more horrible death.

Even as he thought that, he felt a plump, moist hand on his forehead. Fingernails dug into the skin of his right temple just a little. His mind presented a vision from his nightmares: a scaly clawed hand about to dig in and rip his head open. The scent of Madame Flaubert's cologne mingled with the imagined stench of a reptilian, toothy maw; he wanted to retch and could not move.

"You may *go*," she said again, somewhere near his left shoulder. Evidently Sam had not gone; Ford hoped fervently he would stay, but he could not move even a toe to signal him.

"Sorry, Madame," said Sam sounding more determined than sorry. "I think it would be better for us all if I stayed." Something in his tone made Ford wish he could smile, a hint of staunch rectitude that implied Madame Flaubert had known — proclivities, perhaps? At the thought of her hands on his body, he actually shuddered.

"Your voice hurts him," Madame Flaubert said. Quietly, venomously, a voice to cause the same shudders. "You saw that twitch. You had better go, or I will be compelled to speak to your mistress."

No sound of movement. Ford struggled again with his eyelids, and felt one almost part. Then that hand drifted down his forehead and he felt a thumb on his lid. "Madame gave me permission; *she* agreed it was best."

An actual hiss followed, a sound he had read about but never heard a woman make. The thumb on his eyelid pressed; he saw sparkling whorls, Then it released, with a last little flick that seemed a warning, and the hand fell heavily on his shoulder.

"I can't imagine what she means by it." Now Madame Flaubert sounded almost petulant, a woman wronged by false suspicions.

"She has such . . . such *notions* sometimes."

A soft scrape across the room; the sound of someone settling in a chair. "She has not forgotten why you are here. Nor have I."

Madame Flaubert sniffed, a sound as literary as the hiss, and as false. "You forget yourself, Sam. A servant —"

"Madam's cook." The emphasis was unmistakable. Madam's cook — her loyal servant. Not Madame Flaubert's. And she was someone he tolerated on his mistress' behalf?

Ford wished he could think clearly. He knew too little about whatever loyalties might exist in such situations. If this were

Fleet, those overtones in Sam's voice would belong to the trust-worthy NCO of a good officer. But he could hardly imagine his Auntie Q as a good officer. Or could he? And why *was* Madame Flaubert here, if neither Auntie nor her faithful servant wanted her?

"Well. You can scarcely object to my seeking healing for him."

"As long as that's all it is." Sam's voice had flattened slightly. Warning? Fear?

"Those who live by violence die of its refuse," Madame Flaubert intoned. Ford felt something fragile touch his face, and had just decided it was a scarf or veil when Madame Flaubert drew it away. "I see pain in this aura. I see violence and grief. I see the shadow of wickedness in the past, and its unborn child in darkness . . ." Her voice had taken on a curious quality, not quite musical, that seemed to bore into Ford's head and prevent thought. He could almost feel himself floating on it, as if it were a heavy stream of honey.

"What're you trying to do, make him feel guilty?" Sam's voice cut through hers and Ford felt as if he'd been dropped bodily from several feet up. A spasm went through his foot; he felt the covers drag at it. Before Madame Flaubert could move, Sam's strong hands were kneading it, relaxing the cramp.

"Don't touch him!" she said. "You'll interfere with the healing flow, if it comes at all with you here."

"He's been still too long. He needs massage." Where Sam's hands rubbed, Ford felt warmth, felt he could almost move himself.

"Impossible!" Her hand left his shoulder; he heard the rustle as she stood. "I can't be expected to do anything with you treating his legs like bread dough, stirring his aura, mixing the signs. *When* you're quite finished, you will have the kindness to inform me! If he's still alive, that is." An odd sound followed, a complex rustle, then she said, "And I'll leave this protective symbol with him."

It was cold on his forehead, icy cold that struck straight into his brain; his breath came short. But she was leaving, the rustle diminishing, and he heard the door open and close. Instantly a warm hand removed the thing, whatever it was, and a warm finger pried up one eyelid. He could see, somewhat to his surprise. Sam's face stared down at him. The man shook his head.

"You're a sick man, and no mistake. You should never have tried to outfox your great-aunt, laddie . . . you aren't in her league."

✦ CHAPTER FIVE

"This was *not* a good idea," muttered one of the medical team as they stumped wearily off the shuttle at Diplo's only fully equipped port. Lunzie didn't care who'd said it: she agreed. Her variable-pressure-support garment clasped her like an allover girdle. When the control circuitry worked correctly, it applied a pressure gradient from toes to neck without impeding joint movement . . . much. Over it, she wore the recommended outerwear for Diplo's severe winter, light and warm on a one-G world, but (she grumbled to herself) heavy and bulky here. She could feel her feet sinking into the extra-thick padded bootliners they had to wear, every separate bone complaining slightly of the extra burden.

"Winter on Diplo," said Conigan, waving a padded arm at the view out the round windows of the terminal. Wind splashed a gout of snow against the building and it shuddered. Snow, Lunzie reminded herself, would feel more like sleet or hail. Their shuttle had slewed violently in the storm coming in. She had heard something rattle on the hull.

At least they were through Customs. First on the orbiting Station, and then in the terminal, they'd been scrutinized by heavyworlders who might have been chosen to star in lightweight nightmares. Huge, bulky, their heavy faces masks of hostility and contempt, their uniforms emphasizing bulging muscle and bulk, they'd been arrogantly thorough in their examination of the team's authorization and equipment. Lunzie felt a momentary rush of terror when she realized how openly arrogant these heavyworlders were, but her Discipline reasserted itself, and she had relaxed almost at once. They had done nothing yet but be rude, and rudeness was not her concern.

But that rudeness made the minimal courtesy shown them

now seem almost welcoming. A cargo van for their gear, the offer of a ride to the main research facility. None of them felt slighted that their escort was only a graduate student and not, as it should have been, one of the faculty.

If Lunzie had hoped that Diplo had not yet heard about her experience on Ireta, she was soon undeceived. The graduate student, having checked their names on a list, actually smiled at her.

"Doctor Lunzie! Or do you use Mespil? You're the one who's had all the cold sleep experience, right? But the heavyworlders in that expedition put *you* under, didn't they?"

Lunzie had not discussed her experience much with the others on the team; she was conscious of their curiosity.

"No," she said, as calmly as if discussing variant ways of doing a data search. "I was the doctor; I put our lightweights under."

"But there were heavyworlders on Ireta . . ." the student began. He was young, by his voice, but his bulky body made him seem older than his years.

"They mutinied," Lunzie said, still calmly. If he had heard the other, he should have heard that. But perhaps the Governor had changed the facts to suit his people.

"Oh." He gave her a quick glance over his shoulder before steering the van into a tunnel. "Are you sure? There wasn't some mistake?"

The others were rigidly quiet. She could tell they wanted her version of the story, and didn't want her to tell it here. The graduate student seemed innocent, but who could tell?

"I can't talk about it," she said, trying for a tone of friendly firmness. "It's going to trial, and I've been told not to discuss it until afterwards."

"But that's *Federation* law," he said airily. "It's not binding here. You could talk about it here, and they'd never know."

Lunzie suppressed a grin. Graduate students everywhere! They never thought the law was binding on them, not if they wanted to know something. Of course, it might be that the rest of Diplo felt that way about Federation law, which was something the FSP suspected, but just as likely it was pure student curiosity.

"Sorry," she said, not sounding sorry at all. "I promised, and I don't break promises." Only after it was out did she remember something Zebara had repeated as a heavyworlder saying: *Don't break promises! Break bones!* She shivered. She had no intention of breaking bones — or having her own broken — if she could avoid it.

Their first days on Diplo were a constant struggle against the higher gravity and the measures they took to survive it. Lunzie hated the daily effort to worm her way into a clean pressure garment, the intimate adjustments necessary for bodily functions, the clinging grip that made her feel trapped all the time. Discipline could banish in her some of the fatigue that her colleagues Tailler and Bias felt, at least for awhile, so that her fingers did not slip on the instruments or tremble when she ate. But by the end of a working day they were all tired, and trying not to be grumpy.

To add to their discomfort, Diplo's natural rotation and political "day," were just enough longer than standard to exhaust them, without justifying adherence to Standard measures.

Lunzie found the research fascinating, and had to remind herself that her real reason for coming had nothing to do with heavyworlder response to cold sleep. Especially as she only had a limited time to make contact with Zebara. She had been able to establish that he was still alive, and on Diplo. Contacting him might be difficult and enlisting his aid was problematic. But Zebara was the only option. He'd be at least 80, she reminded herself, even if living on ships and low-G worlds would have improved his probable life expectancy. They had trusted each other at one point: would that old trust suffice for the information she required of him? If, that is, he was in a position to help at all.

At the end of the first week, the team had its first official recognition: an invitation to a formal reception and dance at the Governor's Palace. The team quit work early. Lunzie spent an hour soaking in a hot tub before she dressed. The need to wear pressure garments constantly meant that "formal dress" for the women would be more concealing than usual. Lunzie had packed a green gown, long-sleeved and high-necked, that covered the protective garment but clung to her torso. Wide-floating skirts hung unevenly in Diplo's heavy gravity. She'd been warned, so this had only enough flare to make walking and dancing easy. She looked in her mirror and smiled. She looked more fragile than she was, less dangerous: exactly right.

The team gathered in Tailler's room to await their transport to the festivities. Lunzie asked about the Governor's compound.

"It *is* a palace," said Tailler, who had been there before. "It's under its own dome, so they could use thinner plexi in the windows. With the gardens outside, colorful even in this season. It's a spectacle. Of course, the resources used to make it all work are outrageous, considering the general poverty."

"It wasn't so bad before," Bias interrupted. "After all, it's the recent population growth that makes resources so short."

Tailler frowned. "They've been hungry a long time, Bias. Life on Diplo's never been easy."

"But you have to admit they don't seem to mind. They certainly don't blame the Governor."

"No, and that's what's unfair. They blame *us*, the Federation, when it's their own waste —"

"Shhh." Lunzie thought she heard someone in the corridor outside. She waited; after a long pause, someone knocked on the door. She opened it to find a uniformed heavyworlder, resplendent in ribbons and medals and knots of gold braid. She could read nothing on that expressionless face, but she had a feeling that he had heard at least some of what had been said.

"If you're ready, we should leave for the Palace," he said.

"Thank you," said Lunzie. She could hear the others gathering their outer wraps. Her own silvery parka was in her hand.

Within the dome, the Governor's Palace glittered as opulently as promised. Around it, broad lawns and formal flowerbeds glowed in the light of carefully placed spotlights. The medical team walked on a narrow strip of silvery stuff that looked like steel mesh, but felt soft underfoot, like carpet. A news service crew turned blinding lights on them as they came to the massive doors and the head of the receiving line.

"Smile! You're about to be famous," muttered Bias.

Lunzie had not anticipated this, but smiled serenely into the camera anyway. Others blinked away from the light and missed the first of many introductions. Lunzie grinned to herself hearing them stumble in their responses. Such lines were simple, really, as long as you remembered to alternate any two of the five or six acceptable greeting phrases and smile steadily. By the time she was halfway down the line, well into the swing of it, with "How *very* nice" and "*So* pleased to meet you," tripping easily off her lips, the back of her mind was busy with commentary.

Why, she wondered, did the heavyworlder women try to copy

lightweight fashions *here*, when everywhere else on Diplo they wore garments far better suited to their size and strength. Formal gowns could have been designed for them, taking into account the differences in proportion. But no heavyworlder should wear tight satin with flounces at the hip, or a dress whose side slit looked as if it had simply given way from internal pressure.

One of the men — the Lieutenant Governor, she noted as she was introduced and put her hand into his massive fist — had also opted for lightweight high fashion. And if there was anything sillier than a massive heavyworlder leg with a knot of hot pink and lime-green ribbons at the knee, she could not imagine it. The full shirt with voluminous sleeves made more sense, but those tight short pants! Lunzie controlled herself with an effort and moved on down the line. The Governor himself wore more conservative dark blue, the sort of coverall that she'd seen so much of since she arrived.

Refreshments covered two long tables angled across the upper corners of the great hall. Lunzie accepted a massive silver goblet of pale liquid from a servant and sipped it cautiously. She'd have to be careful, nurse it along, but she didn't think it was potent enough to drop her in her tracks. She took a cracker with a bit of something orange on it and two green nubbins that she hoped were candy, and passed on, smiling and nodding to the heavyworlders around her. Besides the medical team, the only lightweights were the FSP consul and a few consulate staff.

She recognized some of the heavyworlders: scientists and doctors from the medical center where they'd been working. These clumped together to talk shop, while the political guests — high government officials, members of the Diplo Parliament (which Lunzie had heard was firmly under the Governor's broad thumb) — did a great deal of "mingling."

The green nubbins turned out to be salty, not sweet, and the orange dollop on the cracker was not cheese at all, but some kind of fruit. Across the room a premonitory squawk from an elevated platform warned of music to come. Lunzie could not see over the taller shoulders around her. As the room filled she felt more and more like a child who had sneaked into a grownup party.

"Lunzie!" That was the Lieutenant Governor, his wide white sleeves billowing, the ribbons at his knee jiggling. He took her free hand in his. "Let me introduce you to my niece, Colgara."

Colgara was not as tall as her uncle, but still taller than Lunzie, and built along the usual massive lines. Her pale yellow dress had rows of apricot ruffles down both sides and a flounce of apricot at the hem. She bowed over Lunzie's hand. The Lieutenant Governor went on, patting his niece on the shoulder.

"She wants to be a doctor, but of course that's just adolescent enthusiasm. She'll marry the Governor's son in a year, when he's back from . . ." His voice trailed away as someone tapped him on the shoulder. He turned away, and the two men began to talk.

Lunzie smiled at the girl who towered over her. "So? You're interested in medicine?"

"Yes. I have done very well at my studies." Colgara swiped at the ruffles down the side of her dress, a nervous gesture that made her seem a true adolescent. "I — I wanted to come to see your team at work, but you are too busy, I know. Uncle said you must not be bothered, and besides I am not to go to medical school." She glowered at that, clearly not through fighting for it.

Lunzie was not sure how to handle this. The last thing she needed was to get involved in a family quarrel, particularly a family of this rank. But the girl looked so miserable.

"Perhaps you could do both," she said.

"Go to school *and* marry?" Colgara stared. "But I must have children. I couldn't go to school and have babies."

Lunzie chuckled. "People do," she said. "Happens all the time."

"Not here." Colgara lowered her voice. "You don't understand how it is with us. It's so difficult, with our genes and this environment."

Before Lunzie realized it, she was being treated to a blow-by-blow account of heavyworlder pregnancy: Colgara's mother's experience, and then her aunt's, and then her older sister's. It would have been interesting, somewhere else, but not at a formal reception, with all the gory details mingling with other overheard conversations about politics, agricultural production, light and heavy industry, trade relations. Finally at great length, Colgara ended up with "So you see, I couldn't possibly go to medical school and have babies."

"I see your point," said Lunzie, wondering how to escape. The Lieutenant Governor had disappeared into a sea of tall heavy shoulders and broad backs. She saw no one she knew and no one she could claim a need to speak to.

"I've bored you, haven't I?" Colgara's voice was mournful; her lower lip stuck out in a pout.

Lunzie struggled for tact, and came up short. "Not really, I just . . ." She could not say, *just want to get away from you.*

"I thought since you were a doctor you'd be interested in all the medical problems . . ."

"Well, I am, but . . ." Inspiration came. "You see, obstetrics is really not my field. I don't have the background to appreciate a lot of what you told me." That seemed to work; Colgara's pouting lower lip went back in place. "Most of my work is in occupational rehab. That's why I focus on making it possible to do the work you want to do. People always have reasons why they can't. We look for ways to make it possible."

Colgara nodded slowly, smiling now. Lunzie wasn't sure which of the things she'd said had done the trick, but at least the girl wasn't glowering at her. Colgara leaned closer.

"This is my first formal reception — I begged and begged Uncle, and he finally let me come because his wife's sick." Lunzie braced herself for another detailed medical recitation but fortunately Colgara was now on a different tack. "He insisted that I had to wear offworld styles. This is really my cousin Jayce's dress. I think it's awful but I suppose you're used to it."

"Not really." Lunzie didn't want to explain to this innocent that she had been forty-three years in one suit of workclothes, cold sleeping longer than Colgara had been alive. "I have few formal clothes. Doctors generally don't have time to be social."

She could not resist looking around, hoping to find something — someone, anything — in that mass of shoulders and backs, to give her an excuse to move away.

"Want something more to eat?" asked Colgara. "I'm starved." Without waiting for Lunzie's response she turned and headed for the refreshment tables.

Lunzie followed in her wake. At least on this side of the room, people were sitting down at tables and she could see around. Then Lunzie was caught up by the ornate center arrangement on the nearest table, pink and red whorls surrounded by flowers and fruit. Surely it wasn't? But her nose confirmed that it was and some was uncooked. She glanced at Colgara. The girl had reached across and was filling her plate with the whorls. Didn't she know? Or was it deliberate insult? Slightly nauseated by such a blatant display, Lunzie fastidiously took a few slices of some yellowish fruit, more crackers, and moved away.

"Is it true you lightweights can't eat meat?" asked Colgara. Her tone held no hidden contempt, only curiosity. Lunzie wondered how to answer *that* one.

"It's a philosophical viewpoint," she said finally. Colgara, her mouth stuffed with what had to be slices of meat, looked confused. Lunzie sighed, and said, "We don't think it's right to eat creatures that might be sentient."

Colgara looked even more confused as she chewed and swallowed. "But . . . but muskies aren't people. They're animals and not even smart ones. They don't talk, or anything." She put another slice of meat into her mouth and talked through it. "Besides, we need the complex proteins. It's part of our adaptation."

Lunzie opened her mouth to say that any protein compound could be synthesized without the need to kill and eat sentient creatures, but realized it would do no good. She forced a smile, "My dear, it's a philosophical position, as I said. Enjoy your . . . uh . . . muskie."

She turned away and found herself face to face with a white-haired man whose great bulk had twisted with age, bringing his massive face almost down to her level. For a moment she simply saw him as he was, exceptionally old for a heavyworlder in high-G conditions, someone of obvious intelligence and wit (for his eyes twinkled at her), and then her memory retrieved his younger face.

"Zebara!"

It was half joy and half shock. She had halfway wanted to find him, had not wanted to search the databases and find that he'd died while she slept, had not wanted to see what was now before her: a vigorous man aged to weakness. He smiled, the same warm smile.

"Lunzie! I saw your name on the list, and hardly dared believe it was you. And then there you were on the cameras! I had to come down and see you."

Conflicting thoughts cluttered her mind. She wanted to ask him what he'd done in the years she'd lost. She wanted to tell him all that had happened to her. But she had no time for a long, leisurely chat, even if he'd been able to join her. She was here with two missions already, and at the moment, she had to concentrate on Sassinak's needs.

"You're looking surprisingly . . . well . . ." he was saying.

"Another forty-three years of cold sleep," said Lunzie, wondering why he didn't know already, when some of the heavyworlders certainly did. "And you, you look . . ."

"Old," said Zebara, chuckling. "Don't try to flatter me. I'm lucky to be alive but I've changed a lot. It's been an interesting life and I wish we had time to discuss it." Lunzie looked a question at him and one of his heavy eyebrows went up. "You know we don't, dear girl. And yes, I can condescend to you because I have *lived* those forty-three years." He reached out and took the plate from her hand. "Come here."

Lunzie looked around, seeing only the same roomful of massive bodies, none of the other lightweights in sight. Across the serving table, one of the servants was watching her with a smirk.

"Come on," said Zebara, with a touch of impatience. "You don't really think I'm going to rape you."

She didn't, of course. But she wished she could find someone, a lightweight on the Team, to let them know she was going with him. She managed not to flinch when Zebara took her wrist and led her along the serving table toward the short end of the hall. The servant was still smirking, grinning openly finally, as Zebara led her through a double doorway into a wide, carpeted passage. Here the crush was less, but still heavyworlder men and women walked by in both directions.

"Restrooms," said Zebara, still holding her wrist and leading her right along a side corridor, then left along another. He opened a door, and pulled Lunzie into a room lined with glass-fronted shelves. Broad, heavy couches clustered around a massive glass-topped table. "Here! Sit down and we'll have a chat."

"Are you sure this is a good idea?" Lunzie began as Zebara turned to look around the room, his eyelids drooping. He waved a hand, which she took as a signal for silence.

The couch was too deep for her comfort; her feet did not reach the floor if she relaxed against the backrest. She felt like a child in an adult's room. Zebara walked around the room slowly, obviously intent on something Lunzie could neither see nor hear. She could not relax while he was so tense. Finally he sighed, shrugged, and came to sit beside her.

"We must take the chance. If anyone comes, Lunzie, pretend to be struggling with me. They'll understand *that*. They know that I was fond of you, that I considered you a 'pet' lightweight. That is their term for it."

"But . . ."

"Don't argue that with me. We haven't time." He kept scanning the room. This close, Lunzie could recognize the slight tremor that age had imposed on him; she grieved for the man he had been. "I know about Ireta, though I didn't know beforehand, and couldn't have stopped it anyway. Please believe that."

"I do, of course. You aren't the kind . . ."

"I don't know what kind I am any more." That stopped her cold, not only the words but the deadly quiet tone of voice. "I am a heavyworlder, I am dying. Yes, within the year, they tell me, and nothing to be done. I've been luckier than most. My children and grandchildren are heavyworlders, who face the same constraints I do. So while I agree that mutiny is wrong, and piracy is wrong, that we must not make enemies of all you lightweights, I wish the Federation would face facts about us. We are not dumb animals, just as you say that the subhuman animals that all once ate are not 'dumb animals.' How can I convince my children that they should watch their children starve, just to preserve the sensitivities, the 'philosophical viewpoint' of those who don't *need* meat but do want our strength to serve them?"

Shaken, Lunzie could only stare at him. She had been so sure, for so long, that Zebara was the best example of a good heavyworlder: trustworthy, idealistic, selfless. Had she been wrong?

"You didn't mistake me," Zebara said, as if she'd spoken aloud. Was her expression that obvious? But he wasn't really looking at her; he was staring across the room. "Back then, I was what you saw. I tried! You can't know how hard, to change others to my viewpoint. But you don't know what else I've seen since, while you were sleeping the years away. I don't want war, Lunzie, as much because my people would lose it as because I think it is wrong." He sighed, heavily, and patted her arm as a grandfather might pat a child. "And I don't like being that way. I don't like thinking that way."

"I'm sorry," said Lunzie. It was all she could think of. She had trusted Zebara; he had been a good man. If something had changed him, it must have been a powerful force. She let herself think it might have convinced her if she'd been exposed to it.

"No, *I'm* sorry," said Zebara, smiling directly at her again. "I often wished to talk with you, share my feelings. You would have understood and helped me stay true to my ideals. So here I've poisoned our meeting, a meeting I dreamed of, with my doubts and senile fears, and you're sitting there vibrating like a harpstring, afraid of me. And no wonder. I always knew you were a brave woman, but to come to Diplo when you'd had such vicious treatment from heavyworlders? That's incredible, Lunzie."

"You taught me that all heavyworlders were not alike," said Lunzie, managing a smile in return.

He mimed a flinch and grinned. "A palpable hit! My dear, if trusting me let you be hurt by others, I'm sorry indeed. But if you mean that it helped you gather courage to come here and help our people, after what you'd been through, I'm flattered." His face sobered. "But seriously, I need your help on something, and it may be dangerous."

"You need *my* help?"

"Yes, and that . . ." He suddenly lunged toward her, and flattened her to the couch.

"What!" His face smothered her. She beat a tattoo on his back. Behind her, she heard a chuckle.

"Good start, Zebara!" said someone she could not see. "But don't be *too* long. You'll miss the Governor's speech."

"Go away, Follard!" Zebara said, past her ear. "I'm busy and I don't care about the Governor's speech."

A snort of laughter. "Bedrooms upstairs, unless you're also working on blackmail."

Zebara looked up. Lunzie couldn't decide whether to scream or pretend acquiescence. "When I need advice, Follard, I'll ask for it."

"All right, all right; I'm going."

Lunzie heard the thump of the door closing and counted a careful five while Zebara sat back up.

"I'm glad you warned me! Or I'd be wondering why you wanted my help."

"I do." Zebara was tense, obviously worried. "Lunzie, we can't talk here, but we must talk. I do need your help, and I need you to pretend your old affection for me."

"Here? For Follard's benefit?"

"Not his! This is important, for you and the Federation as well
as for me. So, *please*, just act as if you . . ." A loud clanging interrupted him. He muttered a curseword Lunzie had not heard in
years, and stood up. "That does it. Someone's hit the proximity
alarm in the Governor's office and this place'll be swarming with
police and internal security guards. Lunzie, you've got to trust
me, at least for this. As we leave, lean on me. Act a little befud-
dled."

"I am."

"And then meet me tomorrow, when you're off work. Tell your
colleagues it's for dinner with an old friend. Will you?"

"It won't be a lie," she replied with a wry smile.

Then he was pulling her up, his arms still stronger than hers.
He put one around her shoulders, his fingers in her hair. She
leaned back against him, trying to conquer a renaissant fear. At
that moment the door opened, letting in a clamor from the alarm
and two uniformed police. Lunzie hoped her expression was that
of a woman surprised in a compromising position. She dared not
look at Zebara.

But whatever he was, whoever he was in his own world, his
name carried weight with the police, who merely checked his ID
on a handcomp and went on their way. Then Zebara led her back
to the main hall where most of the guests were clumped at one
end, with the lightweights in a smaller clump to one side. The
other members of the medical team, Lunzie noticed, were first
relieved to see her, then shocked. She was trying to look like
someone struggling against infatuation, and she must be succeed-
ing.

Zebara brought her up to that group, gave her a final hug, and
murmured, "Tomorrow. Don't forget!" before giving her a nudge
that sent her toward them.

"Well!" That almost simultaneous huff by two of the team
members at once made Lunzie laugh. She couldn't help it.

"What's the alarm about?" she asked, fighting the laugh back
down to her diaphragm where it belonged.

"Supposedly someone tried to break into the Governor's working office." Bias' voice was still primly disapproving. "Since you
didn't show up at once, we were afraid you were involved." A
pause, during which Lunzie almost asked why *she* would want to
break into the Governor's office, then Bias continued. "I see you

were involved, so to speak."

"Meow," said Lunzie. "I've told you about Zebara before. He saved my life, years ago, and even though it's been longer for him, I was glad to see him. . . ."

"We could tell." Lunzie had never suspected Bias of prudery, but the tone was still icily contemptuous. "I might remind you, Doctor, that we are here on a mission of medical research, not to reunite old lovers. Especially those who should have the common sense to realize how *unsuited* they are." The word unsuited caught Lunzie's funnybone and she almost laughed again. That showed in her face, for Bias glowered. "You might *try* to be professional!" he said, and turned away.

Lunzie caught Conigan's eye, and shrugged. The other woman grinned and shook her head: no accounting for Bias, in anything but his own field. Brilliancy hath its perks. Lunzie noticed that Jarl was watching her with a curious expression that made him seem very much the heavyworlder at the moment.

As the guards moved through the crowd, checking IDs, Jarl shifted until he was next to her, between her and the other team members. His voice was low enough to be covered by the uneven mutter of the crowd.

"It's none of my business, and I have none of the, er, scruples of someone like Bias, but . . . you *do* know, don't you, that Zebara is now head of External Security?"

She had not known; she didn't know how Jarl knew.

"We were just *friends*," she said as quietly.

"Security has no friends," said Jarl. His face was expressionless, but the statement had the finality of death.

"Thanks for the warning," said Lunzie.

She could feel her heart beating faster and controlled the rush of blood to her face with a touch of Discipline. Why hadn't he told her himself? Would he have told her if they'd had more time? Would he tell her at their next meeting? Or as he killed her?

She wanted to shiver, and dared not. What was going on here?

By the end of the workshift the next day, she was still wondering. All the way back to their quarters, Bias had made barbed remarks about oversexed female researchers until Conigan finally threatened to turn him in for harassment. That silenced him, but the team separated in unhappy silence when they arrived. The morning began with a setback in the research; someone had mistakenly wiped the wrong data cube and they had to re-enter it from patient records. Lunzie offered to do this, hoping it would soothe Bias, but it did not.

"You are not a data entry clerk," he said angrily. "You're a doctor. Unless you are responsible for the data loss, you have no business wasting your valuable time re-entering it."

"Tell you what," said Tailler, putting an arm around Bias' shoulders, "why don't we let Lunzie be responsible for scaring up a data clerk? You know you don't have time to do that. Nor do I. I've got surgery this morning and you're supposed to be checking the interpretation of those cardiac muscle cultures. Conigan's busy in the lab, and Jarl's already over at the archives, while Lunzie doesn't have a scheduled procedure for a couple of hours."

"But she shouldn't be wasting her time," fumed Bias. Tailler's arm grew visibly heavier and the smaller biologist quieted.

"I'm not asking her to *do* it," said Tailler, giving Lunzie a friendly but commanding grin. "I'm asking her to see that it's done. Lunzie's good at administrative work. She'll do it. Come on. Let's leave her with it; you don't want to be late."

And he steered Bias away even as the biologist said, "But she's a *doctor . . .*" one last time. Tailler winked over his shoulder at Lunzie, who grinned back.

It was easy enough ᵗ find a clerk willing to enter the data. Lunzie stayed to watch long enough to be sure the clerk really understood his task, then went on to her first appointment. She waited until well after the local noon break for her lunch, hoping to miss Bias. Sure enough, he'd already left the dining hall when she arrived, but Conigan and Jarl were eating together. Lunzie joined them.

"Did you get the data re-entered?" asked Jarl, grinning.

Lunzie rolled her eyes. "I did not, I swear, enter it myself. Thanks to Tailler, and a clerk out of the university secretarial pool, it was no problem. Just checked, and found that it's complete, properly labelled, and on file."

Jarl chuckled. "Tailler told us when we came in for lunch about Bias' little fit. He says Bias is like this by the second week of any expedition, to Diplo or anywhere else. He's worked with him six or seven times."

"I'm glad to know it's not just my aura," said Lunzie.

"No, and Tailler says he's going to talk to you about last night. Seems there's some reason Bias is upset by women associates having anything to do with local males."

"Alpha male herd instinct," muttered Conigan.

Jarl shook his head. "Tailler says not. Something happened on one of his expeditions, and he was blamed for it. Tailler wouldn't tell us, but he said he'd tell you, so you'd understand."

Lunzie did not look forward to that explanation. If Bias had peculiar notions, she could deal with them; she didn't have to be coaxed into sympathy. But she suspected that avoiding Tailler would prove difficult. Still, she could try.

"I'm having dinner with Zebara tonight," she said. "Bias will just have to live with it."

Jarl gave her a long look. "Not that I agree with Bias, but is that wise? You know?"

"I know what you told me, but I also know what Zebara did for me over forty years ago. It's worth embarrassing Bias, and worth risking whatever *you* fear."

"I don't like *anyone's* Security, external, internal, or military. Never been one yet that didn't turn into someone's private enforcement agency. You've had a negative contact with heavy-worlders before. You have a near relative in Fleet: reason enough to detain and question you if they're so minded."

"Not Zebara!" Lunzie hoped her voice carried conviction. Far below the surface, she feared precisely this.

"Just be careful," Jarl said. "I don't want to have to risk my neck on your behalf. Nor do I want to answer a lot of questions back home if you disappear."

Lunzie almost laughed, then realized he was being perfectly honest. He accorded her the moderate respect due a fellow professional, but he felt no particular friendship for her (for anyone?) and would not stir himself to help if she got into trouble. She could change quickly from "fellow professional" to "major annoyance" which in his value system would remove her from his list of acquaintances.

To add to her uneasiness, Tailler did indeed manage to catch her before she left the center and insisted on explaining at length the incident which had made Bias so sensitive to "relationships" between research staff and locals. A sordid little tale, Lunzie thought: nothing spectacular, nothing to really justify Bias' continuing reaction. He must have had a streak of prudery before that happened to give him the excuse to indulge it.

✦ CHAPTER SIX

Dupaynil, hustled through the scarred and echoing corridors of the transfer station to the control center where the *Claw*'s captain met him with the suggestion that he "put a leg in it" and get himself out to the escort's docking bay, had no chance to think things over until he was strapped safely into the escort's tiny reserve cabin. He had not been a passenger on anything smaller than a light cruiser for years; he had never been aboard an escort-class vessel. It seemed impossibly tiny after the *Zaid-Dayan*. His quarters for however long the journey might be was this single tiny space, a minute slice of a meager pie, hardly big enough to lie down in. He heard a loud clang, felt something rattle the hull outside, and then the escort's insystem drive nudged him against one side of his safety restraints. The little ship had artificial gravity, of a sort, but nothing like the overriding power that made Main Deck on the *Zaid-Dayan* feel as solid as a planet.

The glowing numbers on the readout overhead told him two Standard hours had passed when he felt a curious twinge and realized they'd shifted into FTL drive. Although he'd had basic training in astrogation, he'd never used it, and had only the vaguest idea what FTL travel really meant. Or where, in real terms, they might be. Somewhere behind (as he thought of it) was the cruiser he had left, with its now-familiar crew and its most attractive captain. Its *very angry* and most attractive captain. He wished she had not been so transparently suspicious of his motives. *She* was no planet pirate nor agent of slavers. She had nothing to fear from him. And he would gladly have spent more time with her. He let himself imagine the nights they could have shared.

"Sir, we're safely in FTL, if you want to come up to Main."

Dupaynil sighed as the voice over the comm broke into that fantasy and thumbed the control.

"I'll be there."

He had messages to send, messages he had had no time to send from the transfer station. And with the angry Commander Sassinak sitting on the other end of the block, so to speak, he would not have sent them from the station anyway. He rediscovered what he had once been taught about escort-class vessels in a few miserable minutes. They were small, overpowered for their mass, and understaffed. No one bunked on Main but the captain who was the pilot. Crew consisted of a round dozen: one other officer, the Jig Executive, eleven enlisted, from Weapons to Environmental. No cook: all the food was either loaded prepackaged, to be reconstituted and heated in automatic units, or synthesized from the Environmental excess.

Dupaynil shuddered; one of the best things about the *Zaid-Dayan* had been the cooking. With a full crew and one supercargo, the escort had to ration water: limited bathing. The head was cramped: the slots designed to discourage meditation. There was no gym, but the uneven artificial gravity and shiplong access tubing offered opportunity for informal exercise. For those who liked climbing very long ladders against variable G. Worst of all, the ship had no IFTL link.

"'Course we don't have IFTL," said the captain, a Major Ollery whose face seemed to brighten every time Dupaynil found something else to dislike. "We don't have a Ssli interface, do we?"

"But I thought . . ." He stopped himself in mid-argument. He had seen a briefing item, mention of the ship classes that had IFTL, mention of those which would not get it because of "inherent design constraints." And escorts were too small to carry a Ssli habitat. "That . . . that *stinker!*" he said, as he realized suddenly what Sassinak had done.

"What?" asked Ollery.

"Nothing." Dupaynil hoped his face didn't show how he felt, torn between anger and admiration. That incredible woman had fooled *him*. Had fooled an experienced Security Officer whose entire life had been spent fooling others. He had had a tap on her communications lines, a tap he was sure she'd never find, and somehow she'd found out. Decided to get rid of him. And *how* in Mulvaney's Ghost had she managed to fake an incoming IFTL message? With that originating code?

He sank down on the one vacant seat in the escort's bridge,

and thought about it. Of course she could fake the code, if she could fake the message. That much was easy, if the other was possible. But nothing he'd been taught, in a long and devious life full of such instruction, suggested that an IFTL message could be faked. It would take . . . he frowned, trying to think it through. It would take the cooperation of a Ssli: of *two* Ssli, at least. How would the captain of one ship enlist the aid of the Ssli on another? What kind of hold did Sassinak have on her resident Ssli? It had never occurred to him that the Ssli were capable of anything like friendship with humans. Once installed, the sessile Ssli never experienced another environment, never "met" anyone except through a computer interface. Or so he'd thought.

He felt as if he'd sat down on an anthill. He fairly itched with new knowledge and had no way to convey it to anyone. Ssli could have relationships with humans beyond mere duty. Could they with other races? With Wefts? Were Ssli perhaps telepathic? No one had suspected that. Dupaynil glanced around the escort bridge and saw only human faces, now bent over their own work. He cleared his throat, and the captain looked up.

"Do you . . . mmm . . . have any Wefts aboard?"

An odd expression in reply. "Wefts? No, why?" Then before he could answer, Ollery's face cleared. "Oh! You've been with Sassinak, I know. She's got a thing about Wefts, doesn't she? They say it started back in the Academy. She had a Weft lover or something. That true?" Ollery's voice had the incipient snigger of those who hope the worst about their seniors.

Dupaynil suppressed a surge of rage. As a Security Officer, he listened to gossip professionally; idle gossip, malicious gossip, juicy gossip, boring gossip. He found it generally dull, and sometimes disgusting: a necessary but unpleasant part of his career. But here, applied to Sassinak, it was infuriating.

"So far as I know," he said as smoothly as he could, "that story was started by a cadet expelled for stealing and harassing women cadets." He knew the truth of that; he'd seen the files. "*Captain* Sassinak" — he emphasized the rank a little, intentionally, and enjoyed seeing Ollery's face pale — "keeps her sex life in her own cabin, where it belongs, and where I intend to leave it."

A muffled snort behind him meant that either someone else thought the captain had been out of line, or that Dupaynil's

defense implied personal knowledge. He left that alone, too, and
hoped no one would ask.

Silence settled over the bridge; he went on with his thoughts.
Telepathic Wefts, and a ship's captain who could sometimes talk
that way with them. He'd seen the reports on Sassinak's first tour
of duty. A Ssli who — he suddenly remembered something from
the tour before he joined the *Zaid-Dayan*. Sassinak had reported
it as part of her testimony before the Board of Inquiry. Her Ssli,
this same Ssli, had taken control of the ship momentarily and
flipped it in and out of FTL space. A move which she had
described as "unprecedented, but undoubtedly the reason I am
here today."

He was beginning to think that Fleet knew far too little about
the capabilities of Ssli. But he had no way to find out more at the
moment so he moved his concentration to Sassinak herself.
When he thought of it, her actions were entirely probable. He
could have kicked himself for not realizing that she would react
quickly and strongly to any perceived threat. She had never liked
having him aboard; she had never really trusted him. So his inter-
ception of her classified messages, once she found out, would
naturally result in some action. Her history suggested a genius for
quick response, for instantly recognizing danger and reacting
effectively in novel ways.

And so he was here, out of communication until the escort
reached its destination. No way to check the validity of his orders
(though he was quite sure now where they had come from) and
no way to tell anyone what he'd found out. It occurred to him
then, and only then, that Sassinak might have planned even more
than getting him off her ship before he could "do something."
Perhaps she had other plans. Perhaps she was not going to take
the *Zaid-Dayan* tamely into Federation Central space, with all its
weaponry disabled and all its shuttles locked down.

For a long moment he fought off panic. She might do *anything*. Then he settled again. The woman was brilliant, not crazy:
aggressive in defending her own, responsive to danger, but not
disloyal to Fleet or Federation, not likely to do anything stupid,
like bombing FedCentral. He hoped.

"Panis, take the helm." Ollery pushed himself back, gave
Dupaynil a challenging glance, and stretched.

"Sir." Panis, the Executive Officer, had slid forward to the main control panel. He, too, glanced at Dupaynil before looking back at the screen.

"I'm going on a round," Ollery said. "Want to come along, Major?" A round of inspection, through all those long access tubes.

Dupaynil shook his head. "Not this time, thanks. I'll just . . ." *What?* he wondered. There was nothing to do on the tiny bridge but stare at the back of Panis' head or the side of the Weapons Control master mate's thick neck. A swingaway facescreen hid his face as he tinkered delicately with something in the weapons systems. At least, that's what Dupaynil assumed he was doing with a tiny joystick and something that looked like a silver toothpick. Maybe he was playing a game.

"You'll get tired of it," warned Ollery. Then he was gone, easing through the narrow hatch.

A lengthy silence, in which Dupaynil noted the scuffmarks on the decking by the captain's seat, the faded blue covers of the Fleet manuals racked for reference below the Exec's workstation. Finally Jig Panis looked over his shoulder and gave Dupaynil a shy smile.

"The captain's ticked," he said softly. "We got into the supply station a day early."

"Ollery reporting: Environmental, section forty-three, number-two scrubber's up a half-degree."

"Logged, sir." Panis entered the report, thumbed a control, and sent "Spec Zigran" off to check on the errant scrubber. Then he turned back to Dupaynil. "We'd had a long run without liberty," he said. "The captain said we'd have a couple of days off-schedule, sort of rest up and then get ready for inspection."

Dupaynil nodded. "So . . . my orders upset your party-time, eh?"

"Yes. *Playtak* was supposed to be in at the same time."

With a loud click, the Weapons Control mate flicked the facescreen back into place. Dupaynil caught the look he gave the young officer; he had seen senior noncoms dispense that "You talk too much!" warning glance at every rank up to admiral.

Panis turned red, and focussed on his board. Dupaynil asked no more; he'd heard enough to know why Ollery was hostile. Presumably *Playtak*'s captain was a friend of Ollery's and they'd agreed to meet at the supply station and celebrate. Quite against regulations, because he had no doubt that they had stretched their orders to make that overlap. It might be innocent, just friendship, or it might have been more. Smuggling, spying, who knows what? And he had been dumped into the middle of it, forcing them to leave ahead of schedule.

"Too bad," he said casually. "It certainly wasn't my idea. But Fleet's Fleet and orders are orders."

"Right, sir." Panis did not look up. Dupaynil looked over at the Weapons Control mate whose lowering expression did not ease although it was not overtly hostile.

"You're Fleet Security, sir?" asked the mate.

"That right. Major Dupaynil."

"And we're taking you into Seti space?"

"Right." He wondered who'd told the man that. Ollery had had to know, but hadn't he realized those orders were secret? Of course they weren't really secret, since they were faked orders, but . . . He pushed that away. It was too complicated to think about now.

"Huh. Nasty critters." The mate put the toothpicklike tool he'd been using into a toolcase, and settled back in his seat. "Always get the feeling they're hoping for trouble."

Dupaynil had the same feeling about the mate. Those scarred knuckles had broken more than a few teeth, he was sure. "I was there with a diplomatic team once," he said. "I suppose that's why they're sending me."

"Yeah. Well, don't let the toads sit on you." The mate lumbered up, and with a casual wave at the Exec, left the bridge.

Dupaynil looked after him, a little startled. He had not considered Sassinak strict on etiquette, but no one would have left *her* bridge without a proper salute to the officer in charge, and permission to withdraw. Of course, this was a smaller ship than he'd ever been on. Was it *healthy* to have such a casual relationship?

Then the term "toads" which wasn't at all an accurate description of the Seti, but conveyed the kind of racial contempt that put Dupaynil on alert. Everyone knew the Federation combined races and cultures that preferred separation, but some hardly remembered force had compelled the Seti and humans both to sign agreements against aggression. And, for the most part, abide by them. As professional keepers of this fragile peace, Fleet personnel were expected to have a more dispassionate view. Besides, he always thought of the Seti as "lizards."

. " 'Scuse me, sir." That was another crewman, squeezing past him to get to a control panel on his left.

Dupaynil felt very much in the way, and very much unwanted. Blast Sassinak! The woman might at least have dumped him onto something *comfortable.* He looked over at Panis who was determinedly not looking at him. If he remembered correctly, the shortest route to Seti space was going to take weeks and he could not endure this kind of thing for weeks.

The crew had worked off their bad humor in less than a week. Dupaynil exerted his considerable charm, let Ollery win several card games, and entertained them with some of the safer racy anecdotes from his last assignment in a political realm. He had read Ollery correctly; the man liked to find flaws in those above him; preferably blackmailable flaws. Given a story about an ambassador's lady addicted to drugs or a wealthy senior bureaucrat who preferred cross-cultural divertissements, his eyes glistened and his cheeks flushed.

Dupaynil concealed his own contempt. Those who best liked to hear such things usually had their own similar appetites to hide.

Panis, however, was of very different stripe. He had tittered nervously at the story of the bureaucrat and turned brick red when Ollery and the senior mate sneered at him. It was clear that he had no close friends among the crew. When Dupaynil checked, he found that Panis had replaced the previous Exec only a few months before, while the rest of the crew had been unchanged for almost five years. And the previous Exec had left the ship because of an injury in a dockside brawl. It was odd, and more than odd: regular rotation of crew was especially important on small ships. Fleet policy insisted on it. No matter how efficient a crew seemed to be, they were never left unchanged too long.

Dupaynil had not been able to bring all his tools along, but he always had some. He placed his sensors carefully, as carefully as he had in the larger ship, and slid his probe into the datalinks very delicately indeed. He had the feeling that carelessness here would get him more than a chewing out by the captain.

In the meantime, as the days wore on, the crew loosened up with him and played endless hands of every card game he knew, and a few he'd never seen. Crutch was a pirate's game, he'd been told once by the merchanter who taught it to him; he wondered where the crew had learned it. Poker, blind-eye, sin on toast, at which he won back all he'd lost so far, having learned that on Bretagne, where it began.

He sweated up and down the access tube ladders, learning to respond quickly to the shifting artificial-G, keeping his muscles supple. He discovered a storage bay full of water ice which made the restrictions on bathing ridiculous. There was enough to last a crew twice that size all the way to Seti space and *back* but he kept his mouth shut. It seemed safer.

For all their friendliness, all their casual demeanor, he'd noticed that Ollery or the senior mate were always in any compartment he happened into. Except his own tiny cabin. And he was sure they'd been there when he found evidence that his things had been searched. He had time to wonder if Sassinak had known just what kind of ship she'd sent him to. He thought not. She had probably done a fast scan of locations, looking for the nearest docked escort vessel, some way to keep him from communicating while he was in FTL.

"I say he's spying on *us*, and I say dump him." That was the mate. Dupaynil shivered at the quietly deadly tone.

"He's got IG orders. They'll want to know what happened." That was Ollery, not nearly so sure of himself.

"We can't just space him. We have to figure out a way."

"Emergency drill. Blow the pod. Say it was an accident." The mate's voice carried the shrug he would give when questioned later.

"What if he figures it out?"

"What can he do? Pod's got no engine, no decent long-range radio, no scan. Dump him where he'll fall down a well, into a star or something else big. Disable the radio and beacon. That way no one'll know he's ever been there. 'Sides, I don't think his orders are real. Think about it, sir. Would the IG haul someone off a big cruiser like the *Zaid-Dayan* — an IFTL message, that'd have to be — and stick 'em on a little bitty escort? To go to Seti space? C'mon. You send a special envoy to the Seti, you send a damn flotilla in with 'em, not an escort. No, you mark my words, sir, he's here to spy on *us* and this proves it."

Dupaynil could not tell through the audio link which of his taps had been found, but he wished ardently that he had not planted it, whatever it was. Once again he had outsmarted himself, as he had with Sassinak. Never underestimate the enemy and be damned sure you know who the enemy is; a very basic rule he had somehow violated.

He felt a trickle of sweat run down his ribs. Sassinak had been dumped in an evac pod, rescued by the combined efforts of Wefts and a Ssli. He had no Wefts or Ssli to back him up; he would have to figure this out himself.

"You're sure he hasn't got the good stuff out of comp yet?"

"Pretty sure." The mate's voice was even grimmer. "Security's got good tools, though. Give him all the time between here and Seti space, and he'll have not only the basics but enough to mind-fry the lot of us, all the way up to Lady Luisa herself."

Dupaynil almost forgot his fear. *Lady* Luisa? Luisa *Paraden*? He had always been able to put two and two together and find more interesting things than four. Now he felt an almost physical jolt as his mind connected everything he'd ever heard or seen; including all the information Sassinak had gathered.

As bright as a diagram projected on the screen of a strategy meeting, all connections marked out in glowing red or yellow . . . Luisa to Randolph, who had ample reason to loathe Sassinak. That had been *Randolph* Paraden's vengeance, through his aunt's henchman, a brainwashed Fleet officer once held captive on the same slaver outpost as an orphan girl. Dupaynil spared a moment to pity that doomed lieutenant: Sassinak never would, even if she learned the whole story. Luisa would never do something that potentially dangerous just for Randolph, though. It must have been vengeance for Abe's part in disrupting her operation, a warning to others. Perhaps fear that he would cause her more trouble.

Abe to Sassinak, Sassinak to Randolph, Randolph to Luisa, whose first henchman partially failed. Where was Randolph *now*, Dupaynil wondered suddenly. He should know and he did not know. He realized that he had not ever seen one bit of information on Randolph in the system since that arrogant young man had left the Academy. Unnatural. A Paraden, wealthy, with connections: he should have done *something*. He should have been in the society news or been an officer in one of Aunt Luisa's companies.

Unless he changed his identity some way. It could be done, though it was expensive. Not that that would bother a Paraden. And why had they stopped with one attack on Sassinak? Dupaynil wished he had her file in hand. They would have been covert attempts, but knowing what to look for he might be able to see it. But of course! The Wefts. The Wefts she had saved from Paraden's accusations in the Academy; the Wefts who had saved her from death in the pod. Wefts might have foiled any number of plots without bothering to tell *her*.

Or perhaps she knew, but never made the connection, or never bothered to report it, rules or no. She was not known for following the rules. He leaned on the wall of his cubicle, sweating and furious, as much with himself as the various conspirators. This was his *job*, this was what he had trained for, what he had thought he was good at; finding things out, making connections, sifting the data, interpreting it. And here he was, with all the threads woven into the pattern and no possible way to get that information *out*.

You're so smart, he thought bitterly. You're going to your death having won the war but lost the brawl. He knew — it was in her file and she had confided it as well — that Sassinak still wondered about the real reason Abe had been killed. She had never forgotten it, never laid it to rest. And he had that to offer her, more than enough to get her forgiveness for that earlier misunderstanding. But too late!

Thinking of Sassinak reminded him again of her experience in the escape pod. It had made chilling reading, even in the remote prose her captain had used. She had gone right up to the limit of the pod's oxygen capacity, hoping to be conscious to give her evidence. He shuddered. He would have put himself into cold sleep as soon as he realized what happened, and he'd probably have died of it. Or, like Lunzie, been found decades later. He didn't like that scenario either. He fairly itched to get his newly acquired insights where they could do the most good.

Sassinak, now. What would she do, cooped in an escort full of renegades? He had trouble imagining her on anything but the bridge of the *Zaid-Dayan*, but she had served in smaller ships. Would she find a weapon (where?) and threaten them from the bridge? Would she take off in an escape pod before she was jettisoned, with a functioning radio, and hope to be found in time?

(In time for what? Life? The trial?) The one thing she wouldn't do, he was sure, was slouch on a bunk wondering what to do. She would have thought of something, and given her luck it would probably have worked.

The idea, when it finally came to him hours later (miserable, sweaty hours when he was supposed to be sleeping), seemed simple. Presumably they would have a ship evacuation drill at the occasion of his murder. The others would be going into pods as well, just to make it seem normal. They had found one of his taps, but not all (or surely they'd have blocked the audio so he couldn't hear). And therefore he could tap the links again, reset the evac pod controls, and trap *them* — or most of them — in the pods. They would not be able to fire his pod; he could fire theirs.

He was partway through the reprogramming of the pod controls when he realized why this was not such a simple solution. Fleet had a name for someone who took illegal control of a ship and killed the captain and crew. An old, nasty name leading to a court-martial which he might well lose.

I am not contemplating mutiny, he told himself firmly. They are the criminals. But they were not convicted yet, and until then what he planned was, by all the laws and regulations, not merely mutiny but also murder. And piracy. And probably a dozen or so lesser crimes to be tacked onto the charge sheet(s), including the things Sassinak might say about his tap into her comm shack. And his present unauthorized reprogramming of emergency equipment. Not to mention his supposed orders to proceed into Seti space: faked orders, which no one (after he pirated a ship and killed the crew) would believe he had not faked for himself.

What would Sassinak do about *that*, he wondered. He remembered the holo of the *Zaid-Dayan* with its patched hull, with the scars of the pirate boarding party. She had let the enemy onto her ship to trap them. Could he think of anything as devastating? All things considered, forty-three years of cold sleep might be the easy way out, he thought, finishing off the new switching sequences.

Sassinak's great-great-great might complain, but a little time in the freezer could keep you out of big trouble. His mind bumped him again, hard. Of course. Cold sleep *them*, the nasties. Drop the charges to mere mutiny and piracy and et cetera, but not murder (mandatory mindwipe for murder), and he might merely spend the next twenty years cleaning toilet fixtures with a bent toothbrush.

Of course it still wasn't simple. For all his exercise up and down the ladders, he had no more idea than a space-opera hero how to operate this ship. He'd had only the basics, years back; he'd flown a comp-desk, not a ship. He could chip away at that compartment of water ice and not die of thirst, but he couldn't convert it and take a shower. Or even get the ship down out of FTL space. Sassinak could probably do it, but all he could do was trigger the Fleet distress beacon and hope the pickup ship wasn't part of the same corrupt group. He wouldn't even do that, if he didn't quit jittering and get to it.

✧ CHAPTER SEVEN

Diplo

Zebara led her through the maze of streets around the university complex at a fast pace. For all his age and apparent physical losses, he was still amazingly fit. She was aware of eyes following them, startled glances. She could not tell if it was Zebara himself, or his having a lightweight companion. She was puffing when he finally stopped outside a storefront much like the others she'd seen.

"Giri's Place," Zebara said. "Best chooli stew in the city, a very liberal crowd, *and* a noisy set of half-bad musicians. You'll love it."

Lunzie hoped so. Chooli stew conformed to Federation law by having no meat in it, but she had not acquired a taste for the odd spices that flavored the mix of starchy vegetables.

Inside, hardly anyone looked at her. The "liberal crowd" were all engrossed in their own food and conversation. She smelled meat, but saw none she recognized. The half-bad musicians played with enthusiasm but little skill, covering their blats and blurps with high-pitched cries of joy or anguish. She could not tell which, but it did make an effective sonic screen. She and Zebara settled into one of the booths along the side, and ordered chooli stew with figgerunds, the green nuts she'd had at the reception, Zebara explained.

"You need to know some things," he began when the chooli stew had arrived, and Lunzie was taking a first tentative bite of something yellowish.

"I heard you were head of External Security," she said quietly.

He looked startled. "Where'd you hear? No, it doesn't matter. It's true, although not generally known." He sighed. "I can see this makes it more difficult for you. . . ."

"Makes what more difficult?"

"Trusting me." His eyes flicked around the room, as anyone's might, but Lunzie could not believe it was the usual casual glance. Then he looked back at her. "You don't, and I can't blame you, but we must work together or . . . or things could get very bad indeed."

"Isn't your involvement with an offworlder going to be a little conspicuous?" She let a little sarcasm edge her voice; how naive did he think she was?

"Of course. That doesn't matter." He ate a few bites while she digested the implications of that statement. It could only "not matter" if policymakers knew and approved. When he looked up and swallowed, she nodded at him. "Good! You understand. Your name on the medical team was a little conspicuous, if you'd had any ulterior motive for coming here . . ." He let that trail away, and Lunzie said nothing. Whatever motives she had had, the important thing now was to find out what Zebara was talking about. She took another bite of stew; it was better than the same dish in the research complex's dining hall.

"I saw the list," Zebara went on. "One of the things my department does is screen such delegations, looking for possible troublemakers. Nothing unusual. Most planets do the same. There was your name, and I wondered if it was the same Lunzie. Found out that it was you and then the rocks started falling."

"Rocks?"

"My . . . employers. They wanted me to contact you, renew our friendship. More than friendship, if possible. Enlist your aid in getting vital data offplanet."

"But your employers . . . that's the Governor, right?" Lunzie was not sure, despite having read about it, just where political power was on this planet.

"Not precisely. The Governor knows them, and that's part of the problem. I have to assume that you, with what's happened to you, are like any normal Federation citizen. About piracy, for instance."

His voice had lowered to a muffled growl she could barely follow. The half-bad musicians were perched on their tall stools, gulping some amber liquid from tall glass mugs. She hoped it would mellow their music as well as their minds.

"*My* ethics haven't changed," she said, with the slightest emphasis on the pronoun.

"Good. That's what they counted on, and I, in my own way, counted on the same thing." He took a long swallow of his drink.

"Are you suggesting," Lunzie spoke slowly, phrasing it carefully, "that your goals and your employers' goals both depend on my steadfast opinions, even if they are . . . divergent?"

"You could say it that way." Zebara grinned at her, and slightly raised his mug.

And what other way, with what other meaning, could I say it? Lunzie wondered. She sipped from her own mug, tasting only the water she'd asked for, and said, "That's all very well, but what does it mean?"

"That, I'm afraid, we cannot discuss here. I will tell you what I can, and then we'll make plans to meet again." At her frown, he nodded. "That much is necessary, Lunzie, to keep immediate trouble at bay. We are watched. Of course we are, and I'm aware of it so we must continue our friendly association."

"Just how friendly?"

That slipped out before she meant it. She had not meant to ask that until later, if ever. He chuckled, but it sounded slightly forced.

"You know how friendly we *were*. You probably remember it better than I do since you slept peacefully for over forty of the intervening years."

She felt the blood rushing to her face and let it. Any watchers would assume that was genuine emotion.

"You! I have to admit that I haven't forgotten you, not one . . . single . . . thing."

This time, he was the one to blush. She hoped it satisfied whoever was doing the surveillance but she thought the actual transcript would prove deadly.

As if he could read her thoughts, he said, "Don't worry! At this stage they're still letting me arrange the surveillance. We're relatively safe as long as we don't do something outside their plans."

Their plans or your plans, she wondered. She wanted to trust Zebara: she *did* trust the Zebara she'd known. But this new Zebara, this old man with the hooded eyes, the grandchildren he wanted to save, the head of External Security, could she trust *this* Zebara? And how far?

Still when he reached for her hand, she let him take it. His fingers stroked her palm and she wondered if he would try something as simple as dot code. Cameras might pick that up. Instead, a fingernail lightly drew the logo on the FSP banner, then letter by letter traced her name. She smiled at him, squeezed his hand, and hoped she was right.

The next day's work at the Center went well. Whatever Bias thought, he managed not to say and no one else asked uncomfortable questions. Lunzie came back to her quarters, feeling slightly uneasy that she hadn't heard from Zebara but her message light was blinking as she came in. She put in a call to the number she was given, and was not surprised to hear his voice.

"You said once you'd like to hear our native music," he began. "There's a performance tonight of Zilmach's epic work. Would you come with me?"

"Formal dress, or informal?" asked Lunzie.

"Not formal like the Governor's reception, but nice."

She was sure he was laughing underneath at her interest in clothes. But she agreed to be ready in an hour without commenting on it. Dinner before the performance was at an obviously classy restaurant. The other diners wore expensive jewels in addition to fancy clothes. Lunzie felt subdued in her simple dark green dress with the copper-and-enamel necklace that served her for all occasions. Zebara wore a uniform she did not recognize. Did External Security really go for that matte black or did they intend it to intimidate offworlders? He looked the perfect foil for Sassinak. She let herself remember Sassinak in her dress whites, with the vivid alert expression that made her beautiful. Zebara sat there like a black lump of rough stone, heavy and sullen. Then he smiled.

"Dear Lunzie, you're glaring at me. Why?"

"I was thinking of my great-great-great-granddaughter," she said, combining honesty and obliqueness at once. "You have grandchildren, you said? Then surely they cross your mind at the oddest times, intruding, but you'd never wish them away."

"That's true." He shook his head with a rueful smile. "And since mine are here in person, they can intrude physically as well. Little Pog, the youngest, got loose from his mother in my office one time. Darted past my secretary straight through the door and into my conference room. Set off alarms and thoroughly annoyed the Lieutenant Governor and the Chiefs of Staff. He'd grabbed me by the leg and was howling because the siren scared him. He made so much noise the guards were sure someone was really hurt." His smile had broadened; now he chuckled. "By the time I had peeled him off my leg, found his mother, and convinced the guards that it was not an exceptionally clever assassination scheme using a midget or a robot, none of us could get our minds back on the problem. Worst of all, I had to listen to a lecture by the Lieutenant Governor on the way he disciplines *his* family. What he didn't know, and I couldn't tell him, was that his eldest son was about to be arrested for sedition. This is, as you might suspect, the *former* Lieutenant Governor, not the one you met the other night."

The revelation about his job did nothing to quiet Lunzie's nerves. Anyone who could pretend not to know that someone's child was about to be arrested had more than enough talent in lying to confuse *her*. She forced herself to concentrate on his feelings for his children and grandchildren. That, at least, she could understand and sympathize with.

"So what happened to little . . . Pog, was it?"

"Yes, short for Poglin. Family name on his mother's side. Well, I counseled leniency since he'd been frightened so badly by the alarms and the subsequent chaos, but his mother felt guilty that he'd gotten away from her. She promised him a good thrashing when they got home. I hope that was mostly for my benefit. She's very . . . aware of rank, that one." It was obvious that he didn't like his daughter-in-law much. Lunzie wondered if he'd meant to reveal that to her. "And have you caught up with all your family after your long sleep?" he was asking.

Lunzie shook her head, and sipped cautiously at the steaming soup that had appeared in front of them. Pale orange, spicy, not bad at all.

"My great-great, Sassinak, gave me Fleet transport to Sector Headquarters. She's an orphan. She's never met the others."

"Oh. Isn't that unusual? Wouldn't they take her in?" His eyelids had sagged again, hiding his expression. Lunzie suspected he knew a lot more about her and her family, including Sassinak, than he pretended.

"They didn't know." Quickly, she told him what little Sassinak had told her and added her own interpretation of Sassinak's failure to seek out her parents' relatives. "She's still afraid of rejection, I think. Fleet took her in. She considers it her family. I had one grandson, Dougal, in Fleet, and I remember the others complaining that he was almost a stranger to them. Even when he visited, he seemed attached somewhere else."

"Will you introduce her?"

"I've thought about that. Forty-three more years. I don't know who's alive, where they are, although it won't be hard to find out. But she may not want to meet them, even with me. I'm still trying to figure out whose she is, for that matter. I haven't really had time." At the startled look on his face, she laughed. "Zebara, you've been *with* your family all this time. Of course nothing is more important to you. But I've had one long separation after another. I've had to make my connections where and when I could. The first thing was to get my certification back, get some kind of job."

"Surely your great-great, this Sassinak, wouldn't have tossed you out to starve!"

"She's Fleet, remember? Under orders. I'm civilian." *Sort of*, she thought to herself, wondering just what status she did have. Coromell had recruited her: was that official? The Venerable Master Adept seemed to have connections to Fleet she had never quite understood. But surely *he* wasn't a Fleet agent? Sassinak had sent her to Liaka with the same assurance she'd have sent one of her own officers. "I wouldn't have starved, no. You're right about that. But by the time I left Liaka, I still didn't have my accumulated back pay. It would come, they assured me, but it was sticking in someone's craw to pay me for forty-three years of cold sleep. All I really wanted was the credit for time awake, but . . ." She shrugged. "Bureaucrats."

"We are difficult sometimes." He was smiling, but she wondered why he had intruded his position again.

They finished dinner with little more conversation, then went to the concert. Zebara's rank meant excellent seats, a respectful usher, and a well of silence around them, beyond which Lunzie could just hear curious murmurs. She glanced down at the program. She had never heard of Zilmach or his (her?) epic work. The program cover showed two brawny heavyworlders lifting a spaceship overhead. She didn't know if that was a scene from the work she would hear or the logo of the Diplo Academy of Music. She nudged Zebara.

"Tell me about this."

"Zilmach, a composer you won't have heard of, spent twenty years on this, working from the series of poems Rudrik wrote in the first Long Freeze on Diplo. Rudrik, by the way, died of starvation, along with some forty thousand of those early colonists. It's called *Bitter Destiny* and the theme is exploitation of our strength to provide riches for the weak. You won't like the libretto, but the music is extraordinary." He nuzzled her neck and Lunzie managed not to jump. "Besides, it's loud, and we can talk if we're careful."

"It's not rude?"

"Yes," he said quietly into her ear, "but there are segments in which almost everyone gets affectionate; you'll know."

Zilmach's epic work began with a low moaning of strings and woodwinds, plus a rhythmic banging on some instrument Lunzie had never heard before: rather like someone whacking a heavy chain with a hammer. She ventured a murmured question to Zebara who explained that it represented the pioneers chipping ice off their machinery. Zilmach had invented the instrument in the course of writing the music.

After the overture, a massed chorus marched in singing. Lunzie felt goosebumps break out on her arms. Although she had told herself that the heavyworlders must have creative capacity, she had never truly believed it. She had never seen any of their art, or heard their music. Now, listening to those resonant voices filling the hall easily, she admitted to herself just how narrow-minded she'd been. The best she'd been able to imagine was "kind" or "gentle." But this was magnificent.

She did not enjoy the stage presentation of the lightweight "exploiters." Although seeing massive heavyworlders pretending to be tiny fragile lightweights cringing from each other had the humor of incongruity. She remembered having seen a cube of an Old Earth opera in which a large lady with sagging jowls was being serenaded as a "nymph."

But the voices! She had imagined heavyworlder music as heavy, thumping, unmelodic . . . and she'd been wrong.

"It's *beautiful*," she murmured to Zebara, in a pause between scenes.

"You're surprised." It was not a question. She apologized with her expression as the music began again. He leaned closer. "Don't worry. I thought you'd be surprised. And there's more."

"More" included a display of gymnastics representing shifting alliances in the commercial consortium that had (according to the script) dumped ill-prepared heavyworlder colonists on a planet that suffered predictable, but infrequent, "triple winters." Complex gong music apparently intimated the heartless weighting of profit and loss (a balance loaded with "gold" bars on one side and limp heavyworlder bodies on the other) while the corporate factions pushed on the balance and each other, and leapt about in oddly graceful contortions.

Diplo's gravity prevented any of the soaring leaps of classical ballet but quick flips were possible and used to great effect. A scene showing the luxurious life of lightweights in space was simply ludicrous. Lunzie had never seen anyone aboard a spaceship lounging in a scented fountain while a heavyworlder servant knelt with a tray of fruit. But overall she remained amazed with the lush, melodic sound and the quality of the voices.

Those segments in which, as Zebara promised, "everyone gets affectionate" depicted the colonists fighting off the depression of that long winter with song and love. Or lust. Lunzie wasn't sure. Perhaps the colonists hadn't been sure, either. But they had been determined to survive and have descendants.

Duet followed duet, combined into a quartet praising "love of life that warms the heart." Then a soprano aria from a singer whose deep, dark, resonant voice throbbed with despair before rising slowly, impossibly, through three octaves to end in a crystalline flourish which the singer emphasized by a massive fist, shaking at the wicked lightweights in their distant ships.

Finally the male chorus of colonists, who had chosen to starve voluntarily so that children and pregnant women might have a chance to survive, made their final vows, led by a tenor whose voice soared to nearly the same dynamic height as the soprano.

"To you, the children of our dreams, we leave the bread of life!" Lunzie felt tears stinging her eyes. "We ask but this! That you remember . . ."

The voices faded, slowly dropping to a complex chant. The music and the rich incense flowing from the censers onstage were enough to get anyone's hormones moving. She let her head sag toward Zebara's shoulder.

"Good girl," he murmured.

Around them, rustling indicated that others, too, were changing their positions. Suddenly Lunzie felt something bump her legs and realized that the seats in this section reclined *completely*. The armrest between hers and Zebara's retracted. Onstage, the music swelled as the lights dimmed. Clearly, an invitation to Zilmach's epic meant more than just listening to the music.

At the same moment that she wondered how she was going to get out of what was clearly intended, she remembered her pressure garment, and sniggered.

"What?" he ask. His arm lay heavily on her shoulders; his broad hand stroked her back.

"An element of lightweight weakness your producers forgot to show," Lunzie said, trying to control her laughter. "This thing we have to wear. Very inefficient at moments like this."

Zebara chuckled. "Dear Lunzie, I have no intention of forcing you. You might get pregnant. You're young enough. You don't want my child, and I don't want the responsibility. But we *are* expected to whisper sweet nothings in each other's ears. If the sweets are not nothings, who's to know?"

This was no time to ask if Diplo External Security had the same kind of electronics Fleet used, which could have picked up the rumbles from dinner in her stomach, let alone anything she and Zebara might whisper. If they didn't, they didn't need to know about it. If they did, she had to hope Zebara had only one double-cross in mind.

"So, how long does this last?"

"Several *looong* minutes. Don't worry. We'll have plenty of warning before it's over. There's the funeral scene coming up and the decision whether or not to eat the bodies. So let's use this interval to find out the things I must know. Who sent you here and what are you trying to find?"

Lunzie could not answer at once. She had not thought that even a heavyworlder could mention cannibalism so calmly. Another blow to her wish to trust him. His tongue flicked her ear, gaining all her attention easily.

"Lunzie, you cannot expect me to believe you came here just to get over your fear of heavyworlders. Ireta would have left you even worse. You could not care that much how we experience cold sleep or what it does to us. You are here for a purpose. Either your own, or someone else's, and I must know that if I am to keep you safe."

"You've told me your government wants you to use our old relationship. How can you ask me to confide in you first?" That was lame, but the best she could do with cannibalism still on her mind.

"I want my grandchildren to live! Really live. I want them to have enough food, freedom to travel, to get education, to work where they want. You want that for your descendants. In that we agree. If war breaks out between our peoples, none of our descendants will have the lives we want for them. Can't you see that?"

Lunzie nodded slowly. "Yes, but unless your people quit working with planet pirates I don't see what's to stop it."

"Which they won't do, unless they see a better future. Lunzie, I want you to be our advocate, our spokeswoman to the Council. You have suffered from us but you have also seen, perhaps understood, what we are, what we could be. I want you to say, 'Give the heavyworlders hope! Give them access to normal-G worlds they can live on, worlds like Ireta. Then they won't have reason to steal them.' But as long as you are here to collect evidence proving how bad we are."

"Not all of you."

Lunzie caught a flicker of movement near them, above them, and curled into Zebara's embrace. Perhaps someone needed the restrooms, sidling along between the seat sections. Or perhaps someone wanted to know what they were saying.

"You're different. The patients I've met here are not like those who hurt me." She felt under her hands his slight tension. He, too, had noticed that shadowy form edging past them.

"Dear Lunzie." That ended in a kiss, a curiously grandfatherly kiss of dry lips. Then he sighed, moved as if slightly cramped, and laid his hand back on her hair.

"Who? Please tell me!"

She decided to give him a little, what he might have tapped from Fleet communications if his people were good enough.

"Sassinak. She wanted to know if the Governor was officially involved in Ireta. Captain Cruss, the heavyworlder on that colony ship, thought so. The Theks got it out of him. With Tanegli's trial coming up, she wanted to know whether to suggest that the Fleet subpoena the Governor."

"Ahhh. About what we thought. But how were you, a physician, supposed to find out such things?"

"I'd told her about you. She said I should come." That wasn't quite accurate, but if he believed she had been pushed into it, he might be sympathetic.

"I see. Your descendant, being a professional, does not consider your feelings, your natural reluctance. Not very sensitive, our Sassinak."

"Oh, she is," Lunzie said quickly. "She is sensitive, she just . . . she just thinks of duty first."

"Commendable in a Fleet officer, no doubt, but not in a great-great-great granddaughter. She should have more respect."

"It's a problem," Lunzie admitted. "But she's actually older than I am — real time, at least — and she has trouble seeing me as her elder. We both do." She squirmed a little getting a stiff wrinkle out from under her hip. "But that's why I came . . . really."

"And I am to offer you just the information you seek, and ask you to smuggle out more. But you will be found to have instead information of great commercial value. You will be discredited as a commercial spy, detained long enough that you cannot testify against Tanegli. Your taped evidence will not be nearly as effective, and if Kai and Varian are not there . . ."

"Why shouldn't they be?"

"Contract scientists with EEC? Easy enough to send an all too special ship to collect them to attend the Assizes. It should not be hard for those with adequate resources to be sure they arrive late. Or not at all."

Lunzie shivered. How could she warn Kai and Varian? Why hadn't she thought of them before? She had assumed that, as civilians, they would be allowed to go about their new responsibilities on Ireta. She should have known better.

"It is not just heavyworlders," Zebara murmured, as if he'd read her mind. "You know there are others?" Lunzie nodded.

Any of the commercial entities would find greater profit in resource development without regulation. Humans and aliens both. She had heard of no society so idealistic that it had no criminals among it. Perhaps the Ssli, she amended: once sessile, how could they do anything wrong, in anyone's terms? But here and now?

"Seti!" came Zebara's murmur. "They've used us, pretended sympathy for our fate, for having been genetically altered. But they despise us for it, as well."

She nodded against his chest, trying to think. The Seti pre-dated human membership in the FSP, though not by much. They were difficult, far more alien-seeming, and less amusing, than the Ryxi or Wefts. They had destroyed a Weft planet and later claimed to have done so accidentally, not knowing of the Wefts they killed. And the Thek!

"It's three-cornered, really." Zebara nuzzled her hair a long moment and she felt the draft of someone's movement past them again. "Our Governor's worked for the Pralungan Combine for over twenty years. He's been paid off in money, shares, and posi-tions for his relatives. The Combine gets strong backs for its internal security forces, industrial enforcers. Even private troops. Crew for illegally armed vessels to fight Fleet interference. Your Sassinak's been a major problem for us, by the way. She gets along too well with her heavyworlder marines. That word's spread and we have too many youngsters thinking of Fleet as a future. Not to mention the number of ships she's blown up in her career. Also, the Seti have some gain of their own we haven't quite fig-ured out. They want some of the planets we've taken: mostly those unsuitable for human settlement. They're funneling money into the Combine and the Combine funnels some, as little as they can, to us."

It was almost too much to take in. "What do you want me to do?" asked Lunzie.

"Get the real data out. Not the faked stuff you're supposed to be caught with. You'll have to leave before your team. It's sup-posed to look as if you're fleeing with stolen information. And if you don't, they'll know I didn't convince you. But you can leave before even they expect it. I can say you double-crossed me, used the pass you were given too soon."

It sounded most unlikely. No lightweight could get offplanet unnoticed. Surely they would be watching her. If she tried to bolt, they would simply call Zebara to check. And then find on her the real data, dooming both of them. She said this, very fast and very softly, into his ear. He held her close, a steady grip that would have been calming if her mind had not gone on ahead to the obvious conclusion.

He did not mean her to escape as a lightweight: as someone walking up the ramp, opening her papers for inspection at the port, climbing into her seat in the shuttle. He had something else in mind, something that would not be so obvious. The possibilities scrolled through her mind as if on a screen. As cargo? But an infrared scan would find her. As — She stiffened, pulled her head back, and tried to see his face in the darkened hall.

"*Not* in cold sleep." She meant it to be non-negotiable.

"I'm sorry," he said, into her hair.

"No." Quietly, but firmly, and with no intention of being talked into it. "Not again."

At that very inopportune moment, the softly passionate music stopped, leaving the hall in sudden silence interspersed with rustling clothing. The silence lengthened. A single drumbeat, slow inexorable, signalled a dire event, and the back of her seat shoved her up, away from Zebara. The armrest slid upward between them. The footrest dropped. Another drum joined the first, heavy, sodden with grief. Muted brass, one grave note after another followed the drums. Onstage, lights showed the barest outline of a heap of bodies, of sufferers still alive and starving. The sacrifice had not been enough. They would all die after all. A child's soprano, piercing as a needle, cried out for food, and Lunzie flinched. The alto's voice replying held all history's bitterness.

Surely it had not really been this bad! It could not have been! The rigid arm of the man beside her insisted it was, it had been. He believed it so, at least, and he believed the future might be as bleak. Lunzie swallowed, fighting nausea. If they actually *showed* cannibalism onstage . . . but they did not. A chorus of grieving women, of hungry children. One suggested, the others cried out in protest, and this went on (as so often in operas) somewhat longer than was necessary to convince everyone that both sides were sincere.

One after another came over to the side of horror, for the children's sake, but it was, in the end, a child who raised a shaking arm to point at the new element in the crisis. The new element, presented onstage as a furcoated robot of sorts, was the native grazer of the tundra. Shaggy, uncouth, and providentially stupid, it had been drawn by the warmth of the colonists' huts from its usual path of migration. The same woman who had been ready to put the dead into a synthesizer now wrestled the shaggy beast and killed it: not without being gored by two of its six horns. Whereupon the survival of the colony was assured so long as they were willing to kill and eat the animals.

One alone stood fast by the Federation's prohibition, and threatened to reveal what they'd done. She was prevented from sending any message and died by her own hand after a lengthy aria explaining why she was willing to kill not only herself but her unborn child.

"That none of my blood shed sentient blood, so precious is to me . . ."

Lunzie found herself more moved by this than she had expected. Whether it was true or not, whether it had happened at all, or for these reasons, the story itself commanded respect and pity. And it explained a *lot* about the heavyworlders. If you believed this, if you had grown up seeing this, hearing this gorgeous music put to the purpose of explaining that the lightweights would let forty thousand people die of cold and starvation because it was inconvenient to rescue them, because it would lower the profit margin, then you would naturally distrust the lightweights, and despise their dietary whims.

Would I have eaten meat even after it had been through the synthesizer? she asked herself. She let herself remember being pregnant, and the years when Fiona had been a round-faced toddler. She would not have let Fiona starve.

In a grand crashing conclusion, the lightweights returned in a warm season to remonstrate with the colonists about their birthrate and their eating habits. The lead soprano, now white-haired and many times a grandmother, the children clustered around her as she sang, told them off in ringing phrases, dizzying swoops of melody that seemed impossible to bring from one throat. The colonists repudiated the lightweights' claims, refused to submit to their rules, their laws, demanded justice in the courts or they would seek it in their own way.

The lightweights flourished weapons and two heavyweights lifted them contemptuously overhead, tossing them — the smallest cast members Lunzie had yet seen — until they tumbled shaken to the ground. Then the two picked up the "spaceship," stuffed the lightweight emissaries inside, and threw the whole assemblage into space. Or so it appeared. Actually, Lunzie was sure, some stage mechanism pulled it up out of sight.

Curtain down! Lights up! Zebara turned to her.

"Well? What do you think of Zilmach?" Then his blunt finger touched her cheek. "You cried."

"Of course I did." Her voice was still rough with emotion. To her own ears she sounded peevish. "If that's true . . ." She shook her head, started again. "It's magnificent, it's terrible, and tears are the only proper response." What she wanted to say would either start a riot or make no sense. She said, "What voices! And to think I've never heard of this. Why isn't it known?"

"We don't export this. It's just our judgment that your people would have no interest in it."

"Music is music."

"And politics is politics. Come! Would you like to meet Ertrid, the one who brought those tears to your eyes?"

Clearly the only answer was yes, so she said yes. Zebara's rank got them backstage quickly, where Ertrid proved to have a speaking voice as lovely as her singing. Lunzie had had little experience with performers. She hardly knew what to expect. Ertrid smiled, if coolly, and thanked Lunzie for her compliments, with an air of needing nothing from a lightweight. But she purred for Zebara, almost sleeking herself against him. Lunzie felt a stab of wholly unreasonable jealousy. Ertrid's smile widened.

"You must not mind, Lunzie. He has so *many* friends!"

She fingered the necklace she wore, which Lunzie had admired without considering its origins. Zebara gave the singer a quick hug and guided Lunzie away. When they were out of earshot, he leaned to speak in her ear.

"I could have said, so does she, but I would not embarrass such a great artist on a night like this. She does not like to see me with another woman, and particularly not a lightweight."

"And particularly not after that role," said Lunzie, trying to stifle her jealousy and be reasonable. She didn't want Zebara now, if she ever had. The emotion was ridiculous.

"And I *didn't* buy her that necklace," Zebara went on, as if proving himself to her. "That was the former Lieutenant Governor's son, the one I spoke of."

"It's all *right.*

Lunzie wished he would quit talking about it. She did not care, she told herself firmly, what Zebara had done with the singer, or who had bought what jewelry seen and unseen, or what the Lieutenant Governor's son had done. All that mattered was her mission, and his mission, and finding some other way to accomplish it than enduring another bout of cold sleep.

✧ CHAPTER EIGHT

FedCentral, Fleet Headquarters

"And that's the last of the crew depositions?" Sassinak asked. The 'Tenant behind the desk nodded.

"Yes, ma'am. The Prosecutor's office said they didn't need anyone else. Apparently the defense lawyers aren't going to call any of the enlisted crew as witnesses either."

So we've just spent weeks of this nonsense for nothing, Sassinak thought. Dragging my people up and down in ridiculous civilian shuttles, for hours of boring questioning which only repeats what we taped on the ship before. She didn't say any of this. Both the Chief Prosecutor's office and the defense lawyers had been furious that Lunzie, Dupaynil, and Ford were not aboard. For one thing, Kai and Varian had also failed to appear for depositions. No one knew if the fast barque sent to collect them from Ireta had found them on the planet's surface for no message had been received on either count.

She herself was sure that Ford and Lunzie would be back in time. Dupaynil? Dupaynil might or might not arrive, although she considered him more resourceful than most desk-bound Security people. If he hadn't made her so furious, she'd have enjoyed more of his company.

She would certainly have preferred him to Aygar as an assistant researcher. True, Aygar could go search the various databases without arousing suspicion. Anyone would expect him to. The Prosecutor's office had arranged a University card, a Library card, all the access he could possibly want. And he was eager enough.

But he had no practice in doing research; no background of scholarship. Sassinak had to explain exactly where he should look and for what. Even then he would come back empty-handed, confused, because he didn't understand how little bits of disparate knowledge could fit together to mean anything. He would spend all day looking up the genealogy of the heavy-worlder mutineers, or haring after some interest of his own. Dupaynil, with all his smug suavity, would have been a relief.

She strolled back along the main shopping avenues of the city, in no hurry. She was to meet Aygar for the evening shuttle flight. She had time to wander around. A window display caught her eye, bright with the colors she favored. She admired the jeweled jacket over a royal-blue skirt that flashed turquoise in shifts of light. She glanced at the elegant calligraphy above the glossy black door. No wonder! "Fleur de Paris" was only the outstanding fashion designer for the upper classes. Her mouth quirked: at least she had good taste.

The door, its sensors reporting that someone stood outside it longer than the moment necessary to walk past, swung inward. A human guard, in livery, stood just inside.

"Madame wishes to enter?"

The sidewalk burned her feet even through the uniform shoes. Her head ached. She had never in her life visited a place like this. But why not? It could do no harm to look.

"Thank you," she said, and walked in.

Inside, she found a cool oasis: soft colors, soft carpets, a recording of harp music just loud enough to cover the street's murmur. A well-dressed woman who came forward, assessing her from top to toe, and, to Sassinak's surprise, approving.

"Commander . . . Sassinak, is it not?"

"I'm surprised," she said. The woman smiled.

"We do watch the news programs, you know. How serendipitous! Fleur will want to meet you."

Sassinak almost let her jaw drop. She had heard a little about such places as this. The designer herself did not come out and meet everyone who came through the door.

"Won't you have a seat?" the woman went on. "And you'll have something cool, I hope?" She led Sassinak to a padded chair next to a graceful little table on which rested a tall pitcher, its sides beaded, and a crystal glass. Sassinak eyed it doubtfully. "Fruit juice," the woman said. "Although if you'd prefer another beverage?"

"No, thank you. This is fine."

She took the glass she was offered and sipped it to cover her confusion. The woman went away, leaving her to look around. She had been in shops, in some very good shops, with elegant displays of a few pieces of jewelry or a single silk dress. But here nothing marked the room as part of a shop. It might have been the sitting room of some wealthy matron: comfortable chairs grouped around small tables, fresh flowers, soft music. She relaxed, slowly, enjoying the tart fruit juice. If they knew she was a Fleet officer, they undoubtedly knew her salary didn't stretch to original creations. But if they were willing to have her rest in their comfortable chair, she wasn't about to walk out.

"My dear!" The silver-haired woman who smiled at her might have been any elegant great-grandmother who had kept her figure. Seventies? Eighties? Sassinak wasn't sure. "What a delightful surprise. Mirelle told you we'd seen you on the news, didn't she? And of course we'd seen you walk by. I must confess." This with a throaty chuckle that Sassinak could not resist. "I've been putting one thing after another in the window to see if we could entice you." She turned to the first woman. "And you see, Mirelle, I was right: the jeweled jacket did it."

Mirelle shrugged gracefully. "And I will wager that if you asked her, she'd remember seeing that sea-green number."

"Yes, I did," said Sassinak, half-confused by their banter. "But what . . ."

"Mirelle, I think perhaps a light snack." Her voice was gentle, but still commanding. Mirelle smiled and withdrew, and the older woman smiled at Sassinak. "My dear Sassinak, I must apologize. It's . . . it's hard to think what to say. You don't realize what you mean to people like us."

Thoroughly confused now, Sassinak murmured something indistinct. Did famous designers daydream about flying spaceships? She couldn't believe that, but what else was going on?

"I am known to the world as Fleur," the woman said, sitting down across the table from Sassinak. "Fleur de Paris, which is a joke, although very few know it. I cannot tell you what my name was, even now. But I can tell you that we had a friend in common. A very dear friend."

"Yes?" Sassinak rummaged in her memory for any wealthy or socially prominent woman she might have known. An admiral, or an admiral's wife? And came up short.

"Your mentor, my dear, when you were a girl, Abe."

She could not have been more startled if Fleur had poured a bucket of ice over her. "Abe? You knew *Abe?*"

The older woman nodded. "Yes, indeed. I knew him before he was captured, and after. Although I never met you, I would have, in time. But as it was . . ."

"I know." The grief broke over her again, as startling in its intensity as the surprise that this woman — this old woman — had known Abe. But Abe, if he'd lived, would be old. That, too, shocked her. In her memory, he'd stayed the same, an age she gradually learned was not so old as the child had thought.

"I'm sorry to distress you, but I needed to speak to you. About Abe, about his past and mine. And about your future."

"My future?" What could this woman possibly have to do with her future? It must have shown on her face, because Fleur shook her head.

"A silly old woman, you think, intruding on your life. You admire the clothes I design, but you don't need a rich woman's sycophant reminding you of Abe. Yes?"

It was uncomfortably close to what she'd been thinking. "I'm sorry," she said, apologizing for being obvious, if nothing else.

"That's all right. He said you were practical, tenacious, clear-headed, and so you must be. But there are things you should know. Since we may be interrupted at any time — after all, this is a business — first let me suggest that if you find yourself in need of help, in any difficult situation in the city, mention my name. I have contacts. Perhaps Abe mentioned Samizdat?"

"Yes, he did." Sassinak came fully alert at that. She had never found any trace of the organization Abe had told her about once she was out of the Academy. Did it still exist?

"Good. Had Abe lived, he would have made sure you knew how to contact some of its members. But, as it was, no one knew you well enough to trust you, even with your background. This meeting should remedy that."

"But then you . . ."

Fleur's smile this time had an edge of bitterness. "I have my own story. We all do. If there's time, you'll hear mine. For now, know that I knew Abe, and loved him dearly, and I have watched your career, as it appears in the news, with great interest."

"But how . . ." As she spoke, the door opened again, and three women came in, chattering gaily. Fleur stood at once and greeted them, smiling. Sassinak, uncertain, sat where she was. The women, it seemed, had come in hopes of finding Fleur free. They glanced at Sassinak, than away, saying that they simply *must* have Fleur's advice on something of great importance.

"Why of course," she said. "Do come into my sitting room." One of them must have murmured something about Sassinak, for she said, "No, no. Mirelle will be right back to speak to the commander."

Mirelle reappeared, as if by magic, bearing a tray with tiny sandwiches and cookies in fanciful shapes. "Fleur says you're quite welcome to stay, but she doesn't think she'll be free for several hours. That's an old customer, with her daughters-in-law, and they come to gossip as much as for advice. She's very sorry. You will have a snack, won't you?"

For courtesy's sake, Sassinak took a sandwich. Mirelle hovered, clearly uneasy about something. When Sassinak insisted on leaving, Mirelle exhibited both disappointment and relief.

"You will come again?"

"When I can. Please tell Fleur I was honored to meet her, but I can't say when I'll be able to come onplanet again."

That should give Sassinak time to think, and if she hadn't made a decision by the next required conference, she could always go by a different street. Outside, she found herself thinking again of Dupaynil, simply because of his specialties. She wished she had some way of getting into the databases herself, without going through Aygar, and without being detected. She would like very much to know who "Fleur de Paris" was, and why her name was supposed to be a joke.

In his days on the *Zaid-Dayan*, Dupaynil would have sworn that he was capable of intercepting any data link and resetting any control panel on any ship. All he had to do was reconfigure the controls on the escort vessel's fifteen escape pods so that he could control them. It should have been simple. It was not simple. He had not slept but for the briefest naps. He dared not sleep until it was done. And yet he had to appear to sleep, as he appeared to eat, to play cards, to chat idly, to take the exercise that had become regular to him, up and down the ladders.

He had no access to the ship's computer, no time to himself in the compartments where his sabotage would have been easiest.

He had to do it all from his tiny cabin, in the few hours he could legitimately be alone, "sleeping."

And they had already found one of his taps. It frightened him in a way he had never been frightened before. He was good at the minutiae of his work, one of the neatest, his instructors had said, a natural. To have a lout like Ollery find one of his taps meant that he had been clumsy and careless. Or he had misjudged them, another way of being clumsy and careless.

He would not have lived this long had he really been clumsy or careless, but he had depended on the confusion, the complexity, of large ships. Fear only made his hands shake. Coldly, he considered himself as if he were a new trainee in Methods of Surveillance. *Think*, he told himself, the nervous trainee. You have the brains or they wouldn't have assigned you here. Use your wits. He set aside the odds against him. Beyond "high," what good were precise percentages? He considered the whole problem. He simply had to get those escape pods slaved to his control.

A crew which had spent five years together on a ship this small would know everything, would notice everything, especially as they now suspected him. But since they were already planning to space him, would they really worry about his taps? Wouldn't they, instead, snigger to each other about his apparent progress, enjoy letting him think he was spying on them, while knowing that nothing he found would ever be seen? He thought they would.

The question was, when would they spring their trap, and could he spring his before? And assuming he did gain control of the escape pods, so that they could not eject his, and he could eject theirs, he still had to get them all *into* the pods. They would know — at least the captain and mate would know — that the evacuation drill was a fake. So there was a chance, a good chance, that they would not be in pods at all. But thinking this far had quieted the tremor in his hands and cured his dry mouth.

Wiring diagrams and logic relays flicked through his mind, along with the possible modifications a renegade crew might have made. His audio tap into the captain's cabin still functioned. Listening on a still operative tap, he learned that the one that the mate had discovered had fallen victim to a rare bout of cleaning. As far as he knew, and as far as they said, they had not found any of the others. On the other hand, he had found two of theirs. He left them alone, unworried.

The personal kit he always had with him included the very best antisurveillance chip, bonded to his shaver. Through his own taps, he picked his way delicately toward control functions. Some were too well guarded for his limited set of tools. He could not lock the captain in his cabin, or shut off air circulation to any crew compartment. He could not override the captain's control of bridge access. He knew they were watching, suspecting just such a trick. He could not roam the computer's files too broadly, either. But he could get into such open files as the maintenance and repair records, and find that the galley hatch had repeatedly jammed. As an experiment, to see if he could do it without anyone noticing, Dupaynil changed the pressure of the upper hatch runner. It should jam, and be repaired, with only a few cusswords for the pesky thing.

Sure enough, one of the crew complained bitterly through breakfast that the galley hatch was catching again. It was probably that double-damned pressure sensor on the upper runner. The mate nodded and assigned someone to fix it.

On such a small vessel, the escape pods were studded along either side of the main axis: three opening directly from the bridge, and the others aft, six accessed from the main and six from the alternate passage. Escape drill required each crew member to find an assigned pod, even if working near another. Pod assignments were posted in both bridge and galley.

Dupaynil tried to remember if anyone had actually survived a hull-breach on an escort, and couldn't think of an instance. The pods were there because regulations said every ship would carry them. That didn't make them practical. Pod controls on escort ships were the old-fashioned electro-mechanical relays; proof against magnetic surges from EM weapons which could disable more sophisticated controls by scrambling the wits of their controlling chips.

This simplicity meant that the tools he had were enough. Although, if someone looked, the changes would be more obvious than a reprogrammed or replacement chip. Fiddling with the switches and relays also took longer than changing a chip, and he found it difficult to stay suave and smiling when a crew member happened by as he was finishing one of the links.

The final step, slaving all the pod controls to one, and that one to his handcomp, tested the limits of his ability. He was almost *sure* the system would work. Unhappily, he would not know until he tried it. He was ready, as ready as he could be. He would have preferred to set off the alarm himself, but he dared not risk it. He played his usual round of cards with Ollery and the mate, making sure that he played neither too well nor too badly, and declined a dice game.

"Tomorrow," he said, with the blithe assurance of one who expects the morrow to arrive on schedule. "I can't stand all this excitement in one night."

They chuckled, the easy chuckle of the predator whose prey is in the trap. He went out wondering when they'd spring it. He really wanted a full shift's sleep.

The shattering noise of the alarm and the flashing lights woke him from the uneasy doze he'd allowed himself. He pulled on his pressure suit, lurched into the bulkhead, cursing, and staggered out into the passage. There was the mate, grinning. It was not a friendly grin.

"Escape pod drill, Lieutenant Commander! Remember your assignment?"

"Fourteen, starboard, next hatch but one."

"Right, sir. Go on now!" The mate had a handcomp, and appeared to be logging the response to the drill.

It could not be that. The computer automatically logged crew into and out of the escape pods. Dupaynil moved quickly down the passage, hearing the thumps and snarled curses of others on their way to the pods. He let himself into the next hatch but one, the pod he hoped was not only safely under his control, but now gave him control of the others.

On such a small ship, the drill required everyone to stay in the pods until all had reported in. Dupaynil listened to the ship's comm as the pods filled. He hoped that the captain would preserve the fiction of a real drill. If nothing else, to cover his tracks with his Exec, and actually enter and lock off his own pod.

Things could get very sticky indeed if the captain discovered before entering his own pod, that Dupaynil had some of his crew locked away. Four were already "podded" when Dupaynil checked in. He secured their pods. It might be better to wait until everyone was in. But if some came out, then he'd be in worse trouble. If they obeyed the drill procedures, they wouldn't know they were locked in until he had full control.

One after another, so quickly he had trouble to keep up with them, the others made it into their pods and dogged the hatches. Eight, nine (the senior mate, he was glad to notice). Only the officers and one enlisted left.

"Captain! There's something . . ."

The senior mate. Naturally. Dupaynil had not been able to interfere with the ship's intercom *and* reconfigure the pod controls. The mate must have planned to duck into his pod just long enough to register his presence on the computer, then come out to help the captain space Dupaynil.

Even as the mate spoke, Dupaynil activated all his latent sensors. Detection be damned! They knew he was onto them, and he needed all the data he could get. His control locks had better work! He was out of his own escape pod, with a tiny button-phone in his ear and his hand-held control panel.

Ollery and Panis were on the bridge. Even as Dupaynil moved forward, the last crewman checked into his pod and Dupaynil locked it down. Apparently he hadn't heard the mate.

That left the captain and that very new executive officer who would probably believe whatever the captain told him. He dogged down the hatch of his escape pod manually. From the corridor, it would look as if he were in it.

Go forward and confront the captain? No. He had to ensure that the others, especially the mate, stayed locked in. His fix might hold against a manual unlocking, but might not. So his first move was to the adjoining pods where he smashed the control panels beside each hatch. Pod fourteen, his own, was aftmost on the main corridor side, which meant he could ensure that no enemy appeared *behind* him. He would have to work his way back and forth between corridors though. Luckily the fifteenth pod was empty, and so was the thirteenth. Although the pods were numbered without using traditionally unlucky thirteen, most crews avoided the one that would have been thirteen. Stupid superstition, Dupaynil thought, but it helped him now.

Although he was sure he remembered which crew members were where, he checked on his handcomp and disabled the mate's pod controls next. Pod nine was off the alternate passage. He'd had to squeeze through a connecting passage and go forward past "14A" (the unlucky one) and pod eleven. From there he went back to disable pod eleven and checked to be sure the other two on that side were actually empty. It was not unknown for a lazy crewmember to check into the nearest unassigned pod.

He wondered all the while just what the captain was doing. Not to mention the Exec. If only he'd been able to get a full-channel tap on the bridge! He had just edged into the narrow cross passage between the main and alternate passages when he heard a faint noise and saw an emergency hatch slide across in front of him. Ollery had put the ship on alert, with full partitioning.

I should have foreseen that, Dupaynil thought. With a frantic lurch, he got his hands on its edge. The safety valve hissed at him but held the door still while he wriggled through the narrow gap. Now he was in the main corridor. Across from him he could see the recesses for pods ten and eight. He disabled their manual controls, one after another, working as quickly as he could but not worrying about noise. Just aft, another partition had come down, gray steel barrier between him and the pods further aft. But, when he first got out, he had disabled pod twelve. Just forward, another.

A thin hiss, almost at the edge of his hearing, stopped him just as he reached it. None of the possibilities looked good. He knew that Ollery could evacuate the air from each compartment and his pressure suit had only a two-hour supply. Less, if he was active. Explosive decompression wasn't likely, though he had no idea just how fast emergency decomp was. He had not sealed his bubble-helmet. He'd wanted to hear whatever was there to be heard. That hiss could be Ollery or Panis cutting through the partition with a weapon, something like a needler.

In the short stretch of corridor between the partitions, he had no place to hide. All compartment hatches sealed when the ship was on alert. Even if he had been able to get into the galley, it offered no concealment. Two steps forward, one back. What would Sassinak have done in his place? Found an access hatch, no doubt, or known something about the ship's controls that would have let her get out of this trap and ensnare Ollery at the same time. She would certainly have known where every pipe went and what was in it, what each wire and switch was for. Dupaynil could think of nothing.

It was interesting, if you looked at it that way, that Ollery hadn't tried to contact him on the ship's intercom. Did he even know Dupaynil was out of the pod? He must. He had normal ship's scans available in every compartment. Dupaynil's own sensors showed that the pods he had sealed were still sealed, their occupants safely out of the fight. Two blobs of light on a tiny screen were the captain and Panis on the bridge, right where they should be. Then one of them started down the alternate passage, slowly. He could not tell which it was, but logic said the captain had told Panis to investigate. Logic smirked when Ollery's voice came over the intercom only moments later.

"Check every compartment. I want voice report on anything out of the ordinary."

He could not hear the Jig's reply. He must be wearing a pressure suit and using its comm unit to report. Didn't the captain realize that Dupaynil could hear the intercom? Or didn't he care? Meanwhile there was his own problem: that emergency partition. Dupaynil decided that the hissing was merely an air leak between compartments, an ill-fitting partition, and set to work to override its controls.

Several hot, sweaty minutes later, he had the thing shoved back in its recess, and edged past. The main passage forward looked deceptively ordinary, all visible hatches closed, nothing moving on the scarred tiles of the deck, no movement shimmering on the gleaming green bulkheads. Ahead, he could see another partition. Beyond it, he knew, the passage curved inboard and went up a half-flight of steps to reach Main Deck and access to the bridge and three escape pods there.

Dupaynil stopped to disable the manual controls on pods six and four. Now only three pods might still be a problem: five and seven, the two most forward on the alternate passage, and pod three, accessible from the bridge and assigned to the weapons tech. That one he could disable on his way to the bridge, assuming he could get through the next partition. Five and seven? Panis might be able to open them from outside, although the controls would not work normally.

How long would it take him? Would he even think of it? Would the captain try to free the man in pod three? At least the odds against him had dropped. Even if they got all three out, it would still be only five to one, rather than twelve to one. With this much success came returning confidence, almost ebullience. He reminded himself that he had not won the war yet. Not even the first battle. Just a preliminary skirmish, which could all come undone if he lost the next bit.

"I don't care if it looks normal," he heard on the intercom. "Try to undog those hatches and let Siris out."

Blast. Ollery was not entirely stupid. Panis must be looking at pod five. Siris: data tech, the specialist in computers, sensors, all that. Dupaynil worked at the forward partition, hoping Ollery would be more interested in following his Exec's progress, would trust to the partition to hold him back. A long pause, in which his own breathing sounded ragged and loud in the empty, silent passage.

Then: "I don't care what it takes, *open it!*"

At least some of his reworking held against outside tampering. Dupaynil spared no time for smugness, as the forward partition was giving him more trouble than the one before. If he'd only had his complete kit . . . But there, it gave, sliding back into its slot with almost sentient reluctance to disobey the computer. Here the passage curved and he could not get all the way to the steps. Dupaynil flattened himself along the inside bulkhead, looking at the gleaming surface across from him for any moving reflections. Lucky for him that Ollery insisted on Fleet-like order and cleanliness. Dupaynil found it surprising. He'd always assumed that renegades would be dirty and disorderly. But the ship would have to pass Fleet inspections, whether its crew were loyal or not.

He waited. Nothing moved. He edged cautiously forward, with frequent glances at his handcomp. The captain's blob stayed where it had been. Panis' was still in the alternate passage near the hatch of pod five. At the foot of the steps, he paused. Above was the landing outside the bridge proper, with the hatches of three pods on his left. One and two would be open: the assigned pods for captain and Exec. Three would be closed, with the weapons tech inside. The hatch to the bridge would be closed, unless Panis had left it open when he went hunting trouble. If it was open, the captain would not fail to hear Dupaynil coming. Even if he weren't monitoring his sensors, and he would be, he'd know exactly where Dupaynil was. And once Dupaynil came to the landing, he could see him out the open hatch. If it was open.

Had Panis left the bridge hatch open? Had he left the partition into the alternate corridor open? It would make sense to do so.

Even though the captain could control the partitions individually from the bridge, overriding the computer's programming, that would take a few seconds. If the captain suspected he might need help, he would want those partitions back so that Panis and any freed crewman had easy access.

He started up the steps, reminding himself to breathe deeply. One. Two. No sound from above, and he could not see the bridge hatch without being visible from it. If he had had time, if he had had his entire toolkit, he would have had taps in place and would know if that hatch . . .

A clamor broke out on the other side of the ship, crashing metal, cries. And, above him and around the curve, the captain's voice both live and over the intercom.

"Go *on*, Siris!"

Then the clatter of feet, as the captain left the bridge (no sound of the hatch opening: it had been open) and headed down the alternate passage. Dupaynil had no idea what was going on, but he shot up the last few steps, and poked his head into the upper end of the alternate corridor. And saw the captain's back, headed aft, with some weapon, probably a needler, in his clenched fist. There were yells from both Panis and the man he had freed.

It burst on Dupaynil suddenly that Ollery intended to kill his Exec. Either because he thought he was in league with Dupaynil or was using this excuse to claim he'd mutinied. Dupaynil launched himself after the captain, hoping that the crewman wasn't armed. Panis and Siris were still thrashing on the floor. Dupaynil could see only a whirling confusion of suit-clad bodies. Their cries and the sound of the blows covered his own approach. Ollery stood above them, clearly waiting his chance to shoot. Dupaynil saw the young officer's face recognize his captain, and his captain's intent. His expression changed from astonishment to horror.

Then Dupaynil flipped his slim black wire around the captain's neck and *pulled*. The captain bucked, sagged, and dropped, still twitching but harmless. Dupaynil caught up the needler that the crewman reached for, stepping on the man's wrist with deceptive grace. He could feel the bones grate beneath his heel.

"But what? But who?" Panis, disheveled, one eye already blackening, had the presence of mind to keep a firm controlling grip on the crewman's other arm.

Dupaynil smiled. "Let's get this one under control first," he said.

"I don't know what happened," Panis went on. "Something's wrong with the escape pod hatches. It took forever to get this one open, and then Siris jumped me, and the captain —" His voice trailed away as he glanced at the captain lying purple-faced on the deck.

Siris tried a quick heave but the Jig held on. Dupaynil let his heel settle more firmly on the wrist. The man cursed viciously.

"Don't do that," Dupaynil said to him, waving the needler in front of him. "If you should get loose from Jig Panis, I would simply kill you. Although you might prefer that to trial. Would you?"

Siris lay still, breathing heavily. Panis had planted a few good ones on him, too. His face was bruised and he had a split lip which he licked nervously. Dupaynil felt no sympathy. Still watching Siris for trouble, he spoke to Panis.

"Your captain was engaged in illegal activities. He planned to kill both of us." Even as he spoke, he wondered if he could possibly convince a Board of Inquiry that the entire scheme, including the rewired escape pod controls, had been the captain's. Probably not, but it was worth considering in the days ahead.

"I can't believe . . ." Again Panis' voice trailed away. He *could* believe; he had seen that needler in his captain's hand, heard what the captain said. "And you're —?"

"Fleet Security, as you know. Apparently that spooked Major Ollery, convinced him that I was on his trail. I wasn't as a matter of fact."

"Liar!" said Siris.

Dupaynil favored him with a smile that he hoped combined injured innocence with predatory glee. It must have succeeded for the man paled and gulped.

"I don't bother to lie," he said quietly, "when the truth is so useful." He went on with his explanation. "When I found that the captain planned to kill me and that you were not a part of the conspiracy, I assumed he'd kill you, too, so he wouldn't have to worry about any unfriendly witness. Now. As the officer next in command, you are now technically captain of this ship, which means that *you* decide what we do with Siris here. I would not recommend just letting him go!"

"No." The Jig's face had a curious inward expression that

Dupaynil took to mean he was trying to catch up to events. "No, I can see that. But," and he looked at Dupaynil, taking in his rank insignia. "But, sir, you're senior."

"Not on this vessel." Curse the boy! Couldn't he see that he had to take command? Sassinak would have in a flash.

"Right." It had taken him longer, but he came to the same decision; Dupaynil had to applaud that. "Then we need to get his fellow — Siris — into confinement."

"May I suggest the escape pod he just came out of? As you know, the controls no longer respond normally. He won't be able to get out, and he won't be able to eject from the ship."

"NO!" Dupaynil could not tell if it was fury or fright. "I'm not going back in there. I'd die before you get anywhere!"

"Frankly, I don't much care," Dupaynil said. "But you will have access to cold sleep. You know there's a cabinet built in."

Siris let fly the usual stream of curses, vicious and unimaginative. Dupaynil thought the senior mate would have done better, although he had no intention of letting him loose to try. Panis squirmed out of his awkward position, half-under the crewman, without losing his grip on the man's shoulder and arm or getting between Dupaynil's needler and Siris. Then he rolled clear, evading a last frantic snatch at his ankles. Dupaynil put all his weight on the trapped wrist for an instant, bringing a gasp of pain from Siris, then stepped back, covering him with the weapon. In any event, Siris went into the escape pod without more struggle, though threatening them both with the worst that his illicit colleagues could do.

"They'll get you!" he said, as Panis closed the hatch. Dupaynil aiming through the narrowing crack just in case. "You don't even know who it'll be. They're in the Fleet, all through it, all the way up, and you'll wish you'd never . . ."

With a solid chunk, the hatch closed and Panis followed Dupaynil's instructions in securing it. Then he met Dupaynil's eyes, with only the barest glance at the needler still in Dupaynil's hand.

"Well, Commander, either you're honest and I'm safe, or you're about to plug me and make up your own story about what happened. Or you still have doubts about *me*."

Dupaynil laughed. "Not after seeing the captain ready to kill you, I don't. But I'm sure you have questions of your own and will be a lot more comfortable when I'm not holding a weapon on you. Here." He handed over the needler, butt first.

Panis took it, thumbed off the power, and stuck it through one of the loops of his pressure suit.

"Thanks." Panis ran one bruised hand over his battered face. "This is not . . . quite . . . like anything they taught us." He took another long breath, with a pause in the middle as if his ribs hurt. "I suppose I'd better get to the bridge and log all this." His gaze dropped to the motionless crumpled shape of Ollery on the deck. "Is he?"

"He'd better be," said Dupaynil, kneeling to feel Ollery's neck for a pulse. Nothing, now. That solved the problem of what to do if he'd been alive but critically injured. "Dead," he went on.

"You . . . uh . . ."

"Strangled him, yes. Not a gentlemanly thing to do, but I had no other weapon and he was about to kill you."

"I'm not complaining." Panis looked steadier now and met Dupaynil's eyes. "Well. If I'm in command — and you're right, I'm supposed to be — I'd best log this. Then we'll come back and put his body . . ." he finished lamely, "somewhere."

✧ CHAPTER NINE

Diplo

Although Zebara had said that few offworlders knew about, had ever seen or heard, Zilmach's opera, Lunzie found the next morning that some of the medical team had heard more than enough. Bias waylaid her in the entrance of the medical building where they worked. Before Lunzie could even say "Good morning," he was off.

"I don't know what you think you're doing," he said in a savage tone that brought heads around, though his voice was low. "I don't know if it's an aberration induced by your protracted cold sleep or a perverse desire to appease those who hurt you on Ireta . . ."

"Bias!" Lunzie tried to shake his hand away from her arm but he would not let go.

"I don't care *what* it is," he said, more loudly. Lunzie felt herself going red. Around them people tried to pretend that nothing was going on, although ears flapped almost visibly. Bias pushed her along, as if she weren't willing, and stabbed the lift button with the elbow of his free arm. "But I'll tell you, it's disgraceful. Disgraceful! A medical professional, a researcher, someone who ought to have a minimal knowledge of professional ethics and proper behavior . . ."

Lunzie's anger finally caught up with her surprise. She yanked her arm free.

"Which does *not* include grabbing my arm and scolding me in public as if you were my father. Which you're not. May I remind you that I am considerably older than you, and if I choose to . . ."

To what? She hadn't done what Bias thought she had done. In some respect, she agreed with him. If she *had* been having a torrid affair with the head of External Security, it would have been unprofessional and stupid. In Bias' place, in charge of a younger (older?) woman doing something like that, she'd have been irritated, too. She'd been irritated enough when she thought Varian was attracted to the young Iretan, Aygar. Her anger left as quickly as it had come, replaced by her sense of humor. She struggled for a moment with these contradictory feelings, and then laughed. Bias was white-faced, his mouth pinched tight.

"Bias, I am not sleeping with Zebara. He's an old friend."

"Everyone *knows* what happens at that opera!"

"I didn't." That much was true. "And how did you know?"

This time it was Bias who reddened, in unattractive blotches. "The last time I came I . . . ah. Um. I've always liked music. I try to learn about the native music anywhere I go. A performance was advertised. I bought a ticket, I went. And they wouldn't let me in. No one admitted without a partner, they said."

Lunzie hadn't known that. After a moment's shock, she realized that it made sense. Bias, it seemed, had argued that he had already paid for the ticket. He had been given his money back, with the contemptuous suggestion that he put his ticket where it would do him more good than the performance would. He finally found a heavyworlder doctor, at the medical center, willing to explain what the opera was about, and why no one wanted him there.

"So you see I know that no matter what you say . . ."

Lunzie stopped that with a laugh. They entered the lift with a crowd of first-shift medical personnel and Bias kept silence until they reached their floor. He opened his mouth but she waved him to silence.

"Bias, it came as a surprise to me, too. But they don't . . . mmm . . . check on it. Besides which," and she cocked her head at him, "there's the problem of a pressure suit."

Bias turned beet-red from scalp to neck. His mouth opened and closed as if he were gasping for air, but formed no words.

"It's all right, Bias," she said, patting his head as if he were a nervous boy about to go onstage. "I'm over a hundred years old and I didn't live this long by risking an unexpected pregnancy."

Then, before she lost control of her wayward humor, she strode quickly down the corridor to her own first chore.

But Bias was not the only to broach the subject.

"I've heard that heavyworlder opera is really something, hmmm? *Different* . . ." said Conigan. She did not quite smirk.

Lunzie managed placidity. "Different is hardly the word, but you may have heard more than I saw."

"Or felt?"

"Please. I may be ancient and shriveled by cold sleep but I know I don't want to have a half-heavyworlder child. The opera reenacts a time of great tragedy. I'm an outsider, an observer, and I have the sense to know it."

"That's something, at least. But is it really that good?"

"The music is. Unbelievable; I'm ashamed to admit I was surprised by the quality."

Conigan appeared satisfied. If not, she had the sense to let Lunzie alone. More troubling were the odd looks she now got from the other team members, and from one of the heavyworlder doctors they'd been working with. She could not say she had no feeling for Zebara. Even had it been true, their tentative cooperation required that she appear friendly. She wondered if she should have feigned a more emotional response to the opera.

And on the edge of her mind, kept firmly away from its center during the working day, was the question of cold sleep. Not again! She wanted to scream at Zebara and anyone else who thought she should use it. I'd rather die. But that was not true. More particularly, she did not want to die on Diplo, in the hands of their Security or in their prisons. In fact, with the renewed strength and health of her refresher course in Discipline, she did not want to die anywhere, any time soon. She had a century of healthy life ahead of her, if she stayed off high-G worlds. She wanted to enjoy it.

The Venerable Master Adept had said she might need to use cold sleep again. She had trained for that possibility. She knew she *could* do it. But I don't want to, wailed one part of her mind to another. She squashed that thought down and hoped it would not be necessary. Surely she and Zebara could find some other way. That night she had no message, and slept gratefully, catching up on much-needed rest.

The next step in Zebara's campaign came two days later, when he invited her to spend her next rest day with him.

"The team's supposed to get together for a progress evaluation." Lunzie wrinkled her nose; she expected it to be a waste of time. "If I go off with you, I'll get in trouble with them."

She was already in trouble with them, but saw no reason to tell Zebara. And that kind of trouble would make it seem his employers' plot was working well. Surely a lightweight alienated from her own kind would be easier to manipulate. She shivered, wondering who was manipulating whom.

Zebara's image grimaced. "We have so little time, Lunzie. Your research tour is almost half over. We both know it's unlikely you'll come back and even if you did, I would not be here."

"Bias has told me, very firmly, that the purpose of this medical mission was *not* to reunite old lovers."

"*His* purpose, no. And I respect your professional work, Lunzie. I always did. We know it could not be a real relationship. You must go and I will not live long. But I want to see you again, for more than a few minutes in public."

Lunzie flinched, thinking of the agents who would, no doubt, snicker when they got to that point in the tapes being made of this conversation. If they weren't listening now, in real-time surveillance. She glanced at the schedule on her wall. Only one rest day after this one. Time had fled away from them, and even if she had not had the additional problem of Zebara and her undercover assignment, she would have been surprised at how short a 30-day assignment could be.

"Please," Zebara said, interrupting her thoughts. Was he really that eager? Did he know of some additional reason she must meet him now, and not later. "I can't wait."

"Bias will have a flaming fit," Lunzie said. His face relaxed, as if he'd heard more in her voice than she intended. "I'll have to talk to Tailler. I don't see why you couldn't wait until the next rest day. Only eight days."

"Thank you, Lunzie. I'll send someone for you right after breakfast."

"But what about?" That was to an empty screen. He had cut the connection. Damn the man. Lunzie glowered at the screen and let herself consider ignoring his messenger in the morning. But that would be too dangerous. Whatever was going on, in his mind, or that of his employers, she had to play along.

❖   ❖   ❖

When she told him, Tailler heaved a great sigh and braced his arms against his workbench.

"Are you trying to give Bias a stroke, or what? I thought you understood. Granted he's not entirely rational, but that makes it our responsibility to keep from knocking him lopsided."

Lunzie spread her hands. If the whole team turned against her, she could lose any chance of a good position after the mission. And after the mission you could be one frozen lump of dead meat, she reminded herself.

"I'm sorry," she said and meant it. That genuine distaste for hurting others got through to Tailler. "I think they should have studied *me* for the effects of prolonged cold sleep, instead of stuffing me full of current trends in medicine and shipping me out here. But they said they were desperate, that no one else had my background. Perhaps my reaction to Zebara is partly that, although I think no one who hasn't been through it *can* understand what it's like to wake up and find that thirty or forty years have gone by. Did you know I have a great-great-great-granddaughter who's older than I am in elapsed time? That makes us both feel strange. Zebara knew me *then*. Though to me that's the self I am *now*. Yet he's dying of old age. I know that personal feelings aren't supposed to intrude on the mission, but these are, in a sense, relevant to the work I'm doing. My normal lifespan, without cold sleep, would be twelve to fourteen decades, right?"

"Yes. Perhaps even longer, these days. I think the rates for women with your genetic background are up around fifteen or sixteen decades."

Lunzie shrugged. "See? Even the lifespans have changed since I was last awake. But my point is that each time I've come out of a prolonged cold sleep, I've battled severe depression over the relationships I've lost. The kind of depression which we know impairs the immune system, makes people more susceptible to premature aging and disease. This depression, this despair and chaos, will affect the heavyworlders even more, because their lifespan is naturally shorter, especially on high-G worlds. My feelings — my personal experiences — are what got me scheduled for this mission. While I can't claim that I consciously chose to consider Zebara as part of a research topic, his reaction to my lack of aging and my reaction to his physical decay, are not matters I can ignore."

Tailler stood, stretched, and leaned against the bench behind him. "I see your point. Emotions and intellect are both engaged and so tangled that you can't decide which part of this is most important. Would you say, on the whole, that you are an intuitive or patterned thinker?"

"Intuitive, according to my early psych profiles, but with strong logical skills as well."

"You must have or I'd have said intuitive without asking. It sounds as if your mind is trying to put something together which you can't yet articulate. On that basis, meeting Zebara, spending a day with him, might give you enough data to come to some conclusions. But the rest of us are going to have a terrible time with Bias."

"I know. I'm sorry, truly I am."

"If I didn't believe you were, I'd be strongly tempted to play heavyhanded leader and forbid your going. I presume that if your mind finds its gestalt solution in the middle of the night, you will stay with us instead?"

"Yes — but I don't think it will."

Tailler sighed. "Probably not. Some rest day this is going to be. At least stay out of Bias' way today and let me tell him tomorrow. Otherwise, we'll get nothing done."

When she answered the summons early the next morning, Zebara's escort hardly reassured her. Uniformed, armed — at least she assumed the bulging black leather at his hip meant a weapon — stern-faced, he checked her identity cards before leading her to a chunky conveyance almost as large as the medical center's utility van. Inside, it was upholstered in a fabric Lunzie had never seen, something smooth and tan. She ran her fingers over it, unable to decide what it was, and wishing the broad seat were not quite so large. Across from her, the escort managed to suggest decadent lounging while sitting upright. The driver in the front compartment was only a dark blur through tinted plex.

"It's leather," he said, when she continued to stroke the seat.

"Leather?" She should know the word, but it escaped her. She saw by the smirk on the man's face that he expected to shock her.

"Muskie hide," he said. "Tans well. Strong and smooth. We use a lot of it."

Lunzie had her face well under control. She was not about to give him the satisfaction of knowing that she was disgusted.

"I thought they were hairy," she said. "More like fur."

His face changed slightly; a glimmer of respect came into the cold blue eyes.

"The underfur's sometimes used, but it's not considered high quality. The tanning process removes the hair."

"Mmm." Lunzie made herself touch the seat again, though she wished she didn't have to sit on it. "Is it all this color? Can it be dyed?"

Contempt had given way now to real respect. His voice relaxed as he became informative.

"Most of it's easily tanned this color; some is naturally black. It's commonly dyed for clothing. But if you dye upholstery, it's likely to come off on the person sitting on it."

"Clothing? I'd think it would be uncomfortable, compared to cloth." Lunzie gave herself points for the unconcerned tone of voice, the casual glance out the tinted window.

"No, ma'am. As boots, now," and he indicated his own shining boots. "They're hard to keep polished, but they don't make your feet sweat as bad."

Lunzie thought of the way her feet felt in the special padded boots she wore most of the day. By evening, it was as if she stood in a puddle. Of course it was barbaric, wearing the skins of dead sentient creatures. But if you were going to eat them, you might as well use the rest of them, she supposed.

"Less frostbite," the man was saying now, still extolling the virtues of "leather" over the usual synthetic materials.

Outside the vehicle, an icy wind buffeted them with chunks of ice. Lunzie could see little through the windows; the dim shapes of unfamiliar buildings, none very tall. Little vehicular traffic: in fact, little sign of anyone else on the streets. Lunzie presumed that most people used the underground walkways and slideways she and Zebara had used their two previous meetings.

"The ride takes more than an hour," the escort said. "You might as well relax." He was smirking again, though not quite so offensively as before.

Lunzie wracked her brain to think of some harmless topic of conversation. Nothing was harmless with a heavyworlder. But surely it couldn't hurt to ask his name.

"I'm sorry," she began politely, "but I don't know what your insignia means, nor what your name is."

The smirk turned wolfish. "I doubt you'd really want to know. But my rank would translate in your Fleet to major. I'm not at liberty to disclose my name."

So much for that. Lunzie did not miss the significance of *"your Fleet."* She did not want to think what "not at liberty to disclose my name" might mean.

Did Zebara not trust her, after all? Or was he planning to turn her over to another branch of his organization and wanted to keep himself in the clear?

Time passed, marked off only by the slithering and crunching of the vehicle's wheels on icy roadway.

"The Director said he knew you many years ago. Is that true?" There could be no harm in answering a question to which so many knew the answer.

"Yes, over forty years ago."

"A long time. Many things have changed here in forty years."

"I'm sure of it," Lunzie said.

"I was not yet born when the Director knew you." The escort said that as if his own birth had been the most significant change in those decades. Lunzie stifled a snort of amusement. If he still thought he was that important, he wouldn't have much humor. "I have been in his department for only eight years." Pride showed there, too, and a touch of something that might have been affection. "He is a remarkable man, the Director. Worthy of great loyalty."

Lunzie said nothing; it didn't seem needed.

"We need men like him at the top. It saddens me that he has lost strength this past year. He will not say, but I have heard that the doctors are telling him the snow is falling." The man stared at her, obviously hoping she knew more, and would tell it. She fixed on the figure of speech.

"Snow is falling? Is that how you say sickness?"

"It is how we say death is coming. You should know that. You saw *Bitter Destiny.*"

Now she remembered. The phrase had been repeated in more than one aria, but with the same melodic line. So it had come to be a cultural standard, had it?

"You are doing medical research on the physiological response of our people to long-term cold sleep, I understand. Hasn't somebody told you what our people call cold sleep, how they think of it?"

This was professional ground, on which she could stand firmly and calmly.

"No, and I've asked. They avoid it. After the opera, I wondered if they associated cold sleep with that tragedy. It's one of the things I wanted to ask Zebara. He said we would talk about it today."

"Ah. Well, perhaps I should let him tell you. But as you might expect, death by cold is both the most degrading and the most honorable of deaths we know: degrading because our people were forced into it. It is the symbol of our political weakness. And honorable because so many chose it to save others. To compel another to die of cold or starvation is the worst of crimes, worse than any torture. But to voluntarily take the White Way, the walk into snow, is the best of deaths, an affirmation of the values that enabled us to survive." The man paused, ran a finger around his collar as if to loosen it, and went on. "Thus cold sleep is for us a peculiar parody of our fears and hopes. It is the little cold death. If prolonged, as I understand you have endured, it is the death of the past, the loss of friends and family as in actual death — except that you are alive to know it. But it also cheats the long death of winter. It is like being the seed of a chranghal — one of our plants that springs first from the ground after a Long Winter. Asleep, not dreaming, almost dead! And then awake again, fresh and green.

"When our people travel, and know they will be placed in cold sleep, they undergo the rituals for the dying and carry with them the three fruits we all eat to celebrate spring and rebirth."

"But your death rate in cold sleep, for anything beyond a couple of months, is much higher than normal," said Lunzie. "And the lifespan after tends to be shorter."

"True. Perhaps you are finding out why, in physical terms. I think myself that those who consent to prolonged cold sleep have consented to death itself. They are reliving that first sacrifice and, even if they live, are less committed to life. After all, with our generally shorter lifespans, we would outlive our friends sooner than you. And you, the Director has told me, did not find it easy to pick up your life decades later."

"No."

Lunzie looked down, then out the blurred windows, thinking

of that first black despair when she realized that Fiona was grown and gone, that she would never see her child as a child again. And each time it had been a shock, to find people aged whom she'd known in their youth, to find a great-great-great-granddaughter older than she herself.

He was silent after that. They rode the rest of the way without speaking, but without hostility. Zebara's place, when they finally arrived and drove into the sheltered entrance, was a low mound of heavy dark granite, like a cross between a fortress and a lair.

Zebara met her as she stepped out, said a cool "Thank you, Major," to the escort, and led her through a double-glass door into a circular hall beneath a low dome. Its floor was of some amber-colored stone, veined with browns and reds; the dome gleamed, dull bronze, from lights recessed around the rim. All around, between the four arching doorways, were stone benches against the curving walls. In the center two steps led down to a firepit in which flames flickered, burning cleanly with little smoke.

She followed Zebara down the steps, and at his gesture sat on the lowest padded seat; she could feel the heat of that small fire. He reached under the seat on his side, and brought out a translucent bead.

"Incense," he said, before he put it on the fire. "Be welcome to our hall, Lunzie. Peace, health, prosperity to you, and to the children of your children."

It was so formal, so strange, that she had no idea what to say, and instead bowed her head a moment. When she looked up, a circle of heavyworlders enclosed her, on the floor of the hall above. Zebara raised his voice.

"My children and their children. You are known to them, Lunzie, and they are known to you."

They were a stolid, lumpish group to look at, Zebara's sons and their wives, the grandchildren, even the youngest, broad as wrestlers. She wondered which was the little boy who had interrupted his meeting. How long ago had that been? But she could not guess.

He was introducing them now. Each bowed from the waist, without speaking, and Lunzie nodded, murmuring a greeting. Then Zebara waved them away and they trooped off through one of the arched doorways.

"Family quarters that way," he said. "Sleeping rooms, nurseries, schoolrooms for the children."

"Schoolrooms? You don't have public schooling?"

"We do, but not for those this far out. And anyone with enough children in the household can hire a tutor and have them schooled. It saves tax money for those who can't afford private tutors. You met only the older children. There are fifty here altogether."

Lunzie found the thought disturbing, another proof that the heavyworlder culture diverged from FSP policy. She had known there was overcrowding and uncontrolled breeding. But Zebara had always seemed so *civilized*.

Now, as he took her arm to guide her up the steps from the firepit and across the echoing hall to a door, she felt she did not know him at all. He was wearing neither the ominous black uniform nor the workaday coverall she had seen on most of the citizens. A long loose robe, so dark she could not tell its color in the dimly lit passage, low boots embroidered with bright patterns along the sides. He looked as massive as ever, but also comfortable, completely at ease.

"In here," he said at last, and ushered her into another, smaller, circular room. "This is my private study."

Lunzie took the low, thickly cushioned seat he offered, and looked around. Curved shelving lined the walls: cube files, film files, old-fashioned books, stacks of paper. There were a few ornaments: a graceful swirl of what looked like blue-green glass, stiff human figures in brown pottery, an amateurish but very bright painting, a lopsided lump that could only be a favorite child's or grandchild's first effort at a craft. A large flatscreen monitor, control panels. Above was another of the shallow domes, this one lined with what looked like one sheet of white ceramic. The low couch she sat on was upholstered with a nubbly cloth. She was absurdly glad to be sure it was not leather. Fluffy pillows had been piled, making it comfortable for her shorter legs.

Zebara had seated himself across from her, behind a broad curving desk. He touched some control on it and the desk sank down to knee height, becoming less a barrier and more a convenience. Another touch, and the room lights brightened, their reflection from the dome a clear unshadowed radiance like daylight.

"It's . . . lovely," said Lunzie.

She could not think of anything else. Zebara gave her a surprisingly sweet smile, touched with sadness.

"Did your team give you trouble about visiting me?"

"Yes." She told him about Bias and found herself almost resenting Zebara's obvious amusement. "He's just trying to be conscientious," she finished up. She felt she had to make Bias sound reasonable, although she didn't think he was.

"He's being an idiot," Zebara said. "You are not a silly adolescent with a crush on some muscular stud. You're a grown woman."

"Yes, but, in a way, he's right, you know. I'm not sure myself that my encounters with cold sleep have left me completely . . . rational." She wondered whether to use any of what the young officer had told her, and decided to venture it. "It's like dying, and being born, only not a real start — everything over birth. Leftovers from the past life keep showing up. Like missing my daughter . . . I told you about that, before. Like discovering Sassinak. People say, 'Get on with your life, just put it behind you.' And it *is* behind me, impossibly past. But it's also right there with me. Consequences that most people don't live to see, don't have to worry about."

"Ah. Just what I wanted to talk to you about. For I will take the long walk soon, die the death that has no waking, and it occurs to me that for you my younger self — the self you knew — is still alive. Still young. That self no one here remembers as clearly as you do. Tell me, Lunzie, will *this* self," and he thumped himself on the chest, "destroy in your memory the self I was? The self you knew?"

She shook her head. "If I only squint a little, I can see you as you were. It's hard to believe, even now, that you . . . I'm sorry . . ."

"No. That's all right. I understand, and this is what I wanted." He was breathing a little faster, as if he'd been working hard, but he didn't look distressed, only excited. "Lunzie, it is a sentimental thing, a foolish wish, and I do not like myself for revealing it. For having it. But I know how fast memories fade. I had thought, all these years, that I remembered you perfectly. The reality of you showed me I had not. I had forgotten that fleck of gold in your right eye, and the way you crook that finger." He pointed, and Lunzie looked down, surprised to see a gesture she had never noticed. "So I know I will be forgotten — myself, my present self — as my younger self has already been forgotten. This happens to all, I know. But . . . but you, you hold my younger self in your mind, and you will live . . . what? Another century, perhaps? Then I will be only a name to my great-grandchildren, and all the stories will be gone. Except with you."

"Are you . . . are you asking me to remember you? Because you must know I will."

"Yes . . . but more, too. I'm asking you to remember me as I was, the young heavyworlder you trusted, the younger man you loved, however briefly and lightly. I'm asking you to hold that memory brightly in mind whenever you consider my people. Cold sleep has a special meaning for our people."

"I know. The escort you sent was telling me."

Zebara's eyebrows rose, then he shook his head. "I shouldn't be surprised. You're a very easy person to talk to. But if anyone had asked me whether Major Hessik would discuss such things with a lightweight, I'd have said never."

"I had to do something to get away from the subject of leather," said Lunzie, wrinkling her nose. "And from there, somehow . . ."

She went on to tell him what Hessik had explained. Zebara listened without interrupting.

"That's right," he said, when she finished. "A symbolic death and rebirth, which you have endured several times now. And which I ask you to endure once more, for me and my people."

The absolute *no* she had meant to utter stuck in her throat.

"I . . . never liked it," she said, wondering if it sounded as ridiculous to him as it did to her.

"Of course not. Lunzie, I brought you here today for several reasons. First, I want to remember you . . . and have you remember me . . . as I near my own death. I want to relive that short happy time we shared, through your memories. That's indulgence, an old man's indulgence. Second, I want to talk to you about my people, their history, their customs, in the hope that you can feel some sympathy for us and our dilemma. That you will speak for us where you can do so honestly. I'm not asking you to forget or forgive criminal acts. You could not do it and I would not ask. But not all are guilty, as you know. And finally, I must give you what we talked of before, if you are willing to carry it."

He sat hunched slightly forward, the dark soft robe hiding his hands. Lunzie said nothing for a moment, trying to compare his aged face, with all the ugly marks of a hard life in high G, to the younger man's blunt but healthy features. She had done that before. She would do it, she thought, even after he died, trying to reconcile what he had lost in those forty-odd years with her own losses.

He sighed, smiled at her, and said, "May I sit with you? It is not . . . what you might think."

Even as she nodded, she felt a slight revulsion. As a doctor, she knew she should not. That age did not change feelings. But *his* age changed *her* feelings, even as a similar lapse had changed Tee's feelings for her. What she and Zebara had shared, of danger and passion, no longer existed. With that awareness, her feelings about Tee changed from resignation to real understanding. How it must have hurt him, too, to have to admit that he had changed. And now Zebara.

He sat beside her, and reached for her hands. What must it be like for him, seeing her still young, feeling her strength, to know his own was running out, water from a cracked jug?

"The evidence you would believe, about our people's history," he began, "is far too great to take in quickly. You will either trust me, or not, when I say that it is there, incontrovertible. Those who sent the first colonists knew of the Long Winters that come at intervals: knew, and did not tell the colonists. We do not know all their reasons. Perhaps they thought that two years would be enough time to establish adequate food stores to survive. Perhaps those who made the decision didn't believe how bad it would be. I like to think they intended no worse than inconvenience. But what *is* known is that when our colony called for help, no help came."

"Was the call received?"

"Yes. No FTL communications existed in those days, you may recall. So when the winter did not abate and it became obvious it would not, the colonists realized that even an answered call might come too late. They expected nothing soon. But there was supposed to be a transfer pod only two light months out, with an FTL pod pre-programmed for the nearest Fleet sector headquarters. That's how emergency calls went out: sublight to the transfer point, which launched the pod, and the pod carried only a standard message, plus its originating transfer code."

Lunzie wrinkled her nose, trying to think when they might have expected an answer. "Two months, then. How long to the Fleet headquarters?"

"Should have been perhaps four months in all. An FTL response, a rescue attempt, could have been back within another two or three. Certainly within twelve Standard months, allowing decel and maneuvering time on both ends. The colonists would have had a hard time lasting that long. They'd have to eat all their seed grain and supplies. But most of them would have made it. Instead —" and he sighed again, spreading his big gnarled hands.

"I can't believe Fleet ignored a signal like that." Unless someone intercepted it, Lunzie thought suddenly. Someone within Fleet who for some reason wanted the colony to fail.

"It didn't!" Zebara gave her hands a squeeze, then stood, the robe swirling around him. "Let me fix you something. I'm thirsty a lot these days." He waved at the selection revealed behind one panel of his desk. "Fruit juices? Peppers?"

"Juice, please." Lunzie watched as he poured two glasses, and gave her the choice of them. Did he really think she worried about him drugging her? And if he did, should she be worried? But she sipped, finding nothing but the pleasant tang of juice as he settled beside her once more.

He took a long swallow, then went on. "It was not Fleet, as near as we can tell. At least, not they that ignored an emergency pod. There was no emergency pod."

"What!"

"We did find, buried in the file,the notation that the expense of an FTL emergency pod was not justified since Diplo was no more than twelve Standard light months from a major communications nexus which could pass on any necessary material. Colonists had wasted, the report said, such expensive resources before on minor matters that required no response. If colonists could not take care of themselves for twelve months, and I can just hear some desk-bound bureaucrat sniff at this point, they hardly qualified as colonists." He took another swallow. "You see what this means."

"Of course. The message didn't arrive somewhere useful in four months. It arrived at a commercial telecom station in twelve months by which time the colonists were expecting a rescue mission."

"And from there," Zebara said, "it was . . . re-routed. It never reached Fleet."

"But that's . . ."

"It was already embarrassing. The contract under which the colonists signed on specified the placement of the emergency pod. When that message arrived at the station, it was proof that no pod had been provided. And twelve months already? Suppose they had sent a mission then. What would they have found? From this point we have no direct proof, but we expect that someone made the decision to deepsix the whole file. To wait until the next scheduled delivery of factory parts, which was another two Standard years, by which time they expected to find everyone dead. So sad, but this happens to colonies. It's a dangerous business!"

Lunzie felt cold all over, than a white-hot rage. "It's . . . it's *murder*. Intentional murder!"

"Not under the laws of FSP at the time. Or even now. We couldn't prove it. I say 'we,' but you know I mean those in Diplo's government at the time. Anyway, when the ships came again, they found the survivors; the women, the children, and a few young men who had been children in the Long Winter. The first ship down affected not to know that anything had happened. To be surprised! But one of the Company reps on the second ship got drunk and let some of this out."

She could think of nothing adequate to say. Luckily he didn't seem to expect anything. After a few moments, he went back to family matters, telling her of his hopes for them. Gradually her mind quieted. By the time they parted, she carried away another memory as sweet as her first. It had no longer seemed perverse to have an old man's hands touching her, an old man's love still urgent after all those years.

✧ CHAPTER TEN

FSP Escort Claw

Dupaynil led the way back toward the bridge, walking steadily and slowly. The young officer would still be wondering, might still wish he had Dupaynil under guard. Except that there was no guard. He would feel safer with Dupaynil in front of him, calm and unhurried. At the landing outside the bridge, Dupaynil said over his shoulder, "If you don't mind, I'd like to finish disabling the pod locks on pod three."

"Who's in there?"

"Your weapons tech. So far as I know, all the crew were in this with Ollery. They're all dangerous, but this one particularly so."

Panis frowned. "Suppose we run into something we need to fight?"

"We'd better not. We can't trust him. I don't think he can get out by himself. At least not without your help. But he and Siris had the best chance of figuring out what I did and undoing it, even with the minimal toolkits standard in pods."

"You may be right, but, look, I want to log at least some of this first. And I want you with me."

Dupaynil shrugged and moved onto the bridge. He thought it would be hours before the weapons tech could possibly get out. At the moment, gaining Panis' confidence took precedence. They settled in uneasy silence, Panis in the command seat and Dupaynil in the one in which he'd first seen the master mate.

He said nothing while Panis made a formal entry in the ship's computer, stating the date and time that he assumed command, and the code under which he would file a complete report. The computer's response to change of command, Dupaynil noticed, was to recheck Panis' retinal scans, palmprint, and voiceprint against its memory of him. Dupaynil would have had a hard time taking over if something had happened to Panis. He asked about that.

"Not as ship commander, no, sir. You might have convinced it that you were a disaster survivor. You were logged in as a legitimate passenger. But you wouldn't have been given access to secure files or allowed to make any course changes. It would've given you life-support access: water, food, kept the main compartments aired up. That's all. And the ship would have launched an automatic distress signal when it dropped out of FTL."

"I see. There are files in the computer, Captain, which will provide evidence needed to confirm Ollery's treachery."

Dupaynil noticed that Panis reacted to the use of his new title with minute straightening; a good sign. He did not mention that he had penetrated some of the computer's secure files already. Maintenance wasn't what he would call secure. Panis glanced over.

"I suppose you'd like me to access them. Although I'd think that would be a matter for Fleet Security." Dupaynil said nothing and waited. Panis suddenly grimaced. "Of course. You *are* Fleet Security, at least part of it. Or so you say." Wariness became him. He seemed to mature almost visibly as Dupaynil watched.

"Yes, I am. On the other hand, since I am the officer involved, the one who killed Ollery, you have a natural reluctance to let me meddle in the files, just in case. Right?"

"Right." Panis shook his head. "And I thought I was lucky to be yanked off a battle platform where I was one of a hundred Jigs, to be Executive Officer on an escort! Maybe something will happen, I said."

"Something did." Dupaynil grinned at him, the easy smile that had won over more than one who had had suspicions of him. "And you survived, acquitted yourself well. I assure you, if you can bring in the *evidence* that shows just where the agents of piracy are in Fleet, you'll have made your mark."

"Piracy!" Panis started to say more, then held up his hand. "No, not this moment. Let me log the first of it, and we'll get into that later."

This was a ship's captain speaking, however inexperienced. Dupaynil nodded and waited. The Jig's verbal report was surprisingly orderly and concise for someone who had narrowly escaped death and still had ripening bruises on his face. Dupaynil's opinion of him went up another two notches, and then a third when Panis waved him over to the command input station.

"I'd like your report, too, sir. Lieutenant Commander Dupaynil, taken aboard *Claw* on resupply station 64, Fleet Standard dating . . . Computer?" The computer checked the date and time, and flashed it on Panis' screen. "Right! 23.05.34.0247. Transfer from the cruiser *Zaid-Dayan*, Commander Sassinak commanding, with orders from Inspector-General Parchandri to proceed to Seti space on a secret mission. Is that right, sir?"

"Right," said Dupaynil. Was this the time to mention that he thought those orders were faked? Probably not. At least, not without thinking about it a bit more. He didn't think Sassinak had intended to tangle him with planet pirates or their allies. If he said his orders were faked, that would drag her into it.

"Then if you'll give your report, Commander," and Panis handed him the microphone.

Carefully, trying to think ahead to the implications of his report, Dupaynil told how his suspicions had been aroused by the length of time the crew had been together and the captain's attitude.

"Escort and crews are never left unshuffled for more than one twenty-four-month tour," he said. "Precisely because these ships are hard to track and very dangerous, and small enough for one or two mutineers to take over. Five years without a shuffle is simply impossible. Someone in Personnel had to be in the plot, to cover the records." He went on to tell about setting some surveillance taps and hearing the senior mate and captain discuss his murder. "They said enough about their contacts in both Fleet and certain politically powerful families to convince me that information we've been seeking for years could well be on this ship. Agents aren't supposed to write things down, but they all do it. Names, dates, places to meet, codes: no one can remember all of it. Either in hardcopy or in the computer. And they knew it, because they were afraid I'd get access to those files." He finished with a brief account of his sabotage of the escape pods, and his actions during and after the drill.

"Do you have any evidence now to support these allegations?" asked Panis.

"I have the recording from that audio tap. There may be data in the other taps. I haven't had time to look at them."

"I'd like to hear what you have," Panis said.

"It's in my cabin." At Panis' expression, Dupaynil shrugged. "Either I would make it through alive to retrieve it or I'd be dead and it might, just might, survive me. Not on my body, which they'd search. May I get it for you?"

He could see uncertainty and sympathized. Panis had had a lot to adjust to in less than an hour. And to him, Dupaynil was still a stranger, hardly to be trusted. But he made the decision and nodded permission. Dupaynil left the bridge quickly, noting that all the partitions were retracted. He went directly to his cabin, retrieved the data cube, and returned. Panis was waiting, facing the bridge hatch. Without saying anything, Dupaynil slipped the cube into a player and turned it on. As it played, Panis' expression changed through suspicion to surprise to, at the end, anger.

"Bastards!" he said, when the sound ceased and Dupaynil picked up the cube again. "I knew they didn't like you, but I never thought . . . And then to be in league with planet pirates! Who's that Lady Luisa they were talking about?"

"Luisa Paraden. Aunt, by the way, of the Randolph Paraden who was expelled from the Academy because Commander Sassinak proved he was involved in theft, sexual harassment, and racial discrimination against Wefts. They were cadets at the same time."

"I never heard that."

Dupaynil smiled sardonically. "Of course not. It wasn't advertised. But, if you ever wonder why Commander Sassinak has a Weft following, that's one reason. When Ollery was trying to get me to gossip about her, that's one of the things he mentioned. And it made me suspicious: he shouldn't have known. It was kept very quiet."

"And you think there's more evidence in the ship's computer?"

"Yes, you heard what they said. Probably even more in their personal gear. But you're the captain, Panis. You're in legal command. I believe that you recognize we're both in a very tricky situation. We have one dead former captain and eleven live crew imprisoned in escape pods. If we should run into some of the other renegades, especially some of Ollery's friends, we could be shot for mutiny and murder before we ever got that evidence to a court-martial."

Panis touched his swelling face gingerly, then grinned. "Then we'd better not get caught."

In the time it took to lug Ollery's body to a storage bay and to disable the controls on the last occupied pod, Dupaynil figured out what to do about his faked orders. He could blame them on the Inspector General's office. Sassinak would never reveal the real source. He was fairly sure he could never get Ssli testimony incriminating *her*. In fact, it was only a guess that she had done it. It was not in the interest of Fleet or the FSP that she be blamed, even though she'd done it. But it was entirely in the interests of the Fleet to bring as many charges as possible against those guilty of conniving at planet piracy.

He thought through the whole chain of events. Would it have made sense for such a traitor to assign him to *Claw* and get him killed? Certainly, if they considered Sassinak a threat and they knew he'd been with her. They'd disrupted a profitable scam on Ireta. He'd uncovered one of their agents on the *Zaid-Dayan*. He was dangerous to them in himself, and they'd taken the opportunity to get him away from Sassinak.

He could almost believe that. It made sense, criminal sense. But if it were true, Ollery or the mate who he suspected of being the senior within the criminal organization, should have known from the beginning about him, should not have needed to discover his taps to suspect him. Of course, there were always glitches in the transfer of data within an organization. Perhaps the message explaining him to Ollery was even now back at the supply station.

Panis had let him do a bit of first aid, a sign of trust that Dupaynil valued. The Jig's bruised face wasn't all the damage. He had a massive bruise along his ribs on one side.

"Ollery," he said when Dupaynil raised his eyebrows at it. "That's when I realized, or at least, I didn't know what was going on. Siris had me down, and then I saw the captain with the needler. He yelled for Siris to roll aside, and kicked me, and then you . . ."

"Yes," said Dupaynil, interrupting that. "And it's going to hurt you to breathe for awhile. We'll have to keep an eye on your color, make sure you don't start collecting fluid in that lung. Why don't you start teaching me what I need to know to do the heavy work while we're going wherever we're going? You don't need to be hauling up and down ladders."

He had had Panis fetch a clean uniform from his quarters, and now helped him into it. Ice for the bruises. At least they had plenty of that. He mentioned the bay full of water ice and suggested thawing some for showers.

"I'll tell you another thing that bothers me," Dupaynil said with disarming frankness when they were back on the bridge. "I'm no longer sure that my orders to leave the *Zaid-Dayan* and board this ship were genuine."

"What? You think someone sent false orders?"

Dupaynil nodded. "My orders carried an initiation code that really upset Commander Sassinak. She claimed she'd seen it before, years ago, right before someone tried to kill her, on her first cruise. I always thought that initiation code simply meant the Inspector General's office. One particular comp station, say, or a particular officer. But even she thought it was strange that she had to put in at a supply station. That I was being yanked off her ship when she had previous orders that all of us were to appear as witnesses in the Ireta trial." He had explained the bare outline of that to Panis. "I could hardly believe it, but they'd come by IFTL link. No chance of interference. But you heard what they said on tape and what Siris said. If there are high-placed traitors in Fleet, especially in Personnel Assignment, and there'd almost have to be for this crew to have stayed together so long, it would be no trick at all to have me transferred."

"Hard to prove," Panis said, sipping a mug of hot soup.

"Worse than that." Dupaynil spread his hands. "Say that's what happened and they expected me to be killed, with a good excuse, like that malfunctioning escape pod. They still might take the precaution of wiping all records of those orders out of the computers. Suppose they try to claim Commander Sassinak or I faked those orders. Then, if I turn up alive, they can get me on that. If I don't, they can go after her. She's caused them a lot of trouble over the years, and I'd bet Randy Paraden still holds a big, prickly grudge where she's concerned. Faking orders or interfering with an IFTL link is big enough to get even a well-known cruiser captain in serious trouble."

"I see. It does make sense they'd want you away from her, with the evidence you'd gathered. And if they could discredit her later . . ."

"I wonder how many other people they've managed to finagle

away from her crew." Dupaynil went on, embroidering for the mere fun of it. "If we find out that one officer's been called away for a family crisis, and another's been given an urgent assignment? Well, I think that would prove it."

Panis, he was glad to see, accepted all this without difficulty. It did, after all, make sense. Whereas what Sassinak had done, and Dupaynil was still convinced she had done it, made sense only in personal terms: he had trespassed on her hospitality. At least his new explanation might clear her and laid guilt only on those already coated with it.

"So what do you think we should do, aside from avoiding all the unknown friends of the late Major Ollery?"

Dupaynil smiled at him. He liked the way the young man referred to Ollery, and he liked the dry humor.

"I think we should find out who they are, preferably by raiding Ollery's files. And then it would be most helpful if we'd turn up at the Ireta trial. Tanegli's trial, I should say. Then we ought to do something about your prisoners before their pod air supplies run out."

"I forgot about that." Panis' eyes flicked to the computer. "Oh, they're still on ship's air. Unless you did something to that, too."

"Didn't have time. But they don't have recycling capacity for more than a hundred hours or so, do they? I don't think either of us wants to let them out, even one by one."

"No. But I can't . . ."

"You can offer them cold sleep, you know. The drugs are there, and the cabinets. They'd be perfectly safe for as long as it takes us to get them to a Fleet facility."

Panis nodded slowly. "That's a better alternative than what I thought of. But what if they won't do it?"

"Warn them. Wait twelve hours. Warn them again and cut off ship's air. That'll give them hours to decide and prepare themselves. Are these the standard pods, with just over one hundred hours of air?"

"Yes. But what if they still refuse?"

Dupaynil shrugged. "If they want to die of suffocation rather than face a court-martial, that's their choice. We can't stop it without opening the pods and I can't advise that. Only Siris has any injuries, and his aren't bad enough to prevent his taking the induction medications."

❖   ❖   ❖

When push came to shove, though most of them blustered, only three waited until the ship ventilators cut out. The senior mate, Dupaynil noticed, was one of them. All the crew put themselves into cold sleep well before the pod air was gone. When the last one's bioscans went down, Dupaynil and Panis celebrated with the best the galley offered.

Dupaynil had found that the crew kept special treats in their quarters. Nothing as good as fresh food, but a tin of sticky fruitcake and a squat jar of expensive liquor made a party.

"I suppose I should have insisted on sealing the crew quarters," Panis said around a chunk of cake.

"But you needed to search them for evidence."

"Which I'm finding." Dupaynil poured for both of them with a flourish. "The mate kept a little book. Genuine pulp paper, if you can believe that. I'm not sure what all the entries mean . . . yet . . . but I doubt very much they're innocent. Ollery's personal kit had items far out of line for his Fleet salary, not to mention that nonissue set of duelling pistols. We're lucky he didn't blow a hole in you with one of those."

"You sound like a mosquito in a bloodbank," Panis grumbled. "Fairly gloating over all the data you might find."

"I am," Dupaynil agreed. "You're quite right; even without this," and he raised his glass, "I'd be drunk with delight at the possibilities. Do you have any idea how hard we normally work for each little smidgen of information? How many times we have to check and recheck it? The hours we burn out our eyes trying to find correlations even computers can't see?"

"My heart bleeds," said Panis, his mouth twitching.

"And you're only a Jig. Mulvaney's Ghost, but you're going to make one formidable commodore."

"If I survive. I suppose you'll want to tap into the computer tomorrow?"

"With your permission." Dupaynil sketched a bow from his seat. "We have to hope they were complacent enough to have only simple safeguards on the ticklish files. If Ollery thought to have them self-destruct if a new officer took command . . ."

Panis paled. "I hadn't thought of that."

"I had. But then I thought of Ollery. That kind of smugness never anticipates its own fall. Besides, you had to log a command change. It was regulation."

"Which you always follow." Panis let that lie, a challenge of sorts.

Dupaynil wondered what he was driving at, precisely. They'd worked well together so far. The younger man had seemed to enjoy his banter. But he reminded himself that he did not really *know* Panis. He let his face show the fatigue he felt and sag into its age and his usually hidden cynicism.

"If you mean Security doesn't always follow the letter of regulations, then you're right. I freely admit that planting taps on this ship was both against regulations and discourteous. Under the circumstances . . . ." Dupaynil spread his hands in resignation to the inevitable.

Panis flushed but pursued the issue. "Not that so much. You had reasons for suspicion that I didn't know. Anyway it saved our lives. But I'd heard about Commander Sassinak, that she didn't follow regulations as often as not. If this is some ploy of hers?"

Blast. The boy was too smart. He'd seen through the screen. Dupaynil let the worry he felt edge his voice.

"Who'd you hear that from?"

"Admiral Spirak. He captained the battle platform I . . ."

"Spirak!" Relief and contempt mixed gave that more force than he'd intended. Dupaynil lowered his voice and kept it even. "Panis, your admiral is the last person who should complain of someone else's lack of respect for regulations. I won't tell you *why* he's still spouting venom about Sassinak, even though she saved his career once. Gossip was Ollery's specialty. But if you ever wondered why he's got only two stars at his age and why he's commanding Fleet's only *non*operational battle platform, there's a damn good reason. I've seen Commander Sassinak's files, and it's true she doesn't always fight an engagement by the book. But she's come out clean from encounters that cost other commanders ships. The only regulations she bends are those that interfere with accomplishing the mission. She's far more a stickler for ship discipline than anyone on this ship was."

Now Panis looked as if he'd been dipped in boiling water.

"Sorry, sir. But he'd said if I ever *did* end up serving with one of her officers, look out. That she had a following, but more loyal to her than to Fleet."

"I don't suppose he told you about the promotion party he gave himself? And nobody came? It's useless to tell you, Panis.

You'll have to decide for yourself. She's popular, but she's also smart and a good commander. As for regulations, I felt that my duties entitled me to bend a few on her ship and she straightened me out in short order."

"What'd you do? Put a tap on *her*?"

Dupaynil gave that a hard look, and Panis suddenly realized what that could mean and turned even redder than before.

"I didn't mean . . . That's not what . . ."

"Good." Dupaynil gave no ground with that tone. "I did attempt to monitor some communications traffic without giving her proper notice. We were looking for a saboteur, as I told you. I thought a little snooping along the corridors, in the crew's gym, and so on, wouldn't hurt. She felt differently." That this was only distantly related to what had really happened bothered him not at all. She had been angry. He had put in surveillance devices without her permission. That much was true. "I don't consider myself one of Commander Sassinak's officers," Dupaynil went on. "My assignment to her ship was temporary duty only, a special mission to unearth this saboteur."

He could not tell if this satisfied Panis, and he didn't really care. He had liked the younger officer but suggestive questions about Sassinak rubbed him the wrong way. Why? He wasn't sure. He had not been tempted to involve himself with her. Her relationship with Ford was clear enough. So why did he feel such rage when someone criticized? It was worth thinking over later, when they'd found or not found the evidence he needed, and decided what to do with it.

Dupaynil's excursions into the ship's computers yielded all he could have wished for. He knew his satisfaction showed. He insisted on sharing his findings with Panis so the younger officer would know why.

"Besides," he said, "if someone scrags me successfully, you'll still have a chance to break up the conspiracy."

"How?" Panis looked up from the hardcopy of one of the more startling files, and tapped it with his finger. "If all these people are really part of it, then Fleet itself is hopeless."

"Not at all." Dupaynil put his fingertips together. "Do you know how many officers Fleet has? This is less than five percent. Your reaction is as dangerous as they are. If you assume that five percent rotten means the whole thing's rotten, then you've done their work for them."

"I hadn't thought of it that way."

"No. Most people don't. But let's be very glad we have to evade only five percent. And let's figure out how to get this information back to some of the ninety-five percent who *aren't* involved in it."

Panis had an odd expression on his face. "I'm not really . . . I mean, my skills in navigation are only average. And the computer in this ship holds only a limited number of plots."

"Plots?"

"Pre-programmed courses between charted points. I'm not sure I could drop us out of FTL, and then get us somewhere else that's not in the computer."

Dupaynil had assumed that all ship's officers were competent in navigation. He opened his mouth to ask what was Panis' problem, and shut it again. *He* wasn't able to pilot the ship, or even maintain the environmental system without Panis' instructions, so why should he expect everything of a young Jig?

"Does this mean we're stuck with the course and destination Ollery put in?" A worse thought erupted into his mind with the force of an explosion. "Do we even *know* where we're going?"

"Yes, we do. The computer's perfectly willing to tell me that. We're headed for Seti space, just as your orders specified." Panis frowned. "Where did you think we might be going?"

"It suddenly occurred to me that Ollery might never have entered that course, or might have changed it, since he was planning to kill me. Seti space! I don't know whether to laugh or cry," Dupaynil said. "Assuming my orders were faked, was that chosen as a random destination, or for some reason?"

Panis fiddled with his seat controls and glanced at something on the command screen next to him.

"Well . . . from where we were, that gives the longest stretch in FTL. Time enough for Ollery to figure out what to do with you and how. Perhaps it was that. Or maybe they had a chore for him in Seti space, in addition to scragging you."

"So, you're saying that we have to go where we're going before we can go anywhere else?"

"If you want to be sure of getting anywhere anytime soon," Panis said. "We've been in undefined space — FTL mode — for a long time, and if we drop out before the node, I have no idea where we might end up. We do have the extra supplies that the crew would have needed, but . . ."

"All right. On to Seti space. I suppose I could find something to do there, in the way of digging up dirt, although what we have already is more than enough." Dupaynil stretched. "But you do realize that while the personnel listed as on duty with the embassy to the Sek are *not* on Ollery's list of helpers, this means nothing. They could be part of the same conspiracy without Ollery having any knowledge of it."

The outer beacon to the Seti systems had all the courteous tact of a boot in the face.

"Intruders be warned!" it bleated in a cycle of all the languages known in FSP. "Intruders not tolerated. Intruders will be destroyed, if not properly naming selves immediately."

Panis set *Claw*'s transmitter to the correct setting and initiated the standard Fleet recognition sequence. He was recovering nicely, Dupaynil thought, from the shock of his original captain's treachery and the necessity of helping in a mutiny. He did not blurt out everything to the Fleet officer who was military attaché at the embassy nor did he request an immediate conference with the Ambassador. Instead, he simply reported that he had an officer with urgent orders insystem and let Dupaynil handle it from there.

"I'm not sure I understand, Commander Dupaynil, just what your purpose here is."

That diplomatic smoothness had once seemed innocuous. Now, he could not be sure if it was habit or conspiracy.

"My orders," Dupaynil said, keeping his own tone as light and unconcerned as the other's, "are to check the shipping records of the main Seti commercial firms involved in trade with Sector Eighteen human worlds. You know how this works. I haven't the foggiest notion what someone is looking at, or for, or why they couldn't do this long distance."

"It has nothing to do with that Iretan mess?"

Again, it might be only ordinary curiosity. Or something much more dangerous. Dupaynil shrugged, ran his finger along the bridge of his nose and hoped he passed for a dandified Bretagnan.

"It might, I suppose. Or it might not. How would I know? There I was happily ensconced on one of the better-run cruisers in Fleet, with a woman commander of considerable personal ah . . . charm. . . ." He made it definitely singular, but with a tonal implication that the plural would have been more natural, and decided that a knowing wink would overdo his act. "I would have been quite satisfied to finish the cruise with her . . . her *ship*." He shrugged again, and gave a deep sigh. "And then I find myself shipped out here, just because I have had contact with the Seti before, without arousing an incident, I suppose, to spend days making carefully polite inquiries to which they will make carefully impolite replies. That is all I know, except that if I had an enemy at headquarters, he could hardly have changed my plans in a way I would like less."

That came out with a touch more force than he'd intended, but it seemed to convince the fellow that he was sincere. The man's face did not change but he could feel a subtle lessening of tension.

"Well. I suppose I can introduce you to the Seti Commissioner of Commerce. That's a cabinet level position in the Sek's court. It'll know where else you should go."

"That would be very kind of you," said Dupaynil. He never minded handing out meaningless courtesies to lubricate the daily work.

"Not at all," the other said, already looking down at the pile of work on his desk. "The Commissioner's a bigot of the worst sort, even for a Seti. If this is a plot of your worst enemy at headquarters, he's planning to make you suffer."

The conventions of Seti interaction with other races had been designed to place the inferior of the universe securely and obviously in that inferior position and keep them there. To Seti, the inferior of the universe included those who tampered with "Holy Luck" by medical means (especially including genetic engineering), and those too cowardly (as they put it) to gamble. Humans were known to practice genetic engineering. Many of them changed their features for mere fashion — the Seti view of makeup and hair styling. Very few wished to gamble, as Seti did, by entering a room through the Door of Honor which might, or might not, drop a guillotine on those who passed through it . . . depending on a computer's random number generator.

Dupaynil did not enjoy his crawl through the Tunnel of Cowardly Certainty but he had known what to expect. Seated awkwardly on the hard mushroom-shaped stool allowed the ungodly foreigner, he kept his eyes politely lowered as the Commissioner of Commerce continued its midmorning snack. He didn't want to watch anyway. On their own worlds, the Seti ignored FSP prohibitions and dined freely on such abominations as those now writhing in the Commissioner's bowl. The Commissioner gave a final crunch and burp, exhaled a gust of rank breath, and leaned comfortably against its cushioned couch.

"Ahhh. And now, Misss-ter Du-paay-nil. You wish to ask a favor of the Seti?"

"With all due respect to the honor of the Sek and the eggbearers," and Dupaynil continued with a memorized string of formalities before coming to the point. "And, if it please the Commissioner, merely to place the gaze of the eye upon the trade records pertaining to the human worlds in Sector Eighteen."

Another long blast of smelly breath; the Commissioner yawned extravagantly, showing teeth that desperately needed cleaning, although Dupaynil didn't know if the Seti ever got decay or gum disease.

"Sector Eighteen," it said and slapped its tail heavily on the floor.

A Seti servant scuttled in bearing a tray piled with data cubes. Dupaynil wondered if the Door of Honor ignored servants or if they, too, had to take their chances with death. The servant withdrew, and the Commissioner ran its tongue lightly over the cubes. Dupaynil stared, then realized they must be labelled with chemcodes that the Commissioner could taste. It plucked one of the cubes from the pile, and inserted it into a player.

"Ah! What the *human*-dominated Fleet calls Sector Eighteen, the Flower of Luck in Disguise. Trade with human worlds? It is meager, not worth your time."

"Illustrious and most fortunate scion of a fortunate family," Dupaynil said, "it is my unlucky fate to be at the mercy of admirals."

This amused the Commissioner who laughed immoderately.

"Sso! It is a matter of luck, you would have me think? Unlucky in rank, unlucky in the admiral who sent you? But you do not believe in luck, so your people say. You believe in . . . What is that obscenity? Probabilities? Statistics?"

The old saying about "lies, damn lies, and statistics" popped into Dupaynil's mind, but it seemed the wrong moment. Instead, he said, "Of others I cannot speak, but *I* believe in luck. I would not have arrived without it."

He did, indeed, believe in luck. At least at the moment. For without his unwise tapping of Sassinak's comm shack, he would not have had the chance to find the evidence he had found. Now, if he could just get through with this and back to FedCentral in time for Tanegli's trial . . . That would be luck indeed! Apparently even temporary sincerity was convincing. The Seti Commissioner gave him a toothy grin.

"Well. A partial convert. You know what we say about your statistics, don't you? There are lies, damn lies and . . ."

And I'm glad I didn't use that joke, Dupaynil thought to himself, since I don't believe this guy thinks that it is one.

"I will save your eyes the trouble of examining our faultless, but copious, records regarding trade with the Flower of Luck in Disguise. If you were unlucky in your admiral, you shall be lucky in my support. Your clear unwillingness to struggle with this unlucky task shall be rewarded. I refuse permission to examine our records, not because we have anything to conceal, but because this is the Season of Unrepentance, when no such examination is lawful. You are fortunate in my approval for I will give you such a refusal as will satisfy the most unlucky admiral."

Again, a massive tail-slap, combined with a querulous squealing grunt, and the servitor scuttled in with a rolling cart with a bright green box atop. The Commissioner prodded it and it extruded a sheet of translucent lime green, covered with Seti script. Then another, and another.

"This is for the human ambassador, and this for your admiral, and this, O luckiest of humans, is your authorization to the passage in a human-safe compartment aboard the *Grand Luck* to human space. To attend a meeting of the Grand Council, in fact. You will have the great advantage of enjoying the superiority of Seti technology firsthand, an unprecedented opportunity for one of your . . . ah . . . luck."

It reached out with the sheets, and Dupaynil took them almost without thinking, wondering how he was going to get out of *this*.

"My good fortune abounds," he began. "Nonetheless, it is impossible that I should be honored with such a gift of luck. A mere human to take passage with Seti? It is my destined chance to travel more humbly."

A truly wicked chuckle interrupted him. The Commissioner leaned closer, its strong breath sickening.

"Little man," it said, "I think you will travel humbly enough to please whatever god enjoys your crawl through the Tunnel of Cowardly Certainty. With choice, always a chance. But with chance, no choice. The orders are in your hand. Your prints prove your acceptance. You will report to your ambassador, and then to the *Grand Luck* where great chances await you."

✦ CHAPTER ELEVEN

Private Yacht **Adagio**

Ford woke to an argument overhead. It was not the first time he'd wakened, but it was the first time he'd been this clear-headed. Prudence kept his eyelids shut as he listened to the two women's voices.

"It's for his own good," purred Madame Flaubert. "His spiritual state is simply ghastly."

"He looks ghastly." Auntie Quesada rustled. He couldn't tell if it was her dress or something she carried.

"The outward and visible sign of inward spiritual disgrace. Poison, if you will. It must be purged, Quesada, or that evil influence will ruin us all."

A sniff, a sigh. Neither promised him much. He felt no pain, at the moment, but he was sure that either woman could finish him off without his being able to defend himself. And why? Even if they knew what he wanted, that should be no threat to them. Auntie Quesada had even seemed to like him and he had been enchanted by her.

He heard a click, followed by a faint hiss, then a pungent smell began to creep up his nose. A faint yelp, rebuked, reminded him of Madame Flaubert's pet. His nose tickled. He tried to ignore it and failed, convulsing in a huge sneeze.

"Bad spirits," intoned Madame Flaubert.

Now that his eyes were open to the dim light, he could see her fantastic draperies in all their garishness; purples, reds, oranges, a flowered fringed shawl wrapped around those red tresses. Her half-closed eyes glittered at him as she pretended, and he was sure it was pretense, to commune with whatever mediums communed with. He didn't know. He was a rational, well-educated

Fleet officer. He'd had nothing to do with superstitions since his childhood, when he and a friend had convinced themselves that a drop of each one's blood on a rock made it magic.

"May they fly away, the bad spirits, may they leave him safe and free . . ."

Madame Flaubert went on in this vein for awhile longer as Ford wondered what courtesy required. His aunt, as before, looked completely miserable, sitting stiffly on the edge of her chair and staring at him. He wanted to reassure her, but couldn't think how. He felt like a dirty wet rag someone had wiped up a bar with. The pungent smoke of some sort of a floral incense blurred his vision and made his eyes water. Finally Madame Flaubert ran down and simply sat, head thrown back. After a long, dramatic pause, she sighed, rolled her head around as if to ease a stiff neck and stood.

"Coming, Quesada?"

"No . . . I think I'll sit with him a bit."

"You shouldn't. He needs to soak in the healing rays."

Madame Flaubert's face loomed over his. She had her lapdog in hand and it drooled onto him. He shuddered. But she turned away and waddled slowly out of his cabin. His great-aunt simply looked at him.

Ford cleared his throat, more noisily than he could have wished, and said, "I'm sorry, Aunt Quesada . . . this is not what I had in mind."

She shook her head. "Of course not. I simply do not understand."

"What?"

"Why Seraphine is so convinced you're dangerous to me. Of course you didn't really come just to visit. I knew that. But I've always been a good judge of men, young or old, and I cannot believe you mean me harm."

"I don't." His voice wavered, and he struggled to get it under control. "I don't mean you any harm. Why would I?"

"But the BLACK KEY, you see. How can I ignore the evidence of my own eyes?"

"The black key?" Weak he might be but his mind had cleared. She had said those works in capital letters.

His aunt looked away from him, lips pursed. In that pose, she might have been an elderly schoolteacher confronted with a moral dilemma outside her experience.

"I suppose it can't hurt to tell you," she said softly.

The Black Key was, it seemed, one of Madame Flaubert's specialties. It could reveal the truth about people. It could seek out and unlock their hidden malign motives. Ford was sure that any malign motives were Madame Flaubert's, but he merely asked how it worked.

His aunt shrugged. "I don't know. I'm not the medium. But I've *seen* it, my dear. Sliding across the table, rising into the air, turning and turning until it . . . it pointed straight at the guilty party."

Ford could think of several ways to do that, none of them involving magic or "higher spirits." He himself was no expert but he suspected that Dupaynil could have cleared up the Black Key's actions in less than five minutes.

"One of my servants," Auntie Q was saying. "I'd been missing things, just baubles really. But one can't let it go on. Seraphine had them all in and questioned them, and the Black Key revealed it. The girl confessed! Confessed to even more than I'd known about."

"What did the authorities say, when you told them how you'd gotten that confession?"

Auntie Q blushed faintly. "Well, dear, you know I didn't actually *report* it. The poor girl was so upset and, of course I had to dismiss her, and she had had so many troubles in her life already. Seraphine said that the pursuit of vengeance always ends in evil."

I'll bet she did, Ford thought. Just as she had probably arranged the theft in the first place, for the purpose of showing the Black Key's power, to convince Auntie Q.

"As a matter of fact," Auntie Q said, "Seraphine felt a bit guilty, I think. She had been the one to suggest that I needed another maid, with the Season coming on, and she'd given me the name of the agency."

"I see." He saw, indeed. What he did not know yet was just why Seraphine perceived him as a threat — or why his aunt had taken in Madame Flaubert at all. "How long has Madame Flaubert been your companion?"

Auntie Q shifted in her seat, unfolded and refolded her hands. "Since . . . since a few months after . . . after . . ." Her mouth worked but she couldn't seem to get the words out. Finally she said, "I . . . I can't quite talk about that, dear, so please don't ask me."

Ford stared at her, his own miseries forgotten. Whatever else was going on, whatever Auntie Q knew that might help Sassinak against the planet pirates, he had to get Madame Flaubert away from his aunt.

He said as gently as he could, "I'm sorry, Aunt Quesada. I didn't mean to distress you. And whatever the Black Key may have intimated, I promise you I mean you no harm."

"I want to believe you!" Now the old face crumpled. Tears rolled down her cheeks. "You're the first — the only family that's come to see me in years — and I *liked* you!"

He hitched himself up in bed, ignoring the wave of blurred vision.

"My dear, please! I've admitted my father was wrong about you. I think you're marvelous."

"She said you'd flatter me."

Complex in that were the wish to be flattered, and the desire not to be fooled.

"I suppose I have, if praise is flattery. But, dear Aunt, I never knew *anybody* with enough nerve to get two Ryxi tailfeathers! How can I not flatter you?"

Auntie Q sniffed, and wiped her face with a lace-edged kerchief. "She keeps telling me that's a vulgar triumph, that I should be ashamed."

"Poppycock!" The word, out of some forgotten old novel, surprised him. It amused his aunt, who smiled through her tears. "My dear, she's jealous of you, that's all, and it's obvious even to me, a mere male. She doesn't like me because . . . Well, does she like any of the men who work for you?"

"Not really." Now his aunt looked thoughtful. "She says . . . she says it's indecent for an old lady to travel with so many male crew, and only one female maid. You know, I used to have a male valet who left my ex-husband's service when we separated. Madame Flaubert was *so* scathing about it I simply had to dismiss him."

"And then she found you the maid who turned out to be a thief," Ford said. He let that work into her mind. When comprehension brightened those old eyes, he grinned at her.

"That . . . that *contemptible* creature!" Auntie Q angry was as enchanting now as she must have been sixty years back. "Raddled old harridan. And I took her into my bosom!" Metaphorically only, Ford was sure. "Brought her among my friends, and *this* is how she repays me!"

It sounded like a quote from some particularly bad Victorian novel and not entirely sincere. He watched his aunt's face, which had flushed, paled, and then flushed again.

"Still, you know, Ford, she really does have powers. Amazing things, she's been able to tell me, and others. She knows all our secrets, it seems. I . . . I have to confess I'm just a little afraid of her." She tried a giggle at her own foolishness, but it didn't come off.

"You really *are* frightened," he said and reached out a hand. She clutched it, and he felt the tremor in her fingers.

"Oh, not really! How silly!" But she would not meet his eye, and the whites of hers showed like those of a frightened animal.

"Auntie Q, forgive my asking, but . . . but do your friends ever come to visit? Travel with you? From what my father said, I'd had the idea you travelled in a great bevy, this whole yacht full to bursting."

"Well, I used to. But you know how it is. Or I suppose you don't. In the Navy you can't choose your companions. But there were quarrels, and upsets, and some didn't like this, and others didn't like that. . . ."

"And some didn't like Madame Flaubert," Ford said quietly. "And Madame Flaubert didn't like anyone who got between you."

She sat perfectly still, holding his hand, the color on her cheeks coming and going. Then she leaned close and barely whispered in his ear.

"I can't . . . I can't tell you how horrible it's been. That woman! But I can't do anything. I . . . I don't know why. I c-c-can't . . . say . . . anything she doesn't . . . want me to." Her breathing had roughened; her face was almost purple. "Or I'll die!" She sat back up, and would have drawn her hands away but Ford kept his grasp on them.

"Please send Sam to help me to the . . . uh . . . facilities," he said in the most neutral voice he could manage.

His aunt nodded, not looking at him, and stood. Ford felt his strength returning on a wave of mingled rage and pity. Granted, his Aunt Quesada was a rich, foolish old lady, but even foolish old ladies had a right to have friends, to suffer their own follies, and not those of others. Sam, when he appeared, eyed Ford with scant respect.

"You going to live? Or make us all trouble by dying aboard?"

"I intend to live out my normal span and die a long way from here," Ford said.

With Sam's help, he could just make it up and into the bath suite. The face he saw in the mirror looked ghastly, and he shook his head at it.

"Looks don't kill," he said.

Sam gave an approving nod. "You might be getting sense. You tell Madam yet the real reason you came to visit?"

"I've hardly had a chance." He glared at Sam, without effect. "For people who can't believe in my idle curiosity, you're all curious enough yourselves."

"Practice," said Sam, helping him into clean pajamas. "Madame Flaubert keeps us on our toes."

Ford snorted. "I'll bet she does. How long has she been around?"

"Since about six months after Madam and her Paraden husband had the final court ruling on their separation. The one that gave Madam some major blocks of shares in Paraden family holdings," Sam said. At Ford's stare, he winked. "Significant, eh?"

"She's a . . . ?" Ford mouthed the word Paraden without saying it.

Sam shook his head. "Not of the blood royal, so to speak. Maybe not even on the wrong side of the blanket. But in her heart, she does what she's paid to."

"Does my aunt know?"

Sam frowned and pursed his lips. "I've never been sure. She's got some hold on your aunt, but that particular thing, I don't know."

"They want her quiet and out of their way. No noise, no scandals. I'm surprised she's survived this long."

"It's been close a few times." Sam shook his head, as he helped Ford brush his teeth, and handed him a bottle of mouthwash. "It's funny. Your aunt's real cautious about some things but she won't *do* anything, if you follow me."

Scared to do anything, Ford interpreted. Scared altogether, as her friends dropped away year by year, alienated by Madame Flaubert. He smiled at Sam in the mirror, heartened to find that he could smile, that he looked marginally less like death warmed over.

"I think it's about time," he drawled, "that my dear aunt got free of Madame Flaubert."

Sam's peaked eyebrows went up. "Any reason why I should trust *you*, sir?"

Ford grimaced. "If I'm not preferable to Madame Flaubert, then I deserved that, but I thought you had more sense."

"More sense than to challenge where I can't win. Your aunt trusts me as a servant but no more than that."

"She should know better." Ford looked carefully at Sam, reminded again of the better NCOs he'd known in his time. "Are you *sure* you didn't start off in Fleet?"

A flicker in the eyes that quickly dropped before his. "Perhaps, sir, you're unaware how similar some of the situations are."

That was both equivocal, and the only answer he was going to get. Unaccountably, Ford felt better.

"Perhaps I am," he said absently, thinking ahead to what he could do about Madame Flaubert. His own survival, and Auntie Q's, both depended on that.

"Just don't let her touch you," Sam said. "Don't eat anything she's touched. Don't let her put anything on you."

"Do you know what it is, what she's using?"

Sam shook his head, refusing to say more, and left the cabin silently. Ford stared moodily into the mirror, trying to think it through. If the Paradens were that angry with his aunt, why not just kill her? Were her social and commercial connections *that* powerful? Did she have some kind of hold on them, something they thought to keep at bay, but dared not directly attack? He knew little about the commercial side of politics, and nothing of society except what any experienced Fleet officer of his rank had had to meet in official circles. It didn't seem quite real to him. And that, he knew, was his worst danger.

The confrontation came sooner than he'd expected. He was hardly back in his bed, thinking hard, when Madame Flaubert oozed in, her lapdog panting behind her. She had a net bag of paraphernalia which she began to set up without so much as a word to him. A candlestick with a fat green candle, a handful of different colored stones in a crystal bowl and geometric figures of some shiny stuff. He couldn't tell if they were plastic or metal or painted wood. Gauzy scarves to hang from the light fixtures, and drape across the door.

"Don't you think all that's a little excessive?" Ford asked, arms crossed over his chest. He might as well start as he meant to go on. "It's my aunt who believes in this stuff."

"You can't be expected to understand, with the demonic forces still raging within you," she answered.

"Oh, I don't know. I think I understand demonic forces quite well." That stopped her momentarily. She gave him a long hostile stare.

"You're unwell," she said. "Your mind is deranged."

"I'm sick as a dog," he agreed. "But my mind is clear as your intent."

Red spots showed under her makeup. "Ridiculous. Your wicked past merely asserts itself, trying to unnerve me."

"I would not try to unnerve you, Madame Flaubert, sweet Seraphine, but I would definitely try to dissuade you from actions which you might find unprofitable . . . even . . . dangerous."

"Your aura is disgusting," she said firmly, but her eyes shifted.

"I could say the same," he murmured. Again that shifting of the eyes, that uncertainty.

"You came here for no good! You want to destroy your aunt's life!" Her plump hands shook as she laid out the colored stones on the small bedside table. "You are danger and death! I saw that at once."

Quick as a snake's tongue, her hand darted out to place one of the stones on his chest. Wrapping his hand in the sheet, Ford picked it up and tossed it to the floor. Her face paled, as her dog sniffed at it.

"Get *away*, Frouff! It's contaminated by *his* evil."

The dog looked at Ford, its tail wagging gently. Madame Flaubert leaned over, never taking her eyes off Ford, and picked up the stone. He watched, eerily fascinated, as she held it up before her, crooned to it, and placed it back with the others.

If he had not watched so closely, he would not have seen it. Her hands were hardly visible, what with ruffles drooping from her full sleeves, dozens of bracelets, gaudy rings on every finger. But they were *gloved*. Her fingertips were too shiny, and when she held the stone, one of them *wrinkled*. Ford hoped his face did not reveal his feelings as he watched her fondle the stones, squeeze them. And watching with that dazed fascination, he saw the squeeze that sent something from one of those massive rings, to be spread on the stones.

Contact poison. He had thought of injections, when Sam

warned against letting her touch him. He had thought of poison in his food, but not of contact poison working through intact skin. Had *that* been the paralyzing agent that had held him motionless before while she claimed to commune with spirits over him? He was no chemist or doctor so he had no idea what kinds of effects could be obtained with poisons working through the skin.

He tried to let his eyelids sag, feigning exhaustion, but when Madame Flaubert reached out, he could not help flinching away from her. Her predatory smile widened.

"Ah! you suspect, do you? Or think you know?"

Ford edged farther away, telling himself that even in his present state he had to be a match for any woman like Madame Flaubert. He didn't believe it. She was big and probably more powerful than she looked. As if she'd read his thoughts, she nodded slowly, still smiling.

"Silly man," she said. "You should have had the sense to wait until you were stronger. Of course, you weren't *going* to be stronger."

He couldn't think of anything to say. His back was against the cabin bulkhead. She was between him and the door, holding up a purple stone and rubbing it slowly. He could feel every square centimeter of his bare skin. After all, how much protection were pajamas?

"All I have to decide," she gloated, "is whether it should look like a heart attack or a stroke. Or perhaps a final spasm of that disgusting intestinal ailment you brought aboard."

He was supposed to be able to kill with his bare hands. He was supposed to be able to take command of any situation. He was not supposed to be cowering in his pajamas, terrified of the touch of an overdressed fake spiritualist with a poison ring. It would sound, if anyone ever heard about it, like something out of the worst possible mass entertainment.

He clenched one hand in the expensively fluffy pillow Auntie Q had provided the invalid. He could use that to shield his hand. What if the murderous old bag had put poison on his bedclothes, too? He felt cold and shaky. Fear? Poison?

"It's a pity," Madame Flaubert said, letting her eyes rove over him. "You're the handsomest young man we've had aboard in years. If you'd only been reasonably stupid, I could have had fun with you before. Or even let you live."

"Fun? With you?" He could not hide his disgust, and she glared at him.

"Yes, me. With you. And you'd have enjoyed it, my pretty young man, with the help of my . . . my *special* arts." She waved, indicating all her paraphernalia. "You'd have been swooning at my feet."

Ford said nothing. He could not reach any of the call buttons without coming within her reach, and he knew the cabins were well soundproofed. Could he make it to the bath suite and hold the door shut? No. Too far, and around furniture. She'd get there first. If he'd been well and strong, he was sure he could do *something*. But another look at those glittering eyes made him wonder.

Her dog yipped suddenly and dashed to the door. Ford drew a breath to yell, if it opened. Madame Flaubert backed slowly from the bed, to press the intercom button.

"Not now," she said. "No matter what . . . ignore!"

Ford leapt and yelled at once. His feet tangled in the bed-clothes and he fell headlong to the floor between the bed and the ornate wardrobe with its mirrored doors. He saw Madame Flaubert's triumphant grin, distorted by the antique mirrors, and rolled aside in time to avoid one swipe with the stone. Her dog broke into a flurry of yips, dancing around her feet with its fluff of a tail wagging. Ford threw his weight against her knees, whirled, and tried again for the bath suite. White-hot pain raked his back, then his vision darkened.

"Idiot!" She stood above him, those over-red curls askew. Then lifted them off to show the bald ugliness of her . . . his? . . . head. "Too bad I can't keep you alive to see what happens to your Captain Sassinak."

The wig plopped back down, still askew. Ford writhed, trying to move away, but one leg would not work. The little dog, wildly excited, bounced up and down, still yipping. The stone she'd used lay on the floor, just out of his reach. Not that he wanted to touch it.

"The green, I think. It has a certain appeal . . ." She had picked up another stone, and without any attempt to hide her act, dripped an oily liquid on it from another of her rings. "Of course, your poor aunt may suffer a shock of her own — even a fatal one — when she sees you lying there, and picks this off your chest."

She sauntered back across the small cabin, smiling that pitiless smile. Ford strained against the effects of the first poison. Sweat poured down his face, but he could *not* move more than a few inches. Then the cabin door opened and his aunt put her head in.

"Ford, I was thinking . . . Seraphine! Whatever are you doing!"

The little dog skittered toward her, still barking, then came back. With a curse, Madame Flaubert whirled, arm cocked.

Ford said, "Look out!" in the loudest voice he could and someone's muscular arm hauled his aunt back out of sight. Madame Flaubert whirled back to him, took a step, and tottered as her lapdog tripped her neatly. She fell in a tangle of skirts and shawls, arms wide to catch herself.

Ford prayed for someone to come in before she could get up. But she didn't get up. She lay sprawled, facedown, that murderous stone still clutched in one hand. The little dog trembled, crouched with its nose to the floor, and then lifted it to howl eerily.

I don't believe this, Ford thought muzzily. He thought it as Sam came in and as he was put back in his bed. As he drifted off, he was convinced it was a last dream in the course of dying.

But he believed it when he woke.

Auntie Q out from under the influence of Madame Flaubert was even more herself than Ford would have guessed. It had taken him three days to shake off the effects of that poison. In that period she had sacked most of her crew and staff except for Sam. In fact, anyone hired since Madame Flaubert's arrival.

Now Auntie Q spent her hours engaged in tapestry, gossip, and reminiscence. She refused to talk much about Madame Flaubert on the grounds that one should put unpleasantness out of one's mind as quickly as possible.

Ford had found out from Sam that Madame Flaubert's ornate rings had torn her surgical gloves, allowing the poison to contact her bare skin. Exactly what she deserved, but he still had cold chills when he thought about his close call. No wonder his aunt didn't want to talk about that.

But Auntie Q had plenty to say about the Paraden Family. Ford had confessed his official reason for visiting her and she took it in better part than he expected.

"After all," she said with a shrug that made the Ryxi tailfeathers dance above her head, "when you get to be my age, handsome young men don't come visiting for one's own sake. And you *are* good company, and you did get that . . . that *frightful* person out of my establishment. Ask what you will, dear. I'll be glad to tell you. Only tell me more of that captain of yours, the one that makes your blood move. Yes, I can tell. I may be old, but I'm a woman still, and I want to know if she's good enough for you."

When Ford was done, having told more about Sassinak than he'd intended, his aunt nodded briskly.

"I want to meet her, dear. When all this is over, bring her to visit. You say she likes good food. Well, as you know, Sam's capable of cooking for an emperor."

Ford tried to imagine Sassinak and Auntie Q in the same room and failed utterly. But his aunt waited with her bright smile for his answer and, at last, he agreed.

✧ CHAPTER TWELVE

FedCentral

Lunzie heard someone scolding her, or so it seemed, before she could even get her eyes open. Bias, she decided. Furious that I stayed too late with Zebara. Why can't that man understand that a woman over two hundred years old is capable of making her own decisions? Then she felt a prick in her arm and a warm surge of returning feeling.

With it came memory, and then rage. That liar, that cheat, that conniving bastard Zebara had sold her! Probably literally and gods only knew where she was! She opened her eyes to find a tired-faced man in medical greens leaning over her, saying, "Wake up, now. Come on. Open your eyes. . . ."

"They *are* open," said Lunzie. Her voice was rough and it sounded almost as grouchy as she felt.

"You'd better drink this," he said in the same quiet voice. "You need the fluid."

Lunzie wanted to argue, but whatever it was she might as well drink it, or they could pump it in a vein. It tasted like any one of the standard restoratives: fruity, sweet, with an undertaste of bitter salt. She could feel her throat slicking back down. The next time she spoke, she had control of her tone.

"Since I've been informed that you don't exist," the man went on, his mouth quirking now in a half-grin, "I won't check your response to the standard mental status exam: no person, place, and time. I'm authorized to tell you that you are presently in a secure medical facility on FedCentral, that you have been in cold sleep approximately four Standard months, and that your personal gear, what there is of it, is in that locker!" He pointed. "You will be provided meals in your quarters until you have satisfied someone . . . I'm not supposed to ask who . . . of your identity and the reason you chose to arrive as a shipment of muskie-fur carpets. *Do* you remember who you are? Or are you suffering disorientation?"

"I know who I am," said Lunzie, grimly. "And I know who got me into this. Is this a Fleet facility, or civilian FSP?"

"I'm sorry. I'm not allowed to say. Your physical parameters are now within normal limits. Telemetry has transmitted that fact to . . . to those making decisions and I am required to withdraw." He sketched a wave and smiled, this time with no apparent irony. "I hope you're feeling better and that you have a happy stay here." Then he was gone, closing behind him a heavy door with a suspiciously decided clunk-click.

Lunzie lay still a moment, trying to think her way through it all. Telemetry? That meant she was still being monitored. She had on not the outfit she last remembered, the pressure suit and coverall she had worn on Diplo, but a hospital gown with ridiculous yellow daisies, printed white crinkled stuff that felt like plastic. Someone's idea of cheerful: it wasn't hers. She saw no wires, felt no tubes, so the telemetry must be remote. A "smart" hospital bed could keep track of a patient's heart and respiration rate, temperature, activity, and even bowel sounds, without anything being attached to the patient.

She sat up, carefully easing her arms and legs into motion again. No dizziness, no nausea, no pounding headache. She wasn't sure why she was surprised. After all, they'd had forty-three years to come up with better drugs than the ones she'd had available on Ireta.

Wherever she was, her quarters included a complete array of refreshment options. She chose the shower, yelping when the mysterious control handle switched to cold pulses when she tried to turn it off. *That* was an effective final wake-up step, to be sure. She wrapped herself in the thick, heavy towelling provided and looked around the small room. Her own personal kit, the green fabric no more scuffed than she remembered, still contained her own partly used containers of cosmetics and scents and lotions. Drawers beneath the counter held others and remedies for any minor illness or emergency. She frowned thoughtfully. It would be difficult to commit suicide with the variety of medications provided, but possible if you took them all at once on an empty stomach. Weren't people in confinement usually kept without drugs?

Drawers on one side held neatly folded garments she did not recognize even when she shook them out. Pajamas, lounging wear, all her size, and in colors she favored, but she'd never bought these. She chose an outfit she could even have worn in public, loose plush pants and a pullover top — and felt much better. That ridiculous hospital gown made anyone feel helpless and submissive. Dressed, with her hair clean and brushed, and her feet in sensible shoes, she was ready to take on the world. Whatever world this happened to be.

Back in the other room, she found the bed remade and rolled to one side. Now a small table centered the room, with a meal laid ready on it. Soup, fruit, bread: exactly what she would have chosen. But the room was empty, silent. Had she taken that long to clean up? She looked but found no clock.

She wondered whether the food was drugged, and then realized that it made no difference. If they . . . whoever they were . . . wanted to drug her, it would be easy enough to do it in other ways. She ate the excellent meal with full appreciation of its excellence. Then she investigated the locker the attendant had first pointed out. There were the rest of her clothes from the Diplo trip and all the other personal gear she'd taken along. Everything seemed to be freshly cleaned, but otherwise untouched.

FedCentral. The man had said she was on FedCentral. She'd never been there and knew nothing of it except for the standard media shots of the Council sessions. *Who* had secure medical facilities on FedCentral? Fleet? But if she was in Fleet's hands, surely Sassinak could identify her and get her out of here? Unless something had happened to Sassinak . . . and she didn't even want to think about that possibility.

Instead she tried to add up the elapsed time since she'd left the *Zaid-Dayan*. It must be very close to Tanegli's trial date when she would be called to give evidence. Unless, of course, she was still cooped up here. Was that what someone wanted? Had that been Zebara's plan all along? She rooted through her personal gear, looking for anything that might be the proof Zebara had promised her of the Diplo end of the conspiracy, but found nothing. Her clothes were all there and the one or two pieces of jewelry she had taken to Diplo.

Her little computer held only its software. Nothing stored in files with mysterious names and nothing new in the files she'd initiated. No mysterious lumps in her clothing, nothing tucked into a pocket of her duffel. Even the clutter was still there. She wondered why no one had tossed out the copy of the program from *Bitter Destinies* or the baggage claim receipt from Diplo or the ragged scrap on which she'd jotted the room number on Liaka where the medical team would assemble. An advertising card from a dress shop she'd never had time to visit. She couldn't even remember if that was from before Ireta or after. Another torn scrap of paper with the numbers of the cases that needed to be re-entered on cubes, the ones Bias had thrown that fit about. But nothing resembling Zebara's promised evidence. Finally, frustrated, she threw herself into the softly padded chair and glared at the door. With suspicious quickness, it opened.

She did not recognize the old man who stood there. He clearly knew her, but waited, at ease, until she acknowledged him with a nod.

"May I come in?" he asked then.

As if I could stop you, she thought, but tried for a gracious smile and said, "Of course. Do come in."

Her voice carried more edge than she intended, but it didn't bother him. He shut the door carefully behind him as she tried to figure out who, or what, he was.

Although he wore no uniform, she felt a uniform would look more natural on him. With that bearing, he would be an officer. At that age, for his silvery hair and lined brow put him into his sixties at least, he should have stars. Tall, much taller than average, piercing blue eyes. If his hair had been yellow or black or brown . . . a warm honey-brown . . .

It was always a shock, and it was going to stay a shock, as it had with Zebara. At least this man was healthy, his white hair a sign of age, but not decay.

"Admiral Coromell," she murmured softly. He smiled, the same charming smile she remembered on a much younger face. Not in his sixties, but upper eighties, at least. "Your father?" He must be dead, but . . .

"He died about two decades ago, painlessly in his sleep," Coromell said. "And you have survived another long sleep! Remarkable."

Not remarkable, Lunzie thought, but disgusting. "I'm beginning to think myself that those superstitious sailors were right! I'm a Jonah."

He snorted, a curiously youthful snort. "Ireta's a planet. It doesn't count. My dear, much as I'd like to chat with you and play verbal games, I can't allow either of us the luxury. We have a problem."

Lunzie contented herself with a raised eyebrow. As far as she was concerned they had many more than one problem. He could say what he would.

"It's your descendant."

She had not expected *that*. "Descendant?" Fiona must be dead by now. Who could he mean? But of course! "Sassinak?" He nodded. She felt a surge of fear. "What's happened to her? Where is she?"

"That's what we don't know. She was here. I mean, on Fed-Central, while I was on leave over on Six, hunting. Unfortunately. Now she's gone. Disappeared. She and an Iretan native, by the name of Aygar. . . ."

"Aygar!"

Lunzie felt foolish, repeating it, but could think of nothing else to say. Why was Sassinak going anywhere with Aygar? Unless she . . . but Lunzie did not believe that for a moment. Sassinak had never, for one moment, thought of anything but her ship first and Fleet second. She would not take off on a recreational jaunt with Aygar when Tanegli's trial was coming up.

"According to the ranking officer aboard the *Zaid-Dayan*, Arly . . ." He paused to see if she knew the name. She nodded. "Commander Sassinak sent you to Diplo to some source you knew about, to get information on Diplo's connection to the Iretan mess. Is that right?"

"Yes, it is."

Quickly, Lunzie outlined Sassinak's thoughts, and her decision to offer to go to Diplo.

"I was best suited, in many ways. . . ."

"I wouldn't have thought so, not after your experience with the heavyworlders on Ireta," said Coromell. "The last person who should have had to go . . ."

"But I'm glad I did."

She stopped, wondering if she should tell him everything, and filled in with a brief account of her retraining on Liaka and the early part of the expedition.

"I presume, then, that you do have the information you sought?" When she didn't answer at once, he cocked his head and grinned, "Or did they catch you snooping and send you home in a cold sleep pod just to frustrate us?"

"I . . . I'm not sure."

He waited, quiet but curious, in just the attitude of the experienced interrogator who knows the suspect will incriminate herself, given enough rope. She did *not* want to explain Zebara to a Fleet admiral, especially not *this* Fleet admiral, but there was no other way. How best to do it? She remembered Sassinak, chewing out one of the junior officers who had tried to conceal a mistake. . . . "When all else fails, mister, tell the truth." She didn't think she'd made that big a mistake, but she'd still better tell the truth, and all of it.

It took longer than she expected. Although Coromell didn't ask questions until she finished, she could tell by his expression when she'd lost him and needed to backtrack and explain. And her leftover indignation at Bias, plus a natural reluctance to go into her emotional ties to Zebara, kept her ranting at the team leader's prudery far too long. At last she came to an end, trailing off with, " . . . and then I felt terribly sleepy in that stuffy car and, when I woke up, I was here."

A long pause, during which Lunzie endured the gaze of his brilliant blue eyes. Age had not fogged them at all. She felt they were seeing things she had not said. She had not said anything about the opera *Bitter Destinies* except that Zebara had taken her to an opera. He sighed, at last, the first thing he'd done that sounded old.

"So. And did Zebara give you the information he promised? Or will you go to Tanegli's trial with your testimony alone?"

"He hadn't when I left his home," Lunzie said. "He said I was to get it by messenger. And then . . . it was over."

"But he had you put in cold sleep, and safely aboard a transport that brought you here in a cargo of muskie-wool carpets. And I hear that was quite a scene, when Customs found a metallic return on the scan and unrolled the whole mess of them. Your little pod came rolling out like . . . Who was that Old Earth queen? Guinevere or Catherine or Cleopatra . . . someone like that. Rolled in a carpet to present herself to a king she'd fallen in love with. Anyway. So you don't know, do you, whether he passed that information with you or not?"

Lunzie shook her head. "I've looked through my things and found nothing. Surely your people looked, too?"

"I'm afraid they did." His lips pursed. "We found nothing we recognized. We thought perhaps when you woke, you would know what to look for. You don't?"

"No. If he included it, I don't recognize it."

"He gave you nothing at all?" Coromell's voice had a querulous edge now, age roughening it with impatience. He gave me a very good time, Lunzie thought to herself, and a lot of worries.

"Nothing." Then she frowned. He started to speak but she waved him to silence. "No, I think he did after all."

Quickly, she went to the locker and pulled out the duffel, pawing through it. She had not kept her copy of the *Bitter Destinies* program. She had not felt she needed it to remember that powerful work and she had not wanted to chance being teased by the team members if they saw her with it. She had not even been sure that Diplo customs would let her take it out. So Zebara must have put that program among her things. She found it, and brought it to Coromell.

"This isn't mine. I threw mine away. And this is signed. Look! All the singers autographed it."

Thick dark ink, in many different calligraphies, most of them extravagantly individual. Coromell took it gingerly from her hand.

"Ah! Perfect for a rather old-fashioned technology. It would take a dot only this size," and he pointed to one of the ellipsis dots between a performer's name and role, "to hold a great deal of information. We'll have to see. . . ."

He stood, then shook his head at her. "I'm sorry, dear Lunzie, but you must stay here, unknown, awhile longer. Without Sassinak, we must not lose your testimony, no matter what this gives us."

"But I . . ."

He had moved even as he spoke, more swiftly and fluidly than she would have supposed possible, and abruptly she faced a closed door again.

"Blast you!" she said, to that impassive surface. "I am not a stupid child, even if you are an arrogant old goat."

That got the response it deserved! Nothing. But she felt better.

She felt considerably better when Coromell returned very shortly to report that the program had none of the expected microdots.

"I find myself annoyed with your Zebara," he said, slapping the program down on the table between them. "If there's a message in this thing, no one's found it yet. Do you have any idea how many little specks there are in an opera program? Every single person credited with anything in the production has a row of them, and we had to check every one."

"But it has to be this," said Lunzie. She picked up the program, and flipped through it. She still thought the cover design looked pretentious. Even with heavyworlder pride at full blast on this thing, she noticed that the opera had needed corporate sponsorship. The ads covered the inside front and back pages. Then came photographs of the lead singers, then scenes from the opera itself, then the outline of the libretto, and the cast list. More photographs, an interview with the conductor. She realized she was reading the Diplo dialect much better than she ever had. It almost seemed natural. She found herself humming the aria of the suicide who refused to eat even re-synthesized meat. Coromell looked at her oddly.

"I don't know . . ." she said. She didn't want to speak Standard! She wanted to sing! Sing? Something fluttered in her mind like great feathered wings and the alternative slang meaning of "sing" popped up, along with the anagram "sign." Suddenly she knew. "Sing a song of sixpence . . . sing a sign . . . good heavens, that man is so devious a corkscrew would get lost in him."

"What!" Coromell fairly barked at her, his patience gone, looking now very like his boisterously bossy father.

"It's here, but it's . . . it's in my head. It's a key . . . an implant, keyed to this program. I think . . . Just be patient!"

She looked a bit longer, let her mind drift with the internal forces. Zebara had known she was a Disciple. She had eased his pain, she had touched his mind just a little, and his heart somewhat more. She looked on through the program, not knowing exactly what she was to find, but knowing she would find it. On the final page, the star's sprawling signature half covered her face, her broad bosom, the necklace . . . the necklace Zebara had . . . had *not* given her. So he said. A gift of the former Lieutenant Governor's son . . . no . . . that was not the link.

The necklace Zebara had not given her . . . her! He had not

given *her* a necklace, and the necklace he had not given her lay innocently among her things. Cheap but a good design, she'd bought it . . . she'd bought it before the Ireta voyage, hadn't she? She couldn't remember, now. Did it matter? It did.

She snapped out of that near-trance and without a word to Coromell dove back into her duffel, coming up with the necklace. An innocent enough accessory, itemized among her effects on her way *into* Diplo. She remembered filling out the form. Not expensive enough to require duty on any world, but handy for formal occasions, a pattern of linked leaves in coppertoned metal, with streaks of enamel in blues and greens.

She laid it on the table, and pushed Coromell's hand back when he reached for it. She gave it her whole attention. Did it have the same number of links? She wasn't sure. Was it the same clasp? She wasn't sure. She prodded it with a finger, hoping for inspiration. She had worn it that last day. It had caught on something in Zebara's house. That fluffy pillow? He had unsnagged it for her, unhooking the clasp and refastening it later. She remembered being afraid of his hands so near her neck, and hating herself for that fear. The clasp it had now screwed together, making a little cylinder. Before, it had had an elegant hook, shaped like a tendril of the vine those leaves were taken from.

"The clasp," she said, quietly, without looking up at Coromell. "It's the clasp. It's not the same."

"Shall I?" he asked, reaching.

She shook her head. "No. I want to see." Carefully, as if it might explode for she felt a trickle of icy fear, she took it up and worked at the tiny clasp. Most such things unscrewed easily, two or three turns. This one was stuck, cross-threaded or not threaded at all. She heard Coromell shift restlessly in his chair. "Patience," she said.

Discipline focussed her attention. The real join was not in the middle, where a groove suggested it, but at the end. It required not a twist, but a pull — a straight pull, pinching the last link hard — and out came a delicate pin with its tip caught in a lump of something dark. She pulled the pin free and held on her hand that tiny, waxy cylinder.

"This has to be it. Whatever it is."

What it was, she heard later, was a complete record of Diplo's dealings with the Paradens and the Seti for the past century:

names, dates, codes, the whole thing. Everything that Zebara had promised, and more.

"Enough," Coromell said, "to bring their government down . . . even revoke their charter."

"No." Lunzie shook her head. "It's not just the heavyworlders. They were the victims first. We can't take vengeance on the innocent, the ones who aren't part of it."

"You know something I don't?" He was giving her a look that had no doubt quelled generations of junior officers. Lunzie felt what he intended her to feel, but fought against it.

"I do," she said firmly, against the pressure of the stars on his uniform and his age. "I've been there myself. I've been to their opera."

"Opera!" That came out as a bark of amusement.

Lunzie glared and he choked it back. "Their very, very, beautiful opera, Admiral Coromell. With singers better than I've heard in most systems. Composed by heavyworlders to dramatize poems written by heavyworlders, and for all its political bias, we don't come off very well. Tell me — what do you know about the early settlement of Diplo?"

He shrugged, clearly baffled at the intent of the question. "Not much. Heavyworlders settled it because it was too dense for the rest of us without protective gear. It's cold, isn't it? And it was one of the first pure-heavyworlder colony worlds. It still is the richest." The lift of his eyebrows said *so what?*

"It's cold, yes." Lunzie shivered, remembering that cold, and what it had meant. "And in the first winter, the colonists had heavy losses."

He shrugged again. "Colonies always have heavy casualties at first."

She was furious. Zebara had reason for his bitterness, his anger, his near despair. Coromell had no reason for this complacency but ignorance.

"Forty thousand casualties, Admiral, out of ninety thousand."

"What?" That had his attention. He stared at her.

"Forty thousand *men*, who died of starvation and cold because their death was the only hope for the women and children to survive. And even so, not all of them did. Because no one bothered to warn the colonists about the periodic long winter cycles, or provide food for them."

"Are you . . . are you *sure*? Didn't they complain to FSP?"

"To the best of my knowledge, it happened, and what I was told, what I believe is also on that chip along with Paraden and Seti conspiracy, is why the FSP never heard about it officially. Major commercial consortia, Admiral, found it inexpedient to bother about Diplo. And then, because the colonists had turned in desperation to eating indigenous animals, these same consortia threatened to have Fleet down on them. Blackmailed them, to put it simply. The whole long conspiracy, the conscription of heavyworlders into private military forces by Paraden and Parchandri families . . . all that results from the original betrayal."

"But why didn't anyone ever tell us? It's been decades . . . centuries . . . no one can keep a secret that long!"

"They can if they're frightened enough. Once begun, it suited the power-hungry on both sides to keep Diplo's population convinced that the FSP would be nothing but trouble. Think of it. Those the consortia dealt with had power. Had that power as long as those they ruled believed no one else could intervene, or would intervene, to bring justice. These chose others, equally ambitious and unscrupulous, to follow them. It was to no one's advantage in the Diplo government *or* the guilty families to have Diplo citizens confiding in the FSP. No one could come out of the Diplo educational system believing FSP would do anything but interdict the planet for meat-eating and lack of population control." She paused, watching Ccromell's face change as he thought about it. "Of course, they *do* eat meat, and they *don't* control their population." His eyes widened again.

"You don't mean? You're serious! But that means . . ."

"It means they remember that only meat-eating saved them, and that they'd promised the men who died to carry on their names. They are as serious, as *devout*, I suppose you'd say, as any upright citizen of FSP who gags at the thought of eating a sentient being. They've broken the law, and they expect all of us to despise them. But they see the law as a weapon which nearly killed them all — for some died rather than eat the muskies — and which we use merely to keep them down."

"But not all the heavyworlder troublemakers are from Diplo."

"No, that's true. Though I have no direct evidence, I would imagine that the one place the *secret* did get out was to other heavyworlders in the form of a warning. Some would believe it, and some wouldn't. And so you have Separationists, Integration-ists, the whole complicated mess that we have here."

"I think I see." He stared past her for a long moment. "If you're right, Lunzie — and I must say you present a compelling case — then we are dealing not only with today's conspirators, but with long-developed plans out of the past. If only Sassinak hadn't disappeared!"

"And you still haven't told me how that happened."

"Because we don't know." Coromell smacked his fist into his other hand. "I wasn't here and no one admits to knowing any-thing about it. She told her Weapons Officer that she had an appointment with me, that she was taking Aygar along, and, in essence, not to wait up for her. No one on my staff knows of any such appointment. She had been informed that I was on leave and not due back for three more days. The last anyone saw — anyone whose accounts I trust — she and Aygar walked off the down shuttle and into the usual crowd at the shuttleport. Passed customs, their prints are on file, and then nothing."

✧ CHAPTER THIRTEEN

FSP Cruiser Zaid-Dayan, *FedCentral*

Sassinak frowned at the carefully worded communication. She did not need to consult the codebook to figure out what it meant. It was in the common senior officers' slang that made its origin very definitely Fleet. Almost impossible to fake slang and the topical references. She had used something like this herself, though rarely. Not something a junior would send to a senior but a senior's discrete way of hinting to the more alert junior.

If she could believe a senior admiral would want a clandestine meeting, would return from leave early, this would be a likely way to signal the officer he wanted to meet. Padalyan reefed her sails, indeed! The reference to the ship she'd served on before the *Zaid-Dayan* almost removed her doubts. But it meant leaving the *Zaid-Dayan* again, and she had not expected to go back onplanet until Coromell returned just before the trial. There was nothing illegal about it, with her ship secured in the FedCentral Docking Station. She still didn't like it.

If Ford had been here . . . but Ford was not only not here, he had not reported anything, anything at all. She should have heard from him by now. Another worry. It had seemed so neat, months ago, sending Ford to find out about the Paradens from a social contact, and Lunzie to Diplo, and dumping Dupaynil on the Seti. Her mouth quirked. She would bet on Dupaynil to come through with something useful, even if he did figure out his orders were faked. He was too smart for his own good, but a challenge would be good for him.

She realized she was tapping her stylus on the console and made herself put it down. She could think of a dozen good reasons why neither Ford nor Lunzie had shown up yet. And two dozen bad ones. She flicked on one of the screens, calling up a view of the planet below. The fact was that she simply did not want to leave her ship. Here she felt safe, confident, in control. Down on a planet — any planet — she felt lost and alone, a potential victim.

Once recognized, the fear itself drove her to action. She wasn't a frightened child any more. She was a Fleet commander who would finish with more than one star on her shoulders. Earned, not inherited. And she could not afford to be panicked by going downside. Admirals couldn't spend all their time in space. Besides, she had promised to share her memories of Abe with that remarkable designer woman.

Even after all these years, thinking of Abe made her feel safer. She shook her head at herself, then went to the bridge to give Arly her orders.

"I can't tell you more than what I know," she said, keeping her voice low. She trusted her crew, but no sense in their having to work to keep secrets. "Coromell wants a meeting out of his office. I'm taking Aygar along as being less obvious than one of the crew. Don't know how long it will take, or when we'll surface, but stay alert. If you can, monitor their longscans. I have an uneasy feeling that something may be out there, 'way out, and if that happens, you know what to do."

Arly looked unhappy. "I'm not breaking the *Zaid-Dayan* out of here without you, Captain."

"Don't expect you'll have to. But it won't do me any good if someone slams the planet while I'm on it. I'll carry a comm unit, of course. Buzz me on the ship's line if Ford or Lunzie show up."

"You're wearing a link?"

"No! They're too easy for someone else to track. I know the comm's signal is hard to home on, but it's better than advertising where the admiral is, since he wants the meeting secret."

"Are you sure?"

"Sure enough to risk my neck." Sassinak glanced around the bridge, and leaned closer. "To tell you the truth, *something's* got my hackles up straight, but I can't tell what. Ford's overdue. Lunzie, too. I don't know. Something. I hate to leave the ship, but I can't ignore the message. Just be careful."

"And you." Arly snapped a salute. Sassinak went back to her

quarters and changed into civilian clothes, as requested. Another
worry; in civilian clothes, she had no excuse for the "ceremonial"
weapons she could carry in uniform.

She was aware that her bearing would hint Fleet to any really
good observer. Why not simply wear her uniform? But orders,
assuming these to be genuine, were orders. She stopped by her
office and picked up the things she could carry in one of the
pouches currently in style. Aygar should be waiting at the access
port. He, at least, had sounded eager enough to go back to the
planet. Of course, he had spent only these few months in space;
he was a landsman at heart.

She was surprised to see Ensign Timran waiting with Aygar
when she came into the access bay. She nodded in answer to his
swift salute.

"Ensign." That should send him away quickly. To her surprise,
it did not. Her brows raised.

"Captain . . . ma'am . . ."

"Yes, Ensign?"

"Is there any chance that . . . uh . . . that Aygar and I could . . ."
Now what was *this*?

"Spit it out, Ensign, and hurry. We have a shuttle to catch."

"Could go downside together? I mean, you're going to be busy,
and he really needs someone along who . . ."

She saw in his face that her expression had changed.

"And just how do you know that I will be 'busy'?"

He reddened and said nothing, but his eyes flicked to Aygar.
Sassinak sighed.

"Ensign, if our guest has shared confidential information, you
should have the wit to pretend he did not. You surely heard the
announcement I made: no liberty, no leaves. Not my decision,
but FedCentral regulations. They don't trust Fleet here. And, if
by some mischance you *did* end up on the surface, that very distrust could get you in serious trouble."

"Yes, ma'am."

"Nor was I aware that you and Aygar were friends."

This time Aygar spoke up, with almost Tim's eagerness.

"He's stronger than he looks, this little one. We began working
out in the gym together, at the marine commander's suggestion."
Clever Currald, Sassinak thought. These two might even do each
other good.

"Even so, he can't come downside. Sorry. And you're going with me. You'll be busy enough yourself."

Timran still looked disconsolate. Sassinak grinned at him.

"Come now. I need the best shuttle-jockeys up *here*, just in case something breaks loose."

He brightened at once and Sassinak led Aygar through the access tube toward the Station shuttle bay.

They had met nothing to arouse suspicion, but Sassinak felt as tight-drawn as a strangling wire. Aygar had long since quit pointing out interesting shops or odd costumes. He'd lapsed into an almost sullen silence. Sassinak was more annoyed by this than she wanted to be. He was not, after all, Fleet. He could not be expected to react as a trained sailor or marine would.

They had walked out of the shuttle port with no visible tail, into a stifling afternoon made worse by the stinging brown haze over the city. Sassinak was no expert but she had made full use of the gleaming show windows of the shuttleport shopping mall. No one seemed to be following them. No one paused repeatedly to look in the windows when she did. She had been downside with Aygar before. Unless someone knew specifically of the meeting with Coromell, this ought to look very much like the previous trips.

She would be expected to take him to one of the monotonous gray buildings in which the prosecution attorneys were working up the case against Tanegli, or to Fleet's own gray precincts. Then on yet another walking tour of the sights, such as they were.

She had started as if for the Fleet offices, then, as instructed boarded one of the express subways bound for Ceylar East, one of the suburbs. None of those who boarded with them were still in their module when they got off and transferred to another line. They had zigged and zagged back and forth under the vast city until Sassinak herself was hardly sure exactly where they were.

Now, only a short distance from the designated meeting place, she wished she'd been born a Weft, with the ability to make eyes in the back of her head. The hot sun and smog made her head ache. She wanted to call Engineering and complain. There. Eklarik's Fantasies and Creations. Its sign was purple curlicues on green with mythical beasts in the corners. Not the sort of place she would ever go on her own; a signal to any follower, as far as she was concerned.

Did Admiral Coromell have a secret passion for historical costumes or antique musical instruments? She gave Aygar a nudge. His shoulders twitched, but he moved across the slideway traffic that way. Sassinak pushed aside the bead curtain and let it rattle closed behind her.

Inside, the shop smelled of potpourri and incense. A thread of smoke rose to a blue haze overhead. Close on either hand were two suits of armor, one smoothly burnished as if it were but iron skin, and the other worked into fantastic peaks and points, decorated with red silk tassels. Racks of costumes, topped with what Sassinak supposed were the appropriate headgear. Floppy hats, spiked helms, flat straw circles, bonnets drowned in ruffles and bows, a row of tiny red enameled cylinders like oversized pillboxes.

She took a step forward, kicked something that clattered, and realized that she had bumped a tall ceramic jar filled with swords. Swords? She lifted one, then realized it had neither edge nor point — a stage sword? It was not steel; the metal made a flat, unpromising sound when she tapped it with her finger. Cluttering the narrow aisles were toppling piles of boots, shoes, sandals; the footgear for the racked costumes, no doubt. Suspended overhead were masks, dozens — no, hundreds — in shapes and colors Sassinak had never imagined. She blinked. Aygar bumped into her from behind.

"What *is* this?" he began, as Sassinak caught a glimpse of someone moving toward them from the back of the shop. She raised her hand, and he quieted, though she could practically feel his resentment.

"May I help?" asked a breathy voice from the dimness. "I'm afraid Eklarik's not here right now, but if it's just normal rental?"

"I'm . . . I'm not sure." The message from Coromell had not specified whether Eklarik's shop assistant would do as well as the man himself. "It's about the *Pirates of Penzance*," she said, feeling like an idiot.

Her knowledge of musical productions was small. She'd had to look up that reference, and although it told her Gilbert and Sullivan were contemporaneous with Kipling, she knew nothing about the work itself. Or what result should follow from the mention of it.

"Ah," said the colorless little person who now came into view between another pair of mounted costumes, these obviously meant for the female form. One was white, a clinging drapery that left one shoulder bare, the other, a vast pouf of pale blue, heavily ornamented with bows, braid, ruching, buttons as if the maker had to prove that he knew how to do all that, bulged half-way across the aisle.

The assistant, between the two, looked so meek and unimportant, that Sassinak was instantly alarmed. No one could be that self-effacing.

"A policeman's lot . . ." said the assistant.

"Is not a happy one," Sassinak replied dutifully, thinking the same thing about the lot of Fleet commanders stuck onplanet in civilian clothes trying to play spy.

"You are the dark lady," said the assistant. Sassinak was still not sure what sex — and was beginning to wonder what race — the assistant might be. Short, slim, dressed in something darkish that rippled. "Your star is shining."

That had to refer to Admiral Coromell. She opened her mouth to say something, but found herself confronted with a crystal sphere slightly larger than she could have held in one hand. The assistant had two hands under it. The crystal gleamed.

"The star you follow," the assistant was saying in a tone that Sassinak would have assumed meant drunk, if one of her crew had used it. "It is dimly seen, in dark places, and often occluded by maleficent planets."

"You have a message for me?" prompted Sassinak when a long silence had followed that after the crystal globe had vanished again into the dimness.

"That *was* your message." A quizzical expression crossed that face, followed by: "You are familiar with the local bars, aren't you? You a sailor?"

Behind her, Aygar choked and Sassinak barely managed not to gulp herself.

"No," she said gently. "I'm not any more familiar with local bars than with . . . uh . . . costumes."

"Oh." Another long silence, during which Sassinak realized that the assistant's pupils were elliptical, and that the dark costume was actually fur. "I thought you would be. Try the Eclipse, two blocks down, and order a Planetwiper."

That was clear enough, but Sassinak wasn't sure she believed it was genuine.

"You . . ." she began.

The assistant withdrew behind the billowing blue satin skirt, and opened its mouth fully, revealing a double row of pointed teeth.

"I'm an orphan, too," it said, and vanished.

Sassinak shook her head.

"What *was* that?" breathed Aygar.

"I don't know. Let's go."

She didn't like admitting she'd never seen an alien like that before. She didn't like this whole setup.

The Eclipse displayed a violently pink and yellow sign, which at night must have made sleep difficult for anyone across the street. Sassinak glanced that way and saw only blank walls above the street-level shops. No beaded curtain here but a heavy door that opened to a hard shove and closed solidly behind them. A heavyworlder in gleaming gray plastic armor stood at one side — evidence of potential trouble, and its cure, all in one. A glance around showed Sassinak that her clothes did not quite fit in. Except for the overdressed trio at one table, clearly there to prey on customers, the women wore merchant-spacers' coveralls, good quality but not stylish. Most of the men wore the same, although two men had on business clothes, one with the crumpled gown of an attorney at court piled on the seat beside him. Sassinak supposed the little gray coil atop it was his ceremonial wig.

She was aware of sideways glances, but conversation did not stop. These people were too experienced for that. She led Aygar to one of the booths and dialled their order. Planetwipers had never been her favorite but, of course, she didn't have to drink the thing. Aygar leaned massive elbows on the table.

"Can you tell me what is going on, or are you trying to drive me crazy?"

"I'm not, and I don't know. I presume that at some point our party will arrive. At least I know what he looks like."

She was trying not to be too obvious about looking around. No one here of Coromell's age, or close to it. Surely they wouldn't have a third meeting place to find. Aygar took a long swallow of his drink.

"That's potent," she said quietly. "Best be careful."

He glowered at her. "I'm not a child. I don't even know why you . . ."

He stopped as someone stopped by their table. Tall silver-haired, erect. If Sassinak had not known Coromell, she might have believed this was he.

"Commander," he said quietly. "May I sit down?"

"Do join us," Sassinak said. She gestured to Aygar. "The young Iretan you may have heard so much about."

The older man nodded, but did not offer to shake hands. He wore an impeccable blue coverall, what she would have expected of a merchanter captain off-duty. One hand bore a ring that might have been an Academy ring, but the face was turned under where she could not see it. And his movements, his assurance, came from years of command, some kind of command. If he was not Admiral Coromell — and he wasn't — then who or what was he?

"There's been a slight misunderstanding," he said. "It is necessary to stay out of reach of compromised surveillance devices until . . ."

Sassinak never saw the flicker of light, only the surprised look on his face and the neat, crisped holes, five of them, in his face.

Instinct had her under the table and scrambling before the first blood oozed out. She heard a bellow and crash as Aygar tossed the table aside and came after her. Something sizzled and Aygar yelped. Then the whole place erupted in noise and motion.

Like all fights, it was over in less time than she could have described it. The experienced hit the floor and scuttled for shelter. The inexperienced screamed, flailed, and threw things that crashed and tinkled. Fumes from the shattered bottles stung her nose and eyes. Glass shards pricked her palms and knees.

Sassinak bumped into other scuttlers, caught sight of Aygar and yanked him down just as a pink streak ripped the air where he'd been and burst the windows out. She jerked hard on his wrist, trusting him to follow, as she worked her way through the undergrowth of the fight. Table standards, chair legs, bodies. Through the service door, and into a white-tiled kitchen. She was surprised to realize that the place sold food as well. More noise behind her, following. She slipped on the greasy wet floor, staggered, and yanked Aygar again.

"Come *on*, dammit!"

"But . . ." He threw a last glance over his shoulder, and whatever he saw propelled him in a great leap that ended with Aygar and Sassinak tangled out the back door, and flames bursting out behind them. "Snarks in a *bucket*!"

Sassinak struggled out from under the younger man and shook her head. Screams, more sounds of mayhem. She looked down the alley they'd landed in. She hated planets . . . living on them, at least. No one to keep things really shipshape. On the other hand, this filthy and disreputable bit of real estate offered hiding places no clean ship would. Aygar, she noted, had a bleeding gash down his face and several rips in his coverall, but no serious injury.

He was already up on one knee, looking surprisingly relaxed and comfortable for someone who had narrowly escaped death. He had probably saved her life with that last lunge for the back door.

"Thanks," she said, trying to figure out what to do with him. She'd thought of him more as deterrence than serious help if things turned nasty. And at the moment, they were about as nasty as she had seen in awhile.

"We should go," he pointed out. "I was told only Insystem had that sort of weaponry."

"We're going."

Another quick glance, and she chose the shorter end of the alley. Nothing happened on the first quick dash to cover behind a stinking trash bin with rusty streaks down its sides. Sassinak eyed the other back doors opening on the alley. Surely someone should have peeked? Unless the neighborhood were really that tough, in which case . . .

"There's someone behind the next one of these," Aygar said softly in her ear.

She eyed him with respect. "How d'you know?"

He shrugged. "I lived by hunting, remember? On Ireta, the things you didn't notice would hunt you. I heard something wrong."

"Great."

No weapons. No armor. And all her tricks were back in childhood, the tricks that worked on screen, and not in real life. Real life worked a lot better with real weapons.

"I can take them," Aygar went on.

She looked at him: all the eagerness appropriate to a young male in the prime of his pride and no military training whatever. And he wasn't hers, the way young Timran would have been. He was a civilian, under her oath of protection. She started to shake her head, but he hadn't waited.

Even knowing about the great strength his genes and his upbringing had developed, she was still surprised. Aygar picked up the entire trash bin with all its clinking, rattling, dripping, smelling contents, and hurled it down the alley to crash into the next. Someone yelped. Sassinak heard the flat crack of small-arms fire, then nothing.

Aygar was moving, rushing the barrier of the two trash bins crunched together. With a quick shrug, she followed, vaulting neatly into the mash of rotten vegetables and fruit peels on the far side. Aygar had neatly broken the neck of the ambusher. Sassinak picked herself out of the disgusting mess carefully and smiled at Aygar.

"Try not to kill them unless you have to," she heard herself say.

"I did," he said seriously. "Look!"

And sure enough, the Insystem guard had managed to hang onto his weapon even with a trash bin pinning him by the legs.

"Right. There are times . . . good job." At least she wouldn't have to worry about this one having post-combat hysterics. "Let's get out of this."

Aygar hesitated. "Should I take his weapon?"

"No, it's illegal. We'll be in enough trouble." We're already in enough trouble, she thought. "On second thought, yes. Take it. Why should the bad guys have all the advantages?"

Aygar pried it out of the man's hand and courteously offered it to her. Surprised, Sassinak let her eyebrows rise as she took it and tucked it into a side pocket. Then, swiping futilely at the stains on her coverall, she led them down the alley to the street.

By this time, sirens wailed nearby. With any luck, they would be on the other street. Sassinak motioned Aygar back. With that blood dripping down his face, he'd be better in hiding. Cautiously, she put her head around the corner. As if he'd been waiting for her, a stocky man in bright orange uniform bellowed and then blew a piercing whistle. Sassinak muttered a curse, and yanked Aygar into a run. No good going back into the alley. They'd have someone at the other end.

They pelted down the street, dodging oncoming pedestrians. Sassinak expected at least one of them to try stopping them, but none did. Behind them, the whistle-blower fell steadily behind. Sassinak led them right at the first corner, slowing to an almost-polite jog as she stepped on the first slideway. Aygar, beside her, wasn't even breathing hard.

Then he gripped her wrist. Across the street they were on, ahead, was a cordon of orange uniforms on the pedestrian overpass above the slideways. They carried something that looked uncomfortably like riot-control weapons. Sassinak and Aygar edged back off the slideway. This street, like the other, had a miscellany of small shops and bars.

No time to choose. Sassinak ducked into the first she saw, hoping it had a useful back entrance.

"You look terrible, dearie," said someone out of the dimness.

Sassinak started to answer when she realized the young woman was looking at Aygar. Who was looking at her.

"We don't have time for this," she said, tugging at Aygar's suddenly immobile bulk.

"Men always have time for this," said the young woman, setting her various fringes in motion. "As for you, hon, why don't you take a look in the other room."

Someone from there had already come to the archway. Sassinak ignored him and tried the only thing she could think of.

"We need to find Fleur. Now. It's an emergency."

"Fleur! What do you know about her?"

An older woman stormed through the draperies of another archway. Somewhat to Sassinak's surprise, she had the trim, brisk appearance of a successful professional which, in a sense, she was. "Who are you, anyway?"

"I need to find her. That's all I can say."

"Security after you?" When Sassinak didn't answer immediately, the woman moved past them to peer through the outer window. "They're after somebody and you've got bloodstains and gods know what stinking up your clothes. Tell me now! You?"

"Yes. I'm . . ."

"Don't tell me."

Sassinak obeyed. Here, in this place, someone else commanded.

"Come." When Aygar cast a last look after the young woman who had greeted him, their guide snorted. "Listen, laddy-o, you're looking at a week's salary, unless you're ranked higher than I think, and you'd be dead before you enjoyed it if we don't get you under cover."

Then, as she led them down a passage, she shouted back to her household, "Lee, get yourself in there with Ell. I don't think the locals know you yet. Pearl, you saw Lee come in. The woman with him, if they think they saw one, was our street tout." She muttered over her shoulder to Sassinak. "Not that that'll hold five minutes if they really saw you, but they might not have. It's getting to our busy time of day, so there's a chance. In here."

In here was a tiny square office, crowded with a desk and two chairs. The woman pulled open a drawer and slapped an aid kit down on the surface.

"He won't pass anywhere, with all that blood. Clean him up. I'll be back with another coverall for you."

Aygar sat in one of the chairs while Sassinak cleaned the shallow gash and put a sticker over it. He did look less conspicuous with the blood off his face. She used several more stickers to hold the rents in his coverall together. The scratches under them had long stopped bleeding.

The woman came back with a cheap working coverall of tough tan fabric and tossed it to Sassinak.

"Get that smelly thing off so I can run it through the shredder in the kitchen. What'd you do, camp out in a grocer's trash bin?"

"Not exactly." Sassinak didn't want to explain. She handed Aygar the gun out of her pocket before peeling off her coverall and slipping into the other one. Aygar, she noticed, was trying not to watch while the woman stared at her.

"You must be Fleet," she said, more quietly. "You've got muscles, for a woman your age. Over forty, aren't you?"

"A little, yes."

The tan coverall was a bit short in the arms and legs, but ample in the body. Sassinak transferred her ID and the handcom into its pockets and then took the gun back from Aygar.

"Ever heard of Samizdat?" The woman's voice was even lower, barely above a murmur.

Sassinak stared, remembering that bleak afternoon when Abe had told her a tiny bit about that organization.

"A little," she said cautiously.

"Hmm. Fleet. Samizdat. Fleur. Tell you what, honey, you'd better be honest, or I swear I'll hunt you to the last corner of the galaxy, my own self, and stake your gizzard in the light of some alien sun, so I will. That Fleur's a lady, saved my life more'n once, and never thinks the worse of a girl for doing what she has to."

"She's a Fleet captain," said Aygar.

Both women glared at him.

"I didn't want to know that," said the woman. "A Fleet captain with undisciplined crew . . ."

Before Aygar could say anything, Sassinak said, "He's not crew; he's civilian, an important witness against planet pirates, and they're trying to silence him. We were supposed to have a quiet meeting but it didn't stay quiet."

"Ah. Then you *do* know about Samizdat. Well, we'll have to get you out of here later, and I'll send word to Fleur. . . ." She stopped, as voices erupted down the passage. "Rats. Up out of that chair, laddy-o, and quick about it."

Aygar stood, and the woman shoved until he flattened against the wall. Sassinak, guessing what she wanted, lifted the chairs onto the desk. Beneath the worn carpet was the outline of a trapdoor. The woman didn't have to urge quickness, not with the words "search" and "illegal aliens" and "renegade posing as Fleet" booming down the hall.

First came a straight drop down five feet to a landing above a short stair. Aygar had scarcely bent to get his head below floor level when the trap banged down, leaving them in complete darkness. Sassinak could hear muffled thumps and scrapes as the rug and chairs went back atop it. She had made it almost to the next level, but stopped where she was, afraid to move in the darkness lest she trip and make a noise. Aygar crept down three steps and touched her shoulder.

"What now?" he asked.

"Shhh. We hope the searchers don't know about the trapdoor."

For the first time since trouble started, Sassinak had leisure to think about it and about her ship. She had been fooled by the original communication because it was in Fleet slang. That implied, but did not prove, that someone in Fleet was trying to get her killed. Whoever it was knew enough about Coromell to suspect that his name would lure her and that she would know only his general appearance. He was famous enough. It wouldn't be hard for anyone to know his height, his age, and find someone reasonably close to impersonate him.

But why all the complexity? Why not simply have someone assassinate her, or Aygar, or both, as they were on their way out of the shuttleport, or any place between? And assuming those orange uniforms were the police, why were the authorities on the side of the attackers?

She tried to think what someone might have said to convince the local police that she and Aygar were dangerous criminals causing trouble. Fleeing a bar fight was only common sense. She'd originally thought to call in to Coromell's office as soon as she found a telecom booth. And what was happening to her ship, topside? She wanted to pull out the comm unit and find out, but dared not with searchers after them.

Time waiting in the darkness had strange dimensions. Endless, seamless, compressed by fear and stretched by anticipation: she had no idea how long it was before she dared extend a cautious foot to the next lower step. She edged down, drawing Aygar after her. Just in case they found the trapdoor, she'd rather be around a corner, behind something, under something. Another step, and another.

When the lights went on, her vision blanked for a moment. Aygar gasped. Now she could see the long narrow room. She ran down the last few steps, Aygar behind her, and looked for a place to hide. There? An angle of wall, perhaps a support for something overhead? She ducked around it, out of sight of the stairs. Then a voice crackled from some hidden speaker.

" . . . know you have a basement, Sera Vanlis, and you'd better cooperate. This is nothing to play games about."

"I still don't see a warrant." Not quite defiance, but not calm confidence, either. "I've nothing to hide, but I'm not setting precedent by letting you search without one."

"I'll call for one."

A pause, then the sound of speech Sassinak could not distinguish. Did the sound go both ways? She had to trust not, had to hope the woman had hit some hidden switch to give them both warning and a way out. But nothing looked like a way out. No doors, in the long opposite wall, or the far end. No door at either end. A fat column of cables and pipes came out of the ceiling, entered and exited a massive meter box covered with dials, and disappeared into a grated opening in the floor.

Aygar nodded toward it. Sassinak looked closer. Not big enough for Aygar and she wasn't sure she could slither alongside the bundled utilities, but it gave her an idea. If this were a ship, there'd be some kind of repair access to the utility conduits. She couldn't find it, and the conversation overhead could have only one ending.

Then Aygar picked up a filing cabinet, one of a row along the far wall, but in line with the path of the cables, and there it was. A flat circle of metal, with a pop-up handle, and under it a vertical shaft with a ladder fixed to one side. She would have had trouble getting the cover free, and up, but Aygar's powerful fingers lifted it as easily as a piece of toast on a tray.

Sassinak eeled into the hole, slipped easily down the ladder to give Aygar room, and murmured "How're you going to cover it after us?"

"Don't worry."

Nonetheless, she did worry as he slipped the access cover behind the next file cabinet over, and backed down into the hole, dragging the file cabinet with him. Surely he couldn't possibly move it all the way into place, just with his hands? He could.

They were in the dark again, the top of the shaft sealed with the file cabinet, but she could hear the proud grin in his voice when he said, "Unless they heard that, they won't know. And I think it's been used that way before. That cabinet's not as heavy as a full one would be."

"Good job."

She patted his leg and backed on down the ladder. They ought to come to a cross-shaft . . . and her foot felt nothing below, then something uneven. She ran her foot over it in the dark, momentarily wondering why she'd been stupid enough not to bring along a handlight. Lumpy, long, slick . . . probably the bundled utilities. She couldn't quite reach them with her hand while clinging to the ladder. She'd have to drop. Aygar's foot tapped her head, and she touched his ankle, a slight sideways shove that she hoped he would understand as "Wait!"

✧ CHAPTER FOURTEEN

"What about a light?" asked Aygar softly.

Sassinak counted to ten, reminding herself that he was not, despite his talents, a trained soldier. He would not have thought to tell her before that he had a light.

"Fine."

Above her, a dim light came on, bright enough to dark-adapted eyes. Shadows danced crazily as he passed it down. Below, the cross tunnel was twice the diameter of theirs, its center full of pipes, with a narrow catwalk along one side. Sassinak eased down, swung her legs onto the catwalk, and guided Aygar's feet. She had to crouch a little; he was bent uncomfortably. She touched his arm and jerked her head to one side. They would move some distance before they dared talk much.

Twenty meters down the tunnel, Sassinak paused and doused the handlight. No sound or sight of pursuit. She closed her eyes, letting them adapt to darkness again, and wishing she had even the helmet to her armor. Even without the link to the cruiser's big computers, the helmet onboard with sensors could have told her exactly what lay ahead, line-of-sight.

She opened her eyes to darkness. Complete . . . no. Not complete. Ahead, so dim she could hardly make it out, a distant red-orange point. She squinted, then remembered to shift her gaze off-center and back across. *Two* red-orange points. She leaned out to peer back past Aygar. Another, and another beyond that.

Marker lights for maintenance workers. That would be the most harmless. Alternatives included automatic cameras that could send their images straight to some police station without ever giving them enough light to see. Or automatic lasers, linked to heat and motion sensors, designed to rid the tunnels of vermin.

She hated planets. There might even *be* vermin in these tunnels. But when there were no choices, only fools refused chances . . . so Abe had said. She edged sideways along the catwalk, moving with ship-trained neatness in that unhandy space. Aygar had more trouble. She could hear him thumping and stumbling, and had to hope that there were no sound sensors down here. She used the handlight as seldom as she could.

Moving past the first dim light in the tunnel's roof set off no alarms she could sense, but then a good system wouldn't tell *her*. She was sweating now in the tunnel's unmoving air, and wondering just how good that air was. Between the first and second lights, she felt a sudden draft along her side, and turned the light on the tunnel wall. Waist high, another grill, this one rectangular. A silent, slightly cooler breath came from it. She could hear no fan, not even the hiss of air movement. Then for an instant it changed, sucking against the back of her hand, then stilled, then returned as before.

Nothing but a pressure-equalizing connector, probably from the subway system, she thought. Nice to know they were connected to something else with air, though she'd rather have found a route to the surface. She tapped Aygar's arm, and they crouched beneath the vent to rest briefly.

"I'm not sure who's after us," she said. "That wasn't the man I was supposed to meet, back there, just someone the right age and size, but not the same.

Aygar ignored this. "Do you know where we are? Can we get back?"

"Not the right questions. To get back, we have to figure out who's trying to kill us. At this point we don't know if they're after you, me, or both. And why."

She could think of reasons both ways. All three ways, and even a few more. Why send her to meet a fake Coromell and then kill *him*? It could hardly have been a mistake; the difference between a white-haired old man and a dark-haired woman was clear to the stupidest assassin. It couldn't have been bad marksmanship, not with the cluster that had destroyed the man's face. Had there been two different sets of conspirators whose plots intersected in wild confusion?

"You said that wasn't Coromell." Aygar's voice was quiet, his tone alert but not anxious. "Did the one who killed him know that?"

"I'm not sure." She was not sure of a lot, except that she wished she'd stayed on her ship. So much for confronting old fears. "If that had been Coromell, and if I'd also been killed, perhaps the next round of fire, you'd have been the ranking witness for Tanegli's trial. And, as you've said often enough, you don't know anything about the dealings Tanegli had with the other conspirators. All you could do is testify that he lied to you, led you to believe that Ireta was yours. If there were some way Coromell's death could be blamed on me . . ."

"And why were all those other people waiting for us outside?" Aygar asked.

Clearly his mind ran on a different track. Natural, with his background. But it was still a good question.

"Hmm. Suppose they plan to kill Coromell in the bar. They expect me to run, with you, just as I did. The only smart thing to do in something like that is get out. So they've got others outside, to kill us. Or me. Then they could pin Coromell's death on me, discredit Fleet, and any testimony I bring to the trial."

"What would happen to the *Zaid-Dayan*? Who is your heir?"

"Heir? Ships aren't personal property! Fleet would assign another . . ." She stopped short, struck by another possibility. "Aygar, you're a genius, and you don't even know it. Testimony is one thing: a ship of the line is another. My *Zaid* is possibly the most dangerous ship of its class. If it's the *ship* they fear and want to render helpless, then by taking me out or even keeping me onplanet while Coromell's death is investigated, that would do it. It would be Standard weeks before another captain arrived. They might even seal the ship in dock."

And why would someone be that upset about a cruiser at the orbital station, a cruiser whose weapons were locked down? What did someone fear that cruiser could do? Cruisers weren't precision instruments. Despite her actions on Ireta, cruisers were designed as strategic platforms, capable of dealing with, say, a planetary rebellion, or an invasion from space. Or both.

Sassinak was up again before she realized she was going to move. "Come on," she said. "We've got to get back to the ship."

As if that were going to be easy. She started looking for another access port. Soon enough this tunnel would come to someone's attention, even if they didn't find the escape hatch from that . . . place. Her mind was working now, full-speed,

running the possibilities of several sets of plotters. It could reduce
to one set, if they had some way to interfere with Coromell's return and thought the singed corpse could pass as his for long
enough to get her in legal trouble. Or suppose they'd captured
the real Coromell and could produce his body.

Not her problem. Not now. Now all she had to do was find a
way out, to the surface, call Arly and get a shuttle to pick them up.
She no longer cared about the legal aspects of action.

The next access port led them down, deeper into the city's
underground warren of service tunnels. This one was lighted and
the single rail down the middle of the floor indicated regular
maintenance monorail service. Plastic housings covered the bundled cables along one wall, the pipes running along the other.
Sassinak noted that the symbols seemed to be the same as those
used in Fleet vessels, the colored stripes and logos she knew so
well, but she didn't try to tap a water pipe to make sure. Not yet.
They could walk along the catwalk beside the monorail without
stooping. With the light, they could move far more quickly.

That didn't help if they didn't know where they were going,
Sassinak thought grimly. The port they'd come out of had a number on the reverse: useless information without the map
reference.

"We're still going the same way," Aygar said.

She stared at him, surprised again. He was taking all this much
better than she would have predicted.

"It's easy to lose one's way without references," she began, but
he was holding up a little button. "What's that?"

"It's a mapper," Aygar said. "One of the students I met at the
Library said I should have one or I'd get lost."

"A locator transmitter?" Her heart sank. If he was carrying
that, their unknown enemies could simply wait, watching the
trace on a computer, until they came up again.

"No. He said there were two kinds, the kind that told people
where you were so they could find you and help you, and the kind
that told you where you were for yourself. Tourists carry the first
kind, he said, and rich people who expect their servants to come
pick them up, but students like the second. So that's what I
bought."

She had not realized he'd been on his own long enough to do
anything like that. Thinking back . . . there were hours and hours

in which he'd been left at the Library entrance. She'd taken him there, or the FSP prosecutors had, between depositions or conferences. She hadn't even known he'd met anyone else.

"How does it work?"

"Like this." He flicked it with a thumbnail and a city map, distorted by the casing of the cables, appeared on the wall of the tunnel. A pulsing red dot must be their position. The map seemed to zoom closer, and letters and numbers replaced part of the crisscross of lines. "E-84, RR-72." Aygar flicked the thing again and a network of yellow lines appeared. There they were, in what was labelled *Maintenance access tunnel* 66-43-V. "Where do we want to go?"

"I'm . . . not sure." Until she knew who their enemies were, she didn't know where it might be safe to surface and call Arly. Or if even that would be a good idea. "Where's the nearest surface access?"

The red dot distorted into a line that crept along the yellow of their tunnel, then turned orange.

"That means go up," Aygar said. "If we have to go down to get somewhere, our line will turn purple." It made sense, in a way.

"Let's go, then."

She let him lead the way. He seemed to know how the mapper worked. She certainly did not. She wanted to ask about scale, but they'd been in one place too long already. Her neck itched with the certainty that pursuit was close behind.

"If you have any more little goodies, like the light, or the mapper, why not tell me now?" It came out a bit more waspish than she intended.

"I'm sorry," he said. He actually sounded abashed. "I didn't know . . . There hasn't been time."

"Never mind. I'm just very glad you opted for this kind of mapper and not the other."

"I didn't think I'd need it, really," he said. "I don't get lost easily. But Gerstan was being so friendly." He shrugged.

Sassinak felt another bubble of worry swell up beside the cluster that already filled her head. A friendly student who just happened to take an interest in the well-being of a foreigner?

"Tell me more about Gerstan," she said as calmly as she could.

Gerstan, it seemed, was "a lot like Tim." Sassinak managed not to say what she thought and hoped Aygar had made a mistake.

Gerstan had been friendly, open, helpful. He had sympathized
with Aygar's position. Because, of course, Aygar had explained all
about Ireta. Sassinak swallowed hard and let Aygar go on talking
as they walked. Gerstan had helped him use the Library computers to access the databases, and he had even said that it was
possible to bypass the restriction codes.

"Really?" said Sassinak, hoping her ears weren't standing right
straight out. "That's pretty hard, I'd always heard."

Aygar's explanation did not reassure her. Gerstan, it seemed,
had friends. He had never explained just who they were: just
friends whose specialty was intercepting data transmissions and
diverting them.

"What kind of transmissions?"

"He didn't say, exactly." Aygar sounded slightly grumpy about
that, as if in retrospect Gerstan didn't seem quite as helpful. "He
just said that if I ever needed to get into the databases, or . . . or
slip a loop. whatever that is, he could help. Said it was easy, if you
had the knack. All the way up to the Parchandri, he said."

An icy spike went straight down Sassinak's back at that. "Are
you sure?" she said, before she could stop it.

"Sure of what?" Aygar was lolloping ahead, apparently quite
relaxed.

"That he said 'all the way up to Parchandri'?"

"The *Parchandri*. Yes that's what he said. Why?"

He glanced back over his shoulder and Sassinak hoped her
face revealed nothing but calm interest. Parchandri. Inspector
General Parchandri? Who should not be here anyway, but at
Fleet Headquarters. As if they were printed in the fiery letters in
the air before her, she could see that initiation code, supposedly
coming from the Inspector General's office. . . .

"I'm just trying to figure things out," she said to Aygar who had
glanced back again.

Should she explain any of this to Aygar? His own problems
were complicated enough, and besides he had no real right to
Fleet's darker secrets. But if something happened . . . She shook
her head fiercely. What was going to happen was that she would
be laughing at the Parchandri's funeral. If, in fact, the Parchandri
was guilty of Abe's murder.

At intervals they passed access ports on either side, above,
below. Each had a number stenciled on it. Each looked much the

same as the others. Had it not been for Aygar's mapper, Sassinak would have had no idea which way to go.

She had been hearing the faint whine for some moments before it registered, and then she jumped forward and tapped Aygar's shoulder.

"Listen."

He shrugged. "This whole planet makes noise," he said. "No one can hear anything in a city. Nothing that means anything, that is."

"How far to where we go up?" asked Sassinak. The whine was marginally louder.

"Half a kilometer, perhaps, if I'm reading this right."

"Too far." She looked around and saw an access hatch less than twenty meters ahead, on their side of the monorail, below the cable housing. "We'll take that one."

"But why?"

The whine had sharpened and a soft brush of air touched his face. He whirled at once and raced for the hatch. Sassinak caught up with him, helped wrestle it open. At once, an alarm rang out, and a flashing orange light. Sassinak bit back a curse. If she ever got off this planet, she would never, under any circumstances, go downside again! Aygar was dropping his legs through the hatch, but Sassinak spotted another, only five meters farther on.

"I'll open that one, too. Then they won't know which."

She could not hear the whine of the approaching monorail car over the clamoring alarm, but the air pressure shifts were clear enough. She ran as she had not had to run for years, scrabbled at the hatch cover, threw it back, and winced as another alarm siren and light came on. Then back to the first, and in. Aygar had wisely retreated down the ladder, giving her room. A quick yank and the hatch closed over them. They were in darkness again. She could still hear the siren whooping. From this one? From the other? Both?

All the way down that ladder, much longer than any they'd taken before, she scolded herself. She didn't even know the monorail car was manned. It might have no windows, no sensors. They might have been able to stand quietly, watch it go by, and then walk out following Aygar's mapper. Then again maybe not. Second-guessing didn't help deal with consequences. She took a long, calming breath, and reminded herself not to tighten up. Although one thing after another had gone wrong, they *were* alive, unwounded, and uncaught. That had to be worth something. Her foot touched Aygar's head. He had reached the bottom of the ladder.

"I can't find a hatch," he said. His voice rang softly in the echoing dark chamber. "I'll try light."

Sassinak closed her eyes, and opened them when she saw pink against her lids. They were at the bottom of a slightly curving, near-vertical shaft, and nothing marked the sides at the bottom. Not so much as a roughly welded seam. Aygar's breath was loud and ragged.

"We . . . have to find a way out. There has to be a way out!"

"We will."

She felt almost comfortable in shafts and tunnels, but Aygar had had a wilderness to run in until he boarded the *Zaid-Dayan*, He'd done remarkably well for someone with no ship training, but this dead end in a narrow shaft was too much. She could smell his sudden nervous sweat; his hand on her leg trembled.

"It's all right," she said, the voice she might have used on a nervous youngster on his first cruise. "We passed it, that's all. Follow me up but *quietly*."

It was not that far up, a circular hatch in the shaft across from the ladder, easily reached. Sassinak just had her hand firmly on the locking ring, ready to turn it, when it was yanked away from her, and she found herself pinned in a beam of brilliant light.

"Well." The voice was gruff, and only slightly surprised. "And what have we here? Not the Pollys, this time."

Squinting against the brilliance, Sassinak could just see a dark form outlined by more light beyond, and the gleam of light down a narrow tube: a weapon, no doubt.

"How many?" demanded the voice.

Sassinak wondered if Aygar could hide below, but realized he couldn't, not in the grip of claustrophobia.

"Two," she said crisply.

"Y'all come on outa there, then," said the voice.

The light withdrew just enough to give them room. Sassinak slid through feet-first, and found herself coming out of a waist-high hatch in a horizontal tunnel. Aygar followed her, his tanned face pale around the mouth and eyes, and dripping with sweat. Carefully, as if she were doing this on her own ship, Sassinak closed the hatch and pushed the locking mechanism.

Facing them were five rough-looking figures in much-patched jumpsuits. Two held obvious weapons that looked like infantry assault rifles, one had a long knife spliced to a section of metal conduit, and one held the light that still blinded them. The last lounged against the tunnel wall, eyeing them with something between greed and disgust. "Y'all rang the doorbell, up there?" that one asked. The same husky voice, from a stocky frame that might be man or woman — impossible to tell, with layers of ragged clothes concealing its real shape.

"Didn't mean to," said Sassinak. "Got a little lost."

"More'n a little. Douse the light, Jemi."

The spotlight blinked off, and Sassinak closed her eyes a moment to let them adjust. When she opened them again, the woman who had held the spotlight was stuffing it in a backpack. The two rifles had not moved. Neither had Sassinak. Aygar made an indeterminate sound behind her, not quite a growl. She suspected that he liked the look of the homemade spear. The person who had spoken pushed off the wall and stood watching them.

"Can you give me one good reason why we shouldn't slit and strip you right now?"

Sassinak grinned; that had been bravado, not decision.

"It'd make a big mess next to the shaft we came out of," she said. "If someone does follow down here . . ."

"They will," growled one of the rifle-bearers. The muzzle shifted a hair to one side. "Should be goin', Cor. . . ."

"Wait. You're not the usual trash we get down here, and there's plenty of trouble up top. Who are you?"

"Who are the Pollys?" Sassinak countered.

"You got the Insystem Federation Security Police after you, and you don't know who they are?"

A twin of the jolt she'd felt hearing Parchandri's name went down her spine. Insystem Security's active arm was supposed to confine itself to ensuring the safety of governmental functions. She'd assumed their pursuers were planet pirate hired guns, or (at worst) a section of city police.

"I didn't know that's who we had after us. Orange uniforms?"

"Riot squads. Special action teams. Sheee! All right. You tell us who you are or you're dead right here, mess and all."

The rifles were steady again, and Sassinak thought the one with the spear probably knew how to use it.

"Commander Sassinak," she said. "Fleet, captain of the heavy cruiser *Zaid-Dayan*, docked in orbit . . ."

"And I'm Luisa Paraden's hairdresser! You'll do better than that or . . ."

"She really is," Aygar broke in. The other's eyes narrowed as she heard his unfamiliar accent. "She brought me . . ."

Sassinak had a hand on the hatch rim; a distant vibration thrummed in her fingers.

"Silence," she said, not loudly but with command.

All movement ceased. The silence seemed to quiver.

"They're coming. I can feel a vibration." The one who'd spoken growled out a low curse, then said. "Come on, then! Hurry! We'll straighten you later."

They followed along the tunnel, a bare chill tube of gray-green metal floored with something resilient. Under that, Sassinak thought, must be whatever the tunnel was actually for. She was aware of the man behind her with a rifle, of Aygar's growing confusion and panic, of the ache in her own legs.

She quickly lost track of their backtrail. They moved too fast, through too many shafts and tunnels, with no time to stop and fix references. She wondered if Aygar was doing any better. His hunting experience might help. Her ears popped once, then again, by which she judged they were now deep beneath the planet's surface. Not where she wanted to be, at all. But alive. She reminded herself of that; they might easily have been dead.

Finally their captors halted. They had come to a well-lit barnlike space opening off one of the smaller tunnels. Crates and metal drums filled one end to the low ceiling. In the open space, ragged blankets and piles of rags marked sleeping places on the floor; battered plastic carriers held water and food. Several huddled forms were asleep, others hunched in small groups, a few paced restlessly. The murmur of voices stopped and Sassinak saw pale faces turn toward them, stiff with fear and anger.

"Brought us in some uptowners," said the leader of their group. "One of 'em claims to be a Fleet captain."

Raucous laughter at that, more strained than humorous.

"That big hunk?" asked someone.

"Nah. The . . . *lady*." Sassinak had never heard the word used as an insult before, but the meaning was clear. "Got the Pollys after her, and didn't even know what an orange uniform meant."

A big-framed man carrying too little flesh for his bones shrugged and stepped forward. "An offworlder wouldn't. Maybe she is . . ."

"Offworlder? Could be. But Fleet? Fleet don't rummage in the basement. They don't come off their fancy ships and get their feet dirty. Sit up in space, clean and free, and let us rot in slavery, that's Fleet!" The leader spat juicily past Sassinak's foot, then smirked at her.

"I suspect I know as much about slavery as most of you," Sassinak said quietly.

"From claiming to chase slavers while taking Parchandri bribes?" This was someone else, a skinny hunched little man whose face was seamed with old scars.

"From being one," said Sassinak. Silence, amazement on those tense faces. Now they were all listening; she had one chance, she reckoned. She met each pair of eyes in turn, nodding slowly, holding their attention. "Yes, it's true. When I was a child, the colony I lived in was raided. I saw my parents die. I held my sister's body. I never saw my little brother again. They left him behind. He was too young. . . ." Her voice trembled; even now, even here. She forced steadiness into it. "And so I was a slave." She paused, scanning those faces again. No hostility now, less certainty. "For some years, I'm not sure how many. Then the ship I'd been sold to was captured by Fleet and I had a chance to finish school, go to the Academy, and chase pirates myself. That's why."

"*If* that's true, that's why the Pollys are after you," said the group leader.

"But how can we know?"

"Because she's telling the truth," said Aygar. Everyone looked at him, and Sassinak was surprised to see him blush. "She came to my world, Ireta. She brought me here on her cruiser for the trial."

"And you were born incapable of lying?" asked the leader.

Aygar seemed to swell with rage at such a sarcasm. Sassinak held up her hand and hoped he'd obey the signal.

"This is my Academy ring," she said, stripping it from her finger and holding it out. "My name's engraved inside, and the graduation date's on the outside."

"Sas-sin-ak," the leader said, reading it slowly. "Well it's evidence though I'm not sure of what."

Sassinak took the ring back, and the leader might have said more, but a newcomer jogged into the room from the tunnel, carrying a flat black case that looked like a wide-band communications tap. Without preamble, he came up to the leader and started talking.

"The Pollys have an all-stations out for a renegade fleet captain, name of Sassinak, and a big guy, civilian. They've murdered an Admiral Coromell. . . ."

The leader turned to Sassinak. The messenger seemed to notice them for the first time, and his eyes widened.

"Is that true?"

"No."

"No which? You didn't murder anyone, or you didn't murder Coromell?"

"We didn't murder anyone and the dead man isn't Admiral Coromell."

"How do you — oh."

Sassinak smiled. "We were there, supposedly meeting Admiral Coromell, when someone of his age and general appearance sat down with us and promptly got holes in the head. We left in a hurry, and trouble followed us. Whoever killed him may think that was Coromell. It'll take a careful autopsy to prove it's not. Or the real Coromell showing up. I don't know who sent us a fake Coromell, or why, or who killed the fake Coromell, or why. Unless they just wanted to get us into trouble. Aygar's testimony, and mine, could be crucial in the trial coming up."

Blank looks indicated that no one had heard of, or cared about, any trial coming up.

"His name Aygar?" asked the messenger. " 'Cause that's who they're after, besides Sassinak."

Now a buzz of conversation rose from the others; no one would meet Sassinak's eyes. She could feel their fear prickling the air.

"You mentioned Parchandri," she said, regaining their attention. "Who is this Parchandri?"

To her surprise, the leader relaxed with a bark of laughter. "Good question! Who is *this* Parchandri? Who is *which* Parchandri would do as well. If you're Fleet, and have never been touched . . ."

"Well, she wouldn't, not if she'd been a slave," said the big man. "They'd know better." He turned to Sassinak. "Parchandri's a family, got rich in civil service and Fleet just like the Paradens did in commerce. *Just* like — takin' bribes and giving 'em, blackmailing, kidnapping, slicin' the law as thin as they could, and pilin' the profits on thick."

"I know there was a Parchandri Inspector General," Sassinak said slowly.

"Oh, that one. Yeah, but that's not all. Not even in Fleet. You got three Parchandris in the IG's staff alone, and two in Procurement, and five in Personnel. That's main family: using the surname openly. Doesn't count the cousins and all who use other names. There's a nest of Parchandri in the EEC, controls all the colony applications, that sort of thing. There's a Parchandri in Insystem Security, for that matter. And the head of the family is right here on FedCentral, making sure that what goes on in Council doesn't cause the family any trouble."

His casual delivery made it more real. Sassinak asked the first question that popped into her head.

"Are they connected to the Paradens?"

"Sure thing. But not by blood. They're right careful not to intermarry or anything that would show up on the computers. Even though they've got people in Central Data. Say a Paraden family company wants to open a colony somewhere but they're down the list. Somehow those other applications get lost, or something's found wrong with 'em. Complaints against a Paraden subsidiary get lost real easy, too."

"Are other families involved?" Sassinak noticed the sudden shifting of eyes. She waited. Finally the leader nodded.

"There have been. Not all the big families. The Chinese stay out of it; they don't need it. But a few smaller ones, mostly in transport. Any that gets in a little ways has to stay in for the whole trip. They don't like whistle-blowers, the Parchandri. Things happen." The leader took a deep breath. "You're getting into stuff I can't answer unless I know . . . something more. You say you were a slave, and Fleet got you out so you joined Fleet . . ."

"That's right."

"Well, did you ever hear, while you were a slave, of a . . . a kind of group? People that . . . knew things?"

Sassinak nodded. "Samizdat," she said very softly.

The leader's tense face relaxed slightly.

"I'll chance it." A broad, strong hand reached out to shake hers in a firm grip. "I'm Coris. That was my wife who speared you with the spotlight." He grinned, a suddenly mischievous grin. "Did I fool you?"

"Fool me?"

"With all this padding. We find it useful to disguise our body outlines. I've been listed in official reports as a 'slightly obese middle-aged woman of medium stature.'" He had reached under his outer coverall to remove layers of rag stuffing, suddenly looking many pounds lighter and much more masculine. Off came a wig that Sassinak realized looked just like those in the costume shop, revealing a balding pate. "They don't worry as much about stray women in the tunnels. Although you, a Fleet commander, may give them a heart attack."

"I hope to," said Sassinak. She wasn't sure what to make of someone who cheerfully pretended to be the opposite sex. "But I'm a little . . . confused."

Coris chuckled. "Why shouldn't you be? Sit over here and have some of our delicious native cuisine and exquisite wine, and we'll talk about it."

He led her to an empty pile of blankets and gestured. She and Aygar sat. She was glad to let her aching legs relax.

"Delicious native cuisine" turned out to be a nearly tasteless cream-colored mush. "Straight from the food processors," someone explained. "Much easier to liberate before they put the flavorings or texture in . . . nasty stuff, but nutritious." The wine was water, tapped from a water main and tepid, but drinkable.

"Let's hear your side of it," suggested Coris.

Sassinak swallowed the last of the mush she'd been given and took a swallow of water to clear her throat. Around her, the ragged band had settled down, relaxed but alert.

"What if they are searching for us?" she asked. "Shouldn't we . . . ?"

He waved his hand, dismissing the problem.

"They are looking, of course, but they haven't passed any of our sensors. And we do have scouts out. Go on."

Sassinak gave a concise report on what had happened from the arrival of Coromell's message. Highly irregular, but she judged it necessary. If she died down here, not that she intended to, someone had to know the truth. They listened attentively, not interrupting, until she told about entering the pleasure-house.

"You went to *Vanlis*?" That sounded both surprised and angry.

"I didn't know what it was," said Sassinak, hoping that didn't sound critical. "It was the nearest door, and she helped us."

She told about that, about the woman's reaction to Fleur's name. She felt the prickling tension of this group's reaction. But no one said anything so she went on with the story until the group had "caught" them.

"Trouble, trouble, trouble," muttered Coris, now far less cocky.

"Sorry."

And she was, though she felt much better now that the taste-less food, the water and the short rest had done their work. She glanced at Aygar, who was picking moodily at the bandage on his face. He seemed to be over his fright.

"You're like a thread sewing together things we hoped they'd never connect," Jemi said softly. Coris' wife was a thin blonde. She looked older than either Sassinak or Coris, but it might be only worry. "Eklarik's shop . . . Varis' place . . . Fleur . . . Samizdat . . . they aren't stupid, you know. They'll put it together fast enough when they have time to think. I hope Varis has warned Fleur. Otherwise . . ."

She didn't need to finish that. Sassinak shivered. She could feel their initial interest fading now into a haze of fear and hostility. She had endangered their precarious existence. It was all so stupid. She had suspected trouble, hadn't she? She had known better than to go haring off into the unknown to meet some admiral whose staff insisted he was off hunting. And because she'd been a fool, she and Aygar would die, and these people, who had already suffered enough, would die. And her ship? A vision of the *Zaid-Dayan* as it hung in orbit, clean and powerful, filled her eyes with tears for a moment. NO.

She was not going to die down here, not going to let the Paradens and Parchandris of the universe get away with their vicious schemes. She was a Fleet *commander*, by Kipling's corns, and it was about time she started acting like it. The old familiar routines seemed to waken her mind as she referred to them, like lights coming on in a dark ship, compartment by compartment. Status report: resources: personnel: equipment: enemy situation . . .

She was not aware of her spine straightening until she saw the effect in their faces. They were staring at her as if she had suddenly appeared in her white battle armor instead of the stained civilian coverall. Their response heightened her excitement.

"Well, then," she said, the confidence in her voice ringing through the chamber. "We'd better sew up their shrouds first."

✧ CHAPTER FIFTEEN

Dupaynil stared at the bulkhead across from his bunk, and thought that luck was highly overrated. Human space aboard the *Grand Luck* meant this tiny stateroom, adjoining plumbing that made the *Claw*'s spartan head look and feel like a spa, and one small bare chamber he could use for eating, exercise, and what recreation his own mind provided. Most people thought the Seti had no sense of humor; he disagreed. The Commissioner's comments about the humbleness with which he would travel argued for a keen sense of irony, at the least.

He had had a brief and unhelpful interview with the Ambassador. The Fleet attaché lurking in the background of that interview had looked unbearably smug. The Ambassador saw no reason why he should undertake to have Fleet messages transmitted to FedCentral when Dupaynil was headed there himself. He saw no reason why redundancy might be advisable. Was Dupaynil suggesting that the Seti, allies within the Federation, might interfere with Dupaynil's own delivery of those messages? That would be a grave accusation, one which he would not advise Dupaynil to put in writing. And of course Dupaynil could not have a final interview with Panis. Quite against the Ambassador's advice, that precipitous young man had already departed, destination unknown.

It occurred to Dupaynil that this Ambassador, of all the human diplomats, surely had to be in the pay of the conspirators. He could not be *that* stupid. Looking again, at the florid face and blurred eyes, he was not sure. He glanced at the Fleet attaché and intercepted a knowing look to the Ambassador's private secretary. So. The Seti probably supplied the drugs, which his own staff fed him, to keep him so safely docile.

And I thought my troubles were over, Dupaynil thought,

making his final very correct bow and withdrawing to pack his kit for the long trip. Not surprisingly, the Fleet attaché insisted that anything Dupaynil asked for was unavailable.

And now he had leisure to reflect on the Ambassador's possible slow poisoning while the Seti ship bore him to an unknown destination; he did not believe for a moment they were really headed for FedCentral. He forced himself to get up and move into the little exercise space. Whatever was coming, he might as well be fit for it. He stripped off the dress uniform that courtesy demanded and went through the exercises recommended for all Fleet officers. Designed, as he recalled, by a Fleet marine sergeant-major who had retired and become a consultant for adventure films. There were only so many ways you could twist, bend, and stretch. He had worked up a sweat when the intercom burped at him.

"Du-paay-nil. Prepare for inspection by Safety Officer."

Of course they'd chosen this time. Dupaynil smiled sweetly into the shiny lens of the surveillance video, and finished with a double-tuck-roll that took him back into the minute sanitation cabinet. No shower, of course. A blast of hot air, then fine grit, then hot air again. Had he been covered with scales, like a proper liz . . . Seti, they'd have been polished. As a human, he felt sticky and gritty and altogether unclean. He would come off this ship smelling like a derelict from the gutter of an unimproved frontier world . . . no doubt their intent.

He had his uniform almost fastened when the hatch to his compartment swung back, and a large Seti snout intruded. They timed it so well. No matter when he took exercise or was using the sanitary facilities, they announced an inspection. No matter how quickly he tried to dress, they always arrived before he was finished. He found it curious that they didn't interrupt meals or sleep, but he appreciated even that minimal courtesy.

"Aaahh . . . Commaanderrr . . ." The Safety Officer had a slightly off-center gap between front teeth. Dupaynil could now recognize it as an individual. "Iss necesssary that airrr tesst be con-duct-ted."

They did this every few inspections, supposedly to be sure that his pressure suit would work. It meant a miserable struggle into the thing, and a hot sweaty interval while they sucked the air out of his quarters and the suit ballooned around him. Dupaynil reached into the narrow recess and pulled out the suit. Not his choice of suits but, the Fleet attaché had assured him with a smile, the only one in his size at the embassy. At least it had held up, so far, with only one minor leak, easily patched.

He pushed and wriggled his way into it, aware of the Seti's amusement. Seti faced the uncertainties of space travel without pressure suits. While they had such suits for those who might need to work on the outer surface of a ship, they did not stock suits for the whole crew. It made sense. Most of the time when a Fleet vessel lost hull integrity, the crew never made it into their suits anyway. And of course a Seti would have been disgraced for insisting on a way of cheating chance. Still Dupaynil was glad to have a suit, even though the Seti considered it another example of human inferiority.

He dogged the helmet down snugly and checked the seals of the seam that ran from throat to crotch. The suit had an internal comm unit which allowed him to speak, or more often listen, to the Seti. This time, he heard the Safety Officer's instructions with amazement.

"Come to the bridge?"

Humans were never invited to the bridge of Seti ships. No human had ever seen the navigational devices by which the gamblers of the universe convinced themselves they were being obedient to chance while keeping shipping schedules.

"At once."

Dupaynil followed, sweating and grunting. He had not had to put on his suit for this. Seti kept breathable, if smelly, atmosphere in their ships. No doubt they intended to make him look even more ridiculous. He had heard, repeatedly, what the Seti thought of human upright posture. It occurred to him that they might have insisted on his suit simply to spare themselves the indignity of a human's smell.

When he reached the bridge, it bore no resemblance whatever to that of a Fleet ship of the same mass. It was a triangular chamber — room for the tails, he realized — with cushioned walls and thickly carpeted floor, not at all shiplike. Two Seti, one with the glittering neck-ring and tail ornament that he had been told signified ship's captain, were crouched over a small, circular, polished table, tossing many-sided dice, while one standing in the remaining corner recited what seemed to be a list of unrelated numbers.

He felt cramped between the table and the hatch that had admitted him and then slammed behind him. The Seti ignored Dupaynil and he ignored that, finally trying to figure out what kind of game they were playing.

The dice landed with one face flat up, horizontal. Three dice at one time, usually, but occasionally only two. He didn't recognize the markings. From where he stood he could see three or four faces of each die and he amused himself trying to figure out what the squiggles meant. Green here, with a kind of tail going down. All three dice had this on the top face for a moment. Purple blotch, red square-in-square, a yellow blotch, two blue dots. The dice rose and fell, bouncing slightly, then coming to stillness. Green squiggles again, and on the other faces purple, blue dots, more red squares-in-squares.

The Seti calling out numbers paused through two throws. Dupaynil's attention slid from the dice to the Seti, wondering what the purple blotch on the napkinlike cloth around his neck meant. When he looked back at the board, the green squiggles were on top again.

Surely that couldn't be right, and surely they didn't just want an observer for the captain's nightly gambling spree. He watched the dice closely. In another two throws, he was sure of it. They were loaded, as surely as any set of dice that ever cheated some poor innocent in a dockside bar. Time after time the green squiggles came up on top. So why throw them? His mind wandered. Probably this wasn't the bridge at all. Some bored Seti officers had just wanted to bait their captive human. Then a fourth die joined the group in the air and down came three green squiggles and one purple blotch.

Three Seti heads swung his way, toothy jaws slightly open. He shivered, in his suit. If that was bad luck, and they thought he had brought it . . .

"Ahhh! Humann!" The captain's voice, through his comm unit, had only the usual Seti accent. "It wass explained to me that you were ssent here by very sspecial luck. Sso your luck continuess. As the luck fallss, you sshall be told, though it makess danger to usss."

Dupaynil could not bow. The suit gave him no room for it.

"Illustrious bringer of luck," he began, for that was part of the captain's title. "If chance favors your wish to share precious knowledge, my luck is great indeed."

"Indeed!" The captain reared back on massive hind legs, and snapped its jaws. A sign of amusement, Dupaynil remembered from handbooks. Sometimes species-specific. "Well, o lucky one, we ssshall sssee how you call your chance when you know all. We ssshall arrive even sssooner than you thought. And we ssshall arrive in forccce."

The Seti could not mean that the way a human would, Dupaynil thought. Surely not . . .

"Do you grasssp the flying ring of truth from tossssed baubles?" the Seti asked. Dupaynil tried to remember what *that* meant, but the Seti captain went on. "You ssshall sssee the ruin of your unlucky admiral, he who tossed your life against the wissdom of our Sek, in the person of the Commissioner of Commerce, and you shall see the ruin of your Fleet . . . and of the Federation itself, and all the verminous races who prize certainty over Holy Luck. Sssee it from the flagship, as you would say, of our fleet, invincible unless chance changes. And then, O human, we ssshall enjoy your flesh, flavored with the smoke of defeat." The captain's massive snout bumped the screen of Dupaynil's helmet.

From the frying pan of Sassinak's displeasure, to the fire of the conspirators on *Claw*, he had come to the Seti furnace. If this was luck, he would take absolute determinism from now on. It couldn't be worse. He hoped the Seti could not detect the trickles of sweat down his back. He could smell his own fear, a depressing stench. He tried for a tone of unconcern.

"How can you be certain of this destination by throwing dice?" Not real thought, but the first words that came into his mouth, idle curiosity.

"Ahhh . . ." The captain's tail slapped the floor gently, and its tail ornament jingled. "Not pleass or argumentss, but ssense. As chance favors, I sshall answer."

His explanation of the proceedings made the kind of oblique sense Dupaynil expected from aliens. Chance was holy, and only those who dared fate deserved respect, but the amount of risk inherent in each endeavor determined the degree of additional risk which the Seti felt compelled to add by throwing dice or using random number generators. "The Glorious Chaos," as they named that indeterminate state in which ships travelled or seemed to travel faster than light, had sufficient uncertainty to require no assistance. So they tossed loaded dice, as a token of respect, and to allow the gods of chance to interfere if they were determined.

"War, as well," the captain continued, "has its own uncertainties, so that within the field of battle, a worthy commander may be guided by its own great wisdom and intuition. Occasionally one will resort to the dice or the throwing sticks, a gesture of courage all respect, but the more parts to the battle, the less likely. But you . . ." A toothy grin did not reassure Dupaynil at all. "You were another matter and judged sufficiently certain of unsuccess without our chance to place you in the toss. As your luck held, in the unmatched dice, so now I offer to chaos this chance for you to thwart us. I told you our plan, and you may ask what you will. You will not return to your quarters."

Dupaynil fought down a vision of himself as Seti snack-food. If he could ask questions, he would ask *many* questions.

"Is this venture a chance occurrence, or has some change in Federation policy prompted it?"

The captain uttered a wordless roar, then went into a long disjointed tirade about the Federation allies. Heavyworlder humans, as victims of forced genetic manipulation, roused some sympathy in the Seti. Besides, a few heavyworlders had shown the proper attitude by daring feats of chance: entering a Hall of Dispute through the Door of Honor, for instance. Some humans were gamblers: entrepreneurs, willing to risk whole fortunes on the chance of a mining claim, or colonial venture. That the Seti could respect. The Paradens, for instance, deserved to lay eggs. (Dupaynil could imagine what the elegant Paraden ladies would think of *that*.) But the mass of humans craved security. Born slaves, they deserved the outward condition of it.

As for the allied aliens . . . The captain spat something that Dupaynil was glad he could not smell. Cowardly Wefts, the shifters who would not dare the limits of any shape . . . Bronthin, with their insistence on mathematical limits to chaos and chance, their preference for statistical analyses. Ryxi, who were unworthy to be egglayers since they not only sexed their unhatched chicks, but performed surgical procedures through the shell. The Seti had the decency, the captain snarled, to let their eggs hatch as they would and take the consequences. The Ssli, who insisted on giving up their mobile larval form to become sessile, bound to one location throughout life: a refusal to dare change.

Dupaynil opened his mouth to say that Ssli anchored to warships in space could hardly be considered "bound to one location," remembered that not everyone knew about the Ssli in Fleet ships and instead asked, "And the Thek?"

This time the captain's tail hit the floor so hard its ornament shattered.

"Thek!" it roared. "Disgusting lumps of geometrical regularity. Undifferentiated. Choiceless, chanceless, obscene . . ." The ranting went on in a Seti dialect Dupaynil could not begin to follow. Finally it ran down and gave Dupaynil a sour glance. "It is my good fortune that you will flavor my stew, miserable one, for you irritate me extremely. Leave at once."

He had no chance to leave under his own power. At some point, the captain must have called for Seti guards because they grabbed the arms of his suit and towed him along strange corridors much faster than he could have gone by himself.

When they finally stopped and released his arms, he was crammed in a smallish chamber with an assortment of aliens. The Bronthin took up the most cubage, its chunky horselike body and heavy head impossible to compress. A couple of Lethi were stuck together like the large yellow burrs which they greatly resembled. A Ryxi huddled in one corner, fluffing and flattening its feathers, and in a translucent tank, two Ssli larvae flutter-kicked from end to end. On one wall, a viewscreen displayed sickening swirls of violent color: the best an exterior monitor could do in FTL space. Beside it, a fairly obvious dial gave the pressure of various atmospheric components. Breathable, but not pleasant.

So the Seti had collected an array of alien observers to gloat over, had they? Dupaynil wondered who the human would have been, if he and Panis had not show up. Certainly not the Fleet attaché. Probably the Ambassador. Had they all been told what was going on? He cracked the seal of his helmet cautiously and sniffed. A tang of sulfur, a bit too humid and warm and clearly no shower in sight. With an internal sigh, he took off his helmet and attempted a greeting to his new companions.

No one answered. The Ryxi offered a gaping beak, which Dupaynil remembered from a training manual meant something like "Forget it, I don't want to talk to you unless you've got the money." He had never learned Bronthin (no human ever had) and the tubby blue mathematicians preferred equations to any other form of discourse anyway. Lethi had no audible communications mode: they talked to each other in chemical packages and could not interface with a biolink until they formed a clump of at least eight. That left the Ssli larvae, who, without a biolink, also had no way of communicating. In fact, no one was sure how intelligent the larvae actually were. They were in the Fleet Academy to learn navigational theory but Dupaynil had never heard of one communicating with an instructor.

He could try writing them a message, except that he had nothing to write with, or on. The Seti had not brought any of his kit from his compartment; he had only the clothes and pressure suit he stood up in.

It really wasn't so bad, he told himself, forcing cheerfulness. The Seti hadn't killed them yet. Didn't seem to be starving them, though he wondered if that slab of elementary sulfur was really enough for the Lethi clinging to it. He found a water dispenser, and even a recessed cabinet with oddly shaped bowls to put the water in. He poured himself a bowl and drank it down. Something nudged his arm and he found the Bronthin looking sorrowfully at the bowl. It gave a low, grunting moo.

Ah. Bronthin had never been good with small tools. He poured water for the Bronthin and held the bowl for it to drink. It swiped his face with a rough, corrugated lavender tongue when it was done, leaving behind a faintly sweet odor. A nervous chitter across the compartment was the Ryxi, standing now with feathers afluff and stubby wings outspread. Dupaynil interpreted this as a request and filled another bowl. The Ryxi snatched it away from him with its wing-claws and drank thirstily.

"They for us water pour but one time daily," the Ryxi twittered, dropping the empty bowl. Dupaynil picked it up with less graciousness than he'd filled it. He had never been the nurturing type. Still, it was communication. The Ryxi went on. "Food at that time, only enough for life. Waste removal."

"Did they tell you where we're headed?"

An ear-splitting screech made him wince. The Ryxi began bouncing off the walls, crashing into one after another of them, shrieking something in Ryxi. The Bronthin huddled down in a large lump, leaving Dupaynil in the Ryxi's path. He tried to tackle it but a knobbed foot got him in the ribs. The Ryxi flipped its crest up and down, keening, and drew back for another kick, but Dupaynil rolled behind the Ssli tank.

"Take it easy," he said, knowing it would do no good. Ryxi never took it easy. This one calmed slightly, sides heaving, crest only halfway up.

"They told," came the sorrowful low groan of the Bronthin. Dupaynil had never heard one speak Standard before. "Wickedly dangerous meat-eaters. We told Theks what would come of it. Those who sweep tails across the sand of reason, where proofs of wisdom abound." The Bronthin had accomplished advanced mathematics without paper or computers, using smooth stretches of sand or clay to scribe their equations. Although their three stubby fingers could not manipulate fine tools, they had developed an elegant mathematical calligraphy. And a very formal courtesy involving the use of the "sands of reason." A colt (the human term) who used its whisk of a tail on someone else's calculations would be severely punished. Bronthin were also strict vegetarians — browsers on their world which had small and witless carnivores. They were pacifists.

Dupaynil eyed the calming Ryxi warily. His ribs hurt. He didn't need another kick. "Do you have any plan?" he asked the Bronthin.

"The probability of escape from this ship, in a nonviable state, is less than 0.1 percent. The probability of escape from this ship in a viable state is less than 0.0001 percent. The factors used to arrive at this include the . . ."

"Never mind," said Dupaynil, softening it with an apology. "My mathematical skill is insufficient to appreciate the beauty of your calculations."

"How kind to save me the trouble of converting to Standard that which can only be properly expressed in the language of eternal law." The Bronthin heaved a sigh, which Dupaynil took to mean the conversation was over.

The Ryxi, however, was eager to talk, once it had calmed enough to remember its Standard.

"Unspeakable reptiles," it twittered. "Unworthy to be egg-layers!" Not again, thought Dupaynil, not anticipating the Ryxi side of that argument. "Thick-shelled, they are. You can't even *see* a Seti in its shell. Not that it makes any difference, because even if something's wrong, they won't do anything. Just let the hatch-lings die if they can't make it on their own. Some of them don't even tend their nests. Not even to warn away predators. They say that's giving Holy Luck the choice. I'd call it criminal negligence."

"Despicable," said Dupaynil, edging farther away from the dance of those powerful feet. Then a bell-like voice rang out, its source unidentifiable.

<Sassinak friend?>

Dupaynil tried to control his start of surprise, and glanced around. The Bronthin looked half-asleep which is the way Bronthins usually looked and the Ryxi had begun grooming its feathers with jerky strokes of its beak. The two Lethi were still stuck to each other and the slab of sulfur.

<Do not look . . . in the tank.> He managed to stare at the blank space above the Bronthin, while the voice continued and his own mind shivered away from it. He had never like descrip-tions of telepathy and he liked the reality less. <Sassinak friend you are. We greet you. We are more and less than we seem.>

Of course. Ssli. So Ssli larvae could communicate! He could not "feel" anything in his mind when the voice fell silent, but that didn't mean it, or they, were not reading him.

<No time to investigate your dark secrets. We must plan.>

They were reading his surface thoughts, at least, to have picked up that distaste for internal snooping. He recognized the irony of that, someone whose profession was snooping on others, now being turned inside out by aliens. He tried to organize his thoughts, make a clear message.

"You stare at wall for a reason?" the Ryxi asked, its feathers now sleeked down.

Dupaynil could have strangled the Ryxi for breaking his con-centration, and then he *did* feel a featherlight touch, soothing, and a bubble of amusement.

"I'm very tired," he said honestly. "I need to rest."

With that, he found a clear space of floor, between the wall and the Ssli tank, and curled up, helmet cradled in his arms. The Ryxi sniffed, then tucked its head back over its shoulders into the back feathers. Dupaynil closed his eyes and projected against the screen of his eyelids.

<What can you do?>

<Nothing alone. We hoped they would bring a human.>

<What did you mean, 'more and less'?>

Again the mental gurgle of amusement. <We are not both Ssli.>

The voice said nothing more and Dupaynil thought about it. If they were reading his thoughts, they were welcome. Not both Ssli? Another alien marine race? Suddenly he realized what it had to be and almost laughed aloud.

<A Weft?>

<Seemed safer this way. Seti hate Wefts enough to kill them before the coup. But with this form come certain . . . limitations.>

<Which humans don't have?>

<Precisely.>

<Sorry, but I don't think they'll let me push that tank to wherever they keep the escape pods. Assuming they have any.>

<Not the plan. May we share?>

It seemed an odd question from beings who could force mental intimacy, and already had, but Dupaynil was in the mood to accept any courtesy offered.

<Go ahead.>

He tensed, bracing himself for some unimaginable sensation, and felt nothing. Only information began to knit itself into his existing cognitive matrix, as if he were learning it so fast that it was safely in long-term memory before it passed his eyes. The Bronthin, he learned, had been hired by the Seti to provide them with mathematical expertise. On the basis of its calculations and models, they had defined the best time to attempt the coup.

And the Bronthin had had no way to warn the Federation. Bronthins could not manipulate Seti communications equipment, were not telepathic, and suffered severe depression when kept isolated from their social herds. As for the Ssli, it had been delivered, in its tank after it had been stolen from a Fleet recruit depot. The Weft, a Fleet guard at the depot, had been shot in the burglary and survived only by shapechanging into the Ssli tank in a larval form. The thieves had not known the difference between Weft and Ssli larvae and had apparently supposed that two or more larvae were in each tank, in case one died.

<But what can we *do*?> Dupaynil asked.

<You can talk to the Bronthin, and find out more of what it knows about this fleet. It had the information to make models with. It must know. It's depressed. That's why it won't talk. Later,

when we drop out of FTL, you can see the viewscreen. We have no such eyes. But the Ssli can link with other Ssli on a Fleet vessel, and that Ssli has a biolink to the captain.>

Cheering up the Bronthin took all of Dupaynil's considerable charm. It turned away at first, muttering number series, but the offer of another bowl of water helped. He watered the Ryxi, too, automatically, and this time the feathered alien handed the bowl back rather than dropping it. But it took many bowls of water, and a couple of sessions of picking the burrs from the dry grass the Seti tossed in for its feed, before the alien showed much response.

Finally it scrubbed its heavy head up and down his arm, took his hand in its muscular lips, and said, "I . . . will try to speak Standard . . . in thanks for your kindness. . . ."

"Inaccurate as Standard is, and unsuited to your genius, would it be possible to recall how many ships this size the Seti have with them?"

The Bronthin flopped a long upper lip, and sighed.

"The ratio of such ships to those next smaller to those next smaller to the smallest is 1.2:3.4:5.6:5:4. An interesting ratio, chosen by the Seti for its ragged harmony, if I understood them." It shook its long head. "Alas . . . never again to roll in the green sweet fields of home or be granted the tail's whisk across the sands in the company of my peers."

"Such courage in loneliness," Dupaynil murmured. In his experience, praising the timid for courage sometimes produced a momentary flare of it. "And the total to which such a ratio applies?"

With something akin to a snort, the Bronthin's lovely periwinkle eyes opened completely.

"Ah! You understand that the ratio is theoretical. The fleet itself made up of actual ships, of which at any time some fraction is out of service for maintenance and the like. Of those actually *here*, in the sense that here has any meaning . . . are you at all familiar with Sere-kleth-vladin's transformational series and its application to hyperspace flux variations?"

"Alas, no," said Dupaynil, who didn't know such things existed —whatever they were.

"Unhhh . . . one hundred four. Eight similar to this, which

would of course make you expect 22.6, 37.3, 35.9 ships of the other classes, but fractional ships are nonfunctional. Twenty-three of the next class, then thirty-seven, then thirty-six. And since it would be the logical next question," the Bronthin went on, its eyes beginning to sparkle, "I will explain that the passive defenses of the Federation Central System, if not tampered with, could be expected to destroy at least eighty-two percent of the total. Those remaining would be unlikely to succeed at reducing the planets or disrupting the Grand Council. But the Seti count on tampering, which will reduce the efficiency of the distant passive scans by forty-one percent, and on specific aid whose nature I do not know, to disable additional defenses. This incursion is timed to coincide with the meeting of the Grand Council and the Winter Assizes, at which the presence of many ships could well cause confusion."

"They expect no resistance from Fleet?"

The Bronthin opened its mouth wide, revealing the square grinding teeth of a herbivore, and gave a long sound somewhat between a moo an a bray. "My apologies," it said then. "Our long misunderstanding of the nature of humans; our votes have long gone to reducing appropriations for what we saw as a means of territorial aggrandizement. These Seti expect that any Fleet vessels in Federation Central Systems space will be neutralized. And once again, we aided this, voting to require that all Fleet vessels disarm lest they overpower the Grand Council."

"A most natural error for any lover of peace," Dupaynil murmured soothingly.

Sassinak would be there with the *Zaid-Dayan*. Would she have disarmed completely, trusting in the disarmament of others to keep her ship safe? Somehow he doubted it. But with the surveillance by the FSP local government, she wouldn't be able to have all the ship's scans on . . . and without warning . . . he realized he had no idea how fast the *Zaid-Dayan* could get into action.

<We do appreciate the difficulty.>

If mental speech could have tones, that would be dry wit, Dupaynil thought. He sent a mental flick of the fingers to the Ssli and Weft, still swimming with apparent unconcern in the tank. Easy for them, he thought sourly, and then realized it wasn't. He would be even more miserable if he'd been stuck in a tank like that.

❖   ❖   ❖

Despite the rising tension, he had actually fallen asleep when a screech from the Ryxi brought him upright, blinking. The viewscreen showed what he presumed to be the real outer view, although he had no way of knowing which of the ship's outer sensors had produced the image. Darkness, points of light, some visibly moving. A Seti voice from the wallspeaker interrupted the Ryxi's tantrum.

"Captives, observe," it began, with typical Seti tact. "See your feeble hopes destroyed."

The view shown shifted from one angle to another. The outside of the *Grand Luck*, with a long pointed snout oozing from a recess to slide past, aimed at some distant enemy. A zooming view of nearby ships, lifting them from points of light to toylike shapes against a dark background. Then another view, of the star around which the Federation Central Zone planets swung, a star which now looked scarcely bigger than any of the others.

<Share again!>

Dupaynil tried to relax. He had already passed on all he'd learned from the Bronthin. Now he watched the screen, listened to the Seti boastful commentary and hoped the Ssli/Weft pair could contact another Ssli. Time passed. The view shifted every few minutes, from one sensor to another.

<Contact.>

Dupaynil wasn't sure if the triumphant tone came from the Ssli or his own reaction. He expected to hear more, but the Ssli did not include him in whatever link it and the Weft had formed with that distant Ssli. They Ryxi clattered its beak, shifted from one great knobby foot to another, fluffed and sleeked its feathers, staring wide-eyed at the viewscreen. The Bronthin refused to look. Its closed eyes and monotonous hum could be either sleep or despair. And the Lethi, as before, simply stuck to each other and the sulfur.

Dupaynil had the feeling that he should do something to prepare for the coming battle. Now that the Ssli had warned its fellow. Now surely that alarm was being passed on. He felt free to consider more immediate problems. Could they possibly break free of this compartment? Could they steal weapons? Find some kind of escape vehicle? Or, failing escape, do something disastrous to this ship and destroy it? He and the Ryxi were the only two who might actually *do* something, for no one had ever heard of a Bronthin being violent. He edged over to the hatch, and prodded its complicated-looking lock.

A roar of Seti profanity from outside made it clear that wouldn't work. He was looking around for something else to investigate, when the viewscreen blurred, cleared, blurred, and cleared again after a couple of short FTL skips. Then it grayed to a pearly haze and the ship trembled.

"Battle started!" came the announcement in Standard over the speaker. Then a long complicated gabble of Seti that must be orders.

<Sassinak is not aboard her ship.> That fell into his mind like a lump of ice. <She disappeared onplanet. Wefts can't land to find her.>

<Other ships?>

He had assumed she would be aboard her ship. He had assumed she would be wary, as alert as he'd always known her. What was she doing, playing around onplanet with her ship helpless above, with its weapons locked down, with no captain? Without at least taking Wefts with her?

<No other ships larger than escort Insystem.>

"Stupid woman!"

He didn't realize he'd said it aloud until he saw the Bronthin's eyes flick open, heard the Ryxi's agitated chirp.

"Never *mind*!" he said to them, glaring.

Here he had gone through one miserable hell after another, all to get her information she desperately needed, and she wasn't where she was supposed to be.

<*Zaid-Dayan* moving.>

That stopped his mental ranting. Then the *Grand Luck* lurched sharply, as if it had run into a brick wall, and as his feet skidded on the floor he realized his head had nowhere to go but the corner of the Ssli transport tank.

✧ CHAPTER SIXTEEN

FedCentral

"You're joking." Coris stared at her. "You don't realize . . ."

"I realize precisely what will happen to all of us if we *don't* take the initiative." Sassinak was on her feet now and the others were stirring restlessly, not committed to either side of this argument. "If you'd wanted death, or a mindwipe, and the rest of your life at hard labor, you'd have managed it before now. It's easy enough, even yet. Just wait for them to come after me. Because Jemi is quite right. They will. I'm too dangerous, even by myself." She paused a careful measure, then added, "But with *you*, I could be dangerous enough to win."

"But we don't . . . We aren't . . ." Jemi's nervous looks around got no support. Most were staring fascinated at Sassinak.

"Aren't what? Strong enough? Brave enough? You've been strong and brave enough to survive and stay free. How long, Coris?"

"I been here eight years. Jemi, six. Fostin was here when I came. . . ."

"Years of your lives," Sassinak said, almost purring it. "You survived capture, slavery, prison, all the disasters. And you survived this life below the city. Now you can end it. End the hiding, end the fear. End the suffering, your own and others."

They stirred. She could feel their need for her to be right, their need for her to be strong for them. Give them time and they'd revert, but she had this instant.

"Come on," she said. "Show me what you've got. Right now."

Slowly, they stood, eyeing her and each other with hope that was clearly unfamiliar.

"Any weapons? We've got this." She pulled out the snub-nosed weapon Aygar had taken from the first row. "How many are you, altogether?"

They had weapons, but not many and most, they explained, were carried by their roving scouts. Nor did they have an accurate count of their own numbers. Twenty here, a dozen there, stray couples and individuals, a large band whose territory they overlapped in one direction, and a scattering of bands in another. They had specialists, of a sort. Some were best at milking the mass-service food processors without detection and some had a knack for tapping into the datalinks.

"Good," Sassinak said. "Where's this godlike Parchandri you say is running the backscenes on FedCentral?"

"You're not going after *him!*" Coris' shock was mirrored on every face. "There'll be guards — troops — we can't do that! It's like starting a war."

"Coris, this became a war the second a warrior dropped into it. Me. I'm fighting a war. War means strategy, tactics, victory conditions." She tapped these off on her fingers. "You people can squat here and get wiped out as the enemy chases me or you can be my troops and have a chance. I don't promise more than that. But *if* we win, you won't have to live down here, eating tasteless mush and drinking bilgewater. It'll be your world again. Your lives! Your freedom!"

The big-framed man she'd noticed before shrugged and came up beside Coris. "Might's well, Coris. They'll be after her, after us. Using gas again, most likely. I'm with her."

"And me!"

More than one of the others; Coris gave a quick side-to-side glance, shrugged, and grinned.

"I should've slit you back up there," he said, jerking his chin in what Sassinak assumed was the right direction.

Aygar growled, but Sassinak waved him to silence. "You're right, Coris. If you're going to take out a threat, do it right away. Next time you'll know."

You can't wage war without a plan, one of the Command Staff instructors had insisted. *But you can lose with one.* Sassinak found this no help at all as she chivvied her ragged troops through the tunnels to the boundary of their territory. She had no plan but survival, and she knew it was not enough. Find the

Parchandri and . . . And what? Her fingers ached to fasten around his throat and force the truth testimony out of him. Would that do any good? They didn't really need it, not for Tanegli's trial. Even if she didn't make it back, even if Aygar didn't, there was evidence enough to convict the old heavyworlder. As for the status of Ireta, she doubted any non-Thek court would dare to question the Thek ruling she'd received which was already in official files.

Official files to which a powerful Parchandri might gain access. She almost stumbled, thinking that. Was nothing safe? She glanced around at her new fighting companions and mentally shook her head. Not these people, who were about as far from Fleet marines as she could imagine. Give them credit for having lived so long. But would they hold up in real combat?

Ahead, a quick exchange of whistled signals. The group slowed, flattened against the tunnel walls. Sassinak wondered if the battle would begin now, but it turned out to be the territorial boundary. She went forward with Coris to meet this second group. To her surprise, "her" people were now holding themselves more like soldiers. They seemed to have purpose, and the others were visibly impressed.

"What goes?" asked the second gang's leader. He was her age or older, his broad face heavily scarred. His eyes focussed somewhere past her ear, and a lot of his teeth were missing. So was one finger.

"Samizdat." The code answer.

"Whose friend?"

"Fleur's. And Coris'."

"Heh. You'd better be Fleur's friend. We'll check that. You have a name, Fleur's friend?"

"Sassinak."

His eyes widened. "She's got a call out for you. Fleur and the cops both. What you done, eh?"

"Not everything you've heard, and some things you haven't. You have a name?"

He grinned at that, but quickly sobered. "I'm Kelgar. Ever'body knows me. Twice bitten, most shy. Twice lucky, to be free from slavers twice." He paused, and she nodded. What could she say to someone like that, but acknowledge bad experience shared. "Come! We'll see what she says."

"She's down *here*?"

"She goes slumming sometimes, though she doesn't call it that. 'Sides, where she is, is pretty near topside, over 'cross a ways, through two more territories. We don't fight, eh?" That was thrown back to Coris, who flung out his open hand.

"We good children," he said.

"Like always," said Kelgar. "For all the flamin' good it does."

He led the way this time and Sassinak followed with Coris' group. She could tell that Kelgar had more snakes in his attic than were strictly healthy, but if paranoid he was smart paranoid. They saw no patrols while passing through his territory, and into the next. There she met another gangleader, this one a whip-thin woman who went dead-white at the sight of Sassinak's face. A Fleet deserter? Her gang had the edge of almost military discipline, and after that first shocked reaction, the woman handled them with crisp efficiency. Definitely military, probably Fleet. Rare to lose one that good. Sassinak couldn't help wondering what had happened, but she knew she'd get no answers if she asked.

They passed another boundary and Sassinak found herself being introduced to yet another leader. Black hair, dark eyes, brownish skin, and the facial features she thought of as Chinese. Most of his followers looked much the same, and she caught some angry glances at Aygar. All she didn't need was racial trouble; she hoped this leader had control of his people.

"Sassinak . . ." the man said slowly. "You had an ancestress Lunzie?" This was something new. How would he know? Sassinak nodded. The man went on, "I believe we are distantly related."

"I doubt it," Sassinak said warily. What was this about?

"Let me explain," he said, as if they had settled down in a club with all afternoon to chat. "Your grandfather Dougal was Fleet, as you are, and he married into a merchanter family . . . but Chinese. Quite against the custom of both his people and hers. He never told his family about the marriage, and she eventually left him to return to her family, with her daughters. His son they liked less, and when he married your mother and decided to join a new colony, it seemed the best solution for everyone. But your grandmother's family kept track of your father, of course, and when I was a child I learned your name, and that of your siblings, in family prayers."

"They . . . knew about us?"

"Yes, of course. When your colony was raided, your grandmother's ship was hung with white flags. When they heard you had survived . . . ."

"But how could they?"

"You were honor graduate in the Academy. Surely you realized that an orphan rising to honor graduate would be featured in news programs."

"I never thought." She might have, if Abe's death had not come on the heels of that triumph, and her grief filled every moment until her first posting.

"The name is unusual. It had made your grandmother very angry for her son to choose a name like that. So they searched the databases, found your original ID. They assumed you had done the same, and would make contact if and when you chose." He shrugged, and smiled at her. "It has nothing to do with your purpose here, but I thought you might like to know, since circumstances brought us together."

If she had a later. "I . . . see." She had no idea what etiquette applied; clearly he expected something more from her than he would of another stranded Fleet officer. "I'm sorry. I don't know what obligations I would have under your customs. . . ."

"You? It is our family that did not protect you. Our family that did not make sure you knew of us. What I am trying to say is that you have a claim on us, if you are not ashamed of the connection."

"I'm not ashamed." That much she could say honestly, with utter conviction. To have another segment of her family accept her brought her close to tears, but not with shame. "I'm . . . amazed, surprised, stunned. But not ashamed."

"Then, if it pleases you, we should go this way for you to meet Fleur again. She, too, was insistent that you must know about our family bond before you talked to her."

She tried to reorganize her thoughts as they went on. A family, at least her father's side. Now, why had she always thought her mother was the connection to Lunzie? Chinese didn't bother her. Why would it? And what kind of family had Dougal had, that he hadn't told them about his wife? Lunzie had said something about finding Fiona's children stuffy. She tried to remember, as she usually tried to forget, her parents. They had both been dark-haired, and she did remember that her father had once kidded her mother about her "Assyrian" nose, whatever that meant.

Her relative, in whatever degree, led her into a large room in which great cylinders hissed softly at one another. Pipes as thick as her waist connected them, code-striped for hot and cold water, steam, gas. Something thrummed in the distance. A narrow door marked "Storage" opened into a surprisingly large chamber that had evidently been used by the group for some time. Battered but comfortable chairs, stacks of pillows, strips of faded carpet. Sassinak wished she could collapse into the pillows and sleep for a day. But Fleur was waiting, as elegant as she had been in her own shop, in soft blues and lavenders, her silvery hair haloed around her head.

"Dear girl," she said, extending a hand with such elegance that Sassinak could not for a moment reply. "You look worn out. You know, you didn't have to get in this amount of trouble just to talk to me again."

"I didn't intend to."

Sassinak took the chair she was offered. Her newfound relative grinned at her and shut the door. She and Fleur were alone. She eyed the older woman, not quite sure what she was looking for.

"I suppose you could say that things . . . took off." Sitting down, in a real chair, she could feel every tired muscle. She fought back a yawn.

"I'll be as brief as I can." Fleur shifted a little in her seat and then stared at a space on the floor between them. "In the hopes that we will have time later to fill in what I leave out now." Sassinak nodded. "When Abe first met me, I had been captured, held hostage for my family's behavior and finally sold into prostitution." As a start, that got Sassinak's attention. She sat bolt upright.

"You?"

"My family were wealthy merchanters, rivals of the Paradens. Or so the Paradens thought. I'd been brought up to wealth, luxury, society: probably spoiled rotten, though I didn't know it. The perfect hostage, if you look at it that way." Another pause. Sassinak began to feel a growing horror, and the certainty that she knew what was coming. "We were taken," Fleur said, biting off each word. "Me and my husband. Supposedly, it was independent pirates. That's what our families were told. But we knew, from the moment we were locked in the Paraden House security wing. I never knew the exact details, but I do know they asked for a ransom that neither my family nor his could have survived independently. His family . . . his family paid. And the Paradens sent him back, whole and healthy of body, but mindwiped. They made me watch."

Sassinak drew in a shaky breath to speak, but Fleur shook her head.

"Let me finish, all at once. My family thought they had proof of the Paraden connection. They tried to bring them to justice in the courts. In the end, my family lost everything, in court costs and countersuit damages. My father died, of a stroke; my mother's heart failed; my brothers . . . well, one went to prison for a 'vicious unprincipled assault' on the judge the Paradens had bribed so well. The other they had killed, just for insurance. And they sold me to a planet where none of my family had ever traded."

Sassinak's eyes burned with tears for the young woman Fleur had been. Before she realized it, she'd moved over to grip her hands.

"Abe saved me," Fleur went on. "He came, like any other young man, but he saw . . . something. I don't know. He used to kid me that whatever training my governess had given me couldn't be hidden. So he asked questions, and I was wild enough to answer, for I'd just heard of my sister-in-law's death. The Paradens took care to keep me informed. And he swore he would get me out, somehow. In less than a year, he had saved out my purchase price. How, on his salary, I'll never know. He wanted to marry me but I knew Fleet was strict about identity checks. I was terrified that the Paradens would find me again. So he helped me set up my first dress shop, and from there . . ."

She waved her arm, and Sassinak thought of the years of grinding work it must have taken, to go from that first tiny shop to the fashionable designer.

"Eventually I designed for the best families, including, of course, the Paradens. None of my friends recognized me. I had gray hair, I looked older, and, of course, I took care to look like a dressmaker, not a customer.

"Abe and I stayed in contact, when we could. He was sure there had to be a way to bring the crime home to the Paradens, and started digging. That was really the beginning of Samizdat. I knew a few people. I helped those I could. Passed him information, when it came to me, and he passed some back. We built up a network, on one planet after another. Then he was taken, and I thought . . . I thought I'd never survive his loss. So I swore that if he came back alive, I'd marry him, if he still wanted me."

She patted Sassinak's hands gently.

"And that's where you came in. When he came back, he had you: an orphan, in shock from all that had happened. I heard through our nets that he was back. I came to Regg to talk to him. And he explained that until you were on your way, he dared not risk your future with any more disruption."

"But I wouldn't have minded," Sassinak said. "How could he think I would?"

"I'm not sure, but we decided to wait, on marriage, that is, until after your graduation. And that, dear Sassinak, is what he wanted to tell you that night. I don't know whether you noticed anything . . ."

"I did! So — so *you* were his big secret."

"You sound almost disappointed."

"I'm not . . . but it hadn't occurred to me. I thought perhaps he'd found out more about the planet pirates."

"He might have. But he'd decided to tell you about me on graduation night. If all had gone well, he'd have brought you to the hotel where I was staying. We'd have met, and you'd have been the witness at our wedding before you went off on your first cruise."

Like light pouring into a darkened house as shutter after shutter came off the windows — she had wondered so long, so darkly, about the secret of that night.

"Did you come to his funeral? I don't remember any civilians at all."

Fleur's head drooped; Sassinak could not see her face.

"I was frightened again. I thought it was the Paradens, that they'd found me, and killed Abe because of me. You didn't need that and you didn't know about me; you wouldn't even have known why I was there. So I left. You can call it cowardice, if you like. I kept track of your career, but I never could find the right time to try telling you. . . ."

Sassinak threw her arms around the older woman and hugged her as she cried.

"It's all right," she vowed. "I'll get the job done this time."

She could hear the steely edge in her voice herself. Fleur

pulled away.

"Sass! You must not let it fill you with bitterness."

"But he *deserved* to get you!" Now she had tears in her eyes, too. "Abe deserved some pleasure. He worked so hard to save me . . . and you, and others, and then they *killed* him just when . . ."

She had not cried for Abe since her few tears the night of his death. She had been the contained, controlled officer he would have wanted her to be. Now that old loss stabbed her again. Through her sobs she heard Fleur talking.

"If you turn bitter, you've let them win. Whether you kill them or not, that's not the main thing. The main thing is to live as yourself; the self you can respect. Abe would not let me despair, the other kind of defeat, but he told me he worried that you might stay bitter."

"But they killed him. And my parents, and your family, and all the others. . . ."

Fleur sighed. "Sassinak, I'm nearly forty years older than you, and I know that sort of comment makes prickles go up your spine." Sassinak had to chuckle. Fleur was so right. "And I know you don't want to hear that another forty years of experience means additional understanding. But!" Her beautifully manicured finger levelled at Sassinak's eyes. "Did Abe know more than you in the slave depot?"

"Of course. I was just a child."

"And if he were alive now, would you still respect his greater age and experience?"

"Well . . ." She could see it coming, but she didn't have to like it. Her expression must have shown that, because Fleur laughed aloud, a silvery bell-like peal that brought an answering laugh from Sassinak.

"So please trust me now," Fleur said, once more serious. "You have become what Abe dreamed of. I have kept an eye on you in the media; I know. But the higher you go in Fleet, the more you will need unclouded judgment. If you allow the bitterness, the unfairness, of your childhood and Abe's death, to overwhelm your natural warmth, you will become unfair in your own way. You must be *more* than a pirate chaser, more than vengeance personified. Fleet tends to shape its members toward narrow interests, rigid reactions, even in the best. Haven't you found that some of your difficulties down here arise from that?"

Put that way, some of them certainly had. She had developed the typical spacefarer's distaste for planets. She had not bothered to cultivate the skills needed to enjoy them. The various gangs in the tunnels seemed alien, even as she tried to mold them into a working unit.

"Abe used to say to me," Fleur said, now patting at her hair, "that growth and development can't stop for stars, rank, or travel. You keep growing and keep Abe's memory green. Don't let the Paradens shape the rest of your life, as they shaped the first of it."

"Yes, ma'am."

"Now tell me, what do you plan to do with all this scruffy crowd?"

Sassinak grinned at her, half-rueful and half-determined.

"Chase pirates, ma'am, and *then* worry about whether I've gotten too rigid."

But when it came down to it, none of them actually knew where the Parchandri was located in a physical sense. Sassinak frowned.

"We ought to be able to get that from the data systems, with the right codes," she said. "You said you had people good at that."

"But we don't have any of the current codes. The only times we've tried to tap into the secure datalines, anything but the public ones, they've sent police after us. They can tell where our tap is, an' everything."

"Sassinak?" Aygar tapped her shoulder. She started to brush him aside, but remembered his previous good surprises. "Yes?"

"My friend, that student . . ."

"The one who boasted to you he could skip through the datalinks without getting caught? Yes. But he's not here and how would we find him?"

"I have his callcode. From any public comsite, he said."

"But there aren't any — are there? Down here?"

She glanced at the ragged group. Some of them nodded and Coris answered her.

"Yes, up in the public tunnels. There's a few we might get to, without being spotted. Not all of us, of course."

"There's that illegal one in the 248 vertical," someone else said. "This maintenance worker put it in, patched it to the regular public lines so he could call in bets during his shift. We used to listen to him."

"Where's the 248 vertical?" Sassinak asked.

Not that far away, although it took several hours of careful zig-ging about to get to it. Twice they saw hunting patrols, one in the blue-gray of the city police, and one in the Pollys' orange. Their careless sweep of the tunnels did not impress Sassinak. They seemed to be content to walk through, without investigating all hatches and side tunnels. When she mentioned this to Coris, he hunched his shoulders.

"Bet they're planning to gas the system. Now they're looking for easy prey, girls down on their luck, kids . . . something to have fun with."

"Gas! You mean poison gas? Or knockout gas?"

"They've used both, before. 'Bout three years ago, they must've killed a thousand or more, over toward the shuttle station area. I was clear out here, and all it did to us was make us heave everything for a day or so. But I heard there'd been street crime, subways hijacked, that kind of thing."

Sassinak fingered the small kit in her pocket. She had brought along the detox membrane and primer that Fleet used against riot control gas, but would it work against everything? She didn't want to find out by using it, and she had only the one. She put that thought away and briefed Aygar on what to tell, and what not to tell, his student friend. If only she'd had a chance to evaluate that friend for herself. No telling whose agent he was, unless he was just a student playing pretend spy games. If so, he'd soon find out how exciting the real ones could be.

Two of the group went through the hatch into 248 vertical ahead of Aygar, and then called him through. This shaft, they'd explained, had enough regular traffic to keep the group out of it, except on special occasions.

Sassinak waited, wishing she could make the call. Aygar was only a boy, really, from a backwoods world: he knew nothing about intrigue. It would be like him to call up this "friend" and blurt out everything on an unsecured line. She kept herself from fidgeting with difficulty. She must not increase their nervousness. How many hours had slipped by? Would Arly be worried yet? Would anyone?

Aygar bounded back through the hatch, his youthful strength and health a vivid contrast to the underworlders' air of desperation.

"He wants to meet me," Aygar said. "He says the students would like to help."

"Help? Help what?"

Sassinak knew nothing of civilian students, except what the media reported. It was clear they weren't anything like cadets.

"Help with the coup," Aygar said as if that should explain it. "End the tyranny of greed and power, he says."

"We aren't starting a coup," Sassinak said, then thought about it.

While in one sense she didn't think she was overthrowing a government, the government had certainly sent riot squads after her, as if she were. Did they think she was working with a bunch of renegade students? Did someone else have a coup planned . . . and had they stumbled into it, and was *that* . . . ?

Her brain seemed to explode, as intuition and logic both flared. Aygar was giving her a puzzled look, as she went on, more quietly.

"At least, not the one he's thinking about. Exactly. Now, what kind of help can he give us? Can he find the Parchandri?"

"He just said to meet him. And where." Aygar was looking stubborn again; he could not fail to realize that he was being used, and no one liked that.

"In public territory. Great. And you're about as easy to disguise as a torn uniform at inspection."

"Fleur's the one who taught us all about disguises," Coris said. "Although, it won't be easy with *that* one."

Sassinak felt almost too tired to think, but she had to. She pulled herself together and said, "We'll go ask her. We certainly can't stroll out looking like that. *And* we'll get some rest before we go anywhere, because I notice that Aygar looks almost as exhausted as I feel. In the meantime, Coris, if you have any maps of the underground areas, I'd like to see them."

She hoped that would give them all the idea that she had a specific plan in mind.

❖ CHAPTER SEVENTEEN

***FSP heavy cruiser* Zaid-Dayan**

"I do not like this." Arly tapped her fingers on the edge of the command console. One of its screens displayed the local news channel. "How could anyone think Sassinak would murder an admiral?"

The senior officers, including Major Currald, were ranged around her while the bridge crew pretended to pay strict attention to their monitors.

"Civilians." Bures looked almost as disgusted as she felt. "You know, if they're so scared of Fleet that they won't let us use our own shuttles up and down, then they probably think we're all born with blood in our mouths and fangs down to here." He gestured at his chin. "Long pointed ones. We go around covered with weapons, just looking for a chance to kill someone."

"News said the guy might not have been Coromell after all," said Mayerd who had come up to the bridge to watch the news with them. "Not that that helps. Good thing we don't have trouble in the neighborhood. It'd be worse if we had action coming."

Arly frowned at her. Doctors were the next thing to civilian, as far as she was concerned. "You know what she said. She thought there might be trouble. . . ."

"Like what? An invasion of mysterious green-tentacled slime monsters? We're at the center of as big a volume of peaceful space as anyone's ever known. Barring a few planet pirates, and I'm not minimizing that. But the last big stuff was decades back. Even the Seti haven't dared Fleet reprisals since the Tonagai Reef encounters. They may be gamblers, but they aren't stupid. I suppose, if the Paradens got all their pirate buddies to come blowing into FedCentral at once, they might cause us trouble, but they're not stupid either. They need a fat, peaceful culture to prey on. A shark has no advantages in a school of sharks."

Arly and Bures had crossed glances above Mayerd. Arly had to admit she had never considered a whole pirate *fleet*. They just didn't operate that way. Two or three raiders at once, more only in defense of an illegal installation. But now, with Sassinak lost somewhere below, the whole weight of the ship rested on her shoulders. She wished Ford would show up from wherever he'd been. She wished Sassinak would come back. *Blast that admiral*, she thought. Coromell, or whoever it had been, luring her away. And why? The trial? To have the *Zaid-Dayan* helpless?

The Fleet comm line blinked at her, and she put the button in her ear. "Lieutenant Commander Arly, acting captain of *Zaid-Dayan*."

"Arly, it's Lunzie. Do you recognize my voice?"

Of course she did. She'd enjoyed meeting Sassinak's astonishing young ancestor. But why was Lunzie calling on the Fleet line? "Yes. Why?"

"You need to know I'm who I say I am. I'm on FedCentral. I can't tell you where."

Arly's heart skipped a beat. Could she be with the captain? Were they in hiding?

"Sass — Commander Sassinak?" She heard the rough edge to her own voice, and hoped it would not carry.

"We don't know. Arly, the *real* Admiral Coromell wants to speak to you. I know he's the real Coromell because I knew him years ago. Before my last session of cold sleep. Do you trust me?"

Something in the voice sounded different; something had changed since Arly had said goodbye as Lunzie left the ship back at Sector HQ. Arly considered. Lunzie sounded more mature, more confident. Did that matter? Did it mean anything at all? And even if she didn't trust Lunzie, she still wanted to hear what this mysterious Coromell had to say. She gestured to Bures, who bent close and tapped out a message on her console: get Flag Officer Directory. Bures nodded. Arly spoke, hoping her voice sounded calm.

"I believe you're Lunzie if that's what you mean."

"It's not, but it'll do. Here he is.

A silence, then a deep voice that certainly had the expectation of command.

"This is Admiral Coromell. You're Lieutenant Commander Arly?"

"Yes, sir."

Bures handed her the Directory, and she flipped through it. Coromell: tall, silver-haired, bright blue eyes. A handsome man, even approaching old age. He had probably been very handsome when Lunzie knew him before. She wondered whether they'd had anything going, and forced herself to listen to him.

"As you no doubt realize, the situation is critical. Your captain has disappeared and the local law enforcement agencies were, until a few hours ago, convinced that she had killed *me*. I've been unable to find out what's going on, and some of my own staff have vanished as well."

"Sir, I thought the admiral was hunting over on Six. That's what Commander Sassinak was told."

"I was. I had an urgent message to return, and my return was complicated by Lunzie's . . ."

A flashing light on the console yanked Arly's attention away from Coromell; the Ssli biolink alarm. Could she interrupt an admiral?

"Excuse me, sir," she said, as firmly as she could. "Our Ssli has a critical message."

He didn't quite snort, but the sound he made conveyed irritation barely withheld. "Check it, then."

Arly touched the controls and the Ssli's message began scrolling across the console's upper screen.

"Enemy approaching. Seti fleet entering system, down-warping from FTL, expecting assistance in evading detection and system defenses."

Her hands trembled as she acknowledged that much. The message continued with details of the incoming menace. Number of ships, mass, weapons as known, probable crew, and troop levels.

Bures, craning his neck to read this sideways, let out a long, low whistle. Mayerd, then Currald, joined him, their faces paling as they watched the long lists grow.

"Commander Arly?" That was the admiral, impatient of the long silence.

Arly answered, surprised that her voice was steadier than her hands.

"Sir, our Ssli reports an incoming Seti fleet, definitely hostile." She heard a gasp, but did not stop. "Apparently they've got Insystem help that's supposed to disable some of the system defenses. They're timed to arrive here during the Grand Council session. There's some kind of coup planned." The display had stopped. She tapped in a question to the Ssli, asking for the source of all this.

"But how do they know?" Coromell asked. The answer came up on the screen even as he asked.

"Sir, our Ssli says there's a Ssli larva, captive, on the Seti flagship, and a Fleet officer . . . *Dupaynil*." Her own surprise carried to him.

"Who's that?"

"A Fleet Security officer assigned to us a few months ago. Then he was transferred, I think to go look up something in Seti space."

"Which he quite evidently found. Well, Commander, you have my permission to leave orbit and make life difficult for those Seti ships."

She opened her mouth to ask what about Sassinak and realized the futility. Even if the captain had been at the shuttle port, they couldn't have waited for her. Not knowing where she was, they certainly couldn't delay.

"Yes, sir," she said. Then, "Request permission to drop a shuttle and pilot in case Commander Sassinak shows up. She may need it."

"Granted," he said.

That was all. She was now more than acting captain: she had command of a warship about to fight an alien fleet. *This is impossible*, she thought, touching the button that set red lights flashing throughout the ship. She punched the ship's intercom.

"Ensign Timran to the bridge." And, off intercom, to Bures, "Get one of Sassinak's spare uniforms from her quarters and whatever else she might need. Get it up to Flight Two, fast."

More orders to give, evicting the Insystem Security monitor teams that had the weapons locked down, to Engineering to bring up the drives.

"Ensign Timran reporting, ma'am!"

He was very quick or he'd been lurking in the passage outside. She hoped he would be both quick and lucky with the shuttle.

"Report to Flight Deck Two. You'll be taking a small unit to the surface."

The admiral had said nothing about an escort, but whatever had happened to Sassinak, a few Wefts and marines couldn't make things worse. When she looked at Currald he nodded.

"Ten should do it," he said. "Leave room for her and that Aygar, coming back." He picked up another comm set and called his own adjutant.

"Yes, ma'am!" said Tim, eyes gleaming. "Do I have permission . . . ?"

"You have permission to do whatever is necessary to assist Captain Sassinak and get her safely offplanet at her command. Bures will have some things for you to take. Check with him."

He saluted and was off at a run. She hoped she'd done the right thing. Whatever had happened to Sassinak, if she was still alive, she would think she had a cruiser waiting for her. And now *we're* leaving — *I'm* leaving, taking her ship, leaving her nothing but a shuttle.

Arly couldn't believe this was happening, not so fast, but it was. Through her disbelief, she heard her own voice giving orders in the same calm, steady tone she'd cultivated for years. Longscans on, undocking procedures to begin immediately, two junior Weft officers to report to Flight Two. A loud squawk from the Station Dockmaster, demanding to know why the *Zaid-Dayan* was beginning undock without permission.

"Orders of Admiral Coromell," said Arly. Should she tell them about the Seti fleet? "We'll be releasing one planetary shuttle."

"You can't *do* that!"

"We're releasing one planetary shuttle," she went on, as if she had not heard, "and request navigational assistance to clear your Station without damage." She punched the all-ship intercom and said, "Ensign Gori to the bridge."

"But our scans are showing live weapons . . ."

That voice abruptly stopped, and an Insystems Security Force uniform appeared on one of the viewscreens.

"You are in violation of regulations. You are requested to cease and desist, or measures will be taken . . ."

"Ensign Gori reporting, ma'am."

Not as quick as Tim, but eager in his own way.

"Ensign, the cap — Commander Sassinak said you knew

regulations forwards and backwards." He didn't answer, but he didn't look worried, either. "You will discuss regulations with Insystems Security. We are withdrawing under threat of enemy attack, at the orders of a higher officer not in our direct chain of command." Gori's face brightened and his mouth opened. Arly pushed him toward one of the working boards, and said, "Don't tell *me*, tell *him*."

Yet another screen showed Flight Two, with the hatch closing on one of the shuttles. As the launch hatch opened, the elevator began raising the shuttle. Arly could just see some part of the Station through the open hatch.

" . . . no authorization for such deliberate violation," the Insystem voice droned on. "Return to inactive status at once or regulations will require that force be used."

Arly's temper flared. "You have a hostile Seti fleet incoming," she said slowly, biting off each word. "You have traitors letting them past the defenses. Don't threaten me. So far I haven't hurt the Station."

Perhaps not all the Insystem Security were in the plot. This one looked as if he'd just been slugged.

"But . . . but there's no evidence. None of the detector nets have gone off. . . ."

"Maybe someone's got his finger on the buzzer."

The shuttle cleared the *Zaid-Dayan's* hull, and disappeared. Arly sent a silent prayer after it.

"If I were you, I'd start looking at the systems with redundancies."

By now, the *Zaid-Dayan's* own powerful scans were unlocked. Nothing would show, yet. The enemy was too far out. Arly glanced around and saw that the regular bridge crew was now in place. It felt very strange to be in Sassinak's place, while 'Tenant Yulyin sat at "her" board, and stranger to see that board mostly dark, after a ship's alert. She pointed to Gori, who transferred the Insystems Security channel to his board.

"Ensign Gori will stay in contact with you."

"Fleet Regulations, Volume 21, article 14, grants authorization to commanding officers of vessels on temporary duty away from normal Sector assignment . . ." Gori sounded confident, and as smooth as any diplomat.

Arly left him to it. The combination of a surprise Seti fleet *and* Gori's zeal for regulations should keep trigger-happy fingers off the buttons until they could get away and raise shields.

"Docking bay secure, Captain."

"Weapons still locked down," Yulyin reported, at the two-minute tick.

"Right. Sassinak and I did some fancy stuff that should unkink by the time we can use them —" She wondered if this Ssli and that distant one were still in contact. And what was Dupaynil doing there? No time for that, though: her weapons had to come first.

She keyed in the code Sassinak had left with her, the captain's access to the command computers, the master controls of all weaponry. Then she explained what they'd done, and as quickly crew and marines began scurrying around the ship to restore it to full fighting capability. One hundred kilometers from the Station, Arly notched up the insystem drive.

So far, if the invaders were getting scan on her, she would look predictable. A rising spiral, the usual departure of a large ship from anything as massive as a planet. Then she engaged the stealth gear, and the *Zaid-Dayan* passed into darkness and silence, an owl hunting across the night.

FedCentral: Fleet Headquarters

Coromell swung to face Lunzie. "I never thought of *that*! My mind must be slowing!"

"What?" Lunzie hadn't heard what Arly said, had only seen its effect in the changes on Coromell's face.

"A Seti fleet, inbound —" He told her the rest, and began linking it to what they'd learned elsewhere. "This Iretan thing . . . you must have come very close to the bone somehow."

"Unless they had it planned and we just showed up in the middle of it."

"True. I keep forgetting you were sleeping away the past forty-three years. Like a time bomb for them. Come to think about it, without the Iretan's trial, the Winter Assizes were mostly commercial cases this time. And nothing coming up before Grand Council but a final vote on some financial rules affecting terra-forming. Not my field: I don't know a stock from a bond."

"So if they wanted a quiet session, they could have arranged that . . . and we really *are* a time bomb."

"Which they set for themselves, I remind you. Very fitting, all this is."

"If they don't blow us away," said Lunzie. "That's not Sassinak up there."

"She'd have left the ship to her most competent combat officer. The best we can do now is make sure whatever was planned down *here* doesn't work."

Lunzie was unconvinced. "But what can one cruiser do against a whole fleet?"

"Buy us time, if nothing else. Don't worry about what you can't change. What we'll have to do is make sure Insystem has the alarm, and believes it, and gets Sassinak out of whatever trap she's in."

The tiny clinic attached to Fleet Central Systems Command had but one corridor that opened directly into the back offices of the Command building. Lunzie followed Coromell, noticing that the enlisted personnel looked as stunned to see him as he had looked when he heard about the Seti fleet.

"Sir? When did the admiral arrive?" asked one, almost but not quite barring the way to the lift marked "Admiral's use only."

"About thirty hours ago. Apparently our security confused at least a few people." He punched the controls and the lift door sighed open.

"But, sir, that commander . . . the murder . . ."

"Put a lock on it, Algin. Who's been speaking for us?"

"Lt. Commander Dallish, sir. He's up . . ."

But Coromell had closed the lift door, and now gave Lunzie a rueful smile.

"I knew that. But he doesn't know that Dallish is the one officer here I really trust. His father and I were close friends, years ago. Dallish has been covering for me."

"Shouldn't you have stayed under cover longer?"

"With Sassinak still accused of murdering me? No. Showing up alive should shake them up just as much as you shook the conspirators by waking up in the midst of their plot. Whoever *thought* he killed me will wonder who the victim was. And whoever sent the victim to take my place will wonder if we're on to him. We soon will be."

Lunzie found Coromell's office a relief after the pastel-walled, determinedly soothing atmosphere of the clinic suite. A great arc of desk took the place of the command module onboard a ship. He grinned when he saw her expression.

"Yes, it's an indulgence. But one which keeps me thinking like a deepspace admiral, and not a planet-dweller."

A younger man, whom Lunzie assumed was "Dallish," stood aside as they entered, then handed Coromell a sheaf of thin plastic strips. One wall had a window looking out across the city — Lunzie's first live view of the hub of interplanetary government. It looked, to her, like any other large city. Below, a broad street had both slideways and vehicular traffic: bright blue and green monorail trains. She glanced around Coromell's office again. The dark-blue flat-piled carpet that seemed to be favored by Fleet officers, a bank of viewscreens on the opposite wall, racks of datacubes, fichefiles, even a row of books bound in plain blue.

"Lunzie!"

She looked away from a row cf exquisitely detailed model ships, displayed against a painted starscape. Coromell and Dallish had tuned in one of the civilian news programs, now showing a view that Lunzie realized was the docking tube of a ship at Station. At first she did not hear whatever the news commentator was saying. Over the tube, the electronic display had gone from green to orange; the ship's name *Zaid-Dayan* and status "Undock: Warning" blinked on and off.

A commentator stepped in front of the vicam, and Lunzie made herself listen to the sleek-haired woman with the professional frown.

"Most unusual behavior has prompted some to suggest that the missing captain of this dangerous ship may have been contaminated with a psychoactive agent, even a disease which has spread to crew members. We have just been informed that the Insystem Federation Security teams whose duty it is to ensure that these warships cannot fire their weapons at innocent civilians, these teams are being evicted from this ship. Even now," and the commentator's head turned slightly so that Lunzie could see out-of-focus movement behind her, up the tube toward the ship. "I believe, yes, here they are, quite against their will. . . ."

Hands on heads, the men and women clumping down the length of the tube looked unhappy enough. Behind them were figures in ominous gray and green armor, helmets locked down, and very impressive-looking weapons in hand.

"Security team weapons," Coromell commented to Dallish. "Notice that? Their own are probably still locked up. They disarmed the warden teams." He sounded almost gleeful. "Probably Wefts, shifting on 'em."

"Excuse me," the commentator was saying, thrusting her microphone into the faces of the first to exit, while the camera zoomed at them. "Could you comment on the mental stability of the crew of this ship? Is there any danger that they might turn . . ."

"Bunch of flippin' maniacs!" snarled one of the men. He had a ripening bruise over one eye, and a split lip. "Gone totally bonkers, they have, hallucinatin' about invaders from the deep!"

"Krims!" Dallish glanced at Lunzie and back to the screen. "If they take that line . . ."

Coromell was already punching commands on his desk. Lunzie's gaze flicked back and forth between him and the newscast. She found it hard to concentrate on either. Those exiting the ship had clumped around the newscaster and her crew; behind them, the camera barely showed something moving again in the tube.

Suddenly a loud squeal made everyone on the screen jump and they moved back. The camera focussed on a large red hatch sliding across the tube opening, as the status board changed to "Undock: ACCESS CLOSED." The news program shifted to someone in a studio.

"Thank you, Cerise," said a male 'caster who then turned to the front. "As you can see, something ominous is going on with the Fleet heavy cruiser *Zaid-Dayan*, whose former captain, a Fleet officer named Sassinak, is sought in connection with a murder investigation on the surface of this planet. We have no explanation for the expulsion of the security teams or for the cruiser's apparent intention to undock from the Station. We have learned from sources close to the Federation Justice Department Prosecutor's office that valuable evidence and a witness in the upcoming trial of the heavyworlder conspirator Tanegli are also missing. Although we cannot speculate at this time on any connection between the two, our correspondent Li Tsan is standing by at the office of the Justice Department Chief Prosecutor, Ser Branik. Li, what can you tell us about the Justice Department's reaction to this latest Fleet outrage?"

"Well, the Prosecutor isn't saying anything. This situation is still too new. But we have heard suggestions that the *Zaid-Dayan* became contaminated with some kind of spore or viral particle, on the proscribed planet Ireta, which is affecting the mental processes of anyone exposed."

"And would that apply as well to the witnesses expected to arrive in the next day or so from the EEC vessel . . . the . . . uh . . . former co-governors, Kai and Varian?"

"It certainly could. We expect to hear that they may be quarantined and their transmitted testimony might well be scrutinized more closely. if such a disease did cause mental instability, that might even be a defense for the original alleged conspirators. Certainly Tanegli hasn't appeared normally healthy in any of the interviews we've seen."

"NO!" Lunzie startled herself as well as Coromell and Dallish with that explosion. They stared at her. She got her voice back under control, choked down the less acceptable phrases she wanted to use, and said, "It's ridiculous nonsense, and any doctor would know that at once. There's no disease that could make Sassinak and Arly crazy after a brief exposure, that wouldn't have affected the rest of us all those years. To the point where we couldn't have survived. Tanegli is *not* some innocent overcome by alien spores. He's as guilty as anyone could be, and I'll see him convicted."

"Not if this goes on," Dallish said, pointing to the screen. He had turned the sound down, but Lunzie could see that the mouths were still moving.

"He's right," Coromell said, putting down the comm unit he'd been holding. "I can't convince *anyone* to listen to me. Even those who believe I'm who I say I am. Someone's put a lock on this thing, hard and fast. That," and he nodded at the unit, "was the Assistant Longscan Supervisor, and as far as he's concerned there's not a ship within a couple of light-years that he didn't have logged for scheduled arrival months ago. That's one I trust, normally as suspicious as I am, but he's believing his machines and his outstation crews. And someone had already reached him, insisting that it was his duty to squelch any panic in the week before the Grand Council and Winter Assizes open."

"Who?" asked Dallish. "I've never seen anything blocked that fast. It was as if they had everything in place."

"Of course they would have," Coromell said. "Once they knew

about their time bomb, about Ireta, they'd start setting up ways to counter anything we could do. I'm suddenly becoming very suspicious about that hunting trip."

"But, sir, you always go rhuch hunting."

"True, but you remember I thought of not going, with Sassinak coming in and the trial approaching. Then they had that 'cancellation' in Bakli Lodge. Well, no matter now. We can dig into that later, assuming we ensure a later."

"Sir, if I may suggest?" Dallish looked both embarrassed and determined.

"Go ahead."

"Lunzie's now the single witness in the Iretan case. She's an obvious target even if she hadn't brought back all that from Diplo."

"She ought to be safe enough here. . . ." Coromell began, and then he shook his head. "Except that we've already passed word to the Prosecutor's office that she's onplanet."

"And we have to assume a leak in that office. Yes, sir."

"Mmm. We'll just have to make sure we have none here." His comm unit buzzed and Coromell picked it up. "Ah . . . Mr. Justice Vrix. Yes, as a matter of fact, but you have her taped deposition on file. No. No, that's impossible. Because . . . yes. Precisely. And until that time, I'm not risking the government's remaining witness." He flipped a toggle and smiled at Lunzie. "You see? We must not let you out of our sight between now and the trial."

Fleet shuttle Seeker

This time, Ensign Timran told himself, he would do everything right the first time. Not by accident, but by the exercise of cool judgment and keen intelligence. He knew that he'd been chosen for this mission because he had a habit of being lucky. But *this* time he had a team of marines, a pair of Weft officers (that they outranked him hardly mattered: while he piloted the shuttle, he ranked everyone) and authorization to rescue his revered captain. He was going to do everything right. He would make *no* mistakes.

Tongue caught between his teeth, he eased the shuttle off its platform, remembered to key in the appropriate signal to the *Zaid-Dayan* to confirm liftoff, remembered to check the low-link and high-link connections with the cruiser's comm shack. From this vantage, the Station looked as if a mischievous child had taken three or four sets of TekiLink toys and mismatched half the connections. As a habitat for gerbils, it might have a certain charm but it lacked the clean functional lines Timran approved of in Fleet installations. The cruiser had been docked at the outer end of one long arm; he had another such to dodge, with a row of boxy insystem transports.

Then he was clear, with an easy drop trajectory down to the shuttleport. Except that he was not going to the shuttleport. He hadn't told Arly: she was busy enough. And his orders said nothing specific about the shuttleport, just that he was to go render assistance to Sassinak. He was sure she wasn't at the shuttleport. If she had been, she'd have contacted the cruiser before now. So going to the shuttleport would only involve a lot of hashing around with civilians who didn't want a Fleet shuttle in their airspace anyway.

Beside him, one of the Wefts had tuned in the civilian newscast. Tim almost glanced at it when he heard the commentator's question to the evicted Security team and the answers, but he remembered what had happened last time he got distracted. More to the point were the angry questions from Airspace Control. They seemed to think he would interfere with scheduled traffic. He smiled to himself. Military shuttles would not have survived in service if they'd been blind to other craft. He knew where everything around him was at least as well as Airspace Control. And all of them knew, from hearing the smug Security teams brag about it, that FedCentral had no inner air defenses. The Bronthin had refused to allow them. From Tim's point of view, the only weapons down there were little stuff.

"We're not goin' to the 'port?" asked the Weft. Kiksi, her name was. If she was a she . . . Tim had never bothered to find out much about Wefts. He didn't dislike them, he just found his own amusements far more interesting than theoretical knowledge about aliens.

"No," Tim said. "They'll just try to impound us. And Commander Sassinak can't be there, or she'd have contacted us."

"Good thought," said the Weft. "Do you *know* where she is?"

"Nobody does," said Tim. He had punched up the mapping function and was now trying to decide just where he did want to

land. FedCentral offered little open land close to where he
thought Sassinak might be.

"Not strictly true," said the other Weft, 'Tenant Sricka. "Sassinak is not where the shuttle can reach her."

This time he did look away, though he kept his hands steady.
"You know where she is? Why didn't you tell Arly?"

"She kept moving. She was under surface. We had no return
contact."

"Under surface . . . like in a submarine?" FedCentral had only
one ocean and Tim had not suspected it of submarine transport.

A chuckle from Kiksi, that made his ears burn. "No . . . under
the city. Subways? Maintenance tunnels? We don't know. We
don't *talk* with her in human shape. We're not made for it. It's
direction sense only. When we are nearer, I can *shift*, and then
perhaps touch her mind more directly. But you, where are you
planning to land the shuttle? And how to prevent detection?"

"I'm not sure."

He knew his ears were bright red and the back of his neck,
under his uniform. It had seemed like a good idea, and even
before Arly called on him, he'd daydreamed about rescuing Sassinak, poring over the maps of the vast complex. The shuttle could
land on unprepared ground, could even make a direct vertical
drop of fifty to a hundred feet, although he'd never done it. But
he couldn't land on the roofs of ordinary buildings or on slideways
or monorail tracks.

Sricka reached over and tapped the map-control console; the
area he'd been watching slid aside, and another came up. Open,
not too rough, and fairly near the city. He didn't recognize the
code.

"Land fill," the Weft said. "That end's already covered, and the
replanting cycle's only up to grass. And that yellow line there,
that's a subway tunnel for returning workers to their housing. It's
your decision, but if I were flying this thing, that's where I'd go."

He had no better ideas, and he was not about to ask for a vote.
He could almost feel the marines' amusement tickling his backbone.

"Looks good," he said trying to sound casual. "And thanks."

"Will it alarm you if I *shift*?"

"No. Of course not."

Nonetheless, he had to gulp hard when the ordinary human

figure beside him turned into a mass of extra joints, spiky protu-
berances, and all too many legs. And a row of bright blue eyes.
Instead of staring, he entered his desired destination in the shuttle's navigational computer and saw to it that the course changes
all went as planned. By the time he neared the landfill, flying the
shuttle as if were any aircraft, he knew that the *Zaid-Dayan* was
long gone. He had to do it right this time. If he messed up, there
would be no rescue.

✧ CHAPTER EIGHTEEN

For a moment, following Aygar up into the more public tunnels, Sassinak thought how she could explain all this to a Board of Inquiry, if she survived long enough. There were no *Rules of Engagement* covering this sort of thing. She remembered something about "accepting civilian volunteers into a military mission" — not recommended, but it did happen — and more than one passage strongly cautioning Fleet officers from involving themselves in local politics. And this was hardly local politics. She had taken on some part of the Federation itself and even though she considered the people involved to be traitors, they could say the same of her.

She dared not think too far ahead or the weight of it would crush her. A single Fleet captain against the most powerful families in the Federations, against the massed pirates, plus the Seti? And with nothing but a ragged bunch of crazies and losers? How could she even be thinking of this? Yet the thought daunted her for only a moment. She had survived the raid on her home, against odds as high. She had survived battle after battle in space where any mistake could have killed her, and some nearly had. She had survived the jealousy of other officers, a hundred mischances, to be where she was now. *If not you, who?* Abe had said more than once.

No time for letting her mind drift, not even to the things Fleur had told her. She would have time later for more such talks, for long reminiscences, for shared tears and laughter, or they would both be dead. For now, she had Aygar to get safely to the rendezvous with his student friend, and whatever came after. She patted her midsection where the extra bulk Fleur had insisted she stuff into the pale blue worksuit felt itchy and unfamiliar. Even worse was the slight dowager's hump that prickled when she twitched her shoulders, trying to remember to slump. Although she'd seen in the mirror that the gray streaks Fleur had added to her hair as well as decidedly wrong makeup made her look years older, she kept thinking a more complete disguise would have been better. Aygar, whose height and shoulders made him unmistakable, had been turned into a male fashion plate. A voluminous magenta shirt unlaced halfway down his chest and tucked into tight gray shorts made him look like anything but fugitive. His mapper button now looked like one of the jewels studding a large medallion hung on a stout chain around his neck.

The first "uptowners" they saw hardly glanced at them. The upsloping tunnel, linking one subway level with another, had streams of pedestrians scurrying in both directions. Most wore one-piece worksuits in grays, browns, and blues; the others were dressed as flamboyantly as Aygar. Homebound workers, Fleur had said, mingling with the pleasure-hunters who also tended to "change shifts" at rush hours. Sassinak trailed him, trying to look as if she merely happened to be going in the same direction. In that brief time below, she'd forgotten how noisy large groups could be. Announcements no one could have understood boomed from the levels below and above; the scurrying feet were overlaid by a constant roar of conversation. A flare of Ryxi screeched, threatening, and the humans parted around them. A gray uniform approached at a jog.

At the next level, the upbound stream bifurcated, a third veering left and two-thirds right. Even more noise broke over them. The synthesized voice of the transportation computers announcing train arrivals and departures, warning passengers away from the rails, repeating the same list of safety rules over and over. Friends met on the platforms with squeals of delight as if they had not seen each other at rush hour the day before. Less demonstrative workers glared at them or muttered brief curses. Aygar and Sassinak both turned right. Here, service booths backed the subway platforms: fountains, restrooms, public call-booths, even a few food booths. As he'd been directed, Aygar turned into the third of these. Sassinak paused as if to look over the menu displayed, then ducked in after him.

He was already shaking the hand of a much smaller young man with a milder version of the same outfit; small-flowered purple print shirt, and looser green shorts but higher-heeled boots.

Backing him were two other young men, similarly dressed, and a girl who seemed to have stepped out of a Carin Coldae rerun. Her silvery snugsuit clung to the right curves, all the way down to sleek black boots, and her emerald green scarf was knotted casually on the left shoulder. Across the back of the bodysuit ran a stenciled black chain design and short lengths of minute black chain hung from her earlobes.

Sassinak managed not to snicker. Innocent bravado deserved a passing nod of respect, although she could have told the young woman that carrying a real weapon where she'd stashed her emerald-green plastic imitation needler would make it hard to draw in time for practical use. Her own hand checked the weapon Aygar had taken from the dead man behind the bar. She moved past them, up to the counter, and ordered a bowl of fried twists that were supposed to be real vegetables, not processor output. Whatever it was, it would taste better than her last meal. She paid for it from the money Fleur had given her and sat down at a largish table near the clump of young people. They were talking busily, waving their arms and looking like any other group of young people in a public place. Now they were moving up, ordering their own food, and then Aygar led them to the table she'd chosen.

"Can we sit here?" asked the darkest of the young men. He was sitting already. "We need a big table."

Sassinak nodded, hoping she looked like a slightly intimidated middle-aged office worker. She ate a couple of fries and decided that it didn't matter if they were real veggies or processed: they were delicious.

"I'm Jonlik," he said smiling brightly at her. "This is Gerstan, and this is Bilis, and our Coldae clone is Erdra." The girl gave Sassinak a long stare intended to impress.

"I thought you were supposed to be a cruiser captain."

"I am," Sassinak said very quietly. "Did you never hear of disguises?"

They all looked unimpressed and she sighed inwardly. Had she ever been this young?

"I wore this for you," the girl said. "I thought . . ."

Sassinak laid a hand over the girl's wrist with strength enough to get a startled look. "I had a Coldae poster in silver, when I was a girl. But that was a picture. Reality's different."

"Well, of course, but . . ."

Sassinak released the girl's wrist and leaned back, giving her stare for stare. The girl reddened suddenly.

"Erdra, you wouldn't have lasted a week in the slave pens. Most of my friends didn't."

Now their stares had a different expression. Jonlik's bottle of *drelz* sauce was dripping on his lap.

"Best wipe that up," she said, in the tone she used aboard ship.

He gaped, looked down, and mopped at his shorts with one flowing sleeve.

"I told you," Aygar growled. She wondered what else he'd told them. At least he was keeping his voice low.

Sassinak turned to Gerstan. "Is it true, what Aygar said, that you can patch into the secure links without being caught?"

Gerstan nodded, and gulped down his mouthful of fries.

"So far. We've gotten all the way up to H-Level, and there's really tricky stuff from F-level on up. I've never been as far as H by myself. Erdra's done it, though."

"What's on H-level?"

Erdra tossed her head in a gesture not quite like Coldae's but close enough.

"Well, it lets you play model games with the lower levels. Like, what if all the water in the auxiliary reservoir is gone suddenly and the pumps on that line are about to seize. That's one thing, but it's not just games, because it's realtime, using their data, bollixing their sensors, overriding the safety interlocks. I've never done anything dangerous . . ." The tone was that of someone who had indeed done something criminal, if not dangerous, but who wasn't about to admit it.

Bilis snorted. "What abut the time you convinced the Transport Authority a train had derailed out on the Yellow Meadow line?"

"That wasn't *dangerous*. They had time to stop the following trains. I set it up that way."

"Cost the taxpayers 80,000 credits, they said," Bilis said to Sassinak. "Lost time, damage from the emergency halts, hours of hunting the 'bases, looking for tampering. Never did find her."

"Never did find the tap at all," said Erdra who sounded much smugger than someone faking a train derailment should. "And if something blows when a train has to make an emergency stop, it needs finding. If there *had* been a wreck, that number 43 would've plowed right into it. They should thank me for finding their problems."

Sassinak eyed the girl, wishing she had her on the *Zaid-Dayan* for a few weeks. With all that talent, she needed someone to straighten her out.

"By the way," Erdra said sweetly, popping a couple of fries into her mouth and crunching them. "How come your ship left without you?"

"I beg your pardon?" It was the only alternative to the scream that wanted to erupt from her gut.

"Your ship. That cruiser. Newscast says it broke away from the Station and went zipping off blathering about an invading fleet. The captain or whoever you left up there is supposed to be crazy with whatever drug or spore or something you caught on Ireta. Whatever made you kill that admiral."

For a moment the whirl of Sassinak's thoughts found no verbal form. Rage: how dare they leave her! Fear: she had been so sure that if she could get a signal out, Arly would be there for her. Exultation: she had been *right*! There was more going on than anyone had thought and those blasted smug Internal Security fops were going to find something worse than a Fleet cruiser's guns to worry about.

She controlled all that, and her breathing, with an effort and said, "I didn't kill any admiral." But I could cheerfully kill *you*, she thought at Erdra who clearly had no telepathic ability at all because she kept right on smiling.

"You nearly finished?" That came from an irritated clump of men in business jumpers, their fry packets leaking grease onto their fingers.

"Oh, sure." Gerstan stood up as quickly as the others did. "Let's go on to somewhere else and talk, huh?"

Sassinak felt very much the drab peahen among the flock but dealt with that by taking the lead. She trusted Aygar to keep them following.

Back down the sloping connecting tunnel to the narrow service tube and the unobtrusive door. Their last protest had been some distance back. Sassinak paid no mind to it. She had enough to think of. Arly would not have taken the *Zaid-Dayan* out without good reason. That she knew. But on top of her own concern, her own burning desire to *be there* when anything happened to her ship, the words "court-martial" burned in her mind. There was no excuse short of death for a captain who was downside when her ship went into action.

She gave the signal knock to the door, and it opened at once. She led the others in, and when the door shut behind them, they faced the same weapons she had.

"What *is* this?" Gerstan demanded.

"Caution," Sassinak said. And to Coris, "No one noticed us and we had no problems. Some of these were fairly loose-tongued in a fry bar but the place was jammed with commuters. Shouldn't be a problem." She turned back to the students. "You wanted a conspiracy? You've just found one. These," and she waved an arm at her motley troop, "are fellow-conspirators. Refugees. Ex-slaves. The poor and homeless of this city which, according to Aygar, you hope to help by plotting a coup."

From their expressions, none of the students had actually *met* any of the undergrounders before. To their credit, none of them tried to bolt.

"You're sure about these four?" Coris asked.

"Not entirely, yet, but let's go down a bit and see if Erdra's as good as Gerstan says."

Coris nodded, and waved Sassinak through the group. She spoke over her shoulder to Erdra. "Did they give any specifics about the ship leaving? Say *what* it was after?"

"Uh . . . not really." Erdra sounded much less smug. Perhaps the girl had recognized that those weapons were real. "Just that they — the people aboard — threw off the Security teams that make sure no weapons are usable. A shuttle was sent off and then the ship left the Station. They'd said something about an invasion, but there's been no word. But that got squashed. It's been confirmed that nothing's out there that shouldn't be."

"And *you* believe that?" Sassinak didn't wait for an answer, but let her annoyance work itself out. "You, who created a fake train wreck? Who could've hidden a real one as easily?"

"But I didn't. And that means someone *else* . . ."

"Is as smart as you are. Right."

"Then is there *really* something out there?" That was Gerstan, bouncing up alongside her. Sassinak refrained from slapping him back into place.

"Arly would not take the *Zaid-Dayan* without good reason.

She's not any crazier than I am. So I think something's out there. What, I couldn't guess."

Actually, she could: a pirate incursion or a Seti fleet. Either one might be part of a larger conspiracy and she had to hope only one of them had materialized. Her mind reverted to something else Erdra had said. A shuttle? Why had Arly released a shuttle?

Then she grinned: obvious. And she would wager she could name the pilot aboard, but not what that very brash young man would do next.

"So you're saying," Gerstan went on, "that the Federation itself is involved in concealing the approach of some danger from deepspace?"

Sassinak nodded. "Yes, because some faction thinks that will give it control. In such cases you have two possibilities. The present rulers want to use force to give themselves absolute power because they fear a challenge, or a faction not quite in control wants to tip the balance its way."

"Which is it?"

"I don't know." She grinned at their confusion. "It doesn't really matter. If Arly detected the incoming fleet at the edge of the *Zaid-Dayan*'s scan range, it can't be here for days. It won't just launch missiles at the planet. To do that it could have lobbed a passive from far outside scan." Their faces were blank. Sassinak reminded herself that none of these people had military training. "Never mind," she said gently. "The point is that whatever's going on up there isn't our problem. *Our* problem is the group here that's concealing it. *That*, we can do something about, if we're quick enough. Then the existing defense systems should be able to handle the invaders." She wasn't at all sure she believed that. Would Arly think to call for more Fleet aid? Or would she be worried that what came might not be on their side?

"Now," she said, putting enough bite in it that they all, students and undergrounders alike, gave her their full attention. "First we must locate The Parchandri and neutralize him. That's your task, Erdra. Get into the links and 'bases, and find out where his hidey-hole is. Get control of the life-support and communications lines. I'd wager next year's pay that he'll be underground but not completely self-contained."

"But . . ." The girl looked around. "Where's an access port? I've always used one of the Library carrels to get in."

"Coris. Take her down and help her get to one of the trunkline 'ports. Bilis can go with her and you'll need a tensquad for guards. If you run into trouble, run! And get her to another 'port. Two runners, for messages, until we get our communications set up. Gerstan, you told Aygar that there were a lot more students who wanted to get involved?"

"Yes, ma'am." That honorific came out slowly as if he hadn't planned it. Sassinak smiled at him.

"Good. We'll find you a 'port and you can let them know. We need communications links topside so we can keep track of what the media's saying and what's going down on the streets. We'll also need some small portable comms, like those the police have." From his expression, he was finding real action scarier than he'd expected. And he hadn't seen real action yet.

"You mean, steal . . . ? Like, from a . . . a policeman? A guard?"

"Whatever it takes. I thought you were eager to start a revolution. Did you think you'd do that without getting crossways with the police?"

"Well, no, but . . . ."

"But talk let you feel brave without doing anything. Sorry, lad, but the time for that's all gone. Now it's time to act or go hide someplace *very* deep until it's over. Can you do it? Will your friends?"

"Well . . . yes. Some of 'em we've even had to sit on, practically, to keep them from doing something stupid."

Sassinak grinned. "Change stupid to useful and get 'em rounded up. Let's go, everyone."

Coris had already left with Erdra and Bilis. Now Sassinak led the others at a good pace back to the lower levels. After the first shock of hearing that the *Zaid-Dayan* had left, she felt an unaccountable lift of spirits. The whole situation was impossible, but it would come out right.

In only a few hours, the fragile bond between the various groups began to strengthen. A trickle of students appeared, from one access tunnel and another, all with necessary equipment. Half a dozen standard 'phone repair kits, with the official connectors that wouldn't trip any alarms no matter where they were plugged in. Two police-issue belt-comps that included both communicators and tiny computers. Nineteen gas-kits similar to the Fleet-issue one Sassinak carried.

"Where'd you get these?" she asked the short, chunky youth who brought them in. He blushed a deep rose and muttered something about the drama department. "Drama department?"

"We did Hostigge's *Breathless* last year and the director wanted realistic props. She's friendly with a guy at the local station who said these weren't really any good without the detox." At which point he handed over a sackful of detox tubes. "Now these I got scrounging around in the junk stores over on Lollipi Street. Most of 'em have been used once, but I thought maybe . . ."

"How long have you been collecting them?" Something about the earnest sweating face impressed Sassinak. He reminded her of the best supply officers: longsided and sticky-fingered.

"Well, even before the play I thought maybe they'd be good for something, if somebody could synthesize the membranes. Then when we got the membrane masks and they didn't take 'em back, I thought . . ." His voice trailed away, as if he still didn't realize what he'd done.

"Good for you," she said.

She hoped he'd survive the coming troubles. He'd be worth recruiting. Of course, nineteen gas kits among hundreds didn't help much, but he'd had the right idea.

Meanwhile, with the communications access to the topside, they knew what the news media were telling everyone. Erdra had tapped into the lower-level secured lines so they knew where the police patrols were. Sassinak found herself yawning again and when she counted the hours, realized she'd run over twenty-four again. Aygar was snoring in a corner of the crowded little maintenance area their group was in. She would have to sleep soon herself.

"Got it," came Erdra's triumphant cry.

Sassinak struggled up. She'd fallen asleep at some point and somebody had covered her with a blanket. She raked her fingers through her hair and wished she could have thirty seconds in her own refresher cabinet.

"Are you sure?" she heard someone else ask.

"Yes, because it's guarded like nothing else we've seen. It's *not* in the central city, though, where I'd have thought, but over here, map coordinates 13-H. Below the main tunnels. But look, it's not directly under any of them. So I got into an archive file and found the building specs." She was waving a hardcopy sheet and Sassinak grabbed it.

"It's a ship!" The others stared at her.

"It can't be," Erdra said. "It's underground."

"Silo construction." From the blank looks, none of them knew what that meant. "Look," and Sassinak pointed to her proof, "the stuff on top's designed to look like real buildings, but it's just shell. Probably even folds back. Down here, this is a lot more than self-contained habitat for a planet . . . this, and this." Her finger stabbed at the plans. "Framing of a standard midsize personal yacht. My guess would be Bollanger Yards, maybe a hundred-fifty years ago. When was that section of the city built up?"

Erdra scowled, fiddled on the keyboard she now carried, and said, "Eighty-two years ago, subdivided for light industry. Before that, nothing but a single warehouse and . . . a derelict shuttle station, from back when private shuttles were legal."

"But a ship couldn't last that long, could it?" asked Gerstan.

"Easily, protected like that. They've maintained it. They'll have replaced obsolete equipment with new. No problem to them. And nothing wrong with the hull design. The question is, do they keep it fitted to launch?"

"Launch? From underground?"

Civilians! Did they not even know that *most* planetary defenses used some silo-sited missiles, often placed on moons or asteroids in the system, safe from random bombardment by stray rocks?

"Launch. As in, 'escape.' If things get too hot. Which is precisely what we were planning to make them."

"How could we tell? And what will it do if it does launch? Will it start a fire?"

"Erdra, do you have a hardcopy of all the connection data?"

Wide-eyed, the girl handed over a sheaf of them. Sassinak began paging through as she talked.

"If it's the hull I think it is, and if it's got the engines it should have, then it will do more than start a fire if it launches. They won't have intended that silo to be used more than once. Its lining will combust to produce part of the initial lift and since they would only do it in an emergency, it's probably set to backblast down any communicating tunnels. Even though that wastes thrust, I doubt they'll care."

Her eyes scanned the sheets, translating into Fleet terms the different civilian notation. Yes. There. Solid chemical fuel, far more efficient than any in the dawn of human space exploration, but still unstable and requiring replacement at intervals. So the hardened access tunnel for that alone, in case anything went wrong, would have blast hatches at both ends. He could still get away.

The old rage burned behind her eyes. So close, and he could still get away. She could almost see them getting near, breaking through one defense after another, only to be met by the blazing flare of the engines as the yacht lifted away from trouble to some luxurious hidey-hole in another system.

<Sassinak!>

Her heart caught, then went on. A Weft — one of *her* Wefts — in range. She sent back an urgent query.

<Ten marines, two of us, Timran piloting the shuttle.>

The shuttle! Virtually helpless against real fighting craft, even a shuttle could take an unarmed yacht. Sassinak felt a rush of excitement. Now she had them trapped; The Parchandri and whoever his main conspirators were. She could block their escape. She could push them into it, make them commit themselves, show themselves. And then destroy them. She realized the others were looking at her oddly.

"Don't worry," she said. "That's not the disaster it seems like. In fact, when you know an enemy's bolthole, it becomes a trap."

"But if the ship goes up, how can we . . ."

Sassinak waved for quiet, and the babble died. "My cruiser dropped a shuttle, remember?" Heads nodded. She went on. "So if I get where I can contact them," and she waved her little comm unit, "they can intercept it." She was not about to tell them she could talk to her Wefts. She'd heard enough racial slurs down here to convince her of that. "But there's plenty of work for the rest of you."

It would take pressure to make them run, pressure in the Grand Council, pressure underground. They must feel threatened every way but that. And she could not use these civilian lives freely. They were not hers to throw away, not even in such a cause.

✧ CHAPTER NINETEEN

FSP Escort* Brightfang, *FedCentral Docking Station

On the bridge of the escort vessel *Brightfang* by the courtesy of his old classmate Killin, Fordeliton had a startling view of the *Zaid-Dayan's* departure as the escort approached the FedCentral Main Station. First he noticed that the Flight Bay was open, then he could see the elevator rising with a shuttle poised on its narrow surface. He wondered briefly if Sassinak were letting Timran run an errand as the shuttle lifted away, the Flight Bay closing in behind it. A few seconds later, the ship itself eased off the docking probe. He felt a great hollow open in his middle. He had counted on reporting to Sassinak the moment he arrived. He was in time for the trial. Why was she leaving? What would he do now?

"What's going on?" he asked.

No one answered. Killin looked angry as he spoke into his comm set, but Ford could not quite hear what he said. The little ship shivered. Someone's tractor beam had swept it. He knew better than to ask anything more, and made himself as invisible as he could. Then Killin turned to him.

"They won't let us dock! They're holding us in position with the tractors and they're threatening worse."

"What's happened?"

"Your captain. According to them, she killed an admiral onplanet and whoever she left in charge of the *Zaid-Dayan* has gone completely bonkers, ghost-hunting. They think it's something catching, probably from Ireta."

"Arly! It'd be Arly if Sassinak left the ship. And Arly's *not* crazy. Patch me over to 'em."

Killin shook his head. "Can't. They've jammed us just in **case.**

So far as they're concerned, Fleet personnel are all crazy until proven otherwise. They're not about to let us spread our damaging lies."

"They said *that*?" With astonishment came the sudden piercing loss. Where *was* Sassinak? In prison? Surely not dead! He realized that he did not want to deal with a world that had no Sassinak in it, not anywhere.

"They said it's worse than that. The Insystem Security officer I spoke to had been thrown off the *Zaid-Dayan*. By Wefts."

"But I've got orders. I've got to get this information down there in time for Tanegli's trial."

Killin shrugged. "Feel like space-swimming the last kilometer? And then I doubt they'll let you go down in a shuttle like a nice, harmless civilian."

"Why are they scared of you? They don't know you've got a deadly Iretan survivor with you."

Killin looked startled. "I forgot. You *were* there, weren't you? Snarks, if they figure that out . . ."

"We don't tell them. We don't tell them I have any connection to the *Zaid-Dayan* or Sassinak. I'm just a humble courier, carrying a sealed satchel from Sector HQ to FedCentral's Justice Center."

"I didn't pick you up at Sector HQ."

"And who knows that? Got a good reason for turning me over to these idiots?"

Killin shrugged. "No. But that still doesn't get you into the Station. If they relent . . ." He broke off as his comm unit blinked at him and he cut the volume onto the cabin speakers.

" . . . assurances that no member of your crew was at any time on the proscribed planet Ireta, which is believed to be the source of a plague affecting mental capacity, you will be allowed to dock and proceed with normal business."

Killin winked at Ford and spoke into the comm. "Sir, this ship has never even been in the same sector as Ireta. We're a scheduled courier run between Sector Eight HQ and the capitol. We have a courier onboard, with urgent sealed messages from Sector to the Justice Center, as I believe your stripsheet will show."

A long pause, then another voice. "Right, Captain. You are on the sheet, listed as courier, with one passenger carrying papers under diplomatic seal. Is that right?"

"Yes, sir. The rest of the crew hasn't changed since the last run."

"Do you . . . ah . . . have any knowledge of the *Zaid-Dayan's* crew? If any debarked at Sector HQ?" Killin raised his eyebrows at Ford, and Ford shook his head quickly, then scribbled a note to him. Killin began drawling his answer as he read.

"Well, only what we heard, you know, back at Sector. Whole crew was ordered to appear here as potential witnesses or something, is what I heard. Certainly didn't hear of any leaving the ship there."

Killin's grin at Ford was wolfish. He didn't like to lie, but this was not a lie. What Ford had told him in the week they'd been together was entirely separate from what he'd heard at Sector. More interesting, too.

"Very well. We will proceed with docking." Killin clicked the comm off, and shook his head at Ford.

"You're going to have to be lucky to get away with this. And that captain of yours shouldn't be so trigger-happy. Admirals! I've known a few I'd like to blow away, but actually doing it gives such a bad impression to the Promotion Board."

Ford maintained the cool reserve expected of a courier all the way through Customs, an ordeal usually reserved for civilians, but in this instance imposed in its full rigor on every Fleet member. He gave his name, his rank, his number, and his current posting: special orders to Fleet Headquarters, FedCentral.

"Last ship posting?" This was almost a snarl.

Ford allowed himself a faint, sad smile. "I'm sorry to say, the *Zaid-Dayan*. I understand it's been a problem to you?"

He dared not try to conceal this, any more than his real identity. But the *Zaid-Dayan* had arrived in port without him, with someone else listed as Sassinak's second-in-command. He had a slight chance.

If the Insystem Security Officer had had movable ears, they'd have pricked. He could feel the interest.

"Ah. And you served with Commander Sassinak?"

"Some time back, yes."

His tone indicated that the further back in time that association slipped, the happier he would be. The Security Officer did not relax, but his eyelids flicked.

"And have you had contact with Commander Sassinak since?"

"No. I had no reason to contact the commander once I left her . . . command." Nothing so blatant as open hostility, just a chill. He had been glad to leave her command, and no backward glances.

"I see." The officer looked down at a datascreen Ford could not see. "This was before the Ireta incident?"

Ford nodded, tight-lipped, and muttered, "Yes."

They would have *his* files, but were unlikely to have the personnel history of the *Zaid-Dayan*.

"We show no ship assignments after that."

"I had special duty." It had indeed been special. "Plainclothes work; I'm afraid I cannot comment on it."

"Ah. Duration?"

"Nor that, I'm sorry." Ford's regret was genuine. He'd have liked to tell someone else about Madame Flaubert and her lapdog. "Some months, I can say."

"And you've had no contact with Iretans since that assignment?"

Really it was too easy, the way the man asked all the wrong questions. He didn't even have to lie.

"No. I reported directly, got my orders, and boarded the next courier."

"Very well, then. We'll escort you to the next shuttle and to the Fleet offices. There's been some unrest because of the . . . unfortunate incidents."

Ford gathered the details of the unfortunate incidents, at least as they were known to the press, on his way downside. His escort, nervous at first but increasingly relaxed as Ford showed no inclination to leap up and act crazy, filled in what the news reports left out without adding any real information.

Sassinak had been onplanet and had killed someone. They were now fairly sure it was *not* Admiral Coromell. Ford let his eyebrows rise. She and the native Iretan had then disappeared, and nothing had been seen of them since.

"Dear me," he said, stifling a yawn. "How tiresome."

His escort delivered him safely to the front door of Fleet offices. Ford noticed that civilians did veer away from him, as if he might be contagious. The marines on guard at the door saluted briskly and let him inside. So far, so good, although he had no real idea what to do next. Still playing innocent courier, he reported to the officer on duty and mentioned that he had important evidence for the Iretan matter.

"You! You're from *her* ship! How in Hades did you get through?" The duty officer, a 'Tenant, had spoken loud enough to turn heads. Ford noticed the quick glances.

"Easy, there," he said quietly, smiling. "I broke no laws and created no ruckus. Shall we keep it that way? And how about announcing me to the admiral?"

"Admiral Coromell?"

"That's right." He glanced around and saw the eyes fall before his like wheat whipped by wind. Something wrong in *this* office, too. "I believe Commander Sassinak would have told him I was coming."

"N-no, sir. The admiral's been offplanet, hunting over on Six. That's why we thought at first . . . why what they said . . . but the dead man wasn't Coromell. . . ."

This made little sense. Ford tried to hack his way through the verbiage.

"Is the admiral aboard *now*?"

"Well, no, sir, he's not. He's en route, I've been told. No ETA yet. He was out hunting at the time of the — of whatever happened. That's why no one could reach him, you see, and . . ."

"I see." Ford would gladly have choked this blatherer, but he still had to find someone to share his information with. "Who's in charge, then?"

"Lieutenant Commander Dallish, but he's not available right now, sir. He was up all night, and he . . ."

Ford thought sourly that Dallish was probably a passed-over goofoff, lounging in bed in midafternoon just because he'd been up all night. Coromell had a good reputation, but if this office was any indication, he had quit earning that reputation some time back. He realized that the day's fatigues and surprises might have something to do with his attitude, but the planetside stinks had given him a headache. He wanted to hand over his highly important information, enjoy a decent fresh-cooked meal, and sleep. Now he could foresee that he was going to have to wait around for a lazy brother officer who would want to sit up and gossip about Sassinak. No. He would not play that game.

"Could you tell me where the Prosecutor's office is, then? I've got a hand delivery there, too."

The 'Tenant's ability to give clear directions met Ford's expectations, which were low. He accepted the offer of a marine guide and escort, and refused the suggestion that he would be less conspicuous in civilian clothes. He would take his evidence to the Prosecutor, he would find his own way back, by way of a decent restaurant. Surely the Prosecutor's staff would know of some.

By then, surely this Dallish would be awake, and if not . . . There was always a bunk in the Transient Officers Quarters. He had the uneasy feeling of being watched as he and his escort stepped into the slideway, but shrugged it off. Of course he was being watched. The news had everyone paranoid about Fleet officers. But if he acted like a big, calm, bored errand boy, nothing should happen to him.

Lunzie recognized his retreating back, but couldn't get Coromell's attention until Ford was out of sight.

"Who?" Coromell said, peering at the crowded slideway.

"Ford!" Lunzie was ready to cry with sheer frustration. It was impossible that *everything* could go so wrong. "Sassinak's Exec, from the *Zaid-Dayan*. He was *here!*"

"Omigod!" Dallish slammed his hand onto the window frame. "It's my fault. You'd told us he was coming, but I was still thinking he'd report to his ship first. He must've gotten to the Station *after . . .*"

"We'll find him. Just call down and ask the duty officer where he went."

But although he told Dallish where Ford was going, they could not find him again. All communications to the Prosecutor's office were blocked.

"Lines engaged. Please call again later" in muted synthetic speech so sweet Lunzie wanted to gag.

"There's got to be a way," she said. "Can't you break into the line?"

"I'm trying. We don't want anyone to know the admiral's here yet," Dallish said, "so I can't use his special code."

By the time they *did* get through, it was after hours as the computer's secretarial function insisted. When they worked their way through the multiple layers of authority and back down through the same layers trying to find the person to whom Ford would have reported if he'd been there, he'd already left. Without an escort. No, nobody knew where he'd gone. He'd been asking around for good places to eat, and the speaker thought he'd talked most to someone who had left even earlier. Sorry.

"He'll come back here," said Coromell, without much conviction. "It's standard procedure."

"Nothing in this entire situation is standard procedure," Lunzie said. "Why should he follow it?"

It came out sharper than she intended, and she realized all at once that she was hungry again and very, very tired.

Despite his confident insistence that he could certainly get something to eat and find his own way back to the Fleet offices, Ford was not entirely sure just where he was. After a long wrangle about what he considered minor matters, he had left the Prosecutor's office. It wasn't anyone's business but his captain's exactly when and where he'd left the *Zaid-Dayan* to visit his great-aunt. They'd had his original taped deposition; he hadn't wanted to repeat it.

The Prosecutor's staff gave him the distinct impression that Sassinak's disappearance with Aygar and Lunzie's non-appearance were somehow his fault. At least he was there to be griped at. He had pointed out that since the first report that the dead man was an admiral had been wrong, the report that Sassinak had anything to do with the murder might be wrong, too.

And where was she? he was asked, and he replied, with what he thought of as massive self-control, that he had no earthly idea, having arrived only that afternoon. He had parted from the staff in no mood to take the precautions they advised. It had been his experience on dozens of worlds that a confident walk, clean fingernails, and the right credit chip would keep him out of avoidable trouble, while good reflexes and a strong right arm would get him out of the rest. So he had walked along, working off the irritation until the right combination of smells led him into a dark little place which had the food its aroma promised.

Hot food, a good drink, and he felt much better about the world. He let himself wonder, for the first time consciously, where Sassinak was. What had *really* happened? He could not believe she was dead, stuffed in a trash bin down some sleazy alley. He wondered where Arly was going with the *Zaid-Dayan*, and what Sassinak thought about *that*, and if Timran had been piloting that shuttle, and who else might be in it.

Thinking about these things, he'd paid his bill with a smile and gone out into the darkening evening where the streets looked subtly different than they had in the sulfurous light of late afternoon. Of course he could stop someone and ask. Or he could go to any of the lighted kiosks and find his location on the display map. But he could always do that later, if he turned out to be really lost. At the moment, he didn't feel lost. He just felt that he wanted a good after-dinner walk.

When he realized that he'd walked far beyond the well-lighted commercial district where he'd had dinner, it was dark enough to make the next lighted transportation access attractive. Ford had walked off most of his ruffled feelings. He realized it would be much smarter to take a subway back to the central square. He was even pleased with himself for being so careful. Only a few dark shapes moved to and from the lighted space above the entrance. Ford ignored them without failing to notice which might turn troublesome as he rode the escalator down.

For a moment, he considered continuing to the lowest level, and seeing if he could find out anything about Sassinak. Every city had its denizens of the night, usually easy enough to find in tunnels and alleys at night. But he wasn't dressed for that. He would hardly fit in, and if Sassinak had plans of her own going forward, he would only get in her way.

At the foot of the escalator, he stood at the back of the platform, waiting for the next train to come. Only a small group, men and women both, who eyed his Fleet uniform and gave him room. When the train came in he checked the number to be sure it would take him all the way in without a transfer, letting the others crowd into the first car. Ford shrugged, and stepped into the second without really looking. He had seen only a few heads in the windows. He was all the way in and the doors had thumped firmly behind him, when he realized what he saw. Thirteen Fleet uniforms, and two very nervous civilians who sat stiffly at one end trying to pretend they saw nothing.

"Ensign Timran," Ford said, as if he'd seen him only a few hours ago. And in a way, he had. "You do get around, don't you?"

He let his eyes rest a moment on each one, and did not miss the very slight relaxation. Whatever they were up to, he had been instantly accepted as a help. Fine. When he found out what they were supposed to be doing, he would help, In the meantime . . . "'Tenant Sricka, I presume you're in charge of this little outing?"

A quick flick of eyes back and forth made it clear what part of the problem had been. Timran, in command as long as he was piloting a ship, had not been quick to relinquish that command on the ground. Sricka, a tactful Weft, had not wanted to risk confusion by confronting him: not on what might be enemy territory, in front of the enlisted marines. Ford acknowledged that tact with a quirk of his mouth. Even Timran wouldn't argue with the Exec of the *Zaid-Dayan*, a lieutenant commander's stripes on his sleeves.

"Suppose I fill you in on a slight change of plans," he said. "After you fill me in on a few necessary details, such as where you left the shuttle and how many you left with it."

Timran leaned forward, keeping his voice low. Ford, who had been unconvinced of Tim's reformation after Ireta, approved.

"Sir, it's under shields on the replanted end of the landfill. 'Tenant Sricka recommended that site because it was remote from the city center but near a subway line. We left no one aboard, because we . . . I . . . we thought that we might need everyone to help the captain. Sir."

Which meant Sricka had tried to explain the stupidity of taking that many uniformed men into a situation where Fleet uniforms might precipitate panic, but Tim hadn't listened and now wished he had. Typical. Ford shifted his gaze to the Weft.

"Do you know where she is?"

"I believe I can find her, sir, given a chance to shift. It's easier that way."

"For which you need privacy, if we don't want to scare the horses. Right! Let me think." He tried to remember how many stops he'd passed during his walk. If only those civilians hadn't been in this car! They'd probably report this concentration of Fleet to someone as soon as they got out. That decided him. "We're getting off at the next stop. Just follow me."

He didn't know where the civilians would get off, but they didn't move when Ford stood and led the others off at the next stop. This one was no larger than the other, with only a narrow bridge to the outbound platform, and no privacy whatever. But if he led them all up the street, they'd be just as noticeable. Unless, of course, he could get those uniforms out of sight. He got them all as far from the others on the platform as he could and explained.

"You marines are MPs, and I'm your commanding officer. These dirtsiders don't know one uniform from another. At least the civilians don't. These others are belligerent drunks that we're trying to get back to the city as quietly as possible."

The Wefts, consummate actors, nodded and grinned. Timran looked both worried and stubborn. Ford leaned closer to him.

"That's not a suggestion, Ensign; that's an order. Now say 'I'm not drunk' and take a swing at the sergeant there."

Timran said it in the startled voice of one who hopes it's not true, swung wildly, and the sergeant, grinning, enacted his role with vigor.

"Don't you bother 'im," Sricka said, tugging ineffectually at the sergeant's arm. "He's not drunk, it's just his birthday!"

"Happy *birthday* to him!" shouted the other Weft, entering into the game gleefully.

The marines grappled, struggled, and started their drunken charges up to street level with difficulty while Ford, still spotless, apologized coolly to the civilians on the platform.

"Sorry. Young officers, a long way from home. No excuse, really, but they're all like this at least once. Get 'em home, let 'em sleep it off, and they'll get their ears peeled in the morning."

With a crisp nod, he followed his noisy troop up the escalator. With any luck, they'd assume that this had nothing to do with the *Zaid-Dayan*. Ford had never found a planet yet that didn't know about drunken young soldiers. On the streetside, his group wavered to a halt, waiting for his direction.

"That way," he said. "Just be prepared to do your act again if I signal. If it's official, let me do all the talking. I landed quite legally this afternoon by the official shuttle and all my papers are in order. Now tell me. Who's got the *Zaid-Dayan*, and what's going on up there?"

Sricka took up the talk, and in a few sentences explained what he knew. Little enough, but Ford agreed that a Ssli would be unlikely to make a mistake.

"If they say a Seti invasion, I'll buy it. What's Fleet have insystem?"

Sricka did not know that. Ford thought about the information lock put on the invasion news, and wished he could talk to his old buddy, Killin. But at least Arly could call for help via the IFTL link. Ford decided not to worry about what he couldn't change. That brought his thoughts back to their uniforms, even more conspicuous as they came into better-lighted streets.

"And your orders?"

"Captain . . . Commander Arly told me to take a shuttle down in case the captain, Commander Sassinak, that is, needed it. To do whatever it took to help her."

"Well, then. First we'll have to find her, then we'll know what help she needs. And to do that, we'll have to look less like what we are. Here, hold up this lamppost for a minute." He had spotted a larger, much busier subway access, the kind that would have shops and other facilities on the platform below. "Sergeant, if anyone asks, tell 'em your officer went down to make a call to the office to get a vehicle."

Back down underground again. He found he was enjoying this much more than he should have. Even the contrast to Auntie Q's luxurious entourage cheered him. He found an automated clothing outlet where commuters who had just spilled something on their suit on the way to a conference could get a replacement. He dared not buy clothes for all of them, but two or three coveralls wouldn't be excessive.

No, four: the least expensive garment came in green, blue, gray, and brown. He inserted his card, punched the buttons, and caught the sealed packets as they came out of the slot. No one seemed to be watching. Back up the escalator, packages in hand, to find the group had put on a small show for a group of late diners who'd stopped to ask questions about Ireta's mysterious plague.

He took control, briskly and firmly, and marched his troops off as if to a definite destination. Half a block later, he slowed them down again. The Wefts wouldn't find much privacy in the subway tunnels of the inner city this early in the night. He glanced back at the marines, and met the wary glance of their sergeant. Who'd picked them? Arly? Currald? Whoever it was had had sense enough to send more than one NCO. Which should he peel off for Sassinak? The old rule held: don't tell 'em how to do it, just tell the sergeant what you need done.

"Sergeant, the Wefts'll need a couple of marines just in case someone comes after 'em while they're hunting the captain." Not that the Wefts couldn't outfight any three humans while in their own shapes, but he suspected that the mental concentration needed for hunting her could take the edge off their other abilities. "Take these clothes and the next dark patch we come to, put 'em on over your uniforms. That'll take care of three of you. One Fleet uniform shouldn't be too dangerous. Then take off. 'Tenant Sricka, you find the captain, and tell her where the shuttle is. Find out what she needs. If she can't contact me, you do or send one of the marines. Can you find *me*, the way you sense her?"

Sricka frowned, then smiled. "I was about to say we couldn't, sir, but you've changed."

"That's what I was told," said Ford, remembering the demise of Madame Flaubert.

"But it would be easier if one of us stayed with you."

Ford shook his head. "I know, but we don't know how bad her situation is. She may need both of you, or it may be harder than you expect to find her in a maze of tunnels. It's not like free space. She must know she has you and a shuttle when she needs it — Which reminds me. Ensign."

"Sir?"

"You've got the toughest assignment. You're going to have to get back out to the shuttle — alone — and be ready for a call. Can't even guess when we're going to need you, or for what, but I know absolutely without a doubt we will, and we won't have time for you to take the subway back out there. D'you have rations on board for several days?"

"Yes, sir, but . . ."

"Ensign, if I could send someone back with you I would. I need all the rest of these in the city, nearby, in case she wants them. This is not an easy assignment for someone your age." That stiffened Tim's backbone, as he'd hoped. "But Commander Sassinak's told me you have potential, and if you do, young man, this is the time to show it."

"Yes, sir. Anything else?"

"Yes. Take this." The last package of civilian clothes. "Put it on first, then go straight to the subway, and back out to the shuttle. Try to look like a young man who's just been told he has to go back to work and fix a problem. Shouldn't be too hard. Get some sleep. Whatever breaks won't break right away. Just be sure you're ready to get that thing up the instant we call for you. I'll try to patch a call to you from the Fleet offices when we get back, in an hour or so, but don't count on it."

"Yes, sir."

In the next darker patch, Ford got them into a huddle. When it opened again, one "civilian" headed back to the subway access, while three others and a marine continued to the next. Ford led the other nine on toward the center of the city. It was a lovely evening for a walk.

✧ CHAPTER TWENTY

Trial day. The early news reports had more speculation about the mysterious shuttle that had disappeared "somewhere near the city" and the strange plague which supposedly afflicted anyone who'd been to Ireta. Riots in the maintenance tunnels were controlled by police with only minor loss of life.

Sassinak winced. She and Aygar and her crew members had just escaped the pitched battle that erupted when the Pollys tried gas on tunnel rats who had gas masks and weapons. She hoped the newssheet was right in reporting so few deaths. Only the knowledge that she *had* to fight the main battle elsewhere let her live with the decision to run for it. The lower third of the page mentioned the trial and Council hearing on Ireta's status.

Sassinak watched Aygar reading, his lips pursed angrily. She already knew what it said. No precedent for overturning a Thek claim. But at least he was alive, and if she could get him into the Council chamber that way, he should have a chance to testify.

Erdra had come back before dawn with a half dozen of the pearly cards that guaranteed admission, each one embossed with the name of its carrier. Sassinak had become "Commander Argray, Fleet Liaison" for the duration, and Aygar was "Blayanth, Federation Citizen." She hoped these faked IDs and the database entries backing them up would let them get into Council without being quarantined as dangerous lunatics. According to the news reports, the lines for public seating had extended across the plaza by midnight. If the "invitations" didn't work, they wouldn't have a chance at open seats. A number of the student activists had been in the lines early, but no one knew which, if any, of those waiting would be admitted.

At least, Sassinak thought, she looked like herself again. Bless Arly for thinking of the clean uniform; familiar in every seam, comforted her almost as much as the bridge of her ship. So did the change in Erdra's eyes when Sassinak appeared in regal white and gold, now suiting the image Erdra had imagined.

"Should be starting now."

Sassinak nodded to their guide without speaking. Aygar shoved the newssheet he'd been reading in a disposal slot, and came along.

"Do you think we'll get in?" he asked for the fourth or fifth time. After that he'd ask what they'd do if this didn't work. She was trying to be patient, but it got harder.

"No good reason it shouldn't work. It . . ." Internal and external communications layered in confusion for a moment. Then she realized that a Weft onplanet had managed to link her with a Weft on the *Zaid-Dayan*, and with its Ssli, and thence to Dupaynil on a Seti ship somewhere at the edge of the system.

"A *Seti* ship!" she muttered aloud, and caught a worried glance from Aygar. "Sorry," she said, and clamped her lips shut. <What are you doing on a Seti ship?> she asked Dupaynil

<Wishing I hadn't ever made you mad.> Whether it was his mind, or the Weft linkage, that sounded both contrite and humble, qualities she'd never associated with Dupaynil.

<Are you alone?>

<No. A Weft, a larval Ssli, two Lethi, a Ryxi, and a Bronthin are my companions in durance vile. The Seti want witnesses to their power. Then they'll eat us.>

<No way. We'll get you out.>

How she was going to do that, while stranded onplanet with Aygar, in the middle of a Grand Council trial and hearing that was expected to turn into a revolution, she did not know. But she couldn't let him think she wouldn't try.

<Don't fret . . . we're sending data to Arly. And I got what you wanted on the Seti, and more. That *Claw* escort was suborned. All but one of the crew were in with the pirates and in pay of the Paradens.>

Sassinak hoped he could interpret the cold wash of amazement that took all the words from her mind. She had been furious with him, but she hadn't intended *that*.

Now his contact carried a thread of amusement. <That's all right. I didn't think you knew. But if I live through this, you may have to fix some charges for me and a young Jig named Panis.>

<What charges?>

<Mutiny, for one. Misappropriation of government property, grievous bodily harm . . . >

<We'll get you out alive. I have *got* to hear this.>

But right now she was too close to the Council buildings and she had to concentrate on her surroundings. Aygar strode along beside her, looking as belligerent as any Diplonian. Her Wefts from the shuttle, and two marines, had faked IDs as well. Would it work?

They came to a checkpoint in the angle between a colonnade and the massive Council building. One heavyworlder in Federation Insystem Security uniform stood behind a short counter. Behind it, lined against the wall, were five others. Sassinak handed over the embossed strip, saw it fed into a machine, and checked against a list. The heavyworlder's gaze came up and lingered on her in a way she did not like.

"Ah! Commander Argray. Your invitation's in order, ma'am. You may enter through that door." He pointed. As they had planned, Sassinak moved on, as if she had no connection with Aygar.

She heard the guard's voice behind her, speaking to Aygar and then Aygar's steps following hers.

The doorway fit the massive building; heavy bronze, centered with the Federation seal. Before Sassinak could reach, it opened flat against the wall for her. She entered the Grand Council chamber through a little alcove off the main room and just below the dais where the eight justices and the Speaker had their seats. Across from her, one wall appeared to be a single massive stone, a warm brown with gold flecks. Delegate seating curved around an open area below the dais, separated from the public seating behind a tall barrier of translucent plastic. Each seat was actually the size of a sentry hut, or more, and in front of each delegate's seat, a colorful seal inlaid in the chamber floor gave the member's race and planet of reference. Sassinak could not see the public seating clearly, but it seemed to rake steeply toward a narrow balcony festooned with the lights and cables of recording and projection equipment.

Seating for invited guests was enclosed in a railing, somewhat like an old-fashioned jury box, although much larger. Already this was filling up, with rather more heavyworlders than Sassinak would have expected. That fit the rumors of an impending coup. She found three seats together, and settled in, with Aygar between her and one of the Wefts. Aygar said nothing to her, and she watched her other crew come in. The other Weft and the two marines found scattered seats where they could catch her eye.

She had never really wondered what the Grand Council chamber was like. The few times she'd seen it on broadcasts, the focus had been on the Speaker's podium backed by the Federation seal. Now she looked up to see a high, ribbed ceiling, with dangling light pods. Behind the Speaker's podium and the justice's high-backed chairs, the great seal stood at least three meters high, its colors muted now in the dimmer light. From her seat, she could see through the plastic behind the delegates' seats more easily and realized that, early as it was, the public seating was nearly full. At the far end of the arc formed by the delegates' places, another enclosed seating area had only a sprinkling of occupants. She wondered if that was for witnesses. She could not see any of them clearly enough to know if Lunzie or Ford were there.

Soon the delegates began to come in, each preceded by an honor guard of Federation Insystem troops. Each delegate's seat, Sassinak realized, was actually an almost self-contained environmental pod with full datalinks. She watched as the delegates tested their seats. Colored lights appeared, to show the vote. A clerk standing by the Speaker's podium murmured into a microphone, confirming to the occupant the practice vote just cast.

A whiff of sulfur made her wrinkle her nose, as a *steth* of Lethi came in, looking like so many pale yellow puffballs stuck together into a vaguely regular geometrical shape. They disappeared completely into their seat, closing a shiny panel behind them. Sassinak assumed they would open a sealed pack of sulfur inside, where it wouldn't foul the air for anyone else. A pair of Bronthin arrived, conversing nose to nose in the breathy whuffles of their native speech. She had never seen Bronthin in real life. They looked even more like pale blue plush horses than their pictures. Hard to believe they were the best mathematicians among the known sentient races. A Ryxi, loaded with ceremonial chains and stepping with exaggerated care, clacked its beak impatiently. A second Ryxi scuttled into the room behind it, carrying a mesh bag in the claw of its right wing and hissing apologies. Or so Sassinak assumed. The Weft delegate arrived in Weft form, to Sassinak's surprise. Then she was surprised at herself for being surprised. After all, as his race's representative, why should he try to look human?

She was surprised again when the Seti came in. She had not expected to see them except in battle armor. But here they were, tail-ornaments jingling and necklaces swaying, their heavy tails sweeping from side to side as they strolled to their seats. She could read nothing of their expressions. Their scaled, snouted faces might have been intended to convey reassurance. Sassinak wondered suddenly if the Seti had politics as humans understood them. Did all Seti support the Sek, were they all involved in this invasion? Could the ambassadors be ignorant of the Sek's plans?

She gave herself a mental shake. Interpreting Seti politics was someone else's responsibility. She had enough to do already. Rightly or wrongly, she had to assume they were part of it. She glanced around. Dark figures on the balcony slipped from one cluster of equipment to another. Lights appeared, narrowed or broadened in focus, changed color, disappeared again. The Speaker's podium suddenly glowed in a sunburst of spotlights, then retreated into the relative dimness of the overhead panels.

The crowd's murmur grew, punctuated by a raised voice, a sneeze, a chain of coughs that began on one side and worked its way to the other. She could feel her skin tighten as the circulation fans went up a notch to maintain an even temperature. Now the legal staffs involved came in, bustling in their dark robes, each with the little gray curl of a wig that looked equally ridiculous on humans and aliens. She wondered who had ever thought up that symbol of legal expertise and why everyone else had adopted it.

Federation Court guards, also heavyworlders, brought in Tanegli who looked as if he could barely walk. Beside her, she felt Aygar stiffen and wished she could take his hand. Anger radiated from him, then slowly faded. Had he realized how useless his hatred of Tanegli was? As useless as her hatred of the Paradens.

She shouldn't think about that, not *now*, but the thought prickled inside her mind anyway. It was one thing to hunt them down for the wrong they had done, and another to let herself be shaped wholly by their malice. She couldn't ignore that. Abe had said it, had told the woman he loved, had urged her to find Sassinak someday and tell her. And Lunzie, who had admired her descendant, the cruiser captain, would not be so happy with an avenging harpy.

The lights flared, then dimmed, and a gong rang out. Spotlights stabbed through the gloom to illuminate the door they'd come in, where two huge heavyworlders now stood with ceremonial staves, which they pounded on the floor.

"All rise!" came the stentorian voice over the sound system. "For the Right Honorable, the Speaker of the Grand Council of the Federation of Sentient Planets, the Most Noble Eriach d'Ertang. And for the Most Honorable Lords Justice. . . ." The floor shook to another ceremonial pounding. The heavyworlder guards led in the procession.

The Speaker, a wiry little Bretagnan who looked dwarfed by the heavyworlders in front of him, and the eight justices behind him were each followed by a clerk of the same race carrying something on a silver tray. Sassinak had no idea what *that* was but overheard another guest explain to someone who asked that these were the justices' credentials, proof that they were each eligible to sit on that bench.

"Of course it's all done by the computers, now," the knowledgeable one murmured on. "But they still carry in the hardcopy as if they needed it."

"And who are those men with the big carved things?"

"Bailiffs," came the explanation. "If I talk much more, they'll be after me. They keep order."

Sassinak found it very different from a military court. She assumed that part of the elaborate ceremony came from its combination with a Grand Council meeting. But there were long, flowery, introductory speeches welcoming the right noble delegate from this, and the most honorable delegate from that, while the lawyers and clerks muttered at one another behind a screen of hands, and the audience yawned and shuffled their feet.

Each justice had an introduction, equally flowery, during which he, she, or it tried not to squirm in the spotlight. Then the Speaker took over. He began with a review of the rules governing spectators, then guests, then witnesses, any infractions of which, he said slowly, would be met with immediate eviction by the bailiffs. "— to the prejudice of that issue to which the unruly individual or individuals appeared to be speaking, if that can be determined."

Very different from court-martials, Sassinak thought. She had never seen unruliness in a military court. Then came a roll call, another check of each delegate's datalink to the Speaker's podium, and the voting displays of all delegates and justices. By now, thought Sassinak, we could have been through with an entire trial.

At last the Speaker read out the agenda on which Tanegli's trial appeared as "In the matter of the Federation of Sentient Planets versus one Tanegli, and the related matter of the status of native-born children of Federation citizens on the planet Ireta!"

Sassinak felt Aygar's shiver of excitement. The moment the Speaker had finished, one of the bewigged and gowned lawyers stood up. This, it seemed, was the renowned defense counsel Pinky Vigal. He seemed tame enough to Sassinak, a mild-mannered older man who hardly deserved the nickname Pinky. But she heard from the industrious explainer behind her that it had nothing to do with his appearance, coming rather from the closing argument in a case he had won many years back. This explanation, long and detailed, finally caught the attention of a bailiff who shook his staff at the guest seating box, instantly hushing the gossiper.

A formal dance of legality ensued, with Defense Counsel and the Chief Prosecutor deferring to one another's expertise with patent insincerity, and the justices inserting nuggets of opinion when asked. Pinky Vigal wanted to sever his client's trial for mutiny, assault, murder, conspiracy, and so on from any consideration of the claims of those born on Ireta, inasmuch as recent evidence indicated that a noxious influence of the planet or its biosphere might be responsible for his behavior. And that evidence was so recent that his client's trial should be put off until the defense had time to consider its import.

The Prosecutor insisted that the fate of Iretan native-borns, and of the planet itself, could not be severed from consideration of the crimes of Tanegli and the other conspirators. Defense insisted that taped depositions from witnesses were not adequate, and must not be admitted into evidence, and the Prosecution insisted that they were admissible.

During all this, Tanegli sat slumped at his attorney's side, hardly moving his head.

This boring and almost irrelevant legal dance seemed likely to take awhile. Sassinak had time to wonder again where the others were. Dupaynil she knew about, at least in outline, but what about Ford? She was sure that if Ford had been on a Seti ship, he'd have somehow taken control and arrived in time for the trial. But where was he? He was supposed to have acquired more backup troops. So far she'd seen nothing but heavyworlders wearing Federation Insystem uniforms.

And Lunzie? Had she not made it back from Diplo? Had something happened to her there? Or here? Aygar could testify about what he'd been told by the heavyworlders who reared him, damning enough to ensure conviction on some of the charges. But they needed Lunzie or Varian or Kai for the original mutiny.

Despite the briefings she'd had in both the local Fleet head-quarters and the Chief Prosecutor's office, Sassinak really did not understand exactly how this case would be tried or whose deci-sion mattered most. A case like this didn't fit neatly into any category although she'd realized that lawyers' perspective would be far different from hers. To them it was not a matter of right and wrong, of guilt and innocence, but of a tangle of competing jurisdictions, competing and conflicting statutes, possibly alterna-tive routes of prosecution and defense: a vast game board in which it was "fun" to stretch all rules to their elastic limit.

She doubted that they ever thought of the realities: those people and places whose realities had no elasticity, whose lives were shattered with the broken laws, the torn social contract. Now the Justices finished handing down decisions on the initial requests and the Prosecutor opened with a history of the Iretan expedition.

Sassinak kept her mind on it with an effort. All the details of the EEC's contracts, decisions, agreements, and subcontracts wafted in one ear and out the other. Lunzie's version had been far more vivid. Display screens lit with the first of the taped testi-mony on datacube videos taken by the original expedition team, before the mutiny. There were the jungles, the golden flyers, the fringes, the dinosaurs . . . a confusion of life-forms. The expedi-tion members going about their tasks. The children trying hard to look appropriately busy for the pictures.

A light came on above one of the delegate's seats and the trans-lators broadcast the question in Standard.

"Are these the native-born Iretan children making claim for the planet?"

"No, Delegate. These children's parents lived aboard the EEC vessel, and were given this furlough onplanet as an educational experience."

The light stayed on, blinking, and another question came over the speaker system.

"Did the native-born Iretan children send a representative?"

Sassinak wondered where that delegate had been for the past several days since Aygar's involvement in her escapades had been all over the news media. The Chief Prosecutor looked as if he'd bitten into something sour and it occurred to Sassinak that the delegate might be already in the defense faction.

"Yes, Delegate, a representative of these children did come, but . . ."

Aygar stood before Sassinak could grab him, and said, "I'm here!"

A chorus of hisses, growls, and the massive heavyworlder bailiff nearest their box slammed his staff on the floor.

"Order!" he said.

Sassinak tugged on Aygar's arm and he sat down slowly. The Speaker glared at the Chief Prosecutor.

"Did you not instruct your witness where he was to go and what the rules of this court are?"

"Yes, Speaker, but he disappeared in . . . ah . . . suspicious circumstances. He was abducted, apparently by a Fleet . . ."

The Chief Prosecutor's voice trailed away when he realized what that gold and white uniform next to Aygar must mean. Sassinak let herself grin, knowing that the media cameras would be zooming in on her face.

"Irregularities of this sort can precipitate mistrials," said Pinky Vigal, with a sweetness of tone that affected Sassinak like honey on a sawblade. "If the Federation Prosecutor has not readied his witnesses, we shall have no objection to a delay."

"No." The Chief Prosecutor glared. Defense Counsel shrugged and sat down. "With the indulgence of the Speaker and justices, and all delegates here assembled" — the ritual courtesy rattled off his tongue so fast Sassinak could hardly follow it — "if I may call the Iretan witness *and any other* from the guest seating?"

Above the justices' seats, blue lights flashed, and the Speaker nodded.

"As long as you remember that it *is* indulgence, Mr. Prosecutor, and refrain from making a habit of it. We are aware of the unusual circumstances. And I suppose this may keep Defense from claiming your witnesses were coached excessively."

Even Pinky Vigal chuckled at that, throwing his hands out in a disarming gesture of surrender that did not fool Sassinak one bit. She felt the rising tension in the chamber. Would Aygar's presence make the conspirators here give their signal earlier or later? They must be wondering what other surprises could turn up. The delegate who had asked the original question had either understood this wrangling, or had given up, because its light was out. The Prosecutor went on, outlining the events of the mutiny, of the attempted murder of the lightweights . . .

"*Alleged* attempted murder," interrupted Pinky Vigal.

The Prosecutor smiled, bowed, and called for "our first witness, Doctor Lunzie Mespil."

Sassinak felt the surge of excitement from the crowd that almost overwhelmed her own. So Lunzie *had* made it! She saw a stir in the witness box, then a slim figure in Medical Corps uniform coming to the stand. Her pulse raced. Lunzie looked so *young*, so vulnerable, just like the younger sister that Sassinak had lost might have looked. Incredible to think that she had been alive a hundred years before Sassinak was born.

Lunzie began to give her evidence in the calm, measured voice that gradually eased the tension Sassinak felt. But a light flashed from one of the delegate's seats, this time with an objection instead of a question.

"This witness has no legal status! This witness is a thief and liar, a fugitive from justice!"

Sassinak stiffened and found that this time Aygar had grabbed her wrist to keep her down. Lunzie, white-faced, had turned to the accusing delegate's place.

"This witness pretended medical competence to gain entrance to Diplo, and then stole and escaped with valuable information vital to our planetary security. We demand that this witness' testimony be discarded, and that she be returned to the proper authorities for trial on Diplo!"

More lights flashed. As the Prosecutor tried to answer the Diplo delegate, others had questions, comments, discussion. Finally the Speaker got them in order again, and spoke himself to Lunzie.

"Is this accusation true?"

"Not . . . in substance, sir."

"In what way?"

"I did go to Diplo with a medical research team. My specialty and background suited me for the work. While there I was abducted, drugged, and put into cold sleep. I awoke here, on this planet, with no knowledge of the means of my departure from Diplo. I daresay it *was* illegal. I hope it was illegal to do that to a Federation citizen with a valid entrance visa."

"You lie, lightweight!" The Diplo delegate had not waited for the translator. He'd used Standard himself. "You seduced a member of our government, stole datacubes . . ."

"I did nothing of the sort!" Sassinak was amazed at Lunzie's calm. She might have been an experienced teacher dealing with an unruly nine-year-old. "It is true that I met an old friend, who had become a government official, but as for seducing him . . . Remember that I had lost over forty years in cold sleep between our meetings. The handsome young man I remembered was now old and sick, even dying."

"He's dead *now*, yes." That was vicious, in a tone intended to hurt, with implications clear to everyone.

Sassinak peeled Aygar's fingers off her wrist, one by one. He gave her a worried sideways glance and she shook her head slightly. Lunzie still stood calmly, balanced, apparently untouched by the Diplonian's verbal assault. Had she expected it? Sassinak thought not.

The Speaker intervened again. "Did you file a complaint about your alleged abduction?"

"Naturally, I informed the Prosecutor's office. They had me in for illegal entry."

"Well?" The Speaker was looking at the Prosecutor who shrugged.

"We took her information, but since she had no particulars to offer and we have no authority to investigate crimes on Diplo, we considered that she was lucky to be alive and took no action."

Sassinak might have missed the signal if Aygar had not reacted to it with an indrawn breath.

"What?" she murmured, turning to look at him.

"Tanegli's handsign. That guard just gave it and the other one . . ."

"Lying lightweight!" Again the Diplo delegate's bellow attracted all eyes. Or almost all. Sassinak saw the guard nearest the witness stand shift his weight, the reflections from his chestful of medals suddenly moving. What was he . . . Then she recognized the position.

"Lunzie! *DOWN!*" Her voice carried across the chamber effortlessly.

Lunzie dropped just as the guard's massive leg swept across the railing. It could have killed her if he'd connected. Sassinak herself was out of the guest box, with Aygar only an instant behind her. Lunzie popped back up and, with deceptive gentleness, tapped the guard on the side of the neck. He sagged to his knees just as Sassinak met the first bailiff's staff.

"ORDER!" the Speaker yelled into the microphone, but it was far too late for that.

The bailiff had not expected Sassinak's combination of tuck, roll, strike, and pivot, and found his own staff suddenly out of his hands and aimed at his head. Single-minded in his original rage, Aygar had launched himself across the Defense table to grapple with Tanegli. A gaggle of legal clerks flailed at Aygar with papers and briefcases, trying to save their client from summary execution.

The eight justices had rolled out of their exposed seats, and only the Ryxi's head peered out as it chittered furiously in its own language. Most of the delegates had shut themselves into their sealed seats, but the heavyworlders from Diplo and Colrin emerged, clad in space armor which they must have worn under their ceremonial robes.

Sassinak tossed Lunzie the bailiff's staff just as the guard Lunzie had hit came up again. Lunzie slammed the heavy knob onto his head, then swung the length violently to knock a needler free from a guard who aimed at Sassinak. When one of Sassinak's Wefts shifted to Weft shape, a Seti delegate stormed out of its seat, screaming Seti curses that needed no translation. Sassinak snatched at the Seti's neck chain only to be slammed aside by the powerful tail. She rolled over and came up on her feet to face a grinning heavyworlder with a needler who never saw the Weft that landed on his head and broke his neck.

Sassinak caught the needler and tried again to reach Aygar, but he and the defense lawyers were all rolling around in an untidy heap behind the table. She yelled, but doubted he could hear her.

Noise beat at the walls of the chamber as the watching crowd surged up to get a better view, and then discovered its own will.

"Down with the Pollys!" came a scream from the upper rows as the students from the Library tossed paint balloons that splattered uselessly on the plastic screen.

"Lightweight scum!" replied a block of heavyworlders, followed by blows, screams, and the high sustained yelp of the emergency alarm system.

Down below, Sassinak faced worse problems, despite the defensive block she had formed with Lunzie, the Wefts, and the two marines. The Speaker lay dead, his skull smashed by the Diplonian delegate who now bellowed commands into the microphone. Aygar crawled out of the ruins of the table and ducked barely in time to avoid a slug through the head.

"Over here!" Sassinak yelled. His head moved. He finally saw her. "Stay *down*!" She gestured. He nodded. She hoped he understood.

In through the door pounded another squad of Insystem Security heavyworlder marines. Three of the Justices tried to break for the door, falling to merciless arms, as Sassinak's group dived for what cover they could find. It wasn't much and the three staves and one small-bore needler they'd captured so far weren't equivalent weaponry.

This would be a good time for help to arrive, Sassinak thought.

"Yield, hopeless ones!" screamed the Diplonian. "Your fool's reign is over! Now begins the glorious . . ."

"FLEET!"

Something sailed through the air and landed with an uncompromising clunk about three meters from Sassinak's nose; it cracked and leaked a bluish haze. I'm not sure I believe this, she thought, reaching for her gas kit, holding her breath, remembering how to count, checking on Lunzie and Aygar. This is where I came in but that shout had to be Ford's.

The heavyworlder troops would have gas kits, too, of course. How fast could they move? She was already in motion, but again Aygar was faster, the blinding speed of youth and perfect condition. They hit the first heavyworlders before they had their weapons in hand, yanking them away and reversing without slackening speed. Sassinak leaped for the higher ground, the Justices' dais, rolled behind its protective rail just as something splintered it behind her. She crawled rapidly toward the far seat, ignoring the unconscious Justices, and picked off the first trooper who came after her. Where was Lunzie? Which way had Aygar run? And did he even know what to do with that weapon?

A stuttering burst of fire, squeals and crashes, and high pitched screams suggested that he'd found out what to push, but she didn't trust his aim. She saw stealthy movement coming over the rail and fired a short burst: no yell, but no more movement.

"Sassinak!" Ford again, this time nearer. "Pattern six!"

Pattern six was a simple trick, something all cadets learned in the first months of maneuvers. Sassinak moved to her right, flattening to one side of the Federation seal and wondered what he was planning to use for the reinforcements that pattern six sent down the center. The few marines he was supposed to have from the *Zaid-Dayan* wouldn't be enough. Something coughed, and she grinned. How *had* Ford managed to get a Gertrud into the Grand Council? The stubby, squat weapon, designed for riot control on space stations, coughed again, and settled to its normal steady growl. Sassinak put her fingers in her ears and kept her head well down. Behind that growl, Ford and whoever he had conscripted could edge forward, letting the sonic patterns ahead disorient the enemy.

But their enemies were not giving up that easily. One of them must have worn protective headgear, for he put his weapon on full automatic and poured an entire magazine into the Gertrud. Its growl skewed upward, ending in an explosion of bright sound. Sassinak shook her head violently to clear her ears and tried to figure out what next.

She could see through the paint-splashed protective screen from this height. The neat rows of public seating were the scene of a full-bore riot. No help there, even if her former accomplices were winning, and she wasn't at all sure they were. Higher up, she could see struggling figures behind the lights and lenses of the media deck. Down below, she saw the Diplonian delegate begin to twitch, waking up from the gas. Him she could handle and she let off a burst that flung him away from the podium, dead before he waked.

The witness box was empty. She did not see Ford but she assumed he was still in the row below. But the guest box . . . from here, she could see its occupants, some dead or wounded, some frozen in horror and shock, and some all too clearly enjoying the spectacle. These had personal shields, translucent but offering safety from such hazards as the riot gas and small arms fire. Sassinak edged carefully along the upper level of the dais. No one else had come up here after her. Perhaps they'd assume she'd slipped off the far side to join her supporters. She wished she knew how many supporters, and with what arms.

In a momentary lull, one of the shielded guests glanced up and locked eyes with her. Sassinak felt her bones melting with rage. Age and indulgence had left their mark on Randy Paraden, but she knew him. And he, it was clear, knew her. She felt her lips draw back in a snarl. His curled in the same arrogant sneer, gloating in his safety, in her danger. Slowly, arrogantly, he stood, letting his shield push aside those near him and left the guest box. Still watching her, he came nearer, nearer, with that mocking smile, knowing her weapon could not penetrate his personal shield. He raised a hand to signal, no doubt to guide one of the heavyworlders to her.

And then fell, with infinite surprise, that expression she'd seen so often before on others who found reality intruding on dreams. It had happened so quickly the Weft was untangling itself from Paraden's body before she realized it. It had *shifted* across the shield and broken his neck.

<Back to work.> And it was gone, back into the fray.

She caught a glimpse of two other shielded guests departing, in considerable rush, and the Weft message echoed in her head.

<Parchandri.>

"You're sure?"

<Parchandri.>

If they were going, she was sure she knew where. She fished the comm unit out of her pocket and thumbed it on. She had a message to send, and then a fight to finish.

✧ CHAPTER TWENTY-ONE

Timran had ignored the commotion around the shuttle's shields the morning after the landing. Nothing civilians could do would damage them or give access. He could tune in civilian broadcasts and spent the day watching newscasters ask each other questions on the main news channel. He'd rather have watched a back-to-back rerun of Carin Coldae classics, but felt he should exercise self-discipline. His second night alone in the shuttle he spent in catnaps and sudden, dry-mouthed awakenings. Keeping the video channels on did not help. He kept thinking someone had sneaked in to take control.

Morning brought the itchy-eyed state of fatigue. He turned the comm volume up high and dared a fast shower in the shuttle's tiny head. A caffeine tab and breakfast. The news blared on about the trial which would start in a few hours. He had heard nothing from Ford since that brief contact giving him the coordinates to watch, the details of the ship he might encounter. That had been around dawn of the day before. He felt so helpless, and so miserably alone. How could he help the captain, stuck way out here? The memory of the last time he hadn't obeyed orders smacked him on the mental nose. But those had been the captain's orders and these were only the Exec's. He had a sudden memory of Sassinak and Ford coming out of her quarters when he'd been on an errand. On second thought, he had better not antagonize Ford.

He settled down to watch the news coverage of the trial. Another interview with another civilian bureaucrat concerning the Iretan plague. Tim snorted, squirming in his seat. They asked the stupidest questions and the experts gave the stupidest answers. He wished he could be interviewed. He'd do a lot better. None of them would ever say, "I don't know" and stick to it.

Of course, they'd probably quit asking the ones who did know.

When the coverage of the Grand Council finally began, with the speaker formally greeting each delegate, Tim sat up straight. He had stowed all the litter of his solitary occupation, prepped the shuttle for emergency liftoff, and made sure that every system was working perfectly. What he didn't have was any kind of effective weapon, unless the ship he expected to meet had neither shields nor guns. He was trying not to think about that. He had his helmet beside him, just in case. Outside the shuttle's shields, a thin line of police kept the curious away. They would be safe at that distance when he lifted.

The view on screen flicked from one location in the chamber to another. He saw Lunzie and an admiral sitting together in the seats reserved for witnesses, then Ford coming in. The view shifted and he saw Sassinak on the other side of the chamber. Why over there? he wondered. Aygar, beside her, looked unhappy. Tim wanted to be there worse than he'd ever wanted anything. He liked the big Iretan and hoped he'd decide to join Fleet in some capacity. And everything was happening *there*! Not here.

When the trouble began, he sat forward, hardly breathing. He'd often said he wished he'd been there to see other fights, other adventures, but he found that watching was far worse. He couldn't see what he wanted, only what the camera showed, and it was all a lot messier than the stories. Then the screen blanked, streaked, and finally returned as an exterior view of the Grand Council hall with a rioting crowd outside. Again the views shifted; first one streetful of people screaming, then another of people marching in step, waving flags, then of orange-uniformed police firing into the crowd.

He glanced outside. The police there shifted about, looking edgy. No doubt they had communication with the inner city, and wondered what to do about him. Suddenly one of them whirled, and fired point-blank at the shield. His companions pulled him away, yanked the weapon from him, and moved back. Tim did nothing. He was trembling, he found, far worse than he had been that time on Ireta, but he managed to keep his fingers off the controls. His mind clung to the thought that Sassinak would call for him, would need him: he must be ready.

Yet when the call came, he hardly believed it.

❖   ❖   ❖

"*Zaid-Dayan* shuttle!" came the second time before he got his fingers and his voice working and thumbed the control.

"Shuttle here!" His voice sounded like his kid brother's. He swallowed and hoped it would steady the next time.

"Fugitives en route. As planned, launch and intercept."

Did that mean the others weren't coming? Was he really supposed to take off without them?

"Are you —?"

"Now!"

That was definitely Sassinak, no doubt about it. This is not like I imagined it would be, he thought. His memory reminded him that so far it never had been. Helmet on, connections made. He looked at the fat red button and pushed it, then got his hands on the other controls just as the shuttle surged up, sucking a good bit of the landfill's carefully planted grass in its wake.

He was high over the city in moments, balancing on a delicate combination of atmospheric and insystem drives. He had time to enjoy the knowledge that he had made a perfect liftoff and was doing a superb job now in precisely the right position.

The coordinates he'd been given, entered into the shuttle's nav computer, now showed a red circle on a displayed map that matched what he could see below. Hard to believe that beneath that vast warehouse a silo poked into the ground ready to launch a fast yacht. But the displays were changing color. The IR scan showed the change first as the warehouse roof sections lifted away. Then the targeting lasers picked up the vibrations, translated as seismic activity.

The inner barriers lifted and the yacht's nose poked out, rising slowly, slowly. As if on an elevator lift, then faster, then . . . Tim remembered he was supposed to give one official warning and poked the button to turn on the pre-recorded tape. Sassinak had not wanted to trust his impromptu style.

"FSP Shuttlecraft *Seeker* to ship in liftoff. You are under arrest. Proceed directly to shuttleport. You have been warned."

Sassinak had said they *could* divert to the shuttleport, even immediately after liftoff. But she didn't think they would.

"Don't even try it, Tiny!" came the reply from the yacht. "You haven't got a chance."

He hoped that wasn't true. Supposedly, the constraints of

taking off from a silo meant that the most common weapons systems couldn't be mounted until after the yacht was out of the atmosphere in steady flight. And his shields should deflect all but heavy assaults. The problem was how to stop the yacht. Shuttles were just that — shuttles — not fighter craft. He had a tractor beam which was not nearly powerful enough to slow the yacht and a midrange beamer designed to clear brush when landing in uncleared terrain. Could he disable the yacht's instrument cone? That's what Ford had suggested.

He got the targeting lasers fixed on the yacht's bow and he kept the shuttle in alignment, and pressed the firing stud. A line of light appeared, splashed harmlessly along the yacht's shields. It wasn't supposed to have shields. They were high in the atmosphere now. His displays told him the yacht should be planning to release its massive solid-fuel engine. This didn't worry him because the more massive yacht, with its limited drive system, could not possibly outmaneuver a Fleet shuttle as long as it stayed below lightspeed. But he still could not figure out how to stop it. If it made the transition to FTL, he could not follow.

Of course he could ram it. No shields on a ship that size could withstand the strain if he intercepted at high velocity. But what if he *missed*? How could he keep track of it, keep it from going into FTL, if he couldn't stop it cold? The yacht's booster separated and it surged higher. Tim sent the shuttle after it. What if it had more power than they'd thought? What if it *could* distance the shuttle? Then it would be free to go into FTL and disappear forever and he . . . *he* would get to explain his failure to Commander Sassinak.

Who had not explained, this time, exactly what to do. Who was not in her cruiser, this time, ready to come to his rescue. He found he was sweating, his breath short. He had to do *something* and, except by a kind of blind instinct, he had never been good at picking alternatives. The yacht opened a margin on him. Tim uttered a silent prayer to gods he couldn't name and redlined the shuttle to catch back up to it. If he was right . . . if he could remember how to do this . . . if nothing went wrong, there was a way to keep that yacht from making a jump. If things *did* go wrong, he wouldn't know it.

❖   ❖   ❖

Sassinak picked herself out of the tangle of bodies with a groan. A dull ache in her leg promised to develop into real pain as soon as she paid attention to it. Tim should be on his way. Arly was out there somewhere doing something with the invasion fleet. And here . . . here was death and pain and carnage. One Lethi delegate smashed into amber splinters and dust that stank of sulfur compounds. A Ryxi whimpering as its broken leg twitched repeatedly. The singed feathers on its back added another noxious reek to the chamber. Aygar? Aygar lay sprawled, motionless, but Lunzie knelt beside him and nodded encouragingly as she looked up. Ford, gray around the mouth, held out his blistered hands for the medics as they sprayed a pale-green foam on them.

Sassinak limped over to Lunzie and thought about sitting down beside her. Better not. She didn't think she could get back up. "How bad is he?"

"Near as I can tell, a stunner beam got him. Not too badly. He should wake up miserable within an hour. What else?" Lunzie still had that intense stare of someone in full Discipline.

"The Paraden representatives here, the ones in the guest box, got away. To their yacht."

"*Blast* it!" Lunzie looked ready to smash through walls barehanded.

"Never mind. I had a trap for them."

"You . . . ?"

Sassinak explained briefly, looking round as she did. The surviving delegates were safely sealed into their places. She could just see them watching her. What must they be thinking? And what should she do?

"Sassinak. A statement?" One of the students had come down to the floor, with a camera on his shoulder. So they had secured the newslines. She frowned, trying to clear her mind, to think. She felt the weight of it all on her. She glanced around for Coromell who should, as the senior, make any statements. Then she saw his crumpled body in the unmistakable posture of the dead.

"I . . . Just a moment." Had Lunzie seen? What would she do? She touched Lunzie's shoulder. "Did you know? Coromell?"

Lunzie nodded. "Yes. I saw it. I'd just gone to full Discipline. Couldn't save him . . . and he was so *decent*." She blinked back tears. "I can't cry now, and besides . . ."

"Right."

Coromell dead. The Speaker dead. The justices, if not dead, at least unable to take over. Someone had to do it. She limped up the step to the Speaker's podium and stepped gingerly between the bodies that lay at its foot: the Speaker, who had reminded her of her first captain, and the Diplonian delegate she herself had killed. The Speaker's podium had had status screens, an array of controls to record votes, and grant the right to speak. But none of that worked. Her own shots, most likely, had shattered the screens. Still, it was the right place, and she stood behind it as the student with the camera moved in for a close shot. She could imagine what it looked like. A tired, rumpled Fleet officer in front of the Federation shield, the very image of a military coup, the end of peace and freedom. But she would do better than that.

"Delegates, justices, citizens of the Federation of Sentient Planets," she began. "This Federation, this peaceful alliance of many races, will survive . . ."

Arly, in the command seat on *Zaid-Dayan's* bridge, had the best view of what happened next. Although the Central System's defenses were concentrated along the three most common approaches from other sectors, the Seti had not chosen an alternative route. They had counted on most of the defenses being knocked out by collaborators. Once she realized that their approach was in fact along a mapped path, she had been able to use the *Zaid-Dayan's* capabilities against them.

At first she had used the defense satellites as cover, taking out two of the flanking escorts, and one medium cruiser as if the satellites had been active. So far, the Seti commanders had assumed that the losses were, in fact, due to passive defense systems that had escaped inactivation. At least, that's what her Ssli told her they were thinking. She hoped they were also wondering if their human allies were double-crossing them.

When that got too dangerous — for the Seti clearly knew exactly where such installations were and they began attacking them — she used the stealth capability and the Ssli's precision control of tiny FTL hops to disappear and reappear unpredictably, firing off a few missiles each time at the nearest ship, and then vanishing again. She could not actually destroy the invaders, not with one cruiser, but she could inflict serious losses.

Now they were well into the system, inside the outer ranks of defenses, still in numbers large enough to threaten all the inhabited planets. It would be another day or more before any Fleet vessels could arrive, assuming the nearest had come at once on receipt of the mayday. By then FedCentral might be in range of the Seti ships.

She was just considering whether to sacrifice the ship by going in for close combat for she thought she might do the Seti flagship enough damage to force the invaders to slow, when the scans went crazy, doppler displays racing through color sequences, alarms flashing. Then the ship's drive indicators rose slowly from green to yellow with some strain as if a massive object had appeared not far off.

"Thek," said the very pale Weft, its form wavering before it steadied back to human.

"Thek?"

She had seen before the way Thek moved, and how it seemed to violate a lifetime's assumptions about matter and space. She had just not realized that her instruments felt the same way about it.

"Many, many Thek. They . . . more or less vacuum-packed the Seti fleet."

The sensors reported the right density and mass for more Thek than Arly had ever seen, but what she thought of was Dupaynil. Dupaynil being squashed by granite pyramids.

"No," said the Weft, shaking his head. "Not *that* ship. That one's whole, but can't maneuver. The Thek made it quite clear to the Seti that their prisoners had best stay healthy."

"What about us?" After all, humans had been involved in the plot, too.

"We're free to go, although they'd prefer that we picked up the prisoners from that Seti ship."

"Fine with me. I'm not arguing with flying rocks." She hoped the Thek wouldn't consider that disrespectful. "Are you . . . *talking* with them?"

He looked surprised. "Of course. You know we're special to them. They think we're . . . I suppose you'd say, cute."

"No one ever told *me* that you Wefts could talk to Thek."

"Not that many know we're telepathic with some humans, or most Ssli."

"Mmm. Right. So where does this Thek want us to go to pick up passengers?"

In the event, they sent a shuttle which the Thek guided through the interstices of the trap they'd shut on the Seti. While it was on its way, Arly remembered to prepare quarters for the alien guests, including a sealed compartment for the Lethi where the fumes from their obligatory sulfur wouldn't bother anyone else.

Arly decided the shuttle's arrival required a formal reception to reassure the allied aliens that Fleet was loyal to the FSP and not part of the plot. With the crisis over, she left the bridge to a junior officer and came to Flight Deck herself, with a squad of marines in dress uniform.

The *Zaid-Dayan* had no military band, but she had a recording of the FSP anthem piped in as more suitable to aliens than anything else. The shuttle hatch opened and two of the crew came out, carrying the Lethi. The Ryxi bobbed out on its own, fluffing feathers nervously, and chittered vigorously before greeting her in Standard with effusive thanks. Then came the Bronthin, its normal pastel blue fur almost gray with exhaustion and fear. Two more of the shuttle crew, with the larval Ssli's environmental tank. Finally, Dupaynil emerged. Arly stared at him in frank shock. The dapper, elegant officer she remembered was a filthy, shambling wreck, red-rimmed eyes sunken.

"Commander!"

"Is Sassinak aboard?" That had an intensity she couldn't quite interpret.

"No. She's onplanet."

"Thank the . . ." He paused. "The luck, I suppose. Or whatever. I . . ." He staggered and the waiting medics came forward. He waved them off. "I don't need anything but a shower — a *long* shower — and some rest."

"But what happened to you?"

Dupaynil gave her a look somewhere between anger and exhaustion. "One damn thing after another, Arly, and the worst of it is it's all my fault for thinking I was smarter than your Sassinak. Now please?"

"Of course."

He did reek and she felt her nostrils dilate as he passed her. She wondered how long he'd been in that pressure suit. She hardly had all the survivors settled when the Weft liaison to the Thek called her back to the bridge. One last chore remained. The humans most responsible had escaped the planet in a fast yacht, and although a Fleet vessel had kept it in sight, it could not stop it.

"Tim and that shuttle!" Arly said. "I forgot him. Comm, get us a link!"

Tim had the yacht's position and the Ssli flicked the cruiser in and out of FTL space in a minute jump that put them well in range. Her Weapons Officer reported that the yacht lacked anything to penetrate the cruiser's shields. Too bad Sassinak wasn't here. She would enjoy this. But she'd had the onplanet fun. Arly put their message on an all-frequency transmission.

"FSP Cruiser *Zaid-Dayan* to private vessel *Celestial Fortune*. Going somewhere?"

"Let us alone, or you'll regret it!" came the reply. "You're nothin' but a lousy little short-range shuttle tryin' to play big shot."

"Take another look," suggested Arly and cut back the visual screens. "Do you want to argue with *this*?"

She sent a missile past their bows, and heard a yelp from Tim on one of the incoming lines. A spurt of annoyance. He should have had sense enough to get out of the way.

"Get that shuttle back in here," she told him.

"Sorry, ma'am."

"What do you mean, *sorry*?"

"I . . . uh . . . It was the only way I could think of."

"What did you do?"

"I . . . locked shields with 'em."

Arly closed her eyes and counted to ten. So *that's* why they hadn't gone into FTL yet. But it meant that blowing the yacht would mean blowing the shuttle, and Tim. Nor could he pull away. Locking shields was hard enough going in. She'd never heard of anyone getting back out, unless both ships agreed to damp the shields simultaneously.

"Who's with you?" asked Arly.

"Nobody," came the reply.

From his tone he knew exactly what that meant. If Sassinak had been aboard . . . but one ensign, who had been unable to think of any way to impede the enemy but bonding to it? He was very expendable.

"You suited up?"

"Yes. But . . ." But what good would it do?

Shuttles had no escape pods, for the very good reason that in normal operation they were useless. And being blown out of an exploding shuttle was a little more than hazardous.

"I can flutter their shields, Commander. Give you a better chance of getting 'em with the first shot."

"Dammit, Tim, don't be so eager to die."

It would help, though, and she knew it.

"I'm not," he said. Was that a quaver in his voice?

He was not going to die if she could help it. But the yacht had meanwhile refused to cut its acceleration outsystem or change course. Its captain seemed sure he could make his FTL jump anyway.

"Even if I do scrape a louse off our hide."

"Do that and you're dead for sure. We've followed more than one through FTL flux." She flipped the channel off. "And why can't the blasted Thek help us now?" Arly demanded of the Weft at her side. "I hate the way they pick and choose. If these are the bigshots . . ."

The *Zaid-Dayan's* proximity alarms blared. The artificial gravity pulsed. Arly swallowed hastily, clutching the arms of her chair. Small objects tumbled about and a dust haze rose, to be sucked rapidly away by the fans.

"Do me a favor, Captain, and don't bad-mouth the Theks any more," said the Weft.

This time he'd shifted completely and hung now from the overhead, bright blue eyes gleaming at Arly. Then he shifted back, leaving a mental image of strings of innards trailing down in a most abnormal way to reassemble into a living person.

"I just said . . ."

"I know. But you people complain all the time about how slow the Thek are and how they don't pay attention. You should rejoice that they're now paying attention and you've had a demonstration of how they can move."

"Right. Sorry. But the yacht . . ."

The Thek had absorbed all the yacht's considerable inertia, flicking Tim and his shuttle off as a housewife might flick an ant off a plate. When he hailed them, Arly could hear astonished relief in his voice.

"Permission to land shuttle?"

Should she bring him in or send him back to FedCentral? A glance at the readouts told her the shuttle wouldn't make it back safely.

"Permission granted. Bring 'er aboard, Ensign."

And he did, without any hotdog flourishes.

Arly looked around the bridge, and wondered if she looked as disheveled as the others. Far more ragged than Sassinak ever looked, she thought. We'll have to get this place cleaned up before she sees it and everyone rested. But we still have to get back down there just in case.

Convincing the Dockmaster at the FedCentral Station that the *Zaid-Dayan* was not an agent of doom required the rough side of Arly's tongue.

"We saved your tails from a 'catenated Seti *fleet*. And you're going to gripe at me because I left without your fardling permission?"

"It was highly irregular."

"So it was, and so were the Seti. So were the traitors in your system that wanted to let 'em in. It's not my fault you wouldn't believe the truth. Now you can let us dock or watch us sit out here using your station for target practice."

"That's a threat!" he said.

"Right. Going to take us up on it?"

"I'll file a complaint." Then his face sagged as he realized to whom that complaint would go: Sassinak. Now in command of the loyal Federation forces onplanet. Acting Governor. "It's all *very* irregular . . ." His voice trailed away into a sigh. "All right. Bays twelve through twenty, orange arm."

"Thank you," said Arly, careful to keep her voice neutral. Never push your luck, Sassinak always said, and she felt her luck had been working overtime lately. "If you have any fresh forage for Bronthin, we have an individual in bad shape who's been a Seti prisoner."

This the Dockmaster could handle. "Of course. With so much diplomatic traffic, we pride ourselves on keeping full supplies for every race in the FSP. Any other requirements?"

"A Ryxi which is suffering from 'feather pit,' whatever that is, and a pair of Lethi who seem all right, although our medical team isn't familiar with Lethi."

"Only *two* Lethi? That's very bad. Lethi need to cluster in larger numbers."

"Plus a larval Ssli," Arly said. "It's complained that its tank needs recharging."

"No problem with *any* of that," said the Dockmaster, suddenly cordial. "If you'll send the allied races to bay sixteen, that'll be the quickest access for our specialty medical services."

"Will do." Arly shook her head as she looked around the bridge. "Can you believe that? He was willing to stand us off as if we were pirates, but he's got specialty medical teams for our aliens."

Arly had been in communication with Sassinak for the past several hours. The situation onplanet had stabilized with the loyalists firmly in control, and only scattered pockets of resistance.

"And I think most of that's confusion," Sassinak had said. "We're finding that many of the Parchandri/Paraden supporters had been blackmailed into it. Others just didn't know any better. Right now the Thek are calling for a formal trial."

"Not another one!"

"Not like that one, no. A Thek trial." Sassinak had looked exhausted. Arly wondered if she'd had any rest at all since her disappearance. "Another Thek cathedral is all I need! But considering what they've done, we really can't argue. They want those prisoners you rescued from the Seti, especially the Bronthin, Ssli, Weft, and Dupaynil."

So now, docked at the Station, Arly saw these turned over to special medical teams. Soon they'd be on their way to the Thek trial. She wondered about the crew and passengers of the yacht Tim had trapped. But she wasn't going to ask any questions. Two experiences with fast-moving Thek were quite enough.

It was impossible to overestimate the civilizing influence of cleanliness, rest, and good cooking, Sassinak thought. Back on the *Zaid-Dayan*, back in a clean uniform, with a stomach full of the best her favorite cook could do, with a full shift's sleep, she was ready to forgive almost anyone. Particularly since the Thek, in their unyielding fashion, had satisfied any remaining desire for vengeance.

For a moment, she felt again the pressure of those most alien minds. And marveled that she had survived *two* terms in a Thek cathedral. Never again, she hoped. The judgment process might be exhausting but it served its purpose admirably.

The guilty Seti were to be confined to one interdicted planet, guarded by installations whose crews were former pirate prisoners. Paraden family lost all its possessions, from shipping lines to private moonlets. Paradens and Parchandris alike were given basic survival and tool supplies, the same they had sold to many a colony starting up, and deposited on a barely habitable planet.

With the single exception of Ford's Auntie Q. She lost nothing, for the Thek considered her a victim, not a Paraden, despite her name.

And, thanks to Lunzie's partisanship and fierce arguments, heavyworlders were also considered victims. After all, they had been cheated by the wealthy lightweights who then blackmailed them into service. So the Thek required only that those conspirators in the governments of heavyworlder planets be expelled. The others, informed of the complex plot, were given shares in the liquidation of Paraden assets. They could use that to ease their lives.

In addition, FSP regulations changed to allow heavyworlder migration to any world open to humans. But that did not include Ireta: the Thek would not change their earlier decision. Aygar had been consoled, finally, by the knowledge that he would have a chance to see many equally fascinating worlds. And enough money to enjoy them.

Now the original team relaxed in Sassinak's office, with most of the tales untold and a long night ahead for telling them. Restored by a couple of sessions in the tank to heal his burns, Ford crunched another of the crispy fries. Sassinak met his eyes and felt indecently smug. They had private plans when the party broke up. He had told her just enough about Auntie Q and the Ryxi tailfeathers to whet her appetite.

Dupaynil, though, had lost some of his polish. Specklessly clean, as usual, perfectly groomed, he still had a hangdog tentative quality that she found almost as irritating as his former blithe certainty.

Lunzie, always tactful, had put aside her grief for Coromell to try to cheer Dupaynil up, but so far it hadn't worked. Timran, on the other hand, was indecently gleeful. He had taken the mild commendation she'd given him as if he'd been awarded the Federation's highest honor in front of the Grand Council. Now he sat stiffly in the corner of her office as if he would burst if he moved. She'd better rescue the lad.

"Ensign, there's an errand . . . a fairly special one . . ."

"Yes, *ma'am!*"

"We're having guests; I'd like you to escort a lady from the Flight Deck in here."

If anyone could settle a young man like Tim, it would be Fleur. He'd enjoy Aygar's student friend, too, and Erdra. Sassinak grinned wickedly at the thought of Erdra coming face to face with the reality behind her daydreams. *She* was no Carin Coldae and the sooner she quit playing games and went back to finish that advanced degree in analytical systems, the better. The riot had cured her of any thought that violence and glamor coexisted, and a visit to a working warship ought to clear out the rest of her nonsense.

Lunzie would want to meet her relative-of-sorts, from the Chinese family. It had been extravagant, in several ways, to send her own shuttle down for them, but she felt it important to build respect for Fleet. No more restrictions on the movement of Fleet personnel, and no civilian weapons monitors, either. The *Zaid-Dayan* was, as it always should be, ready for action. Now, while Tim was gone, she could try to penetrate Dupaynil's gloom again.

"I wanted to apologize to you," she began, "for pulling that trick. . . ."

"It *was* a trick, then, with the orders?" He brightened a moment. "I was sure of it. You used the Ssli, right?"

"Right. But it was flat stupid of me not to know more about the ship I tossed you onto. I had no idea . . ."

"I know." He looked glum again.

"You said something about charges?"

"Well, the Exec of the escort and I had to overpower the crew, put 'em in custody. . . ."

"On an *escort*? Where?"

"In the escape pods in cold sleep. They were going to space me."

Sassinak stared at him. He said it in a tone of flat misery entirely out of character for someone who had run a successful mutiny.

"I'm sure we can get the charges dropped. If anyone's dared filed them," she said. "Especially now. I've had contact with

Admiral Vannoy, back at Sector, and he's rooting out the traitors around Fleet."

But that didn't cheer him up as it should have. Clearly impending charges weren't the burden he carried. Lunzie caught her eye and made a significant glance at Ford, at Dupaynil, then at Aygar. Sassinak let one eyelid droop in a near-wink.

"Ford, if you don't mind, I think I'd like a grownup to supervise that reception. Aygar, you might want to be there to greet your friends."

Aygar leaped up while Ford stood more slowly, grinning at Sassinak in a way that almost made her blush.

"You ladies take care," he said, with his own significant glance at Dupaynil. "No squabbling."

Then he left, shepherding Aygar ahead of him.

"Now, then," said Sassinak. "You've been brooding about as if you were about to be stuck in Administration forever. So, what's the problem?" She thought for a long moment he would not answer, then it burst out of him.

"It's ridiculous, and I don't want to talk about it."

Lunzie and Sassinak waited, saying nothing. Dupaynil looked up and met Sassinak's eyes squarely.

"I was so *furious* with you for pulling that trick. For getting *away* with that trick. I dreamed of outfoxing you again, coming back with what you needed, but making you pay for it. Then I had to escape those . . . those pirates on *Claw*, and realized that I didn't know one thing about actually running a ship. Panis had to train me as if I were a raw recruit. But I still thought, with what I'd found, that I'd have a chance of returning in triumph. A good story to tell, all that. But then the Seti . . ." He stopped, shaking his head, and Sassinak and Lunzie stared at each other over his bent head.

"What did they do?" asked Lunzie.

Sassinak was thinking that it was a good thing they'd died before she'd had the opportunity to skin their scaly hide off their live bodies.

"Arly didn't tell you?"

"She said you looked pretty dilapidated when you came aboard, but you wouldn't go to Medical —" Her skin crawled as she thought of reasons why he might not, which could explain his present mood. "Dupaynil! They didn't!"

This time he laughed, a genuine if shaky laugh. "No. No, they didn't actually *do* anything. It was just . . . Have you ever seen a Seti shower?"

What did that have to do with anything? "No," Sassinak said cautiously.

"It sprays you with hot air, grit and more hot air," Dupaynil said with more energy than she'd heard from him yet. Bitter, but alive. "I'm sure it's what keeps their scales so shiny. Probably takes care of itchy little parasites on a Seti. But for a human, day after day . . . And then I had to stay in that blasted pressure suit for *days*." His expression brought a chuckle to Sassinak; she couldn't help it. "I'd planned on strolling in, cool and suave, to hand you what you needed. Instead, I was stuck in a stinking pressure suit in a crowded compartment full of terrified aliens where I could do not one damn thing, and had to be rescued like any silly princess in a fairy tale."

"But you did," said Sassinak.

"Did what?"

"Did do something. Kipling's corns, Dupaynil, *you* got the warning to us. You had the evidence the Thek used."

"They could have got it straight from those slime-buckets' minds."

"Well, if the Thek hadn't been there, we'd have needed it. After all, they asked for you at the trial. They needed your evidence, too. I don't know what more you could want. You escaped one death trap after another, you got vital information, you saved the world. Did you really think anyone could do that without getting dirty?" She thought of herself in the tunnels, even before Fleur's disguise.

"I wanted to impress you," he said softly, looking at his linked hands.

"Well, you did." Sassinak cocked her head at him. "Impress me? Was that all?"

"No." She would never have suspected that Dupaynil could blush, but what else were those red patches on his cheeks. "When I was on *Claw*, when I realized what you'd done, and I was so mad . . . I also realized I wanted . . ."

It was clear enough, though he couldn't say it.

"I'm sorry." That was genuine. He had earned it. She couldn't offer more. Her joyful reunion with Ford had revealed too much to both of them.

"Sorry!" Lunzie fairly exploded, her eyes sparkling. "You nearly get the man killed, he has to take over a whole *ship*, and then he saves us all from a Seti invasion, and you're just *sorry!*" She looked at Dupaynil. "She may be my descendant, but that doesn't mean we agree. I think she ought to give you a medal."

"Lunzie!"

"You wouldn't think so if you'd seen me getting off that shuttle," Dupaynil said. "Ask Arly."

"I don't have to ask Arly. I can see for myself." That came out in a sensuous purr. Under Lunzie's bright gaze, Dupaynil's grin began to revive.

Sassinak regarded her great-great-great with affectionate disdain. "Lunzie, I know where I inherited *some* of my propensities." If Lunzie stayed interested, she gave Dupaynil only a few more hours of freedom.

"Meow!" Lunzie stuck out her tongue, then leaned closer to Dupaynil.

Whatever else she might have said was interrupted by the arrival of the others: Fleur, who had worn one of her own creations in lavender and silver, Aygar and Timran in the midst of the students. Erdra, Sassinak noticed, wore the same kind of colorful shirt and leggings as the others. Perhaps she had grown out of her wishful thinking already.

"Have you?" Fleur asked, drifting close a little later, as the conversation rose and fell around them.

"What?"

"Grown out of your past?"

Sassinak snorted. "I grew out of Carin Coldae a long way back."

"You know that's not what I mean."

Sassinak thought of Randy Paraden's face, the instant before the Weft killed him, and of the faces of the other conspirators in the Thek cathedral. She had looked long in her mirror when she came back aboard, hoping not to find any of the marks of that kind of character.

"Yes," she said slowly. "I think I have. I can't change what they did to me, but I can change what I do about it. It's time to be more than a pirate-chaser. But not less."

THE END

Natural numbers, 543, 941
Naval Ordnance Laboratory, 102
**NAVAL ORDNANCE RESEARCH CALCULATOR (NORC),
917–919**, 334, 456, 492, 588, 1489
Naval Proving Ground, 456
Naval Research Laboratory, 122, 1285
NBS, 369, 445, 611, 766, 1331
NCR Corporation, 123, 304, 431, 452, 919, 644, 680, 1428,
1493
NCR COMPUTERS, 919–920
Century series, 919, 1491
Criterion series, 919
Tower series, 919, 920
nCube 2, 905, 1024, 1323, 1325
Nearest neighbor rule, 1038, 1039, 1177
Nebraska, University of, 522
NEC (Nippon Electric Corporation), 147, 287, 457, 644,
734, 737, 997, 1322, 1323
NEC SX-2,3, 1322–1324, 1492
NEC UltraLite, 739
Negation as finite failure (NFF), 425, 778, 782, 786
Negative acknowledgment, 385, 596, 1068
Negative feedback, 49, 65
Negative number, 210, 211
Neliac, 1224, 1472, 1473, 1475
Nested block structure, 727
Nested loops, 68, 1251
Netlib, 1232
Network
  computer. *See* **NETWORKS, COMPUTER.**
  local area. *See* **LOCAL AREA NETWORK (LAN).**
  metropolitan area. *See* **METROPOLITAN AREA
    NETWORK (MAN).**
  wide area (WAN), 198, 477, 870, 904
  semantic, 721
Network access protocol, 382
Network analyzer, 43, 148
NETWORK ARCHITECTURE, 920–921, 392
Network degree, 1018
Network File System (NFS), Sun, 967, 974, 987
Network model, 400
Network processor, 197
NETWORK PROTOCOLS, 921–923, 618, 973, 1136
Network Systems Corp, 360
NETWORKS FOR LEARNING, 923–924
NETWORKS, COMPUTER, 924–929, 476, 578, 986
NEURAL NETWORKS, 929–934, 108, 129, 185, 187, 332,
847, 955, 977, 1211, 1266, 1490
Neuromancer, 626
Neuron, 931
New Jersey Institute of Technology, 923
New Mexico State University, CP-10
New School for Social Research, 145
New York at Albany, State University of, 1465
New York at Binghamton, University of, 1465
New York at Buffalo, State University of, 177, 293, 1465
New York at Stony Brook, State University of, 286, 1465
New York Institute of Technology, 244
New York Times Information Bank, 175
New York University, 1196
Newark College of Engineering, 615
Newline character [C], 152
NeWS, 1435
News Election Service (NES), 1067
Newsgroup, 623
NewsNet, 1056
Newton divided difference polynomial, 950

Newton-Cotes formulas, 953
Newton-Raphson method, 28, 173, 534, 712, 827, 949,
1004, 1184, CP-11
NewWave, 1362
Nexis [on-line law service], 742
NeXT, Inc., 70, 235, 520, 525, 1056
nFET, 272
Nibble, 181
NIL pointer, 408, 757, 758, 780, 1259
Nim, 285, 291
Nine's complement, 211
Nine-track tape, 856
Nintendo, 287, 289, 290
Nixdorf Corporation, 123
Nixie tube, 180
NKK Steel Co., 537
NLM medical project, 632
NLS [text editor], 1356
nMOS gate, 273
NMR scanner, 126, 128, 130, CP-9
NO-OP, 934, 971, 95
Node firing, 416
Node, 35, 36, 409, 416, 193, 199, 584, 586, 754, 755, 771, 780,
864, 1014, 1015, 1177, 1188, 1196, 1237, 1323, 1390
Nominal bandwidth, 116
Nomography, 1384
Non-executable statement, 424
Nondeterminism, 166, 589, 726, 780, 791, 938, 1015, 1109,
1195, 1420
Nondeterministic automaton, 108
Nondeterministic Polynomial (NP), 938, 939
Nonexecutable statement, 536, 1282
Nonlinear programming, 820, 1004
Nonmonotonic inference, 721
NONPROCEDURAL LANGUAGES, 934–938, 1123
Nonterminal symbol, 115, 175, 209, 562, 581, 870
Nonvolatile memory, 324, 850, 859, 877
NOR gate, 80, 273, 776, 1003
NOR operator, 272, 276
NORAD, 336
NORC. *See* **NAVAL ORDNANCE RESEARCH
  CALCULATOR.**
Norm [matrix], 527, 740, 741
Normalized floating-point number, 410, 531, 1320
North American Aviation, 1226, 1227, 1409, 1410, 1490
North Carolina State University, 1229
Northgate Corporation, 644
Northrup Aircraft Corporation, 433, 834
Northwest Airlines, 999
Northwestern University, 269
Norwegian Computing Center, 992, 1209
Notebook computer, 72, 235, 459, 519, 623, 738, 881, 1056
Notebook [Mathematica], 761
NoteCards, 632, 633
Notepad system, 145
Nottingham Algorithms Group (NAG), 236, 1229, 1231
Novis, 163
NP-COMPLETE PROBLEMS, 938–941, 213, 564, 586, 656,
1335, 1405, 1491
NSA. *See* National Security Agency.
NSF. *See* National Science Foundation.
NSFnet, 923, 928, 1327
NTSC Television, 166
NU-Bus, 147
Nu-Prolog, 783, 784, 787, 788
Nucleus, 717
Null byte, 151

explain how the data structure is laid out; rather, it defines the effects of the various operations. As a result, the implementation of the abstract data type, including both the layout of the data structure and the algorithms for the operations, may be modified without requiring modification of user programs. When it has been verified that the implementation performs in accordance with its public specification, the specification may safely be used as the definitive source of information about how higher-level programs may correctly use the module. In one sense, we build up "bigger" definitions out of "smaller" ones; but because a specification alone suffices for understanding, the new definition is in another sense no bigger than the pre-existing components. It is the compression of detail that gives the technique its power.

For example, we might define a data type *Stack*, whose elements are of an arbitrary type *T* and for which operations *Push*, *Pop*, and *Top* are provided. The definition of the abstract data type would be

type *Stack(T:*type);
specifications
    procedure *Push(var S: Stack(T); x:T)*;
        [specification of *Push* in the formal
        notation of choice]
    procedure *Pop(var S: Stack(T))*;
        [specification of *Pop* in the formal
        notation of choice]
    function *Top(S: Stack(T))* **returns** *T*;
        [specification of *Top* in the formal
        notation of choice]
implementation
    [declarations of data structure used to
    represent *Stacks*]
    [bodies of *Push*, *Pop*, and *Top*]
end type.

A program might then declare stacks of integers, reals, or other data types, including types defined by the programmer. For example, after the definition above, the following program fragment would be legal.

declare
    X: Stack(integer);
    Y: Stack(real);
    Z: Stack(MyType);
    j: integer;
    g: real;
    p,q: MyType;
    ....
Push(X,j); *Pop(Y)*; *p := Top(Z)*;
Pop(X); *g := Top(Y)*; *Push(Z,q)*;

The specification techniques used for abstract data types evolved from the predicates used in simple sequential programs. The method for formally verifying that the specification of an abstract data type is consistent with its implementation was originally formulated by Hoare (1972). Additional expressive power was incorporated to deal with the way information is packaged into modules and with the problem of abstracting from an implementa-

tion to a data type (Guttag, 1980). One class of specification techniques defines the properties of a data type as a set of axioms; these techniques draw on the similarity between a data type and the mathematical structure called an *algebra* (Liskov and Guttag, 1986). Another class of techniques explicitly models a newly defined type by defining its properties in terms of the properties of common, well-understood types.

The theory of abstract data types has greatly influenced the relatively recent development of object-oriented programming (*q.v.*) languages, including Smalltalk, C++, and CLOS. In these languages, a *class* (*q.v.*) denotes a concrete realization of an abstract data type. Classes are often organized into a hierarchy so that general properties are shared by classes at high levels of abstraction (the superclasses) and specialized properties are embodied in classes at lower levels of abstraction (the subclasses).

References

1972. Hoare, C.A.R. "Proof of Correctness of Data Representations," *Acta Informatica* **1**, No. 4.
1980. Guttag, J. "Abstract Data Types and the Development of Data Structures," *Programming Language Design*. A. Wasserman, Ed. New York: Computer Society Press of the IEEE.
1980. *Proceedings of the Workshop on Data Abstraction, Databases, and Conceptual Modelling. SIGPLAN Notices*, **16** (1).
1982. Hilfinger, P. *Abstraction Mechanisms and Language Design*. Cambridge, MA: The MIT Press.
1984. Shaw, M. "Abstraction Techniques in Modern Programming Languages," *IEEE Software*, **1** (4). October.
1985. Cardelli, L., and Wegner, P. "On Understanding Types, Data Abstraction, and Polymorphism," *ACM Computing Surveys*, **17**(4). December.
1986. Bishop, J. *Data Abstractions in Programming Languages*. Wokingham, England: Addison-Wesley.
1986. Liskov, B., and Guttag, J. *Abstraction and Specification in Program Development*. Cambridge, MA: The MIT Press.

GRADY E. BOOCH AND MARY SHAW

ACCESS METHODS

For articles on related subjects *see* ACCESS TIME; DATABASE MANAGEMENT SYSTEM; DIRECT ACCESS; FILE, and RECORD.

An *access method* is a technique for accessing data that has been placed on some kind of mass storage device, most often a disk. While the term "access method" is used to describe the method used to retrieve the data, the process is frequently closely related to the structure of the data as it resides on the disk. As a result, the term is sometimes loosely used to describe the structure of the data itself and, often, "access method" is used as a synonym for the program or routine that implements the method.

All modern computer manufacturers provide service routines to implement access methods, generally as a component of the operating system (*q.v.*). Instead of access method, terms such as data management, file control program, and I/O (input or output) supervisor are sometimes used, depending on the manufacturer. The terminology used in this discussion is common to several manufacturers, including IBM. However, the evolution and concepts of access methods apply to all manufacturers, although not all manufacturers support every variant described below.

Evolution of Access Methods In the earliest days of computers and programming, each programmer had to program the flow of data to and from I/O devices, including auxiliary storage units such as disks, drums, and tapes. This required that the programmer be familiar with the characteristics of particular devices and write code for functions such as testing for available channels (*q.v.*), testing for I/O errors, and programming error recovery. Many of these functions were time dependent. Programming I/O in this manner tended to bind the programs to a particular device. When the storage device changed, the programming had to be substantially modified.

Since I/O programming tended to be fairly similar from one program to the next, it was not long before utility service programs (or access methods) were developed. Such programs perform, in a generalized manner, all of the interactions with the storage device. The programmer need merely be concerned with requesting a record and providing a location in storage for it. The division of functions is depicted in Fig. 1. Note the assumption in this figure that the application program can continue processing while data is being transferred, a point to which we return below.

The interface between the application program and the access method tends to be fairly simple and standardized and is generally reducible to a set of parameters. The technique usually used is to place the input and/or output parameters in a table. This table may be called (among other names) the DTF (Define The File), DD (Data Definition), or FCT (File Control Table). The parameters include a pointer to an area of storage to and from which the data transfer is to be made (i.e. the record buffer), the size of the record, whether labels are to be written or exist at the front of the file, whether a tape is to be rewound at the end of the file, and pointers to special error-handling routines (provided by the application). The application program need only place the necessary data into the table. This is a far easier task than having the programmer write an I/O

routine. The access method, when invoked by the application, uses the contents of the table to perform the task requested. This technique has the advantage that, when a new storage device becomes available, the access method rather than the application programs can be modified. Thus, all programs using the access method are able to use the new device without significant modification, and frequently without any modification. When access methods were first used, they rarely provided complete transparency (i.e. independence) from the device, because new devices provided new characteristics that required the addition of new variables to the parameter table. Today, most variables are known or have been anticipated. Thus, it is now commonplace for existing applications to utilize new devices without any change to the application. Applications thereby have achieved *physical device independence* and are transparent to the introduction of new devices.

On early computers without multiprogramming (*q.v.*), it was important to use the central processing unit (CPU) as efficiently as possible. Fig. 1 illustrates an application that continues processing while data transfer takes place. This is achieved by having the access method return control to the application program after it starts the data transfer. When data transfer is complete, the interrupt mechanism gives control to the access method again. The access method performs checking for data transfer errors and, assuming no problem, "posts" or flags the file parameter table that the data transfer is complete. Control is then returned to the application program. The responsibility of ensuring that processing of data does not begin until the data transfer is complete is left to the application program, which must check the parameter table for completion of the data transfer.

The most popular auxiliary storage device on pre-multiprogrammed computers was magnetic tape. Because records are stored sequentially, one after the other, on magnetic tape, they must be processed sequentially for most efficient processing. The standard access method thus became known as SAM (Sequential Access Method). Using SAM, there was little processing that an application program could do on input while waiting for the next record (although, on output, it could start to generate the next record). A better method was needed to take advantage of the predictability that the next one of the sequentially stored records would be read. Thus, a

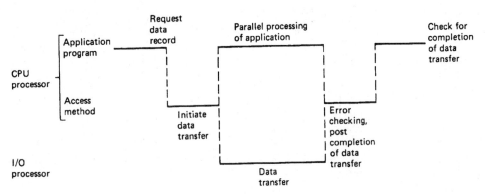

FIG. 1. Division of functions.

new access method was designed to achieve what the application program generally could not—namely, to overlap processing with data transfer. When reading data, this is achieved by looking ahead and performing the access for the next record while the application program is processing the last (or current) record. This modification of the model of Fig. 1 is illustrated in Fig. 2.

As Fig. 2 illustrates, the data transmission proceeds in parallel with the application processing, with a brief time-out at the end of the transmission for the access method to handle the details of error checking. In this case, the access method does not have to post the completion of data transfer to the application, since the application is still working with the last record. Fig. 2 illustrates the normal situation, but clearly there are situations where the application finishes its work before the data transfer is complete. In this case, some waiting is necessary, but nevertheless some overlap of processing and data transfer has been achieved that otherwise would not have been. This access method is known as QSAM (Queued Sequential Access Method) and the sequential access method of Fig. 1 became known as BSAM (Basic Sequential Access Method). QSAM has been illustrated above for input, but applies equally well to output. On output, QSAM also absorbs the responsibility of blocking records—whereby several application program records are batched together to the same physical record on disk (*see* BLOCK AND BLOCKING FACTOR).

BSAM and QSAM were well suited to handling tape files that are inherently sequential. With the advent of direct (random) access storage devices, the need arose to support direct access of a record without passing (and inspecting) all previous records in the file. This need gave rise to two additional access methods.

In the first of these, it is assumed that the application program has the ability to compute the location of the data on the direct access device relative to the beginning of the file and to instruct the access method to retrieve (or replace) the data at that location. This access method is known as DAM (Direct Access Method) or BDAM (Basic Direct Access Method). As with BSAM, the application program is required to check that the input (or output) is complete before using the data. Since the location of the data is computed by the application program, there can be no "lookahead" by the access method. However, overall computer efficiency can still be maintained if BDAM is

used in multiprogramming systems so that while one application is waiting another is executing.

The second direct access method introduced combined the advantages of sequential and direct access. This access method is known as ISAM (Indexed Sequential Access Method). It combines the two modes of basic and queued access, depending upon whether the operation demands the application check for completion (Basic) or permits "lookahead" by the access method (Queued). Thus, when we speak generically of ISAM, we mean both BISAM (Basic ISAM) and QISAM (Queued ISAM). ISAM permits the application to process records sequentially, by the key within the record, or directly, by means of maintaining a separate index of keys (or list of pointers) to all records.

With ISAM, therefore, record keys become important. Typical examples of record keys are employee names in an alphabetized file or social security numbers in a file ordered numerically. QSAM always gets the next record and, thus, for QSAM (or BSAM), the key has no significance in accessing the record. In the case of ISAM, unlike QSAM, the records are not necessarily stored next to each other and the key becomes important as a means for locating the record. ISAM, in principle, keeps a list of keys and pointers to the appropriate records. In this manner, working from the index list, the records can be presented back to the application program in sequence by key (when all or a significant portion of the file is to be processed) or a unique record can be obtained directly without having to "pass over" any of the records logically preceding it. While ISAM doesn't always read the next record, because of the characteristics of disk storage devices, data transfer is most efficient when the records are adjacent. A great deal of effort goes into handling the organization of records on the device for optimum performance.

Since records in a file accessed by ISAM need not be stored in sequential order, the insertion of a new record in a large file is much more efficient than for files accessed by QSAM or BSAM, since a record can be placed anywhere and the index of the key list updated so that it may be found subsequently.

An example of how ISAM use indexes is shown in Table 1. Since use of a single index sometimes results in a search of a quite long list, it is common to use a hierarchy of indexes, as shown in the table. The table assumes that an exployee file with 10,000 records is stored in 100 blocks

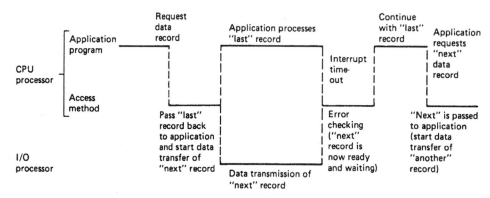

FIG. 2. Overlap of processing with data transfer.

TABLE 1. A Hierarchical Block-Oriented Index

Index Level 1	Index Level 2	Block Number	Block Starting Address
	00000-00713	1	46217
	00718-01426	2	46337
00000-08756	.	.	.
	.	.	.
	.	.	.
	07823-08756	10	47395
	41063–42217	41	50362
41063-52071	.	.	.
	.	.	.
	49278-50593	49	51612
	50614-52071	50	51738
	.	.	
	.	.	

on a disk, with the first block starting at disk address 46217. Each block would store an average of 100 employee records, but would have the capacity to store more than 100 records so that change to, and growth of, the file would be possible before it is reorganized and the indexes updated. Table 1 also assumes that employee numbers are in the range 00000-99999. To retrieve the record for the employee whose number is 49731, the first level index would be searched until the fifth entry (41063-52071) was found; then the second level would be searched, starting at 41063-42217, until the ninth entry (49278-50593) was found; finally, address 51612 (the start of block 49) on the disk would be searched sequentially until the record with key 49731 was found. Note how much more efficient this is than searching the entire file sequentially. Note also how much more efficient a two-level index is than a single index search would be.

The next advance in access methods was the Virtual Storage Access Method (VSAM), which was introduced in conjunction with the introduction of Virtual Storage Operating Systems by IBM, although such operating systems were in use by Burroughs and several other manufacturers prior to IBM's adoption of the concept. VSAM combines many of the features of ISAM, QSAM, and BDAM into one comprehensive access method. It also incorporates improved techniques for the positioning of records on the disk and for increasing the degree of overlap of computation and I/O processing (buffering).

VSAM can operate like ISAM in that records can be accessed by keys, like QSAM in that records can be accessed by the order on the storage device, or like BDAM, where the record is accessed by a "relative" position in the file. However, the current state of the art permits it to operate in only one of these modes for any one file. Thus, if ISAM mode is chosen for a file, that file must always be accessed by VSAM in "ISAM mode."

A further step in the evolution of data organization is the advent of the concept of the Database Manager, a system software program that manages the data resources for a series of programs. An access method is concerned only with moving data back and forth from main storage to a peripheral storage device (generally disk or tape). A Database Manager has a wider spectrum of concerns, including maintaining relationships between different sets of data, converting the data format to fit that required by the application programs, and simultaneous use of the same data by different application programs. As organizations move towards a database environment, applications are using Database Managers where they formerly used access methods. Most Database Managers call upon the established access methods to perform input and output. The access methods used are generally based on BDAM or, occasionally, on VSAM.

Another aspect of access methods is related to the advent of on-line processing in which there is a need for the application program to interact with an on-line terminal. Many of the traditional problems solved by access methods are also apparent here: blocking, buffering, error recovery, protocols of communicating with the devices, etc. But there are differences, since there is no storage medium involved and the devices are intended for interacting with people. Communication with such devices is heavily influenced by communications (e.g. phone line) capabilities. Just as device access methods evolved in parallel with operating systems, so telecommunication access methods evolved in parallel with telecommunication monitors. Telecommunication access methods are, however, far less standard than mass storage device access methods.

Storage device access methods evolved to enable the application to process data stored on a variety of devices in a variety of ways in an efficient manner and to isolate the application from the physical characteristics of the device; telecommunication access methods evolved to allow the application to communicate with a variety of terminal devices and in a variety of ways in an efficient manner and to isolate it from the physical characteristics of the device. Thus, terminal access methods have evolved from BTAM (Basic Telecommunications Access Methods), whereby a terminal is locked to an application under a specific communications monitor, to VTAM (Virtual Telecommunications Access Method), where a terminal may be connected to any application under a variety of telecommunications monitors.

FRED BRADDOCK

ACCESS TIME

For articles on related subjects *see* CYLINDER; DIRECT ACCESS; FLOPPY DISK; HARD DISK; LATENCY; and MEMORY: AUXILIARY.

Access time is the elapsed time between the initiation of a request for data and receipt of the first bit or byte of that data.

Direct access devices require varying times to position a read/write head over a particular record. In the case of a moving-head hard disk drive, this involves positioning the *comb* (head assembly, as in Fig. 1) to the designated cylinder, plus rotation of the selected track to the desired record. Comb-movement times for a typical medium-sized disk drive are shown in Fig. 2.

For a disk, total access time is the sum of comb-movement and rotational times to reach a particular record (plus the time to switch from reading or writing one surface to another, but, since this is done at electronic speeds, it contributes almost nothing to the access time). There is a different access time for each record retrieved at random from a disk drive, since it is necessary to move from cylinder C_1 to cylinder C_2 (Fig. 2), and then await rotational positioning of record R. Suppose the disk drive, whose comb-movement time is shown in Fig. 2, rotates at 3,600 rpm, which is equivalent to 16.7 ms per rotation. Then the *maximum access time* for this device is 87 ms (70 ms for the comb movement, plus 17 ms for the rotation), the *average access time* is about 43 ms (35 + 8) and the *minimum access time* is 12 ms. The latter time, which is the time required to move the comb to an adjacent cylinder is also called the *track-to-track access time*. Of course, if successive records are on the same cylinder, the access time can be zero.

Average access time is an important parameter for analytical planning of a real-time computer application, e.g. an on-line inquiry system. Minimum access time is more important for sequential usage of disk drives. The dominant component of delay for sequential retrieval of records from a disk drive is the average time for a half-rotation (8.3 ms for the drive described in Figs. 1 and 3).

During the past 30 years, rotational speeds for hard

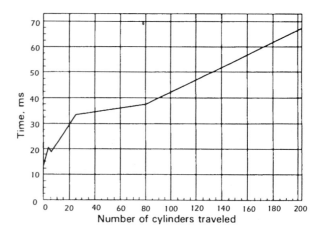

FIG. 2. Comb-movement times for typical disk drive.

disk drives have improved relatively little: 3,600 rpm is typical. But bit densities per track have increased fivefold in this same period, so that average transfer speeds have increased even if track-to-track access times have not diminished. During this period, average access times have been halved as a result of a widespread changeover from hydraulic actuators to "voice coil" actuators for moving the comb mechanism.

For a floppy disk drive, the average access time is 25 ms; the access times for compact disc read-only memories (CD-ROMs) are approximately twice as long as for floppy disks.

For a drum or fixed-head disk, average access time is a half-revolution and maximum access time is a full revolution, since both have heads that are fixed over the data areas. Average access times for drums are 5 to 10 ms.

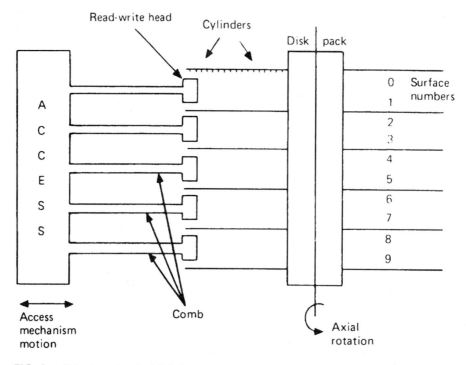

FIG. 1. Side view of typical disk drive.

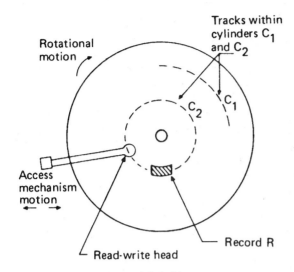

FIG. 3.   Top view of typical disk drive.

For "honeycomb" lattices of videotape cartridges and similar mass storage systems, average access times depend on movement of the medium to a read/write head. For tape-cartridge mass storage systems, average access time is approximately 15 sec and minimum access time to a new cartridge is approximately 12 sec.

DAVID N. FREEMAN

ACCOUNTING SYSTEM, COMPUTER

For articles on related subjects *see* BENCHMARK; COMPUTING CENTER; DATA SECURITY; OPERATING SYSTEMS; and SOFTWARE MONITOR.

As computer/software systems have developed, there has been a corresponding need to develop an accounting system for the resources of the system. As with any accounting system, the goal of this capability must be to charge the user for the cost of services rendered in such a fashion that the user is motivated to evaluate the benefits of those services. Furthermore, the resources used by any one user must be limited in order to prevent that user from degrading the total effective services available to others.

Accountability is important both to the computing center staff and to its users. In order to perform their duties as financial planners for the center, the administrators require some form of an accounting system. Such a system may be expected to yield statistics on hardware utilization and individual spending. These statistics can then be used to form the basis for monthly and yearly reports.

A completely automated accounting and resource control system does the following.

- It provides minute details concerning both hardware and software utilization along with job statistics on account spending.

- It prevents unauthorized users from accessing hardware and software facilities for which they have not received permission.
- It prevents users from exceeding their allocated funds or other account limits.
- It enforces job limitations on such things as page or line limits, computer time, memory size, and disk file space.
- It assists the operating system in providing more effective control of resources such as main memory, auxiliary memory, peripheral devices, etc.

Development of Accounting and Resource Control Systems

Early Computer Systems   Since early computer systems consisted of hardware with little or no software support, automated accounting was almost non-existent. The accounting that did exist was done by user sign-up sheets, time clocks, or a flat-rate charge per computer run.

The idea of basing charges on the value of resources used was not very important either. Because the entire computer was dedicated to the current user, there was little reason to charge less if the program used only half of the memory or no tape units, etc. Besides, the hardware could not usually support an accounting system because there was no hardware-readable clock and it was often not practical for the machine operator to type in the date and time for each job logged on the machine. (Interestingly, personal computer systems have put the user back into this mode of operation!)

Early Automated Accounting Systems   As Rosin (1969) points out, the first accounting systems were often nothing more than system logs produced by the "on-line" printing facility. Since the purpose of such a log was to record the use of major system components, the log was more useful for measuring system behavior than for actual user accounting.

Some systems were enhanced by a hardware-readable clock, which made it possible to log the time along with the system component in use. However, the content of each entry in the log was a function of the sophistication of the resident monitor and often provided only such information as log-on and log-off time. Thus, user accounting was still based on total machine time used, with the hardware clock now providing a more accurate method for recording that time.

Executive Systems and Automated Accounting   With the introduction of channels (*q.v.*) and interrupts (*q.v.*), the establishment of resident monitors or supervisors became an accepted fact. These supervisors were complex routines that could process interrupts, software requests, and a new language called the *command and job control language* (*q.v.*). Thus, the computer user could communicate with the system via command language control cards that provided such information as name and account number, job limitations on time, pages, and cards to be used, and special resources (tapes, plotter, etc.) required.

Utilizing a hardware clock, most user interactions with the system were recorded, detailing what commands the system had received. The purpose of the accounting system was to monitor the individual user's interaction with the system and not simply the system performance.

Still, until the introduction of disk files, it was not feasible to verify each user's identification against some master file of valid users. Nor was it possible to determine user limits as to funds available, privileges, etc. Instead, accounting information was collected on magnetic tape or punched cards for later processing on an after-the-fact basis.

Disk Files The introduction of disk files added another step in automated accounting. The disk file was sufficiently fast to provide for an on-line verification of valid user identification. The accounting information could be made resident within the system, available only to the accounting programs and to those with sufficient access privilege.

The accounting system could record each job transition or step, print out job charges at the completion of a job, and accumulate monthly statistics. By maintaining the accounting information in an on-line fashion, users could be prevented from using more than their current funds or exceeding their current account limits.

Multiprogramming and Time Sharing The next step in computer hardware/software development—namely, multiprogramming (*q.v.*) and time sharing (*q.v.*)—produced the greatest impact on automated accounting. Because these advantages have made it feasible to allocate and share the multiple resources of a computing system, it is possible to have multiple users on the system at the same time.

For each user of the system, the accounting system must know (1) who is responsible for the charges, (2) what type of service this user is entitled to (and with what constraints), (3) what resources have been allocated to the user, and (4) what price schedules apply. Further, the pricing structure must allow the user to estimate easily and predict costs, and should require only small amounts of system resources for the accounting.

Proprietary Software Time sharing (*q.v.*) has brought new problems in automated accounting. Where it was previously possible to simply charge the proprietary system user for computer time used, more complex multi-user systems have made it possible to allow one user to provide service to another. The result is that users are billed by both the computing center (for hardware use, expendable supplies, etc.) and other users (for proprietary software use). Thus, the accounting system must be cognizant of the use of such proprietary software and should, in fact, allow some "higher-order" user to suballocate resources to another user. For instance, it should be possible for one user to develop and maintain a subsystem, fully consistent with the operating and accounting

systems, which bills the individual users for actual resources used (both hardware and software).

Another example might be the instructor who allocates fixed amounts of time or money to each student in a course in such a fashion that no student can use more than a fair share. Obviously, the person responsible for the account must be able to reallocate the resources without exceeding the total allotted. In addition, it should be possible to place limits, which may not be uniform, on each student account so that special projects may use extra memory or disk space, special hardware, etc.

Since some software can be charged only on a "value received" or transaction basis (such as ledger entries in an accounting system or students scheduled in an automated scheduling system), the accounting system must be flexible in terms of the algorithm used to calculate actual charges.

Costs of an Automated Accounting System and Charges Levied

The costs of an automated accounting system are directly a function of the resources used to gather and maintain the accounting information. In order that the overhead of collecting the information not interfere with normal system operation, the charges themselves must reflect the unique characteristics of the system. Normally, charges are based on such things as:

1. CPU time used.
2. Memory residence time (e.g. number of pages referenced or amount of memory occupied by a job).
3. Connect time and/or port cost.
4. I/O operations performed (e.g. disk reads and writes).
5. Physical I/O units used:
   a. Cards read/punched;
   b. Lines printed;
   c. Magnetic tapes mounted; and
   d. File space used.

However, these charges must relate to the characteristics of the operating system if they are to be easily collected. They should also relate to the allocation scheme for the resources if they are to be fairly levied (i.e. disk space should not be charged on a bit or character basis if it is allocated on a track or sector basis).

An on-line system where each user has an active account, although costly in terms of disk space required, allows the accounting system to:

1. Encumber funds on a per-job basis so as to prevent deficit spending.
2. Set dynamic limits on controlled privileges as a function of time, geographic entry point, and system load.
3. Maintain flexible and dynamic pricing, with actual cost information available to users on demand.
4. Maintain up-to-the-minute accounting for each

user and periodically inform users of their accumulated computer resource utilization.

As described, automated systems can be fairly costly. However, the benefits provided both to the computing center operations staff (e.g. current resource use, system load, operating difficulties) and to the users (e.g. current pricing structure, resources available, job flow) generally outweigh the costs. Indeed, by knowing the state of the computing system, both operators and users are able to optimize their interaction with it so as to increase its effective utilization.

Reference

1969. Rosin, R.F. "Supervisory and Monitor Systems," *Computing Surveys* **1**:37-54.
1987. Milenkovic, M. *Operating Systems: Concepts and Design.* New York: McGraw-Hill.

RICHARD H. ECKHOUSE

ACM. *See* ASSOCIATION FOR COMPUTING MACHINERY.

ACTIVATION RECORD

For articles on related subjects *see* BLOCK STRUCTURE; CALLING SEQUENCE; and PARAMETER PASSING.

An *activation record* consists of all of the information pushed onto the system stack (*q.v.*) during execution of a procedure call in a high-level block structured language. The activation record has only transient existence during execution of the called procedure. Typically, the record contains arguments used by the programmer as part of the procedure's *calling sequence*, current contents of important system registers (*q.v.*) pushed by the machine command used to invoke the procedure, and local variables pushed by the procedure itself.

Suppose that, on the Digital Equipment Corporation VAX, a main program calls *proc1*, which then calls *proc2*, which in turn calls *proc3*. Fig. 1 shows how the stack would then appear. Each activation record results from execution of a procedure call, and each called procedure terminates execution by executing a *return* command, which removes the topmost activation record from the stack (by merely resetting the stack pointer, SP in the figure). As first *proc3* and then *proc2* and finally *proc1* finish, their corresponding activation records will be removed from the stack, and thus the stack will return to its status prior to the call of *proc1*. Among the important registers saved by each procedure call are the PC, the program counter, which is needed so that the corresponding *return* can transfer control to exactly the right place in the calling routine. The registers labeled AP and FP, called the Argument Pointer and the Frame Pointer, are used by the procedure in order to reference procedure arguments and local variables, respectively.

On some systems, the terms *activation record* and

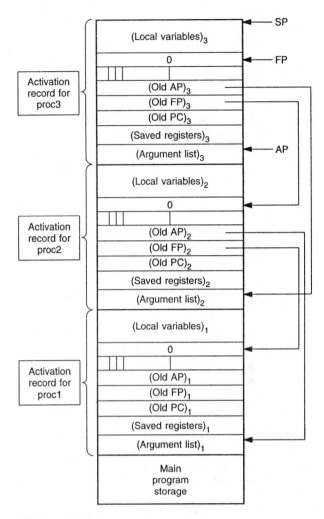

FIG. 1.   Activation records on a stack.

stack frame are synonyms, but VAX terminology is that a stack frame consists of just that part of the activation record that is created by the command that invoked the procedure, not those parts consisting of arguments pushed by the calling procedure and local variables pushed by the called procedure. For the topmost activation record, the FP at the top right of the diagram points to the beginning of the stack frame, and the AP below it points just beyond the end of the frame.

In the figure, the second and third nested procedures are called *proc1* and *proc2*, but the essence of the figure would be no different if those procedures happened to be later activations of *proc1* itself. This is equivalent to picturing how the stack would look just after recursive procedure *proc1* has called itself twice. As far as the recursive logic is concerned, additional activation records may be created indefinitely, bounded only by the amount of memory available to enlarge the stack. But lack of such a resource is exactly what usually causes a runaway recursive procedure to abort. A properly written recursive routine will contain terminal conditions and an inductive step that relates to those conditions in such a way that the stack will accumulate activation records only until a terminal condition is reached, and then recede to its original status as each successive stage feeds information back to the stage that called it.

Reference

1989. Sethi, R. *Programming Languages: Concepts and Structures.* Reading, MA: Addison-Wesley.
1991. Federighi, F. D. and Reilly, E. D. *VAX Assembly Language Programming.* New York, NY: Macmillan.

EDWIN D. REILLY

ADA

For articles on related subjects *see* CONCURRENT PROGRAMMING; ABSTRACT DATA TYPE; EMBEDDED SYSTEM; INFORMATION HIDING; PROGRAMMING LANGUAGES; and STRUCTURED PROGRAMMING

Ada is a programming language developed under the auspices of the United States Department of Defense (DoD) for the purpose of reducing software development and maintenance costs, especially for large, constantly changing programs with long lifetimes. It was designed during the period 1975–1980, and it was specifically intended to support modern programming techniques such as structured programming, information hiding, abstract data types, and concurrent processing.

The original motivation for the Ada development stemmed from military command-and-control applications, particularly for computers "embedded" in weapons, airplanes, or other military equipment (*see* EMBEDDED SYSTEM). Although these applications have some special requirements, such as real-time processing, concurrency, and nonstandard I/O, the requirements that emerged are suitable for a general-purpose programming language. The design proceeded in that spirit, and as a result Ada has found wide use in industrial, business, and university facilities as well as in the military.

History   The impetus for the Ada development effort came in the early 1970s, when it became clear that DoD was supporting an enormous number of programming languages (estimates on the number range from a few hundred to a few thousand). In 1976, DoD issued a directive on the use of advanced computer technology in defense systems in order to halt the proliferation of similar languages. This directive required most new software to be developed in one of a small number of approved languages. The initial list of approved languages contained seven programming languages in which DoD had already made significant investment; these languages are CMS-2, SPL/1, TACPOL, Jovial J3, Jovial J73, Cobol, and Fortran.

At the same time, DoD initiated an effort to develop a modern language to add to this list. An initial draft of requirements for such a language, the "Strawman" proposal, was circulated in 1975. This was revised in response to the comments received, and a series of requirements proposals called "Woodenman," "Tinman,"

"Ironman," and "Steelman" resulted. The actual language design (DoD, 1980) was obtained through an international design competition, combined with extensive public review of the winning initial design, which was done by a Cii Honeywell Bull design team led by Jean Ichbiah.

The language was named Ada in honor of Lady Augusta Ada Byron, the Countess of Lovelace (*q.v.*). She programmed Babbage's Analytical Engine (*q.v.*) in the 1830s, and she is often called the world's first computer programmer.

Ada compilers are currently available for virtually every hardware architecture, from personal computers (*q.v.*) to supercomputers (*q.v.*).

Language Characteristics   Although the early Ada development was heavily influenced by Pascal, extensive syntactic changes and semantic extensions make it a very different language. The major additions include:

- Module structures and interface specifications for large-program organizations and separate compilation;
- Encapsulation (*q.v.*) facilities and generic definitions to support abstract data types;
- Support for parallel processing; and
- Control over low-level implementation issues related to the architecture of object machines.

There are three major abstraction tools in Ada. The *package* is used for encapsulating a set of related definitions and isolating them from the rest of the program. The *type* determines the values a variable (or data structure) may take on and how it can be manipulated. The *generic* definition allows many similar instances of a definition to be generated from a single template. Support for parallel processing includes concurrently executable procedures called *tasks* and language facilities for synchronization. Support for low-level matters includes control over a type's storage layout and a loophole mechanism that provides access to machine-dependent features.

The following example, taken from Shaw (1980), illustrates some of the important features of Ada. The purpose of the example program is to produce the data needed to print an internal telephone list for a division of a small company. A database containing information about all employees, including their names, divisions, telephone numbers, and salaries, is assumed to be available. The program must produce a data structure containing a sorted list of the employees in a selected division and their telephone extensions.

An Ada program to solve this problem is organized in three components: 1) a definition of the record for each employee (Fig. 1); 2) declarations of the data needed by the program (Fig. 2); and 3) code for construction of the telephone list (Fig. 3).

The **package** of information about employees whose specification is shown in Fig. 1 illustrates one of Ada's major additions to our tool kit of abstraction facilities. This definition establishes EmpRec as a data type with a small set of privileged operations. Only the specification of the package is presented here. Ada does not require the

```
package Employee is
   type PrivStuff is limited private;
   type EmpRec is
      record
         Name: string(1..24);
         Phone: integer;
         PrivPart: PrivStuff;
      end record;
   procedure SetSalary(Who: in out EmpRec;
      Sal: float);
   function GetSalary(Who: EmpRec) return
      float;
   procedure SetDiv(Who: in out EmpRec; Div:
      string(1.8));
   function GetDiv(Who: EmpRec) return
      string(1.8);
private
   type PrivStuff is
      record
         Salary: float;
         Division: string(1.8);
      end record;
   end Employee;
```

FIG. 1. Ada package definition for employee records.

module body (i.e. the implementation of the procedures and functions) to accompany the specification (though it must be defined before the program can be executed); moreover, programmers should rely only on the specifications, not on the body of a package. This makes it possible to compile programs that use this package before the code of the package is actually compiled. The specification itself is divided into a visible part (everything from **package** to **private**) and a private part (from **private** to **end**). The private part is intended only to provide information needed by the compiler to generate code, but not needed by the programmer.

Assume that the policy for using EmpRec's is that the Name and Phone fields are accessible to anyone, that it is permissible for anyone to read but not to write the Division field, and that access to the Salary field and modification of the Division field are supposed to be done only by authorized programs. The scope rules prevent any portion of the program outside a package from accessing any names except the ones listed in the visible part of the specification. In the particular case of the Employee package, this means that the Salary and Division fields of an EmpRec cannot be directly read or written outside the package, but can only be accessed using the routines declared inside the package. Therefore, the integrity of the data can be controlled by verifying that the routines that are exported from the package are correct. Presumably, the routines SetSalary, GetSalary, SetDiv, and GetDiv perform reads and writes as their names suggest; they might also keep records showing who made changes and when, or a password could be added as a parameter to the sensitive routines.

Although the field name PrivPart is exported from the Employee package along with Name and Phone,

there is no danger in doing so. An auxiliary type was defined to protect the salary and division information; the declaration

type PrivStuff is limited private

indicates not only that the content and organization of the data structure are hidden from the user (private), but also that all operations on data of type PrivStuff are forbidden except for calls on the routines exported from the package. For limited private types, (i.e. if variables p and q are declared outside **package** Employee to be type PrivStuff, both "$p := 1$" and "**if** $p = q$ **then**..." are prohibited). Naturally, the code inside the body of the Employee package may manipulate these hidden fields; the purpose of the packaging is to guarantee that *only* the code inside the package body can do so.

The ability to force manipulation of a data structure to be carried out only through a known set of routines is central to the support of abstract data types. It is useful not only in examples such as the one given here, but also for cases in which the representation may change radically from time to time and for cases in which some kind of internal consistency among fields, such as checksums, must be maintained. Support for *secure* computation is not among Ada's goals. It can be achieved in this case, but only through a combination of an extra level of packaging and some management control. Even without guarantees about security, however, the packaging of information about how employee data is handled provides a useful structure for the development and maintenance of the program.

The declarations of Fig. 2 illustrate the use of abstract data types. One new type (PhoneRec) is defined; the type defined in Fig. 1 is used, and another non-primitive type, String, is used. The Employee package is used instead of a simple record. The clause

use Employee;

says that all the visible names of the Employee package are available in the current block.

The type definitions for EmpRec and PhoneRec abstract from specific data items to the notions "record

```
declare
   use Employee;

   type PhoneRec is
      record
         Name: string(1..24);
         Phone: integer;
      end record;

   Staff: array (1..1000) of EmpRec;
   Phones: array (1..1000) of PhoneRec;
   StaffSize, DivSize, i,j: integer range 1..1000;
   WhichDiv: string(1..8);
   q: PhoneRec;
```

FIG. 2. Declarations for Ada version of telephone list program.

—Get data for division WhichDiv only

```
DivSize := 0;
for i in 1..StaffSize loop
   if GetDiv(Staff(i)) = WhichDiv then
      DivSize := DivSize + 1;
      Phones(DivSize) := (Staff(i).Name,
                          Staff(i).Phone);
   end if;
end loop;
```

—Sort telephone list*

```
for i in 1..DivSize loop
   for j in i+1..DivSize loop
      if Phones(i).Name > Phones(j).Name then
         q := Phones(i);
         Phones(i) := Phones(j);
         Phones(j) := q;
      end if;
   end loop;
end loop;
```

FIG. 3.   Code for Ada version of telephone list program.

*This example uses a simple selection sort, not as an endorsement of this method but because many readers will recognize it.

of information about an employee" and "record of information for a telephone list." Both the employee database and the telephone list can thus be represented as vectors whose elements are records of the appropriate types.

The declarations of Staff and Phones have the effect of indicating that all the components are related to the same information structure. In addition, the definition is organized as a collection of records, one for each employee—so the primary organization of the data structure is by employee.

The telephone list is constructed in two stages (Fig. 3). Note that Ada's ability to operate on strings and records as single units substantially simplifies the manipulation of names and the interchange step of the selection sort used compared with a language such as Fortran where each element of the record would have to be processed separately. Ada also provides a way to create a complete record value and assign it with a single statement; thus, the assignment Phones(DivSize) := (Staff(i).Name, Staff(i).Phone); sets both fields of the PhoneRec at once.

Ada = 9X Ada is an ANSI standard language, and under the ANSI requirements, this standard must be reviewed every few years. This is not a reflection on any inadequacies in the language. Rather, this revision process is useful in keeping the language up to date with the needs of real users.

For these reasons, the DoD has recently established the Ada = 9X project, to solicit revision requests and incorporate these changes in an orderly manner. This process will take a few years to complete. It is expected that Ada = 9X will be largely upward-compatible with the existing language definition. Some language facilities will be simplified, and some new features will be added.

References

1981. Hibbard, P., Hisgen, A., Rosenbers, J., Shaw, M., and Sherman, M. *Studies in Ada Style.* New York: Springer-Verlag.

1983. U.S. Department of Defense. *Reference Manual for the Ada Programming Language.* Washington, D.C.: Ada Joint Program Office.

1984. Buhr, R. *System Design with Ada.* Englewood Cliffs, NJ: Prentice Hall.

1986. Booch, G. *Software Engineering with Ada.* Menlo Park, CA: Benjamin/Cummings.

1986. Cohen, N. *Ada as a Second Language.* New York: McGraw-Hill.

GRADY R. BOOCH AND MARY SHAW

ADA, AUGUSTA.   *See* COUNTLESS OF LOVELACE

ADDER

For articles on related subjects *see* ARITHMETIC, COMPUTER; ARITHMETIC-LOGIC UNIT; LOGIC DESIGN; and SUPERCOMPUTERS.

An *adder* is a logic circuit that forms the sum of two or more numbers represented in digital form. The simplest adder is the binary one-position adder, or *full adder* (see Fig. 1), in which the ith bits of two summands and the carry from the (previous) stage $(i - 1)$ are added to form the ith sum bit and the carry to the (next) stage $(i + 1)$. A

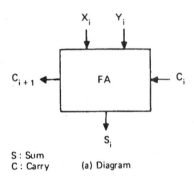

S : Sum
C : Carry   (a) Diagram

X_i	Y_i	C_i	S_i	C_{i+1}
0	0	0	0	0
0	0	1	1	0
0	1	0	1	0
0	1	1	0	1
1	0	0	1	0
1	0	1	0	1
1	1	0	0	1
1	1	1	1	1

(b) Truth table

FIG. 1.   The binary full adder (FA).

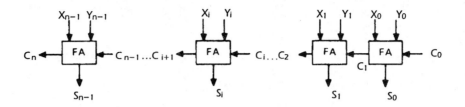

FIG. 2. Binary ripple-carry adder.

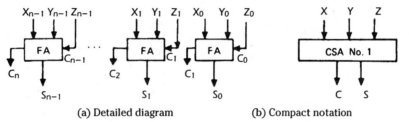

(a) Detailed diagram   (b) Compact notation

FIG. 3. Three-operand binary carry-save adder.

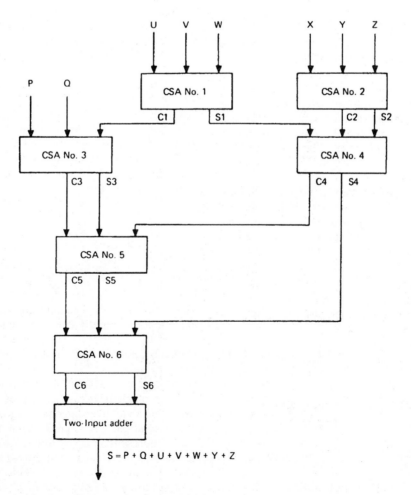

$$S = P + Q + U + V + W + Y + Z$$

FIG. 4. CSA summation of eight operands.

ripple-carry adder for two n-bit binary numbers is formed by connecting n full adders in cascade (Fig. 2). The addition time of the ripple-carry adder corresponds to the worst-case delay, which is n times the time required to form the C_{i+1} (carry) output by one full adder, plus the time to form the S_i output, given the C_i input.

Higher speeds of two-operand addition can be attained by the use of *carry-completion sensing, carry-look-ahead*, and *conditional-sum* techniques (Garner, 1965). In these techniques, additional logic circuitry is employed to reduce the total delay in the adder circuits.

One-position adders for a higher radix r (for example, 4, 8, 10, or 16) are similar to the full adder of Fig. 1. The digits X_i and Y_i assume values 0 to $r - 1$, and they are represented by two or more binary variables. The values of the bits in S_i are easily described by a truth table; carry signals (C_i and C_{i+1}) remain two-valued (0 and 1). The adder speed-up techniques discussed for radix 2 also apply to two-operand addition of higher radix numbers.

Fast summation of three or more operands can be accomplished by the use of *carry-save* adders (CSA). A binary three-operand n-bit CSA is shown in Fig. 3. The third n-bit operand Z is entered on the C_i inputs of n binary full adders. The C_{i+1} outputs form a second output word $C = (C_n \cdots C_1)$ and the sum of the three input words X, Y, Z is represented by two output words, C and $S = (S_{n-1} \cdots S_0)$. The time required to form C and S is equal to the time required by one binary full adder. The final sum, which is the sum of C and S, is then obtained in a two-operand adder, which may employ any of the speed-up techniques discussed above.

The summation of more than three operands uses CSAs in a similar manner to reduce the sum to two words. Fig. 4 illustrates the CSA configuration for eight operands P, Q, U, V, W, X, Y, Z. The abbreviated notation of Fig. 3(b) is employed. The time required to form the words $C6$ and $S6$ (representing the sum of the eight input operands) is equal to four full-adder operation times, regardless of the length of the operands.

Carry-save adders are frequently employed to implement fast multiplication by means of multiple-operand summation. The technique of *pipelining* may be employed to further improve the effective speed of CSA utilization (*see* SUPERCOMPUTERS).

Reference

1965. Garner, H.L. "Number Systems and Arithmetic," in Alt, F. and Rubinoff, M. (Eds.), *Advances in Computers* **6**: 131-194. New York: Academic Press.

ALGIRDAS AVIŽIENIS

ADDRESS, INDIRECT. *See* INDIRECT ADDRESS.

ADDRESSING

For articles on related subjects *see* BASE REGISTER; COMPUT-ERS, MULTIPLE ADDRESS; GENERAL REGISTER; INDEX REGISTER; IN-DIRECT ADDRESS; INSTRUCTION SET; MACHINE AND ASSEMBLY LAN-GUAGE PROGRAMMING; and VIRTUAL MEMORY.

BASIC TERMINOLOGY AND HARDWARE CONCEPTS

A typical computer instruction must indicate not only the operation to be performed but also the location of one or more operands, the location where the result of the computation is to be deposited, and, sometimes, the location where the next instruction is to be found. Of course, in certain kinds of instructions, such as those involved in decision making, there may be no computational operands but only a determination of the next instruction to be executed. Normally, however, all parts of the instruction are either explicitly or implicitly given. We will first consider the hardware techniques by which an address (or location) in the computer may be specified. In what follows, we shall consider primarily storage in which each location has associated with it a sequentially assigned address. An alternative method of method of determining a desired storage location will be considered briefly in the later section "Content-Addressable Storage."

Historically and presently, computer hardware allows addresses to be specified in a variety of ways. The most straightforward approach would be to put the entire address directly into the instruction, representing a specific location of a word or part of a word in storage. Thus, on the IBM 650, an early decimal computer, the 2-digit operation code and the two 4-digit addresses, representing the location of the data and the location of the next instruction, respectively, were represented in the instruction itself. (On modern computers, except for the case of decision-making instructions, the address of the next instruction is always taken implicitly to be the location after that of the instruction being executed.) The operation code in the 650 (as on modern computers) implied the location of one of the operands and the location of the result.

Op Code	Data Address	Next Inst. Address
2 digit	4 digit	4 digit

For example, the operation code AU (add to upper) implied that the upper half of the accumulator register was one of the operands, along with the explicitly named operand, and the result was to remain in the upper half of the accumulator.

As the amount of storage increases, however, and the number of digits (either binary or decimal) needed to represent an address becomes large relative to the size of the instruction, it becomes clear that it is no longer feasible to represent an entire address each time it occurs in an instruction. This is especially true when the address part of an instruction must be able to accommodate the largest possible storage that might be attached to a particular model of computer, even though an individual installation might have only a small part of that storage. In such cases, the addresses actually occurring would use only a small portion of that part of the instruction set aside for addresses. The remaining portion must always contain zeros, representing a waste of a valuable resource.

Several hardware devices have been and are employed to obtain, from one of a small number of larger registers, most of the information needed to specify an address, with the instruction itself containing only the information needed to complete the address. A number of these methods were employed in the Control Data Corp. (CDC) 160 and 160A computers, early small machines that started out with 4,096 12-bit words of storage. In the CDC 160, which dates back to 1959, six bits were used for the operation code, while the other six bits (with only 64 possible values) were used in the determination of an address. By choosing an appropriate operation code, the address would be interpreted to be in one of five modes: direct address (d); indirect address (i); relative address forward (f) and backward (b); and no address (n).

The direct addressing mode (d-mode) corresponds to the IBM 650 situation discussed above, in that the address referred to a 12-bit operand in one of the first 64 words of storage.

Relative addressing provided for operand addresses and jump addresses that were near the storage location containing the current instruction. In relative addressing forward (f), the six-bit address portion was added to the current contents of the program counter (PC - *q.v.*). This register held the full 12-bit address of the current instruction. The new value was then used for obtaining the operand or to jump to one of the 63 addresses forward from the address holding the instruction that was being executed. For relative addressing backward (b), the operand or jump address was obtained by subtracting the six-bit address from the current contents of the PC.

In the no-address mode (n), which is usually now referred to as the *immediate address* mode, the six-bit address part was not treated as an address, but as a constant to be used in the actual computation.

In the CDC 160A, seven banks of 4,096 words each were added to the storage, thus complicating the specification of an address. The modes of addressing already available were retained, but several three-bit registers were added to contain the number of the bank (0–7) in which a designated address would be found, and different operations referred to different bank registers. Additional operations were provided so that the programmer could set the values of these registers as necessary. This later machine also provided for two-word instructions in which the second word might be a 12-bit immediate operand as well.

Indirect Addressing One way to address a memory larger than the address part of an instruction allows is to have the instruction address point to another address that stores the operand address. This facility, called *indirect addressing* or *deferred addressing*, was available on the CDC 160 and is available on most contemporary computers. Fig. 1 illustrates this situation on a hypothetical 16-bit computer with a 7-bit instruction field and a 9-bit address field that permits the direct addressing of only 512 ($= 2^9$) memory locations. Indirect addressing can be used to address a memory of up to 65,536 words. In the example in Fig. 1, the program has placed the operand address 021326 (where we express addresses in octal for convenience) at a specific address (125) in the first 512 words of memory. If the instruction is, for example, an "add indirect" instruction, the address 125 is interpreted as an indirect address or pointer to the actual operand at location 021326. The address stored at 125 (namely, 021326) becomes the *effective address*.

Some systems allow multilevel indirect addressing. Thus, the number stored at 021326 may have a bit set that

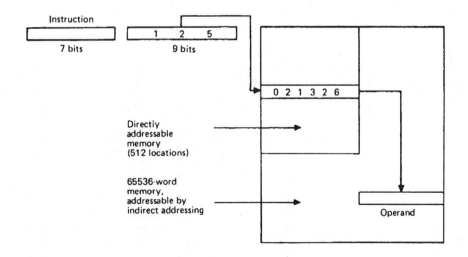

FIG. 1. Extension of addressing through indirect addressing.

indicates that it, itself, is an indirect address that points to another location that contains the operand address. Indirect addressing may be combined in various ways with the use of index registers to produce complex addressing chains.

Index Registers The concept of an index register, sometimes called a "tally register" or "base register" (see below), grew out of the B-line or B-register introduced on some of the earliest computers developed in England at the University of Manchester (*see* Manchester University Computers). This represented a major advance in computer design. Index registers are hardware registers that can be set, incremented, tested, etc., by machine instructions. Each instruction contains an indication as to whether its address is to be added to (or subtracted from) the contents of a designated index register to form the effective address. One of the main purposes, as suggested by the name, was to allow the effective address to be used as an index into a set of contiguous storage registers commonly referred to as a "vector." Without changing the part of the address that was in the instruction itself, one could refer to one after another of the contiguous registers merely by changing the contents of the index register successively. This replaced the more time- and space-consuming sequence of instructions that would normally put an instruction containing an address into an arithmetic register, modify it by ordinary addition, and then store it back to replace its former value. (This modified instruction was then executed, and it would refer to a different storage location.)

The use of index registers eliminated the need for modification of the instruction itself by allowing the index register to be modified by special instructions added to the computer for that purpose. With the advent of newer

systems in which more than one task may be executing the same instructions at the same time, it has become very important that instructions not be modified during execution, since the modification by one task might be inappropriate for another task executing the same set of instructions (*see* Reentrant Program).

General Registers The use of variable-length instructions has also become much more widespread in recent years. The IBM System/360/370/390 (*q.v.*), for example, uses instructions that may take one, two, or three half-words for their representation. In the System/360, 16 *general registers* are provided, each capable of acting as an arithmetic register, a base register for relative addressing, or as an index register. (The fact that one cannot tell by looking at one of these registers whether its contents represents an ordinary number or an address has sometimes led to other problems, but this degree of flexibility is very useful.) An instruction might refer only to one or two of these registers, in which case only four bits would be needed in the instruction for each one, and it could fit in a half-word (16 bits).

A full-word instruction could accommodate one reference to a general register (4 bits) and a reference to a storage address. The latter could be a combination of a base register (4 bits), an index register designation (4 bits), and a 12-bit *displacement*, which could be used as a local offset from the contents of the base register. Fig. 2 illustrates the determination of an effective address from a System/360 instruction.

Relocation Registers Many computers have one or more hardware *relocation registers*, which aid in the implementation and running of multiprogramming (*q.v.*) systems. An example is the CDC Cyber series. A number of

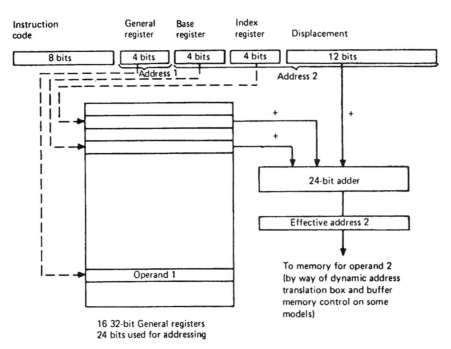

FIG. 2. Effective address calculation on the IBM 360.

different programs may be in the computer memory, each occupying a contiguous area. Thus, program A might occupy the area from 40,000 to 67,777, but this program (as well as all other programs in memory) is written and loaded into memory as if the area it occupies actually has the addresses 0 to 27,777. When program A is given control, the address 40,000 is stored in the hardware relocation register, and this constant is automatically added to all memory reference addresses while program A is running. The program could have been loaded anywhere else in memory, and can be loaded into different areas at different times. It will always produce the correct memory addresses, since all addressing is automatically made relative to the starting address of the area into which the program has been loaded.

In computers of this type, another hardware register will contain the *field length* or program size. Any attempt to reference beyond the area occupied by the program will be trapped, and an error condition will be signaled.

In a machine with two relocation registers, like the Univac 1100, a program may consist of two segments: for example, a program segment and a data segment, which can be placed independently anywhere in memory. The starting addresses of each of the two segments are placed in the two relocation registers, and every effective address has an associated bit that specifies which relocation register is to be added.

A relocation register is quite different in nature from an index register or a register used as a base for relative addressing. The relocation register is a special hardware register whose contents can be accessed and changed only through the use of privileged instructions (*q.v.*) under control of the operating system.

Content-Addressable Storage

Content-addressable or associative memories (*q.v.*) are quite different in concept from the more conventionally addressed memories described above. In a content-addressable memory, the data item itself contains a key, usually in a specified field. This key is, in effect, the address of the item. The key may be the whole data item itself. The desired data item is located by means of an examination of all relevant keys. This could be done by software in a computer system with conventional memory addressing, but it would be quite slow.

In an associative or content-addressable memory, comparison circuits are used to provide a hardware-assisted and presumably very fast search through all data items to find the one that matches the key. Small memories of this type have been used to speed up address translation in virtual memory (*q.v.*) systems. Larger systems in which all addressing is associative have been proposed and some experimental models have been built.

The use of content-addressable memory was very expensive in terms of earlier technologies, but may prove practical with modern very large-scale integration (VLSI) technology. There are a number of important application areas in which associative memories would be very useful.

Bernard A. Galler and Saul Rosen

SOFTWARE ASPECTS

Corresponding to each hardware aspect of addressing, there must be one or more techniques by which the programmer specifies addresses in the program.

Absolute Addressing In the earliest and most elementary programming systems, a programmer would assign instructions and data to locations in memory, and instructions would refer to absolute locations in memory. Thus, using a decimal computer for convenience, a programmer might write

```
267 ADD 3256
```

and, as a result of the eventual loading process, the instruction ADD 3256 would appear in location 267. It was the responsibility of the programmer to make sure that the appropriate data word was in location 3256 at the time the program was to be run. These are absolute addresses in that 267 always represents the same physical location in memory and 3256 similarly represents a specific physical location.

Relative Addressing Some of the first advances in programming involved permitting the programmer to write programs or parts of programs without having to be aware of the absolute physical locations in which the instructions and data were to be stored. One of the early approaches to this goal was by way of regional or relative programming. A programmer, or several programmers, might decide that the program would be divided into a number of regions, A, B, C, D, etc. Addresses would then be relative to the start of a region. A programmer might write

```
A5 ADD B15
```

to specify that an instruction located in the fifth location in region A is to add (to the accumulator) the data located in the fifteenth location in region B. A translator and loader would eventually take all regional addresses and convert them into absolute addresses.

There are a number of important advantages to this procedure. The programmer does not have to make arbitrary decisions about how large the regions are going to be. Separate sections of the program can be written independently, and unexpected or undesirable interactions can be avoided.

Symbolic Addressing It was a relatively short step from regional addressing to free symbolic addressing. In the typical assembly system the programmer may write

```
INCR ADD ALPHA
```

and leave it up to an assembler to decide where the instruction INCR is to be placed. Somewhere else in the program, he or she would have a data item named ALPHA.

Indirect Addressing In a computer that allows indirect addressing, the assembly language programmer typically indicates an indirect address by adding a character such as *, to the absolute or symbolic address. Thus,

```
INCR ADD ALPHA*
```

would indicate that the effective address is not ALPHA, but is in the location specified by ALPHA.

Indexing   If an index register is to be used in calculating an effective address, this is normally specified following the instruction address. For example,

```
ADD A,4
```

indicates that the contents of index register 4 is to be added (subtracted on some computers) to A to determine the effective address. Indexing can be combined with indirect addressing so that

```
ADD A*,4
```

would specify the effective address as the sum of the contents of location A and index register 4.

Higher-Level Languages   The development of higher-level programming languages has relieved the programmer of the responsibility for many aspects of memory management. However, that responsibility must reside somewhere: Either the programmer or the language processor and operating system must take on the responsibility for allocating space for instructions and data and for producing the programs that make appropriate use of the addressing structure of the computer. The software features of addressing discussed in this article are therefore mainly of interest to the assembly language programmer. The programmer who writes in a higher-level language such as Pascal or C does not have to be aware of the details of memory addressing in the computer on which a program will run, but may be sure that the compiler being used is very much aware of these details, and usually expends a great deal of effort to take advantage of the memory-addressing hardware features provided on the computer.

SAUL ROSEN

VIRTUAL MEMORY

Overlays   Many programs are too long to fit into the space in main memory that can be allocated to them at run time. In a uniprogramming system, this will be true when the amount of space required by the program is greater than the total memory available to problem programs. In a multiprogramming system it may be true because the amount of space that is needed is more than the operating system is willing to allocate to this particular program. In either case, it becomes necessary to break the program up into sections, segments, or overlays so that the entire program need not be in main memory at

the same time. The term *folding* has sometimes been used for this process.

In many older systems, the programmer had the responsibility for breaking the program into overlays and for providing the loading instructions that bring necessary overlays into main memory as they are needed. Many software systems provide aids to overlay planning. The user can name the overlays so that all symbolic addresses in an overlay will be automatically tagged with a special identifier that indicates which overlay they belong to.

A loader (*q.v.*) or linker (*q.v.*) creates an object program organized as a set of overlays and a root segment containing information about the overlay structure. The root segment is loaded into main memory along with the segments needed to get the program started. Any reference to a symbolic address in a segment that is not in main memory causes a call on the supervisor to load the required segment, overlaying other segments if necessary.

There have been a number of efforts to produce software systems that provide automatic folding of programs. In such systems, a programmer would write a program as if there were enough main memory to contain the whole program, and the software system would organize the program into overlays to fit the actual amount of storage that would be available. Efforts to produce software systems of this type date back to the earliest computers, but none was particularly successful until the advent of so-called *virtual memory* systems that first made their appearance around 1959 and that have become increasingly popular since the 1970s.

The Atlas System   The Atlas (*q.v.*) computer was probably the first virtual memory system. Its designers called it a single-level storage system. The idea was that a programmer would program as if all available memory were on a single level and directly addressable, whereas in fact memory was on two levels. In the Atlas, the two levels were drum and core.

A program for the Atlas could be written as if it were to run in a homogeneous memory consisting of $2^{20} = 1,048,576$ words. Memory was organized into *pages* of $2^9 = 512$ words each. The physical core memory might consist of only 32 or 64 such pages. However, the "address space" (i.e. the addresses that a user could address) consisted of $2^{11} = 2,048$ such pages. Thus, an address in the Atlas consisted of an 11-bit page number and a 9-bit number indicating the location within the page.

A hardware page-address register is associated with each physical page (or *page frame*, as it is sometimes called). A typical running program might consist of 50 pages, of which 20 pages at a particular time would be located in core memory and the other 30 located on the drum.

Each page of the program represents a set of 512 consecutive addresses with the same page number (i.e. the same 11 leftmost bits). The program page number is kept in the page address register of the physical page that is occupied by that program page. Thus, any program (or logical) page may occupy any physical page, and it may occupy different physical pages at different times during the running of the program.

Assume now (see Fig. 3) that the next instruction to be executed refers to an operand whose address (in octal) is 0231443. This is a reference to location 443 in page 231. Note that core memory of the machine contains nowhere near 231 pages, and there are only 50 pages in the program being executed. The programmer does not have to confine the program to the first 50 pages or to any contiguous block of 50 pages. He or she can use any areas in virtual memory that are convenient. Thus, the programmer does not have to know beforehand how long the code areas and data areas are going to be. The program can be broken up into segments and placed far enough apart in virtual memory so that their memory allocations will not overlap. There is no point at all to scattering a program at random over a large virtual memory; in fact, such programs will usually perform very inefficiently. One wants a very large virtual memory in order to be able to assign areas, whose ultimate size is not necessarily known in advance, to program and data modules that do not overlap and that form the structural units of a program. The segmented, two-dimensional virtual memories discussed below were introduced to make this type of modular programming (*q.v.*) more automatic and more convenient.

The page address registers form an associative or content-addressable memory. They are subject to a very rapid hardware scan to determine if one of them is page 231. If it is (say, if page 231 is in physical page 12, as in Fig. 3), then the operand sought is in physical location 12443, and the operand is fetched from that location. If, on the other hand, page 231 of this program is not in core memory, it must be fetched from the drum. An interrupt called a *page fault* occurs, and the operating system initiates a transfer of that page from drum into core. Assume that physical page 16 is available. The supervisor will cause program page 231 to be loaded into physical page 16, and will place the number 231 in the corresponding page address register. It then returns control to the program, which tries again to access an operand in virtual location 231443. This time it finds logical page 231 in physical page 16 and translates the address 231443 to 16443.

Segments and Pages The Atlas system is an example of a one-dimensional or single-segment virtual memory system. The programmer or the language processor must provide symbolic or absolute addresses in the one-dimensional virtual memory. Many of the classical storage allocation problems remain, although they are helped considerably by the fact that the virtual memory is much larger than the actual central memory of the computer on which the program is run.

From the point of view of program organization, there are a number of advantages to a two-dimensional organization of virtual memory. Although two-dimensional virtual memory systems usually are multiprogrammed systems, it is convenient to think of each program in the multiprogrammed environment as if it were running in its own virtual memory.

In such a system, a program runs in a large virtual memory consisting of a number of segments. An address then consists of a segment name (or number) and a displacement relative to the beginning of the segment. This is somewhat analogous to the regional organization of programs in earlier computer generations and has some of the same advantages. The programmer or the language processor can assign programs and data to different segments without worrying about the relative posi-

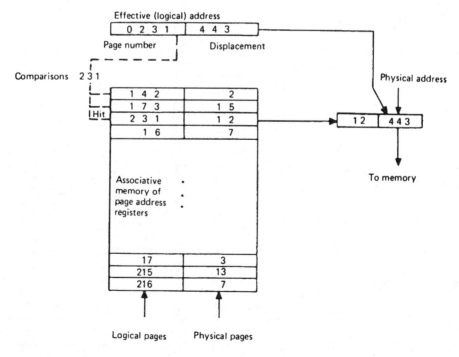

FIG. 3. Address translation on the Atlas computer.

tion of the segments in the total addressing space. This is especially true if the segments are large enough so that possible segment overflow is not a problem. The segments themselves may be organized into pages.

A *job* (or *process*) is then represented in central memory by a segment table that provides a set of pointers (*q.v.*) to page tables corresponding to the active segments of the process. Each active segment will usually have one or more pages in memory. The actual address space or virtual memory is very large, and in most practical situations it consists mostly of unused space. Of the part of virtual memory that is actually used by a program, only a relatively few pages will be in central memory; the rest will reside on a paging drum (or disk) or in a backup mass storage system (usually disk storage). The segment may serve as a unit of sharing among programs. The same segment (i.e. a pointer to the same page table) may ap-

pear in several segment tables that correspond to several jobs that are simultaneously active. The possibility of sharing segments was one of the strong motivations for the development of the segmented virtual memory systems.

The first and perhaps the only complete implementation of this type of virtual memory system was attempted in the Multics system developed at M.I.T. on the General Electric (later Honeywell) 645 computer and its successors. The actual addressing and address translation scheme used is too complicated to be discussed here. The reader is referred to Organick (1972).

IBM Virtual Memory Systems The IBM 360/67 introduced in 1965, and later the IBM 370 series introduced in 1972, helped to popularize some of the concepts of virtual memory. In the standard 370 systems, the vir-

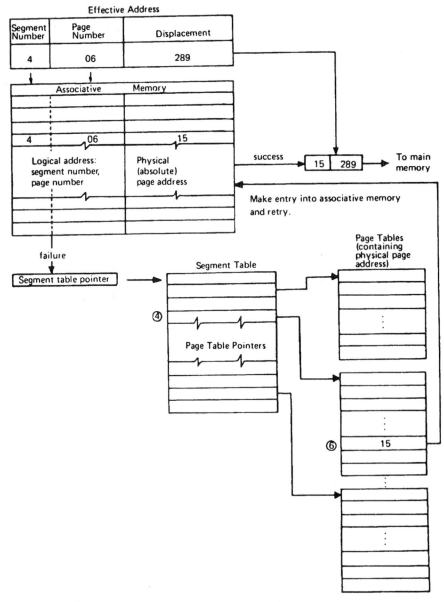

FIG. 4. Address translation of a virtual memory machine (IBM 370).